THE COMPLETE SERIES

VOLUME 3

CONTAINING THE NEXT FOUR STORIES:
SERVANTS OF THE SKULL
THE MURDER MONSTER
THE SINISTER SCOURGE
CURSE OF THE WAITING DEATH

WRITTEN BY
EMILE C. TEPPERMAN & PAUL CHADWICK

BOSTON
ALTUS PRESS
2009

© 2009 Altus Press

Servants of the Skull originally appeared in
SECRET AGENT "X" (November 1934)

The Murder Monster originally appeared in
SECRET AGENT "X" (December 1934)

The Sinister Scourge originally appeared in
SECRET AGENT "X" (January 1935)

Curse of the Waiting Death originally appeared in
SECRET AGENT "X" (February 1935)

Printed in the United States of America

First Edition — 2009

Visit AltusPress.com for more books like this.

EDITED AND DESIGNED BY
Matthew Moring

THANKS TO
*Brian Earl Brown, Stephen Payne,
Ray Riethmeier & Bill Thom.*

ALL RIGHTS RESERVED

No part of this book may be reproduced or utilized in any form or by any means, electronic or mechanical, without permission in writing from the publisher.

BOOK

3

TABLE OF CONTENTS

Introduction .... *by Stephen Payne* i

Servants of the Skull .... *by Emile C. Tepperman* 1

The Murder Monster .... *by Emile C. Tepperman* 145

The Sinister Scourge .... *by Paul Chadwick* 277

Curse of the Waiting Death .... *by Paul Chadwick* 425

INTRODUCTION

STEPHEN PAYNE

EDUCATED GUESSES BASED on observation, converted to hypotheses, tested as experiments, analyzed for conclusions: Such is the basis of the scientific method and even trial and error logic. And such an approach, though probably not as formal, determined whether a particular pulp magazine, especially a hero or character book, achieved success—or died on the vine. The more astute pulp editors, practiced at such thinking, intentionally sought writers who had developed proven track records, those who could pen tales crackling with excitement and pulsing with energy. These were the wordsmiths who commanded the attention of armies of readers and who earned fortunes for their editors and publishers. These were the folk like editor John Nanovic and writer Lester Dent on *Doc Savage* and Nanovic (again) and Walter Gibson on *The Shadow;* boss Harry Steeger and Norvell Page of *The Spider* and Steeger once more and Robert Hogan of *G-8 and His Battle Aces.*

Less perceptive editors struggled to find effective tale spinners for their publications, and readers rewarded those magazines accordingly. Among others, these books included such "masterpieces" as *Captain Satan,* by William O'Sullivan; the initial novels in *Bill Barnes, Air Adventurer,* by Major Malcolm Wheeler Nicholson; *The Black Hood,* by G.T. Fleming Roberts; and far too many others. It is obvious that being a "big name" like Street & Smith or Popular did not guarantee success for a book, nor did the lack of a name. And the usual "market forces" greatly affected the chances of a pulp's success. But the editors' "smarts," that awareness of readers' preferences and a willingness to experiment, profoundly influenced a book's chances in the marketplace. And here is the place that Rose Wyn of Periodical House/Ace Publishers found herself in 1934: her imprint, at best a third-tier operation, printed few hero

INTRODUCTION

periodicals of any note, outside of *Ten Detective Aces, Flying Aces,* and *Western Aces*. Frankly these were not exactly stars in the heavens. Oh, and then there was a little book entitled *Secret Agent "X."* It was, at the time, Wyn's only single character book.

The wife of publisher A.A. Wyn, Rose herself was a pulp editor. She had launched the adventures of the Secret Agent, at best a derivative character, to compete against Doc Savage, the Shadow, the Phantom Detective, and the Spider. With the majority of her "big guns" being snatched away by better paying pulp houses, Wyn had assigned fictioneer Paul Chadwick to scribble the adventures of the Man of a Thousand Faces. But he just was not working out. Maybe it was the imitative way he handled the Agent; maybe it was, frankly, his style of writing, at best "faux creepy," that Chadwick employed. Whatever the case, Wyn had to do something, quickly, to salvage her publication. For some reason unknown today, she gave a young Emile Tepperman the opportunity to write a group of stories. Had she hired him as a permanent replacement for Chadwick? Or had she assigned him as a stopgap before she could find a permanent scribe? Unless more evidence turns up, we will probably never know the answer to this question. The questions we *can* answer, however, are twofold: How effectively did Tepperman handle the Secret Agent's adventures? And how much influence did he exert on the future of *Secret Agent "X?"* To answer the first question, we will examine, briefly, Tepperman's first *X* novel, "Hand of Horror" (August 1934), then look closely at the duo of Tepperman entries in this volume, "Servants of the Skull" (November 1934) and "The Murder Monster" (December 1934). We will see that with his understanding of style, plot, characters, and settings, Tepperman could have performed a creditable job on *Secret Agent "X."* Further, we will find that far from being a "failed" experiment, Tepperman' brought a new humanity, a new "realism" (if such existed in the early hero pulps) to the character of Secret Agent "X." Indeed Emile Tepperman paved the way for Wyn to hire a young G. T. Fleming-Roberts, who would become the most effective and talented writer to handle the character.

To launch his time on the magazine, Tepperman wrote "Hand of Horror," a decent though not noteworthy tale with the usual Chadwickian trappings. Our new Brant House develops the narrative around a ruthless master criminal with political ambitions and a weird method of murdering his enemies, the so-called "bloated death." This is actually an exotic venom, always a favorite of Tepperman's predecessor, Chadwick. Couple this with a femme fatale, constant focus on the Agent, and spooky atmosphere, and we see a narrative not much distinguished from one by Chadwick himself. Then comes Tepperman's next entry, "Servants of the Skull." Here we see what he really might have accomplished with the series, and it is remarkable, both for its realism and its innovation.

The prose alone is critical to realizing that we have a new writer on our hands. Tepperman composes his stories with a leaner, less pretentious, less melodramatic approach to the subject matter. At the most atomistic level the reader notices this quality particularly in Tepperman's diction. It is a distinct contrast to the work by Paul Chadwick. Consider this opening scene from "Servants of the Skull," the first of the Tepperman entries in this volume:

> The thirty-odd men in the artificially lighted room looked up from their various occupations with tense expectancy when the heavy iron-bound door swung open. These men represented a strange conglomeration of criminal types; crafty, hard, ruthless, their predatory natures were reflected in the very manner in which they moved and talked. It would have seemed, at first glance, that there existed no power on earth that could control these men, no power to make them toe the mark. Yet, when that door opened, they all, without exception, froze in their places. The eyes of many reflected a nameless fear; others exhibited a sort of sullen defiance. Not one of them smiled or laughed.

Here we see few of the Gothic images that Chadwick so often used. Tepperman is direct, even blunt in his word choice. There is precious little of the Gothic effects we see in Chadwick. Indeed, juxtapose this sample of Tepperman's work with two from Chadwick, this one from the first *Secret Agent "X"* novel, "The Torture Trust" (February 1934):

> The prison guard's feet made ghostly echoes along the dimly lighted corridor of the State Penitentiary. The sound whispered weirdly through the barred chambers, dying away in the steel rafters overhead. The guard's electric torch probed the cells as he passed, playing over the forms of the sleeping men. It was after midnight. All seemed quiet within the great, gloomy building that was one of society's bulwarks against a rising tide of crime.

This passage from the opener of Paul Chadwick's "The Spectral Strangler" (March 1934) presents a similar tone of Gothic melodrama:

> [Federal Detective] Bill Scanlon stood waiting. Then he relaxed.

INTRODUCTION

> A cat with coal black fur and glowing green eyes spat at him and slunk away. It might have been an evil omen, but Scanlon wasn't superstitious. He thought it was only the cat he had seen... A shadow detached itself from the blackness of a house stoop opposite the maple. Slinking spiderlike, the shadow moved after Scanlon, stalking from tree to tree, hedge to hedge, and stoop to stoop, drawing closer—always closer.

What a different way of using language that the two writers employ! Paul Chadwick's diction is meant to convey a sense of weirdness and foreboding. However, its real effect is to cause readers to roll their eyes at the narrator's melodramatic overkill. It is like watching *really bad* Vincent Price (actually a capable thespian) or, better, Bela Lugosi at his most extravagant (Think *White Zombie* and Lugosi's notorious work for filmmaker Ed Wood). Emile Tepperman, on the other hand, employs the language in a much more crisp fashion, yet keeps his diction evocative. Here is realism, not Gothic melodrama. In the future career of Tepperman, it will become the hallmark of a prose style that will eventually seem to celebrate the brutal, the cruel in life.

Yet this begs the question: In popular literature, especially in the pulps, why should this kind of tougher, more realistic diction have any advantages over a more melodramatic kind? It certainly does— and it did even during the Depression. In the first place it is more in tune with the style that would become the industry standard by the mid-to-late 1930s. Second, Tepperman's mode of expression is frankly more efficient in portraying the story. In other words his word choice is unencumbered by the unnecessary "special effects" recorded in the above passages by Paul Chadwick. Last, such word choice more effectively engages the readers' interest. It inspires them to move more deeply into the text, not to ridicule it.

In the same vein is Tepperman's syntax, his manner of arranging phrases, clauses, sentences, and paragraphs. As the lines from "Servants of the Skull" illustrate, Tepperman composes in a "rat-a-tat" kind of style perfectly suited to the subject matter that his fiction portrays. Note this section from the same narrative, wherein the eponymous villain threatens X's companion Betty Dale:

> The Skull went on: "What will you say, Miss Dale, when I tell you that this electric chair *does not kill!* It will maim you! Maim you mentally and physically, will make you an imbecile within five seconds of the moment I pull this switch... That, Miss Dale, is what will happen to you. You will be thrown out into the street to be found

INTRODUCTION

by your friend and protector, Secret Agent 'X'! I shall send you as a challenge to him—a challenge from the one man who is his match!"

Like the writer's diction, a less melodramatic style tends to move the storyline, and of a necessity the readers' eyes', with much greater speed over the page. Also it more realistically depicts the way people would speak (if the pulps can be said to portray realism!).

If the styles of the Tepperman and Chadwick show obvious differences, then so too do their plots. In Chadwick's hands the Man of a Thousand Faces battles all manner of pulp super criminals wielding terrifying death weapons. In "The Torture Trust" it may be the Masters of Death, who seek money and power and who use acid to attain their goals. The devious Black Master, a Shadowesque villain, lusts after vast wealth, his method for gaining it being a new asphyxiating gas ("The Spectral Strangler"). With Chadwick's other early "X" yarns, the Agent encounters a super flame thrower, the Flammenwurfer ("The Death-Torch Terror"), and an opportunistic master spy, the Green Mask ("Ambassador of Doom"), selling military secrets. And then there is the group of medical extortionists from the notorious "City of the Living Dead," a story which merits no response, save, "What the hell were they thinking?" With the exception of this final entry, this is pretty standard pulp fare, if not derivative stuff, as far as Chadwick's handling of plot goes. Every one of the villains is out for power or wealth, with little to distinguish miscreant A's goals from those of miscreant B. Only their *modus operandi* might differ. In addition the order of events from one month's adventure is nearly always the same as the next one. The Agent will investigate a criminal mastermind's machinations, only to be exposed at a crucial time. Then he will effect a daring escape from the criminal's clutches (or from those of the police), a la the Shadow, don a new disguise, and recommence his investigation. Altering his features like most people change socks, he will move through the remainder of the story until the final battle with the resident fiend. Here the Secret Agent will expose the man's real identity, then, whistling his eerie call, disappear to the amazement of the police or other onlookers. This is strict adherence to a formula, plain and simple.

In Chadwick's defense it was difficult to come up with a new menace, month after month. This may explain why his fictional threats to society had to grow ever more deadly and horrible, ever more paranoid. Though it may seem counterintuitive, this may also

INTRODUCTION

account for editor Rose Wyn's likely problems with Chadwick's narratives. Wyn, as editor, would clearly see where the book was going with Chadwick as scribe. If a plot requires a new horror every month, then the next month's number and the next will necessitate ever more horror and fear, along with a villain just as horrible and fearsome to perpetrate it. This type of narrative circumstance will then force the writer, especially the formulaic one, to grope for plots more desperately each time. Eventually he will move in the direction of diminishing returns. Readers, too, will become satiated with such material, desensitized to the point that the pulpster's work will have little or no impact.

Very likely, then, switching gears was uppermost in Rose Wyn's mind when she assigned *Secret Agent "X"* to Emile Tepperman. He, in contrast, would bring a new kind of plot angle to the mysteries. I've mentioned his first *"X,"* "Hand of Horror," which is not much different from one of Chadwick's fictions. With Tepperman's next story, "Servants of the Skull," we see a rather imitative effort, true enough, one possibly inspired by Walter Gibson's work on *The Shadow*. But in comparison to an early piece by Paul Chadwick, Tepperman executes the plot with class and style. Agent "X," instead of being exposed early on, remains ingeniously hidden in disguise until... well, you'll have to read this for yourself! And the resident villain, the Skull, is equally adept at maintaining his own masquerade, not being revealed until Tepperman is good and ready to unmask him—not any earlier. The point is this: here is a writer who knows how to plot a story. He gives just enough information to tantalize the readers, then compels them to move deeper into the plot. In doing so, he encourages mystery about both story and characters until the very end of the proceedings.

The same is true of Tepperman's next novel, "The Murder Monster." The plot revolves around a bizarre group of mute, lookalike robots who shoot flames from their fingertips, thereby murdering their victims. The Murder Monster, their weird master, is another Gibsonesque villain. And he is almost as strong an opponent for Agent "X" as is the Monster's predecessor, the Skull. Equally as original is the explanation that Tepperman provides for the villain's minions. A well-plotted story, "The Murder Master" moves with a relentless pace that never lets up until the final exciting scene. Lest I forget, the narrative's plot contains an interesting sidelight that amounts to pulp social commentary, in this case regarding the treatment of criminals.

Today many of us think that more humane policies towards the incarcerated are the product of our more "enlightened" age. And we know that pulp novels are the last place to see such progressive ideas because all pulps were racist and classist, if not fascistic in their ideology. Such is far from true. Tepperman's Brant House has a conscience of sorts, as this early section of "The Murder Monster" reveals. Here a group of university men from Ervinton College are playing an exhibition football game against felons from State Prison:

> The visiting team deployed from the field, trotted into the basement through the side entrance of the main building, where showers and a locker room had been set up for them. The convicts watched them gloomily, in marked contrast to the hilarity of the college boys. For they were not going home to well-cooked meals in comfortable dining rooms, to the fond glances of proud parents, to the arms of sweethearts. They were going in to a dreary supper and dismal cells, to their lonely thoughts and gnawing memories.

It is as though Tepperman is acknowledging that these men's identities are not *what they have done;* rather their identity is wrapped up in *who they are,* that is, human beings. And because they are human, they deserve to be treated with respect and dignity, even if they are criminals and (especially if they are most likely from the lower classes). Of course, it does not hurt that this particular bunch from "The Murder Monster" apparently has a sense of its past criminal behavior. Those without lacking a conscience are treated with open contempt, in line with most pulp fiction of the day.

This portrayal of characters is another feature distinguishing Tepperman's work from that of Paul Chadwick, being most obvious in the men's treatment of felons. The original Brant House depicted criminals as a shabby, dirty class of people, "lowlifes" who are tough with their guns, but cowardly without them. Further, they are animalistic, with wolf imagery predominating as Chadwick's means of describing them. This traditional portrayal dates all the way back to ancient writers like Pliny the Elder and even to writers of the Hebrew and Christian Scriptures. It is shorthand for the person who is predatory, ravenous, ruthless. The novel "Curse of the Waiting Death" states that a masked bandit is "like a hungry wolf," for example. "The Torture Trust" declares thugs to be "slavering, red-jawed wolves." And last, Chadwick paints one "Fat" Hickman of "The Sinister Scourge" as a man with "lips drawn back in a wolfish leer." In each instance, these criminals (and for that matter, most of Chadwick's criminals) are predators who deserve *anything* that happens to them. And it makes sense that a man hunter like Secret Agent "X" would have to track and eliminate them. He is a virtual avenger of God (or, in this case, the State) who, in this early period, stoically and relentlessly pursues his foes, in order to protect the innocent (us).

Of course, the Man of a Thousand Faces is not completely emotionless. He does show signs of horror at his enemies' plans (as "The Torture Trust" notes) and friendliness towards allies like Jim Hobart and Betty Dale—but not much more. It is as if he does not want to become too close to people, not even to those who should be dearest to him. Here we see a distinct problem with Chadwick's earliest *"X"* work: the originator of Secret Agent "X" missed a terrific opportunity to imbue his fictional creations with life. As a consequence, readers could not identify with (read "root for") a protagonist and supporting players of such shallow characterization. They and the master of disguise become figures with as much life as a casket.

In contrast, Emile Tepperman, with his fresh ideas on characterization, offers us a more believable Man of a Thousand Faces. In "Hand of Horror," "X" is human enough to walk onstage, whistling a tune from *H.M.S. Pinafore,* as Will Murray and Tom Johnson have noted *(The Secret Agent X Companion* 89). This is lightheartedness personified! On the opposite end of the spectrum, "Servants of the Skull" presents us with an Agent equally as human. In one episode from this one, he shows more than a little pessimism, if not fatalism. It is a prefigurement of the mindset Operator #5, Jimmy Christopher, will later express during Tepperman's Purple Invasion cycle. Here in "Servants" the situation is dire: The Man of a Thousand Faces and Betty Dale are trying to escape certain death in the Skull's lair. To Betty's exclamation that she and the Agent are free from the Skull's clutches, the Agent replies, "We're not out yet... This is going to be a grueling ordeal, Betty. You must keep a stiff upper lip. I—have doubts now about our ever getting out alive" ("Servants of the Skull"). Later in "The Murder Monster," the Man of a Thousand Faces "[feels] a surge of bitter repugnance" at the fate of the robots in the story. It is extremely doubtful if Chadwick would have depicted Secret Agent "X" in such terms. And it is as questionable that Chadwick would have given as much care to the "X"-Betty Dale dynamic.

In Chadwick's initial series entries we see Betty as a young woman who enjoys a friendship with the Secret Agent, but their connection is stiff, formal. She "loves him from afar," so to speak. So the series' legend goes, he cannot become too deeply involved with her because it would endanger her life. In other words, criminals would strike at him through Betty. Also it would divert "X" from his war on crime and criminals. What really happens, from a narrative perspective, is the fact that Chadwick fumbles the ball again, failing to explore the relationship with Betty and Secret Agent "X." She thus becomes little more than a plot device to advance the story, an all-purpose damsel in distress and all around cliché of the Thirties professional woman. In comparison to Doc Savage's cousin Pat Savage, a prototype for the modern woman, Betty Dale's development is shallow, in Chadwick's depiction.

Tepperman's vision of Betty metamorphoses into something warmer, more human, as does her connection with the Secret Agent. It is clear that the two experience something like love, though she never sees his true face (not until "City of Madness" by Fleming-Roberts, in fact). Furthermore she has become one of his "lieutenants," Tepperman's narrator informs in "The Murder Monster," as though to say the Secret Agent has pulled her deeper into his service. She suffers agony when she does not hear "X's" voice, the same entry tells us, and feels calmed again only when he calls her. Moreover, as this new Brant House expresses in a text note in "The Murder Monster": "And Betty had grown *to care more than she liked to admit for this strange man* [emphasis added]..." Something is going on here, and it is not mere infatuation. Apparently, Betty is really falling for the Agent, and the feeling for him is mutual. In reality this is a new direction Emile Tepperman was taking the series, one Chadwick could not have envisioned. Secret Agent "X" was gaining much more emotional depth.

If Betty Dale changed subtly under Tepperman, so too did the corps of the Secret Agent's operatives, with the introduction of Harvey Bates to the series. Here in "The Murder Monster" he is merely "Bates," head of the Agent's other detective agency. Interestingly he sounds like an intelligent, if not educated man, much different from Jim Hobart, the redheaded ex-cop. Also Tepperman's version of Bates gives G. T. Fleming-Roberts a springboard from which to launch, as much as Chadwick's take does. As far as the portrayal of Jim Hobart goes, the owner and operator of the Hobart Detective Agency alters a bit, as well. Chadwick's Brant House had always maintained that Hobart worked for A. J. Martin, but that he, Hobart, never realized his boss was actually the Man of Mystery. With Tepperman, Jim Hobart has strong suspicions in this direction, as the following text note from "The Murder Monster" discloses:

> Jim sometimes wondered if the orders he received from Mr. Martin had not originated with someone else who was using Martin as a go-between. If that was so, Jim had a good idea, or thought he had, who that "someone else" was. But he was thoroughly satisfied to continue, because he was in a position to know, the opinion of the police to the contrary, that the "someone else" was emphatically on the side of law and order.

Who could the "someone else" be but the Man of a Thousand faces himself? Perhaps this new treatment of Hobart signals a change in his relationship with the Agent. But alas, we will never know, given that this new Brant House scribbled only one more entry, "Talons of Terror," for the magazine. Doctor Blood, its sinister mastermind, is as horrible a villain as "X" ever encountered, being a character from the weird menace tradition. And like the other three "X" stories by Tepperman, it deserves another reading.

Examined superficially, this final contribution might seem to have ended the influence of Emile Tepperman on *Secret Agent "X."* It might even cause us to regard his labor on the magazine as an experiment that failed. Yet his tenure there was not futile. Quite the contrary, he penned some entertaining fiction for the Secret Agent; and he did so in many ways. Born from a willingness to take narrative risks, his new insights lent vitality to the characters. His leaner, innovative plots more effectively moved the stories forward. And his more realistic style brought dynamism to a series in danger of stagnation. *Secret Agent "X"* was primed to move into its next and greatest phase, the G. T. Fleming-Roberts era. Who would have thought four stories could do so much? Truly Secret Agent "X" remains the Man of a Thousand Faces, a Thousand Disguises—and a Thousand Surprises!

BOOK IX

SERVANTS OF THE SKULL

From the macabre maze of a labyrinthian world, the Skull, master of murder, reached out and destroyed the brains of mighty financiers. Money kings were his meat. And the law could not protect them... Only one man could match brains with the sinister Skull—and that man was Secret Agent "X." But the Skull did not fear "X." For "X"—the Man of a Thousand Faces, a thousand personalities, a thousand tricks—had one vulnerable spot. And the Skull knew where it lay.

CHAPTER I

MEET THE "SKULL"

THE THIRTY-ODD MEN in the artificially lighted room looked up from their various occupations with tense expectancy when the heavy, iron-bound, door swung open. These men represented a strange conglomeration of criminal types; crafty, hard, ruthless, their predatory natures were reflected in the very manner in which they moved and talked. It would have seemed, at first glance, that there existed no power on earth that could control these men, no power to make them toe the mark. Yet, when that door opened they all, without exception, froze in their places. The eyes of many reflected a nameless fear; others exhibited a sort of sullen defiance. Not one of them smiled or laughed.

A distinct rustle of interest swept through the room as the opening door disclosed two figures standing in the corridor. One was a tall, slender man whose hair was graying slightly at the temples. This man had a blindfold over his eyes, and he was resting one hand, with long, tapering, sensitive fingers on the shoulder of the other man, who was guiding him.

The other man was far from a prepossessing sight. He was dressed in nondescript, soiled clothing. The sleeves were too short for the long arms, and the coat seemed too small for the barrel of a chest in the squat, powerful body. This man had been endowed with great physical strength, but there his endowment had stopped; for his face clearly indicated that he was lacking in mental balance. And in addition, that face was horribly scarred as if by a terrible disease.

They entered the room, and the one with the scarred face closed the door behind them, then turned to the other and said in a high-pitched, cackling voice:

"All right, Fannon, you can take off the blindfold." A black shock

of wild, disordered hair falling low, almost obscured his scars as he faced the men in the room. "Well, boys, the boss is right on the job. Here's another one to take Tyler's place. An' he's the goods, too—Frank Fannon, the best safe man in the world."

The newcomer removed the blindfold and stared coolly around the room. He returned the nods of several men who greeted him, surveyed the room with interest. His guide sidled close to him and said:

"The boss's orders is, you wait here till he sends for you. He'll tell you all the rules of the place. My name is Binks. Anything you want, you ask me for it. I'm the 'Skull's' handy man."

The gunman tumbled backward, groggy from the straight-arm jab.

Fannon merely nodded, and watched Binks go out. The door snapped shut after him. Fannon noted that there was no handle on the inside of the door; it could only be opened from the corridor.

He frowned, cast an inquiring glance at the men in the room. One of them, a heavy-set man with thick, gnarled hands, burst into harsh laughter. "Whatsamatter, Fannon? Don't you like the idea o' bein' a prisoner? You oughtta be used to it by now!"

Fannon, still frowning, crossed the room to the heavy-set man who was sitting at a table with four others where they had been playing stud poker when the door opened. Fannon looked down at him thoughtfully, remarked, "I seem to know you from somewhere."

The heavy-set man guffawed heartily, turned to the others at the table. "Can you beat that? He seems to know me from somewhere!

They used to call him 'Dude' Fannon where we came from. His manners is like the Prince o' Wales!" He poked a finger up at Fannon. "Sure you know me from somewhere. Don't you remember the stretch we did together at Folsom ten years ago? You oughtta remember me—Nate Frisch. We was together for five years."

Fannon smiled. "Quite so. Now I remember perfectly." He gazed around the room. "There seem to be quite a few other old friends of mine here."

"Sure," said Nate Frisch. "Let's get intro—"

He stopped, looking fearfully toward the door. A sudden terror had come into his eyes.

The door had opened soundlessly again, and Binks stood there. "My, my," he croaked, grinning at Frisch with his gruesomely mutilated face. "I see you been forgettin' the rules, Nate."

FRISCH was shivering violently, his face a pasty hue. "I—I didn't mean nothin' by it, Binks. Fannon is just an old friend o' mine, an' I was kinda recallin' old times with him." His voice was almost pleading now. "It ain't nothin' to report to the Skull, Binks. Sure I know the rules—no talkin' to new men till they been passed by the Skull. But I just forgot it for a minute. You won't mention it to him, will you? Be a regular guy for once."

Binks resembled a gargoyle when he laughed. "I'll think about it, Nate, I'll think about it. Maybe I'll toss a coin. Got a coin fer me to toss?"

"Sure, sure," Frisch said eagerly. He took out a half dollar and flipped it to Binks who caught it dexterously. "Thanks, Nate. Maybe I'll forget about it, like you said." He motioned to Fannon. "Come on. The Skull will see you now."

Fannon followed him out into the corridor, watched him swing the big door shut, heard it click. The corridor was long, dimly lit by a single weak bulb at the far end.

"We won't need no blindfold now," Binks said as he proceeded toward the illuminated end. "You couldn't get out of here in a million years unless I took you. I'm the only one," he added proudly, "outside of the Skull, that knows the way out."

"I don't even know where we are," Fannon said. "What's this, a cellar?"

Binks cackled. "Maybe the Skull will tell you. I ain't sayin' a word. It ain't healthy to talk out o' place in here."

They reached the end of the corridor. There was no door here, only a blank wall. Binks bent down, fumbled in the corner, and suddenly the wall at the end of the corridor seemed to slide away, leaving a dark opening. Binks stepped into it, and Fannon followed. Binks bent down, manipulated something again, and the panel through which they had stepped slid to, leaving them in utter blackness.

Fannon could tell that Binks was once more bending to the floor. In a moment Binks straightened up, there was a *whirring* of well-oiled machinery, and they began to rise. They were in some sort of elevator that moved smoothly and noiselessly. When it stopped, Binks reached down, pulled a lever. Fannon's eyes, more accustomed to the darkness now, noted the exact position of the lever, but he said nothing.

In response to Binks' manipulation of the lever, the panel slid open again, revealing another long corridor similar to the one below. Fannon estimated that they had come up one flight in the elevator. He said, as they went along this second corridor, "What's all the mystery about? You'd think the Skull was another Fu-Manchu with all these secret passages and things."

"Nobody's ever seen his face," Binks told him. "Not even me. An' he trusts me more than anybody else—I guess because I ain't got the brains to do him dirt. Ha, ha!"

There was a note of insanity in Binks' laughter; a suggestion of sadistic cruelty that made his listener shudder. Fannon tried to pump him, without seeming to do so. "What happened to this chap, Tyler, whose place I'm supposed to take?"

Binks half turned, looked up at him queerly. "You want to know? I'll show you. Wait a minute." He stopped under a dim electric light bulb set in the wall that lined the corridor. Fannon could see a narrow slot, waist high, in the wall, about a half inch long. Binks took a peculiarly shaped key from his pocket. This key was flat, just wide enough to fit into the slot.

When he slipped it in a crack appeared in the wall. The crack widened; a panel was sliding open, disclosing another passageway at right angles to the one they were in. As soon as they stepped into this passageway, the panel closed behind them. This corridor, though wider than the others, was also lit by only a single bulb at the end. On either side were heavy doors similar to the one in the room below.

Binks stopped before the second door on the left from the end.

He turned the knob, opened it slowly. It was pitch dark inside, and the faint illumination from the hall failed to help. Fannon could feel an uneasy stirring from within, and then a slight groan. Binks produced a flashlight from his pocket, threw its beam into the interior of the room, illuminating the gaunt, cadaverous body of a man chained with his face to the wall.

THE man had a stubble of beard a week old, and there was a mad, fearsome light in his eyes as he blinked at the flashlight, over his shoulder. He was so chained, Fannon saw, that his toes barely touched the floor. The strain upon his arms after any considerable period of time would be unbearable.

Binks said with mock solicitude, "How do you feel, Tyler? You been gettin' plenty time to think?"

The chained prisoner only succeeded in croaking a few unintelligible syllables.

Binks remarked conversationally to Fannon, "He's been here three days now. We been havin' some fun." He lowered the flashlight so that it showed the man's naked torso, and Fannon gasped. It was criss-crossed with long bloody gashes that had been made with a whip. The man's back was a raw mass of bloody flesh. Binks continued, "But that's only the beginning. Tomorrow the Skull is gonna give him the works. Tomorrow is execution day."

Tyler managed to gasp out, "For God's sake, help me!"

Fannon restrained himself with difficulty. He threw a significant glance at the poor victim as he followed Binks out into the corridor, watched him slam the door. He had noted that this door, too, had no handle on the inside. He noted, also, that none of the doors was equipped with a lock. It was only necessary to turn the knob from the outside to open them.

As they went down the hall past a number of other closed doors, Fannon asked, "What did Tyler ever do to merit such punishment?"

Binks only laughed. "The Skull will tell you."

Fannon said nothing further. He was busy going over in his mind every inch of the route they had covered, in an effort to remember it so that he could traverse the same route alone. They passed through another of the queer sliding panels, and stood in a square anteroom. Opposite them was a door with no handle on it, while at the left was another door that did have a handle.

Binks indicated the door without the handle. "The Skull will let you in through that door," he said. "I'm not supposed to be around when he talks to you fellers. I'm not supposed to know what his plans are." He laughed idiotically. "Not much, I don't!"

Fannon watched him go out through the door at the left, saw the last grinning leer that he cast behind him before the door closed. Then Fannon went to the one chair in the anteroom, sat down, and lit a cigarette. His face was calm, betrayed no emotion, no sign of fear or perturbation. If anyone was watching him through secret peepholes, his face told nothing except, perhaps, that there was a criminal of higher type than average, who was supremely self-assured.

After a few moments, the door opposite began to open slowly. There was utter darkness beyond it. Through the doorway came a stocky man, wide-shouldered, with a square chin and a low forehead. He grinned at Fannon, showing discolored teeth. "So you're the new man, huh? Glad to know you."

FANNON did not rise. He allowed the smoke to trickle slowly from his nostrils, then said drawlingly, "I thought I was here to talk to the Skull."

The stocky man asked, frowning, "What makes you think I'm not the Skull?"

Fannon slowly shook his head. "I don't want to hurt your feelings, but you haven't got the brains to be the boss of this outfit."

The stocky man grinned again. "You win, brother. I'm Rufe Linson, second in command. The Skull always likes to test men out this way. He's watching us now. Before you can see him, I'll have to search you. Stand up."

"I was searched once, before coming in," Fannon protested, though complying.

Rufe made a derogatory gesture. "By that halfwit, Binks. I do a regular job. See, the Skull has got wind that there's a certain guy tryin' to squirm into this place—a guy called Secret Agent 'X.' You might be him for all we know. So we gotta search every man right down to the skin. This 'X' guy always has special trick stunts on him; and if we ever found gas guns or trick cigarettes or things like that on a new guy, believe me it would be tough for him."

While he talked, he searched the new man's clothing with a thoroughness that overlooked nothing. He ripped the lining of Fannon's coat, turned down the cuffs of his trousers, took the ribbon off the hat, ripped open the tie.

In the pockets he found a few coins, a package of cigarettes, and a box of matches. He broke every one of the cigarettes, then made Fannon remove his shoes. He pried open the soles to see if there was anything hidden there.

"It's all right," he assured Fannon. "When you go back to the main room, you'll find new clothing to put on. The Skull always keeps his men well dressed."

When he had finally satisfied himself that there was not a thing on the new man that might be suspicious, he said, "Okay. Put your shoes on. The Skull will see you now. Here's where you get a chance to make some real dough. I guess you can use it?"

Fannon nodded bitterly. "They made me work for almost nothing in the prison shop for five years. Now I want to make them pay me for it."

"You'll get your chance, boy. The Skull will show you how." He was watching closely while Fannon laced his shoes, fascinated by the swift movement of the long, dexterous fingers. "Boy," he admired, "no wonder you're the best safe man in the country—with them fingers. Can you open any kind of safe at all?"

"I've never hit one I couldn't," Fannon told him. He finished lacing his shoes and stood up, "What now?"

"You go inside. I guess you're okay. Be careful how you talk to the Skull. Act respectful. He don't take any lip, and he don't stand for jokes."

Fannon nodded, said, "See you later." He walked across the anteroom with a firm step, shoulders back, as if going in to face an unavoidable ordeal. He stepped from the lighted anteroom into the pitch blackness of the next room, and heard the door slam behind him. In the darkness he put his hand out behind him, felt for the knob which should be on the inside. There was none. This door had no knob on either side. It was evidently operated from another room. He was locked in there in the darkness—with the Skull.

CHAPTER II

EXPOSED

HE STOOD STILL, waiting. Soon he heard a rumbling noise from the floor directly in front of him. A trap door of some sort had opened, and from the aperture thus formed a platform was rising. On the platform was the weirdest figure that the eyes of man had yet beheld.

A faint glow of light came up through the trapdoor, and it illuminated the form that was rising. Clad from head to foot in a bright vermilion cloak, it wore a hood of the same material and color. The face was exposed, but it was not the face of a human being. No flesh showed. There was only the grinning outline of a skull—the skull of a skeleton. There was a strange sort of glow about it that seemed to emphasize the bony structure of the fleshless head.

Fannon stood quietly in the darkness, not a muscle of his face moving, as he watched the ghostly rise of the vermilion figure. Suddenly the platform stopped moving, and a spotlight alongside the figure burst into light, flaring directly into Fannon's face. Fannon blinked once or twice, then lowered his lids.

The figure spoke, but Fannon could not see it now, because of the spotlight. "You have no doubt now, Mr. Fannon, as to whether you are talking to the Skull?"

Fannon shook his head. "No."

The Skull chuckled. "No doubt you are anxious to learn why you are being admitted to the ranks of the Servants of the Skull?"

"Because you need me," said Fannon.

The Skull grunted impatiently. "I need no one. I could get along without you very well. But your particular knowledge will help me to expand my operations. The man who preceded you was only an amateur compared to yourself in the business of opening safes. He thought himself indispensable, however, and acted disrespectfully to me. He even entertained notions of supplanting me in command here. Binks showed you how far he succeeded. Take warning from his fate."

Fannon remained silent, and after a moment the Skull continued, "Before you were released from prison you were approached with an offer of employment. You were ignorant of the nature of that employment, but you knew that its nature was criminal. Am I right?"

Fannon answered tonelessly, "You are right."

"Now that you know that it is the Skull who is employing you, are you still eager to go on?"

"I am," Fannon said. "In jail we managed to get news of every one of your exploits. We knew that you were recruiting, for we heard of several disappearances from the underworld, which were followed by crimes that only the missing men could have accomplished. These crimes were attributed to the genius of the Skull, so we knew those men had been drafted to serve you."

"That is true," said the Skull in a pleased tone. "What particular crimes did you hear of?"

"Well, the last I heard of, was the kidnaping of Ainsworth Clegg, the oil man. There had been several kidnapings before that. Then I heard that Clegg, like the others, had been found on the streets of the city, with their mentality destroyed, their bodies wrecked in some horrible manner, so that the doctors gave them only a few days longer to live. We wondered what terrible thing could have done that to them."

The Skull chuckled. "You shall have a chance to see how it is done. Now, I wish to tell you this—every man who is selected by me to become a servant of the Skull will be able to retire a wealthy man when his term of service is over. But—" the Skull's voice became hard, brittle—"in return he must give me blind obedience. He must carry out every order I give, or suffer the consequences. If you are ordered to kill your brother or your sister, *you must obey!*" The Skull was silent for a long minute, then asked slowly, "Are you ready to take service with me?"

And Fannon answered tersely, "Yes!"

"That is good," the Skull said, "You will now go back to the main room. For one week you will be on probation. During that week you will be assigned one task. If you carry it out successfully, you will be admitted as an equal to the ranks of the Servants of the Skull. You will be just in time to participate in the greatest coup in the history of crime which I am now planning. It will be something to astound the world, something which will net us a huge profit.

"One thing more—" as Fannon turned to the door—"no one is allowed to leave this place while in my service. You will be conducted in and out on expeditions, blindfolded, by Binks, who is the only one besides myself that knows the way out. At night, do not try to leave the main room. It is dangerous."

FANNON nodded, his eyes still veiled from the spotlight. Suddenly the spotlight clicked off, and as his eyes became accustomed once more to the gloom, he saw the hideous vermilion-cloaked Skull descending slowly on his movable platform. Then the trapdoor closed, and he was left in pitch darkness.

There was a click behind him, and the door swung open. He stepped into the lighted anteroom, and the door swung shut once more.

The anteroom was empty. He was kept waiting for almost ten minutes, which seemed an hour, before the door at the left opened and Binks reappeared. Binks said little now, seemed to be sulky. He led Fannon back through the maze of passages along which they had come. This time Fannon's keen eyes darted here and there on the return trip, noting angles of corridors, little points about the passages that would enable him to find his way through them alone.

At one spot Fannon suddenly stopped and ripped loose leather from the sole of his shoe where Rufe had cut it. Binks glowered at him suspiciously, but Fannon explained. "Rufe cut my shoes up, and the leather bunches. Makes it hard to walk."

Binks grunted, and went on; he did not notice that Fannon, instead of throwing the leather away, rolled it in the palm of his hand until it was a soft ball. At another time, just as they were passing through one of the sliding panels, Fannon tripped, and nested heavily on the halfwit. In that instant Fannon's long, dexterous fingers darted into Binks' pocket, and came out with the special key he had used to get from one corridor to another.

Binks said, "Can't you keep your feet? What's the trouble, tired?"

"I guess I need some rest," Fannon grumbled, as he palmed the key and slid it into his own pocket.

In the main room some of the men were playing cards or shooting dice; some were reading. Nate Frisch was perusing a magazine with intense interest. He put it down when Binks and Fannon came in, started to say something, but changed his mind and continued his reading. He evidently remembered the halfwit's previous warning.

Binks said, "Come on through; I'll show you your bunk."

Binks had not noticed the swift movement with which Fannon, as they came in, had inserted the rolled piece of leather into the lock of the corridor door to keep it from locking when the door was closed. He led him into a dormitory just beyond the main room. Here there were rows of cots against the walls, each with a number painted in black on the wall above it. Binks stopped before number seventeen.

"This was Tyler's," he explained. "Now it's yours." He pointed to a pile of clothes on the cot. "All new. The Skull takes care of his servants. Ha, ha!"

Fannon watched him go out through the main room, wondering how his face had become so evilly scarred. All over the place the lights were extremely dim, so that it had been impossible to examine those scars closely. Fannon wondered if the man was as silly as he appeared to be, or whether it was a pose. If a pose, what was the purpose?

He watched through the open door while Binks went through the main room and out into the corridor, watched the heavy, iron-bound door slam shut. He breathed a sigh of relief. Binks had not discovered the leather jammed into the lock. The way was open to get out of there later.

Now he undressed, went into the lavatory and washed, then returned to his cot and lay down. In less than five minutes he was sound asleep.

Two hours later he awoke, almost as if he had set an alarm clock somewhere inside his head to arouse him at that moment. He was refreshed by his sleep, cautious and wary. All around him men were sleeping. Loud snores came from many of them. Only a single night light was burning at one end of the room, and by its glow he distinguished the features of Nate Frisch asleep in the cot next to his.

Soundlessly he arose, and without waiting to dress, he stole out into the main room. It was empty. Evidently there was a curfew hour here, a compulsory bedtime. In his bare feet he was as silent as a cat. He pushed at the heavy door, and it gave under his pressure. The piece of leather had done its work.

HE stole along the outer corridor without encountering a soul, until he came to the wall at the end. He knelt as he had seen Binks do, found a short lever protruding only three inches from the wall.

He pulled this downward, and saw the panel in front of him slide out. He stepped into the elevator, found the lever that closed the panel, as well as another one beside it. In a moment he was ascending, and when the cage stopped, he opened the panel, stepped out into the upper corridor.

In the middle, where the dull bulb glowed, he inserted the key he had taken from Binks' pocket in the little slot, and stepped through the opening when the panel slid out. He decided that the panel was set in motion by an electrical circuit that was closed when the metal key was inserted in the slot. He was now in the passage with the doors, one of which was the room where Tyler was confined. He had carefully counted the doors, knew it was the second one from the end.

He proceeded cautiously now, fully aware that there must be some sort of trap here for the intruder. In front of Tyler's door he paused a moment, then, standing to one side of the door, he touched the knob with his thumb and index finger, and turned it gently.

His caution saved his life.

For from a cunningly concealed hole in the center of the knob, there catapulted a small needle. A spring had ejected the needle with tremendous force. Anybody seizing the knob to turn it in the natural manner would have received the needle in the palm of his hand. As it was, the needle fell harmlessly to the floor. Fannon picked it up, and his lips set in a grim line as he noted that the tip of the needle was coated with a brownish substance. Probably a deadly poison.

But he was given no time for cogitation. For the turning of that knob had done something else besides eject that needle; it had set off some sort of alarm; for somewhere in the maze of passages, a bell began to ring with clangorous insistence. Fannon realized that he was trapped. So clever a man as the Skull would not have left doors unguarded without setting a trap of some kind for the unwary.

Without trying to get into Tyler's room, Fannon darted down to the end of the passage, toward the sliding panel he had come through. Quickly he inserted the key, watched the panel slide away underneath the dim electric bulb directly above it. The panel opened, and Fannon started to step through it, then stopped suddenly, halfway across. For on the other side stood Rufe, grinning evilly, a heavy revolver leveled at his heart.

"Lift up your hands!" Rufe grated. "High! Over your head!"

Fannon hesitated, but Rufe thrust the gun forward, finger tense on the trigger, lips snarling.

Fannon raised his hands, stood still.

Rufe taunted him. "I figured there was something phony about you, *Mister* Fannon! If you was really Frank Fannon, you would of recognized me as the guy that did a job with you ten years ago. But I thought maybe your time in stir kinda ruined your memory. Now I know different. Won't the Skull be glad to find out that Mister Fannon is—Secret Agent 'X!'"[1]

---

1 AUTHOR'S NOTE: *The man who is known as Secret Agent "X" needs no introduction to the regular readers of this magazine. His masterful impersonation of Fannon is only another evidence of the superb skill in disguise that he is master of, indicates fully how he acquired the nickname of "The Man of a Thousand Faces." In his constant battle with crime, he has risked his life on numerous occasions, and, just as in this case, if he met death his body would rot, forgotten in some unknown grave, where it would not even be claimed by the government which, unofficially, made frequent use of his services. How he managed to substitute himself for Fannon will be seen in the next chapter.*

CHAPTER III

THE MYSTERIOUS MR. POND

THE CASE OF Ainsworth Clegg, mentioned by Secret Agent "X," posing as Fannon, in his interview with the Skull, had stirred the city as it had seldom been stirred before.

Clegg was an extremely wealthy man, the Chairman of the Board of Paramount Oil. His kidnaping by the Servants of the Skull had been an audacious bit of business in itself, taking place in broad daylight right in front of the Paramount Oil Building on Broad Street. Clegg, a man in his early fifties, was descending from his automobile at ten A. M.

The chauffeur was holding the door for him, when three cars drove into the street, stopping one in front, one behind, and one double-parked alongside Clegg's limousine, thus blocking it off from view on three sides. From these cars there erupted a score of men armed with machine guns. They did not threaten; they acted.

Two of the gunners raked the street in both directions, clearing it of living beings. Twenty people were killed by that fusillade. Other men struck down the chauffeur, while four of their number seized Clegg and bundled him into the double-parked car.

Then the horde of criminals leaped back into the automobiles and sped away, delivering a parting volley at a radio car that just turned into the street. The radio car was wrecked, the two policemen in it killed.

Pursuit picked them up within three minutes, but the cars separated. Each one was followed for a while, but a strange thing happened in each case. At one point in the chase, each of the cars seemed to have disappeared from the face of the earth. One minute they had turned a corner, and the next minute, when the pursuers had come around the same corner, the quarry was gone.

The police conducted a thorough search of the streets where

*"For God's sake, save me!"
he managed to gasp.*

the disappearance had taken place, but with no success. It seemed as if some mighty power of magic had waved a wand and caused the cars, with their vicious occupants and their prisoner, to vanish into thin air.

The hue and cry was tremendous. But the next day it increased in intensity when there was delivered by mail at police headquarters an envelope containing nothing but a single card. On one side of this card was the picture of a Skull. On the other side was a message; a message so preposterous in its demands that it must have been written by a madman. It required that the sum of four million dollars in gold be raised by midnight the same day, as ransom for Clegg. It made no threats, merely contained the one sentence. And it was signed—The Skull.

The newspapers printed an appeal that afternoon, from Clegg's family, addressed to the Skull, stating that it was a physical impossibility to raise four million dollars by midnight, let alone in gold. It appealed to the Skull to set a more moderate ransom, one that it would be possible to pay. Not even a millionaire, the notice stated, could pay four million dollars, or even one million. People just didn't keep their assets in liquid cash.

It was hoped that there would be some response to this appeal, some sort of word from the kidnapers. To the consternation of Clegg's family and business associates, not a word was forthcoming. For one week they waited in anxiety and dread, until the day that Mr. Elisha Pond found Ainsworth Clegg in the street.

MR. ELISHA POND, whose means no one questioned, was himself a rather mysterious personage, whose goings and comings had long ago become the despair of society matrons. For months at a time he might not be heard from at all, and then, with no notice of his coming, he would drop into the Bankers' Club and spend a few hours with a particular group of men who usually congregated there after dinner. Among these were Pelham Grier, the stock broker, Jonathan Jewett, head of one of the largest insurance companies in America, and Commissioner Foster, at present head of the police department.

Subsequently, Mr. Pond might be seen around town for as much as a month at a time, or else he might drop out of sight again the very next day. He had long been an enigma to his friends, and they had given up speculating as to what he did with his unaccounted for time.

Mr. Pond first saw Ainsworth Clegg as he was crossing the street on the way to the club. He was standing listlessly on one of the crosswalks of the subway construction job that had caused the whole street and many others in the vicinity to be ripped up for many months now.

At first Mr. Pond thought the man was a beggar, from his dejected attitude. But a closer inspection showed that here was something far different from a casual mendicant. The man's eyes were vacant. He seemed to have no control over his muscles; for his jaw hung open.

The man's whole frame seemed to sag and shake, as if he were an automaton without any guiding control. He was resting against the railing of the crosswalk, and seemed on the point of slipping underneath the railing into the deep subway cut below.

Pond reached out a supporting hand, helped him across the street to the opposite sidewalk. The man did not walk, he shuffled. Apparently he had not enough muscular control of his body to lift his feet. Once across, Mr. Pond said to him, "You should be in a hospital. Do you want to be taken to one?"

His only answer was a vacant stare from eyes that seemed devoid of human intelligence. Pond himself was a graduate of a recognized medical college, had, in fact, at one time practiced medicine. But he was at a loss to diagnose the cause of this man's condition. And then, as he gazed more carefully at the man's countenance, he stiffened, and allowed a little gasp of amazement to escape his lips. For he recognized in this broken hulk of a man devoid of human intelligence, the once brilliant, masterful business executive, Ainsworth Clegg, Chairman of the Board of Paramount Oil.

IT was, perhaps, three quarters of an hour later that Mr. Elisha Pond sat with a group of six other distinguished gentlemen in a corner of the Bankers' Club.

Pond had brought the hulk of Ainsworth Clegg into the staff physician's room at the club, where he had been carefully examined without discovering what had caused his condition. Commissioner Foster had been at the club, and he had arranged for Clegg to be removed to a hospital without making his return known to the general public.

Now, the group of men was seriously discussing the problem. Arnold Hilary, the newspaper publisher, shifted uneasily in his seat. "Suppose," he muttered, "that this Skull, as he calls himself, should take a notion to snatch all of us who are here. What would stop him?"

Commissioner Foster, who sat next to Pond, clenched a fist and brought it down on his own knee with such vehemence that he winced. "Damn it, nothing would stop him—that's the rub! I've got every available man out, trying to pick up a lead. We place the guards on those men who might be marked as possible victims. And what happens?" He paused, and glared around at the circle of friends. "This Skull snatches them right out from under our noses! And he leaves his damned card, too! But we'll get—I swear we'll get him if I have to appoint every citizen of the city a special officer!"

Pelham Grier, the stockbroker, big, portly, red-faced, chewed a cigar thoughtfully. "Even at that, Foster, you might be appointing the Skull himself a special officer. You admit that you haven't got the faintest notion who he is. Can't you even make a guess as to his identity?"

Pond looked from one to the other. These men, titans of finance and business, were like little children when faced by a situation such as this, indulging in idle threats and guesses when there was serious work to do. Harrison Dennett, the construction man, ventured to say, "Maybe it's this criminal that's known as Secret Agent 'X.' I understand he's been able to outsmart the police every time." He cast a malicious sideglance at Foster.

The commissioner shook his head. "This Secret Agent 'X' may be a criminal. In fact, if I should lay my hands on him he'd be sent away for the rest of his natural life, and then some. But I'll say this for him—I've never known him to kill."

Dennett shuddered. "I should never have taken that subway job. It's been hoodooed from the very beginning. Four men were killed on the job in the first month, and the whole crew went on strike. They said there was a jinx around, and I almost believed them. Those four casualties happened in very peculiar ways. The rest of the men wouldn't go back to work, so I had to hire help in Philadelphia and pay their fare in. Now, Clegg is found right outside the job. I bet the men get scared again, and quit on me. I'll lose my shirt on that job!"

Dennett looked defiantly from one to the other. "There's been sabotage on that contract ever since I got the award. It almost seems as if some one is deliberately trying to ruin me so he can take the job away from me. But I tell you all right now—" his chin jutted obstinately "—I don't give up easy!"

Jonathan Jewett, the gaunt, hard-headed president of the Northern Continent Insurance Company, who had sat silent through the conversation so far, said to Dennett in a manner strangely kindly for so forbidding an old man, "I understand that you're strapped for money on account of all these delays. Why don't you stop in to see me some time at the office? I may be able to work out a program where the Northern Continent could lend you sufficient on a bond issue to pull through."

"Yes," said Dennett bitterly. "And then the Northern Continent would own the job. I'd be out in the cold." He forced a smile. "I like you personally, Jewett, but you drive a hard bargain. No, thanks. I'll try to pull through without mortgaging my soul to you!"

JEWETT shrugged. "As you please, Dennett. But remember, I offered to help."

The remaining two members of the group had listened with rapt interest. They were Pierre Laurens, proprietor of the largest jewelry store in the city, and Arnold Hilary, publisher of the *Herald*.

Pond, observing all of them, noted that Hilary seemed strangely nervous, while Laurens, a thin dark, lean-jawed man slightly under medium height, was quite at ease. It was Laurens whose jewelry store had been raided by the Servants of the Skull recently, and a fortune in stones taken.

Mr. Pond leaned forward. "Perhaps you have noted," he said, "that all the crimes that have been committed by this Skull have the earmarks of perfect workmanship. Take the robbery of your store, for instance, Laurens. It was perfectly timed with the time lock, was it not?"

Laurens nodded. "Not only that. In addition to the time lock I had an inner door on the safe that was supposed to be proof against dynamite. Well, one of those men knelt before the safe and twirled the dials, listening for the tumblers to drop. I had thought it was impossible to open a modern safe that way, but I saw it with my own eyes. That man opened the inner door inside of ten minutes while those ruffians held everybody at bay with machine guns, and practically took possession of the street outside!"

Commissioner Foster hitched forward in his seat. "Look here," he said. "I've a damn good idea as to who that man was that opened the safe. Tell you why." He stopped, took a drink from the long glass at his elbow, while the others waited eagerly. "There are only two men in the country could open a safe like that. One of them is Frank Fannon, who is coming out of jail tomorrow; the other is Ben Tyler.

"Naturally, it couldn't have been Fannon, since he won't be released till tomorrow morning. That leaves Tyler. Now, as to Tyler—he came out of jail three weeks ago. For a while we knew where he was, then he suddenly disappeared. Two days later, Laurens was robbed. I tell you, this Skull is recruiting criminals, experts in their line, from the underworld. He is building up an organization that it will be impossible for us to break up if we let it grow any longer."

He looked down his nose at the glass he held in his hand, then added as an afterthought, "I wish I could somehow get in touch with this Secret Agent 'X'—unofficially, of course. I'd sick him onto the Skull. He's the only one with brains enough to make it an even battle; and if they destroyed each other, I wouldn't feel too bad!"

Elisha Pond had suddenly become very thoughtful. "This Frank Fannon," he asked. "I am interested in the name. What jail is he coming out of tomorrow?"

"Folsom. He's finishing up a federal stretch for robbing a post office."

"I see," said Mr. Pond.

CHAPTER IV

ROAD OF PERIL

THE MAN WHO was known at the Bankers' Club as Elisha Pond had many unusual resources at his command, and he made brilliant use of them. It is, therefore, not surprising that when he drove up to the gates of Folsom Penitentiary the next morning, he in no wise resembled the clubman of the evening before.

His car bore on the radiator the insignia of the United States Army. His driver was a red-haired young man in military uniform, who was known in his usual haunts as Jim Hobart.[2] At this time, Jim Hobart was arrayed in chauffeur's habiliments, and played the part to perfection.

Mr. Pond himself was dressed in the snappy whipcord of a lieutenant colonel of the United States Intelligence Service,[3] a uniform to which, by the way, he was entitled.

As he swaggered up the steps of the administration building,

---

2   AUTHOR'S NOTE: *Readers of previous chronicles will recall that Jim Hobart is the young ex-patrolman whom Secret Agent "X" befriended, and employed as one of his agents. Jim, it will be recalled, had been the victim of an unjust frame-up, had been dismissed from the force, and subsequently taken in hand by the Agent who knew the circumstances of the case and was convinced of his innocence.*

3   AUTHOR'S NOTE: *As has been mentioned in other stories, Secret Agent "X" spent several years during the World War in the United States Intelligence Service, where the brilliant feats which he accomplished earned him recognition in the highest places. As a result of his Intelligence career, ten of the wealthiest men in the country were induced to place on deposit to his account, under the name of Elisha Pond, in the First National Bank, an unlimited credit which is replenished as he uses it, and for which he is never asked to account. He does not know the names of these men, nor do they know his true name. The only stipulation is that he use his courage, his wide knowledge, and the resources which have been placed at his command, to fight crime wherever it appears. Only one man in Washington knows his true identity, and that man does not even know how the Secret Agent operates. He can only tell that "X" has been on a case by reading the results in the papers.*

and then into the warden's office, he looked for all the world like a grumpy old martinet of sixty who had been soured by a lifetime of military service.

In the warden's office he deposited his cap and swagger stick on the desk, and introduced himself. "Lieutenant Colonel Delevan, U. S. Intelligence Service, sir. I am here in connection with a prisoner by the name of Frank Fannon who is being released this morning."

The warden shook hands with him respectfully, asked in a puzzled manner, "Fannon? What can the Intelligence Service have to do with him? Of course," he added hastily, "I shall be glad to assist you—"

"Naturally, sir." The colonel produced a folded document which he neglected to open, merely holding it up in the air. "I have here a warrant of arrest for Fannon, sir. It has come to our attention that Fannon was connected with an international spy ring, and it becomes my duty to take him to Washington for questioning. Will you be good enough to see that he is turned over to me upon his discharge?"

The warden was surprised, but far from suspicious. "Of course, colonel. Fannon is almost ready now. I will go myself and bring him here. If you don't mind waiting—"

"Not at all, sir. And thank you for your cooperation."

When the colonel was left alone, he stepped to the window which overlooked the driveway outside. Jim Hobart stood beside the sedan in which they had come. He saw the colonel, nodded imperceptibly, and jerked his head toward the gate. The colonel glanced in that direction, and tensed.

Just outside the gate was a long, black, closed car. It had every appearance of hidden power, and seemed to be waiting for some one. The colonel inspected it for a long time, trying to pierce the gloom of its interior through the closed windows with his keen eyes. Satisfied finally, he turned away from the window without looking again at Jim Hobart.

IN another moment the door opened and the warden entered with the prisoner, Frank Fannon. Fannon was tall, thin, his hair graying at the temples. Prison life had embittered him, as indicated by the grim twist of his lips.

The warden said, "Here he is, colonel."

Colonel Delevan said pompously, "Fannon, I hereby place you under military arrest. You will come with me." At the same time he drew his heavy service revolver from the holster at his side, and covered the prisoner.

Fannon was surprised and angry. "Military arrest!" he exclaimed. "What for? I've been out of the army for fifteen years!"

"You will be duly informed of the charges against you after you have been questioned, and before the court-martial. Now, about face and march!"

"You're crazy!" Fannon snarled. "I won't go. It's a frame of some kind!"

The warden was about to say something when Colonel Delevan raised a hand. "If you will leave me alone for a moment with this prisoner, sir, I believe I can show him the folly of resisting an officer of the United States Army."

"Of course, of course," the warden mumbled, and went out of the room looking very puzzled.

As soon as they were alone, the colonel stepped close to Fannon, spoke very low. "You fool! Do you want to queer the whole business? Play up to me!"

Suddenly Fannon's defiant expression gave way to one of understanding. He exclaimed, "I get you. You're from the Skull! I didn't know you'd go to such lengths—"

"Never mind what you didn't know. You are going to learn a lot that you never knew before. Now, let's go."

"Sure, sure," Fannon said. "I'm sorry I didn't understand. I thought the arrangement was that the Skull was going to have a private car waiting for me at the gate."

As they left the room, the colonel's eyes lighted with triumph. His suspicions about that black car were being verified. He showed nothing of his elation, however, merely said, "Plans often have to be changed."

They met the warden in the hall. The colonel said to him, "Fannon realizes now that it is futile to offer resistance. Thank you again, sir, for your cooperation."

"Not at all, colonel. I'm always glad to be of assistance." The warden accompanied them to the main door, watched them get into the sedan, the colonel still holding his revolver in plain sight. To anyone watching the scene from that black car at the gate, it was evident that Fannon was being arrested and taken away.

Jim Hobart got behind the wheel, and without a word of instruction, turned the sedan around, drove through the gate. As they passed the black car, Fannon noted it and said, "Look, there's the car that was supposed to pick me up. I was told it would have a letter 'S' monogrammed on the door."

The colonel did not answer him, but sat silently while Jim Hobart increased their speed until they were doing seventy-five. After another minute or two, Jim glanced in the rear vision mirror, said over his shoulder, "They're following us, sir."

The colonel smiled in satisfaction. "That's fine." He holstered his revolver and took from a hip pocket a peculiarly shaped gun.[4]

Fannon's eyes widened in sudden apprehension as the colonel raised the gun and fired it full in his face. He had no time to utter the frantic protest that rose to his lips, for the gas took immediate effect, and he slumped in the seat, unconscious.

The colonel immediately opened the windows to allow the fumes to escape.

"Now," he said crisply to Jim, "raise your rear vision mirror so you can't look in back here. And don't turn around!"

Jim did as directed. "I won't look, sir," he said. "Those are the orders that Mr. Martin gave me when he sent me on this job."[5] He drove at the same swift pace as before, with his eyes straight ahead.

And then the colonel began to work with a smooth efficiency that would have astonished any one who beheld him. At frequent intervals he glanced through the rear window at the pursuing car. The speed with which they were traveling made it impossible for the black car to close up the distance between them.

In no time at all the colonel had removed his own uniform and donned the clothing of the unconscious Fannon. Then he opened a box that had lain in the bottom of the sedan, and set up on the seat

---

4   AUTHOR'S NOTE: *It is well known, as evidenced by the comment of the police commissioner, that Secret Agent "X" never kills when he can help it. Since it often becomes necessary for him to defend himself, he carries the gas gun which he used here. It contains a highly volatile anaesthetic gas which renders a man unconscious with lightning speed, but has no harmful effects.*

5   AUTHOR'S NOTE: *As has been explained in previous books, Secret Agent "X" never showed his true face, or disclosed his true identity, even to those he trusted the most. This was not so much that he was afraid of his judgment, which had never gone wrong in a matter involving human nature, as that he did not want them to be in a position where they could be compelled to divulge information by means of inhuman torture. Thus, when he hired Jim Hobart, he did it under the guise of A. J. Martin, an Associated Press correspondent. In this case, acting as Martin, he had merely directed Jim to place himself under the orders of Colonel Delevan. and not to be curious as to who Colonel Delevan really was.*

a collapsible mirror. The box contained pigments, paints, plastic material, mouth and nose plates; in fact everything that was needed for a consummate artist to create a perfect disguise.

THE colonel removed his own wig of gray hair and substituted for it one which he had previously prepared and which exactly matched Fannon's hair. Then he removed the make-up from his own face, revealing for an instant the firm, masterful, though almost boyish, features that no one in the world could boast of having seen—the features of that man of mystery, that man of a thousand faces, Secret Agent "X."

Then his fingers went to work, building up ridges, contours of cheek bones, changing the shape and length of teeth by means of caps, not passing over the slightest detail of Fannon's physiognomy.

If Jim Hobart had disobeyed orders and cast his eyes behind him for one second as he drove, he would have been amazed at the miraculous transformation that was taking place in the back of the sedan.

Within twelve minutes of the time he had begun, Secret Agent "X" sat up in the rear seat beside the body of Fannon, after putting away the make-up box and mirror.

He tested his throat muscles for a moment, then said, "All right, Jim, you can lower the rear vision mirror."

Jim Hobart started perceptibly, and gasped. For the voice that had just uttered those words had been the voice of the ex-convict, Frank Fannon. Every inflection, every modulation of tone, had been faithfully duplicated.

Quickly, Jim lowered the mirror, looked into it. And he clawed for the emergency brake even as his other hand deserted the wheel to reach his gun. For he was startled to see Frank Fannon sitting there behind him, smiling.

But "X" quieted him by speaking once more in Colonel Delevan's old voice. "It's all right, Hobart. Fannon is right here—still unconscious."

Jim breathed a sigh of relief that was mingled with wonder.

"I—I didn't know a thing like that could be done," he stammered. "I—I've heard of such impersonations, but I never believed them."

"Never mind about that now," the Secret Agent said crisply. "Listen carefully to what you must do now." He glanced back at the black car ploughing on behind them. "In a couple of minutes you

Rufe went into the air, over "X's" shoulder. At the same time a gun barked behind them.

will slow up to give our friends a chance to come closer to us. When you are down to about fifteen miles, I will open the door and leap out to the side of the road, taking my revolver. You will then stop, and fire at me—but be sure to miss." He chuckled. "You think you can shoot well enough to miss me?"

Jim grinned. "I think so, sir."

"All right. I will fire back at you, and you will act as if you were wounded. According to my plans, the next thing that should happen is that our friends in the black car will storm up and attack you. When they do, you must give your car all the gas she can take, and drive away from here. Is everything plain?"

"I've got it, sir," said Jim,

"Fine. You will drive to the abandoned farmhouse that I showed you on the way up, take Fannon in, and hide the car in the barn. You will keep Fannon a prisoner there, not letting him out, *and not letting him be seen by a soul!* Remember that. If he should be seen, my life might be placed in deadly danger. Do you understand?"

"I do, sir, and you can depend on me."

"Very well then. Let's go!"

The thing could not have gone off more smoothly if it had been rehearsed. When "X" leaped from the car, sprawling in the road and firing in Jim Hobart's direction, the pursuing sedan, with the letter "S" monogrammed on the door speeded up; and from it there came a fusillade that would have blasted the pretended army car into a burning wreck if it had not been built of bullet-proof steel and glass.

Jim Hobart, after sending a couple of shots backward, stepped on the accelerator and left the scene in a spurt of speed.

The Skull's car did not pursue him farther, but stopped to pick up the man they thought was Fannon. So well did "X" act that the four men in that car were completely taken in. They congratulated him on his daring escape, and looked on him with new respect when he told them that he had killed the colonel who was arresting him.

They took him to the headquarters of their master, the Skull, where we saw him conducted, blindfolded, into the main room by Binks, then later, interviewed by the Skull; and subsequently, after making a daring attempt to reach Tyler, trapped in the corridor by Rufe Linson, the Skull's second in command.

Now, as he stood with his hands in the air under the menacing muzzle of Rufe's gun, it seemed as if all the trouble he had taken to work his way in here had gone for nothing.

RUFE licked his lips in triumph. "The Skull will be here in a minute. And then you'll wish you was dead—the way Tyler does!"

"X" said nothing. His hands were in the air, his ears keenly attuned for any sounds coming from the corridor behind him where he knew the Skull's room was located. And suddenly he smiled grimly. For his fingers, high in the air, had transmitted a message to his brain—a message of hope and escape!

His hands, raised high above his head, had come in contact with the dim electric light bulb on his side of the doorway. Rufe could not see the bulb, for he was standing on the other side.

Slowly, "X" began to turn the bulb in its socket, listening for sound. And then it came—a door opening down the end of the passage, behind him.

Rufe said, "Here comes some one. That'll be Binks."

At the same time "X" gave the last turn to the bulb, tore it out of the socket. The corridor was plunged in darkness.

Rufe shouted angrily, but his voice was drowned by the crash of the bulb, which "X" had dashed on the floor. From behind the Agent came a muttered oath in the voice of Binks.

"X" reached out, met Rufe's gun arm. Rufe's fingers were just contracting on the trigger when "X" seized his hand, jerked it up. The gun exploded into the ceiling. Behind them came the sound of running feet.

Rufe clinched with "X," at the same time shouting, "Don't shoot, Binks! I got him!"

The Secret Agent bent his knees, seized Rufe by the legs, and heaved.

Rufe went into the air, over "X's" shoulder. At the same time a gun barked behind them. Rufe's body was just coming down behind "X" when the shots sounded; "X" sprang through the opening in the wall, inserted the metal key in the slot. The panel started to close.

Rufe's voice came from the floor, in a bubbling groan. "Damn you, you halfwit! You got me instead o' him. I'm—dying!"

Binks' cackling tones demanded, "Who was it, Rufe? It's too bad yore dyin', but you ought to thank me. The Skull'd fry you for missin' up like this, an' lettin' him git away. Who was it?" Rufe's only answer was a weak groan.

The panel slid shut with a click. "X" was left on the other side, not knowing whether Rufe had lived long enough to utter his name, or not. He shrugged. The chance had to be taken. He twisted the metal key in the slot until it jammed there. The panel wouldn't open now without trouble.

Then he silently made his way along the corridor to the concealed elevator, and down to the passage below. The alarm hadn't spread to this part—the walls were apparently sound-proof. "X" encountered no one on his return trip to the main room. He stopped long enough to remove the piece of leather he had jammed into the lock, then stole into the dormitory after shutting the door. The men were all asleep. He crept into bed silently, composed himself in an attitude of slumber. Some one would surely be down soon to check on them.

He turned on his left side, so he could watch the door out of half closed lids. Soon the outer door opened, padded footsteps sounded, and Binks entered. "X" closed his eyes, pretended to breathe stertorously. He heard Binks prowling about the room, felt more at ease; if Rufe had uttered his name, Binks wouldn't be prowling—he would have reported to the Skull.

Binks had stopped at the outer door as he came in to examine the lock. "X" reflected that Binks could not be imbecilic as he looked, if he was cagey enough to have surmised that the lock might have been jammed in some fashion.

Binks wandered from cot to cot, stopping at each for a moment. "X" wondered what he was doing. Soon he discovered. The halfwit had paused at Nate Frisch's cot, next to his, then he came over to stand beside him. He risked opening one eye, and saw that Binks was feeling his clothes.

It was clever—too clever for Binks. He must be acting on instructions from the Skull. "X" was glad that he had not donned his clothes when he went out; for the clothes would still retain the warmth from his body, thus betraying him.

The halfwit went through "X's" pockets, finding nothing. Finally, he uttered a harsh, discordant laugh, and stepped over to Frisch's cot, shook him roughly until he awoke. He said, "Wake up, Frisch, the Skull wants to see you!"

Frisch didn't answer for a moment. He was still full of sleep. Then, as he realized what the message might mean, he stammered in abject fear, "W-what's he want of me? I told you I didn't mean nothin' by talkin' to Fannon. For God's sake—"

Binks interrupted him, cackling wickedly. "It ain't about that; it's somethin' else. If you got a coin fer me, maybe I could tell you what."

"Here," Nate exclaimed, pressing a coin into his hand that he took from his trousers pocket. "What is it?"

"I'll tell you," said Binks. "You're goin' to be the Skull's new second in command. Rufe Linson just kicked off!"

Several of the men were awake by this time, and "X" thought it safe to do the same. He sat up with a pretense of rubbing his eyes, yawning widely. He turned around, saw Nate dressing hastily, and then looked up to see Binks grinning down at him.

He said, "Hello, there. What's up?"

Nate said, "What d'ya know? Rufe's had somethin' happen to him, an' I'm gonna take his place. I never expected nothin' like that!" He looked up at Binks, suddenly suspicious. "You ain't stringin' me, Binks, are you? What you said is right?"

Binks shrugged. The action was weird, for it raised his deformed shoulder higher than ever, making him look like a grotesque caricature of some evil god. "I'm only tellin' you what the Skull told me."

Nate finished dressing, and they started to go out. At the doorway, Binks turned, surveyed the room with a sardonic grin. Then his eyes came to rest on "X" and there was a wicked twinkle in them. "Did you sleep well your first night, Mr. Fannon?"

"X" nodded. "Pretty good—till you came in and woke me up."

"That's fine, that's fine!" said Binks, rubbing his hands. "Some people are troubled with sleepwalking. You ain't troubled with that, are you, Mr. Fannon?"

"What do you mean?" "X" sat up, rigid.

"Oh, nothing. Nothing at all. I just thought you mighta been having some dreams—about sliding panels an' so forth!"

The door closed on Binks' evilly grinning face.

CHAPTER V

CHAMBER OF DREAD

THE MEN IN the room engaged in some low-voiced, desultory conversation, then began to drop off to sleep. "X" remained awake for a short while after the last of them had begun to snore. Then he finally went to sleep.

He awoke in the morning, washed and dressed with the men, and went with them into the main room where they sat around waiting to be conducted to breakfast. The room was still lit by the dim bulbs. The only way they had of telling it was morning was the muted gong that rang somewhere in the place; for no natural light came into the room. The windows were all closely shuttered, airtight and light-proof. Over each window was stretched a fine wire mesh, and when "X" approached one of the windows he saw that there was a small card fastened on the mesh. It read:

> Do not try to penetrate the screen or open the windows. The shutters are of steel and are charged with a high voltage of electricity. To touch them means death!

After a short wait, the corridor door opened, and Binks entered. The halfwit avoided looking at "X." He announced, "Breakfast's ready, boys, come along. You better eat well—I hear there's plenty work on the books for today." He turned back to the door, leering.

They trooped out after him.

The dining room was reached by traversing an entirely different set of corridors, in the other direction from the concealed elevator. "X" was compelled to admit that the Skull made his men as comfortable as possible in their enforced confinement.

There were ten tables, each set for four. Quiet-footed Jap waiters served them, anticipating their every need. "X" found himself seated at a table with Nate Frisch, a man named Elles, who had done several stretches for forgery, and a thin, dangerous-looking fellow whom Nate addressed as Gilly. Gilly, it developed, was an expert machine gunner, a former member of a nationally notorious bootleg gang in Chicago.

Nate was swelled up with his new importance. "I'm second in command now," he boasted. "I'll be gettin' two shares instead o' one. Believe me, boys, big doin's is scheduled."

Gilly, the gunner, appeared morose. "How come you was picked? There's better guys than you here."

Nate put down his knife and fork and glared at him. "You lay off that stuff, or I'll break your stinking neck. You better be careful how you talk to me from now on!"

"All right, all right," Gilly said quickly. "If the Skull picked you, I guess he knows what he's doing. I ain't lookin' fer any trouble."

"You bet he knows what he's doin'!" Nate growled. "The Skull said to me last night in that dark room, he says, 'I'm choosing you to take Rufe's place because I know you don't hesitate to kill. I need men like you.'"

A cackling voice behind him broke in. "Ha, ha! Tell 'em what else the Skull said to you, Nate." They turned to see Binks grinning at them. The halfwit came up close, his ugly, scarred face leering at Nate. "Tell 'em the rest of it, Nate."

Nate fidgeted in the chair. "Aw—"

Binks turned to the others. "You know what else the Skull said? He said to Nate, 'I'm also pickin' you because yore too dumb to try to double-cross me!' Too dumb! Ha, ha!"

An idea suddenly occurred to Nate. He pointed a finger at Binks. "How do you know what the Skull said? We was supposed to be alone in there!"

Binks only laughed again. "There's lots o' things I know about around this place. If I wanted to, I could hang the whole lot of you!" He came around the table, alongside "X." His teeth were bared in an ugly grimace. "Did you hear that, Mr. Fannon? Too dumb to doublecross him!" Binks, face came closer to "X." "Now you, Mister Fannon, you ain't dumb, are you?"

"X" looked at him impassively without replying. The halfwit did not wait for an answer, but walked away toward the kitchen.

WHEN they finished breakfast, Binks reappeared from the kitchen and led them out. "The Skull," he announced, "wants ev-

The gunman snarled, raised his gun.

erybody in the execution room this morning. There's gonna be a show put on, an' Tyler is the main actor. He'll squeal swell."

Binks waited till they had all passed out of the dining room, then closed the door, locking in the Jap waiters and cook. They, as the others, were prisoners.

The halfwit said to "X" as they went down the corridor, "Tyler is the guy I showed you last night; the guy whose place yore takin'. The Skull ain't got much luck with his safe men, has he?"

"X" frowned down at the ugly halfwit. "What do you mean?"

"Nothin', nothin'," Binks cackled, and hurried up ahead. He led them through a maze of passages, through which it would have been hopeless for anyone to try to find his way alone. Finally they reached a narrow, dark passage that sloped downward. This was very long, and as they proceeded it got darker and damper. The slope became sharper. "X" estimated that they must be at least a hundred feet below the street level.

The passage ended in a heavy barred door. Binks removed the bars, tugged at the door until it swung open. "Go on in, boys, go on in. I gotta tell the Skull that ever'thing is ready."

They filed past him into a room that was in utter darkness. Though it was impossible to see anything here, "X" estimated that it must be a room of tremendous size, for though there were over thirty men in the group, they weren't at all crowded. The heavy door slammed shut, with Binks on the outside, and "X" heard the iron bars being replaced.

The men shuffled, talked in low, nervous tones. "X" began to feel his way around the room, along the wall. He collided with one or two of the men, but they were not in the mood to fight. "X" knew that there would be some instrument here for inflicting death or worse upon Tyler, wondered if it was the same instrument that had turned Ainsworth Clegg into a mental and physical wreck. If possible, he wanted to save Tyler—not only out of any feeling of compassion, but because Tyler would be a well of information.

He worked his way to a corner in the dark, felt his way along the wall until he was stopped by what appeared to be another wire screen like the one on the windows upstairs. He followed this screen clear across the room, realizing that it divided the room in two parts.

Suddenly there was a muffled gasp from the assembled men. A dim red light had appeared on the other side of the screen. Looking through the mesh, "X" could see a niche in the far wall in the other half of the room. This niche was the size of a large man, and was about halfway up in the wall. Apparently there must be some way of entering it from outside, for it was too high for a man to reach it from the floor.

The thing that had made the men gasp was the figure in the

niche. It was the same vermilion-cloaked figure that "X" had met the night before, with the same hideously glowing skull in lieu of a face.

There was a low hum of fear-ridden voices which ended in abrupt silence as the Skull raised a vermilion-gloved hand. "Gentlemen," he said in a brittle, mocking voice, "before we proceed with the festivities, I have an announcement to make. Last night my lieutenant, Rufe Linson, met with an unfortunate accident. In his place I have appointed Nate Frisch, who will be in charge of expeditions in the future. When you are on the outside, his word will be supreme, as mine is here. The accident to Rufe is regrettable, and I am taking steps to punish the responsible party. However, I believe Nate Frisch will be able to fill the job satisfactorily."

The Skull raised his hand once more "Now, gentlemen, we will proceed."

Another light, bright and glaring, went on below the niche. It illuminated a ghastly sight. Tyler, the traitor, was strapped in a chair. It was not an ordinary chair, and he was not strapped there in the ordinary way.

THE other men on "X's" side of the wire mesh seemed to have known what to expect; but the Secret Agent, though in superb control of his nerves, barely restrained a gasp of horror.

For the chair was an exact replica of the electric chair at the state prison. And Tyler had metal electrodes strapped to his ankles, his wrists, and to the back of his neck. He was still stripped to the waist, and in spite of the straps that held him tight, he shook in a palsy of terror.

The red light in the niche went out, and the figure of the Skull was shrouded in darkness. But his voice came to them. "For the benefit of our new member I will explain that this is our method of punishment. It is a slight innovation on the legal method in use in our state prison, in that the victim is not killed. Our electrician has stepped down the current so that there is just enough to cause an intense shock to the nervous system, resulting in a paralysis of all the nerves, as well as a deadening of the brain cells."

He paused, then said, "Tyler! Do you understand what is going to happen to you?"

Tyler squirmed in the chair, tried to raise his eyes toward the niche. "For God's sake!" he babbled. "Don't do that to me! Anything! Anything! Kill me! But not that! Oh, God, save me!" His words lost themselves in a shrill scream of terror.

The Skull's brittle laughter floated down from above. "You call on God! I am God here!"

"X" thought he detected a note of insanity in the sonorous tones of the Skull. He felt a faint stir of eagerness ripple through the crowd of men in the room. They were getting ready to enjoy the spectacle.

Once more the Skull spoke from his niche. "Tyler! This is your last moment of sanity. I am about to throw the switch. This—is—your—end!"

Tyler strained against the straps, his throat working though no sound came from his lips.

From above came a blinding flash as the switch was thrown in. Tyler's body seemed to jerk in the chair. His hands spread out clawlike, spasmodically. Blood spurted from his nose. His mouth opened wide in a soundless scream, his eyes widened, almost popping from their sockets. His head was raised, his Adam's apple working frantically.

The Secret Agent had seen many gruesome sights in his career; he had seen men in Flanders who took ten hours to die, lying on the shell-pitted battlefields with their entrails squirming out of gaping wounds in their stomachs while they moaned continuously till they died. But the picture of Tyler as the current raced through his body, twisting him into horrid, incredible contortions, was one that rivaled any horror conceivable by man.

"X" shuddered in revulsion as a long sigh went up from the assembled men. They were enjoying each moment of Tyler's suffering. A long minute it lasted, while Tyler squirmed and strained in the chair.

And then it was over. The Skull must have pulled the switch, for suddenly Tyler's body relaxed, sagged in the chair. His head hung on his breast, but the quick, heavy breathing attested to the fact that he still lived.

"Tomorrow, gentlemen," the Skull said to them in the same steady voice, "Tyler will be able to get about again. His condition will no doubt be amusing to you. We will keep him around for you to play with for a day or two, then send him out into the street as a warning to those who defy the Skull!"

The light over the chair went out, leaving the room once more in utter darkness.

CHAPTER VI

DEVIL'S MISSION

A LOW MURMUR swept through the room as the men began to comment to each other on the scene they had just witnessed. Low, incoherent moans began to come from the other side of the mesh screen where Tyler was still strapped in the chair. "X" waited silently, bitterly. He could do nothing for Tyler, and now he would be unable to learn anything from him. The man's mind had been destroyed by the ordeal. Through the mind of Secret Agent "X" there flashed a picture of Ainsworth Clegg, one day a brilliant, shrewd businessman; and the next, a doddering idiot. Now it was clear how the man's condition had been brought about. If those men at the Bankers' Club—Dennett, Grier, Hilary, Jewett—could see this diabolical means by which Clegg had been robbed of his sanity, they would hardly credit their senses.

His thoughts were interrupted by the opening of the outer door. Binks, more horrible in appearance than ever, stood there. The light from the corridor cast an evil reflection on his vacuous, scarred countenance.

"All right, boys," he announced. "The show's over. All out." He cackled, "Ha, ha—just like a movie—all out. Ha, ha!"

He waited while the men filed out past him. Five of the men he tapped on the shoulder, whispered to. Those five men stayed in the room. Among them were Nate Frisch, and Gilly, the gunman. When the Secret Agent passed him, he tapped him on the shoulder, too. "Stay here till I take these boys back," he whispered. "Then I'll take you to the Skull. He wants to see you."

"X" nodded, waited with the others. Binks closed the door on them, leaving them in utter darkness once more. "X" debated the chances of breaking out of there. He wondered if those others had been told to guard him.

Soon the door opened once more, and Binks beckoned to them. Out in the corridor he said nothing to them, but led them through a new series of passages, to another anteroom similar to the one where Rufe had searched him.

Binks left him alone, going out through the side door, giving them a last leering grin.

While they waited, the men lit cigarettes, engaged in desultory conversation. Nate Frisch, though he had been appointed second in command, seemed to know as little about the reason for their presence there as the others. "Maybe it's a new job," he said. "The Skull has been planning something extra big for a long while."

Gelter, a coarse brute of a man, who had escaped from the state prison where he had been serving a life term for kidnaping, said, "If it's a snatch job, it's right up my alley. This is good stuff, pullin' jobs an' bein' able to disappear so the cops think you got magic or something!"

They relapsed into moody silence, watching the door opposite them—the door that had no handle. They were kept waiting a long time, so long that the Secret Agent began to think it was deliberately done for the purpose of increasing their nervousness. Finally there was a click and the door began to swing open, revealing an inner room without any lights. The men strained their eyes to pierce the gloom of that inner room, but without success.

When the door had opened wide, a voice from within, the voice of the Skull, called out, "Fannon and Gilly! Come in first."

Gilly looked apprehensively at the others, wet his lips and went in. "X" followed him. The door closed behind them, and clicked as the lock caught. "X" could hear Gilly breathing hard close beside him, could hear the little gunman's body shivering close to his own. But he also sensed another presence in the room—a sinister presence that seemed to exude an aura of evil.

A soft glow began to appear in the room, bathing it in a sort of dull, uncertain luminance. It was accomplished by a system of indirect lighting, of course, but the effect was uncanny.

As the light grew stronger, there became visible at the other side of the room, the figure of the Skull, seated at a desk, facing them. The glowing outline of the skeleton head grinned at them in weird, macabre brilliance.

Secret Agent "X" inspected the room through veiled eyes. It was a large room, perhaps twenty feet square, and absolutely bare except for the desk and the chair where the Skull was seated. The floor was of varnished hardwood except for a strip about four feet wide that ran clear across the middle, between the Skull and his visitors.

The Skull noted "X's" eyes inspecting the place, and said mockingly, "You seem to be interested in my layout here, Fannon. What do you think of it?"

"It strikes me," the Secret Agent answered, "that you have gone to a great deal of trouble to make this headquarters invulnerable. It looks as if you have built a permanent place here—secret panels, electric chair, a maze of passages. Is it all necessary?"

The Skull chuckled. "You have seen only a small portion of my arrangements here, Fannon. But I assure you that every bit of it is necessary, thoroughly planned. Think, for instance—you have been here a whole day; have you any idea where you are?

"Frankly, no," said "X," "I confess that I don't know whether we are above or below ground. I don't even know what portion of the city we are in. I can see that this place takes up a good deal of space, but I can't imagine where it could be."

THE Skull chuckled. "The location of this headquarters is nothing short of a stroke of genius, Fannon. And you see how efficient my other precautions are? No one of you can find his way out of here. No one of you can find his way back. Binks and I are the only ones who know the various ways in and out. If, by chance, one of you should be a traitor, he would never be able to lead the police here, because he knows as little as they."

The Skull turned to the little gunman, who had stood silent during the conversation. "What do you think of this set-up, Gilly?"

"Gee, boss," Gilly exclaimed, "you're a wonder! You certainly got things down pat!"

The Skull's voice suddenly became crisp. "X" felt that he was about to learn the real reason for his being there with Gilly.

"Fannon, I am going to send you out on a mission. Every new man must be tested."

"X" breathed easier. The Skull then was not sure that it had been he who had struggled with Rufe in the corridor last night. Perhaps Binks had not reported his suspicions; or perhaps Binks' manner had hinted of suspicions that did not exist in that quirked mind of his. In any event, it was a promise of action, and that was welcome.

The Skull went on. "Gilly will accompany you. Gilly is a very fast man with a gun, and he always goes out with new men. It is so easy for him to place a bullet accurately in the event that he smells treachery. You understand?"

"X" nodded.

Gilly broke in eagerly, "What's the job, boss?"

"You are going to open a safe. Fannon, who is an expert safe man, will do the opening, while you act as lookout"

"Suits me swell," said Gilly.

The Skull looked at "X." "And you?"

"X" nodded, dissembling his emotions. This was what he feared. Though he had made a study of many types of safes, though he had instruments and equipment in his various hideouts which would open any safe door, he certainly did not possess the great degree of skill which the real Fannon had developed in a lifetime of crime. He could not open a safe the way Fannon could, by listening to the fall of the tumblers. He must, in some way, get the use of his own tools. An accomplishment which seemed, on the face of it, impossible.

He said, "What kind of safe is this? Don't forget I've been in stir for five years, and I'm a little rusty. Five years is a long time to be out of practice."

THE Skull's vermilion-gloved hand waved impatiently. "I have allowed for all that. I chose this job with that in mind. The safe is an old model, and should be child's play for an old hand like you—rusty or not rusty."

"X" remained silent, thinking swiftly. There must be some way out of the dilemma. He started at the Skull's next words.

"It is the safe of a man named Harrison Dennett, in his home at number 363 Willow Street. He's the subway construction man. Have you heard of him?"

"X's" face showed no sign of recognition of the name. "We hardly hear about people like that in jail."

"That is true," the Skull said almost banteringly. "It *would* have been peculiar if you *had* heard of him, would it not? Now, as to the job. Dennett is much more than a mere construction man. He is a large scale real estate operator. But his wealth is tied up in real estate, and he has met with many—er—setbacks, on the subway job, so that he is very low on cash at this time. He has been offered loans from various sources, but on terms that would practically take the subway contract away from him."

"X's" mind raced back to that conversation at the Bankers' Club. Dennett had felt then that some one was placing obstacles in his path, trying to ease him out of the contract. It seemed, from the Skull's remarks, that Dennett's intuition had been correct. The Skull was planning another coup against the construction man.

The Skull went on. "Dennett has one source from which he can raise money without losing control of the subway contract. That is by pledging as collateral two matched pearls which he owns, and which are worth a cool half million dollars."

"X" had heard of those pearls, had actually seen them one day, when Harrison Dennett was showing them around at the club. They were a pair of gorgeous stones with a bloody history attached to them, dating back to Florentine times. No ordinary thief would have dared steal them, for they were well-known to connoisseurs of gems throughout the world, and would have been impossible to dispose of.

The Secret Agent listened closely as the Skull continued. "I have information that Dennett has arranged to secure a loan on these gems, that he has taken them out of his safe deposit box and put them in the safe at his home till tomorrow. I want those two pearls. You will open the safe and get them while Gilly watches for you."

Now it was out. There could be no doubt as to the Skull's intent. He wanted to deprive Dennett of the only hope of doing without a loan. And it was up to Secret Agent "X" to get those pearls. He must commit an act which would ruin Dennett in order to gain the confidence of this master of crime. And then came the next problem—how to open a safe. He was not a Fannon; he would need tools.

The Skull was saying, "It's a Roebler Safe Company box, series of 1927, model 42. You should be familiar with that model. It was in use before your—er—enforced retirement. The servants are taken care of for the night, and I have arranged it so that Dennett will be away. You will have a clear field. It shouldn't take you more than ten minutes."

"X" hesitated, then decided to make an effort to get hold of tools. Without them he faced defeat.

"I'm afraid it would take me much longer than that. The Roebler boxes are tough nuts. And my fingers are stiff. Maybe I ought to have some tools."

"Tools?" the Skull's voice carried an edge of sudden suspicion. "You don't want tools. This isn't a nitro job. You've got to use your head and your ears and your fingertips. Aren't those the tools of your trade?"

Gilly, who had been standing silent, snickered. "Tyler never used tools. An' I thought you was better than Tyler."

"X" snapped at him impatiently, "Tyler was in practice!" Then he turned toward the Skull. "Look here, boss, if you let me get a bag of tools I'll guarantee a hundred percent job. You've got to make allowances for me—the first job in five years."

"What kind of tools would you want?" the Skull asked. His voice was low, dangerous. "And where do you have to go to get them?"

"I have a friend in Chinatown from whom I used to borrow tools. I can get a full set from him in no time. He'd still remember me."

"Tell me what things you need, and I will see that you are supplied. There is no need for you to go to this friend in Chinatown."

"X" thought quickly. He wanted other things besides implements for opening a safe. He had come here bare of weapons, without any of the clever devices that had stood him in such good stead in the past. And lucky it was that he had done so, for the strict search to which he had been subjected would have revealed them, betrayed them.

Now he felt that in order to cope properly with the Skull, he must be properly equipped. Not only that, but the particular instrument he had in mind which might aid him in opening the safe in Dennett's house was one of his own devising, an instrument which could not be procured in any store. Its very possession would brand him in the eyes of the Skull as being more than an ordinary safe breaker, for it was a product of a high order of mechanical skill and scientific knowledge.

It was imperative that he gain permission to go for them himself.

"These are special instruments," he said. "My friend is the only one I know of who can supply them."

"All right," said the Skull. "Give me his address and I will send for them."

"He would never give them to anybody but me. I have to go myself. It would take less than a half hour."

"I wonder, Fannon," the Skull said softly, "if you really need these things, or if you are not scheming some way of escaping."

"X" concealed the sudden alarm he felt at the Skull's uncanny instinct. This man, whoever it was behind that ghastly fleshless mask, was far too fiendishly clever to be handled in any ordinary way. "X," keen student of psychology that he was, set himself to sell the Skull the idea of going for the tools. He assumed an appearance of hurt surprise at the motive imputed to him by the Skull.

"Why would I want to escape? Didn't I come here of my own free will in the first place? And then, even if I did escape, where would I go? I'm wanted for murder—for killing Colonel Delevan in the army car. You can't fool around with the government. They'd get me, all right, and I know it. I need you to protect me; I'd be crazy to try any stunts." He paused, then said eloquently, "All I want is a chance to make good."

And suddenly, surprisingly, the Skull capitulated. "All right, Fannon," he snapped. "You can go for them. But Gilly goes along—and at the least sign of treachery, Gilly will empty his gun into you. Is that clear, Gilly?"

"You bet, boss. Seven slugs in the guts!"

"X" was distrustful of the sudden change of mood in the Skull. Had he really been convinced by "X's" eloquence? The Agent doubted. The Skull was playing a deep game here, and it suited his plans to seem to acquiesce. There would no doubt be a trap somewhere along the line that would have to be met.

"X" asked, "What about Nate Frisch and those other men in the outside room? Are they coming with us?"

"No," said the Skull. "Hereafter you must learn that it is unwise to ask questions here. You will be told all you need to know. In this case, however, I was going to make an announcement to the other men after you left, so I will tell you now that I am sending Frisch on another mission of much more importance than yours."

He stopped a moment while Gilly fidgeted, and "X" waited impassively. "There is one obstacle in the path of my plans for the future. Nate Frisch and the others are going out to take steps to remove that obstacle. That is all I will tell you now. By the time Gilly and you return, I will be able to announce the successful completion of their mission, and to outline our future operations—which, by the way, will net us millions of dollars in profit and startle the city by its ingenuity!"

He raised his hand in a gesture of dismissal. "Go now. Get your tools. Then go to 363 Willow Street. The rear door will be unlocked, the house empty. Bring back the pearls. And remember, Fannon, I will accept no excuses, no excuses whatsoever! Failure is punished here severely, as you may guess. And nobody is allowed a second chance!"

THE door swung open, and "X" and Gilly passed out. From within, the Skull called out, "Nate Frisch! Bring those other men in!"

"X" and the little gunman watched them file into the darkened room. The Secret Agent wondered what mission they were being sent on. From what the Skull had said, it was one of paramount importance. The door without the handle started to swing shut. The Skull's voice came to them sepulchrally from the inner room. "Wait there, Fannon and Gilly, until Binks comes. He has his orders to lead you out, and will await your return."

The door clicked shut.

Gilly sprawled in a chair, lit a cigarette, and regarded "X" with narrow, sharp eyes. "I hope you don't try no tricks on this trip, Fannon. I'd hate to have to burn you down. You're a pretty smart guy, an' if you're on the square we'll get along fine."

"Have you ever wondered," the Secret Agent asked him, "who the Skull really is?"

Gilly shrugged. "Nope. I ain't interested as long as he takes care o' us, an' fixes the jobs so they're easy to pull. An' don't forget, it ain't healthy to wonder about things like that in here."

It was twenty minutes before Binks came in. He shuffled through the doorway from the corridor, still with that nasty leer on his face. Out of one pocket of his voluminous coat he produced a thirty-eight automatic, which he handed to Gilly together with a half dozen extra clips of ammunition.

"The Skull said to give you these."

Gilly took them, pocketed the clips, but fondled the automatic lovingly before putting it away. "X" could discern the killer's lust in his eyes.

"X" said to Binks, "How about me—don't I get a gun, too?"

Binks cackled harshly. "Not much, you don't! The Skull never trusts a new man with a gun till he's done at least one job. Gilly'll do all the shootin' you'll need on this trip!"

CHAPTER VII

THE MING TONG

FROM ONE OF his other pockets Binks produced two burlap hoods. Gilly seemed to know what they were for, for he took one and slipped it over his head. There was a slip knot at the bottom around his neck, which Binks tightened and knotted. Then he motioned to "X" to do the same.

"X" put the other hood on, felt Binks' finger jerking the cord tight. He could see nothing. The hood was a perfect blindfold. He felt Binks' fingers tying the knot, then heard Binks say:

"Here, take hold of Gilly's hand. I'll lead Gilly. Don't let go, 'cause if you ever get lost in these here passages you might easy get killed. The Skull's put lots o' traps around in here since last night."

Thus, hand in hand, they traversed an almost interminable series of passages, waiting while the halfwit manipulated sliding panels, opened hidden doors. The Secret Agent tried to memorize the many twists and turns they took, but after a while even his keen mind gave it up. The Skull had planned too well.

Once they went up in an elevator, and "X" estimated that it must have been four flights before they stopped. Once more they proceeded, with the hoods still on their heads. Now "X" sensed that they were passing through a series of rooms. His sharply attuned senses told him that these must be empty rooms, probably in some deserted building. The musty odor that pervaded here registered through his olfactory nerves in spite of the burlap hood.

They descended a creaking wooden staircase, crossed a bare wooden floor, and went down another set of stairs. Now they were in a cellar, "X" could tell. Once more they entered a series of passages. "X" judged that they must have come at least a half mile. He wondered at the thoroughness of the Skull in preparing this complicated means of egress, only to be further astonished when Binks drew back from up ahead.

"This is exit number three. When you come back we'll use another way."

"Number three!" he exclaimed. "How many are there?"

Binks chuckled. "That'd be tellin'. All I can say is, they's more'n six; that is, that I know of. Then maybe they's a couple the Skull ain't told me about."

At last they came to the end of the journey. They walked through a door that Binks held open for them, and "X" smelled fresh air. Binks said, "Now, let go hands. I'm gonna whirl you around." He took hold of "X", turned him around six or seven times, then said, "All right, you can take the hood off."

"X" fumbled with the string, got it off just as Binks was through doing the same for Gilly. Gilly took off his hood, blinked, and said, "Jeez! I never come out this way before!"

They were in a narrow alley between two large apartment houses. Each house had a service entrance on the alley, and "X" saw why Binks had whirled them around. The idea was to prevent their telling from which house they had come.

"All right, boys," Binks told them. "Go ahead an' do yore job. When yore through, you come to number 18 Slocum Street. That's a apartment house. You go through to the rear, an' you'll find a door in the fence. I'll be on the other side o' that door."

"Okay," said "X". "I'll remember the address—18 Slocum Street."

"What time'll you boys be done?"

"I don't know. I have to go to Chinatown and get my tools first. What time is it now?"

Gilly consulted a wrist watch. "Eleven."

"X" figured quickly. "I can't see my Chinese friend till noon. It'll take him about an hour to get the kit for me. Then the job itself shouldn't take more than a few minutes. Make it three o'clock."

Binks nodded. "Three o'clock is right. The other boys with Nate Frisch'll be back by one, an' that'll give me time to meet you. The Skull told me to tell you that the back door of that guy's house that you're goin' to is gonna be left open. He arranged it."

"He sure does things thoroughly," the Secret Agent remarked.

"I'll say he does," Gilly chimed in.

The two of them went out of the alley, leaving Binks behind. When "X" turned back at the mouth of the alley, the halfwit had already disappeared. There was no telling which of the two houses he had gone into. "X" gave up the idea of tricking Gilly, trussing him up and going back to trace his way into the Skull's headquarters. The Skull had taken too many precautions for that. The only other course open was to perform the job he had been assigned, and try to get into the good graces of the master criminal, try to discover enough about him to break up the gang.

THEY found themselves on a side street less than two blocks from the Bankers' Club. As they walked past it, "X" looked into the broad windows, saw Jonathan Jewett, the dyspeptic old insurance president, talking to Laurens, the jeweler, in a pair of easy chairs overlooking the street. He played with the thought of how they would react if they suddenly learned that one of the two men slinking along outside was Elisha Pond, their fellow club member.

Gilly said, "Where do we go from here, Fannon?"

"Let's get something to eat. We might as well, as long as we have the time."

Gilly laughed. "You got guts, Fannon. Here you are, wanted for murder, and here's me, wanted for murder an' plenty more, an' you wanna go in a public restaurant an' eat!"

"X" shrugged. "What of it? We have to eat. Come on, I'll show you how to get away with it."

He led the gunman a block west to where the subway job was under way. There were dozens of men at work here. Some of them were having their lunch in a coffee pot on the corner, and it was here that "X" led his companion.

"This is one place nobody'll look for us," he told Gilly. "Anyway, we'll take the chance."

Sitting next to a couple of laborers, they partook of a hearty lunch, and left.

Gilly looked at "X" with new respect. "I like a guy with guts," he said. "Just play square, an' we'll get along fine."

They took a cab down to Pell Street, and "X" wound his way through the tortuous streets, as if he had been born there.

"Jeez," Gilly wondered. "How come you remember these streets after being in the can for five years?"

"I used to come down here pretty often," the Agent told him. He stopped before a narrow, old brick building sandwiched in between a restaurant and a Chinese theatre. Unhesitatingly, he entered the dark hallway, started to climb the narrow, winding staircase. Gilly came close after him. "Say, Fannon," he wheezed, "what's this joint? What'd that sign say over the doorway?"

"I don't know," the Agent told, him. He could have told him if he had wanted to. The sign read, "Ming Tong."

The Ming Tong was the most powerful tong in America, numbering members all over the country. This was its headquarters.

At the head of the staircase, a tall, raw-boned Chinaman stood with his arms folded in front of him, hands in the voluminous sleeves of his jacket. He stood there impassively, blocking the stairs.

"X" knew that he had an automatic in each of the hands that were hidden.

He stopped when he was about three steps below the Chinaman, and Gilly brought up short behind him. Suddenly he felt Gilly's gun poking into his back.

"Look, Fannon," the gunman muttered, "I don't like this. If it's a trap for me, I'm gonna hand it to you right in the liver!"

"X" said irritably over his shoulder, "Don't be a sap, Gilly. This guy is a guard for my friend. My friend is a big man in Chinatown."

Gilly muttered something, but ceased his protests. He still kept his gun out, however.

"X" looked up at the big Chinaman and said, "Brother, I come in peace, seeking speech with Lo Mong Yung." He said this in fluent Cantonese, the sing-song syllables falling from his lips naturally, as if it were his native tongue.[6]

The Chinaman started perceptibly at the sound of his native tongue spoken so fluently, stared down trying to discern the features of the caller in the uncertain light that filtered in from outside.

Gilly exclaimed, "Jeez, Fannon, you sure can sling that lingo! Where—" He stopped as the Chinaman burst into speech, answering "X" in Cantonese.

"O stranger, who comes here calling my brother, I know not your face. There is only one white man in the world who has earned the

---

6   AUTHOR'S NOTE: Secret Agent "X" once confided to the author that many years of his early manhood were spent in the Far East. He has acquired a mastery of Oriental languages that few white men possess. His initiation into the Brotherhood of the Ming Tong took place after he had aided in the forlorn defense of one of their temples against a band of marauding soldiers under an unscrupulous warlord who was devastating the country. It was his ingenuity which saved the temple and earned him the right of brotherhood—for the first time in history accorded to a non-Chinese. The story of that episode may some day make interesting reading if the author can gather sufficient material on it.

right to be called brother by the men of the Ming Tong, and you are not he. What is your business?"

"X" said quietly, "Look not in my face, O Brother, search my heart and my speech. You say that there is only one white man who may be called your brother. I am that man!"

The Chinaman was skeptical. "O stranger, your words are false. What business have you with Lo Mong Yung, the venerable father of our tong?"

"X" was about to answer, when from an inner room further down on the floor, came the thin voice of an old man. His tone was low, just loud enough to be heard in the hall, but it carried a weight of authority that many a king might have envied. He said, "My old ears know that voice, Sung! Let him come!"

The big Chinaman stepped aside with alacrity, said, "Pass, stranger."

He allowed "X" to pass, but put out an arm to bar the way for Gilly. The gunman snarled, raised his gun.

"X" said quickly, "Let him come, Brother. He is a friend."

From within came the same thin voice of authority, "Let both pass, Sung!"

The big Chinaman glowered at Gilly, called back in Cantonese, "This second one, master, waves a gun, and snarls like a wild animal of the forest."

"Let both pass, Sung, but come behind them."

Sung stood aside, still glowering. "X" went down the hall toward an open door. He stepped inside a brightly lighted room, with Gilly close behind him, and with Sung right in back of Gilly.

Anyone who might have expected to find an orientally furnished room in these surroundings would have received a surprise. "X" knew this room, but Gilly, just behind him, whistled in amazement.

They were now in a completely equipped office. A row of filing cases stood along one wall. Near the door a stenographer was working industriously at a noiseless typewriter. She was a young Chinese girl, and it spoke well for her training that she did not even look up as the visitors entered, but continued with her work.

In the center of the room, at a large, glass-covered desk, sat a Chinaman who might have been ninety years old but for the keen restlessness of his eyes. His face was lined and creased with a thousand wrinkles, and the skin on the shrunken hands that rested on the glass top of the desk resembled yellow parchment. He said nothing, but watched the two visitors sharply.

"X" said, still in the flowing Cantonese that he had used in the hall, "Greetings, Father of the Ming Tong, from a lowly son and brother of the Ming Men!"

Lo Mong Yung remained silent for a long time, inspecting him critically, casting not a single glance at Gilly. Finally he said, "The voice I hear is one I know; yet the face of him who speaks is strange to me. I am an old man, and my eyes are prone to deceive me. But my ears are sharp, and recognize the voice of one who is a brother of the Ming Tong. You are—"

"X" held up his hand. "Let no names be spoken here. Your ears have told you the truth. But this one who is with me knows me by the name of Fannon, and it is the face of Fannon which you behold."

The old man nodded. "I hear and I believe. Yet one thing more. Step close to me, brother of the Ming Tong, and whisper that word which is known only to the Ming Men. Thus shall I be sure that you are he whose voice I hear."

"X" came forward slowly, bent low, and whispered close to the old man's ear. Lo Mong Yung's eyes lighted, and he nodded his head in satisfaction. "You are a master artist, my son. If you can thus confuse your friends, surely you will succeed in confusing your enemies. Now speak your needs. The tong is yours to command, for it is long in your debt."

Gilly stirred restlessly. "Say," he exclaimed suspiciously, "what the hell is all this chinky palaver about? Are you pullin' anything? If you are—"

"Take your time, Gilly," the Secret Agent growled. "I'm trying to talk him in to lending me a kit."

"If he don't want to, you tell me, an' I'll shoot the roof off this place. That's the way to treat Chinks!"

"It's all right. He's almost sold." As "X" turned back to Lo Mong Yung, he noted a humorous light in the old man's eyes.

"My son," he said, "I hear and understand what this one speaks of to you. It seems that he is an enemy. Do you want him removed? I have but to raise a hand to Sung, who is behind him, and the lowly vermin will no longer trouble your footsteps."

"NO, no," the Agent said hastily. "It is important to me that he shall remain alive. He is but a minor tool of the fiend whom I must overcome. But there is something that I would ask of you."

"It is granted, my son."

"At the Belleville Apartments on Twenty-third Street, resides a young lady who is known by the name of—" he paused, then spelled out, slowly and laboriously in Cantonese, an English name. The name he spelled was—B-e-t-t-y D-a-l-e.[7]

"I would ask you, Father," he continued, "to send there one of the tong brothers. Let him say to her that a certain friend of hers is sending for the bag of tools that is in the secret compartment of the closet in her bedroom. To prove to her that he is truly my messenger, let him tell her how that compartment is opened—by pressing upward on the shelf in the closet as one stands with his feet on the threshold. And then let him bring the bag of tools back here as quickly as he can, lest this one who is with me should become suspicious."

Lo Mong Yung nodded, raised his hand and spoke to the big Chinaman at the door. "You have heard, Sung. Go and tell one of the brothers to do this at once. Be sure to remember the name and address of the white lady on Twenty-third Street."

Sung bowed in a dignified manner, glowered at Gilly, and left the room.

"Now, my son, while you are waiting, you will have refreshments. My niece, Anna, will attend to your wants."

As if it had been a command, the girl who had been typewriting stopped her work, and arose from the desk. "If you will please to step this way, honorable sirs," she said in English, with a dainty hint of a lisp, "I shall be happy to serve you."

She led them into an alcove behind a screen at one end of the room. Here was a table beautifully inlaid, with richly lacquered chairs bearing upon their back, a coat-of-arms representing a dragon's head holding a man in its teeth. This was the insignia of the Ming Tong.

Gilly seated opposite "X," saying surlily, "What's the play now?

---

[7] AUTHOR'S NOTE: *The young lady whose name Secret Agent "X" mentions above is the daughter of a friend of the Agent's, a police captain who died in the performance of his duty, leaving Betty Dale an orphan. The Agent had befriended her, seen her secure an important position on the staff of the "Herald," and he often made use of her services. In her apartment was a bag similar to the ones he kept in all his retreats, containing a complete kit of the articles he found invaluable in his business. Since he could not go with Gilly to any of his retreats, he planned to ask his Chinese friends to send to Betty Dale's apartment to get that bag.*

What we waitin' for?" His suspicions had been lulled to the extent that he had put his gun away, but he was not thoroughly at ease.

The Secret Agent explained to him that it was necessary for his Chinese friend to send for the tools, as he did not keep them on the premises.

"How long'll it take?" Gilly demanded, munching one of the soft, buttery almond cakes that Anna had placed on the table.

"About a half hour. We might as well make ourselves comfortable." "X" lit a cigarette, drew a deep lungful and allowed the smoke to exhale slowly from his nostrils. Then he took a sip of tea from a transparent, blue, paper-thin china cup that Anna had placed before him. He was at home here, among friends. Under the name they knew him by, he was a welcome guest in any of the tong's headquarters throughout the country.

Gilly allowed himself to be beguiled by the tea and cakes, and shortly he was in a better humor. After the tea, the Chinese girl served them tiny glasses of a thick amber liquid, sweet and strong and heady. Gilly's eyes began to sparkle. "Boy!" he exclaimed. "This is the real McCoy. Talk about cordials! It's got 'em all beat!"

"X," too, relished the flavor of the drink. It was a cordial distilled in small quantities in China, from macerated poppy-seeds, coriander, and a mixture of rare herbs and perfumes. Nothing like it was available in the Western world because of the limited quantities in which it was produced.

As they were finishing a second glass of the cordial, "X" heard the door open. Lo Mong Yung's voice called to him, "Come in, my son. Our messenger has returned."

He arose from the table, and went around the screen with Gilly. Sung was just placing a black bag on the desk.

"X" asked in Cantonese, "Was the lady home, Sung?"

THE big Chinaman shook his head. "No, O Brother. But there is something strange that I must tell you—the lady's apartment was broken into and searched before I came!"

"X" took a quick step forward, forgetful of the presence of Gilly, seized Sung by the sleeve. "Tell me what you found, quick."

"It was this way, O Brother. I rang the bell of the lady's apartment, but no one answered. The door, however, was open to my touch, and when I entered the apartment I saw that trouble had been there. Every room was upset, seemed to have been thoroughly searched. Pictures were removed from the walls, the couch and chairs were ripped open, the rugs were torn up. There had been a struggle there, I could see, for the telephone lay on the floor where it had been thrown over. Some one must have carried off this lady who is a friend of yours.

"There was nothing I could do, so I went to the closet in the bedroom, followed your instructions, and got the bag from its hiding place. I am sad, O Brother, because I must bring this sad news about one who I can see is dear to you."

Mechanically, "X" nodded his thanks, picked up the black bag.

Gilly said to him, "Do we go now, Fannon?"

But he scarcely heard him. His mind was occupied with the news. Betty Dale had been taken away from her apartment by force. He cast around for possible motives, for a mental clue as to who might be behind it. That it was connected in some way with himself, he was sure. He had many enemies. Some, or one of them, could have learned of her association with him. They would consider it an excellent means of striking at the Secret Agent through her.

There was only one thing to do—get done with the present job as quickly as possible, go to Betty's apartment and see what clues he could pick up there. He started toward the door, followed by Gilly.

Lo Mong Yung called after him, "My son, I see that you walk in sorrow. Remember that the men of the Ming Tong ever stand ready to aid you."

"I will remember, Father of the Ming Men," said Secret Agent "X." "I thank you. But this is a matter that only I can attend to, I am a man who has always thought himself to be sufficient unto himself; but now I learn that no one of us—not even myself, who have trained my body and mind for many years—is above the human instincts that have been planted in our race."

CHAPTER VIII

MATCHED JEWELS

AS THEY SPED uptown in a cab, Secret Agent "X" paid little attention to Gilly. His mind was not on the immediate mission he and Gilly had to accomplish.

He was sorely tempted to stop off at Betty Dale's empty apartment and look the place over. But that would have interfered with, possibly have wrecked, all the elaborate steps he had taken to worm his way into the Skull's organization.

The mind of Secret Agent "X" always worked along clear, logical lines. He refused to jump to conclusions, to indulge in guess work as to who had taken Betty away, unless he had something definite to go on. To speculate at random would only lead to the wrong conclusion, would be a waste of time.

Recently he had engaged in a struggle with an organization known as the DOACs. Some of these DOACs still were at large, and they knew of his connection with Betty. This might be a manifestation of their desire for revenge. There were many others in the past who had reason to remember the Agent with bitterness, and it was futile to try to guess haphazard at the identity of her abductor.

By a deliberate mental effort he turned his thoughts to other things for the time being. And hardly soon enough. For Gilly had been watching him in a peculiar way. Now he said suddenly, "What the hell's eatin' you, Fannon? You ain't said a word since we left the Chink's house!"

"X" was startled. He had not thought that he appeared so preoccupied that Gilly would notice it. Above all he must not arouse the suspicions of Gilly or the Skull. If he did, he might as well drop this business now and go after Betty Dale.

He forced a smite. "Nothing is eating me, Gilly. I always like to figure out a job ahead of time. It's easier to do your thinking before than after."

Gilly looked at him queerly, his hand in the pocket where the automatic rested. "Some guys lose their nerve after bein' in stir, Fannon. I hope you ain't lost yours. Because if you have, you ain't no good to the Skull, an' the best thing would be a slug behind the ear for you."

The eyes of Secret Agent "X" bored into the little gunman's. "Don't worry about me, Gilly," he said softly. "I'm going to pull this job at Dennett's, and pull it right. You take care of your end, and I'll take care of mine." His face came closer to the other's, eyes still fixed on him. "And something else, Gilly, watch your tongue. I'm not used to taking guff from your kind. Do you understand?"

Gilly's eyes were the first to drop from that clash of glances. Sullenly he said, "Oh, all right, Fannon. I didn't mean nothing."

Somehow, Gilly knew that this man who sat beside him was in no fear of the automatic in his pocket. Somehow, he knew that that man would complete successfully anything that he undertook. He had felt the force of intelligence and power behind those eyes that had fascinated him for a moment.

The cab slowed up, pulled in at the curb. The driver called to them, "This is the corner of Willow and Briggs where you told me to stop. Okay?"

They got out and dismissed the cab, "X" carrying his bag. Willow Street was a short street no more than a hundred feet long, off one of the main thoroughfares. It boasted a row of old, rich looking private homes that had survived the feverish days of demolition and construction which had swept the city during the boom days of 1929. The numbers began at 350, and 363, Harrison Dennett's house, was only a few doors from the corner. "X" knew its layout, for he had visited it a number of times as Elisha Pond.

Now, he and Gilly made their way to the street behind Willow with the intention of cutting through the rear. The street behind it, they were surprised to find, was Slocum Street, where they were to meet Binks. In sharp contrast to Willow, it consisted of a row of towering apartment houses, of which number eighteen was the smallest and oldest. The subway spur which Dennett was building started at Briggs Avenue here, and both Briggs and Slocum were all cut up. Men were working, and there was the sound of a steam shovel from one of the excavations.

"Hell!" Gilly exclaimed. "We can't make it on this side. There's too many people around. How come the Skull told us to go in the back way? He musta known there'd be men workin' here."

"It's all right," the Secret Agent told him. "In my business we have ways of getting around that." He opened his bag, took out a gold-plated badge which he pinned inside the lapel of his coat. Gilly grinned in appreciation as he read the inscription on the badge. It said: "Inspector, Department of Water Supply, Gas and Electricity, City of New York."

"These things come in handy in this game," the Agent explained, as he led the way through an alley between two apartment houses, which led into the rear of 363 Willow. "If any one should stop us here, we're inspectors checking up on gas mains and water connections on account of the subway construction. That's the way we turn what seems to be an obstacle into an advantage."

"Jeez!" Gilly exclaimed. "I guess you got the goods, all right, Fannon. The Skull knew what he was doin' when he picked you."

THE back door of Dennett's house was unlocked, as the Skull had promised. Gilly said, "Okay, Fannon, go on in an' do your stuff. I'll cover the outside, an' I'll give you the office if anybody comes, by comin' up an' ringin' the back doorbell three times quick. If you hear that, you know you gotta scram quick. I'll cover you."

He took from his pocket a card which he handed to "X." It bore on its face the facsimile of a hideous looking skull—the trademark of their master.

"Leave that when you finish the job," Gilly grinned. "We always leave 'em our compliments."

"Okay," the Secret Agent said. "See you soon."

He went up the three steps of the back stoop, went in through the unlocked door. He was now unlawfully entering a man's home with the intention of committing robbery.

There was a pantry just inside the door, and "X" went through this into the kitchen. The kitchen was unoccupied, as was the broad, carpeted hallway beyond. The Skull had planned well. The servants were out.

As "X" made his way to the library, he felt that for the first time in his life he was working under a great nervous strain. He could not erase from his mind the thought of Betty Dale in trouble.

At the end of the hall was the library. He knew its location, had often drunk a whiskey-and-soda there with Dennett. Once in the library, he was no longer a prey to worry. He pushed every thought from his mind but the business in hand. He became once more that marvel of selfless efficiency—Secret Agent "X." He had a given task to accomplish.

He knelt before the safe which was in the far wall of the room, between two windows, and opened his black bag. He nodded in satisfaction as he saw that it contained all the instruments that he would need in the next twenty-four hours—not only for this job, but also for his subsequent trip to the Skull's headquarters. There were no weapons in the bag, however. His gas gun, dart equipment and hypo he generally carried about his person, and not in the bag. These he had left, and very wisely, when he went to the Skull's lair in the guise of Fannon.

First he took from the bag a queer framework contraption which fitted under the sole of his shoe. It had clamps around the edges, which held it firmly in place, and when he stood up it was impossible to notice that there was anything attached to the under part of his shoe.

After that he proceeded to stow several items from the bag about his person. That done, he knelt once more before the safe, and delved into the bag.

He did not see the figure of Harrison Dennett which appeared in the open doorway connecting with the inner room; did not see Dennett stop short upon seeing him, glide back into the other room, and reappear with a heavy automatic which he directed at the intruder's back.

"X" worked swiftly.

HE took from the bag a small box with earphone attachment. This was a listening device perfected by himself, which magnified sound.[8] He placed the diaphragm of this box close to the door of the safe, alongside the dial. With the long, sensitive fingers of his right hand, he twirled the dial slowly, listening for the drop of the tumblers which would be magnified so that he could hear it through his ear phones.

---

8   *AUTHOR'S NOTE: This listening device of the Secret Agent's was one which he had found of invaluable assistance on more occasions than one. It is probably the smallest amplifier in the world, with earphones, diaphram and miniature storage batteries that will all fit into the pocket. Any inventor would no doubt be proud to boast of having devised it, and could probably retire for the rest of his life on the royalties from its manufacture and sale. But Secret Agent "X" regarded it only as another tool with which he could combat crime—and a marvelously efficient one at that.*

This was one of the most delicate tasks in the world; a task which the real Frank Fannon could probably perform without the aid of an amplifying instrument. It had been this instrument that "X" had wanted in particular, for without it he would never have been able to tackle the job.

Dennett, holding the gun tight, bent forward interestedly as he saw the use to which that amplifier was being put. He watched tensely, his face in the shadow, as the Secret Agent twirled the dial back and forth; took an involuntary step forward, then checked himself, as "X" gave the dial a final twirl and swung open the door.

Inside was a second door; with a keyhole. "X" put the amplifier down, and picked out of the bag a flat, silk-covered instrument case. He examined the keyhole for a second, then, out of the instrument case which he unfolded, he picked unerringly, a single key, from a collection of perhaps two dozen. A turn of the key, and the inner door was open.

There were stacks of papers in the inner compartment, and in the corner lay a chamois bag. "X" took the bag, opened it, and poured into the palm of his hand two pearls so beautiful that they seemed to live in his hand. They were a perfect pair, and from them emanated rays of a dozen brilliant hues. Truly, they were worth every dollar of the Skull's estimate. Matched pearls—the most priceless jewels in the world.

And then Dennett stepped forward, raising the gun, and said, *"Don't move!"* as "X" started, began to turn. "I've got you covered, and I'll shoot to kill!"

"X" remained frozen on the floor, the pearls in his hand. He had recognized the voice of Harrison Dennett; he was trapped as a common housebreaker.

CHAPTER IX

LOOT FOR THE SKULL

HARRISON DENNETT STAYED in the doorway, keeping a safe distance between himself and the intruder. "Now," he said, "get up slowly, keep your hands in front of you, and turn around. I want to see your face."

"X" obeyed, faced the contractor.

Dennett's gun was steady, centered on "X's" heart. His eyes were hard.

This was the end; "X" was posing here in the guise of Frank Fannon, a hardened ex-convict, caught in the commission of a felony. Prison. If he tried to escape, Dennett would be justified in shooting him without compunction; and he could not, and would not, injure Dennett. It was against his policy to kill even dangerous criminals.

It would not be any better—perhaps be even worse—if he disclosed his identity as Secret Agent "X." Commissioner Foster and Inspector Burks would each give much to arrest Secret Agent "X"—would free ten Fannons to do it.

Dennett's mouth was grim. He said, "You were after those pearls, and nothing else. And you're an expert, I can see that by the instrument you were using to listen for the tumblers. No expert would go after those pearls for their own value. You could never sell them. *What did you want them for?*"

"X" assumed a sulky appearance. "What difference does it make? You got me cold. What're you going to do?"

There flashed through his mind the disturbing realization that Gilly had not warned him of Dennett's approach. Gilly wasn't yellow—he would have made sure to sound a warning. Which meant that Dennett must have been in the house all the time; the Skull had been wrong. Or—had the Skull *intended* to be wrong? Had he deliberately sent him out to be caught here in Dennett's house?

If he had, then he knew that Fannon was not Fannon. It would be death to go back, even if he did succeed in escaping from the menace of Dennett's gun.

He glanced up as he heard the contractor say, "Who sent you here?"

"X" veiled his eyes. "I came on my own."

"That's funny. All my servants happen to be away. Isn't it a coincidence that you should pick this time to break in here?"

"Suppose it is?"

Dennett's cold eyes were on the two pearls which "X" held in his hand. He said coldly, "Some one sent you here to get those pearls. No ordinary thief would go after them. Who sent you? Tell me that and maybe I'll be inclined to go easy on you."

"X" maintained silence, merely shook his head.

"I think," Dennett said, his eyes narrowing, "that I know the answer to that question. You are one of the Servants of the Skull! Speak up, quick! Are you?"

"X" shrugged. "I'm not saying a thing."

"All right," Dennett exclaimed, his jaws snapping shut with an ominous grimness. It's your funeral." He waved the gun. "Put those pearls back in the safe. *Put them back!*" as "X" hesitated.

THE agent's body was taut, his fingers tense. He knelt before the safe, opened the chamois bag, started to pour the two pearls back. The first one slipped to the floor as if he were awkward with his hands. He picked it up. And now, instead of being awkward, his hands moved with lightning speed. It was a little trick of prestidigitation which had deceived shrewder men than Dennett. The pearls seemed to be going into the bag. In reality, what went into it were a couple of keys from the open, silk-covered case on the floor.

"X" palmed the pearls, and slipped the chamois bag into the safe under Dennett's eyes. The safe door clanged shut. Dennett relaxed a bit. He was sure—would have sworn—that those pearls were in the safe. It was as quick a sleight-of-hand trick as had ever been executed on the stage.

Dennett said, "Now hand me that instrument you were listening to the tumblers with. I am interested in it."

"X's" hand felt on the floor, while his eyes locked with the contractor's. He gripped the amplifier, raised it, and hurled it straight at Dennett.

Dennett saw the swift motion of "X's" arm, started back involuntarily, and his finger tightened on the trigger. But his aim had been spoiled. He fired just as the amplifier box struck his shoulder, fell to the floor and was shattered. The shot went wild.

"X" scooped up his bag, leaped from his kneeling position halfway across the room, and was out through the hall door before Dennett had recovered his senses enough to fire another shot.

He sped toward the rear of the hall. As he swung into the kitchen, another shot from the contractor's gun barked through the house, crashed into a shelf of chinaware, smashing several dishes.

But "X" was already out through the back door, dashing across the small strip of yard of the rear. Gilly was running too, just ahead of him, looking back. Gilly stopped, waited for him. "What the hell happened?" he demanded.

"X" kept on running beside the gunman. "Dennett jumped me with a gun," he explained. "I had to take a chance on a fast one to break away from him. And he almost got me at that!"

They were through the alley between the houses now, out on Slocum. Workmen looked up from their work in the subway cut, but none made a motion to interfere with them. Gilly was waving his gun. He shouted to "X," "There's number 18, across the street. Let's get over there!"

They dodged across the crosswalk over the excavation. From behind them came a wild shout.

A policeman down the street saw them and came running, tugging for his gun. Gilly threw a shot in his direction, and just then, as if by pre-arrangement, one of the workmen, down in the excavation started a riveting machine going. The staccato carvings of the riveting machine drowned the sounds of Gilly's shot, and of the policeman's answering blast.

"X" and Gilly dashed into the entrance of number 18, ran through the empty foyer, and out through the rear. They found the door in the back fence, slid through it; but there was no Binks. Gilly consulted his wrist watch, and cursed.

"Hell! It's only half past two. He wasn't supposed to meet us till three. This is a hell of a mess!"

On the other side of the fence they could hear the policeman shouting, could hear many people talking. "X" had noticed a bar in the door through the fence, and he slid this home. "It'll give us another minute," he remarked. "Now we better get out of here."

He looked around, and whistled. They were in an empty lot facing the river. Along the curb stood a black sedan, a driver at the wheel, looking over toward them. When he caught "X's" eye, he motioned toward them. "X" nudged Gilly, who looked in that direction, snarled, and brought his gun around. "X" knocked it up, exclaiming, "You damn fool! Don't you see the 'S' on the door? That's the Skull's car! Let's go."

Gilly shouted, "Jeez, Fannon, you're right!"

They ran down to the curb.

The chauffeur was a stocky, stolid-faced man they had never seen before. He opened the door as they came up, called out, "Get in."

Gilly piled in, "X" after him. The driver slammed the door and stepped on the gas almost in the same motion. As the car jumped away from the curb, "X," looking back, saw the policeman top the fence. He didn't even notice the car, which was already rounding the corner into the river front street.

A FEW blocks down, the driver pulled up at the curb, and turned around grinning. "I bet you guys thought you was forgotten!"

Gilly said, "I hope to tell you, pal. I thought we would have to shoot it out with that dumb cop. How come you was there, pal?"

"Me? My name's Gordon. I drive for the boss. He always has me around when there's a job on the books, in case that nitwit, Binks, can't get there to bring the boys in. Sort of insurance. We'll drive around for a while, then go to another place an' see if Binks is there."

Gordon drove them around for an hour. At the end of that time, he stopped off and made a telephone call. When he came out he said, "Okay. We'll meet Binks now. He says to come to entrance number seven."

Number seven proved to be a pool parlor in a cheap residential section not far from Slocum. "X" and Gilly got out of the car. Gordon said, "Go through the pool room an' you'll find an alley in back, at the right. Go half-way up the alley to where you see a cellar door. Stop there till Binks comes."

He drove off, and they followed his instructions. Binks was waiting for them, his head just above the open cellar door. "Too bad," he crackled. "Too bad, boys. That was an awful flop. Well, come on, we might as well go back."

They stepped down into the cellar, and Gilly closed the door over their heads at Binks' direction. Then the halfwit gave them hoods to put on again, and led them through passage after passage, up and down flights of stairs. "X" was still carrying his black bag, and he had to hold on to Gilly with the other hand.

After what seemed an interminable time, they stopped and Binks said, "Take 'em off, boys."

"X" put the bag down and removed his hood. He saw that they were in the same anteroom where he had waited for his instructions that morning. Binks picked up the bag, saying, "I'll take it now. The Skull will want to keep that till the next time."

"Look here," the Agent protested. "That's only borrowed. I have to return it to my friend."

Binks paid him no attention, but shuffled out. "Tell it to the Skull," he threw back. "His orders was to bring him the bag."

"X" and the gunman were left alone. Gilly said, "Well, it looks bad for us, pal. The Skull don't like guys that flop, no matter how come."

"Flop?" the Agent asked.

"Sure. You was supposed to get them pearls. The guy busted in on you when he wasn't supposed to even be around, but the Skull won't take that for an excuse. He don't take excuses."

"Well, why did we come back then?" The Secret Agent did not tell Gilly that he had the pearls in his pocket.

Gilly laughed harshly. "Where could we go? In the first place, we'd both be picked up in no time wandering around the city. And in the second place, I'd hate to be on the lam from the Skull. Did you see what he did to Tyler? How'd you like to have the same thing happen to you?"

HE stopped as the door facing them started to open. The Skull's voice came through it. "I will see Fannon first."

Gilly looked at "X" and grinned. "Well, so long, pal. You was a good fellow while you lasted. What kind of flowers do you like?"

"X" paid him no attention, but walked in.

The door closed behind him, as before. The room was very faintly lighted, disclosing the Skull seated at a desk at the far end of the room. Once more "X" noted the four foot wide strip running across the floor.

The hideous death's head of the Skull grinned at him out of the vermilion hood. The boss raised one vermilion-gloved hand, motioned him to remain where he was at the door. With the other hand, he indicated a short-wave radio set on the desk at his elbow. "Wait," he said. "I am just getting the police calls on your job."

"X" stood close to the door, measuring the distance between himself and the desk. He was tempted to make a quick leap, lock his hands about the throat of that repulsive figure, and throttle him to death. But he restrained the impulse. It looked too easy. So clever a man as the Skull had not left himself unguarded in this room. He waited. And soon the radio came to life.

"Calling all cars! Be on the lookout for Frank Fannon, ex-convict wanted for burglarious entry into the home of Harrison Dennett. Dennett reports nothing stolen, as he forced Fannon to replace the loot. Fannon escaped with one companion, identified as Jack Gilly, after gunfight with patrolman. Both are dangerous. Exert great care in stopping suspects. Fannon is forty, tall—"

With a vicious gesture, the Skull snapped off the radio. "So you failed?" It was more a statement than a question, low-voiced, ominous. The glowing death's head brooding in the semi-dark seemed to be evolving some Satanic form of punishment "You know how failure is rewarded here?"

Again the Secret Agent measured the distance between himself and the desk. So far the breaks had been with him. With patience he would no doubt prevail. But patience was what he had little of today, with Betty Dale a prisoner in the hands of some unknown enemies. A slight rustling sound at his left diverted his attention for the moment, and he smiled to see that it was a large rat scampering across the floor from one hole to another. He turned back to the Skull.

"What makes you think I've failed?"

"Didn't you hear the radio? Dennett stated to the police that you put the jewels back in the safe. That, my friend, is failure!"

"But you told me that Dennett would be away, that I would have a clear coast. Instead, he surprised me in the middle of the job."

Slowly the Skull's head shook from side to side. "It makes no difference. I make the best preparations for you that I can. Sometimes a little thing miscarries. Then you must use your own wits to save the situation. You thought more of escaping with a whole skin than of my orders. My men learn that it is no good coming back here with a whole skin and empty hands. They would be far better off to die on the job." He paused. "I am sorry that I must treat you as I would treat any of the others, Fannon. I had hoped that you would make good, for you have possibilities. But now—"

He stopped, for "X" had put his hand in his pocket. "If that is a gun, Fannon, it'll do you no good. Keep your hand in your pocket!" Accompanying the words, a blinding spot-light snapped on, no doubt in response to a button the Skull had pressed on his desk. It blared full in "X's" eyes, blinding him, making it impossible for him to shoot even if he had had a gun.

"X" stood still in the light, and forced his lips into a smile. "It is not a gun," he said calmly. "It is the pearls from Harrison Dennett's safe. I got them after all; I wanted to spring them on you as a surprise."

From behind the spotlight came the Skull's vicious snarl. "You lie! You haven't got those pearls. They're in Dennett's safe where he said he made you replace them!"

"X" shrugged. "If you will allow me to take my hand out, I will show them to you."

"All right. Take your hand out. You are helpless under the spotlight anyway. I call your bluff, Fannon. Let me see the pearls, or you go to the chair! Like Tyler!"

SLOWLY, carefully, "X" withdrew his hand from his pocket holding the two gems in his fingers. They glowed with deep, mysterious color under the spotlight. Anyone could see that they were pearls of immense value.

From the Skull there came the wheeze of a sudden, amazed intake of breath. A moment there was silence, then the spotlight clicked off. "X" blinked his eyes, peered through the sudden comparative darkness in which he could see once more.

The Skull said, "Fannon, I hardly believe my eyes. How did you do it?"

"X" explained coolly. "Dennett thought I put them back. But when he opens his safe, he will discover that the hand is quicker than the eye. There's only a worthless key in the safe now."

"Give them to me," the Skull ordered eagerly.

"X" took a step forward, but the Skull exclaimed, "Wait. Do not come closer. Put them in the basket."

The Skull pressed a button, and from the side of his desk there began to slide out a bamboo pole with a hook on the end of it. From this hook there hung suspended a small wicker basket. The basket came to rest about a foot from the Agent, and he deposited the two gems in it. Slowly the pole began to recede. It was operated by some sort of spring attached to the side of the desk.

"X" reflected that the Skull took plenty of precautions. He would not even allow his men to come close enough to the desk to put anything on it. It would be difficult to overcome him—especially when time pressed. Perhaps the best way would be a quick leap across the intervening space. He set himself, poised on the balls of his feet, his body taut. This was the moment. The Skull's attention was away from him for the second, for he was leaning over the desk, reaching eager, vermilion-gloved hands for the pearls.

"X's" knees bent. Three swift steps. Now!

And he stopped. For again there was that scraping sound in the corner of the room. The Skull raised his eyes irritably. The rat was scampering across the room now, directly toward the desk. "X" relaxed. The opportune moment was gone. He must wait for another.

And then his body grew rigid. For the rat, scurrying toward the desk, had reached the four-foot wide strip in the floor. There was a violent flash, the smell of scorching flesh, and the rat seemed to shrivel, curl up. It remained motionless on the edge of that four foot strip, scorched crisp.

"Damn those rats!" the Skull exclaimed. He looked up at "X." "So you know now!" The horrible, flesh-less skull seemed to leer more wickedly than ever. "That is why I did not want you to come closer. Had you tried to attack me, tried to jump me, the same thing would have happened to you that just happened to the rat! That—" he laughed harshly—"is how I treat all rats! Good joke, eh, Fannon?"

"X" tried to imagine how the real Fannon would react to what he had just seen. Frightened? Awed? That was it. Even a hardened, worldly-wise ex-convict like Fannon would be awed at beholding such infernal cleverness.

"Gosh, boss," he said. "I'd never rat on you! Look—I brought you the pearls. You didn't know I had them. I could have taken a powder with them!"

"That is true, Fannon. I will remember it. I need an honest man as lieutenant here. You are intelligent, clever. You have just shown your loyalty. Perhaps you noted that the calibre of the men I have here is not high. You have a good chance to become second in command. Now," he raised a hand and beckoned, "you may come closer to the desk while I talk to you."

"X" looked surprised, hesitated. "You want me to cross the room?"

"Yes."

It was asking much, with the body of the electrocuted rat still on the floor, but "X" squared his shoulders, and without further hesitation, he went toward the desk, stepping full on the strip in the floor. He was staking everything again on his confidence in his own uncanny intuition about human nature.

He had a momentary feeling of coldness along his spine as his foot came down close beside the dead rat, but nothing happened. He came close to the desk, noting that the Skull's hand had come above the glass top now, holding an automatic trained on his stomach.

HE stood there quietly, looking into the cavernous physiognomy of evil that leered up at him.

"Bravo!" exclaimed the Skull. "I wondered if you had confidence in me. There is a switch under the desk here. I shut off the current with my foot. Not many men would have had the courage to cross that strip at my command. You see, I am testing you in many ways, Fannon. You may now step back."

"X" said, "Thank you," and stepped back to the door. He saw the Skull make a movement with his foot under the desk.

"The current is on again, Fannon." The Skull put down the automatic. "The gun was merely a precaution in case you were tempted to attack me in spite of your professed loyalty. It is a habit of mine never to trust anyone fully. I don't even trust Binks entirely, and he is harmless enough."

The Skull seemed now to be in a mellow mood. But "X" waited tensely, silently. He felt there was something else coming, something behind the Skull's new affability. And all the time his thoughts were darting back to that empty apartment of Betty Dale's. When, when would he be able to get to that!

The Skull was talking again. "Frankly, Fannon, I had my doubts about you. Something happened in one of the corridors last night; something that I have not solved yet. One of my men was killed. Rufe—you met him. He had apparently discovered some one in the passage who had no business there. That some one killed Rufe. I entertained some suspicions of you!"

"Why should I want to kill Rufe?" the Secret Agent asked. "It was my first night here. How would I be able to find my way around in those passages?"

"I thought of all that, Fannon, and that is why you are still alive today. It couldn't have been you, or any of my servants; for everybody is locked in at night. And that leads me to the only other logical conclusion—that there is an outsider prowling loose in the corridors. If there is, I have a good idea as to his name. Fannon," the Skull leaned over the desk, emphasizing each word, "have you ever heard of Secret Agent 'X'?"

IF the situation had not been so tense, the Agent could have enjoyed the sardonic humor of being asked whether he had ever heard of himself. As it was, he merely nodded, composing his voice to a casual tone. "I've heard of him. They say he's poison to crooks, and poison to the police also. You think he's the one who's doing the prowling?"

"I believe so. It wouldn't be strange if he interested himself in me. I am now the most powerful man engaged in criminal activities in America, perhaps the only one mentally worthy of the steel of such a man as this Secret Agent 'X'."

"From what I have seen," said "X," "I think you could give him cards and spades."

"Perhaps, Fannon, perhaps." There was a measure of pride to be detected in the Skull's voice now. "It may be that I have him in a tight spot right now."

"X" tensed. Had the Skull been playing with him all along? He told himself that it could not be. He was too keen a judge of people to have been deceived. He would have detected a false note in the Skull's speech before now. Still, the Skull was clever. Every man, even "X" himself, was bound at some time to meet a man who was his mental superior.

The Skull's next words set him at rest on that score. The Skull was not playing with him. But they brought to the Agent a new problem. For the master said, "You will recall, Fannon, that when I sent you to Dennett's, I also sent Nate Frisch with some other men on another mission. Well, that mission has been accomplished successfully. Take this key." He threw across the room a small flat key similar to the one Binks used. "Binks has gone out to meet some of the men, so you will have to guide yourself."

"X's" eyes gleamed. Was this to be the opportunity? He caught the key in the air, and waited.

"Use that key in the slot of the panel at the end of the corridor. Go through the opening, and turn left. You will find a heavy, barred door. Unbar it, then wait till I press the button from the inside, which unlocks it."

The Agent nodded. He was going to be left alone, with a key. Was the Skull growing careless, or was he trusting him?

The Skull went on. "I will need you in that room. Nate Frisch has gone on another errand; and anyway, I think your higher intelligence will be better suited to my needs in this case. For in that room, Fannon, is the answer to the identity of Secret Agent 'X'! It is the master stroke of mine that will remove him from my path! Go now, and wait at the barred door!"

The door behind the Secret Agent opened, and he stepped out into the anteroom. Here was something that required careful action. Without a doubt he must go into that room behind the barred door and see what the Skull's stroke of genius consisted of.

He made his way down the corridor, through the sliding panel, and unbarred the heavy door. As he waited, he searched his subconscious mind, and was amazed to discover that the thought of Betty Dale's possible predicament overshadowed his present task. He had never thought that the emotion of deep friendly regard—almost of protectorship—had grown so strong in him. Perhaps it was the realization that he was here, helpless to aid her at the moment, which preyed so upon him.

His revery was interrupted by a slight *click,* following which the heavy door swung open, revealing a room in utter darkness. "X" entered grimly, and the door swung shut behind him. He couldn't see a foot in front of him now.

SUDDENLY a dull glow began to grow high up along the wall, and "X" started, his lips forming into a thin line as he realized where he was. The glow dimly illuminated the forbidding figure of the Skull standing in a niche in the wall. And below the niche, built into the floor, was the electric chair in which Tyler had been executed. And beside the chair was a trussed-up figure that stirred and uttered a helpless little moan.

The wire mesh that had separated the room into two parts before was now raised so that a man could pass under it. "X" took an involuntary step toward that pitiful figure on the floor, but stopped, restraining himself by an iron exercise of will power.

And suddenly the spotlight from up above burst into brilliant luminance, bathing the chair and the trussed-up figure in a merciless light.

And "X" gasped. For that helpless figure on the floor was the golden-haired figure of Betty Dale.

She was bound and gagged, but her eyes were wide open, reflecting hopeless resignation.

From the niche came the Skull's voice. "This lady, Fannon, is known as Miss Betty Dale. She is in the confidence of Secret Agent 'X,' and should be in a position to supply us with some very interesting information about that gentleman. She is unwilling to talk, but I feel sure we can remedy that."

"X" wet his lips and stepped forward under the brilliant blare of the spotlight.

The Skull said crisply, "Take off her gag, Fannon, and see if she would like to talk before we begin to do things to her."

"X" knelt beside Betty Dale, and his fingers moved clumsily to remove the gag while he looked down into her determined little face. He dared not say a word to her lest it be heard by the Skull in the stillness that had descended upon the room. He tried to make his eyes expressive, but it was no use.

In him now, she saw nothing but a vicious criminal henchman of the master who stood in the niche above. She had never been able to penetrate any of his disguises, and could not be expected to do so now with her nerves in the frayed condition that they must be in before the ordeal which she knew was inevitable.

When the gag was off, the Skull said in the mocking tone which "X" had begun to loathe, "Well, Miss Dale, you must talk now if you wish to avoid the things I have in store for you. Will you give me the information I need?"

She opened her mouth, but gulped, not trusting herself to talk. She clamped her lips tight and shook her head, staring defiantly up into the spotlight.

The Skull sighed, and went on, as if explaining some elementary proposition to a child. "You don't understand, Miss Dale. I am sure, that after I have described to you what I intend to do to you, you will be very glad to tell me all you know." The vermilion-cloaked arm rose, and a gloved finger pointed to the electric chair. "You know what that is, of course, Miss Dale, since you are a newspaper woman; it is an electric chair. You look at it, contemplate death, and feel yourself strong enough to die rather than betray this friend of yours who is known as Secret Agent 'X'."

He uttered a short, mocking laugh. Betty remained silent, her face white, biting her lower lip. "X" felt a surge of blind anger sweep over him at the sight of the girl's mental anguish, at the contemplation of the physical anguish which the Skull planned for her. But his will conquered his instinct. To make a rash move now would gain neither of them anything but death; for the Skull was impregnable in his niche up there, surrounded no doubt, by clever, ingenious defenses.

The Skull went on. "What will you say, Miss Dale, when I tell you that this electric chair *does not kill!* It will maim you! Maim you mentally and physically, will make you an imbecile within five seconds of the moment when I pull the switch. You have heard of the men who were found in the streets—strong men, intelligent men. When they were picked up in the streets, it was found that their bodies and minds were shattered. That, Miss Dale, is what will happen to you. You will be thrown out into the street to be found by your friend and protector, Secret Agent 'X'! I shall send you as a challenge to him—a challenge from the one man who is his match!"

Betty Dale's eyes reflected the horror of the words she had just heard. Her chin trembled.

"X" clenched his fists so that the nails bit into the palms of his hands, in an effort to restrain himself from leaping up at the Skull.

The Skull said to "X," "You were here this morning, Fannon. Tell her how it works."

"X" bent over Betty, said in a clear voice, "It would be better for you to talk, Miss Dale. What the Skull tells you is true—there is just enough current to shatter the nerves, destroy the brain cells. Believe me, it is not pleasant."

Betty turned her eyes from the niche to the face of "X," staring at him in loathing. "You fiends!" she cried huskily. "You wouldn't dare!"

Once more the Skull's horrid, mocking voice addressed him. "She doesn't believe that we'd do it, eh, Fannon? Let's show her." The vermilion-cloaked figure raised a hand and pointed to the opposite wall. "Look!"

At the same moment the spotlight shifted, focusing on a spot in the wall. A small panel, about four feet square slid up, revealing a barred opening.

"Untie her, Fannon, and take her over there. Let her look in."

"X" knelt beside her, fumbled for the knots, and untied Betty Dale. He helped her to her feet silently, though she shrank from him. It was impossible to whisper a word here that would not be overheard by the sinister figure in the niche above him. "X" had noticed already that the acoustic properties of the room were such that the slightest whisper could be heard.

Betty struggled, moaned, "I don't want to look at anything. Leave me alone."

"Make her look, Fannon!"

"X" gripped her arm in his powerful fingers, led her to the barred window. Somehow, his touch seemed to quiet her, for she went with him. The aperture was at the height of a tall man's chest. Betty's eyes barely reached above the ledge, but it was enough to enable her to see that which was in the room beyond. She looked, and "X" felt her whole body grow rigid. But she did not faint. From her throat there came shriek after shriek of horror.

"X" pulled her away from the aperture, and the panel slid down. The spotlight was shifted from the wall, snapped off for an instant, leaving the room in darkness except for the glow that illumined the vermilion Skull in his niche.

"X" let Betty scream. He gripped her arm tightly, as if to reassure her. He had seen something while the wall was flooded with light—something that the Skull had probably never intended that he should see. It was a small lever in the corner, such as was found in all the passages. Its presence meant that there was another panel there, somewhere in the wall—a panel leading to a corridor, perhaps to freedom.

When the light went out, Betty stopped screaming, and leaned weakly on "X." She said hurriedly, in a low, husky whisper, "Please—don't let him do that to me. You are a man. Can you allow such things to be done? Save me!"

The spotlight clicked on, and the Secret Agent could only give her arm a friendly squeeze, which he hoped she would understand, before the Skull's hateful voice addressed them.

"I heard what you just said to Fannon, Miss Dale. You have no chance with him. He is wanted for murder, and is dependent on me for protection. Besides, neither he nor anybody else could get you out of this place against my wishes. So you see, you must do as I ask."

He paused a moment as Betty closed her eyes in despair, then went on. "The sight of what my chair can do has unnerved you, I see. I don't blame you. Tyler is not a pretty sight for even a strong man to see. The man you saw in there was a cunning cracksman yesterday. Today he is a driveling idiot." He paused. "Will you talk now?"

"X," with his hand on Betty's arm, felt a tremor course through her. Her chin jutted, though, and she uttered a single word, "No!"

The Skull's voice crackled with sudden, venomous anger. "Fannon! Strap her in the chair!"

THE Secret Agent looked up into the blinding core of the spotlight. By a supreme effort he kept his voice even. "Isn't there some other way? Do we have to put her in the chair? I—"

He stopped as the Skull's icy cold voice interrupted him. "So you are soft, after all, Fannon? No one who is soft can go far with me. I must have men who stop at nothing—when the Skull commands! If you are soft you are useless to me. And useless men are dangerous men. *Do you know what I mean, Fannon?*"

"X" caught himself up, snapped out of the momentary forgetfulness of his role. The real Fannon would not have uttered that plea. Cold enemy of society that he was, he would have been far from reluctant to inflict torture upon anyone who stood between him and his goal.

"X" said, "It's not that I'm soft, chief. You ought to know that from my record. I only thought that if you sent the current through her, she'd never be able to talk any more. I thought maybe we could try something else on her—something that wouldn't destroy her mind—"

The Skull interrupted him once more. "I see. It seemed to me for a moment that you were trying to intercede for her; and that would have been very bad—for you. Your suggestion may be appropriate, but I have said that she goes to the chair, and to the chair she goes. As a matter of fact, I am glad that she refuses to talk. I have never had a woman in the chair, and I am curious to see if the effects of the current are greater or less than on a man. So—in she goes!"

"X" could no longer afford to hesitate. He swung her around, affecting to treat her with roughness. But Betty, with a surge of desperation, wrenched her arm out of "X's" grip, turned and fled toward the heavy, iron-bound door at the other end of the room. "X" leaped after her. That was not the way to safety. But before Betty had taken two steps, the heavy mesh screen that separated the room into two parts, and which had been raised some six feet up to now, suddenly descended with a clattering bang, right in front of her. Had she been a foot farther toward the door she would have been crushed under it. As it was, she was trapped by the screen.

The Skull said, "It was useless, my dear. You are helpless down there. I enjoy your antics at escape, for all I have to do is move a finger, pull a switch, and you are caught again. Make up your mind that there is no way out. Now," crisply to "X," "begin. My time is valuable."

Betty had wilted with the last opportunity of escape gone. Her head hung, and she offered no resistance as "X" led her to the chair and began to strap her in.

Two electrodes fitted at her wrists, one at the back of her neck, and two at her ankles. If he had any thought of strapping them loosely so that the metal should not come in contact with her body, he was compelled to discard it, for the Skull watched every move, instructing him how to tighten them properly, how to place the electrode at the nape of her neck.

She was following the motions of "X's" hands, now, as if fascinated by them, unable to move. She raised her eyes to his in a mute appeal, and he tried to convey to her a message with his own eyes. But suddenly her lids drooped, and her head lolled on her breast. She had fainted.

CHAPTER X

"ALIAS SECRET AGENT 'X'!"

THE CHAIR HAD a high back, and from his niche in the wall the Skull could not tell that Betty was unconscious. To him she appeared to be drooping with the flight of hope. He asked, "Finished, Fannon?"

"X" nodded. There was a gleam in his eye. He could not speak now, for he was flexing the muscles of his throat, tensing his whole body for the thing that he was about to do. He was about to perform the greatest piece of acting he had ever been called upon to stage in his career—with the lives of Betty Dale and himself as the forfeit if he failed.

The Skull said, "Well, Miss Dale, I am about to throw the switch which will send enough current through your body to make you just like that man you saw in the next room. Have you anything to say?"

But Betty couldn't answer. She was breathing irregularly now, as if a prey to nightmares in her unconscious condition. All the color had fled from her cheeks, and her long lashes lay supine over her eyes.

The Skull repeated impatiently, "Quick! You have one second more!"

And then the miracle took place.

Out of Betty's slack mouth there came words. Low words, mumbled at first, almost incoherent, then gaining clearness—and in Betty's voice. "God! Don't, no! I'll tell you anything!"

But it was not Betty who was talking. Secret Agent "X" was leaning over her, his lips parted, as if intensely eager to hear what she said. And it was he who was uttering those words by a supreme achievement of ventriloquism.⁹

The Skull was deceived. Clever man that he was, the performance deceived him. He clucked in satisfaction. "That is very wise, Miss Dale. Now tell us—" his voice assumed an edge of keen expectancy "—*who is Secret Agent 'X'?*"

Once more the voice of Betty Dale floated up to the niche, emanating by some strange alchemy of skill from the parted, unmoving lips of Secret Agent "X," but appearing to be spoken by the girl. "I—I don't know. I never saw his face. But I know where he is."

"Where?" The Skull rapped out the one word with a sharp eagerness that was full of venom.

Again the throat muscles of Secret Agent "X" began to contract and expand, and Betty Dale seemed to say, "He's right here in your place. He told me he was going to get in under a disguise."

"Who? What's his disguise?"

"He's disguised as a half-wit—a man by the name of Binks!" Betty's voice from the lips of "X" seemed to utter the last word with hesitation, regret. It was a superb piece of acting. On the stage it would have brought down the house. Here it elicited an astounded exclamation from the Skull.

"Binks! Impossible! No one could make up like that halfwit, no matter how clever he is!"

Once more Betty seemed to cry, "That's all I know. Now release me. Let me go!"

The Skull paid no attention to her. He mused, "Binks, eh? What do you think, Fannon? Could she be making it up? Binks is the last one here I would have suspected. To tell you the truth, it might have been anybody else but Binks—even you. I suspected you, too, frankly. But Binks!"

"X" stood erect, said, resuming the voice of Fannon, "Has she ever seen Binks?"

"By Jove!" the Skull exclaimed. "You're right. She's never seen him. She was unconscious when she was brought here, and Binks

---

9   AUTHOR'S NOTE: *The fakirs of India have for centuries made a practice of ventriloquism. In this country it has been extensively used by unscrupulous persons posing as mediums and inducing thousands of gullible people to part with their money by seeming to evoke the voices of the dead from the grave. Never, in the opinion of the author, has ventriloquism been put to a worthier use than that which Secret Agent "X" made of it at this time. The power of ventriloquism is in itself a comparatively easy thing to acquire. It is the ability to mimic a woman's voice by a man, and vice versa, that is extremely difficult. Secret Agent "X" is one of the few people in this country who possess that ability.*

has been out on errands all this time."

"So she couldn't be making it up. Where could she have learned that there is such a person except from this Secret Agent himself?"

"I'll send for him," the Skull said suddenly. It'll be easy to prove if he's Secret Agent 'X.'" He paused, then asked Betty, "First, Miss Dale, suppose you tell us when it was that Secret Agent 'X' informed you he was coming here disguised as Binks?"

Once more "X" bent over Betty Dale. Once more his lips pursed, his throat muscles contracted. "I—" he began in Betty's voice. But that was as far as he got. For suddenly Betty stirred, opened her eyes, and cried, her voice clashing with the voice "X" was using, "I won't talk, I tell you! I won't!"

The effect was weird, as of twins talking at the same time.

From the niche above came an ominous purr, more deadly in portent than the rattle of a snake before striking.

"So-o, Mr. Frank Fannon alias Secret Agent 'X'! You are a master of ventriloquism among your many other accomplishments! Let us see if you can avoid the slugs from my gun which will now break both your legs!"

THE heavy report of the Skull's gun came as an echo of his last word, filling the room with cacophonous detonation. But the Secret Agent had jerked into motion with the first words of Betty Dale. For he realized at once that the game was lost unless he acted swiftly.

His long fingers flew as he unbuckled the straps from her wrists, while the Skull talked, sure of his prey.

As he worked, Betty looked at him, wide-eyed, happy laughter mingling with her tears. "You!" she exclaimed happily.

And even before the report of the Skull's gun boomed through the room, "X" was on his knees beside the electric chair. His hand had gone to his pocket and come out again with a lightning-like motion, holding one of the gadgets which he had transferred from the black bag.

This gadget was an ingeniously constructed pair of nippers, attached to which was a needle capable of piercing a heavy electric wire.

At the spot where "X" knelt, the heavy cable which conducted the powerful current to the electric chair came out of the wall, and branched to each of the electrodes. Into this cable "X" plunged the needle, clamping the nippers around the cable. The short circuit thus effected caused a blinding flash, and plunged the room into darkness.

In the blackness "X" could hear Betty's quick breathing between the resounding explosions of the Skull's automatic. Shots ripped into the framework of the chair, crunched into the cement floor, filled the room with acrid powder stench.

"X" seized Betty by the wrist, dragged her to the corner of the room where he had seen the lever in the wall.

The Skull had stopped shooting, his clip evidently empty. He was not shouting; his silence was more ominous than any cries of rage he might have uttered.

"X" felt about in the darkness until he located the lever, and he pressed it downward quickly.

Somewhere in the place an alarm bell was jangling loudly. "X" heard hoarse shouts as the panel in the wall slid upward exposing a narrow passageway. He dragged Betty through it, pressed the lever on the other side. The panel slid down just as another hail of shots came from the Skull's reloaded automatic. The panel, however, slid to, protecting "X" and the girl from the slugs.

The bell was still raucously clanging its alarm as "X" turned to lead Betty down the passageway. He heard a gasp from Betty, looked ahead, and stopped short. Rushing toward them from the other end where he had just come through a panel, was the gunman, Gilly, drawn gun in his hand.

CHAPTER XI

LABYRINTH OF DANGER

BEHIND GILLY CAME Nate Frisch and three or four others. Frisch and Gilly were the only ones armed.

Gilly shouted, "What's up, Fannon?"

"There's a stranger in the corridors!" the Secret Agent told him hurriedly. "We got to spread out and get him."

"Hey," demanded Nate Frisch. "What you doin' with that girl? That's the dame we brought here."

"The Skull told me to take her out of there. Let me through here."

Frisch had pushed past Gilly, was almost convinced by the Agent, when suddenly another demonstration was given of the Skull's thoroughness. Through the corridor echoed the Skull's voice, carried evidently by some hidden annunciator. He was broadcasting through the passages, just as the police did.

"Stop Fannon. Stop Fannon. He is Secret Agent 'X' in disguise! Kill Fannon! He is Secret Agent 'X' in disguise. All men into the corridors. Stop Fannon! Those who are armed will shoot him on sight. Others will grapple with him and call for help. It is impossible for him to escape, so continue the search until he is found."

As the meaning of the Skull's words became apparent to the group of men in the corridor, Frisch raised his gun, snarling.

"X's" swift movements, however, took him by surprise. Long, crushing, irresistible fingers seized his gun wrist, twisted it sharply. Other long fingers gripped his shoulder, heaved with all the power of "X's" supple body. Frisch went tumbling backward in the narrow corridor, backward into Gilly and the others, catapulting into them with a force that threw them off their balance, tumbling them to the floor in a tangled, confused heap.

And "X," in that moment of respite, under the awe-struck gaze of Betty Dale, produced from a pocket the key that the Skull had given him, inserted it in a slot in the wall at his elbow. A panel slid open, and he thrust her through it, stopped but a second to deliver a straight-arm jab into the jaw of Gilly who was struggling up out of the mess of writhing men on the floor. Gilly was the only dangerous one at the moment, for he still had a gun; Frisch having dropped his under the cruel pressure of "X's" fingers.

Gilly tumbled backward, groggy from the straight-arm jab, and "X" stepped through the opening, inserted his key on the other side, and watched the panel slide closed again.

Betty was waiting for him, white-faced. Her eyes were starry. "I might have known," she said, "that you wouldn't let him—"

He put one hand over her mouth, smiling as he did so. "Of course I wouldn't, Betty. But we'll talk about that later. Now, we must get out of here. Let's see where we are."

They were in another narrow passage branching off at right angles from the one they had just quit. It was, like the others, dimly lit by a single small bulb at the end.

He led her along it, silently.

"But how can we ever get out?" she asked. "That man said that no one—"

"Wait!" was all he told her.

He used his key at the other end to admit them to another corridor, much wider, with doors on either side. "X" thought he recognized this as the corridor along which was the door of Tyler's cell.

He opened the second door on the left and, sure enough, there was the grisly sight of the man who had been the victim of the Skull's fiendish ingenuity. It was this room that Betty had been made to look into through the barred aperture in the "execution room."

Tyler was no longer chained. No needle had sprung from the knob though "X" had taken the precaution to stand at one side, and to keep Betty behind him as he turned the knob. Evidently events had been moving too fast even for the Skull since last night, and he had not had time to replace the needle. But when the door opened a bell began to ring, the same as last night. The alarm was given once more, and the Skull now knew which corridor they were in.

Tyler looked up at them inanely, without the slightest sign of intelligence in his eyes. His hands were shaking as if from palsy, and his lower jaw hung slack, as if out of his control, allowing saliva to dribble down to his chin.

Betty uttered a horrified gasp, leaned against the wall for support.

"X" stepped into the room, gripped Tyler by the arm. "Come on," he said in a gentle voice. "I'll take you out of here."

But Tyler shrank back, uttering an incoherent sound that was between a scream and a moan.

Suddenly the hidden amplifier in the corridors came to life once more, echoing the voice of the Skull. "Fannon is now in corridor H, in Tyler's cell. Every one is to converge on corridor H. Do not let him escape again. Converge on corridor H!"

AT the same moment a panel high up in the wall began to slide up, revealing the same barred aperture through which Betty had been forced to look. As the opening, at first narrow, began to widen, "X" could see the bright light of the powerful spotlight in the execution room focused on it. Once that opening got wide enough, he would be bathed in its rays, helpless against the Skull who was undoubtedly still there.

Shrugging, he relinquished his grip on Tyler, slipped out of the room, and slammed the door. In the corridor Betty was still leaning weakly against the wall. "How terrible!" she murmured. "That man must be destroyed before he does the same thing to more people."

"He will be," the Secret Agent assured her grimly. "Now let's worry about ourselves."

He led the way along the corridor, just as the amplifier announced, "Fools! Can't you find corridor H? Binks has not returned yet. You must find it yourselves. Fannon cannot escape; he must be found and killed; the girl, too."

Betty asked tremulously, "Is there no way out?"

"X" had taken a peculiar, boxlike contraption from his pocket; this was no larger than a package of cigarettes, but it had a hole at either end, in which, Betty could see, there were lenses. He now stooped and removed the framework that had fitted under the sole of his shoe, and which he had worn on the way in with Gilly and Binks. He placed this in his pocket, and examined the floor as they went along. They worked their way through two more passages, and came to an elevator without encountering anybody. As they went down in the elevator, Betty asked, "What is that box—a camera?"

He smiled. "No, but it is the instrument of our salvation. It is a box containing a specially angled series of lenses which I built myself. It is constructed in accordance with a little known theory of light refraction, and shows markings invisible to the naked eye.

The elevator stopped, and they came out into another corridor.

"X" stooped and looked through the lens, then allowed Betty to do so. She saw faint scraping marks on the floor.

"This is one of the passages through which I entered with Binks. I wore a short piece of gray graphite attached to the sole of my shoe when I came in, and particles of the graphite detached themselves as I walked. By following them we will get out!"

She looked up at him, suddenly smiling, suddenly hopeful. "And then?"

"And then," he told her grimly, "I must begin all over again—work my way once more into the ranks of the Servants of the Skull. He must be destroyed!"

They were now following the particles of graphite through a damp tunnel that gave every evidence of being far below the surface of the ground. This was not one of the elaborately constructed passages, but evidently the outlet of route number seven, that by which Binks had brought him and Gilly in. The amplifier did not reach here, but far behind them they could still hear its metallic tones, hear confused shouts as men scurried around in search of them.

This tunnel led them at last into a small room without windows. There was a door at the opposite end which "X" tried, but found locked. There was no light here, but "X" used his thin pocket flash.

Betty waited while he brought out the kit of chromium steel tools which he had taken from the bag. In a few moments he had the lock open, swung the door wide—and Betty gasped behind him. For behind the door was a blank concrete wall.

"X" tapped the wall, and found that it was solid. There was no egress from the room except by the door by which they had come.

Betty asked, "Must we go back?"

"There's something queer here," said the Secret Agent. He stooped and examined the floor with the box-lens. "Here are particles of the graphite leading away from this blank wall. We must have come in through here all right, but this wall is solid, there's no doubt of that."

He went back to the other door, into the tunnel, and opened it a crack, then stopped, rigid. From the tunnel, not a hundred feet away, had come the tread of many feet. Then, as he listened, motioning Betty to silence, Binks' cackling voice came to them.

"If they came along here, they're trapped all righty. There's a room down the end of this tunnel, but he won't know how to get out of it, nohow. The door ain't got no lock on the inside, an' you fellows can just rake that room with your machine guns."

They heard Gilly say, "Boy, gimme a chance at that guy. I'll cut him in half with lead!"

"X" cautiously closed the door, noting as he did so, the truth of Binks' statement—there was no way to lock the door from the inside. He snapped his flash on again, saw Betty gazing at him with trustful eyes. She had every confidence that he would get her out of this impossible situation.

Once more he crossed to the door opening on the concrete wall. He closed it, began to throw his light along the wall of the room, on either side of the door. The approaching footsteps sounded louder outside.

Suddenly "X" uttered an exclamation of satisfaction.

Betty asked, "What is it? Have you found a way out?"

"I think so. See this lever? I believe I remember now what this room must be. I was blindfolded when we came in, and couldn't tell just what was going on. Let's see what happens."

He jerked the lever downward. For a moment nothing happened, then there was a smooth whirring of well-oiled machinery, and the whole room *began to move upward*.

The room was an elevator.

They heard shouts from the tunnel outside, oaths in Binks' cackling voice. Then the stuttering of a machine-gun. But they were already well above the level of the tunnel, and the shots had no effect.

Betty cried, "We're going to escape! We're going to escape!"

"We're not out yet," the Secret Agent said grimly. "As I recall it, the entrance to this route was through a cellar. We still have to reach that. And Binks and his crew know we are on our way and can head us off." He took her hand. "This is going to be a gruelling ordeal, Betty. You must keep a stiff upper lip. I—have doubts now, about our ever getting out of here alive."

Betty's mouth was firm, but her eyes were wet. "I—don't care. If you die—then I should like to die—too."

The Agent gripped her hand, pressed it. They waited together for the elevator to reach the upper level, for whatever lay in store beyond.

CHAPTER XII

THE SKULL'S COUP

THERE WAS A grinding noise, and the elevator came to rest. "X" opened the door which had presented to him only a blank wall before, and found that it now led into a narrow hallway. The quartz markings on the floor appeared under the box-lens, and they followed these.

They were apparently in an empty house of some sort. No light entered here, for the windows were boarded up with steel shutters like those on the windows in the headquarters of the Skull.

The markings led them to another small room, with another door opening on a blank wall. Here the Agent did not hesitate. He sought and found a lever in the wall, pressed it, and the elevator descended swiftly. When it stopped, the agent put his hand on the knob, opened the door a crack, and stopped. Just outside he had caught the sound of whispered words. There were men out there in the darkness, waiting for them. Softly he closed the door, turned to Betty in the dark.

"Binks must have taken a short cut," he told her. "They're out there, waiting for us."

"What are you going to do?"

"They must have heard the noise of the machinery," the Agent told her. "They know we are here and are waiting for the door to open. If we don't come out pretty soon they'll come in after us."

"And then?"

"Too much depends on our getting out. *Nothing must stop us!*"

She couldn't see his face in the dark, but she heard the grim resolve in his tone.

Soon, Binks' voice came to them. "Go on, Gilly, I'll hold the flashlight. You go on in there an' mop 'em up. They ain't got no guns. It'll be a pipe!"

She was trapped by the screen.

"Okay!" Gilly exclaimed. "Here I go!"

"X" crouched beside the door, holding Betty behind him. They were in such a position that they would be screened by the door when it opened.

They heard Gilly approach, felt the door give under his push. A beam of light penetrated the crack. There was a hard push from Gilly and the door swung wide. Gilly had pushed it with the snout of the sub-machine gun which he held at his shoulder. For a second that snout showed in the doorway, and "X," reaching a long arm around the door, gripped it and tugged.

Gilly uttered a shout, came tumbling into the room after the gun, sprawled on the floor. The gun slipped from his hands as he tried frantically to rise. He was in the center of the room, outlined by the beam of the flashlight. For "X" to have stepped out there from behind the door would have meant death from the other guns in the darkness.

Binks shouted, "Go on in there, boys! Blast him before he gets his hands on Gilly's gun!"

There was a rush of feet toward the doorway. But "X" slammed it shut in the faces of the advancing attackers, stooped to the floor, and yanked upward on the lever.

The door heaved inward under the thrust of a heavy shoulder, and the big, brutish form of Gelter, one of the men who had gone on the mission to kidnap Betty, appeared, with a gun in his hand.

But the room had already begun to move upward in response to "X's" touch on the lever. The floor of the room was now higher than the outer floor, and Gelter tripped, sprawled half in and half out. The floor rose to the accompaniment of shouts from the men outside, and Gelter struggled to maintain a hold, with his legs hanging over the edge of the rising floor.

Gilly scrambled to his knees; murderous, slitted eyes on the Secret Agent. He reached for his machine gun. "X" took a quick step forward, brought the edge of his open hand down in a chopping blow to his neck, and the little gunman slumped down, unconscious, his grip on the Thompson relaxing.

And just then Betty Dale shrieked—again and again. "X" looked at her swiftly, turned his eyes to follow the wavering finger that pointed. Gelter had waited too long; the floor had risen to the top of the doorway, clamping his body at the waist. As he felt the inexorable pressure, the big kidnaper's face turned yellow with terror. His big, hairy arms strained against the floor in a futile attempt to stop it from rising. His eyes were on "X" and he shouted hoarsely, "God! Stop it! It's crushing me!"

"X" leaped to the lever, depressed it. The elevator stopped for a moment, then moved downward; but not before there was a horrible crunching of bones, and Gelter screamed shrilly, then became silent as his body slumped on the floor.

The floor, moving downward, released him from the terrible grip, and he slid off, falling into the outer room below. The flashlight was still flaring up at them. "X" picked up the submachine gun, put it to his shoulder, aiming low into the room below, and pressed the trip.

Lead belched from it into the floor of the cellar room below. There were confused shouts, cries of panic, and a rush of feet away from the spraying lead. Binks' voice, raised in a cackling, querulous shout of anger, rose above the stuttering of the gun. "C'mere, you monkeys! He's comin' down. Get him!"

But the flying lead, on top of the sight of Gelter's broken body hurtling down upon them, was too much for the innately cowardly men. They fled, and Binks followed them. His flashlight disappeared, leaving the place in utter darkness. By the time the elevator was down to the level of the cellar room once more, there was no opposition to the egress of "X" and Betty Dale.

The Secret Agent gave Betty his flashlight, told her to keep the pencil of light ahead of them. He advanced before her, the machine gun still at his shoulder. Her light showed they were in a cellar, flicked around and found the door, opening upward. "X" went up the steps first, looked out and saw that the alley above was clear. He stepped up, followed by Betty, and quickly moved into a darker spot, whispering over his shoulder, "Douse the light."

She did so, and not a moment too soon. For a patrolman came running into the alley, no doubt attracted by the shots. He saw the open cellar door, clicked on his flashlight, drew his gun, and stepped down into it. "X" seized the opportunity to grip Betty's arm and dash with her into the back entrance of the pool room through which he had entered that afternoon. The sight of the machine gun at his shoulder cowed the occupants of the pool room, and they shrank out of the way.

The Secret Agent rushed Betty through, out into the street. As he had expected, Binks and the others had not given up the chase so easily. A black car was waiting at the curb. The minute "X" appeared in the doorway of the pool room, the muzzle of a Thompson was thrust out of one of the windows. "X" had his Thompson at his shoulder and spitting fire before the gunner in the car could get set. "X" kept his finger on the trip this time, till the drum was empty. He saw the Thompson in the car drop from a suddenly nerveless hand and clatter to the gutter, saw a close-cropped head loll out of the window as the frightened driver shot the car from there.

Even before the car had disappeared around the corner, "X" had hurried Betty in the opposite direction. Around the near corner he dragged her, dropping the empty Tommy, and down the street until he saw a cruising cab.

He flagged this, bundled her into it, and gave an address uptown. In the cab Betty tried to catch her breath. Finally, when she was breathing more regularly, she said, "I don't know how you did it, but I'm sure no one else in the world could have got out of that nightmare prison! Where are you going now?"

"X" was fingering the radio in the cab, trying to tune in to some station that would be broadcasting news. He said morosely, "First I'm going to take you where you'll be safe. Then I'm going to work on the Skull once more. I'll never feel you're really safe till the Skull is destroyed."

HE found a station, tuned it in, and sat back as the announcer said, "A sensational item of news has just reached me. Harrison Dennett, the noted real estate operator and subway contractor, upon whose home an unsuccessful attempt at robbery was made this afternoon, did not have such good luck this evening. At six-thirty tonight he was kidnaped from his automobile. The kidnapers seemed to have vanished into thin air with their victim, leaving not the slightest trace. In the car was left a card bearing the gruesome reproduction of a skull. This card has been left at most of the major crimes that have been committed in the past few months. There is no doubt that some fiendish master of crime has—"

"X" snapped off the radio, lapsed into thought.

"What does it mean?" asked Betty.

"It means," the Secret Agent said bitterly, "that the Skull is getting himself more patients for that electric chair of his!"

CHAPTER XIII

DOOM TRAP

THE DARKENED ROOM gave off an animal smell; a smell of unwashed bodies. Muted voices buzzed with excited comment. There was the noise of shuffling as nervous men shifted their feet; rustling of clothing; here and there a nervous laugh.

All became still as a dull glow illuminated a niche high up in the wall, limning the horrid figure of the vermilion-garbed Skull. A spotlight flared down in the upturned faces of the expectant men below.

The Skull spoke, his hideous face leering at his listeners.

"I have called you all together," he began, "because I have an important announcement to make. You all know that the man who was known as Fannon was really the person who goes by the name of Secret Agent 'X.' You also know that he was almost trapped here, and escaped only by some extremely lucky accidents. I cannot understand yet how he found his way out of this place, but I assure you he will never find his way in again—except as a prisoner."

The Skull paused a moment, appraising the men below him, as if trying to ascertain how much damage had been done to his prestige by the sensational escape. Utter silence reigned in the room. The men were still evidently as much in awe of him as they had ever been.

Their master surveyed them sardonically for a moment, noting the varied emotions written on the coarse faces below him, mercilessly exposed by the searching beams of the spotlight. He went on.

"I have never made it a practice to announce my plans in advance. This time, however, I am making an exception, for the reason that I want you all to perform enthusiastically the work which I shall assign to each of you. We have already launched the operation which I have been planning for some time; the operation which is going to net us ten million dollars in cash."

He paused to let that sink in, noting the sudden greedy interest that the men began to evince.

"I flatter myself," he continued, "that I have conceived one of the most original methods of prying money loose from the public in the annals of crime. We are going to kidnap ten wealthy men, whose names I have carefully chosen after certain investigations. The first of these, Harrison Dennett, the construction man, is already here, in our power. The other nine will be brought in today. Each of you will be assigned a certain task, which must be performed with the precision of clockwork, for every one of the nine other kidnapings has been timed carefully with the habits of these men, which I have taken great pains to check on.

"As you return with the prisoners, Binks will meet you at the different entrances assigned you, and you will conduct the prisoners to the cell down below. One prisoner, and no more, is to go in each cell. I have a particular reason for that, which you will learn later. Now, are there any questions?"

For a while there was silence as the men digested the peculiar information they had just received. Then Gilly raised a hand, blinking in the spotlight.

"Gilly," said the Skull, "what is your question?"

The little gunman shuffled from one foot to the other. Already he regretted having raised his hand, was astounded at his own temerity.

"Well?" the Skull snapped. "Talk up. What is it?"

GILLY fidgeted, looked sheepishly at the men around him, then up toward the niche which he couldn't see because of the blinding light. "Jeez, boss, I don't mean to be fresh or nothin'. But I been in the snatchin' racket myself, out West; an' I know what these rich guys is like. We once snatched a guy what was supposed to be a millionaire, an' it turned out that all he had was houses an' stocks, but no cash. It took his family almost a month to raise the dough, an' then we had to settle for a hundred grand. That was all they could lay their mitts on." He stopped, licked his lips nervously.

The Skull asked, encouragingly, "What is the point you wish to make, Gilly?"

"Well, boss, I was wonderin' if you could get ten million dollars from those ten guys. How're they gonna raise all that cash?"

The Skull laughed harshly. "I told you that my plan was one of the most original in the history of crime, Gilly. I am glad that you mentioned this matter. It shows that you are wide awake. But I, also, thought of it; and the method I have devised for making it possible to raise the cash is what makes my plan original. You see, Gilly, we shall not ask these men to pay one cent out of their own pockets! There will be no demands for ransom from their families, or from the firms which they head. But—*the money will be forthcoming!*"

Gilly wet his lips again. "How?" he asked in a dry whisper.

"That, men, will remain a secret until tomorrow morning. When we have these ten men safely in the cells, I will send an announcement to the newspapers, and they will print it. And it will open the way for a new kind of crime—wholesale kidnaping, with payment of the ransom money absolutely assured! There will be no hesitation about paying it, for they will have Ainsworth Clegg and the others as examples of my art. You will recall that I told you at the time we seized Clegg and the others, that I did not intend to make any money on them. They were doomed, for I wanted to let it be seen what would happen to those who defied me. So I deliberately set the ransom demand at a preposterous figure. Now, with those examples before them, there will be a rush to make the payment. Tomorrow morning you will learn who is going to pay the ransom!"

Gilly had no more questions. The group of men in the room with him stirred nervously. Their curiosity was piqued. They wondered how their master intended to cause ten million dollars to be raised for ransom. They were no children; many of them, like Gilly, had at one time or another turned their hands to kidnaping, and they knew from bitter experience that large ransoms are more easily demanded than produced. Fresh in their minds was the recent case of a kidnaped upstate politician whose family, it had been supposed, measured its wealth in multiples of millions, but who had been released for a measly ninety thousand dollars. Each was busy trying to solve the puzzle in his own mind.

"Now," said the Skull, "we will once more discuss Secret Agent 'X.' I will admit that he, whoever he may be, is the only man with courage and cleverness enough to be a possible menace to our plans. I will also admit that he succeeded in escaping from what was a perfect trap. But I assure you that I will have him here, in one of the cells downstairs, within twenty-four hours!"

A low murmur of interest was heard from the men.

The Skull went on, emphasizing his words. "I am sure that when be learns of our present operation, he will make a desperate attempt to work his way in here again. In what disguise, I do not know. A man who could successfully deceive me by posing as Fannon may do anything. It is even possible that he may place himself in the role of one of the men who is to be kidnaped. I shall make it easy for him to do so, as you will see when you are given your instructions. But—" the Skull paused to let the words sink in—"whatever disguise he uses, *I shall know him!* Do you want to know why?"

The master's voice rang with evil triumph as he went on swiftly. "Because, my friends, though he may be known as The Man of a Thousand Faces, he has only ten fingers! And—*I have prints of all ten of them!* We will fingerprint every prisoner, every stranger who enters here. And sooner or later Secret Agent 'X' will come into our hands!"[10]

---

10   AUTHOR'S NOTE: *Secret Agent "X" had known that it was impossible for a man to live in any one place for even a single day without leaving his fingerprints. Ordinarily he would have worn gloves, or painted his fingertips with collodion, as he often does. In this case, however, it was not feasible to do so, as either the gloves or the collodion would have aroused the suspicions of an astute criminal like the Skull. "X" did, however, exert every effort to avoid leaving his prints. The Skull, however, made it a practice to secure the prints of every new man's fingertips from the silver with which he ate. These prints the Skull now had.*

CHAPTER XIV

SPIDER AND THE FLY

IN A QUIET section of the city stands the Montgomery mansion, a relic of the old blue-stocking aristocracy. Few know how old the house really is. At one time it was far uptown, almost suburban; until the bustling tide of business and residential buildings swept up around and past it, so that now it is "downtown."

For many years it has stood silent and apparently unused, seeming to reflect upon its ancient grandeur and the wealth of its former owners.

A curious sight-seer would have had difficulty in making his way into the house. For if he successfully climbed the high stone fence, he would have found, upon going up the old porch, that the door and all the windows were boarded up securely. If he wandered around to the rear, through a garden strewn with ancient statuary, if he succeeded in finding the entrance in the back that led into the house through the butler's pantry, and if he made his way along the hall to the front of the ground floor, he would have been surprised to find that the rooms which he supposed un-tenanted were very comfortably equipped. Peeking into one of them, he would have seen a pleasantly furnished bedroom, and on the bed, sleeping the sleep of exhaustion, a very beautiful blonde young lady.

And if this sight-seer were a careful reader of the newspapers he would have uttered a gasp of surprise upon recognizing the features of the young lady as being those of a Miss Betty Dale whose disappearance and suspected abduction were one of the big news items of the evening.

Still more surprised would the uninvited guest have been had he stepped into the alcove adjoining the next room. For here he would have seen another person whose picture was appearing in the evening paper—one Frank Fannon, ex-convict, who was reported to have figured in a series of queer episodes since he was released from jail the day before.

Now, this uninvited sight-seer, if he had remained silent and watched the man in the alcove, would shortly have rubbed his eyes in amazement at what was taking place. For this man, Fannon, was seated before a triple mirror, doing things to his face. Soon the face of Frank Fannon disappeared under the long, agile fingers, revealing for a moment the countenance of a keen-eyed young man with a mobile, restless mouth and an imperious nose—a face which the sightseer would surely not have recognized, for it was a face that no one in the world had ever seen.

And under the eyes of the astounded sight-seer that face would soon have begun to assume an entirely different appearance. The temples became grayed, the lips fuller, the eyebrows thicker; in fact, a complete metamorphosis took place, and instead of Frank Fannon, there sat before the triple mirror the suave, urbane millionaire clubman, Elisha Pond.

After a few careful finishing touches to his face, Mr. Pond arose and proceeded to change to faultless evening attire. When he was finished, he stepped into the next room, took a last look at Betty Dale who was still in deep slumber, induced by the sedative he had given her. She was safe here from the Servants of the Skull.

He had given her the sedative before bringing her here, and, after the peril was over, he would return and take her away before she regained consciousness. She would never know where she had slept, would never know where she had been afforded sanctuary. The less she knew, the better it would be for her.

Mr. Pond left her there, and went out through the hall to the cellar, through the cellar to the back of the house. Here the curious sight-seer would no longer have been able to follow him, for his dark-clad figure merged with the darkness of the night. A tall gate in the stone fence swung open on well-oiled hinges, and Mr. Elisha Pond stepped through it into the garden of the house next door. This house was known to the world as the home of Mr. Pond; but none knew of the excursions that its master made in the night to the Montgomery mansion next door, where he prepared himself to do battle against hideous crime.

Mr. Pond went through the garden and into the garage at the rear of his home. The chauffeur, who lived above the garage, was downstairs tinkering with one of the cars, of which there were four here. He touched his cap respectfully, said, "Good evening, sir. I didn't know you were home, sir. Will you want me to drive you tonight?"

"No, Carl, I will take the small coupe and drive myself."

"It is all ready, sir."

Mr. Elisha Pond nodded genially, got into the car, and drove off. To his servants here he was known as a kindly, wealthy master who treated them considerately and was a snap to work for, since he was away most of the time.

Mr. Pond's first stop was at the Bankers' Club. He had to park a block away because of the subway construction going on. As he crossed the street over the subway cut where he had found Ainsworth Clegg, he wondered if one day shortly, Harrison Dennett would not be found in the same fashion, mind and body wrecked. Dennett was a strong, cool sort of man, and the thought of how he would be after a treatment of the fiendish electric chair was particularly horrible.

At the Bankers' Club there was an undercurrent of uneasiness that was reflected even in the greeting of the doorman who was usually a paragon of stiff respectfulness.

Inside, the club seemed deserted, a pall of gloom lying over it. In the corner by the window where at this hour there usually congregated Commissioner Foster, Pelham Grier, Pierre Laurens, Jonathan Jewett, Dennett and others, there were only Jewett and Commissioner Foster. They sat in silence, as if they were utterly weary. Commissioner Foster appeared harried and worn. He looked up as Pond approached them.

"Hello, Pond," he said. "I'm glad to see that you're here at least. You shouldn't wander around the town unprotected like this—he'll get you, too."

"Who'll get me?" Pond asked lightly, seating himself beside Jewett. The tall, gaunt Insurance Company president barked, "You don't mean to say you don't know what's been happening today?"

"I heard that Dennett was robbed and then kidnaped. I haven't seen a paper since. Has anybody else been abducted?"

JEWETT snorted. "Where've you been tonight—taking a beauty nap? Take a look around here. Do you see Grier? Do you see Laurens? No! I'll tell you why. They've both been abducted by the Skull!"

The eyes of Mr. Elisha Pond became veiled as he glanced from the insurance man to the police commissioner. "The situation," he said slowly, "becomes alarming."

Commissioner Foster looked haggard. "More than alarming, Pond. It is terrifying. That is not all. Grier and Laurens are not the only ones besides Dennett who have been abducted. Five more are gone. I sit here in dread. Every hour I receive reports of more kidnapings. So far there is a total of eight of the wealthiest men in the city in the power of the Skull. I have assigned guards to every one who might be a possible future victim, but I confess that I am helpless. The abductions are performed with great daring, must be carefully planned, for these 'snatchers' disappear with their victims almost under the very eyes of the pursuers."

Mr. Pond asked, "Where is Arnold Hilary?" Hilary was another one of the group that frequented this corner of the Bankers' Club after dinner. He was the proprietor of the *Herald*, the newspaper that Betty Dale worked for, and had, on occasion, received substantial financial assistance from Elisha Pond. The use of his unlimited resources in this way had often aided the Agent in his work, by establishing powerful connections for him. The use of these connections had often meant the difference between success and failure.

In answer to his question Foster told him, "Hilary is keeping close to his home. I've put a guard around it. We think he might be in danger of abduction, too."

"What leads you to believe that?" Pond asked with quick interest.

Foster coughed behind his hand, hesitated a moment, then said, "Look here, Pond, this is strictly confidential. It hasn't been released to the papers. It was reported that a card with a drawing of a skull was found in Dennett's car when he was kidnaped, and that similar cards were found in the homes of Grier, Laurens and the others. That is true. But there was a message on those cards that was not printed in the newspapers."

"Yes?" Pond asked.

"Those cards are downtown at headquarters now, but the message on each was identical. I remember it word for word: 'Do not prepare to raise ransom money. No ransom will be demanded from the family or business connections of my prisoners. Ten men are to be abducted today. Let them not offer resistance, lest they receive the same treatment that Ainsworth Clegg and the others received. Tomorrow I will make known the terms upon which I will release these men. Until then, do nothing.' And it was signed, 'The Skull'!"

Foster finished reciting the message, stopped and lit a long cigar that he extracted from his pocket. The match trembled a little. He did not see the swift gleam in Pond's eyes as he heard the strange wording on the cards.

It was Jewett who broke the silence that followed. "I tell you, Pond, it's like fighting the darkness! This Skull, as he calls himself, is fiendishly clever. And he's Satan himself. Imagine Grier, Laurens, Dennett and the others being in the power of such a being; why, we don't know when we'll find their broken bodies in the street. We don't know what he plans! Why, he even says that he isn't going to ask for ransom from their families! The man must be a maniac!"

"I don't think so," said Elisha Pond. "I think he has a definite plan, which we shall learn tomorrow when he makes his announcement. But why, Jewett, are you so wrought up? You seem to feel that he has done you a personal injury."

Jewett's eyes blazed. "You're damn right, he has! Do you know that every one of those men who've been taken by the Skull is insured to the hilt? Approximately six million dollars of life insurance is the maximum that anybody can get, and each of those men has the maximum. Ten men. Sixty million dollars. Can you understand what that would do to the life insurance companies of the country if they were all killed? Not only that, but if ten men can be kidnaped, why not a hundred? Why not a thousand? It would be disaster for the institution of life insurance, which it has taken decades to build up to its present strength!"

"I see," Elisha Pond said very quietly. "I begin to see more clearly." Suddenly he arose. "I must go now, gentlemen. If there is anything I can do, commissioner, please let me know."

"I will," Foster said glumly. "But I'm afraid we're all helpless. This Skull must be a genius of crime; and I fear the police are not equipped to combat him. It's a bitter admission to make, but there's no use glossing the facts. So far, we've been worse than useless. Take care of yourself. Do you want a guard?"

"Hardly," laughed Pond. "I don't think the Skull is interested in me—not if he's after insured men. I haven't much insurance."

"He can't get it," Jewett explained to Foster. "He lives too dangerous a life—exploring in Africa, flying planes. Why, he's even got the rank of general in the Chinese Army!"

As Pond was at the door, Jewett called after him, "Tell you what you can do, if you want to, Pond. You can stop in at Hilary's hotel and buck him up a bit. He's heavily insured, and he seems to be pretty scared about this business."

"That's an idea," said Elisha Pond. "I was thinking of doing that myself."

CHAPTER XV

THE SKULL STRIKES

SECRET AGENT "X" never underestimated an opponent. He was far too intelligent for that. Therefore he was quite sure that it would be useless to return to the cellar behind the pool room in an effort to win into the Skull's headquarters through entrance number seven. He put himself mentally in the Skull's place, and imagined what the Skull would do. Either he would destroy the entrance as being of no further value since its existence was known, or else he would lay some sort of trap in anticipation of the Agent's attempt to come back that way.

The rear of the apartment house on Slocum Street, where he and Gilly had been originally supposed to meet Links, offered another slender thread that might lead him back into the lair of the Skull, but this too he thrust aside. The Skull would no doubt have taken similar precautions there, and, possibly, at every one of his other entrances.

From the Bankers' Club, "X" had gone to an apartment that he maintained near the waterfront.[11] Here he stepped out of the character of Elisha Pond, and became A. J. Martin, an Associated Press correspondent. Before going to the apartment, he had phoned Jim Hobart at the farm where he was keeping the real Frank Fannon a prisoner, instructed him to give Fannon a dose of a powder which would keep him unconscious for another twenty-four hours. Hobart was then to come to the city and meet "X," whom he knew

---

11 AUTHOR'S NOTE: Secret Agent "X" maintains numerous retreats in various parts of the country, several in each of the larger cities. These are absolutely necessary, since the success of his work may often depend upon the accessibility of a place where he may change his appearance—in fact, his very life may often depend upon it. The author once asked him how much his annual rent bill amounted to, and was rewarded with an enigmatic smile.

only as A. J. Martin.

The Secret Agent paid particular attention to his equipment now, realizing that if his line of reasoning was correct, he would be placing himself in greater jeopardy than ever in his life by doing the thing that he now intended doing.

He left the apartment, went to a near-by garage and got a small sedan which was always kept ready there for him in the name of Martin. He drove in leisurely fashion up to the East Eighties, and parked there for fifteen minutes. Soon a cab drew up at the corner and Jim Hobart alighted from it, minus his army chauffeur's uniform. The young man was bubbling with excitement as he ran to his employer's car.

"Say, Mr. Martin," he exclaimed as "X" drove farther uptown, "that Colonel Delevan that you sent me to do the job for is certainly a wonder. You should have seen him make himself up like Fannon. I turned around, and did I get a jolt when I saw that there were two Fannon's in the back of the car. Why, they might have been twins. He's a genius, that Colonel Delevan!"

"Thank you," the Agent murmured.

"Eh, what did you say, Mr. Martin?"

"Nothing at all," the Secret Agent said hastily. "Now listen carefully, Jim. I'm going to give you a job now that is of the utmost importance. I know I can rely on you."

"You bet your boots, Mr. Martin. I've been having a better time since I met you than I ever had in my life."

"I know that, Jim, and I'm taking advantage of it."

"X" braked the car just then across the street, and about a hundred feet from a large residential hotel. "In that hotel," he said, "is staying a man named Arnold Hilary, who is the proprietor of the *Herald*. I am going to leave you now. If I do not return, I want yon to remain here and watch for him. If he comes out alone, don't bother about him any more, but go back home and wait to hear from me. But—if he comes out with anybody else, I want you to follow them; discreetly. It'll be as much as your life is worth if you should be noticed. So be extremely careful. Do you understand?"

JIM HOBART nodded eagerly. "I understand, Mr. Martin. I'll be careful, all right."

"You will note where they go, and remain on watch there, for an hour. At the end of that time you will go to police headquarters and ask to see either Commissioner Foster or Inspector Burks. You will tell them that you saw where Hilary was taken, and lead them to the place. Tell them to bring along a wrecking crew. Is everything clear now?"

"I got it, Mr. Martin. I'm all set."

"X" got out. "Of course, I may be wrong in my deductions, in which case I'll be right back. Well, good luck." He turned and strode off in the direction of the hotel.

As soon as he got abreast of it, he saw that his deductions had been correct. For parked opposite the entrance was a black sedan, and at the wheel was Nate Frisch. Nate Frisch, dressed in a peculiar gray-green uniform, with a visored cap.

Inside the lobby he saw another one of the Servants of the Skull, a man named Orson, whom he recognized at once. He might be too late; perhaps the Skull was already striking here. Orson was lounging in a corner, smoking a cigarette and surveying the lobby through slitted eyes. He glanced at "X," then allowed his gaze to slide away. He did not recognize in the man who was posing as A. J. Martin, the Frank Fannon who had slept in the same room with him the night before.

"X" hurried up to the desk. Near the desk a uniformed patrolman stood on guard, with a riot gun under the crook of his elbow. He frowned as "X" said to the clerk, "I would like to see Mr. Hilary, please."

Before the clerk could answer, the patrolman came up close, demanded, "What's your name, mister, and what do you want to see Mr. Hilary for?"

"X" took a card from his pocket and handed it to the policeman. It was the card of Mr. Elisha Pond, and on the back was written in ink, "Dear Hilary, This is Mr. A. J. Martin, whom I phoned you about. He has a matter of great importance which he must see you about at once. E. P."

The patrolman said grudgingly, "Yeah. Mr. Hilary phoned down an' said to send you right up when you came. Go ahead. We got to be careful," he explained. "There's another man on guard upstairs. Not a soul is allowed on the fourteenth floor unless we know who he is. This here Skull has got the whole department buffaloed!"

"You don't say so!" Mr. Martin commented. "I'd think you'd arrest him or something, if he's so dangerous. My, what the city is coming to!"

The policeman snorted, and picked up the phone to notify the officer on the fourteenth floor that a visitor was coming up. "X" entered the elevator, noting that the eyes of Orson were now following him with interest. He had noted the conversation with the policeman.

Upstairs, a plainclothes man with a gun openly holstered at his hip met "X" and conducted him to the suite of the newspaper publisher. Hilary was alone in the sitting room of his three-room suite. He was settled comfortably on the sofa, reading, with a whiskey-and-soda beside him. "X" suspected that Hilary had deliberately placed himself there with the book, as a pose, when he learned that he was going to have company. Hilary was distinctly ill at ease, too worried about something or other to have been able to read so quietly.

He rose and shook hands with "X." "I don't know your business with me, Mr. Martin, but Elisha Pond said you were okay, and I'll take his word for anything. Sit down. Here, have a drink. Pour it yourself. It's fourteen-year-old Bourbon." His tone of cordiality seemed forced, with an undertone of nervousness in it.

"Thanks," said the Secret Agent. "I never drink when I'm working."

HILARY eased himself onto the sofa again, picked up his glass with a shrug. There were dark rings under his eyes. "Just as you say, Mr. Martin. Now, what can I do for you?"

"I've come here, Mr. Hilary, about—the Skull." The Agent stopped a moment as Hilary started, then went on. "I have reason to believe that the Skull intends to kidnap you tonight."

Hilary's face went ashen. "How—how do you know?"

"I have means of getting information. It doesn't matter how, but I'm almost sure of what I say."

Hilary gulped down the rest of his drink, put the glass on the table beside the couch. His hand shook so that the glass wobbled and fell to the floor when he released it. It struck the thick carpet on its edge, and did not break, but rolled over. Hilary looked down at it stupidly, then raised his eyes to "X."

"W-why do you come here to tell me this?"

"Because I intend to prevent your kidnaping. I believe that Mr. Pond told you on the phone that you could rely implicitly on me, could do anything I suggest without any fear. How far do you trust Mr. Pond?" He leaned forward in his chair to emphasize the question, his keen eyes burning into the other.

Hilary seemed fascinated by those eyes. "Why, there's nothing I wouldn't do for Mr. Pond. I owe most of my success to him. I'd do anything he asked."

"Would you allow me to change places with you?"

"You mean—you want to be kidnaped instead of me?"

"I mean just that"

"You couldn't get away with it. The Skull's men would know me. They'd know in a minute you weren't I. They'd kill you."

"Suppose you let me worry about that, Mr. Hilary. Now, quickly—there isn't much time, if my guess is correct—will you do it?"

"I'll do it," Hilary agreed. "But I don't understand why you want to. I've got a police guard—"

"So did the others—Grier, Laurens. But the Skull got them. Do you think that if he goes after you those guards outside will be a barrier?"

"You're right, Martin." Hilary was almost eager now. "What must I do?"

"Come into the next room." The Secret Agent picked up the open bottle of Bourbon and the bottle of charged water. "Take your glass, and come on. We must hurry."

As he led the way into the next room, "X's" fingers were busy. From his pocket he extracted a small pellet which he had kept there in readiness.[12] He knew Hilary's habit of drinking when he was alone, and had planned accordingly.

The next room was a bedroom. Hilary came in with him, sat down on the bed, and reached for the bottle. He poured himself a stiff drink, downed it straight, and coughed. "I needed that," he muttered apologetically. "You don't know what a strain it's been today; not knowing whether I was going to be the next victim or not. And I want to tell you that there are plenty more men in the city who've been worried, the same as I. This Skull, nobody knows where he'll strike next. And he's so clever; no precautions—"

His voice trailed off, his head sank to his breast, and in a moment he sprawled on the bed, breathing stertorously, inert and unconscious.

---

12   AUTHOR'S NOTE: *These pellets contain an anaesthetizing substance fully as powerful as the gas which Secret Agent "X" uses. The pellets are quickly soluble, and a half grain dissolved in a pint of liquid is sufficient to render a man unconscious after a single drink. He does not recover consciousness for from ten to fourteen hours, depending upon his physique. The pellets are tasteless, and unlike the ordinary form of "knockout drops," they have absolutely no after effects.*

"X" was already moving swiftly, efficiently. He peeled off his outer clothing, undressed Hilary, and donned the publisher's habiliments. Then he took from his inner pocket the flat black case containing make-up material, and set to work. Within ten minutes there were two Hilarys in the room.

The Secret Agent wasted no time in practicing the speech of the man he was impersonating. He dragged the body of Hilary to the clothes closet, and placed him on the floor there, propping his head up with his discarded clothes.

He had hardly straightened the room up, put away his paraphernalia and carried the bottles and glass back into the living room, before there was a discreet tap on the door. He went to the door and unlocked it. The plainclothes man on duty in the hall pushed his way in.

He said, "Say, Mr. Hilary, do you know anything about extra guards being ordered from the Home Detective Agency?"

"Extra guards?" the Agent asked. "I don't know of any." His voice as he spoke was the voice of Hilary to the last subtle inflection.

"Well, there's four of 'em out here. They've been sent to stay here with you day and night. I phoned the Agency, and their office says the men were ordered by Commissioner Foster. He's using their men because he don't want to take extra patrolmen off their regular work."

"X" was worried by this new development. His whole plan would be ruined if he had too much protection. Foster meant well, no doubt, but by this move the commissioner might be destroying the only possible chance of checkmating the Skull. Everything depended upon "X's" getting back into the Skull's headquarters.

"X" frowned, and said, "Send them in while I phone Foster and have them called off. This is ridiculous. The Skull must certainly feel flattered to know that the whole police department of the city isn't enough to cope with him!"

The detective nodded, and went to the door while "X" picked up the phone. The detective opened the door, and four men in the gray-green uniforms, guns in hand, entered. The first of the men was Nate Frisch, and the second was Gilly.

CHAPTER XVI

JAWS OF THE TRAP

SECRET AGENT "X" cradled the telephone as the four men spread out in the room, shutting the door after them. The detective sensed from the pregnant silence that suddenly permeated the room that something was wrong, and he instinctively went for his gun. But Gilly, who was at his left and a trifle behind him, brought the butt of a heavy automatic down on his head, and the plainclothes man tumbled to the floor in a heap.

The other two men stooped and dragged his inert body to one side, while Frisch advanced upon "X," menacing him with a gun, and grinning savagely.

"All right, Mr. Hilary," he said, "I guess you know who we are. We ain't from any detective agency. We're from the Skull!"

"X" simulated extreme panic, as Hilary might have done. "The Skull!" he cried. "What do you want with me?" He seemed to shrink away from Frisch with just the right degree of fear.

"You're comin' out with us, Mr. Hilary. I'll be on one side o' you, an' that little guy will be on the other. We'll both have guns in our pockets. Our two pals'll be right behind. If you make one single wrong yap we'll let you have it from both sides, right in the liver. You'll take a long time dyin', an' you'll wish you'd have kept your trap shut. Now stand up!"

"X" stood up hesitantly. "You—you're going to take me to the Skull?" He managed to put a quaver in his voice that would have done credit to any Thespian.

"You're damn right we are. An' when that dumb cop in the lobby asks you how come you're goin' out, you'll tell him you're goin' on personal business, an' takin' your private guards along. Get it?"

As "X" marched to the elevators with Frisch on one side and Gilly on the other, he was compelled to admire the daring simplicity of the plan. The Skull had no doubt established this detective agency address, so that when the plainclothes man called, as he was sure to do, they could answer properly, allaying his suspicions.

The Skull was very thorough. On the cap of each of the four men was a gold shield with the lettering, "Home Detective Agency." The uniforms were well-cut and expensive, giving the impression of a solid, respectable agency. "X" recalled now, that he had seen advertisements of the Home Detective Agency in several newspapers for some time past.

The Skull had probably built up the fictitious organization for some such use as this. Probably if the police went there to investigate, now, they would find nothing but an empty office. The person in whose name the license had been obtained would no doubt be out of the country, or dead, by this time.

Down in the lobby, just as Frisch had anticipated, the patrolman stared as he saw them come out of the elevator, then walked over. "Hello, Mr. Hilary," he exclaimed, surprised. "I thought you was staying upstairs!"

"X" felt a hard object poked into his ribs from each side. He could hear Frisch's heavy breathing, so close was the man to him. The threat of death was close.

"I'm going out on business," he said. "I—hope to be back soon. These men are plenty of protection for me."

The policeman was doubtful. "Don't you think you ought to call up headquarters first, Mr. Hilary? My orders—"

Frisch interrupted him harshly. The words he uttered were not in his usual style. The Skull had evidently made him learn them by rote. "See here, officer. Mr. Hilary is not a prisoner. If he chooses to go out, you have no right to detain him. You may report to headquarters yourself if you wish, but Mr. Hilary is in a hurry, and can't wait!"

Frisch's hand on the Secret Agent's arm urged him on, and they stepped past the policeman. The policeman, however, was not looking at Frisch; he was looking at Gilly.

"Sa-a-y!" he exclaimed. "I know your face! You ain't a private guard! Why, I've seen your mug in the lineup! You—"

He stopped, his eyes wide with horror, as he saw guns magically appear in the hands of the four. In the moment of realization, he started to raise the riot gun, but a storm of lead tore into his body from four guns. He dropped the riot gun, clutched at his stomach, cried, "My God!" and collapsed on the tiled floor of the lobby, his lifeblood gushing out of him.

Cries and shouts arose about them. The desk clerk reached for the phone, then dropped it and ducked under the desk as Gilly threw a shot at him. Still holding "X" between them, they rushed out of the lobby, crossed the street on the run, and piled into the black sedan.

Frisch took the wheel, and the car was spurting away from the curb before any of the passers-by knew what was taking place. Gilly and one of the others had "X" between them on the rear seat, while the fourth sat next to Frisch, looking backward out of the open window, with his gun ready.

"X" simulated great terror, he was eager to know if Jim Hobart was following, but dared not risk a glance through the rear window lest he arouse the suspicions of his captors.

THE sedan wound through several streets under Frisch's manipulation. They heard the siren of a radio car on the next block, and Frisch turned right, tore across town for three blocks, then headed south. The truck driveway of a large warehouse yawned open at their left, and Frisch turned into it. The door closed behind them, shutting out, partly, the sound of another police car siren outside. When the police car got to the spot where they had driven into the warehouse, the officers would find no single trace of them. They would begin to search the warehouses on the block, no doubt, and "X" waited to see how the Skull had planned to cover up. He was keenly interested in how the Servants of the Skull always managed to disappear without leaving a clue behind.

He was soon to see. The place had been in darkness when they entered, for Frisch had snapped off his headlamps early in the chase. Now a light sprang up toward the rear, showing the interior of the place, stacked with bales of goods, unlabeled, along the walls. The middle of the floor, where the car stood, was entirely clear. The reason for this became obvious in a moment, when a narrow strip of the floor, upon which the car stood, began to tilt downwards, forming a sort of runway down which Frisch drove the car. He stopped on a sort of platform below the floor level, and the strip of floor rose above them. The garage above was now empty of cars in case it should be searched.

There was a dim bulb down here, similar to the ones used in the corridors of the Skull's headquarters. Slowly the car began to turn. "X" realized that they were on a turntable. The car stopped turning and "X" looked ahead to see that they were facing a long, dark tunnel. Out of this tunnel came the slouching figure of Binks; Binks, the halfwit, with his hideously scarred and mutilated face.

"X" stirred in his seat, and Gilly, beside him, poked him savagely with the gun. "Hold still, you!" he snarled, "if you know what's good for you!"

"X" said nothing, but subsided, watching keenly. Binks came up to the car, peered in, and cackled. "I see you got'm, fellers. That makes number ten. The Skull will be tickled. Everything goin' off like clockwork."

Frisch said, "We had a tough time. Had to slug a dick an' kill a cop."

"Tell that to the Skull," Binks cackled. "Hurry up, now. The boss is waitin'. He wants to see this guy that you got here! Put a blindfold on 'im and let's go!"

Gilly produced a hood from next to him on the seat, and placed it over "X's" head. The Secret Agent offered no resistance. With the hood on his head, he could see nothing, of course, but he felt the car proceeding slowly ahead. After a short while Frisch turned the car, backed it up, then drove ahead some ten feet, and stopped. "X" heard the click of the ignition being turned off, heard the motor die. He waited silently, expecting to be taken from the car. Instead he heard Binks' voice.

"All right, boys, you can all put the hoods on now. From now on you got to follow me blind. You got to trust Binksy!"

"X" heard the men donning their hoods, grumbling as they did so. Frisch said, "It's a wonder the Skull picks a nitwit like you to take us through them passages. Suppose you forgot the way?"

Binks' shrill laughter answered him. "That'd be too damn bad fer you boys. You'd starve to death in them passages, 'cause you'd never get out!"

"I know a guy that got out," Frisch taunted. "This place ain't fool-proof."

THERE was silence for a moment, then Binks said, "I'll tell the Skull what you think about the place, Nate. I bet the Skull'll like to hear that."

"Nix, nix!" Nate pleaded. "I didn't mean nothin', Binks. You wouldn't squeal on a guy, would you?"

"Not if he had a coin to toss in the air that I could catch. I like coins. I save 'em."

"Sure," Frisch cried eagerly. "Here you are. It's a half a buck."

Binks laughed gleefully. "See how I caught it? That's great, Nate. You're a nice feller. If the Skull ever gets tired of you, or mad at you, and puts you in the electric chair, I'll tell you what I'll do for you—I'll put you out of your misery quick, with a knife, afterwards. It'll save you a lot of pain. Would you like me to do that for you?"

"Aw, shut up!" Frisch growled.

Binks laughed shrilly. "X" noted that they were moving again, but the motor was not running! They were on some sort of moving platform. There was a continuous sound of clanking from just behind them; otherwise there was silence. None of the men in the car spoke.

After about fifteen minutes they came to rest slowly. "X" heard Binks open the door of the car and say, "All right, boys, come on out one at a time, and hold hands. Use the cuffs on Hilary."

Gilly snapped a pair of cuffs on "X's" hand, then snapped the other on his own. Frisch did the same with "X's" other hand. The Agent was now in the middle of the living link that was moving toward the lair of the Skull. Binks went first, holding Frisch's hand, and the other two men followed after Gilly.

After negotiating a dozen winding passages, they finally came to a halt. Binks said, "You can take them hoods off, boys, but leave Hilary's on. Cuff his hands behind him."

Gilly and Frisch, after removing their hoods, snapped the handcuffs off their own wrists, and joined the two empty circlets of steel behind "X's" back. He was now handcuffed with two pair of cuffs, with his hands behind him.

He heard a door open in front of him, and was led through it, with Gilly and Frisch still on either side of him.

Binks said, "I'll take the other two boys back to the main room. Gilly and Frisch, you stay here with him till the boss comes."

Frisch growled a sullen "Okay." When the door closed behind Binks, he grumbled to Gilly, "One o' these days I'll take that damn half wit an' break his neck for him—Skull or no Skull."

Gilly snickered. "You're just talkin' big, Nate. You know you're dead afraid of the Skull."

"Who wouldn't be?" Frisch demanded. "But Binks, he's different. We could do without him fine."

Suddenly "X" felt Frisch stiffen beside him. Gilly stirred uneasily. A mocking voice spoke from above them. "Well, well. So we are honored by the company of Mr.—ah—Hilary! Take off the hood, Nate. Let me see his face!"

"X" recognized those hateful tones. The Skull was in the room.

CHAPTER XVII

THE JAWS CLAMP

NATE FRISCH'S FINGERS fumbled with the knot, and in a moment he removed the hood.

Once more Secret Agent "X" faced the Skull across the desk in that room with the four-foot strip of charged flooring. To him it felt as if he had hardly been out of the room; the same leering, fleshless death's-head sat behind the desk. The weak illumination cast a weird shadow upon the vermilion-hooded face of the Skull. Only the dead rat was missing; it had been removed.

Under the influence of the familiar surroundings, he almost reverted, unconsciously, to the role of Fannon, whom he had impersonated here that morning. Almost, he felt as if Betty Dale were still a prisoner, under threat of a hideous fate, and that he must still exert himself to the utmost to snatch her out of the clutches of this master of deviltry.

But the Skull spoke once more, and the words snapped him out of it. "Mr. Hilary, you have been highly honored; you have been chosen by me as one of the first ten men to be kidnaped under my new plan of operations. I am now going to ask you some questions, the answers to which I need; and I counsel you to reply quickly and accurately. You have seen the things that happen to those who arouse my anger. You were acquainted with Ainsworth Clegg, were you not?"

"X" felt the deep, heavy breathing of Frisch, the wheezy breath of Gilly, one on either side of him. He took a step forward, felt his arms seized on either side by Gilly and Frisch. He said, imitating Hilary's voice, "You must be crazy, whoever you are. You gained nothing by what you did to Clegg. Now, you kidnap me and the others, and expect to get millions in ransom. I can tell you now that you won't get it. None of us can raise that much cash. It's impossible!" He wanted to draw out the Skull, to make him talk. He had observed previously that this master of devilish plans had a slight trace of vanity, and he was now playing on it.

The Skull said, "Frisch! Gilly! Let him go. In this room I do not need your protection." He waited a moment until they dropped their grips on "X's" arms, then he said to "X," "My actions, Mr. Hilary, may seem insane to you, but believe me they are not As the old saying goes, 'There is method in my madness.' You think I gained nothing by breaking Ainsworth Clegg, destroying his mind and his body. You are wrong."

The Skull stopped, raised his hand and pointed at "X" to emphasize his words. "Clegg was an investment in horror; an object lesson in advance—a sort of sales talk to stimulate the eagerness of the public to raise large sums to ransom those whom I may kidnap in the future. And it is immaterial to me whether I get ransom for you and those others in the cells, or not; for if I send the ten of you out into the streets, broken hulks of men, I will be able to collect twice as much on the next batch."

The Secret Agent found it difficult to repress a gesture of loathing for the cold-blooded callousness displayed by the Skull. Instead, he allowed his eyes to grow wide in simulated admiration. "A man like you could conquer the world. You have no conscience—no compunctions about anything; there is nothing to stop you!" He could see the skeleton head nodding as if its owner were pleased. "X" had gauged correctly the extent and the nature of the man's vanity. But that was only the first step. His work was still to do. He wanted very much to discover how the Skull proposed to get ten million dollars out of his captives.

The Skull said, "As you say, there will be nothing to stop me from conquering the world. Money, today, is, more powerful than weapons. And I shall have ten million dollars to start with!"

"X" felt Gilly and Frisch stirring restlessly beside him. This sort of talk was beyond their comprehension. He took advantage of the Skull's momentary relaxation of mood to broach the subject uppermost in his mind. "I can't imagine a man like you making a mistake," he began. "But I don't understand how you expect me and the others to raise a million dollars apiece. Frankly, I couldn't raise a hundred thousand in cash; and I know that Grier and Laurens couldn't, either."

The Skull laughed in a pleased manner. "I am making no mistake, Hilary. I realize that you and your friends aren't able to produce any sizable amounts in cash; but I know where the cash can be forthcoming. And it will be, never fear!"

THE Agent waited, hoping that the Skull would elaborate. And he did.

"I might as well tell you now, for it will be public property in a few hours when I release my notice to the newspapers. You see," he leaned forward over the desk as he spoke, eyes gleaming in the half light, under the flap of the vermilion hood, "you see, each of you is insured to the hilt. That means that each of you carries approximately six million dollars of life insurance."

The Secret Agent tensed. He had suspected something like this. Now his suspicions were crystallized into certainty. The plan was devilishly ingenious.

The Skull went on. "Do you understand now where the money will be coming from? I am asking the insurance companies to chip in one million dollars for each of you—a total of ten million dollars, which is less than the sixty million they would have to pay if you all died. The companies will be eager to do it, for they know I mean business. They will have to pay out about five or six million on Clegg when he dies, as he surely will within a day or so. No man can live long after the treatment I give him!"

"X" nodded. He was compelled to admit that the plan was a sound one. The companies would pay. Men like Jonathan Jewett were shrewd, hardheaded business men, but they knew when they were licked. They would pay the ten million to save sixty million, and they would reduce the policies by the amount they paid out, so that in the end they would not be the losers at all.

The Skull was almost sure to get his ransom. And then—what couldn't a super-criminal like him do once he had the resources which ten million dollars could procure for him. There would be no stopping him. Atrocities would pile up with breath-taking rapidity. The city, the nation—the world, possibly—would offer an open field for his vicious depredations.

Only he, a lone man, with his hands manacled behind his back, might, by some lucky break, be able to stem the mushroom growth of this vilest criminal since the Borgias.

The Skull continued arrogantly, "I have already notified the insurance companies of my terms. They must pay me one million dollars a week for ten weeks; and each week, upon payment of the installment, one of you will be released. If the money is not forthcoming one of you will be released anyway—but not until I have played with him awhile. I am sure, my friend, that neither you nor your friends in the cells here wish to be found in the street some gray morning, in the same state that Ainsworth Clegg was found. So you'd better pray that your insurance companies be prompt!"

"X" wondered if the Skull was wholly sane. He asked, "How in the world do you expect to get away with such a sum of money? Don't you know that the numbers of the bills will be recorded? You could never use that money."

The man in vermilion laughed. "I have taken care of that, too, my friend. The money is to be in one-thousand-dollar bills. It is now ten P.M., and I have specified in my ultimatum to the companies that the first million dollars is to be delivered at midnight. Tomorrow morning I shall send out all of my men to change the bills at various banks. They will go in boldly and change them for small bills. They will not be molested, for," he wagged a finger at "X," "I still hold you.

"Every day for a week they will continue to change them. No doubt they will be followed, attempts will be made to locate this place. These attempts will fail, for as you saw, my men are able to disappear at will by entering this place through any one of fifteen entrances—the one you came through is an example." He paused, then snapped, "All right, Hilary! We have had enough of this! Take that pad and pencil, and write the names of all the companies you are insured with, and the amounts."

At the same time he pressed a button, and the bamboo pole slid out from the side of the desk. The basket hooked on its end stopped within a foot of him. In the basket was a small pad of paper, and a pencil.

The Skull ordered, "Frisch! Open his handcuffs the same as you did with the other prisoners. But keep each of his wrists cuffed to your own while he writes."

FRISCH extracted a key from his pocket, opened one set of handcuffs, and snapped the empty bracelet on Gilly's wrist. Then he did the same with the other handcuff, attaching it to his own. Then he swung his hand around, bringing "X's" right hand in front of him. "X" could now move both hands, but only with the wrist of one or the other of the gunman accompanying it. It was awkward, but permitted him to reach the basket and to write. If he tried to escape he would have to carry both gunmen with him.

He reached into the basket and picked out the pad and pencil, appearing to do so reluctantly.

The Skull said, "Do not hesitate, my friend. You seem to be an intelligent man. You can comprehend how terrible it would be for you to have that intelligence—destroyed—like Clegg!"

"X" was in a quandary. He did not know the particulars of Hilary's insurance policies; he knew that the publisher carried a large amount with Jewett's company, and he also knew, by chance, of one other company that covered him for a large sum.

It was possible that the Skull already had some of the information, and would discover at once that he was bluffing. He started to write, saying, "I really don't recall the exact amounts. I leave most of that to my agent. But I'll put it down to the best of my recollection."

He wrote the names of some of the larger companies, setting fictitious sums next to each. He could not be far wrong, for a man like Hilary would have his insurance spread over as many companies as possible.

When he finished, he replaced the pad and pencil in the basket. The Skull pressed another button, and the bamboo pole slid back. Gilly and Frisch swung his hands in behind his back again, but this time they did not leave the two handcuffs. They removed one, and cuffed his hands with the one set, thus leaving the Agent even less play for his hands than he had had before. He offered no resistance.

"X" watched the Skull pick the pad out of the basket. But the Skull did not bother to read what he had written; instead he tore the cardboard back off, holding it carefully by the edges. "Most of the information that you have written here, Mr. Hilary, I already have. What I really wanted was the cardboard back which has been specially treated to take the impressions of your fingerprints. You see, though I do not suspect you of being anybody but yourself, I am very thoroughgoing; it is possible that a certain man may try to work his way in here under a disguise, and I am therefore taking the prints of everyone who enters here."

"X's" eyes narrowed to slits. He had not looked forward to this. He had anticipated, of course, that any new recruit would be fingerprinted, and he had deliberately conceived the idea of entering the stronghold of the Skull as a captive, thus turning suspicion away from himself. But he had not anticipated that the Skull would be so careful as to check on the very men he kidnaped.

He hid his uneasiness with an artful bit of acting. "I must hand it to you, Mr. Skull. You don't leave any loopholes, do you?"

"In this business," the Skull replied didactically, "there must be no loopholes. I am at war with society, and in war a careful general never leaves himself unguarded." The Skull arose. "All right," he snapped at Gilly and Frisch. "Take him away. Put him in cell number ten. And send Griscoll in to check these prints for me."

CHAPTER XVIII

PRISONERS OF SATAN

THE CELL WHERE Frisch and Gilly conducted the Secret Agent was one of the rooms in the corridor where he had first seen Tyler tied to the wall. The doors now all had numbered cards tacked on them. Number ten was the first room on the left as they entered the passage. It was next to Tyler's room, which was nine.

They left the handcuffs on him, and in addition they picked up the end of a chain set in the wall, snapped the padlock at its end onto the links of the cuffs. The chain was less than four feet long, and was attached to a ring in the wall close to the floor. They went out, and Gilly peered back from the corridor to throw him a last taunt before he slammed the heavy door.

"Sorry we ain't got one o' your papers for you to read, Mister Hilary. Would you like breakfast in bed in the morning?"

"X" did not reply. He waited for the door to close, then took a tentative step in the pitch darkness that descended upon the room. He took one more step and found that he had reached the end of the chain. That was as far as he could go.

He realized that he had but five minutes at the most before he would receive visitors. It would not take the Skull longer than that to have the fingerprints checked, and "X" knew that once the Skull learned his identity he would not delay in taking swift action.

"X" wondered if Jim Hobart had succeeded in following them to the garage; he thought it very unlikely. In any event he must depend on his own wits and resources during the next half hour, which would perhaps be the most crucial of his life.

From the room next to his came the sound of groans, then the babbling of a terrified man. "X" recognized the voice. It was that of Laurens, the jeweler. He, too, was one of the prisoners. Laurens suddenly ceased his babbling, and a moment later his voice came again, high-pitched, speaking quickly, slurring words. "X" listened keenly. It was hard to tell what he was saying through the wall, but after a moment the Agent understood. Laurens was praying. Laurens, cool, phlegmatic, hard-headed, was praying. So strongly did the Skull affect men.

"X" reflected that Laurens had probably never uttered those words since his childhood. Now, in the face of terror they came back to him with facility. It was at times like these that men crept back to the bosom of a Deity they had all but forgotten in the turmoil of their crass existence.

Now there arose cries from other rooms in the double row. Men called out hoarsely to each other from room to room. "X" recognized Grier's formerly hearty voice, now thick with fear. They were shouting encouragement to each other, giving their names so that they could know who else shared their danger.

"X" did not call to them. He was laboring swiftly, silently, in the dark. He had twisted his arms around so that the fingers of his right hand came up close to the lining of his coat where lay the flat black case containing his chromium steel tools. His fingertips just reached the lower edge of the pocket where it lay, and he tried to nudge it out, inch by inch, so that it would fall to the floor.

He succeeded partially, had it halfway out, when he found he could move his hand no farther forward. He squirmed, trying to force the case out. He estimated that fully five minutes were gone since he had been taken from the Skull's presence; ample time for the prints to have been checked, and the Skull notified.

"X" clenched his teeth, strained his muscles. His fingers gripped the cloth on the under side of the pocket in the lining, and he wrenched with all his strength. The pocket ripped under the grip, and the case slid out to the floor, struck on its edge, and came to rest in the middle of the room.

It was out of his reach.

With his hands behind his back he had no means of reaching out to pick it up. It lay there, tantalizing, spread open by the fall, the metal instruments which had so often been the keys to safety for him gleaming dully in the dark.

And just then a panel in the wall close beside him slid open, and a blinding spotlight filled the small room. He remembered now, that this was how the Skull had forced Betty to look in on Tyler. There must be such a sliding panel for each of these rooms, so that the Skull could look in on all his prisoners when he chose.

"X" faced the spotlight, blinking. He so placed his body that the kit of tools was hidden from view.

From behind the spotlight came the mocking voice of the Skull. "How do you do, Secret Agent 'X'? You are very clever, my friend; I had never expected to see you here as Hilary. But welcome back in any disguise. You are going to provide me with a half hour of pleasure before I place you in the chair. Under my gentle persuasion you shall disclose to me all the little secrets that you have; and I shall see your face—perhaps show you mine before you are deprived of your sanity!"

THE Skull laughed long and loud. "You made a terrible mistake when you undertook to outwit the Skull. You see, my friend of a Thousand Faces, you have only ten fingers—and they ruined you!" The Skull raised his voice. "Binks! Go and get him. Keep a gun on him every minute, and don't take the handcuffs off him. Bring him here!"

The panel slid down, leaving the cell once more in complete darkness. No sooner was it fully closed than "X" broke into action. He recalled how long it had taken Gilly and Frisch to bring him here, coming through the connecting passages—no more than four or five minutes. That was the length of time he had.

He did not deceive himself that he could overcome the halfwit while he was opening the padlock that linked his handcuffs to the chain; Binks, he told himself, was not as dumb as he looked. He would be wary, knowing that this prisoner was not an ordinary one. He must do whatever he had to do before Binks arrived, must be ready for him.

He stretched out on the floor on his face, his hands suspended in the air behind him by the chain. The floor was of wood, moldy and dank, and he felt a furry creature scurrying over his ankle, then another. Rats. A weaker man might have shuddered in revulsion as those rats reminded him of the one that had been electrocuted in the Skull's office earlier in the day.

"X" set his lips grimly, and not even bothering to shake off the rats, he stretched out his legs toward the instrument case, gripped it with both feet, and turned on his side, straining against his manacled arms. Then he drew up his feet until the instrument case was close beside him.

He let it lie there, squirmed to his knees, then squatted on the floor over the case. His hands were now directly over it, and his fingers flew as he searched it, withdrew a set of keys. In the darkness he felt of them, and unerringly, as always, selected the right one. He twisted his hand, inserted the key in the lock of the handcuffs, just as there came the noise of someone fumbling at the door.

The door began to open, and "X" coughed loudly to cover the click made by the key as it turned in the lock of the cuffs. Binks came into the room, leaving the door wide open. Light streamed into the cell, and Binks saw the open case on the floor. He looked up at "X" in swift suspicion, and stooped for the case. That was a mistake. "X" let the open handcuffs slide to the floor, and seizing the halfwit by both wrists, twisted them behind his back.

Binks emitted a choked cry, attempted to struggle, and then subsided sullenly as the Agent picked up the handcuffs and snapped them on his wrists. Strangely enough he was silent, astute enough to know that a protest would be unavailing.

Yet "X" wondered why he made no outcry. He was prepared for that, ready to spread his hand over the other's mouth if he should open it to call out. A shout could be easily heard by the Skull, for the voices of the imprisoned men in the other cells came clearly enough.

"X" wasted no time in wondering. He placed the instrument case in the outside pocket of his coat, since the inner pocket was torn, and prodded Binks through the door. Out in the corridor he hesitated for a moment. Was it wise to release the other men now? He could not herd them through all the corridors to safety with the Skull still commanding the situation, sending his gunmen after them, directing them through the hidden amplifiers. They would be so many sheep to be slaughtered in the passages. He could not protect them all. It would be wiser to seek out the Skull—fight it out.

THE thought occurred to him suddenly: suppose the Skull overcame him? These men would still be prisoners. He saw that Binks had half-turned, was regarding him quizzically in the semi-gloom left by the single bulb at the end of the corridor.

The halfwit cackled, and asked, "Whatchu worryin' about? It ain't all easy sailin', is it? You better be smart an' go back in that cell o' yo'rn. You can't beat the Skull, Mister Whatever-yore-name-is!"

"X" made no reply. He prodded him on toward the middle of the corridor, called out in a low but urgent voice, "Dennett! Which cell are you in?"

The discordant voices of the prisoners suddenly ceased. There was stillness in the corridor, and no answer to his question. "X" repeated it, this time a little louder.

From one of the cells came a cautious voice, that of Grier, the stockbroker. "Who is that?"

"This is Hilary. Is that you, Grier?"

"Yes. For God's sake, where are you?"

"Out in the corridor. I can't release you all yet, for a certain reason. Where's Dennett?"

"X's" plan was to release Dennett, leave him here with instructions to release all the others if he did not return within a certain time. The reason he had chosen Dennett was because he felt from his experience with him that the contractor was the coolest of them all, the least liable to yield to panic.

Grier's voice came to him. "Dennett's in one of these rooms. We heard him led in. I haven't heard him talk since, though."

The Agent turned to Binks. "Tell me which cell Dennett is in. Quickly, if you want to live."

Binks cackled. "I ain't tellin' you nothin'. An' I ain't afraid o' you, neither. Everybody knows Secret Agent 'X' don't kill!" He said it in a loud voice, and at the mention of the name the voices of the imprisoned men which had arisen in pleas to him to be released at once became hushed.

Grier exclaimed, "God! I could have sworn it was Hilary's voice!"

Binks cried, "He ain't Hilary. He's took Hilary's place. You look out fer him. He's worse than the Skull!"

"X" took hold of the halfwit and shook him roughly, pushed him toward the end of the corridor. His plan was spoiled by Binks. There was no use releasing any of those men now; they would turn upon him, demand explanations of his impersonation of Hilary, impede his actions. He would have to risk leaving them there until he had finished with the Skull.

At the end of the corridor he pressed the lever in the wall, and pushed Binks through the sliding panel. He was worried about Dennett; he wondered if the Skull had done anything to the contractor. He remembered that the Skull had insisted on the pearls being taken from Dennett's safe—an act which could have been expected to ruin him by preventing the loan. Did the Skull have a personal grudge against the contractor, and had he sacrificed him to that hate without waiting for ransom?

As they made their way down the second corridor, Binks unwillingly in the lead, the halfwit seemed to read his mind by some prescience of the mentally afflicted.

"I bet yo're wonderin' about Dennett, huh? Well, the boss gave him some o' that special treatment. He didn't like him nohow. Dennett's gonna be picked up in the street tomorrow morning—just like Clegg was. Ha-ha! It'll be funny. I didn't like that guy neither!"

"X's" eyes smoldered. Another strong man broken mentally and physically. The Skull, wrecker of men, must be destroyed. Anything was warranted now—even the thing that he proposed to do with Binks.

The Secret Agent had learned enough about the layout of the place by this time to be able to find his way to the "execution" room unaided. Binks did not appear to be in any special fear of him; either his mind failed to grasp the fact that he was in the hands of the Skull's greatest enemy, or else he had sublime faith that the Skull would step in at any moment.

In fact, "X" also had the idea that the Skull would undoubtedly become impatient when Binks did not return at once, and be on his guard. He wanted to surprise the Skull in the execution room. No compunctions were going to stand in his way. He was going to kill that monster if necessary. He hoped, however, that he would not be forced to do so. He now had his gas gun, and that should be sufficient to overpower the Skull.

BINKS asked, "Where you takin' me to, mister? You gonna see the Skull?" He turned toward "X" as he asked the question, stopping in his shuffling walk.

The Agent nodded. They were now in the corridor with the execution room. They stood before the heavy door, which had been left partly open by Binks when he went to get "X." There was a dim light in the room, and the Agent could see that it was unoccupied. The wire mesh screen that ordinarily cut it in half was now raised.

"X" propelled Binks into the room. He steeled himself for what he was going to do. He hadn't expected to find the Skull here, had been almost sure that he would have to exert pressure on Binks to make him talk.

He whirled the halfwit around, set him in the electric chair, clamped an electrode around his neck, and fastened it. Then he stooped and examined the cable. It had been repaired where he had cut it. The fatal chair was again in working order.

Binks suddenly whined, terror in his voice, "What you gonna do to me?"

"X" said sternly, "I am going to strap you in and give you a dose of the current that your master has been giving to his victims!"

Binks shouted wildly, "No, no! Don't do that!"

"X's" mouth was grim. "Your boss did this to Clegg and Dennett and Tyler, and God knows how many others, without even giving them a chance to get out of it. I'm going to give you a chance, at least, before turning on the current. I want to know where the Skull went from here. I know he was in this room a few minutes ago."

Binks subsided in the chair. Cunning eyes peered out at the Agent from the horribly distorted face. Panic had given way to scheming. "You couldn't never reach the Skull. He'll get you before you even see him. He knows this place like a book, an' you don't." As he talked he cast a side glance up at the niche as if he were expecting his master to appear at any moment to rescue him.

"X" said impatiently, "You have one more chance before I strap you in. Talk up."

Binks said triumphantly, "You can't turn on the current. The switch is up in the niche, an' you can't reach it from here. I ain't sayin' nothin', mister!"

"X" bent and opened the handcuffs, then swiftly strapped his ankles and wrists. Binks was now helpless in the chair, as Betty Dale had been a few hours before. The Agent turned and made for the door. "You forget," he threw over his shoulder, "that I've been around in this place. I know how to get up to that niche from the outside." He had the door half-opened. "It's too bad you won't talk, Binks." He hoped fervently that the halfwit would weaken.

He was sure that he could never throw that switch, never submit even the vilest creature living to the inhuman punishment of that chair. But it was imperative that he find the Skull, and quickly. Even now the master of the leering death's-head might be approaching along one of the tortuous corridors, planning to take him by surprise. The Skull must certainly know by this time that he had escaped from the cell.

Binks' hoarse, pleading voice stopped him. Binks did not know that he was as safe in that chair as out of it. In the vicious world he lived in it was difficult to understand that anyone would hesitate at inflicting cruel and painful torture upon an enemy. He fully believed that "X" was going to pull that switch.

"Wait, wait!" he begged. "Come back. I'll do what you want."

With a surge of relief, "X" came back into the room and approached the chair. He stood over the other and asked, "All right. Where is the Skull?"

Binks peered up at him, cunning once more now that the immediate danger was over. "The boss is gone to his private room where I was supposed to bring you. Only him an' me knows about that room. If I take you there, an' you put it over on him—" he reminded "X" now of a rat that was deserting a sinking ship "—will you let me go free?"

"X" hesitated only a moment. Binks was small fry compared to his boss. The destruction of the Skull was worth the freedom of a hundred Binkses. "I will," he promised.

Binks seemed almost eager now, to betray his master—too eager, the Agent thought. "Unstrap me!" he pleaded. "I'll take you there. An' you let me go. Remember, you promised!"

"X" bent and opened the straps. Binks hoped to outwit him on the way—that was evident. He was playing both sides; if he didn't succeed in outwitting the Agent, he had his promise to go free. If he did succeed by some ruse in outwitting him, the halfwit would earn the commendation of the Skull.

"X" helped him up, clamped the handcuffs once more on his wrists, behind his back. "Now," he ordered, "get going. And if you try any tricks—" he produced his gas gun and flourished it under Binks' nose "—I'll give you a dose of this."

BINKS' eyes widened. "I won't try no tricks, mister. To tell you the truth, I'll be glad to get rid of the Skull. All the time I been with him, I never know when he's goin' to put me in that chair, like the others. He'd kill his own brother if he took the notion. It ain't been no pleasure, I'm tellin' you!"

"X" did not relax his vigilance as they went through a new set of passages that he had never seen before. They met no one; and "X" reflected that the Skull's system of locking his men in when they were not working was boomeranging against the boss now, for they proceeded unmolested. He wondered that the Skull had permitted Binks to come alone to get him, without assistance.

This might be explained by the fact that the Skull did not want any of the other men to learn of this section of his headquarters; and he might also have felt that "X," handcuffed helplessly, would not be too much for Binks to handle.

The halfwit was strangely silent now, as he preceded the Agent.

They passed from one dimly lit corridor to another, "X" keeping his gas gun in evidence. Binks was unaware that the gun was not a lethal instrument, and probably was in dread of doing anything that might cause his captor to use it on him.

At the end of one corridor, Binks used his key and they stepped into a narrow elevator, descended for what might have been two stories. "X" was keenly observing everything. He was curious as to the location of this headquarters. It was a tribute to the Skull's ingenuity that the Agent had not yet been able to guess just where he had been able to build so complicated a series of passages and rooms in the heart of the city.

"X" was also curious as to the source of the power that fed the electric chair. The voltage used in that heavy cable would require a very large dynamo—and he had not heard any noise such as a dynamo is bound to make.

When the elevator came to rest, Binks stooped and raised the lever that opened the door. "X" asked him, "How far is it now?"

The halfwit said, "It's right close. Better not make any noise now. It's at the end of this here passage." The panel of the elevator slid open revealing another passage that turned at right angles a few feet away. "X" kept his gas gun handy. He would give the Skull no opportunity to use any of the devious defenses that the master of crime had erected about himself. He would give him a quick dose of the gas at first sight.

Binks stepped out of the elevator, and the Agent made to follow him. "X" was carefully watching Binks, expecting that the halfwit might resort to some trick at the last moment. He did not expect what really took place. Binks touched nothing with his hands. He merely took a step forward, and as his foot pressed into one of the boards on the floor, the elevator door slid shut with a bang, closing "X" into the darkness of the small compartment.

"X" understood at once, though too late, that Binks had led him through all these passages merely to get him into this one elevator; he was trapped.

Swiftly he stooped to the lever, pressed it downward. The door did not open. Binks must have disconnected it from the outside. "X" tried the other lever that started the car, but that, too, failed to respond.

And from out in the corridor he heard the sardonic laughter of the Skull.

CHAPTER XIX

THE CREEPING DEATH

"**X**'S" **LIPS CLAMPED** tight. He took out his pencil flash and inspected his narrow prison. The walls were of wood, expertly joined. With his implements, and given time, he could work his way out of here. But he knew that he would not be given time. The Skull had big things on his hands now, and would hasten the end.

From outside the Skull taunted him. "You aren't the only great impersonator, Mister 'X'! My own impersonation fooled you to the end; fooled you so that you let me out of that chair when you had me helpless!"

"Impersonation?" The Agent's head snapped up. In that instant he understood what the Skull meant. He exclaimed, "Then—you are Binks?" talking at the blank walls of the little cubicle.

"Now you know, my friend. But you know too late to do you any good. You made a mistake when you spared the poor, half-witted Binks. It was those scars and mutilations on my face that led you astray. Merely a tight-fitting rubber mask, my friend. And now—"

"X's" mind raced backward, from point to point of his contacts in this place. It was possible. He recalled that Binks had never appeared at the same time as the Skull. Always there had been a period of waiting between the time the halfwit left him and the appearance of the master. And no wonder that no one else in the place had ever been trusted with the secret of the entrances and exits. The Skull had never, in effect, trusted anybody but himself. He had been able to snoop around, to overhear the conversations of his men; always in dim light, so that the rubber mask on his face would not be discovered.

"And now—" the Skull had said.

And now there was a soft whirring of well-oiled machinery, and the elevator started to descend slowly, ominously.

And "X" heard the Skull say, "Do you know where you are going, my friend? You are descending to a chamber on the level of the river. And I am going to open certain valves—" He laughed. "Your body will be found in the river in a few days—bloated, rotted. And in just thirty minutes the poor halfwit, Binks, will go to the main room and let out two of my men who are to go and pick up the first payment of ransom money!" The voice rose to a paean of triumph. "Thirty minutes exactly! And my plan succeeds. Triumph! Triumph! And for you—your death, my friend, shall be unwept, unhonored and unsung!"

The cage descended for a long time. "X" wondered if Jim Hobart had succeeded in following him to the entrance in the garage; and if so, whether the police would believe his story that the car had disappeared into the apparently empty garage. He doubted that they could find their way in here, even if they did believe him; doubted that they could pierce the clever camouflages the Skull had placed in the way—the movable ramp in the interior of the garage, the long trip underground on some sort of moving vehicle while he was blindfolded.

"X" decided that there was little to hope for help from the police. The lives of those men in the cells upstairs depended on him alone. And he was caged here, with the prospect of death by drowning.

The elevator ceased its motion. For several minutes there was silence. "X" reflected bitterly that the Skull had quoted the ancient poet with great aptness: "Unwept, unhonored and unsung!" Truly that would be his fate. None would ever know that the Secret Agent had toiled here mightily to save men from a hideous fate. He would simply vanish from the earth, and the body of an unknown man would be fished out of the river. The papers would report it as the suicide of a derelict.

Elisha Pond and others whom the Agent had created would walk no more in their accustomed haunts, and some would wonder where they had gone. Betty Dale would awake in the old Montgomery Mansion, and make her way home. If she escaped the future attentions of the Skull, she would wonder at "X's" nonappearance, await him, perhaps, for years. And then, at last, she would reluctantly yield to the conclusion that he must be dead. She alone might guess how he had perished. And he knew that her sorrow would be great. He visualized her, waiting from year to year, hoping against hope that he would some day present himself to her in another disguise.

Above everything Secret Agent "X" felt most poignantly the fact that the Skull would remain with a free hand to wreak his insidious will upon helpless men and women—to go on destroying the minds and bodies of intelligent men in his ruthless climb to power.

All these things flashed through his subconscious being with kaleidoscopic swiftness as the cage descended. His conscious intelligence, in the meanwhile, was coping with the problem in hand. For Secret Agent "X" was not one to bow his head and await what seemed to be inevitable. For more times than one the things that had appeared to be inevitable had turned out to be avoidable by the exercise of his keen brain.

Now he was swiftly examining the ceiling of his cage. There was a flat plate screwed into the center of the ceiling, probably the terminal of the cable that lifted the elevator. "X" took a small screwdriver out of the flat black case in his pocket, and raised himself so that he could reach the plate.

It was the only thing that offered itself to work on, and he was not one to remain idle under any circumstances. In order to raise himself, he pressed his knees outward against the sides of the cage, which was no more than two feet wide. Then he rested his back against one wall, pushed the soles of his shoes against the opposite wall. In this manner he managed to raise himself so that he could reach the plate with the screwdriver.

He was off the floor, and working on the first of the screws by the time the cage came to a stop. And it was to this that he owed his life. For he heard the Skull shout from above:

"All right, Mister 'X'! This is a quicker end than I planned for you, but I am short of time. See how you like swimming down there. Good-by forever!" And the Skull's laughter rose cruelly, mercilessly, while the floor of the cage dropped open with a sudden jerk.

Had "X" been standing on the floor he would have been hurled down the shaft that now yawned below!

THE Agent clung to his precarious hold, pressing his feet against the opposite wall, looked down. About fifteen feet below, at the bottom of the shaft, was an opening. And just below the opening he could see the white foam of swirling water. The river was rushing in here, the water making low, grumbling noises as it was forced in by a tremendous pressure from somewhere at the mouth of that tunnel that must lead from the waterfront.

No man could have lived down there. Refuse shot past at express train speed. Even as he looked, a heavy piece of rotten lumber was slammed against a side of the watery tunnel below there; slammed with a crash that would have shattered a man's ribs.

The Skull must just have opened the valves, and the inrush of water was devastating to anything it might catch there. "X" assumed that the Skull would soon open another valve that would lead the water out again through another pipe, back to the river where his body would have been carried had he fallen down there. And while he watched he was afforded another evidence of the Skull's devilish ingenuity.

For, probably in response to another switch or lever, a heavy grating slid over the top of the opening over the rushing water. He smiled grimly. The Skull was taking no chances on his climbing out of there once he fell through the opening.

"X" estimated the distance to the grating below, allowed his body to relax, and jumped straight down through the open trapdoor. He landed on all fours, bending his knees and elbows to take up the shock of the drop. His right hand slipped between the bars, and he went down, his head striking the grating. For a moment he was stunned; the cold, swirling water below licked at his hand, hanging down, and drops cascaded on his cheek.

He rolled over on his back, and breathed deeply to get air into his lungs and drive the dizziness from his head. He lay there for a while with his eyes closed. The right side of his head hurt badly, and he put up a hand to feel blood where the skin had cracked.

His make-up was ruined, rubbed off in spots. He could not pass for Hilary any longer unless he took the time to touch himself up. And that was out of the question. He felt that speed was essential now; the Skull believed him dead, and must be taken by surprise.

He looked up to see the trap door in the elevator above him snap shut with a clang. He watched as the cage rose a little way, then stopped once again. Suddenly he felt the grating upon which he was resting heave. *It was sliding away from under him!* Either the Skull could see that he hadn't fallen through yet, or else he was just making sure.

The water had risen now so that it was bubbling above the grating. In a moment there would be nothing for him to rest upon. He would drop down into that maelstrom.

He glanced upward quickly. The shaft of wood came down flush with the opening here; there was no handhold except the elevator tracks, and these were slippery with grease. "X" tried to brace himself against the opposite wall as he had done in the elevator, but the walls were wet where the water from below had slapped against them, and his feet slipped. The grating was halfway open now. It was sliding into a slot in the wall into which it fitted snugly. He stood on the slowly moving bars, back to the wall, and watched the space in front of him grow wider and wider—the space into which he would be hurled when his foothold slid entirely away from under him.

The moving bars made a rasping sound against his wet rubber heels. He looked down into the water below, watched it foam past, rumbling and roaring as if impatient at being deprived for so long of its prey. He wondered how long a strong swimmer could live down there. A sudden sound above him drew his gaze upward, and he saw that the trapdoor of the cage had opened once more. The cage was descending upon him at express train speed.

IF it didn't stop it would crush him there, or else hurl him into the water. He crouched, ready to dive, and noted something for the first time. The grating had opened wide now, leaving him only about four inches to stand on. He could see clearly now, and noticed that there was a cord of some sort stretched across the opening, fluttering around in the foaming waters.

Barely had his brain grasped the significance of this cord stretched across the opening, before the cage was upon him. Only a half-inch of foothold remained, and he was ready to dive, when that sixth sense of his held him there. And he was not crushed. For the cage had stopped with a sudden lurch, not a foot from his crouched head; it stopped with a jerk that would have dislodged anybody clinging to its sides.

And with that half-inch of foothold remaining to him, "X" did the thing that his sudden understanding of the situation dictated. He stooped far over, gripped that cord, and yanked it upward. At the same tune he reached up and gripped the hanging edge of the open trapdoor in the cage.

His pull on the cord brought instant response in the form of a clamorous bell ringing somewhere above. The last half-inch of grating disappeared from under his feet, and he let go the cord, clung with both hands to the trapdoor.

His quick intuition had grasped the situation instantly. That cord was there to tell the Skull whether or not his man had fallen through the opening. If the bell rang, the Skull knew the job was done; if it didn't he knew that his victim was still clinging to the elevator. So he had dropped the cage with a jerk to dislodge him. And now that "X" had pulled the cord, the Skull would think that he had gone through this time.

And "X" had judged correctly. For the grating started to slide back once more, until it covered the opening again. If the Agent had fallen through, he would be trapped there in the rushing water, unable to climb out. And the water was now a good half-inch above the bars of the grating, rising faster and faster.

"X" did not look down again. He devoted his attention to getting back in the elevator. His hold on the edge of the trapdoor had been precarious, but now he could stand on the grating. He reached up, gripped the lever just inside the cage, lifted himself by that, then managed to scramble up by getting a purchase on the upper edge of the trapdoor for here it was hinged to the wall of the cage.

He raised one foot, then the other, and levered himself up. He was now resting his fingertips on the hinged edge of the trapdoor. He strained his muscles, and inch by inch he moved himself upward.

Now he had his back against one wall, and the soles of his shoes against the other, resting on the lever. He was well within the cage when the trapdoor suddenly swung shut beneath him. With a sigh of relaxing muscles he rested on the floor; if the trapdoor had remained open another half minute he would have been compelled to give up his hold and drop back to the grating.

Slowly, the cage began to rise. The Skull must by now be convinced that he was beneath the grating, carried along by the rushing force of the river water. He had dropped his gas gun and screwdriver in the first mad fall of the elevator. If he should come to grips with the master of murder he must use some other means to fight him.

He waited, breathing deeply, while the cage rose for what he estimated were about three flights. It was dark in the cage; but the Agent did not take out his flashlight. Darkness was his friend now.

When the elevator came to a stop, Secret Agent "X" rose to his feet and tried the lever that controlled the door. It worked. The Skull had apparently hooked up the connection again from the outside, intending no doubt to use the cage when he was through with the valves controlling the river flow.

The panel slid open, and "X" stepped into the corridor. He did not close the panel behind him. It might be necessary to have it conveniently open on the way back.

CHAPTER XX

ALIAS THE SKULL

NOW, THE AGENT proceeded swiftly from passage to passage, his uncanny instinct for direction guiding him right. Yet he was cautious, proceeding soundlessly through the empty passages. For he was unarmed, and the Skull would be fully equipped and dangerous; even though he might be taken by surprise at finding "X" still alive.

The Agent met no one as he retraced his steps and reached the huge barred door of the execution chamber. He did not stop here, but made his way into the next corridor, opened a door and stepped carefully into the anteroom of the Skull's private sanctum. This was where he had originally been searched by Rufe Linson when he came as Fannon. Before him was the door without a handle. The door which led to the inner lair of the Skull.

Quickly, silently, "X" stooped before that door, and laid out at his side the flat black case containing his chromium steel instruments. From this case he extracted a long, thin, tempered steel tool, which he inserted in the crack between the door and the jamb. He knew that the door was opened electrically from within, and being familiar with such mechanisms, he knew exactly what tool to use.

The steel jimmy, a perfect conductor of electricity, closed the circuit which controlled the door, and it swung open on well-oiled hinges.

The room within was utterly dark. Would it be occupied?

The Agent tensed as he saw that the face of the Skull was gleaming at him from the darkness—that luminous face, weird and revolting.

"X" waited tautly. He was in the light, at the mercy of the demoniac master of evil who sat there. Not a word was spoken. The Skull's face did not move.

Suddenly, "X's" eyes began to gleam. He sensed something; no man could sit there so quietly, absolutely immovable. With a quick motion he produced his flashlight, clicked it on, directed its beam at the desk. Its rays bathed the hideous face. And the Agent, with a sigh of relief, scooped up his tools, darted into the room. He stopped short just within; he had been about to dart across to the desk—and in doing so he would have stepped on that four-foot strip of electrically charged floor.

The Agent jumped, cleared the strip, and came close to the desk. The thing that glowed there luminous and ugly was not the head of a man, but a mask—the mask which the Skull used. It was painted with phosphorus to resemble the bony structure of the head, and in the dark the phosphorus gleamed in the semblance of a skull. Over the back of the chair lay the vermilion-hooded cloak of the master of crime.

That mask and cloak could mean only one thing. That the Skull was still out in the guise of Binks. "X" glanced at his watch; ten-thirty. Yes. The Skull had said where he was going. He would be in the main room now, preparing to take some men out to collect the ransom for the first of the millionaires.

The Agent found a shaded lamp on the desk. He turned this on; it cast a dull light, sufficient to illuminate the room. In the wall to the left of the desk there was an open panel. "X" could see a narrow spiral staircase just outside the panel, leading upward. He knew where it went, from his knowledge of the location of the rooms; it led up to the niche in the execution chamber, where the Skull held his cruel rites.

And then the Agent's eyes gleamed as he noted something else—something close to the desk, something which had failed to register with him until that moment. It was a microphone. A microphone on a stand, right beside the Skull's chair. Vividly the Agent recalled the picture of himself and Betty Dale escaping through the passages, while the stentorian voice had bellowed through the hidden amplifiers, directing the pursuit.

And slowly the lips of Secret Agent "X" tightened into a thin smile as he contemplated an idea, grimly ironic in its conception, daringly dangerous in execution.

Swiftly he donned the mask and robe, seated himself, and drew the microphone toward him. He flexed the muscles of his throat, tautened, and spoke into it; and his voice was a perfect imitation of the voice used by the Skull.

"This is the Skull talking!" he called sonorously. "Seize Binks! Seize Binks! Seize Binks! Binks is a traitor! Binks is a traitor!"

HE stopped, and his voice came rolling back to him from the amplifiers in the corridor outside: "—a traitor!"

Once more he spoke into the microphone. "Binks is a traitor! Bring him to my office. I will hold you all responsible if he escapes. Get Binks and bring him to my office at once! Do not fail, as you value your lives! When he is caught, let everybody come to my office!"

He ceased talking, waited tensely. Within a few moments he would know if his trick was successful. The Skull might talk the men out of it. If they did turn on him, he might escape, might come back alone to the office.

"X" waited, his ears keenly attuned for sounds outside that would tell him whether many men were coming, or only one. After what seemed an age of waiting, during which he sat unmoving, not showing by so much as the twitch of a muscle the suspense that he felt, there was the sound of voices in the corridor, and the outside door of the anteroom opened.

The men were all there. In the forefront walked Frisch and Gilly, with Binks, handcuffed, between them.

Their brutish faces suggested puzzlement mingled with awe. Frisch and Gilly stopped, hesitantly, at the threshold of the office, waiting for orders from the man who wore the mask of the Skull.

Binks, who had been expostulating shrilly, became quiet when he saw that an impostor sat in his chair. He gazed with burning eyes through his rubber mask at the Agent, then said, "I see you're hard to kill, Mister 'X'!" There was open venom in his voice, and a tinge of fear.

Frisch said, "We got him, boss. He was in the main room with us, tellin' us that you wanted me and Gilly to go out an' pick up the ransom. When you broadcasted, we grabbed him, an' he's been tryin' to tell us all the way up here that you ain't the Skull. He says you're Secret Agent 'X'! I socked him one, but he wouldn't keep quiet."

The other men were crowding close behind, and "X" could see that none of them looked sorry for Binks. They all more or less hated the apparent halfwit, who had prodded and taunted them. Frisch, especially, took a particular pleasure in buffeting Binks around. He no doubt recalled the half-dollars he had thrown to him, recalled that the halfwit had ridiculed him before all the men.

The Agent said, "Bring him in."

Frisch and Gilly propelled their prisoner toward the desk.

Before they reached the four-foot strip of electrified flooring, "X" said, "That's far enough. Now—"

But the Skull, his hands manacled behind his back, interrupted, shouting at the men who had crowded in behind, "You fools! This isn't the Skull. I tell you, it's Secret Agent 'X'! Rip that mask off his face, an' you'll see it isn't the Skull!"

Gilly laughed wickedly. "You have been half nuts for a long time," he taunted. "Now you're all nuts. Maybe you'll tell us next that you're the Skull!" He looked toward "X" behind the desk, as if wondering whether his levity was going to be rebuked.

The Agent said, "Binks is a traitor, men. He was planning to kill the two men who went for the ransom, and collect it for himself. You know that punishment we have for traitors?"

They shouted, "Put him in the chair. Let's see him wriggle!"

"X" nodded, and the slow motion of his hideous mask must have been impressive to the gathered ruffians. The Skull made another, a desperate attempt to convince them.

"I tell you," he screamed, "That's not the Skull. I'm the Skull!" He stopped as a gale of derisive laughter swept the men. Gilly cried, "See that? Just what I said he'd claim. Can you imagine this here halfwit bein' our boss!"

Binks cried desperately, "I'll prove it, you damned idiots. I know all about you. You, Gilly!" He stopped for a moment, and then continued and his voice had suddenly become the voice that the men had become accustomed to hear from the Skull himself. He had been a little panicky before, but now he realized that he must control himself, prove to these men beyond doubt that he was their leader. The voice of the Skull, coming to them from Binks, would, at least, cause them to waver, would induce them to listen to him.

ONCE he had their ear, he could prove that he was the Skull. He knew things about them that only the Skull could know; if he mentioned those things, they would be convinced. He started to talk again, using the voice of the Skull. "You, Gilly! Do you remember—"

But Secret Agent "X," whose brain was keenly attuned to the least change in the situation, detected the change in the voice with the very first words, before the men did. The Skull's voice was hardly audible above the men's derisive shouts; they had not yet caught the significance of the change of tone.

Before they had a chance to do so, the Agent arose and thundered, "That's enough! We will have an execution at once! It will be a lesson to those who betray the Skull!"

Binks tried to shout, but "X" motioned to Frisch, ordered, "Shut him up. He's said enough!"

Frisch grinned wickedly, raised a fist and brought it down heavily at the side of his prisoner's head. Binks staggered, and cringed. The blow had hurt.

"X" said curtly, "We will have everybody present at the execution. I want to have those millionaires see how our chair works. You, Frisch, take some men and bring them out of the cells. Take them to the execution room; all you other men, go there and wait for me. Leave me alone with Binks. I want a few words with him alone to show him how bad his mistake has been!"

The men did not question the command. They filed out, shutting the outer anteroom door behind them. Binks stood in a corner, his hideous rubber mask seeming the very incarnation of madness. From under that mask his eyes gleamed fiercely, calculatingly, at the Agent. He was by no means ready to acknowledge defeat. He said with a trace of cunning in his voice, "Look here—I know you're 'X.' You're a cleverer man than I thought, to have gotten out of the elevator shaft. Why don't you come in with me? I can make you a rich man. You'd never have to work again—"

He stopped as he saw "X" shake his head slowly in the negative. He burst out, snarling, "You fool! You think you can take my place? You think you can go on with my plans?"

The Agent said softly, "That is not what I intend, Mister Skull."

"Then you must be looking for a reward! I will give you more than you can ever collect in rewards! Come in with me, and I will give you a third of my profits—three million dollars! And who knows how much more—with two clever men like us working together. Come on," he urged, as he saw that "X" was silent, "join me. Every man has a price. Three million dollars for a starter should be enough for anyone!"

His eyes widened as he saw the Agent produce a hypodermic syringe from his pocket, and load it from a small vial of muddy-colored liquid. "I'll make it five million!" he screamed. "Half of my profits!"

The Agent said, as though explaining an elementary lesson to a child, "You have not learned yet, Mister Skull, that all men cannot be bought. There are higher things than money, Mister Skull."

"You're crazy!" the manacled man snarled. "Nobody turns down money. You must be playing a deeper game than I can figure. What is it? You couldn't be fool enough to turn down five million. Don't you understand? *Five million dollars!* There's nothing that it couldn't buy you—ease, comfort, *power!*"

"You are wrong, Mister Skull. There are honor and ease of conscience and the pride of serving humanity. Those are things that you can't understand, Mister Skull."

The Agent finished loading the hypodermic, came around the desk, and jumped the four-foot strip of electrified flooring.

The Skull shrank back against the wall. "What are you going to do?" he demanded hoarsely.

Secret Agent "X" advanced upon him grimly, purposefully. "I'm going to put you to sleep. And then I'm going to rip off that rubber mask, and verify my suspicions as to whose face is really under it. I'm going to see the face of the Skull!"

CHAPTER XXI

FACE OF THE SKULL

THE POLICE AT last had a lead to the headquarters of the Skull. It had come none too soon, for the first installment of the ransom was to be paid at midnight—one million dollars in thousand-dollar bills. The insurance companies had rushed through special agreements with the heirs of the abducted millionaires, whereby the companies were authorized to pay out the money and to reduce the policies by the amounts paid.

Headquarters confessed itself checkmated. There was no possible hope, barring a lucky break, that the lair of the Skull could be located in time to save the millionaires and prevent the payment of the ransom. The terrible prospect presented itself of having the same crime repeated time and time again, with impunity. For there was nothing to prevent the Skull, once he had carried this operation to a successful conclusion, from repeating with another group of heavily insured men. The situation threatened to disrupt the entire insurance institution of the nation. The companies would be chary in the future of issuing large policies, and men would be reluctant to purchase them, lest they become victims of the Skull.

Commissioner Foster and Inspector Burks had been in almost constant conference with insurance company officials, and in telephonic communication with state and national officials. Nothing remained but abject capitulation to the terms of the master criminal; to allow those millionaires to be rendered pitiable wrecks like Ainsworth Clegg was unthinkable. Commissioner Foster reluctantly gave the word that he would cooperate with the companies in the delivery of the ransom money.

And then, just when spirits were at their lowest, came a bright ray of hope. Jim Hobart, former patrolman, informed Inspector Burks that he could lead him to the spot where the car which had kidnaped Hilary had disappeared.

Everything suddenly became bustle and stir. Squad cars were ordered; reserves were called out. Foster himself said to young Jim Hobart, "Look here, young man, if your lead turns out to be the means of breaking this case, I'll see that you are reinstated on the force—no matter what you were ever charged with!"

And sure enough, the false floor in the garage was discovered, the lever that lowered the runway found. Plainclothes men swarmed down, to find themselves faced with an impasse. For here there were no passages, no rooms, no hideouts; there was only a break in the concrete wall, which opened into the new subway cut under construction. They found here the improvised tracks used for hauling material, and a handcar on the tracks.

Jim Hobart could give them no further information. He was as puzzled as they—until he noted that on the wall there was drawn an arrow pointing to the right. The peculiar thing about this arrow was that it showed brightly in the dark.

Inspector Burks, looking at it closely, exclaimed in wonder. "Hell, that's drawn with radium! Look at how it shines!"[13]

They found, as they went in the direction indicated by the arrow, that at every point where there was a choice of directions, there, too, was an arrow. They followed them eagerly, from the subway cut into a maze of complicated passages. Panels were open, and needed no manipulation. It was as if the way had been paved for them by a friend.

At last they came to a heavily barred door, which opened automatically at their approach. And in the room behind that door they witnessed a remarkable scene.

THE room was cut in half by a heavy wire mesh screen that seemed to run from floor to ceiling. On their side of the screen as they entered the room, stood, stupefied at the sudden entrance of the police, some thirty-odd men, all with criminal records. They seemed to have been cut off from the rest of the room by the wire screen.

On the other side of the screen, near the wall, was an electric

---

13   AUTHOR'S NOTE: *In the past it has been the custom of Secret Agent "X" to leave his mark at the close of a successful operation. In view of the danger that always existed of others trying to imitate that mark, the Agent used radium to paint the glowing "X" which was his trade mark. In this way imitation was eliminated, due to the almost prohibitive cost of radium. His own funds, being unlimited, permitted him to use it.*

chair. And near the chair stood the kidnaped millionaires, looks of joy and relief crossing their harassed countenances as they saw the police. They cried, shouted, gesticulated, and then became suddenly silent as one of their number, Grier, the stockbroker, exclaimed, "The Skull! He's still there!" and pointed to the niche above the electric chair.

Inspector Burks followed Grier's pointing finger, and gasped in amazement. For there stood a man garbed in a vermilion cloak and hood, wearing on his face a hideous mask resembling the head of a skeleton. This man had one hand raised, gripping the handle of a switch, and seemed to be leering down at the scene.

There was a slight blur of motion in the semi-darkness of that niche, and suddenly, as if by its own volition, the heavy screen began to rise. The police, who had come into the room behind Burks, trained submachine guns on the thirty-odd ex-convicts who crouched in terror, looking up to the figure of the Skull in his niche, as if seeking aid from him. But the Skull was silent, not moving, seeming to regard the whole scene with leering, sardonic humor.

Burks raised his heavy service revolver, covered the vermilion figure, and bellowed, "Come down from there, or I'll shoot!"

There was no response from the Skull.

The millionaires huddled together, as if fearing some last terrible action from the master of evil, which would wipe them all out. After a moment Burks stepped toward the niche, motioning for a couple of his men to follow him. He came up close under the niche, reached up and pulled at the Skull's robe, shouting, "Come on, there! You're under arrest!"

In answer to the inspector's pull, the figure of the Skull suddenly toppled forward, and fell from the niche, its fall being broken by the three men underneath.

Burks scrambled to his feet, leveled his gun. But the Skull was prostrate on the floor, not moving.

Burks reached down, gripped an edge of the mask, and plucked it away.

A gasp went up from everybody present, including the Servants of the Skull.

For the face that was exposed beneath the mask was the face of Harrison Dennett, the subway contractor.

Grier came up beside Burks, exclaimed, "Good God! We thought Dennett had been killed, and it was he all the time. We were told Dennett had been killed first, so we wouldn't suspect him!"

Burks said grimly, "He's not dead—just unconscious. Looks like someone gave him a shot of some sort of anesthetic."

Laurens, the little jeweler, exclaimed, "Think of it! He was our friend, and he turned out to be such a devil! He was broke, and losing the subway job, so he figured he'd recoup this way!"

Burks said, "I wonder who laid him out here; and who left those arrows for us to follow. It looks like—"

He paused, for just then, from the corridor outside there came a series of incoherent cries, and the sound of wildly stumbling feet. There reeled into the room a young patrolman, one of those who had been assigned to guard the corridors. He staggered in, his hands to his eyes, rubbing them madly.

Burks jumped up, seized him by the shoulder. "What's the matter, O'Brien? You hurt?"

O'Brien rubbed knuckles at his tortured eyes. It was several minutes before he could speak, and then he said, "Some one was in the corridor, inspector. He came through a panel—looked like some sort of a halfwit, with a face that was full of scars. I called to him to stop, but he started to run away, so I pulled my gun. An' then, what does he do but turn around an' throw some sort of a little pellet at me. It burst on the floor—tear gas! I couldn't see a thing, an' he escaped!"

Just then there came an eerie whistle from somewhere out in the maze of passages—a whistle strangely musical in its quality, that seemed to pierce to the very marrow of the bones of the men in that room.

Inspector Burks raised his head, and there was a peculiar light in his eyes. "Now I understand," he said. "I've heard that whistle before. I—think—I know who it is!"

BOOK X

THE MURDER MONSTER

A panic-stricken cities shrank in horror from these death-dealing robots who were immune to bullets. Only Secret Agent "X" dared meet the challenge of these inhuman fiends and their master, The Murder Monster, whose pointed finger turned men and women into flaming agony.

CHAPTER I

STORM CLOUDS OF CRIME

THE SETTING SUN cast a cold, hard glint across the waters of the Hudson. Brittle spearheads of light flashed athwart the waves that rippled at the bank of the river below the somber walls of the State Prison.

The chill of early November dusk was in the air; almost it seemed to reflect a spirit of dreadful foreboding, to presage the approach of calamity. Somehow, the air seemed charged with thunderbolts of doom, poised and waiting to be hurled at the grim walls of the gloomy pile that loomed above the river, imprisoning fifteen hundred bitter men.

It was Sunday afternoon, and the inmates were being given a glimpse of life in the world beyond their cells. They were being treated to a football game between their own team and the team of Ervinton College, an institution that played the State Prison once a year.

The players on the field, convicts and college boys alike, were lost in the excitement of the game.

But the convict spectators displayed only a listless half-interest. Behind the high wire screen that separated their section from that of the visitors, they sat tensely, eyeing each other furtively, shifting nervously in their seats. Over the whole prison there seemed to be an air of tension, of taut expectancy.

That sixth sense that is so highly developed among men who are confined alone for a long time seemed to have divined that death hovered near. Many cast glances backward toward the main building, where were confined the more recalcitrant prisoners—dangerous criminals, untamed by their imprisonment, who were denied the privilege of witnessing the game.

The closing whistle blew, interrupting the play at nothing to nothing. Rousing cheers came from the section set apart for the visiting college spectators. The convicts cheered half-heartedly. They were casting furtive glances around the field and toward the grandstand where the warden sat, entertaining the faculty of Ervinton. The keepers, who were stationed ten feet apart across the front of the prisoners' seats, called out, "Everybody remain seated till the teams are off the field!"

The visiting team deployed from the field, trotted into the basement through the side entrance of the main building, where showers and a locker room had been set up for them. The convicts watched them gloomily, in marked contrast to the hilarity of the college boys. For *they* were not going home to well-cooked meals in comfortable dining rooms, to the fond glances of proud parents, to the arms of sweethearts. They were going in to a dreary supper and dismal cells, to their lonely thoughts and gnawing memories.

AN inch of fiery red sun showed over the top of the wooded hills to the west, across the river. Dusk had come quickly. It was growing dark fast, and the guards now hurried the convicts into a double line and marched them toward the main entrance. The warden, with two of his deputies, stood in the grandstand talking to several of the faculty of Ervinton College who had come down to see the game.

The warden was a tall man, with a lined, wrinkled face topped by iron-gray hair. The weight of responsibility for all these prisoners sat heavily on his shoulders. Moodily, as he talked, his eyes rested on the leading ranks of convicts marching dispiritedly toward the building.

In a moment that front rank would step through the entrance, would be led to the mess hall. Another dreary day would be done, a dreary night would commence.

But that marching line never reached the entrance.

For there erupted, at that moment from the basement exit in the side of the building, a disorderly swarm of men. The Ervinton college players, the substitutes and the coaches, were being herded out, still in their football uniforms. Some stumbled, others ran, and it was evident that something terrible had happened inside.

The warden leaped from the grandstand to the field, started to run toward the basement exit, followed by his deputies. Several guards swung in after him. The long marching line of convicts had halted at a command from the head keeper, and stood silent, watching the strange exodus.

The two sandwich men pumped a rapid, steady stream of lead at that horrible figure—to no avail.

And suddenly the warden, who had been running across the field, stopped short in his tracks, his face white, his hands trembling. For right behind the college players, forcing the boys ahead at the point of submachine guns and rifles, there appeared other men—men who were dressed in the street clothes which the college boys had left in the lockers, but who did not look like college boys.

The warden exclaimed, "God! It's the lifers! They've gotten loose somehow—and they must have broken into the armory; they've all got weapons! Look, there's Gilly, and Furber, and—" he named others of them whom he knew by sight. "Quick, Turner," he addressed the deputy immediately behind him, "signal the gatehouse guard to close the gate. Have the two tower guards enfilade them with machine gun fire!"

The deputy turned to obey. At the same moment, one of the

armed convicts raised a Thompson gun to his shoulder and directed a stream of lead into the gatehouse. The guard there was flung against the wall of his little enclosure, his body riddled by a dozen slugs; the gate, which had been opened to permit the egress of the visitors, remained open.

And now was demonstrated the devilish ingenuity behind this well-planned escape. The convicts, their faces screwed into snarling masks of defiance and hatred, were herding the college players along front of them, pushing them toward the open gate. No shots were fired at them from the wall towers; for the very good reason that the college boys, being in front, would be the first to be hit.

The warden could do nothing. He stood there helpless, his face bleak, and watched the most dangerous criminals in his charge march through that gate to freedom. He said hoarsely to the deputy, "Good God, Turner, they're using the Ervinton boys as shields!" His hands clenched and unclenched spasmodically. "We can't fire at them now. Those innocent boys would be the first to be hit!"

AND Turner did not signal the tower guards. A small group

gathered about the warden, gazed spellbound at the vicious faces of the escaping convicts. Turner and the other deputy flanked their chief, hands hovering over the service revolvers holstered at their hips, not daring to draw them, lest such an overt act provoke the vicious lifers to let loose again with the machine guns and mow down innocent spectators as they had killed the gatehouse guard.

But after that one burst of fire from the Thompson, the escaping convicts rushed grimly across the yard toward the gate.

The long line of marching prisoners proceeding toward the main building had stopped without orders from the keepers who flanked them. The marching convicts cast envious glances at those who were escaping, but they made no move toward a break for freedom themselves. They had no living shields, like the others.

The warden raised his voice, calling hoarsely to some of the armed convicts. "Gilly! Renzor! You can't get away with that. You'll be caught before you get a mile from here. Drop those—"

He stopped as Gilly, one of the two he had addressed, swung snarling toward him, bringing the submachine gun around to bear on the little group. The warden and those with him dropped to the ground to avoid the threatened barrage. But Gilly did not fire, for a tall, heavyset convict who was running alongside him shouted, "Never mind that stuff, Gilly! Keep on goin'!"

Gilly grumbled, but obeyed. The convicts hustled the terrorized college boys along through the gate. Outside, there waited a huge closed truck, with motor running. The convicts piled into this, the motor roared, and the truck sped away, leaving the Ervinton boys with their hands in the air.

Now the guards in the towers directed a withering fire at the swiftly moving truck. But no damage was done; its sides were of sheet metal, and wheels were equipped with solid tires. In less than three minutes it had rounded a bend in the road to the south, and disappeared from view.

Inside the prison grounds, bedlam reigned. The hundreds of excited spectators were shouting and gesticulating, running aimlessly around the ball field. In the yard the keepers were herding the remaining prisoners into the main building, while the warden uttered crisp commands to his deputies.

"Shut the gates! March the men to the cell blocks—we'll feed them later. Turner, go into my office and start the siren; then phone all the towns along the roads; get out the state police." He addressed the other deputy, "You, Seely, see the men safely in their cells, then get out every available keeper and guard, organize a posse. I'll lead it personally."

One of the professors from Ervinton College, who had joined him at the first sign of the break, tapped him on the shoulder. "I am afraid, warden, that you will not be successful in catching those men. This was a well-planned escape."

There was a look of desperation in the warden's face. "We *must* get those men back, Professor Larrabie!" he exclaimed. "They are the most vicious criminals in the state. Gilly, the one that wanted to mow us down with the machine-gun, is a killer many times over. He was about to be transferred to the death house!" The warden went on, his words tumbling out with hysterical speed, "And the others—Dubrot, Renzor, Gerlan—the brainiest, most ruthless fiends we've ever had here! Can you imagine what it means—a gang like that at liberty?" He shuddered. "If I don't bring them back I—" his voice broke, "there'd be nothing left for me. I couldn't face the governor!"

"Nonsense!" the professor retorted. Professor Larrabie was a tall, kindly man. He was extremely wealthy in his own right, but was also an enthusiastic scholar. Though he had no need for the income, he loved his scholastic work. He held the position of associate dean of Ervinton, and was far from a worldly man. But he showed that, for all his unworldliness, he had a well-developed sense of observation. For he said, "I believe this was done by one of the visitors, Warden. Just prior to the end of the game, I noted that someone from the visitors' stand arose and entered the building. He came out immediately before the escape. I believe that person to be responsible. But the sun was in my eyes, and I could not see his features."

JUST then Turner, the deputy, came running out of the main building. He was breathless, and his face was ashen. He exclaimed, "The siren doesn't work, sir—it's been tampered with. And the phone is dead! I can't get a connection to notify anybody!"

The warden turned a haggard face to Professor Larrabie. "Ten minutes ago, Professor, I'd have staked my life that a thing like this was impossible." He seemed to have aged ten years in those ten minutes. "It's a perfect jail break!"

Professor Larrabie nodded. "It would be. The deliverer of those men is very clever. He foresaw everything!" The professor's gaze wandered over the field where the crowd of visiting spectators was milling around, shouting and gesticulating excitedly. He indicated a figure running toward them across the field. "Here comes Harry Pringle, the son of the deputy police commissioner of New York. Harry is a school chum of my own son, Jack. They are both alumni of Ervinton." The professor stared near-sightedly at the running youth. "He seems to have something momentous on his mind!"

Harry Pringle reached them, breathless, greeted the professor, then swung to the warden. "Look here, sir!" His thin, ascetic face was burning with intense excitement. "I saw somebody leave the stand a little while ago and enter the building, then come out in about ten minutes. I've been searching through the crowd for him, but I can't find him now. I thought you ought to know about it."

The warden nodded. "Thanks, Pringle. Professor Larrabie has told me the same thing. But the sun was in his eyes, and he couldn't tell who it was. Did you recognize him?"

Harry Pringle shook his head. "It was nobody I know. But," he added eagerly, "I'd recognize him if I saw him again. I'll never forget that face—now!"

The warden said, "Then I shall have the gates closed and give you an opportunity to examine every person on the grounds. But," he put his hand on young Pringle's shoulder, "I'd advise you to be careful. If the person who aided those criminals to escape should learn that you saw him, your life wouldn't be worth two cents, my boy."

An armed file of guards emerged from the building at this moment. The warden said to Turner, "I'm heading the posse. You take charge in my absence. Nobody is to leave the grounds until Mr. Pringle here has seen his face."

The guards piled into three or four cars, the warden got into the first, and the posse started out. Professor Larrabie watched them go, and shook his head sadly. "He will never catch them," he said to Turner. "They have too much of a start."

The professor was right. Late that night the warden and his men returned. They had not been able to pick up a single trace of the truck. Nobody had seen it. He sighed deeply, tired and worn from the long, fruitless search. He asked Turner, "Did that young fellow Pringle have any luck?"

"No, sir. He looked everybody over, but not a face like the one he saw. The police are going to have him go through the rogues' gallery in the morning on the chance that he may recognize one of the pictures."

The warden looked hopelessly at his deputy. "He won't, Turner, he won't recognize it. Whoever that man was, he's too smart to have his picture in the rogues' gallery. This whole thing has been done too cleverly and ingeniously."

He sank wearily into the chair behind his desk. He seemed to have shrunk within himself. His whole bearing was that of a beaten man.

"I am afraid, Turner," he said, "that there are bad days ahead."

CHAPTER II

MR. VARDIS OF NOWHERE

ON A NIGHT, some four weeks after the sensational escape of the twenty-five convicts from the State Prison, a quiet, strikingly handsome gentleman might have been seen seated alone at a table in the Diamond Club.

The Diamond Club was the swankiest resort of the New York City underworld. During prohibition it had been a carefully conducted speakeasy, so elaborately rigged up with safety devices and complicated alarm systems that, though it had been raided a dozen times by prohibition agents, not a drop of liquor had ever been found on the premises.

The proprietor of the club was "Duke" Marcy, former beer baron. Marcy had always been too clever to get into the toils of the law, and now he was able to secure a liquor license, and to operate the Diamond Club as a legitimate enterprise. He took particular pleasure in exhibiting the various devices by which he had frustrated raids in the old days, and these secret liquor caches, light signals and false doors were a never-ending source of attraction to the crowds which nightly thronged the place.

"Duke" Marcy's floor show was the talk of the town, his prices were exorbitantly high, and he did a thriving business. With it all, people wondered why Marcy, who was said to have reaped a fortune out of his former illegal activities, should bother with comparatively small-time stuff like running a night club; they wondered if its purpose was not to cover up some darker, more insidious operations of the underworld czar.

The handsome gentleman who sat alone at the table near the dance floor watched with detached interest while Leane Manners, the star of the floor show, pirouetted expertly through the steps of a complicated and exquisitely delicate dance, with the spotlight following her every graceful movement.

At the end of the dance a thunder of applause filled the room, mingled with cries of "Encore, encore!"

The dancer's eyes swept over the gay, flashily dressed audience, flickered for an instant as they met the gaze of the quiet gentleman, and then she swept into motion once more as the orchestra swung into the rhythm of the music for her encore.

When the encore was over, she was compelled to take three bows before retiring. She did not go back to the dressing room, but threw a cloak over her shoulders, stepped off the floor. Half a dozen unattached men rose enthusiastically, inviting her to their tables. But she favored the quiet gentleman who had also risen and was bowing to her with the innate courtesy of an old world aristocrat. She made her way toward his table.

"How do you do, Mr. Vardis?" she said. She knew this man only as Mr. Vardis, a quiet, unobtrusive gentleman of wealth, with powerful affiliations. It was he who had been instrumental in bringing her to the attention of influential booking agents, resulting in her engagement by "Duke" Marcy for the Diamond Club.

She was not aware—nor was anybody else in the world, for that matter—that the firm mouth, the aquiline, masterful nose, the high forehead and the coal-black hair of the mysterious Mr. Vardis were an elaborate disguise masking the features of a being even more mysterious. For the person behind that disguise was—Secret Agent "X."[14]

Secret Agent "X" as he became known, fully justified the confidence that had been placed in him. He never betrayed that trust, no matter what personal sacrifice his duty entailed. To finance his activities ten wealthy men, who were unknown to him and to whom

---

14 AUTHOR'S NOTE: *Regular readers of these exploits will need no introduction to Secret Agent "X." The man who hides his identity behind that symbol of the unknown quantity has figured in previous chronicles. Little is known about him personally, except that he saw active service during the War, was wounded in action, and later entered the Intelligence Service. In this branch he so distinguished himself that the value of his special resources and abilities was recognized by the government to be as necessary in peace times as in time of war. Accordingly, after the Armistice, a remarkable proposition was made to him by an official high in government circles. He was made a free-lance agent, commissioned to combat crime wherever it reared its ugly head in the country. It was guaranteed that his anonymity would be preserved, and he was given carte blanche to proceed in any manner that he saw fit, reporting to no one, responsible only to himself. The powers granted to him were unprecedented but they were warranted by the wave of unlawfulness that swept the land after the War, rendering the usual law enforcement agencies almost helpless.*

he was unknown, subscribed an unlimited fund which is on deposit to his credit in the name of Elisha Pond at the First National Bank. As this fund becomes depleted by his necessary expenditures in the battle against crime, it is replenished by these wealthy men, who never ask an accounting, never know how it is used. But they feel that it has been well spent when they read in their newspapers of the destruction of another criminal gang, or of the capture of some vicious master criminal whom the police have been unable to cope with. Always, in these cases, there remains at the end an element of mystery, for the police themselves do not know how the discomfiture of the criminals was brought about, except that some mysterious force entered the situation at the opportune moment. Reading these accounts, those wealthy men smile knowingly, and feel that their money has been put to good use.)

Mr. Vardis courteously held a chair for her.

The orchestra struck into a waltz, the lights were dimmed, and couples left their tables to dance. As a waiter approached within hearing, Mr. Vardis invited Leane to dance, but the beautiful red-haired girl laughingly refused.

"I'd much rather sit and talk to you," she smiled. Her voice was musical, cultured, bore out the impression one somehow got that she was a girl of refinement and education.

Mr. Vardis smiled depreciatingly. "That will be as great a pleasure for me." He seated himself, and gave the hovering waiter an order for wine, selecting it from the wine list with the care of a connoisseur.

LEANE maintained the attitude of a careless young dancer having a good time. She continued to smile at her host; but her voice took on a quick urgency. "I'm so glad you've come, Mr. Vardis. There are some things you'll want to know."

Leane Manners had not been introduced to the Diamond Club by accident—nor had Secret Agent "X" become interested in her by accident. She was the fiancée of another of the Agent's lieutenants, a young man named Jim Hobart. Hobart did not know Mr. Vardis; he knew Secret Agent "X" by another name. The Agent never permitted his assistants to know more than one of the various identities he assumed in his operations.

When Jim Hobart had mentioned that Leane, who lived in a middle western town, wanted to come on to work in New York, "X" had concurred in the idea, had sent for her, referred her to "Mr.

Vardis." As Vardis, he had gotten her the introduction to the booking agents, had maneuvered so that she came to the Diamond Club. In addition to the salary she received here, the Agent maintained her on his own payroll. Her duty was to watch for information that would be useful to him. All over the country he had such representatives, received stray bits of information that often helped him to prevent crime before it was even committed.

Now he nodded somberly. "I expected that you would learn something of interest here." Then casually lighting a cigarette, he threw a side glance at the occupants of the near-by tables who were regarding him and Leane with curiosity, and leaned over the table, his lips smiling as if he were whispering a soft compliment.

In reality he was saying, "So that you will be able to work intelligently for me, I will tell you what brought me here tonight. You have read, of course, about the jail break from State Prison last month?"

She nodded.

"Those escaped convicts," the Agent told her, "have not been seen or heard of since the escape. They were not the average run of criminals. Among them were fiends like Dubrot, who has a giant mentality—perverted strangely toward evil; men like Gilly and Renzor, who take human life without blinking an eyelash.

"And there were twenty-five of them—twenty-five vicious, depraved criminals who can no more rid themselves of the urge to evil than a leopard can change its spots. Those men are loose somewhere in the country, hiding out, planning death and destruction!"

THE Agent had spoken forcefully, eloquently, with a purpose. Now, Leane sat tensely, gripped by the picture of menace that his words had evoked. She listened raptly as he continued.

He was still smiling for the benefit of those at the other tables. But his words were in deadly earnest.

"It goes without saying that they did not escape without outside help. Therefore there must be some one, somewhere, who knows about them, perhaps holds the secret of their present hiding place. So far all the forces of the law haven't turned up a single clue." His voice dropped even lower than before. *"I want to find those men!* I am asking everybody with whom I have contacts to keep their eyes open—to watch for any little hint that may be of help. I am asking you to observe carefully everything that happens here in the Diamond Club; and for a very good reason—Baylor and Nagle, two of the escaped convicts, used to be 'Duke' Marcy's private gunmen. It is just possible that Marcy may have had something to do with the escape. Keep constantly alert, report everything to me, no matter how trivial—"

She interrupted him, her face suddenly flushed.

"I think I can tell you something, Mr. Vardis. Baylor and Nagle—I've heard their names mentioned here, but it slipped my mind until you just brought them up. It was on the very day of the jail break, too. Linky Teagle had come in to see 'Duke' Marcy. You know Linky Teagle?"

"Yes. I've seen him around. He used to be Marcy's pay-off man."

She nodded nervously. "That's right, Mr. Vardis. Teagle and Marcy came out of the private office in back, past the dressing room. I had come in early, and I was resting there. They thought they were alone, and I heard Teagle say, 'Baylor and Nagle are in on it, too, Duke.' Marcy said something I couldn't hear, and then they stepped out of the hall. At the time, the names didn't mean anything to me, so I paid no attention. But now—"

The Agent leaned back in his chair, his fingers drumming on the table. "Teagle!" he repeated. "Teagle would never talk. However, it's worth trying. Thanks, Leane."

"Another thing," she went on swiftly. "Marcy had been staying away from here more and more, until a couple of days ago. Just yesterday he began spending more time here. His old girl friend, Mabel Boling, with whom he's supposed to have broken off, has been here to see him twice today, and twice yesterday. She comes in the back way, and goes right to his office. Everybody is supposed to think they're angry at each other, but it's not so. They're up to something, those two."

The soft music of the waltz hardly made it necessary to raise the voice above a whisper. Leane watched the calm face of Mr. Vardis as he cogitated the information she had just given him. She felt almost as if she were under a spell beneath the keen, penetrating eyes that burned in that otherwise austere face. Though she knew nothing about Mr. Vardis, except that a friend of her fiancé's had recommended him highly.[15] She felt that she could trust him, that the fortunes of herself and her sweetheart were secure in his hands.

She started to speak again. "If Linky Teagle should come here again—" Suddenly she stopped, lowered her eyes, and her voice changed to a casual, conversational tone. "I'm so thankful that I have this job, Mr. Vardis. It's easy work, and the pay is good—"

No muscle of Mr. Vardis' face moved to show that he was aware of the reason for the sudden change of tone. But he had noted as quickly as Leane, the shadows that suddenly stood near the table. One was their waiter, carefully carrying a musty wine bottle which he held in a napkin. The other was a huge man, faultlessly attired in evening clothes—"Duke" Marcy himself.

WHILE the waiter poured the wine, "Duke" Marcy bowed first to Leane, then to Mr. Vardis, as Leane introduced him. Marcy spoke in a soft, unctuous voice that went ill with his tremendous physique. He said, "Forgive me for taking the liberty of stepping over to your table. I was eager to meet this friend of Miss Manners, who displays such an excellent taste in ordering wines." His eyes followed the almost caressing hands of the waiter who handled the bottle. "Only a connoisseur of the first rank would order Montrachet of the vintage of 1904. It is the only bottle we have. I had hoped to preserve it for my own use."

---

15   AUTHOR'S NOTE: *This feeling of Leane's was amply justified by past events. Jim Hobart had been a young policeman, discharged from the force in disgrace when the agent had met him. "X" had known that Hobart was innocent of the charges upon which his dismissal had been predicated, and he had befriended the red-haired, good-natured young man, given him employment. Hobart didn't suspect the true identity of his employer. He knew only that his benefactor was a newspaper man by the name of A. J. Martin, and that Mr. Martin could do wonderful things, and had many strange powers. Only recently, on a case that the Agent had solved, he had so arranged it that Jim Hobart received credit for capturing the criminals. Due to this Hobart had received the commendation of the police commissioner and had been permitted to obtain a license as a private detective. He now operated the Hobart Detective Agency, the most profitable client being Mr. A. J. Martin. It looked very much as if Leane Manners would shortly become Mrs. Jim Hobart. It was thus that the Agent requited faithful services.*

Mr. Vardis, who had arisen, said politely, "You will join us, of course?"

As "Duke" Marcy seated himself in the chair which the waiter brought, he said with a grand gesture, "No, Mr. Vardis, I am not joining you. You are joining me. This bottle of Montrachet comes with the compliments of the house!"

Mr. Vardis accepted graciously. Leane Manners fidgeted as they sipped the exquisite Burgundy. Marcy's eyes were veiled throughout the conversation that followed. As he turned from Vardis to Leane in the course of the talk, the huge muscles of his shoulders and upper arms showed in rippling undulations through his dress

jacket. The corded veins of his thick, squat neck moved as he spoke. He seemed capable, should the occasion arise, of taking a man like Mr. Vardis and breaking him in his hands.

Leane's hand shook as she sought Vardis' eyes. Had Marcy heard her utter the name of Linky Teagle? Was he playing with them?

The waltz ended, and as Marcy turned for a moment to view the next number of the floor show, Leane caught a distinct flicker of the eyelid from Mr. Vardis, and a slight nod of reassurance. She smiled once more, relieved. She trusted him implicitly.

Marcy evinced no disposition to leave. He seemed bent on outstaying Mr. Vardis.

When this became apparent, Mr. Vardis rose, excusing himself. There was no point in his remaining now. The single name that the girl had uttered had been sufficient for him. There were some other things that he wanted to know, but he could get the other information elsewhere. He bowed in courtly fashion over Leane's hand, shook hands with Marcy.

Marcy's huge paw encircled his own hand, and Marcy, grinning, with his eyes narrow-slitted, began to exert pressure. It was his favorite means of instilling respect in men he met. That crushing bear grip of his brought sweat to men's foreheads, left them weak and tingling, with their right hand useless for hours afterwards.

But now, Marcy's brows contracted in surprise. This man was his match.

Leane, who knew that trick of Marcy's, watched breathlessly, helpless to stop the pain she knew was going to be inflicted on her friend. But suddenly she sighed in relief as she saw Mr. Vardis' hand wriggle slightly, clasp itself about Marcy's big paw, and contract.

Mr. Vardis' hands were slim, long fingered and powerful. The tips of the fingers barely met behind Marcy's knuckles, yet Marcy winced. Only a second did Vardis continue the punishing grip, then he suddenly released his hold, still smiling courteously. Once more he bowed to Leane, and made his way leisurely toward the door.

Marcy gazed after him with a puzzled expression. He said to Leane, "Say, girlie, that friend of yours is no slouch." His lower lip protruded slightly, his eyes became pinpoint. "I'll have to pay more attention to him in the future!"

CHAPTER III

LINKY TEAGLE

MR. VARDIS HAD excused himself at the Diamond Club, stating that he had an appointment for which he was late. But upon leaving the place, he no longer seemed to be in a hurry. Instead, he strolled down Broadway in a leisurely manner, and entered a cigar store. He stepped into the telephone booth and dialed a number that was not in any book. Almost at once, a precise voice came over the wire. "Bates talking."

Vardis asked, "Who is on duty tonight, Bates?"

Bates recognized the voice, answered quickly, "Stegman and Oliver, sir. They are here now, awaiting orders."

"Good," said Mr. Vardis. "Have them go out and inquire around cautiously. I want to know where Linky Teagle can be found tonight. I will call back in an hour."[16]

Bates repeated the orders crisply to be sure he had them right. "Information is wanted as to the whereabouts of Linky Teagle. It is wanted within an hour." He paused a moment, and "X" heard him issuing swift instructions at the other end. Then his voice came again. "Okay, sir. Stegman and Oliver have left. Anything else?"

"Yes," said Mr. Vardis. "What reports have you on the robot

---

16 AUTHOR'S NOTE: Secret Agent "X" did not depend on any one organization, such as Jim Hobart's detective agency, for all his information. At a good deal of trouble and expense, he built up the organization headed by Bates. "X" has steadfastly refused to disclose to the author just where the office is, or where Bates is located, or what the telephone number is. Men all over the country report to Bates, who is more or less of a clearing house for news of national importance. That "X" has other agents besides those headed by Bates there is no doubt. He often uses a man from Jim Hobart's outfit, one or two from Bates' office, and, perhaps, others whom I do not yet know about. The reason for this, I understand, is so that they may not be able to check with each other to discover his identity. One thing is very definite: though these men are from every walk in life, they have been thoroughly investigated by the Agent, and are absolutely dependable.

murders?"

"Nothing helpful, sir," regretfully. "All the witnesses of the crimes who have been interviewed by our men swear that the murderers are a strange race of robots. They did not talk, and they walked stiffly, as automatons do. The four murders reported have netted them large sums of cash and were all attended by an absolute lack of mercy. In no case were the victims warned, or threatened. In fact, no word was spoken, The robots merely shot to kill, then walked off with the money."

"I know all that," Mr. Vardis said shortly. "I will call you back every hour from now on. Have the men circulate in the underworld; let them try for any kind of lead to these robots. Any further reports now?"

"Only one, sir. The man who is shadowing 'Duke' Marcy reports that Marcy has done nothing suspicious today, in fact seems to be busy running the Diamond Club. The only thing of possible interest was a short conversation that Marcy had only a few minutes ago with a stranger named Vardis. Our man recommends looking up this Vardis."

"Vardis is all right," said Mr. Vardis. "I know all about him. Proceed with the investigation of the robot murders, and with the matter of Linky Teagle."

Mr. Vardis left the telephone booth and walked east, purchasing an evening paper on the way. He turned in at a dilapidated brownstone house west of Sixth Avenue. This was one of a row that had deteriorated into boarding houses for down-at-heels theatrical people. Mr. Vardis had been able to secure the basement floor at a nominal rental, and he lived here alone, coming at odd times, going as he pleased, with no one to note his actions, which were, at times, more or less surprising. Now, in the seclusion of an inner room, he set himself to scan the paper carefully, studying the reports of the so-called "robot murders."

A great deal of space was devoted to them, for they bore all the qualities of sensational terror that aided in the building of newspaper circulation.

The first of them had occurred the day before yesterday, and had been attended with an exhibition of daring, ingenuity and ruthlessness that had left the city gasping.

At eleven-thirty at night, four figures had strutted stiffly into the office of the cashier on the mezzanine floor of the Grand Central Station. This was the office where all the ticket clerks brought their cash from the ticket windows on the upper level of the station. It was estimated that the cash on hand exceeded twenty thousand dollars.

The four figures might have been men—they had the faces and bodies of men—except for the fact that they moved stiffly, jerkily, like automatons, and never uttered a word. They bore a striking facial resemblance to each other—so much so, that they might have all been cast from a single mould. Their faces were youthful in appearance, pleasant and harmless looking. But they quickly demonstrated that they were far from harmless. For they drew automatics with silencers attached, and shot to death the cashier, the assistant cashier, and a guard on duty in the office.

Then they scooped up the cash in sacks which they produced from under their clothing, and boldly marched out through the lower level exit. It was not until they were well away that the bodies of the murdered men were found in the office. The assistant cashier lived long enough to tell the story to the police.

The police might not have believed the story in its entirety, even though the four robots had attracted attention in their march through the station, had there not come in swiftly upon the heels of this crime, the news of three other robberies committed at almost the same time by men answering the same description. In one case a patrolman on the beat where the robbery took place had seen them escaping with a sack of loot from a local post office, and had emptied his service thirty-eight at them. Bystanders swore that every one of the patrolman's shots had struck the robots, yet they were not wounded. Instead, one of the robots turned as if impelled by some mechanical device, raised its gun and fired at the policeman, killing him instantly.

FOR three days now those robberies had continued with impunity, the robots striking in parts of the city where they were least expected, always avoiding spots where the police had massed to trap them. The city was growing panicky. Deputy Commissioner Pringle, in charge while Commissioner Foster was away in Europe, had cancelled all leaves, had every available man on duty.

Mr. Vardis put down the paper, clenched his hands tightly. His eyes were bleak, almost fathomless. This menace of inhuman robots devoted to crime was a possibility that he had often envisaged with dread—not for himself, but for the community where they would strike. For it was inevitable that at some time or other there would arise a criminal with a mind of such scientific skill, of such devilish ingenuity, that it might develop such robots to do its work.

Such a criminal would be difficult to combat, for he would be clever, dangerous; he would remain hidden in security while his machines robbed and killed. And even if some of those machine-like fiends of man's creative skill should be caught or disabled, the criminal himself would still be free to continue in his diabolical traffic.

If this thing had arisen now, it was a most inopportune time for the agencies of law enforcement, because of the added menace of those twenty-five hard-bitten convicts who were still at large, and who might be heard from at any moment now—also with reports of pillage and murder.

The newspaper flares about these escaped criminals had not died down yet, even after a month. The accounts of the nation-wide search being conducted for them shared honors with the robot murders. In addition to the rewards offered by the government, many individual newspapers were offering large sums for information leading to their capture—dead or alive. But no amount of tempting cash reward had so far succeeded in coaxing a single hint as to their whereabouts. Were they out of the country? The editorial writers hoped so—for, though it might reflect on America's penal institutions that these convicts had been able to make a clean getaway, yet thousands of citizens would sleep easier if they were sure that those vicious men were no longer a hidden menace to their families.

"X" was almost certain that they were still somewhere in the country, hiding in some extremely clever retreat until they were ready to make their presence felt. The task of locating them, however, seemed utterly hopeless. He had reports from his agents everywhere—with not a single helpful hint among them.

So far, the only lead he had was the name which Leane Manners had spoken—that of Linky Teagle, "Duke" Marcy's former pay-off man. "X" knew him as a crook of a low order of intelligence, who, since Marcy had turned from bootlegging to other, possibly more subtly insidious enterprises, had existed as a hanger-on at the fringe of the aristocracy of the underworld.

It was his business to "spot lays" for daring hold-ups, to "put the finger" on likely looking victims for kidnap plans; it was quite likely that a man like him would know where those escaped convicts were hiding out—but very unlikely that he would impart this in-

He saw the uniformed officer burst into flames and came tumbling down right at him.

formation to a casual questioner. His very value to the underworld lay in the fact that he could be relied upon not to talk under any circumstances. Many a time had he been sweated in headquarters, "put through the mill," but never had he uttered a word of betrayal. Teagle must be handled in a skillful manner to be induced to disclose information.

Mr. Vardis opened a cunningly concealed door in the wall of his room. A closet was disclosed, containing a row of filing cabinets. From one of the drawers labeled "G," he took a thick folder, and proceeded to examine its contents carefully.

The name on the edge of this folder was "Gilly"—a name he had good cause to remember. It was also the name of one of those twenty-five vicious criminals who had been released from State Prison.[17]

Delving into the folder, Mr. Vardis picked out several sheets which were clipped together. They were headed, "Friends of Gilly." Among them was a sheet containing photographs, side and back, of one John Harder, once an associate of Gilly's. Harder was a fugitive from justice in the Middle West, and there was very little likelihood of Gilly's having been in touch with him recently.

Mr. Vardis placed these photographs on a little dressing table in one corner, turned on a strong daylight bulb, and spread out the contents of a flat black box which he withdrew from a drawer. This box contained all the material necessary to change the appearance of his face; a wide range of pigments, specially prepared plastic material, face plates of different sizes and degrees of concavity, nose plates, even sets of plates of various sizes to slip over the teeth." [18]

The long, facile fingers worked swiftly. Under their deft manipulation, the face of Mr. Vardis began to melt, finally disappeared, revealing for an instant the true features of that man of mystery—Secret Agent "X." They were young, strong features, expressive of indomitable will, high intelligence, keenness and courage. They were features that no man now living could boast of ever having seen.

Only for a moment did that powerful face remain under the

---

17   AUTHOR'S NOTE: *The name of Gilly will be recalled by those who read the recent exploit of Secret Agent "X" related under the title of "Servants of the Skull." Gilly was one of the vicious gunmen who acknowledged the criminal known as the Skull as his master. Gilly almost caused the Agent's death during those exciting days of hairbreadth adventure: but when the Skull's plans were disrupted, and his headquarters were invaded by the Police under the guidance of the Agent, Gilly had been captured with the others. Gilly had been serving a life sentence for his part in the Skull's crimes, when the jail break took place, and he was one of the twenty-five to escape.*

18   AUTHOR'S NOTE: *To the reader these disguises which the Agent assumes may appear to be simple matters, requiring little effort or expenditure of energy; just as, in hearing a pianist playing a difficult number, we may watch his fingers racing across the keyboard and imagine that it is easy. On the contrary, each disguise that "X" assumes requires a degree of skill, or artistry, of sheer genius that it is impossible to estimate. It is known how difficult is the modeling of a head by a sculptor working at his ease with clay. Imagine then, how much more difficult it is to model upon one's own face the likeness of another man, duplicating facial muscles, pigmentation, and the thousand other details that make the individuality of a man.*

glare of the daylight bulb. The long skillful fingers worked surely, efficiently, and shortly there appeared the face of John Harder—the fugitive from justice, the friend of Gilly, the gunman.

AN hour later of that same evening a man might have been seen making his way west across Times Square, hat brim pulled down and coat collar turned up against the steady drizzle that was slanting downward out of a pitch-black sky. Any policeman in New York would have recognized the features of that man if he had looked into his face; for they were the features of the notorious John Harder, wanted for murder in three states, whose picture had been broadcast in every newspaper in the country.

But Secret Agent "X" passed unmolested across the world's busiest thoroughfare, proving once more the truth of the old adage that the best hiding place is generally in the most conspicuous spot.

The clock on the Paramount Building said ten o'clock. Electric signs flashed all along Forty-second Street, announcing burlesque, movies, legitimate drama, penny arcades, restaurants, special sales, announcing, in fact, every possible attraction to lure pennies, quarters, halves and dollars from the pockets of the amusement seekers who thronged the streets. None of those amusement seekers was aware that here, almost at their very elbows, was being staged a greater, tenser drama than any they could pay their good money to see in the gaudily lit theatres.

Secret Agent "X" made his way over to Eighth Avenue. The rain was increasing in intensity, and he lowered his head to allow the water to slide off his hat brim. But he kept his eyes ever watchful, eyeing passers-by and loiterers, appraising them swiftly, certainly. The unknown foes that he was setting out to pit himself against were diabolically clever. They might even be shadowing him already. At the corner of Eighth Avenue and Forty-second, a man stood looking into the window of a cheap clothing store.

The Agent came up beside this man, but did not look at him. Instead, he glanced in the window, appeared to be interested in the display. After a moment, "X" began to run his forefinger along the front of the window, tracing an idle pattern. He noted that the man was watching now, out of the corner of one eye, and the Agent swiftly wrote the word, "Bates" on the wet pane. The man saw it, but made no motion to indicate that he understood. After a moment, though, he turned and walked unconcernedly around the corner and up Eighth Avenue.

He stopped in the middle of the block before the brightly lit window of Haley's Bar and Grill. There was a colorful display of bottles in the window, accompanied by the sign, "Licensed to serve wines and liquors."

The man who had led "X" around the corner stopped for a moment, nodded almost imperceptibly in the direction of a second man who stood close to the doorway of Haley's, and continued on his walk.

The Secret Agent turned toward the entrance, drawing a cigarette from his pocket. At the door he stopped, asked the man standing there for a light. The man obligingly produced a book of matches, lit one and cupped the flame from the rain while "X" lit his cigarette. He murmured, "Teagle is in the rear room in the third booth on the left. Stegman and I picked him up easy. He's all alone; seems to be waiting for some one."[19]

"X" said, "Good work, Oliver. You and Stegman are relieved for the night. Report back to Bates, then you can go home."

Oliver said, "Right, sir," and left, walking in the direction Stegman had taken. If he recognized the face of the man he had just spoken to, he gave no sign of it. Those who were in the employ of Secret Agent "X" were trained never to ask questions, never to wonder at the sometimes curious things they were ordered to do.

THE Secret Agent, meanwhile, entered the barroom, walked through, past the long bar lined with drinkers, and into the rear room. This was equipped with tables set into booths along both walls.

Linky Teagle sat in the third booth, as Oliver had said. He was glowering moodily at a glass of beer, half empty, on the table before him. Teagle was a man of medium size, with a thin, pinched face, small eyes that never rested and never looked directly at anyone. Sparse, muddy-colored hair was combed back from a low forehead

---

19 *AUTHOR'S NOTE: These two operatives of Bates', like all the others, had no idea who their real employer was, or what was the ultimate purpose of the various queer tasks that they were called upon to perform. All they knew was that their work was dangerous but not illegal, and that they were extremely well paid. Their loyalty to their unknown chief was above suspicion, and they never asked questions. Many of them, like Oliver, were reformed criminals: some like Jim Hobart, were ex-policemen. There were even numbered among those on "X's" payroll a former sword-swallower from a circus sideshow, and a general of the old Imperial Russian Army.*

in an effort to conceal the fact that he was almost bald. He was dressed in a tight fitting double-breasted blue serge suit, and the automatic holstered under his left armpit made a visible bulge under his coat.

He looked up with a start as the Agent slid into the seat opposite him, and frowned when he found it was not the person he apparently expected. His frown changed to a look of consternation as "X" removed his hat, and he recognized the widely advertised features of John Harder. He glanced around furtively, made sure that no one had noticed, and muttered without moving his lips, "Put that hat on, quick! You nuts?"

"X" obeyed, smiling grimly. His ruse was thus far successful. Everything depended now upon whether Linky Teagle was really in possession of any information about those escaped convicts, as Leane Manners had suggested in the hint she had dropped.

Teagle said, "You're Harder. What the hell you doin' in this town? You'll get spotted inside of half an hour!"

"X" said slowly, his voice assuming a toughness that went well with the character he was impersonating, "That's my lookout, Teagle. I got to talk to you."

"Not here, damn it. Wouldn't I look swell, bein' found with you? The cops would ride me for ten years. There's a law in this state about consortin' with known criminals. Who sent you to me?"

"I've heard o' you," said "X." "I got to get in touch with an old pal o' mine by the name o' Gilly—" he watched the other keenly as he mentioned Gilly's name, and detected a quickly suppressed start of alarm. "He broke outta jail a while ago with some more guys, an' I gotta see him. I've been told you know where he is. How about it?"

Teagle made to rise. "We can't talk about that here. Let's get out some place—"

"X" put out a hand, restrained him. He was close to victory. By his very attitude, Teagle had half admitted that he knew where Gilly was. Taken by surprise, his mind had failed to react quickly enough so that he could make immediate denial. By failing to make that denial, he had implied that he knew what "X" wanted to know.

"X" spoke tensely. "We don't need to talk about it. You know me. You know I'm one of the boys. Take me to Gilly."

Teagle's face was pale, but there was a crafty gleam in his eyes. "Forget it. I don't know a thing about it; ain't heard from Gilly since he broke outta State Prison with the rest of the boys. Whoever told you I know where he is was givin' you a sleigh ride." He glanced around the place nervously, and gulped the rest of his beer. "Better scram, big boy. 1 can't help you, an' you'll only make it bad for me if I'm found wit' you. Besides," he added urgently, "I'm expectin' some one here any minute now—an' it wouldn't be so good for you to meet—that person."

The Agent made no move to leave. His eyes bored into the other's as he said slowly, very low, "Teagle, I know you can put me wise where Gilly is. I need to see him bad. If you hold out on me, I'll figure you for a wrong guy. And, Teagle, *you know how I handle wrong guys!*" He waited a moment, watched Linky Teagle's hands move aimlessly, nervously on the table. The go-between knew Harder's reputation, knew that Harder had killed often in the past on very little provocation.

The Agent went on gently, "On the other hand, I'm a great guy to my pals. Anybody who treats me right don't suffer by it. I got plenty of dough, Teagle, an' I'm willing to pay for favors!"

Teagle's hands stopped moving on the table. There was a greedy, appraising look in his eyes. He wet his lips. "How—how much would it be worth to you—supposin' I *could* dig up the dope on Gilly?"

"How does a couple of grand sound to you, Teagle?"

The Agent saw the light of avarice dissipate the sullenness from the other's face.

Teagle hesitated a moment, then said, "I—I think maybe it could be managed. I'd have to get in touch with some people, an' maybe it would take a couple of hours. Tell you what—" he was almost eager now "—you meet me in front of this place at twelve tonight, an' I'll tell you if it's okay. Better go now, before my friend that I'm expectin' gets here."

The Secret Agent rose. "I'll be here at twelve," he said shortly.

Teagle looked up at him, said, "I ain't tryin' to give you advice or nothin', but you better put on some work clothes, an' grease up your face. You're takin' an awful chance walkin' the streets this way."

"I'll worry about that," the Agent told him. He leaned over the table, acting out the character of the tough John Harder. "You wouldn't be thinkin' of any kind of a double-cross, would you, Teagle?"

Linky Teagle stared back into the hard face above him. "I got a reputation," he exclaimed indignantly, keeping his voice low with an effort. "Nobody can say that Linky Teagle ever squealed!"

The Agent nodded. "See that you keep that reputation."

HE walked through the front bar, with his hat brim turned low. Outside, the rain was coming down fast. But the Agent did not hurry away. Instead, he turned into a nearby doorway, and with swift fingers he remodeled the lines of his face. John Harder, the fugitive from justice, disappeared. Working in the dark, by the sense of touch only, the Agent smoothed away the lines of dissipation that had marked the features of Harder, removed the plate from his teeth, inserting another. He discarded the slouch hat, replacing it with a cap which he produced from an inside pocket, and took off the brilliant-hued necktie he had worn, donned, instead, a staid green tie. He reversed his topcoat. The inside became the outside now, and being of waterproofed tweed, gave the appearance of a raincoat.[20]

When he emerged from the doorway, he was no longer John Harder, but a pale, anaemic looking clerk in search of a drink.

Once more he entered Haley's Grill, made his way to the rear, and seated himself in a booth commanding a view of Linky Teagle's table. Teagle's expected guest had already arrived. "X" tensed as he recognized the broad shoulders, the bull neck, and the dominating features of "Duke" Marcy!

Marcy was talking very low, almost inaudibly, and Teagle was bent forward, ears straining to catch his words. When Teagle spoke in reply, his voice was just as low. It was impossible to overhear their conversation, impossible to get any closer without arousing suspicion. The subject of their talk would have to remain their secret for the present.

The Agent ate a few bites of the sandwich he had ordered, drank part of the coffee, and left. He would have given much to know what Marcy and Teagle were discussing, but there were many things he had to do yet tonight. He felt somehow that he was drawing closer to the heart of the mystery surrounding that ruthless jail break. If Teagle kept his appointment at midnight, he might reach to the very core of it. He might, too, be walking into a trap—especially in view of the fact that Teagle was intimate with Marcy. But that was a risk that Secret Agent "X" was always prepared to

---

20   AUTHOR'S NOTE: *For the necessities of quick change, the Secret Agent has several stock disguises which are simpler than most of the other's, and which he has used so often that he can build them even in the dark, by the sense of touch alone.*

take.²¹ If "X" had continued to shadow Linky Teagle, he might have heard a very illuminating conversation. For Teagle, after a short talk with Marcy, arose, while the ex-gangster waited for him, and went outside, crossed the street to a phone booth in a drug store. The rumble of the subway drowned most of his conversation, but some fragmentary phrases were audible. "—wants to join up... not a chance?—how'll I stall him?... what! You sure Harder died last month? Then this guy must be phony... I'm meetin' him at twelve... will you have some men around?... I don't know who he can be—say! There's only one guy I ever heard of who could pull a make-up like that to fool me! I bet it's..."

When Teagle returned to the booth where Marcy awaited him, his cunning little eyes were shining with excitement. He could not repress his news. He leaned over the table, whispered confidentially to the big ex-gangster...

---

21   AUTHOR'S NOTE: *From the very first, upon entering into his strange career, the man who is known as Secret Agent "X" had decided that his life was forfeit to the cause he was espousing. He knew that peril would beset his every step, that there would await him around each corner the danger of a death without honor or acclaim—a death that might be lingering, full of agony. But long ago on a battlefield in France, when he recovered from a wound that should have killed him, he considered that his life was no longer his own; so he risked it daily, feeling that already he was living beyond the span of time allotted to him in the scheme of things. His sole regret upon the contemplation of death would be that he could no longer be of service to humanity in its constant struggle against evil.*

CHAPTER IV

IN THE NAME OF CHARITY

SECRET AGENT "X" was also making a telephone call at a booth not a block away from the drug store where Teagle was talking. "X's" call was to another of his lieutenants, perhaps the most trusted—Betty Dale.[22]

She was always glad to help him, eager to hear his voice.

Often weeks passed during which she did not hear from him, during which she lived in an agony of uncertainty as to whether or not he still lived; for she knew that his chosen career carried him ever into the byways of danger where a man's life is, more often than not, measured by the speed of a lethal bullet or the flashing arc of a sharp-edged knife.

Only when she heard his voice on the wire after such a period did she breathe a sigh of relief, only to give way once more to concern over his safety—for she also knew that when he called her he was again engaged in some stupendous battle with crime and required her services.

She wasted no time in banalities now, for she knew what matter the Agent was working on, recognized the urgency in his voice.

"I haven't been able to dig up a thing on the jail break," she told him regretfully. "My paper is going to increase its offer of a reward to ten thousand dollars; but I'm afraid it won't do any good. If there are people in the underworld who have information, they are too

---

22   AUTHOR'S NOTE: *Betty Dale is already well known to readers of previous annals. The daughter of a police captain who was killed in action, she was left alone in the world but for Secret Agent "X," who was a friend of her father's. "X" aided her to finish her schooling, then saw her well placed as a reporter for a daily newspaper. Many times in the past had he found occasion to enlist her services in his battle with crime. And Betty had grown to care more than she liked to admit for this strange man, whose true features she had never seen.*

The Agent did not appear to notice the shadows which resolved themselves into men.

much in fear of their lives to try to sell it."

"I know, Betty," the Agent said. "But there is another angle I want to look into, and I think you can help."

"What is that?" she asked eagerly.

"Didn't you do some publicity work last year for a Broadway show?"

"Yes. The name of it was, 'Woman in Black.' Mabel Boling was the star."

"Exactly. You got to know Mabel Boling pretty well, didn't you?"

Betty sounded puzzled. "Why, yes. Mabel feels she owes me a lot; her show would have been a failure without the publicity I developed for her. But—what has she got to do with this—"

The Agent's voice interrupted her. "Mabel Boling is very close to 'Duke' Marcy. And there may be a connection there with this matter I'm investigating. I'd like to meet Mabel Boling, Betty."

"You couldn't have called at a better time," Betty told him. "I can arrange for you to meet her tonight if you wish!"

"How?"

"There's a bazaar at the Grand Central Palace. It's a society affair and is being given to raise a fund for the relief of the unemployed. Mabel Boling is going to be there."

"Mabel Boling—at a society bazaar?" the Agent asked.

Betty laughed. "It may sound funny, but Mabel's up in the world these days. She doesn't see 'Duke' Marcy any more—at least, not in public. She hangs out a lot with young Harry Pringle, the deputy commissioner's son—he's crazy about her. And, since Harry is on the bazaar committee, Mabel will be there, too.

"I see," said "X," reflectively.

"I was just dressing to attend the bazaar myself. I am covering it for my paper. If you'll meet me there, I'll introduce you to Mabel."

The Agent figured time quickly. His appointment with Linky Teagle was for midnight. It was not ten-thirty. He'd have ample time to stop in at the bazaar, meet Mabel Boling, and still keep the appointment.

"I'll be there," he said.

Betty's voice was troubled. "How will I know you?" [23]

"Don't worry," he chuckled. "I'll make myself known to you!"

Betty Dale did not know at the moment that by her eager invitation she was unwittingly placing the man she admired most in the world in the greatest danger he had ever faced in his career.

---

23   AUTHOR'S NOTE: *Though Betty Dale was perhaps closer to him than anybody else in the world, she had never been allowed to meet Secret Agent "X" in any of his permanent assumed personalties, such as Elisha Pond or A. J. Martin. Thus, she never knew in what guise he would next present himself to her. This man whose face she had never seen, she admired and loved for his kindliness, his courage, his bravery and strength. And she often wondered if it would ever be vouchsafed her to talk with him for an hour without having the shadow of some horrible crime looming over them, calling him into perilous paths.*

THE 1934 Unemployment Bazaar was the most lavish undertaking in years. Society had subscribed heavily, men and women of wealth entered into the spirit of the affair with the greatest of enthusiasm. It was as if these favored of fortune were seeking by some means to ease their consciences of the burden of the knowledge that thousands of families went without food and clothing while they basked in the lap of luxury.

Limousines were parked down the length of Lexington Avenue and in all the side streets. Fully five thousand people were circulating upstairs in the huge bazaar room, which had been equipped with booths all around the four walls. Manufacturers of everything under the sun had rented booths here, content to display their names, to give out samples of their merchandise, and to have it known that they supported the cause.

Other booths had wheels of chance at a dollar to five dollars a throw. And at these booths the elite of New York's wealthy class amused themselves, winning baby dolls and trinkets of no intrinsic value.

One man, immaculate in his evening clothes, accompanied by two ladies in dresses that must have cost enough to feed a hundred families, spent fifty dollars at one of the wheels before he got a winning number and won a stuffed kewpie. He presented it to one of the ladies with him. She carried it around with her proudly. The man was Roderick Pringle, wealthy banker, who was serving as deputy police commissioner. He was the father of Harry Pringle, the young man whom Betty Dale had mentioned. The lady to whom he had presented the kewpie was his daughter, the other was his wife.

The daughter said, pouting, "It's a wonder, dad, that Harry doesn't pay some attention to us. He's one of the committee here and supposed to be busy, but he does nothing except hang on to the skirts of that Boling woman!"

Roderick Pringle, frowning, followed with his eyes the glance of his daughter, across to where a handsome young man of perhaps twenty-nine or thirty stood in earnest conversation with a beautiful, hard-faced, dark-haired woman at least five years his senior.

The face of the portly deputy commissioner became choleric. "He's at it again, in spite of what I told him! He has no consideration for his official position. The woman's not even a good actress—and she consorts with underworld characters." His voice became caustic. "A fine crowd for the son of the deputy police commissioner to hang out with!" He clenched his fist. "Wait till we get home—I'll give it to that young pup. This has got to stop, once and for all!"

His daughter, perhaps regretting that she had called his attention to Harry's companion, tried to change the subject. She tugged at his sleeve. "Dad! Who's that terribly attractive man who just came in over there? Isn't he handsome? And he looks so dignified!"

Roderick Pringle swung his gaze from his son around to the entrance towards which his daughter was looking. "I don't know the man, Irma. Never saw him around before." He bent bushy brows on his daughter. "Now don't you go getting interested in strange men. I've got enough on my hands with Harry!"

Irma Pringle laughed. "I'm sure he's somebody important, dad. Look, he seems to be coming in our direction!"

The tall, dignified gentleman was indeed approaching them, having noted their presence as he entered. When he came up to them, he bowed in courtly fashion, spoke with the modulated accents of good breeding. "I beg your pardon, sir. You are Commissioner Pringle, are you not?"

Pringle nodded.

"My name is Vardis. I am a stranger in New York, but my friend, Commissioner Foster, wrote me before leaving for Europe that if I visited the city I was to look you up. I took this opportunity of making myself known to you."

Pringle thawed out at mention of Foster's name, and introduced Mr. Vardis to the ladies. The conversation drifted into various channels, and as they talked they moved around, examining the interestingly equipped booths. Mr. Vardis was an engrossing conversationalist when he wanted to be, and his listeners were entranced by the swift flow of anecdote and comment that came from his lips.

They stopped before one booth in the line of brilliantly lit stalls along the wall that was not open. The wooden shutters were still in place. It bore the number, thirteen. Pringle nodded toward it. "There's a generous contributor to the cause of charity. The people who rented that booth contributed five thousand dollars to the bazaar fund."

On the closed shutters was a sign reading as follows:

> This booth donated by anonymous benefactor. It will be opened shortly before midnight, and a surprise is promised to all. Be sure to stay for the opening.

"It's probably the contribution of some manufacturer or department store," Pringle said. "It'll make good advertising for them when it's opened."

Mr. Vardis noted two young men who approached them across the floor. They, like Harry Pringle, bore buttons in their lapels announcing that they were on the bazaar committee.

Irma Pringle exclaimed, "Here come Jack Larrabie and Fred Barton, dad. I wonder where Ranny Coulter is?"

The commissioner grunted. "Probably up to some mischief. It's a wonder Jack and Fred aren't up to some crazy stunts, too!" He turned to Mr. Vardis, explained quickly as the two young men approached, "These two, together with Ranny Coulter, are chums of my boy. The four of them are generally always together. I wish some one would take them in hand and whip some sense into them. They've all graduated from college, mastered professions, but they won't work. It's a sickness—too-much-moneyitis! If I lost all my money, it might be a good thing for my boy, Harry; and the same goes for Jack and Fred, here, and Ranny Coulter."

THE two young men came up, were introduced to Mr. Vardis. He noted that Irma Pringle monopolized young Jack Larrabie in a possessive manner. Vardis smiled at the commissioner. "Engaged?" he asked.

"Hell, no," Pringle returned. "They want to be, but I won't let them till Jack goes in practice for himself. He's studied medicine, but he won't practice—says what's the use, when his dad is worth a couple of million dollars. His father is Professor Larrabie of Ervinton College, you know. A millionaire in his own right."

"I seem to recall the name," said Mr. Vardis. "Wasn't it Professor Larrabie who was present at State Prison at the time of the jail break?"

"The same. My son was also there. Harry actually saw the man who is suspected of having killed the guards and paved the way for the escape. I'm worried about Harry's safety on that score. But the boy's stubborn—won't have a bodyguard; says his three pals are all the protection he needs."

The crowd before booth thirteen had grown much larger now, and there was a buzz of excited comment and speculation as to the identity of the donors of the five thousand dollars.

Fred Barton, who had been left somewhat alone while his chum, Jack Larrabie, was engrossed with Irma Pringle, joined Mr. Vardis and the commissioner, and the talk turned to the news of the day.

Mr. Vardis tried to broach the subject of the escaped convicts, but the commissioner was already answering a question of Fred Barton's about the robot murders.

"I don't think, Fred," the commissioner said with a note of authority "that there is any chance of the robots attacking this bazaar. There are uniformed officers on guard at all the entrances downstairs and at the doors up here. Anybody who looks like a robot wouldn't stand a chance of getting near this place."

"That's a consolation, anyway," Fred Barton remarked. "This would be tempting pickings for them. I bet there's a hundred thousand in cash here tonight."

Mr. Vardis was listening closely now. "Do you believe they are robots or mechanical men?" he asked. "I understand they were shot at, but couldn't be hurt."

"That is true," the commissioner said slowly, "It is a hard thing to imagine, but I am forced to believe that they are robots. In no other way can their peculiar actions be explained."

Fred Barton scoffed. "Impossible!" he declared. "As you know, I've made a thorough study of chemistry and physics. The creation of mechanical men is as far-fetched, as impossible, as the discovery of the legendary Fountain of Youth. It would be physically impossible to exercise remote control, by radio, or by any other device, of the arm, leg and head movements of a mechanical man. These so-called robots act and fight like human beings. They must be human beings."

"And yet," said Commissioner Pringle, with a troubled look in his eyes, "you know that famous line—'There are more things in heaven and earth than the mind of man can conceive of!' Anything is possible in this day and age. How do you feel about it, Mr. Vardis?"

"Naturally," Mr. Vardis replied modestly, "I have not sufficient information on which to base an opinion. However, I am inclined to agree with young Mr. Barton, here. Isn't there a possibility, commissioner, that these robots are, in reality, those twenty-five convicts who escaped from State Prison?"

Pringle shook his head. "Emphatically no. Those robots were seen to touch various articles with their bare hands. They left prints. And those prints match no classification on file anywhere in the world! The only explanation I can see is that they are robots—that they have all been created exactly alike by some master fiend who has acquired more scientific knowledge and skill than our greatest students!"

They were interrupted by the approach of a trimly dressed young lady, hardly more than a girl. Mr. Vardis' eyes grew kindly as they took cognizance of her sparkling blue eyes, of the golden blond hair, showing under the small, chic hat. This was Betty Dale.

She glanced casually at Mr. Vardis, with no hint of recognition, smiled at Fred Barton, but concentrated on Pringle. "I hope you'll pardon the intrusion, commissioner. I am Betty Dale, of the *Herald*. I was wondering if you'd grant me a short interview on the robot murders?"

Pringle smiled. "I remember you well, Miss Dale. You don't need to introduce yourself to me. Do you know Fred Barton? And Mr. Vardis?"

Mr. Vardis bowed. Betty did not know him, did not guess who he was. She asked Pringle a number of questions, making notes on a small pad of paper she produced from her bag. When she had finished, she thanked him.

"I'm sorry, Miss Dale," Pringle told her, "that there is little I can add to the news that appeared in the evening papers. We have no idea where these robots will strike again, but I can assure you that the men of the police department are doing everything in their power to protect the residents of the city—from the commissioner down to the lowliest patrolman!"

SEVERAL other people approached the commissioner, and Mr. Vardis found himself alone with Betty for a moment—rather, he maneuvered so that they were alone. "I think, Miss Dale," he said, "that I know a friend of yours."

She looked at him quickly. He could see that she was not interested in him, that her eyes were restlessly roving over the crowd as if she sought some one. She remarked politely, "Really? That is interesting. Who is it?"

"Someone," he replied in a voice that had suddenly assumed a peculiar inflection—one that he reserved for her alone—"someone who shall be nameless!"

Her face paled, her eyes widened. Emotion struggled for utterance, but was repressed. "You—Mr. Vardis!" she exclaimed. Then her eyes clouded with concern as he led her farther away from the group around booth thirteen, toward the center of the floor. "You're working on these robot murders?"

He nodded. "That—and more. I haven't much time now, Betty. Let's find Mabel Boling so I can have a little talk with her. Right at this time I am interested in her ex-friend, 'Duke' Marcy—and, also, in young Pringle."

Betty's eyes lowered. She uttered a warning sound. "There she is—with Harry Pringle. It'll be easy; she's coming up to talk to me."

Mabel Boling greeted Betty Dale effusively. She still recalled the debt she owed to the pretty, blond newspaper girl. Betty knew Harry Pringle by sight, too; and she performed the introductions.

"X" led them across the floor to a booth where cocktails were being served in the name of charity at one dollar each. He bought drinks for everybody, while he covertly sized up Mabel Boling. She was unquestionably beautiful. In addition she was vivacious, and an actress of parts. "X" could understand how she would be the perfect companion, for a man like "Duke" Marcy. But she lacked culture, poise. "X" wondered what attraction she possessed that could hold a young man of education and refinement like Harry Pringle.

Betty Dale adroitly managed to engross young Pringle in conversation, leaving the Agent more or less tête-à-tête with the actress. "X" skillfully turned the conversation to "Duke" Marcy. Mabel Boling's face went blank. "I haven't seen him for months," she declared emphatically. "He was the great mistake of my life." She glanced fondly at Harry Pringle. "I don't even like to think of those days any more."

Though she was a good actress, "X" felt that underlying her words there was a queer note of insincerity. He sensed that she was on guard more or less; that there was something on her mind. Keen judge of human nature, he felt that she could be drawn out at the proper time and place. So, after a little further conversation, he intrigued her into accepting his invitation to have lunch with him the next day. He was a little surprised at the alacrity with which she accepted the invitation, while she cast a wary eye on Harry Pringle to make sure that he hadn't overheard.

Was it possible that she was as anxious to talk to him as he was to talk to her? There was the chance that "Duke" Marcy had spoken to her of his encounter with Mr. Vardis at the Diamond Club.

The Agent betrayed nothing of his thoughts. His face showed only pleasure at the prospect of lunching with an attractive woman. "Suppose I phone you tomorrow?"

She nodded, and whispered her number. And shortly after, she drifted away on Harry Pringle's arm.

THE bazaar was in full swing now; women shone resplendent in their gorgeous evening gowns and glittering jewels. Men were spending money freely, placing dollar and five dollar bills on the wheels, paying a dollar apiece for drinks. The Agent agreed with Fred Barton's estimate that over a hundred thousand dollars was being spent in the booths that evening.

He turned back to Betty Dale to find her conversing with a short, wiry, hawk-nosed man whose bald head glittered under the sharp electric lights. Though "X" knew this man, he betrayed no sign of recognition as Betty Dale introduced them.

"Mr. Vardis, this is Mr. Runkle." Her eyes flickered slightly as she looked at the Agent in an endeavor to convey some message.

Runkle shook hands enthusiastically, his full red lips expanding in an unctuous smile. "I saw you talking with the commissioner a while ago," he said. "I suppose it was about the subject that is on everybody's tongue these days?"

"If you mean the robot murders," the Agent replied, "you are correct. One couldn't help discussing them."

Runkle's ferret-like eyes probed into the Agent, almost as if he were aware that this was a disguise. "You don't happen to be a police officer, do you?"

"I have no connection with the police whatsoever," "X" told him. "What gave you that impression?"

Runkle shrugged. "One sometimes gets a feeling."

Ed Runkle was a criminal lawyer, probably the shrewdest and most successful in the profession. It was he who had once defended "Duke" Marcy on a charge of income tax evasion and got him an acquittal. Runkle had also handled the cases of many of Marcy's old gang including some of those who had escaped from State Prison in the recent jail break. Runkle was saying, "Look at all these people, enjoying themselves here, while murder and robbery goes on in the city. Just as I came in they were crying an extra about another robot murder." He demanded suddenly, "Are you interested in crime, Mr. Vardis?"

"X" shrugged. "Who wouldn't be—when it is so close to us?" The Agent perceived that, for some reason, Runkle was making an attempt to draw him out. "X" would have enjoyed allowing himself to be drawn out, perhaps even to glean some profitable information for himself in the process. But he consulted his watch and noted that it was eleven-thirty. He must leave if he wanted to keep his appointment with Linky Teagle.

He excused himself, and Betty Dale walked as far as the door with him. She wore a troubled expression. "I don't know what it is," she said, "but I feel a strange kind of nervousness—as if something terrible were brewing. It must be recent events. That awful jail break, and now these robot murders." She shuddered. "It's almost as if some evil super-mind were enfolding the city in a fog of terror. People don't feel safe any more. If things like the robot murders can take place day after day here, and the police be powerless to stop them, unable to find a single clue, people will take to barricading themselves in their homes."

Secret Agent "X" nodded somberly. "It's all you say it is, Betty. And there is no tangible lead by which they can be run down. However," he murmured as he bowed over her hand, "with a little luck, I may run into something tonight."

As Betty Dale watched the Agent cross the corridor to the elevator, she felt a sudden premonition of danger, felt almost as if she had seen for the last time the strange man who was Secret Agent "X." Something seemed to tug at her heart, shouting a warning. But she turned back to the busy bazaar, smothering that feeling in a sudden access of energy. She had work to do; she had to cover the event for her paper.

She stepped inside the doorway, and stopped stock still, frozen at sight of the thing that was happening in the glitteringly lit room.

CHAPTER V

FRANKENSTEIN

BOOTH THIRTEEN—THE MYSTERY booth rented by the anonymous donor of five thousand dollars—had been opened! The crowd of hilarious men and women had stopped their laughter, remained rooted where they stood, gaping aghast at the terrifying figures that swarmed out of the interior of the booth. They were like men, yes. And they were clad like men, all in gray suits and gray slouch hats. But they moved with the quick, jerky strides of automatons.

No word was uttered by them, no sound, except for an occasional unintelligible grunt that might have been expressive of pain or of sadistic pleasure. They seemed to be obscene beings endowed with the shapes of men. Each was armed with a snub-nosed automatic equipped with a silencer, and each walked stiffly to a particular spot in the room. Within a minute every exit was covered. The pleasure-seeking crowd of the bazaar was trapped by these manlike beasts.

And then there stepped to the front of the booth, a hideous, awe-inspiring monster. It walked like a man, but stiffly, as did the others. Yet it differed from the others; for it wore a peculiar contraption like a gas mask. The rest of its body was encased, from the gas mask to the feet in a grayish, rough sort of material that might have been asbestos. Its torso was round, stocky, the shape and size of a large barrel. From its gloved right hand protruded a peculiar sort of tube, ending in a tapering point, not unlike a large hypodermic syringe.

This hideous figure stood for a long minute surveying the crowd, silently, grotesquely, like a frankensteinian monster.

Many of the people in the crowd had not yet noticed this monster, for their eyes were glued in horror to the white, expressionless countenances of the mechanical-appearing men who had swarmed out first; and a slow murmur spread through the throng, tinged with sudden fear.

"The robot murderers!" The word went from one to the other in the amazed throng. These were the beings who had committed the robot murders, emblazoned on the front-page of every newspaper in the city for the past week. No wonder the description was alike in every case. These beings were as alike as peas in a pod—clothes, features, bearing—everything!

The whispered word went around, "automatons!"

Betty Dale felt herself brushed aside by one of these creatures who completely disregarded her as he made for the door, turned and stood on guard, automatic pointed at the crowd.

But she paid him no attention. For her eyes were now focused on that awful figure in the booth—that awkward, ungainly monster that stood silently surveying the room.

The first to regain his wits was a patrolman, one of the twelve assigned to duty in the bazaar. He pushed through the crowd toward the booth, shouting to the other uniformed men, "Let's take 'em, boys! It's the robots!"

He was reaching to his hip pocket as he advanced.

The monster turned its ponderous head toward him as if it were a giant dinosaur noticing a lizard in its path. Its right arm rose, the index finger, lined up with that peculiar hypo-like tube, pointed at the blue-coat.

Only that, and nothing more. No sound, no flash. But suddenly, as if an invisible giant hand had been placed against his chest, the unfortunate policeman was brought to a halt. A look of incredible terror and amazement appeared on his round, moonlike face. And in a moment, fierce, torrid flames were leaping up all about him; sizzling, white-hot flames that scorched the clothes from his body, and the flesh from his face. He screamed again and again—screams of dreadful agony that made the blood of Betty Dale and every one of the spectators run cold with horror.

He rolled on the cement floor, clawed about him frenziedly. No one dared approach for fear of being engulfed in that raging furnace which he had become. A wide circle had been cleared about him. And then, suddenly, he lay still, a pitiful scorched thing, that had just now been a man, an officer of the law, a human being with a love of life, perhaps the father of a family.

Men and women stood silent, petrified by the sudden calamity.

A quietness as of the tomb descended upon the assembled company. And then, strained nerves could stand no more. The sight of that lifeless thing that had been burned to death before their very eyes released hysteric floodgates of emotion.

A woman screamed, shrilly, piercingly, and fainted. It was Mabel Boling. She slid to the floor, inert and unconscious. Harry Pringle, who was still with her, stooped to aid the senseless woman, as echoes of her shriek were taken up by women all over the room. The bazaar suddenly became a bedlam of high-pitched, hysterical voices. People milled about in panic, shrinking from the awful figure in the booth.

Harry Pringle knelt beside Mabel Boling, shouting, "Give her air! Give her air! Some water, somebody!"

And in the midst of that pandemonium, the ungainly monster stirred slowly, and a deep, metallic, cadaverous voice issued from somewhere in the depths of its barrel-like body. "Let nobody move. Stand still with your hands in the air!"

IT was as if some one at a great distance were broadcasting, the voice emanating from a receiving set somewhere in the monstrous shape that dominated the room.

Men and women stiffened to frightened attention as those deep, ominous tones resounded through the place. The uniformed men, cowed by the hideous death of their colleague, obeyed the command with the others. The robot killers who guarded the doors stood motionless, as if they had nothing to do with what was going on. But their automatics were trained upon the crowd. It would have been suicide for anyone to defy the order.

Only Harry Pringle, oblivious to everything, still knelt beside Mabel Boling, striving wildly to bring her back to consciousness.

The macabre being in the booth raised its hand once more, and without warning, without repeating the command, pointed at Pringle. From somewhere in the middle of the room came the agonized cry of Pringle's mother, "Harry! Harry! My boy!"

Too late.

White hot flames sprang up from the young man. The revolting odor of scorched flesh once more pervaded the room. He threshed wildly about, trying to beat out the flames, to no avail. People backed away from him, forming a wide circle. He started to cry, "Damn you—" but his voice was suddenly smothered by the flames, as he twisted horribly in the throes of excruciating agony.

Jack Larrabie, his young friend, was standing close to the far wall. Behind him was a fire extinguisher, hanging ready for use. Stealthily he reached up for it, but the murder monster seemed to have all-seeing eyes. Again that metallic voice, "Don't touch it!"

The gloved hand made a half move toward Larrabie, stopped as the young physician stayed his reaching arm in mid-air. He was glaring murderously at the monster.

All this had taken only a few seconds; and in that short time young Harry Pringle's agony ended in merciful death. He seemed to shrivel up, drop to the floor. Flames still licked his pathetic form, and even though he was dead, his body twitched.

Toward the middle of the room, a white-haired woman struggled frantically in the restraining arms of her husband, the commissioner, moaning in a dead voice, "My boy! My boy!"

Roderick Pringle, his face gray, held desperately to his wife's arms. To let her leap to her son would only mean death for her, too.

Of a sudden, wild, uncontrollable laughter burst from the half-crazed woman—no mother's sanity could help cracking under the strain of witnessing such a sight.

But above her strident shrieks of mad laughter, there rose once more that metallic voice. "Gag her! Stop that noise, or—"

The pointing finger started to swing in her direction warningly.

Frantically, desperately, Roderick Pringle, himself on the point of breaking down, threw his arms about his wife, smothering her cries. At last the surcease of unconsciousness came to the bereaved mother, and she sagged in her husband's arms. Her daughter already lay in a merciful faint on the floor.

Mabel Boling stirred, sighed, and opened her eyes. Her uncomprehending gaze fell on the charred remains of Harry Pringle. She did not realize yet what had befallen him; she was still dazed, and she weakly allowed her head to drop back on the concrete floor.

And now the murder monster and his hellish cohorts had the throng subdued, resistless. From a gay, insouciant gathering, spending money freely in the name of charity, this bazaar had been transformed to a grisly scene of murder and terror, with two smouldering bodies, strangely twisted in death, as mute evidence of the dread horror that had suddenly come among them.

CHAPTER VI

THE BETRAYAL

THE RESONANT VOICE of the gruesome being in the booth now rose in terse, metallic command to its cohorts of robot killers. "Take up the collection!"

The automatons snapped into motion at the order. They swarmed from booth to booth, producing from somewhere in their clothing large canvas bags into which they poured the cash which had been taken in.

The robbery was proceeding with the timed efficiency of a well-rehearsed play, every movement of the automatons seeming to have been carefully planned in advance. The whole thing took very little time. While they were emptying the cash drawers, that ominous voice of the specter in the booth spoke again, addressing the cowering throng.

"Make no resistance and you will be harmed no more. The sooner you learn that resistance is useless; the better off you will be. Remember that for the future when we appear again!"

Betty Dale tried hard to remember every inflection of that voice. But she knew it was useless. The voice was disguised, and besides it was issuing from some sort of metal speaker which made it impossible to identify it.

An outcry from the doorway behind her made her turn suddenly about.

This doorway opened into the hallway close to the stairs and the elevator. She saw the two elevator cages open, with the robot killer who had brushed past her before, standing guard. He had shot the two operators with his silenced gun, and their bodies lay now, one of them huddled in the cage, the other sprawled half in and half out of the other cage, a pool of blood seeping along the cement floor from a wound in the head.

The cry that caused her to turn was uttered by a uniformed man who had come down the stairs from the floor above, no doubt attracted by the screams of the women. He was one of the special policemen employed by the building. His gun was holstered at his side, but he drew it as he noted the situation through the open doorway.

He raised his gun, fired six times through the open door at the barrel-like figure in the booth. The heavy slugs from the thirty-eight whined across the room to the thunderous reverberations of the gun and buried themselves in that unholy being—without effect!

The figure staggered slightly from the smashing impact of the bullets, but recovered its balance, raised a pointing finger at the brave attacker.

But the robot killer at the elevator cages was already in action. He emptied his automatic into the body of the special, who staggered, ran a few steps on the concrete floor, and flung headlong down the stairs leading to the floor below. But the searching finger of the ugly monster in the gas mask had found him too, and his body burst into flames, forming a veritable ball of fire that rolled down the steps.

The metallic voice issued an order to the killer at the elevators. "Guard those stairs. Allow no one up or down. We leave now!"

The robot seemed to understand the order as if it were a human being. It moved stiffly toward the head of the stairs, and took up a position there, then proceeded to insert a new clip in the automatic it had just emptied into the body of the special policeman.

Betty Dale had her hand to her mouth in consternation. She had no eyes now for the swift movement of the horde of robots and their leader. For she had seen something that made her blood chill with sharp concern. Just before the flaming body of the policeman had hurtled downward, carrying fiery destruction for anyone who might be in its path, she had glimpsed a face—the face of a man who was running up the stairs. It was the face of Mr. Vardis—Secret Agent "X"—returning, attracted, as had been the special policeman who was now hurtling down upon him, by the screams of the women.

SECRET AGENT "X" had heard those screams as he stepped from the elevator downstairs and started to cross the lobby to the street. He turned to go back, but the cage was already rising in response to insistent ringing from above, where the robot killer was summoning the operator back to meet his death.

The Agent's sure instinct told him that those screams were not occasioned by any ordinary accident—he caught the edge of frightful terror in them.

He noted from the indicator that the second cage was not descending, and his swiftly roving eyes saw the staircase at the left. Several people were in the lobby, and he shouted to them, "Call headquarters, somebody! Send in a riot call!" Then he dashed for the stairs, sprinted up them with a speed that left those in the lobby agape.

On the way up, as he passed landing after landing on the way to the fourth floor, he heard further cries, then silence, which was even more ominous. He passed the third floor, was approaching the fourth, when he saw the special policeman on the landing, got a swift glimpse of the room with the hideous figure in the booth, saw the uniformed officer burst into flame and come tumbling down right at him.

The stairways was narrow, there was no chance of avoiding that hurtling bundle of fire. It would strike him in a moment, engulf him in its flaming destruction.

His brain worked with the speed of lightning. He seized the banister, vaulted over, and hung by his hands on the outside, as the ball of fire rolled down, thumped on the lower landing, and came to a stop against the wall.

The Agent easily supported himself by his hands. He hung there for a moment longer, while the full import of the situation came to him. He heard the metallic voice from the booth order, "You will all remain quiet while we leave. Keep your hands in the air."

There was silence within that room, then the voice again, "All right, we're leaving. File out the back way."

Hanging there by his hands, "X" saw the shape of the robot who had shot the officer at the head of the stairs.

The Agent realized at once what was taking place. Those beings who had committed the robot murders had struck again, this time at the gay throng assembled here in the name of charity; they had brought terror and frightful death along with them; and now they were making good their escape. That escape could not be prevented. But there was one thing that could be done—one of these so-called robots must be captured if possible.

Without hesitation, "X" leaped into action. He swung over the banister, dashed up the stairs, at the same time drawing a peculiar-shaped gun.[24]

The robot on the landing was just turning to depart. From below came the shrill note of a police whistle, the tramp of many feet on the stairs.

As "X" reached the top landing, he got a glimpse into the bazaar room, saw the ghastly figure of the murder monster moving with ungainly, ponderous motions as it stepped through a doorway at the far end of the room, followed by the horde of robots who marched across the floor in its wake.

The robot who had stood at the head of the stairs was just stepping through the doorway to cross the room and join the others. "X" leveled his gas gun and pulled the trigger. A stream of gas was ejected from the muzzle, enveloping the robot's head. The action was a desperate one, for if the robot were protected and not susceptible to the effects of the gas, it would immediately turn upon the Agent and loose a stream of lead from its automatic, which, at that short range, could mean nothing but death.

"X" poised on the balls of his feet, ready to leap forward at the figure if it swung toward him. But it didn't. Suddenly, as the gas struck, the robot sagged, and crumpled to a heap on the floor!

Pandemonium reigned within the bazaar room as the last of the unholy horde left through the far exit. "X" paid no attention to the riot within. He stooped swiftly beside the unconscious figure, looked deeply into the smooth features. He ran his hand along the inert shape. His fingers encountered metal. The figure was wearing a bullet-proof vest, and leg, thigh and arm guards of the same material. No wonder bullets had no effect! He raised his head sharply as a frantic figure raced up beside him. It was Betty Dale. Her face was flushed with excitement, and her hands shook. Her voice was barely audible above the cacophony of sound from inside the bazaar room. "I—I saw you on the stairs!" she exclaimed. She shuddered, closed her eyes tight as if to shut out some terrible sight, "I thought you'd be burned! God! It's horrible! That—that monster—it killed Harry Pringle, and a policeman. And those robots—"

"X" arose from beside the inert form on the floor. The feet of the police were pounding closer on the stairs. They were on the landing below now.

---

24 AUTHOR'S NOTE: Secret Agent "X" does not use lethal weapons. His gas gun contains a highly volatile, quick-acting anaesthetizing gas of his own compounding, which serves the same purpose as a lethal weapon without inflicting injury or death. It renders the subject instantly unconscious, and leaves no ill effects.

The Agent put a hand on Betty's shoulder that seemed to soothe her as if by magic. His eyes glittered. "That is all over and done with, Betty. The dead are dead. But this man on the floor here will change the situation. From now on the police and the public will know that these are not robots, not mechanical men, not supernatural beings. The police were rapidly becoming demoralized by the feeling that they had to face super-human beings. From now on they will fight with renewed vigor, knowing that their enemies are no more than men."

He drew Betty Dale away before the first of the uniformed men came into sight on the stairs. "It's too bad that I won't have an opportunity to question this man. I am afraid the police won't get anywhere with him," He shrugged. "Perhaps I can arrange to question him later. Now I must get out of here. I have an appointment."

He pressed her hand, left her, and slipped into the throng in the bazaar room. Betty watched him, speechless, while he mingled with the hysterical crowd who still kept a wide space cleared around the smouldering, scorched bodies of Harry Pringle and the unfortunate policeman who had defied the murder monster.

CHAPTER VII

FOUR WHO WAITED

IT WAS TWENTY minutes past midnight when Secret Agent "X" appeared again on Eighth Avenue outside Haley's Bar and Grill. He had been delayed by the police investigation at the bazaar, had been compelled to wait while the names of all those present had been taken. The police had been puzzled at finding the killer's unconscious body, had been at a loss to understand how he had been rendered insensible. But no one except Betty Dale had seen the Agent fire his gas gun at the robot-like killer, and she said nothing.

Haley's Bar and Grill was still doing a rushing business. Outside the rain had stopped, but the sky was cloudy and dark. "X" stood near the curb, away from the light that streamed out of Haley's windows. He was twenty minutes late for his appointment with Linky Teagle.

Once more he was in the role of John Harder, fugitive from justice, friend of Gilly, the gunman. He had confidence in the perfection of his disguise, in his knowledge of the characteristics of the man he was impersonating, for he had studied them thoroughly. He would have felt a good deal less confident, however, had he possessed knowledge of a fact not yet reported to the police—the fact that John Harder, the man he was impersonating tonight, was dead! Harder had accidentally shot himself in the leg while examining a machine gun. Harder had fallen on the Tommy, had for two days lain in the lonely hut where he was hiding out, until two of his gang returned. But Harder was dead when they found him—for gangrene had set in. The two pals took his body and buried it in a barren field near the hut. That was the end of Harder.

Gilly, many miles away in State Prison, got word of that event by means of the grapevine telegraph of the underworld, because he was known to be a one-time pal of Harder's. And so, though Secret Agent "X" did not know that he was impersonating a dead man, others did...

The Agent strolled up and down the street in front of Haley's, wondering whether Linky Teagle had been there and gone, or whether he would soon appear. "X" was not unconscious of the possibility that this appointment might be a trap of some sort. He kept a wary eye out for passing automobiles from which a sub-machine gun might spout lead. He now carried an automatic holstered under his left armpit; and few could use it with a dexterity to equal his. He did not intend to inflict death if he could help it—yet it would come in handy if he were being "put on the spot."

No overt attack was made, however. And soon a shadowy figure approached out of the misty night, came close. It was Linky Teagle. Teagle scanned his face, and grunted. "You got nerve, wandering around the city with a fat reward posted for you in every post office in town!"

"X" brushed the remark aside. "Well?" he demanded "How about Gilly?"

Teagle took his time about answering. "You got that two grand you promised?"

The Agent nodded. "I got it, right here." He tapped the breast pocket of his coat.

Teagle's face was eager. "Okay. Give us it, an' I'll take you to him!"

"X" brought out an envelope and handed it to the other. Teagle almost snatched it from his fingers, opened the flap and drew out the contents. Twenty crisp one hundred dollar bills. He looked up suspiciously. "This ain't—swag from some hold-up, is it? Will I get my neck in a sling if I try to pass it?"

The Agent reassured him. "That ain't hot money, Teagle. It's good cash. You can change it in any bank in the city. Think I'm a sap?"

Teagle pocketed the money. "Okay, Harder. Come along." He turned, proceeded up Eighth Avenue.

The Agent swung in beside him. "Where do we have to go?"

"Don't ask so many questions!" the other growled. "You'll see."

They walked up two blocks, turned the corner and stopped before a small store with windows which had been frosted to prevent passers-by from looking in. The street was deserted, but "X" noted two doorways across the street, where the shadows seemed thicker than elsewhere. Also, as Teagle rang the bell at the door, the Agent saw two men appear out of a hallway several doors down.

These men strolled casually toward the store with frosted windows, their hands in their overcoat pockets. At the same time, the two shadows on the opposite side moved, resolved themselves into men, and started across. The Agent did not appear to notice all this, but he crowded closer to Linky, slid the automatic from his shoulder holster and put it into his coat pocket. He did not take his hand out of the pocket, but he looked significantly at Teagle.

Linky looked down at the bulge the automatic made close to his own side, looked up at "X", and said, "What's the idea, friend?"

"X" laughed harshly. "Just an old habit of mine when I go into strange places. You can never tell what's on the cards."

The door of the store opened to Teagle's ring, and a big, heavy-set man with a walrus moustache looked inquiringly at them, then said, "Oh, hello, Linky. Come on in." He turned and went back down the short, dark hall, motioning them to follow him.

Teagle said to the Agent, "This is where we meet your friend. You don't have to worry about nothin' happening. This joint is okay."

"X" crowded in beside Linky, shut the door behind them so quickly that anybody outside who might have been waiting for a clear potshot at him would have been disappointed.

OUT in the street, the four shadows converged before the door. They did not ring the bell. No word was spoken among them. They seemed to be acting according to prearranged plan, and waited silently.

In a few moments the door opened, and the big man with the walrus moustache appeared again, stood aside for them to enter. They filed in past him and walked down the short hall. The big man closed the door, followed them into the lighted room at the end of the hall.

This was a barroom, with a small bar at one end. Near the bar was another door, which was closed. This other door led into a private room where guests could drink undisturbed, transact whatever private business they had.

The big man stepped behind the bar, saying nothing to the four who had entered. They stood near the wall now, hands in pockets, unmoving, their eyes on the door to the inner room. There was something peculiar about them—something that caused the bartender to shudder. They looked like brothers—and they walked

"You didn't think you would be allowed to live after learning so much of our secret?" came the metallic voice.

stiffly, mechanically. There was nothing to indicate that they were human except four pair of eyes that glittered out of those faces with a merciless light that made the man with the walrus moustache feel, somehow, cold and clammy.

The four men waited stolidly, never speaking.

Presently the door of the inner room opened and Linky Teagle came out—alone. A shadow crossed his face—was it a shadow of fear?—as he saw those four silent figures. He gulped, looked away from them with an effort, and said to the bartender, "He took the doped drink like a fish: he's out cold already."

The bartender grinned nervously, rubbing his hands. "A Mickey Finn always works, Linky. Only I was afraid that guy was too slick to take it. He certainly fell fer the whole lay, just like a sap—expectin' you to lead him to Gilly!" He glanced at the four men. "You can go in an' get him now, boys." He spoke diffidently, as if he almost thought they would not understand him.

But they did. One of them produced from his coat a capacious sugar sack, which he unfolded and shook out. It was large enough to hold an unconscious man. The four of them then advanced into the inner room.

The bartender peered over Teagle's shoulder, glimpsed the inert form that lay with head on table, unconscious. He poured out two stiff jolts of whisky, handed one to Teagle, and downed his own at a gulp, sighed gustily. "I'm glad that's over. Did you scratch his face to see if he had make-up?"

Teagle nodded. "It's make-up all right, and damn clever. If I didn't know for sure that Harder was dead, I'd swear it was him."

The four men closed the inner door behind them as they went about their gruesome task of stuffing the inert form into the sack. The bartender shivered slightly. "God! Those guys give me the heeby-jeebies—they don't seem to have no soul. They don't talk or anything; they just look at you with those killer-eyes!"

Teagle's eyes were on the inner door. He seemed to share some of the walrus-moustached one's feelings, but he said nothing. He appeared tense, alert.

The bartender asked huskily, "What'll they do with that guy in the sack—after they're through asking him questions?"

Linky Teagle shrugged. "Maybe there won't be anything left of him by that time." He moved toward the door. "I wonder what's keeping them so long."

The man with the walrus moustache came around to the front of the bar. He said, uneasily, "I'm wonderin'—whoever their boss is, how come he trusts us to see all this? Suppose—" his voice dropped to a whisper "—suppose he give them orders to knock us off after they finish this job?"

Linky Teagle said, "I was thinking of the same thing. We better take a look in there."

His hand snaked inside his coat, produced a gun. He reached out, opened the door wide. The inner room was empty.

The bartender gasped. "They musta gone out the back way!"

And just then there was the sound of heavy steps in the short hall that led from the front door. There had been no sound of anyone entering, but there was the distinct noise of a ponderous tread in the hall now.

The bartender's face went pale. "They left the outside door unlocked—so they could go around from in back!"

Teagle swung his gun toward the hallway, just as a strange, monstrous figure came into view. It was the same horrid being that had struck terror into the crowds at the bazaar, that had launched invisible death at Harry Pringle and the policeman. Its barrel-like body waddled as it walked, and its ghastly gas-masked head peered through the gloom.

It stopped in the doorway, slowly and ponderously raised its hand, with the finger pointing at the bartender.

The bartender screamed, started to duck behind the bar. Linky Teagle had his gun poised. His finger now contracted on the trigger, and seven slugs—seven livid streams of death streaked from the muzzle straight at the monster. But the heavy figure was unmoved by the hail of lead. It was as if those death-dealing bullets that would have been fatal to any man were no more than pellets from a boy's toy sling.

With a sure, inexorable motion, its pointing finger sought the bartender, and a flash of flame sprang from the screaming man's clothing. In an instant he had become his own fiery funeral pyre. His screams tore through the small room; horrible, hideous screams that mingled with the echoes of Teagle's gun. He swept his arms in a desperate, flail-like motion over the bar, and the whisky bottle was hurled to the floor, shattered. The alcoholic liquid spread, and the dying man rolled across the floor, right into it. Flames spread, fed by the alcohol, and the place became an inferno.

In the meantime, the hellish monster had turned its death-finger toward Teagle. But Teagle, acting with desperate speed, had slipped through the inner door that led to the back room and kicked the door shut.

The room became bright as the flames spread. For a moment the huge, ungainly monster stood there, watching its handiwork. If it entertained any emotion of anger at being balked of its other prey, any disappointment at missing Linky Teagle, there was no way of telling. It turned ponderously and made its way out of the short hall, into the night, where it stepped into the rear of a closed truck that sped away.

CHAPTER VIII

THE LAIR OF THE MONSTER

A SQUARE ROOM, poorly lit. Chairs arranged in a semicircle before a raised platform with curtains at the rear.

Walls of whitewashed brick, with small windows high up near the ceiling—a typical cellar room, converted to its present use.

In the chairs were seated beings that resembled men—rather, shells of men, lacking a human spark. They were awaiting something or someone. They smoked, but did not talk. Their startlingly youthful features bore an uncanny resemblance to each other—as if they were all members of a single family. And in their eyes there was a ruthlessness, a cold-blooded killer lust that it was hard to credit. It was as if they had made a bargain with the devil—raiding their immortal souls for a quality of merciless viciousness beyond human conception.

There were four chairs vacant in the semicircle. None of those strange beings paid any attention to the empty chairs. They did not even stir when four of their fellows entered through a side door, carrying a sack in which something squirmed.

They deposited the sack on the floor, and one of them stooped, cut open the rope that tied it at the top. They helped out the half-conscious man who was within it, stood him on his feet. The doped drink had not yet worn off entirely, and the man was still groggy, wobbling, dazed.

The face of John Harder stared about the room with swollen, uncomprehending eyes. He was no longer the desperate fugitive from justice; he was a man with half his senses deadened by dope, unable to familiarize himself with his surroundings.

No words were spoken by the robot killers who held his arms. There was utter silence in the room for a space of minutes. And then the curtains parted at the back of the narrow platform, and the murder monster stepped out—huge, ungainly, terrifying.

At sight of that monster, the captive wrenched wildly at the hands that held him; but his strength had been sapped by the dope, and he was as a child in the grip of his grinning captors.

The monstrous figure on the platform paid him no attention at first. It stood there, planted solidly, its hideous head moving from side to side as it took stock of those present.

Finally, from somewhere in its bowels there emanated the same sonorous metallic voice that had struck terror into the hearts of the people at the bazaar.

"I have no fault to find with the way you all acted tonight at the bazaar. You were true sons of the monster! Always remember that you must be ruthless, merciless! Do not hesitate to kill—a dead enemy is a harmless enemy; and we have no friends! By striking terror into the hearts of everybody, we eliminate resistance."

The voice paused for a moment, then went on, "In future, however, you must be more careful. Tonight we lost one of you— Number Eight is reported missing, captured by the police. If he had come at once in answer to my order, he would not have been caught. It is imperative now that we release him. My plans are all set for tomorrow morning at eleven o'clock, when he is to be arraigned in court. You will all participate; your instructions will be issued later. Now we must attend to another matter."

The ungainly monster half turned toward the captive, ordered those holding him, "Bring the prisoner forward!" Then it once more addressed the seated audience of killers, "There is one enemy whom I knew all along I would have to eliminate in this campaign, for he was sure to interfere with our progress. That enemy is the man known as Secret Agent 'X.' You have all heard how impossible it is to find him, how dangerous he is. Well, gentlemen, I have the honor to show you—Secret Agent 'X'! He was caught by a simple trick; he practically walked into our hands."

The four men led their struggling captive down to the foot of the platform.

The monster continued, "I am sure that this is Secret Agent 'X' because nobody else in the world could have disguised himself as John Harder. He tried to crash into this organization in that role; gentlemen, John Harder is dead. But this man didn't know it. And there he stands. Look at that disguise. Perfect! It shall now be our pleasure to scrape that putty off his face, and see for the first time the real features of—Secret Agent 'X'! And after we are through asking him a few questions, I will treat him to a bath of fire!"

There was no trace of pity in the eyes of the smooth-faced killers who watched the captive struggle ineffectually with those who held him. He tried to talk, but the powerful drug had paralyzed the muscles of his throat temporarily. It was wearing off slowly, and confused syllables issued from his mouth, syllables that had no coherence or meaning.

He was rapidly searched, and an automatic taken from his shoulder holster, together with a few other papers. Then those who held him proceeded to scratch the plaster and make-up from his face.

WHILE they were doing it, the resonant voice of the monster spoke mockingly, "For once the famous Secret Agent 'X' has nothing to say; for once he is helpless. At last he has met his master! This, gentlemen, is the end of Secret Agent 'X'!" There was a note of proud triumph in that voice now—a note of evil, unmerciful triumph, which ended in a gasp of rage as the last of the make-up was removed, revealing the face of—Linky Teagle!

A rustle of excitement spread among the assembled killers, but even then no word was spoken among them—only, here and there were heard gross, unintelligible grunts, and the wheezy, terror-impregnated breathing of Linky Teagle.

Above the sound of those inhuman grunts rose the metallic, but now enraged voice of the murder monster. "If this is a trick, somebody is going to pay for it! Scratch that face and see if it's another disguise!"

One of the four killers, grinning as a child might grin when it crushes a grasshopper with its foot, drew a knife and scraped the point along the captive's face, eliciting a muted howl of agony. But no plaster came off. Blood ran freely where the knife point had scored into the flesh. It was indeed Linky Teagle.

The monster uttered a single ominous word, "Explain!"

Teagle gulped, tried to talk, and succeeded only in emitting grotesque sounds. He was in the grip of terror, and he tried desperately to talk. Finally, urged by his dread, he managed to get out some words. The dope was wearing off, easing his throat muscles.

"It's no joke, boss. I had this guy 'X' in the back room, and the bartender brought in the doped drink. But he must have got wise. Because—" he stopped, swallowed hard, and found it impossible to continue.

The monster ordered, "Bring him water."

One of the four disappeared through the side door, returned in a moment with a glass of water which Teagle gulped at a single draught. His throat felt better, and he went on.

"He must have got wise, somehow. Because all of a sudden he pulls out a funny shaped gun. I says, 'What's that, Harder?'—makin' believe, see, that I still thought he was Harder. An' he says to me, lookin' kinda funny, 'So you know who I am! Well, I will show you how to make a quick change, only you won't be able to witness it, Linky.' An' with that, he shoots off this funny gun that don't make no noise, an' I feel a sudden kind of sickish sweet feelin', an' that's all I know till I wake up in the sack! So help me, boss, it ain't no joke!"

Several of the killers stirred uneasily in the silence that followed Linky's recital, It was difficult to tell from their impassive countenances what they felt. Only their eyes blazed with a dangerous lust. But they looked tensely at the monster on the platform. Somehow the monster's rage and bafflement seemed to pervade the whole room.

The resonant voice burst from the bowels of the barrel-like shape. "So he put you to sleep, eh, Teagle? And then he changed places with you—made up as you, and made you up as Harder. Then he came out and sent my men in to put you in the sack." The voice paused, then continued ruminatively, "And to think—I almost got him. I wondered that Linky Teagle could be so quick-witted as to escape the fire bath!"

Teagle looked up, sudden fear in his eyes. "What do you mean, boss—escape the fire bath?"

"You didn't think, Teagle, that you would be allowed to live after learning so much of our secret? Well, perhaps you did. So did that foolish bartender. I killed him. I thought I failed with you. This time I shall not fail."

Slowly the ominous finger rose, pointing at Teagle. "Stand away from him!" ordered the metallic voice.

The four smooth-faced killers who had held him now sprang away. Teagle cried out piteously, "What you gonna do to—"

He never ended the sentence, for he was suddenly enveloped in flames...

CHAPTER IX

DESPERATE PLAN

SECRET AGENT "X" did not permit himself to rest after escaping the trap set for him by Linky Teagle.

He knew that the murder monster would quickly discover the ruse by which he had substituted Linky Teagle for himself in the sack. He knew that the murder monster would be spurred to redoubled activity by the realization that it was the Secret Agent, and not Teagle, who had escaped from the menace of the flaming death in the smelly barroom on Eighth Avenue.

And "X," too, was spurred to feverish activity by the knowledge that there was much to be done yet if the monster was to be prevented from striking again with that horrible flaming death. All hope of gaining admittance to the inner ring of the monster's cohorts was now dissipated. He must follow along other lines of inquiry.

The most promising lead was the actress, Mabel Boling. She was a former friend of "Duke" Marcy. She had been with Harry Pringle when he was killed. The Agent was to phone her tomorrow. But that was too long to wait. If she knew anything, she must be made to talk before morning.

It was to see her, therefore, that the Agent was now on his way. He had discarded, temporarily, the personality of Mr. Vardis. To appear before Mabel Boling in that character might make her suspicious now. He was Mr. A. J. Martin, a newspaper man. As such, he had every legitimate reason to approach her; he would be collecting news on the atrocity at the bazaar, and it was certain that she would not be asleep after her harrowing experience—she would probably be home, being interviewed by other representatives of the press.

"X" drove toward the address she had given him in the West

Eighties. On the way he passed a newsboy crying an extra. He pulled in at the curb, bought a copy.

His hands clenched on the paper, his mouth set grimly as he read the screaming headline:

WOMAN IS LATEST VICTIM OF MURDER MONSTER

—

Mabel Boling, Actress, Is Burned to Death in Her Apartment by Mysterious Death Blast

—

TWO-ALARM FIRE RESULTS

—

At one A.M. this morning, the Murder Monster struck again. This time his victim was a beautiful woman, Mabel Boling.

It will be recalled that she recently broke with "Duke" Marcy—

Secret Agent "X" skipped the rest of the account. He ran his eye to the next column where the heading announced that Deputy Commissioner Pringle, on the job despite the death of his son, had issued a call for every detective on vacation to return to active duty until the murder monster was captured or killed.

It added that the police were seeking "Duke" Marcy for questioning, but that he had disappeared from all his known haunts; a general alarm had been issued for him, and it was expected that he would be apprehended shortly.

The Agent put the paper down, headed his car back the way he had come. The murder monster had acted swiftly. There must be a keen brain, indeed, behind that clumsy automaton; for it had foreseen that Mabel might be a possible source of information, had taken immediate, ruthless steps to eliminate her. Every avenue of information that might lead to the murder monster had been blocked.

With bitterness in his heart, the Agent drove to an apartment that he maintained nearby where he kept copious records of the reports of his far-flung operatives. Here he ensconced himself in solitude, and spent the few remaining hours of the night in studying every angle and manifestation of the case. He had long ago discovered what few men have learned—that two or three hours of concentrated thought are often worth days of feverish activity.

He checked through his records of every single one of those twenty-five convicts who had escaped from State Prison, familiarizing himself with the habits and recorded peculiarities of each. He consulted voluminous indexes and cross-indexes, searching down every little detail that came to his attention.

IT was well on in the morning when he laid sway the last record with an air of decisiveness. Purposefully he picked up the newspaper once more and sought for a certain item. He found it, crowded to the second page by the news of Mabel Boling's death. It announced that the so-called robot killer who had been captured the night before at the bazaar would be arraigned at eleven o'clock in the morning before a judge of the Court of General Sessions.

The reason for this quick arraignment, it was stated, was because of a writ of *habeas corpus* which had been secured by the defendant's attorney.

And the name of the attorney, which stared up at "X" out of the printed page with a sinister implication, was the name of the man he had talked to at the bazaar—Edward Runkle! Runkle was defending the murder monster's man—Runkle, the shrewdest criminal lawyer in the city, who boasted that no client of his had ever gone to the chair!

Automatically, the Agent read the last few lines of the item, which stated that though the defendant had been grilled intensely by the police and the district attorney, he had refused to make any kind of statement—had, in fact, sat there without opening his mouth, just like the robot he had been previously supposed to be!

The Agent consulted his wrist watch, noted that it was eight-thirty. He left the apartment, drove to a drug store a few blocks away that was just opening for the morning. Here he entered one of the phone booths and dialed a number. It was the number of the Hobart Detective Agency, a new and highly successful inquiry bureau. Its head was a young, red-headed former patrolman; and though he had only been in business for a short time, he employed more than fifty operatives all over the country. Nobody suspected that Hobart, though ostensibly the boss, took his orders from the obscure newspaperman, A. J. Martin. And Hobart himself did not know that A. J. Martin was—Secret Agent "X."[25]

Though it was only eight-thirty, Hobart was on the job, and his voice came cheerfully over the wire.

When he learned who was on the phone, he said, "Gosh, chief, there's big doings. Did you see the papers?"

"I did. And there's plenty of work for you."

"On the murder monster case?"

"Yes. Here's what I want you to do. Get hold of half a dozen of your men. Be sure they are well armed. Have them ready for duty in the corridor at the Court of General Sessions by ten o'clock, at the opening of court.

"Don't use any local operatives who might be known to the police—phone out of town, have six or seven outside operatives fly in; they should be able to get here by ten o'clock. By the time they get here, you will receive by messenger written instructions as to what to do. *Carry out those instructions to the letter!*"

"Depend on me, chief."

"The orders may sound peculiar, Jim, but it's imperative that you follow them implicitly. It may even seem to you that you are acting in a way to frustrate the law—but you must carry the orders through. Do you understand?"

"I understand perfectly, chief. I ought to know by this time that anything you do is okay. You figuring to take that killer out of court by force? If you say so, I'll do it."

"Not exactly by force, Jim; but I suspect that the 'Murder Monster,' as you call him, will make an attempt to rescue him—or kill him. He has so far succeeded in murdering everybody who might be able to betray him. There is no doubt that he will try to do the same in court today. We must stop him!"

"Okay, chief. By the way—have you seen Leane recently? I've

---

25 AUTHOR'S NOTE: *As has been mentioned before, it was in the role of A. J. Martin that Secret Agent "X" had first befriended Jim Hobart. Jim took his orders, and obeyed them without question. Often he saw from the results of the work he was doing that his employer was a man of unusual capacity. If he was inclined to make any conjectures in that direction, he certainly kept them to himself. In any event, he never doubted that A. J. Martin was the man he represented himself to be. Jim sometimes wondered if the orders he received from Mr. Martin had not originated with someone else who was using Martin as a go-between. If that was so, Jim had a good idea, or thought he had, who that "someone else" was. But he was thoroughly satisfied to continue, because he was in a position to know, the opinion of the police to the contrary, that the "someone else" was emphatically on the side of law and order.*

been so busy I haven't had a chance. And I'm worried about her, working in that fast night club of Marcy's, especially since he's been tied up by the police with this murder monster. Also, I understand that this Mr. Vardis that you recommended her to has been hanging around her a lot. Is he okay?"

"Leane will be all right," the Agent assured him. "She needn't work at the Diamond Club any longer. And Mr. Vardis won't see her any more—he's gone on a long trip. From now on she can work with you, directly under my orders. How's that?"

"Swell, chief!"

CHAPTER X

THE MONSTER'S MAN

THE COURT OF General Sessions was a scene of bustling activity that morning. In Part 1, on the first floor, where the captured robot killer was to be arraigned later that morning, two uniformed guards stood at the door. Nobody was admitted unless he had business in the court room. Spectators were barred because of the dangerous character of the killer.

Inside the court room, though spectators were not admitted, all the seats were filled with attorneys and witnesses in the various cases scheduled on the calendar for the day. The judge had not yet appeared, but Chief Assistant District Attorney Fenton, tall, gaunt, stern, a relentless prosecutor, was already seated at the long table inside the enclosure before the bench. He was going through a sheaf of papers, stopping every few moments to converse with his two clerks who hovered around him.

He looked up, frowning, as the bald-headed, oily Ed Runkle approached him.

"Hello, Joe," Runkle greeted him. "How's tricks?"

Fenton grunted an answer. He had nothing but contempt for Runkle's breed of lawyer, who would accept as a client the most vicious enemy of society, provided a fee accompanied the case. But Runkle's tremendous political connections made it unwise to antagonize him.

"I'm busy, Runkle. Is there anything you want?"

"What time is my client's case coming up this morning?" the lawyer asked.

Fenton ran his finger down the calendar to the line which read: "People vs. John Doe—motion on writ of *habeas corpus*."

"It should be reached about eleven, Runkle—after the call of the calendar and the sentencing of convicted defendants."

"Can't you move it up a little, Fenton?" Runkle was smiling ingratiatingly now. "I have another case on in Brooklyn, and I'd like to get away early."

The D. A. put down his papers, glared up at the little lawyer, and exclaimed impatiently, "Why should I do anything for you? You know damn well that this man is a murderer—he was caught red-handed at the bazaar. Yet you ask for a writ of habeas corpus! You know damn well that you're only doing it so as to prevent the police from grilling him further. You know he'll never be discharged."

Runkle shrugged. "I'm only doing my duty as an attorney." He added unctuously, "Every man is entitled to be considered innocent until he is convicted by a jury; and it's his privilege to be brought before a judge within forty-eight hours."

"Sure, sure!" Fenton said bitterly. "You know the law inside and out. Of course it's your privilege. But did you consider that in forcing us to bring him here out of the security of the jail, you make it possible for his associates to rescue him? For all we know, they may be planning to attack us here the way they attacked the bazaar last night!"

"I'm sorry if you feel that way about it," Runkle said, getting ugly. "If you don't like the law, why don't you get yourself elected to the legislature and change it? You don't care if a man is guilty or innocent—all you want is convictions to build up your record!"

Fenton sprang to his feet, face purple. "You know that's a lie, Runkle! For that matter, how about you? You'd use every quirk of the law to get your client out, even if you knew he was as guilty as hell! How about this case? Who hired you? Who paid your fee?" He shook an apoplectic finger under the little lawyer's nose. "I'm going to put you on the stand and make you tell us who hired you! It's birds like you that make it so easy for criminals!"

Everybody in the court was watching with interest now, attracted by the loud words. The scene might perhaps have ended in a fist fight, if the door at the side of the court room had not just then opened. An attendant stepped through, announced in a brittle voice. "His Honor, the Judge. All rise!"

Fenton turned away from Runkle choking down his rage. The little criminal lawyer, unruffled by the other's burst of irascibility, smiled thinly as he faced the bench, while everybody in the court room stood in deference to the majesty of the law represented here by the black-robed judge who entered behind the attendant and seated himself in the tall chair behind the bench.

Judge Rothmere was one of the oldest of the justices of the court in point of service. He was also the sternest. Criminals and their lawyers tried to avoid him by every possible means, going to extremes to get their cases postponed to times when he was not presiding; for every criminal knew that if he was convicted in Judge Rothmere's court, he would be sentenced to the maximum prescribed by law.

THE judge glanced over the court room while the clerk intoned the usual formula for opening the session. His eyes, under the bushy eyebrows, took cognizance of the strained attitudes of Runkle and Fenton.

Runkle was by far the cooler of the two; he owed his great success as a criminal lawyer to the fact that he never lost his head in the court room. Now, as the judge leaned forward over the bench, he stepped up, speaking in a self-contained, calm manner of injured righteousness.

"If Your Honor please, the district attorney just finished some very disparaging remarks about me before you entered the court room. I am here to argue a motion on a writ of *habeas corpus* for one, John Doe, charged with murder in the first degree: The district attorney has scheduled this motion for eleven o'clock, and has absolutely refused my request to have it called earlier. It is highly important that I leave shortly, as I have a pressing engagement, and I appeal to Your Honor not to permit Mr. Fenton to run this court, but to have the defendant, John Doe, brought here now."

Judge Rothmere, who ordinarily made no concessions to defendants' lawyers, seemed to feel that Runkle deserved special consideration. He turned to Fenton, asked, "What is your objection, Mr. Fenton, to accommodating Mr. Runkle?"

Fenton spluttered. "If the Court please, I don't think Runkle is entitled to any consideration. This writ is entirely uncalled-for. In the ordinary course of events, the defendant would have been indicted some time this week and duly brought to trial. Runkle has taken this action merely to get this killer of his out of the hands of the police before he can be made to talk. It's a shame that any attorney could be got to handle this case, and I intend to question Mr. Runkle as to who retained him!"

The judge nodded, turned to Runkle. He was listening to both sides impartially.

Runkle did not lose his patience. He said, "I am perfectly willing to explain how I was retained. Early this morning, about three A. M., I was awakened by the ringing of the telephone beside my bed. A muffled voice told me that if I went down to my front door I would find ten thousand dollars, and that it was the fee paid to me in advance for defending this man. I was warned that if I did not take the case I would regret it. Then my unknown caller hung up.

"The money was there in front of my door, tied in a neat parcel. I immediately called police headquarters, and the call was traced to a drug store pay station. The bills in the package of ten thousand dollars were checked carefully and found not to correspond to any that were known to have been stolen from the bazaar. Under the circumstances, Your Honor, I felt entirely justified in taking the case, and I at once proceeded to obtain a writ of *habeas corpus*. It is what any other attorney would do under the circumstances. I cooperated fully with the police, and there should be no fault to find with my actions."

Runkle stopped, drew a handkerchief from his pocket, and wiped his lips. He took a deep breath and went on. "I once more ask Your Honor to exercise the discretion of the court, and have this defendant produced now instead of at eleven o'clock."

Judge Rothmere had listened closely to Runkle's explanation. Now he addressed Fenton sternly. "I see nothing wrong in Mr. Runkle's conduct, Mr. District Attorney. The defendant is entitled to the services of counsel, and Mr. Runkle is doing the best he can for his client. I will grant the request of defendant's attorney." He raised his voice; "Bailiff! Bring in the defendant, John Doe. Number—" he glanced down at his copy of the calendar "—Number twenty-seven."

When the bailiff left to obey the order, the judge bent his imposing, bushy eyebrows and looked at the district attorney. "Perhaps this will be a lesson to you, Mr. Fenton, not to attempt, in the future, to assume the prerogatives of the Court. As a matter of fact, for certain other reasons that have been brought to my attention, I had intended having this defendant brought up earlier, even if Mr. Runkle had not requested it."

Fenton gnawed his lower lip, glaring at Runkle, who grinned at him.

There was a stir in the courtroom as the bailiff and two armed guards led in the robot-like killer who was down on the police blotter as John Doe. No trace of emotion or interest showed on his smooth face. Though he had not shaved, his cheeks were still smooth. No beard had grown there. Only his eyes showed a sign of human intelligence. They darted about the courtroom, glittering with expectancy—as if he sought some one he knew should be there. He walked less stiffly now, for he had been divested of his ingeniously contrived bullet-proof under-clothing.

HE was led up to the bar, and the clerk rose, began to intone the usual questions. "Prisoner, what is your name?"

The prisoner remained stolid, did not speak.

The judge leaned forward a little, inspecting him closely, while Runkle stepped to his side, whispered in his ear so that everybody could hear. "I'm your lawyer. It's all right. You can answer the questions."

Still the prisoner said nothing. He stood there like an automaton, or, perhaps, a man in a trance.

Finally the bailiff ventured to say, "If it please Your Honor, that's the way he's been since he was arrested. He was grilled all night but he wouldn't open his mouth. They had to book him as John Doe!"

"All right," the judge snapped. "Enter his name as John Doe. We will leave the other questions till later. Perhaps we can make him realize that he's in real trouble." He turned to Runkle. "Now, sir, what is the purpose of this motion?"

Runkle wiped his lips with his handkerchief—it seemed to be a habit with him whenever he talked—and began a long argument to the effect that his client should be discharged because of lack of evidence. He finished by making the formal request, "I move that this defendant be discharged because there is no evidence that a crime has been committed in this jurisdiction."

It was a motion that is always made as a matter of routine, but never granted. Judge Rothmere, however, seemed to weigh Runkle's argument seriously. He turned to Fenton, asked, "Have the defendant's prints been taken? What is his criminal record?"

The district attorney answered reluctantly, "There is no record at all for him, judge. His fingerprints do not fall into any category on file."

"You see, your honor," Runkle began, "this defendant hasn't even got a record. He's being framed—"

Fenton laughed scornfully. "Framed! That's what Runkle claims about every one of his clients, Your Honor. It's his stock in trade. He'll soon be telling us about this man's poor old mother and father in South Bend, Indiana, or some place!" Fenton gestured eloquently. "Judge, the mere fact that Runkle has been retained here should prove that the defendant has something to worry about. It's common knowledge in the underworld that Runkle can help a criminal to beat any kind of 'rap.' If a defendant can pay Runkle's fee, he can get away with murder!"

Runkle smiled, not deigning to reply. His eyes were on the judge.

And Judge Rothmere suddenly threw a bombshell into the court room. In his august, judicial voice he announced, "Mr. Runkle, I will grant your motion. The defendant is dismissed!"

Nothing that the judge could conceivably have said or done could have caused greater consternation in the courtroom than those four words.

Men stared at each other as if their hearing had suddenly betrayed them. The bailiff and the guards stood speechless. District Attorney Fenton seemed suddenly to choke, then he waved his hands in the air and rushed up to the bench. "You can't do that!" he shouted. "This man is a murderer! Are you crazy?" The unexpectedness of the decision had deprived him of all sense of discretion.

The killer at the bar remained unmoved, unspeaking, as if none of this concerned him in the least.

Runkle seized him by the elbow, urged him toward the door. "You're free, do you understand? Get out of here before they hold you for something else. Beat it!"

Fenton turned from the bench, ran shouting after them. "Stop! Stop! I'll swear out another warrant for him. He can't go free. He's a murderer!"

Judge Rothmere frowned, called out, "Mr. Fenton! Do you forget where you are? This is a courtroom!"

Fenton paid no attention to him, ran after the prisoner, The judge pounded with his gavel. "Bailiff," he shouted, "Seize Mr. Fenton. I declare him in contempt of court!"

The bailiff stared at him uncomprehendingly, too dazed to act.

The judge half rose in his bench, thundered at the unfortunate bailiff, "Did you hear me?"

That official finally came out of his daze, stammered, "Y-yes, Your Honor," and sped after the district attorney, gripping him by the arm. "Sorry, sir, it's the judge's orders!"

Fenton fumed in the bailiff's grip, but the delay was enough to allow the robot killer and his attorney to leave the court room. As the door closed behind them, Fenton turned to the bench. There were tears of rage in his eyes. "Do you know what you've done, Judge? You've released a cold-blooded killer. He'll kill again, as sure as you're sitting there. *Why did you do it?*"

Judge Rothmere rose dignifiedly from the bench, tapped once with the gavel. "Court," he announced quietly, "is adjourned till ten o'clock tomorrow morning! Till then, Mr. Fenton, I will parole you in your own custody to answer to a charge of contempt of this court!"

And the judge turned, left the bench and went out through the side door, leaving the room in a state of seething excitement.

HE was out in the corridor now, but before crossing to his chambers across the hall, he walked down a few paces and peered around the bend. He could now see the front door of the court room through which Runkle and the killer had gone.

They stood there now, faced by five men in plain clothes who wore on the lapels of their coats badges of the Department of Justice. One of these men was saying to the baby-faced killer, "We want you, bo. We have a warrant for the arrest of one, John Doe, now held by the state authorities, for questioning in a kidnaping investigation. I guess you're our man." He turned to the others. "Take him, boys!"

Runkle started to protest, but he suddenly found himself looking into the barrel of a revolver. The officer who had spoken before held that gun, and he said, softly, "We don't want you—yet, mister. But we'll take you along if you open your trap once more. Yeah, we'll take you along—feet first!"

Runkle's face went pale. Before he could collect himself, the other men had snapped handcuffs on the now struggling killer, and were leading him out of the building with a gun stuck in the small of his back.

Runkle started to shout after them, "You're no officers—" but he stopped quickly, cowering, as one of them swung around, raised his gun. The man did not fire. He merely laughed, turned around and followed the others. So quickly and quietly had the thing been done that the few people in the corridor had not even noticed it until Runkle began to shout. Then it was too late, for the five men with their prisoner were gone.

Runkle sped after them, stood in the entrance watching the high-powered car into which they had climbed speeding around the corner on two wheels. He cursed, then shrugged, turned to the small crowd that had gathered behind him; "I got my fee, anyway," he said, grinning. "And nobody can say I'm hiding him from the law, because you all saw him snatched from under my eyes."

Around the bend in the corridor, Judge Rothmere had watched the drama with interest. He now turned and directed his steps toward the chambers. An attendant who had followed him from the court room approached, asked, "Can I help you, sir?"

"No. I won't need you any more today. You may go home."

The judge entered his chambers, using a key, and went into an inner room. Here a man lay on the floor, gagged, glaring up in impotent fury. He was dressed in an ordinary business suit, the judge wore a judicial robe, But there the difference ended. For their faces were exactly alike.

The man in the robe said, "I am sorry, Judge Rothmere, if I caused you inconvenience. It was necessary, in the cause of true justice, that I pose as you for a few minutes. I will leave you bound now, and I will also leave my mark before I go, so that it will be known that it wasn't you who just sat on the bench. Otherwise you might have some difficult explaining to do."

Now the man in the judicial robe left the gagged man, stepped into the outer room. Here he doffed the robes, raised long fingers to his face. Swiftly the features of Judge Rothmere disappeared, only to give place in a few moments to the face of A. J. Martin, newspaper man.

The whole transformation took less than six minutes. Now he spoke to the gagged man in the inner room. "If any one asks you who did this, judge, you can tell them I left my card on the table out here."

As he spoke, he deposited on the small table a card, on which there was the reproduction of a glowing "X."

Then he silently opened the door and stepped into the corridor.

CHAPTER XI

ENTER—BRINZ

WHEN THE FIVE men who wore the federal badges sped away in the car with the robot killer in their custody, the large clock on the City Hall building showed the time to be exactly twenty-nine minutes past ten o'clock. The whole thing was over, thirty-one minutes before the scheduled time for the arraignment.

The car swung around the corner and passed out of the sight and ken of the crowd surrounding Runkle and Fenton. But there were others who were interested in that car. Near the corner, a tan-and-gray cab had been parked all morning, with the flag up. The driver smoked cigarette after cigarette, but never took his eyes off the court house. Once in a while he would turn to say a few words to the sole occupant of the cab, or to answer a curt question. The occupant of the cab was a stocky, sullen sort of man, with a long, thin face that contrasted oddly with his squat body.

He chewed on an unlighted cigar, and leaned forward. "What time, is it, Kardos?" he asked the driver.

"Twenty-five after ten," Kardos replied. "The boss ought to be here soon."

The stocky man with the long face continued to chew nervously on the cigar. "This business is gettin' my goat. Workin' for this guy, Kardos, is dangerous stuff. Linky Teagle works for him—an' he didn't show up this morning. I'm wonderin'—"

He stopped, as Kardos stiffened in his seat, cried hoarsely, "Loo-ka that! Some other crowd is takin' that guy away!"

He pointed to the court house steps, down which were coming the five men with the federal badges, dragging along the prisoner known as John Doe.

The stocky man jerked open the door of the cab, leaped to the sidewalk. His hand went to his armpit, but he didn't draw the gun.

"What's the use?" he said to the driver. "We can't take the whole five of 'em."

Kardos swung to him, "What'll we do, Brinz? We were told not to let any one take him away."

Brinz shrugged. "Tell you what—you tail them in the cab. See where they go—and for the luva Pete, don't lose them. I'll stick around, an' when this boss of ours gets here, I'll break the sad news to him. You call back when they hole out."

The car with the five federal men swung around the corner, passing close to the cab. Kardos called out, "Okay, Brinz, here I go." He shifted into gear, set off in the wake of the escaping car.

Brinz remained at the curb, still chewing his cigar. He appeared oblivious of the crowd that had swarmed out of the court house. But their voices were raised, loudly, excitedly, and he could hear them plainly. He heard Runkle cry, "I tell you, they were no federal men. Their badges were fakes! But they took me by surprise. By the time I knew what it was all about, they had that fellow out of the building!"

Brinz continued to listen worriedly. He heard District Attorney Fenton say bitterly, "So you say, Runkle! I'm willing to bet that you knew all the time what was going to happen!"

Brinz swung his eyes away suddenly from the crowd across the street. For a truck had drawn up quietly at the curb. Its side bore the lettering, "Interstate Express—Deliveries Everywhere."

The driver's compartment of this truck was entirely enclosed so that the man who sat behind the wheel could not be seen. A close inspection of the body would have shown that it was constructed of bullet-proof sheet steel, with a large double door at the back, and a small grilled window on either side.

Brinz stepped close to the grilled window. A deep, metallic voice spoke from the darkness within. "What has happened here? Is everything set?" Brinz shook his head. There was a little awe in his tone, as if he were almost afraid to break the news. "It's all gone haywire, boss. This here John Doe must have been brought up in court ahead of time. Just now he got taken away by five men in a car—practically snatched out of the court room, what it looks like. That crowd across the street is wonderin' what's happened."

The metallic voice carried a note of rage. "Did you find out who those men were?"

"I didn't, boss." Brinz shuddered slightly, for that voice had sounded very ominous to him. He added eagerly, "But I tell you what I did—Kardos was in his cab over at the corner, an' I told him to tail them. Maybe he'll call back an' give us some dope on them." He went on swiftly as there came no answer from the truck, "I done the best I could, boss. I couldn't stop 'em alone, could I? And anyway, Kardos'll probably be calling back pretty soon."

For a moment there was silence. Then the resonant voice said, "Kardos had better call back—for the sake of both of you!"

The side window closed with a snap, and the track rolled away from the curb, disappeared around the corner.

Brinz wiped his face with the sleeve of his coat. There was a fine sweat on his face and on the back of his hands. He had been close to death just now. His broad nose, which had at some time been flattened by a smashing blow, twitched with the reflexes of relief from fright. He stood a moment undecided, then he suddenly nodded to himself and crossed the street.

He elbowed through the crowd in front of the court room until he was close to Runkle, and tapped him on the shoulder. The little attorney turned, said, "Hello, Brinz, where've you been for the last couple of years?"

"Here an' there," he answered evasively. "Can I talk to you—in private—Mr. Runkle?"

"Certainly. Are you in trouble again?"

"Yes. But not with the law. This is something different."

Runkle regarded him curiously. "All right. Let's go over to my office."

He led the way out of the crowd, and down the street, Brinz walking close beside him, and looking furtively about as if he feared being observed.

One man observed them. That was District Attorney Fenton, who watched them speculatively until they turned into the shabby building past the next corner, where Runkle had his office.

Fenton's eyes were veiled as he turned and re-entered the court house without speaking to anyone.

IN the meantime, the car with the five men and the prisoner sped east for two blocks, slowed up and swung into a garage in the middle of one of the East Side slum blocks. The taxi that was following pulled up just beyond the entrance, and waited with its motor running.

Within the garage, the five men bundled their prisoner out. He was handcuffed now, but still silent, though there was growing fear reflected in the black, reptilian eyes.

The men gagged the killer, tied his ankles with wire, and joined the end of the wire to the handcuffs behind his back, rendering him helpless. Then they bundled him into the rear compartment of a showy green coupe that stood in the shadows in the rear.

A young, red-headed man sat at the wheel of this coupe. When the top of the compartment closed over the prisoner, he said to the five men, "All right, boys. You can go now. Get back to your regular jobs and forget all about this. Forget you ever flew to New York this morning!"

They did not notice the figure of Kardos, who had left his cab and stolen to the door, where he peered inside, noting what was taking place.

The pseudo federal men grinned at the red-headed young man. "Don't worry, Mr. Hobart. Our memories are going to be something terrible from now on. As far as we're concerned, we never saw this town in our life!"

Kardos, outside, slipped away from the door as he saw them prepare to leave, and he returned to his taxicab, watched them walking away in different directions.

Inside the garage, the red-headed Jim Hobart issued swift orders to two mechanics, who took the car in which "John Doe" had been brought there, and rolled it on to a circular platform. They set to work upon it at once, removing the license plates first. Within two hours enough work would have been done on that car to make it impossible to recognize it as the one in which Runkle's client had been abducted.

Jim Hobart, in the meantime, locked the rumble compartment of his coupe, in which the killer had been stowed, then drove slowly out of the garage, and turned the corner. He headed north. But he did not see the taxicab that followed him at a discreet distance.

CHAPTER XII

GILLY THE GUNMAN

WHEN SECRET AGENT "X" stepped out of Judge Rothmere's chambers into the corridor of the court house, he made his way without stopping, down the back staircase and out the rear entrance into Lafayette Street. A small sedan was parked near by, and in this he made his way uptown.

On the way he stopped and called the Hobart Detective Agency. Jim Hobart had just got back. "It's okay, Mr. Martin," he reported. "The boys got this John Doe as per orders, and I just delivered him at the apartment on Eighth Avenue at the address you gave me. He's there now, all nicely tied up."

"Good work, Jim," the Agent commended. "I'll get in touch with you later. There'll be more work to do today," he added grimly.

Before leaving the booth, he made one more phone call, to Bates. He ordered Bates to place two men on the task of shadowing Runkle, the lawyer, and of checking up on anybody he might meet.

That done, the Agent returned to his car and drove to the apartment on Eighth Avenue. He could not know that even at that moment, the taxi driver, Kardos, was phoning certain information to a number not listed in any telephone directory.

At the apartment, which was on the third floor of an old, run-down apartment house, the Agent nodded in satisfaction as he saw the bound and blindfolded figure of the robot killer squirming on the floor. Here was his only avenue of approach to the murder monster. By his own daring and ingenuity he had balked the monster in its attempt to rescue this killer; he now had him alone where it might be possible to apply sufficient pressure to draw out certain information.

Before removing the blindfold, the Agent stepped to a mirror and worked swiftly on his own face. The features of A. J. Martin disappeared, were replaced by those of a thin, ascetic looking man in the middle forties. The purpose of this was to save the personality of A. J. Martin for future use; he was not ready to discard it, and if this killer should see him as Martin, the personality of Martin would be helpless.

"X" now stepped to the side of the killer, removed the gag. The killer's features were smooth, expressionless. Only his eyes showed emotion, and they stared up at the Agent with mingled defiance and fear.

"X" examined him closely, stooped and touched his face with long, sensitive fingers. The killer shrank from his touch, looked around the room, for the first time became aware of his surroundings. He tried to roll away from "X's" searching fingers on his face, but the Agent held him firmly with one hand.

Suddenly the Agent uttered an exclamation of surprise. His sensitive, probing fingers had found something that it would have been impossible for anyone whose senses were less keenly on the alert to discover. It was a slight ridge under the chin, so infinitesimal as to be invisible to the naked eye.

The Agent's eyes glittered, as he seized the killer under the arms, dragged him, squirming and struggling, to the opposite side of the room where his make-up table stood. He placed him on the floor, and turned on the powerful lamp that stood beside the table.

The lamp, which the Agent used when he fashioned his careful disguises, bathed the helpless killer's face in a merciless light, illuminating every detail of his features.

Now the Agent went to the cabinet in the corner, brought out a peculiarly shaped magnifying glass. This was constructed along the lines of the lenses used by bacteriologists, but more adaptable to being carried about for handy use. There was little that this instrument did not reveal when applied under a strong light.

"X" held the killer in a viselike grip while he examined his face. The glass showed a tiny line that ran under the chin from ear to ear. It was such a line as might have been left by a healing scar that was perfectly tended. The Agent followed that line from the right ear, up along the fringe of the killer's scalp, and around to the other ear.

For a long time he studied it, maintaining utter silence. Then at last he smiled softly.

"I see, my friend," he said.

But his eyes were clouded with a strange emotion—the emotion of discovering something that has hitherto been considered incredible by the mind of man. For that line, indicative of a healed scar, had given him the clue to a momentous discovery. It had given him a glimpse of a thing so weird, so monstrous, as to stagger the imagination.

The Agent's grip tightened; he held the other helpless in the crook of his arm, while the long, sensitive fingers of his right hand probed further, feeling the contours of the man's head. The brownish, nondescript-colored hair was wiry, unnatural. The Agent pressed with his thumb and forefinger, and the whole scalp seemed to move. The man was wearing a cunningly contrived wig!

The killer's eyes betrayed a venomous hatred as "X" removed the wig. It was fitted with a suction cap that clung to his shaven skull. At one spot on that skull, the Agent's magnifying glass revealed another scar, not more than an inch long, and entirely healed.

The Agent did not examine the scar at this time. His mind was occupied with the horrid, monstrous secret he had discovered.

He said, "My friend, the masquerade is over!"

The killer glared up at him, tried to heave himself upright, and emitted a series of inarticulate, horrible grunts.

"X" studied the killer's eyes. He was interested in them, for they seemed to evoke a memory somewhere within him—a memory of another face, of those same eyes peering out of a face that in no way resembled this one. He went on, watching the other intently.

"Your face has been changed, my friend—changed by a marvelous job of plastic surgery. This monster master of yours has had your face changed to resemble the others whom he uses. You acted like robots to fool the public and the police—and why shouldn't they be fooled, when you were all facsimiles of each other!"

"X" knew he was right in his findings, because the killer bared his teeth in a snarl, threw him a venomous glance.

THE Agent hardly dared to put into concrete thoughts the revolting conclusion suggested by that line around the rim of the killer's face. But now, as he noted the killer's reaction, he was convinced that he had guessed right—this man had had his face transformed by a highly skilled surgeon!

At the urge of a sudden flash of inspiration, Secret Agent "X" twisted the killer's body around, seized the handcuffed wrists, and examined his fingertips. They were smooth, white, soft. Holding the killer's hand firmly, the Agent directed his magnifying glass on the right thumb. And under that glass, which mercilessly showed every line and mark, the Agent was able to detect a minute scar running across the under side of the thumb. Each finger in turn that he examined showed the same scar. A remarkably skillful surgeon had grafted fresh skin onto each finger—skin that had been miraculously provided with a set of loops and whorls!

The Agent's lips set grimly. "Very clever—very clever indeed!" he remarked. "No wonder the police could discover no record for you!"

Once more he turned the killer around facing him. "Your fingertips have also been changed. You have been made into a different man. I wonder if you knew in advance that you were going to be made into a replica of those others—or did your master have that done to you against your will?"

The killer regarded him sullenly, saying nothing.

"X" arose from his knees, stood over him. "All the world knows now that you and your fellows are not robots. Why continue the pretense? Why don't you talk now? Is it because you are afraid to let me hear your voice? *Are you afraid that I will recognize you—Gilly?*"

That last sentence, deliberately spoken with sudden intensity, seemed to have the effect of a charge of electricity upon the killer. His whole body shook with an uncontrollable spasm of terror. His mouth opened, but no sound issued except a short series of horrible inarticulate grunting noises. The man seemed to be straining his larynx to utter words that rebelled at being spoken.

The Agent said to him, "You wonder how I guessed who you are, Gilly?" He smiled grimly. "I wasn't quite sure—but now I see that I am right. It was your eyes that gave you away, Gilly. You could change your face a thousand times, but I would always remember your eyes!"

"X" spoke tautly, quickly now. He wanted to follow up his advantage.

"I can send you back to the death house, Gilly—or I can let you escape, give you enough money to go to another country and change your name. All you have to do is give me the name of your master, tell me where your headquarters are. Which do you choose?"

Gilly's eyes lost their glare of hatred. They seemed to be imbued now with a sort of dumb terror. They looked up at "X" with a note of helpless appeal. He opened his mouth, tried to talk, but nothing resulted—only those horrid animal grunts.

The Agent suddenly knelt beside him again. "I wonder—" he muttered. "It can't be possible. It's too fiendish even for the murder monster." Once more he examined Gilly's shaven skull, his fingers passing over the short scar.

Gilly did not draw away from him now. On the contrary, he bent his head, as if anxious for "X" to see that scar.

The Agent drew in his breath sharply as he suddenly understood its significance. Gilly had had more than his face and fingertips changed—some one had operated on his brain, as well. An incision had been made into the brain cells controlling his power of speech. He had been rendered mute!

CHAPTER XIII

PERILOUS TRAIL

SECRET AGENT "X" never allowed emotion to play a part in his life. But now, as he studied his captive, he felt a surge of bitter repugnance against the unholy being that had conceived this diabolical jest of making veritable robots of his men.

The Agent had sought by every means possible to locate those twenty-five convicts who had escaped from the State Prison. And if he had succeeded in finding them, he would not have hesitated at turning them over to the law, for they constituted a menace to the society he devoted his life to protecting. But nothing the law could have done to them even approached in horror and in pure cruelty the things that this murder monster had done.

"X" should have been elated at discovering this important link between the escaped convicts and the murder monster—for he knew now what the police did not as yet suspect—that the so-called robots were in reality the convicts whom every agency of the law was seeking throughout the country.

But he was far from elated. For he realized now what a stupendous task still faced him. No matter how dangerous those convicts might have been while they were free, the Agent now saw the shadow of a menace infinitely greater. What an inhuman monster this must be, that had freed these men only to chain them by a series of hideous operations in a more horrid slavery than any they had ever known in State Prison!

His thoughts were interrupted by a sudden ominous sound from the hallway outside the apartment. Boards creaked under a heavy, ponderous tread, and a resonant, metallic voice called out, "Number Eight! Where are you? Number Eight! Where are you?

Gilly twisted violently out of the Agent's hands and started to drag himself toward the door in spite of his bound hands. He opened his mouth and uttered a weird, inhuman sound, for all the world like some obscene animal calling to its master.

That sound was heard, for from outside came the mechanical sounding voice of the monster. "Get away from the door, Number Eight. It's going to be smashed in!"

Gilly stopped crawling toward the door. He rested on his back, his face twisted into a grimacing leer of triumph as he stared up at "X." It was difficult to understand how this little gunman of the underworld should be so loyal to a master that had done such inhuman things to him. "X" had offered Gilly freedom, immunity from prosecution, for information. Gilly could not feel that he was in any danger from the Agent. Yet he welcomed the approach of the murder monster, welcomed the prospect of being brought once more under that fiendish domination!

There must be some powerful hold—some powerful attraction—that the monster exerted over these men. "X" wondered if it was possible that the operation on the brains of Gilly and the others—almost certain now that they had all been subjected to the knife—accomplished more than merely depriving them of speech; if it was possible that it had, in fact, converted them all into veritable robots without personal initiative or will of their own.

There came a smashing impact against the door; the monster must have hurled its huge form against it. But the panels were strong, the door was solid, for the Agent always made it a point to provide his retreat with reinforced doors for just such a contingency. Yet, strong as it was, it yielded a little under the impact of that heavy body. "X" saw that it would not stand up long under the attack. If he remained in the room he would become a target for that finger of death. He would go up in flames, leaving his task unfinished, taking with him the secret of the identity of the robots, leaving the city at the mercy of these cohorts of hell.

He never left himself, however, without some means of retreat. Now, he sprang to the window, slid it open while the handcuffed Gilly watched him with narrowed, mad eyes. The Agent counted for escape on the drain pipe which ran up to the roof, close to the window. But the monster had taken care of that, too. For, no sooner had "X" showed himself at the window than there was a wicked spat, and a bullet imbedded itself in the woodwork close to his head. Somewhere outside, a rifleman was stationed with a silenced rifle. Nobody was going to be able to leave that building, by window or otherwise, till the monster had got his man. "X" did not stop to wonder how the monster had learned of the apartment. He immediately set to work.

From a cabinet in the corner, he produced a pot-bellied jar to which was attached a metal hose. This jar was made of dull, burnished metal, and had a sort of stand beneath it, into which was fitted a Bunsen burner.

While the heavy oak door bent under the repeated charges of the monster outside, "X" methodically lit the Bunsen burner and ran the hose close to the window. Then he donned a pair of goggles, and took a hypodermic syringe from the cabinet.

Gilly watched him with a puzzled gaze as he filled the container of the hypodermic with a light-colored liquid. Gilly shrank away from him as he approached, tried to wriggle from his grip. But the Agent held him tight, thrust the needle into his arm, and drove the plunger home.

The whites of Gilly's eyes showed, his lids drooped, he wheezed, and was unconscious within half a minute. The hypodermic had been loaded with a highly potent, quick-acting anaesthetic. The dose was sufficient to keep a man unconscious for at least forty-eight hours. Since the Agent could not take Gilly out of that apartment, he had made sure that the monster would not be able to make use of him for the next two days.

THE blows on the door were telling. Splinters were flying. In a moment there would be a large enough opening for the monster to aim his finger through. "X" turned to the window, observed with satisfaction that the hose from the potbellied jar was now giving off a vapor that thickened as it rose out of the window into heavy clouds of smoke. As the smoke grew in volume, it became impossible to see through it. To the riflemen stationed outside the house, the window would be invisible. This was the latest development in smoke screens—a chemical which the Agent had developed himself and was using now for the first time.

Under the protection of the smoke screen, the Agent swung himself out of the window, clinging to the drain pipe. But instead of descending as he might have been expected to do, he drew himself up, inch by inch, slowly, painfully. The smoke swirled around him, but his eyes were protected by the goggles. Gripping the pipe with taut fingers and tight knees, he worked himself up toward the roof. It was several minutes before he heard a crash from within the apartment he had just left. He heard heavy, lumbering steps, the crash of furniture. That would be the monster feeling his way around in the room, probably unable to see through the smoke which must be filling the place by this time.

Suddenly from below there came a shower of high-powered slugs, as the riflemen stationed outside realized that "X" must be using the smoke screen to escape. The slugs clanged against the drain pipe below the point where the smoke came out. Soon they would raise their sights on the chance that he was working upward instead of down. He could not hope to reach the roof before that; in fact, if he ascended any higher, he would emerge from the protection of the smoke screen and would be a clear target.

He was now alongside the window on the floor directly above his own. Without hesitation he swung his feet over the sill, crashing the glass. He leaped through the jagged opening into the room. It was unfurnished, vacant. His trousers were cut by the glass, there was a long gash in his right hand, and a jagged scratch on his cheek. But he did not stop; he dashed through the room, out into the hall. Doors were opening everywhere, heads were peering out—heads of people who looked bewildered, frightened by the sudden uproar in their house.

On the landing below "X" heard heavy steps, heard the monster ascending the stairs. The monster was quick-witted, had divined what "X" had done to escape, and was coming after him.

The Agent ran up the stairs. People ducked their heads inside at sight of his bloody face, made no move to hinder him as he raced to the roof. He pushed open the skylight, raised himself up, and sped across to the roof of the adjoining house.

He ducked down through the skylight of the next building, just getting a glimpse of the monster's hideous masked head peering after him out of the opening he had left. The monster was too unwieldy to hoist itself through the skylight after him.

"X" sped down four flights of steps to the street. A crowd was milling around, attracted by the strange happenings. "X" mingled with the crowd, listening to comment. "It's the murder monster!" some one said. "He came in that truck across the street and went in this house here. And they're firing out of the truck at the house!"

"X" noted the truck opposite. He could tell that it was armored, an impregnable fortress. He waited until he saw the murder monster appear in the street again. The horrible gas-masked figure was flanked by several of the robots who were carrying the body of Gilly.

From near-by came the sound of a police siren. The Agent hoped fervently that the monster would leave before the police got there, for he knew that the uniformed men wouldn't stand the ghost of a chance against the horrible weapon of fire that the monster wielded.

He himself had fled from it, for he was not yet ready to meet it on even terms; and a senseless attack at this time would not have served the cause of justice—might even have hindered it by removing the only man in existence who knew the secret of the escaped convicts.

"X" breathed a sigh of relief as he saw the monster and the robots pile into the truck, and the truck pull away before the police car rounded the comer. Then he himself turned and walked away from there swiftly. He had retreated before the monster, had, apparently, lost the first encounter with it. But he was far closer to victory than he had yet been, for he now knew much about the monster and the robots that the monster did not suspect him of knowing.

And he proceeded to act upon that knowledge.

CHAPTER XIV

DEVIL'S DRAGNET

THE ACTIONS OF Secret Agent "X" during the next two or three hours might have appeared highly peculiar to an uninformed observer. He went to another of his apartments and changed back to the disguise of Mr. Vardis. Leaving the apartment, his first stop was at the office of a large theatrical supply firm, where he was closeted with the manager for some twenty minutes before he emerged with a large bundle that he deposited in his car. He then drove to a quiet store in the East Fifties, on the window of which appeared the modest lettering, "Corlear & Son, Custom Tailors." He took his package inside, and spent almost an hour in the fitting room with Mr. Corlear himself.

The casual observer would have wondered that a man engaged in so desperate a battle with crime should find time for such apparently frivolous occupations. But Mr. Vardis seemed to have nothing on his mind but securing a perfect fit in the clothing he was ordering. Mr. Corlear finally escorted him to the door personally, saying, "I promise you, Mr. Vardis, that it will be ready for you by tomorrow morning. I will myself work all night on this job."

From Corlear's, Mr. Vardis drove to the nearest pay telephone and phoned Bates. He issued careful instructions. "You will hold the two planes in readiness in the field in Brooklyn. At the first alarm they will go up over the city."

"The planes will be ready, air," Bates replied. "How about our other operations—shall we continue them?"

"Absolutely. Keep Runkle under constant observation. I will continue to call you every half hour for news. Have you been able to pick up any trace of 'Duke' Marcy as yet?"

"No, sir. I have more than a dozen men on his trail, but no success."

"Keep after him. It's important that he be located within the next twenty-four hours."

When he had completed his call to Bates, the Agent called the office of the Hobart Detective Agency. "This is Mr. Martin," he told the girl who answered the phone. "Please let me talk to Mr. Hobart."

That young man was bubbling with excitement when he got on the wire. "I'm glad you called, Mr. Martin. I've been offered a retainer to work on this robot murder case, and I was wondering if I should accept it!"

"A retainer? By whom?"

"They're in my private office now. Young Jack Larrabie, and Randolph Coulter. It seems they expect to be next on the monster's list. Their friend Pringle—"

"Take the case, Jim! Ask them to wait. I'll send up a man to handle it for you—a Mr. Fearson. Give him every co-operation; follow his orders as if they were my own. He'll be there in a half hour!"

He hung up, leaving Jim Hobart slightly bewildered. Now he wasted no time. He returned to his car, and sitting in the back, he set up his portable mirror, worked on his face. In a short time there appeared once more the features of the thin, ascetic looking, middle-aged man who had questioned Gilly a few hours earlier. That completed, he selected a set of cards and papers from a small portfolio. These papers established that he was a Mr. Arvold Fearson, private investigator. He had a license in that name, and the picture attached to that license was a duplicate of his new face. It was only one of a dozen identities which the Agent had prepared in advance for instant use.

Well within the half hour specified, he presented himself to the switchboard girl in the Hobart Detective Agency and gave his name.

The girl flashed him a smile. "Mr. Hobart is expecting you, Mr. Fearson. He has two clients inside, but he told me to let him know the minute you arrived."

"X" nodded and seated himself while the girl called inside, and he surveyed the busy office. There were five girls employed here; one was Jim Hobart's secretary, three were file clerks, and one was the switchboard operator. The office was large, well furnished. Behind the telephone girl was the door of Jim Hobart's sanctum, while to the left was another door leading to a large room where each operative had a desk of his own where he could study material, make out reports, and plan his work.

In the short time that Jim Hobart had been running this agency, he had achieved phenomenal success. This was partly due to the aid which "X" had given him. In his role of Elisha Pond, he had recommended the agency to banks and insurance companies, had helped to secure large and profitable accounts. The Hobart Detective Agency was well known throughout the country now, and it was consulted more and more by people who had heard the name, or seen it mentioned in the papers. This was exactly what "X" wanted, for in this fashion the agency was enabled to build up large files on criminals, on underworld connections, and to keep its pulse on the trend of criminal events.

Sometimes, through cases that came to it, the Agent was apprised of crimes in the making of which the police did not even have an inkling. He had not been surprised, therefore, to learn that young Larrabie and his friend, Ranny Coulter, were consulting the agency.

IN a few moments the door of the inner office opened, and Jim Hobart came out. He smiled at "X," and asked, "Mr. Fearson?"

The Agent nodded. He arose and produced one of his cards, which he handed over. Jim Hobart read the name, "Arvold Fearson, Private Investigator." In the lower left-hand corner there appeared a queer initial, written in ink. Young Hobart said, "That is Mr. Martin's initial, all right."

"X" said, "I am working on this case of the murder monster for him and have acquired a good deal of information. That is why Mr. Martin sent me. He was sure you would not resent having me take charge, since I have all the facts at my fingertips."

Jim Hobart nodded, appraising "X." He did not pierce the disguise, but he was not yet wholly satisfied. "Did Mr. Martin give you any other message for me?"

"Yes. He said to tell you that there is blood on the moon."

Jim smiled. "That's better. Now I'm sure you're okay. We can't be too careful, you know. Now, if you will come inside, Larrabie and Coulter can tell you their story at first hand. I'll introduce you as my chief operative."

The Agent acquiesced, and followed him inside. Jim closed the door carefully, and introduced "X" to the two young men who were waiting with tense, drawn faces. "Doctor Larrabie and Mr. Coulter—this is Mr. Fearson, my best man. I'm giving him charge of your case. Please tell him what you told me."

Young Larrabie was high strung, much more nervous than he had appeared last night when he had seen his friend, Harry Pringle, murdered before his eyes. Ranny Coulter was stouter, more phlegmatic, but he, too, appeared to be laboring under a great strain.

It was young Larrabie who assumed the burden of explaining their difficulty. "You know, of course, about what happened to Harry Pringle last night." At "X's" nod, he continued. "We thought at first that damn monster gave him the works just as an example to the others present. It was bad enough that way, and Ranny here, and Fred Barton and myself decided to work on the thing, try to get that monster. We were all present at the bazaar last night, and we realized it was a tough job. We didn't understand how tough it really was until this morning."

"What happened this morning?" the Agent asked quietly.

Larrabie told him grimly. "Fred Barton's disappeared!"

Ranny Coulter broke in. "It's not just his disappearing—we're sure something's happened to him. We were supposed to get together this morning at Jack's house, but Fred didn't show up. So we phoned, and got no answer. Jack and I drove over to his apartment—he lives alone, you know, away from his family. I have a passkey, and when we got in we found the place had been thoroughly searched, and some of the furniture was upset. An end table had been turned over and smashed—it looked like a struggle had taken place."

Coulter stopped. There was a moment of silence. Jim Hobart, who had been standing behind "X," shifted uneasily. Young Larrabie said slowly, "It looks very much as if this murder monster is after the four of us for some reason—first, Harry Pringle, then Fred. The four of us have always stuck together. It may be our turn next—Ranny's or mine. That's why we've come here."

"Can you think of any reason," the Agent asked, "why this monster should be interested in you four?"

They shook their heads. "Unless," Coulter said, "he figures we'll try to get back at him for murdering Harry that way last night and is eliminating us before we can interfere."

"X" shook his head. "If the murder monster is behind your friend Barton's disappearance, it is not for that reason. The monster has more dangerous enemies whom he would try to eliminate first. Have you notified the police?"

"No," Larrabie told him. "The police have been so helpless in the whole thing, we thought we'd use your agency."

"They will have to be notified soon," said the Agent. "In the meantime I suggest that the first thing to be done is to interview Fred Barton's father. Suppose we do that first, and then decide on the next step in the light of what we may learn from him."

The two young men agreed, placing themselves in the agency's hands. As they were leaving, "X" lagged behind to give Jim Hobart some instructions. "How many operatives have you available in the city now?" he asked.

"I could dig up about fifteen," Jim told him. "There are a few unimportant cases that I could pull them off."

"All right. Round up as many as you can, keep them ready for instant duty. I'll call you back."

As "X" and the two young men drove downtown to the financial district in Ranny Coulter's car, the Agent was careful to look behind frequently. But they were not followed.

CHAPTER XV

SATAN RECRUITS

RANNY COULTER DROVE silently, while Jack Larrabie explained to the Agent, "We ought to catch Fred's father in his office about this time. You've heard of him, of course—Giles Barton, head of the Eastern Steel Institute. That's the clearing house for the eastern branches of all the big steel manufacturing companies." Young Larrabie smiled ruefully. "I hate to break the news to him about Fred; the old man's a terror when he's aroused. I could almost wish we wouldn't find him in."

They did find him in, however, and had no trouble in getting in to see him, for Coulter's and Larrabie's families were quite friendly with the Bartons.

When they were ushered into the old man's luxuriously furnished, richly carpeted office, they found him pacing up and down, his face purple with rage, yet with a hint of apprehension in his eyes.

He was about to burst into a torrent of words at the two young men, but noticed "X," and looked questioningly at them.

"This is Arvold Fearson, Mr. Barton," young Larrabie introduced. "He's all right. We've hired his agency to do some work for us. What's the trouble?"

Barton spluttered. "Trouble! Have you seen Fred today?"

Ranny Coulter lowered his eyes, then glanced at Jack Larrabie. "You tell him."

Young Larrabie said, "I'm sorry, Mr. Barton, but I think—something's happened to Fred."

"You think!" the old man barked. "I damn well know it! You young cubs go chasing around, wasting your lives, and all you can get into is trouble! Here—take a look at this!"

He snatched up a sheet of paper from his desk, thrust it at them.

Larrabie took it, read it in silence, and in silence passed it over to the Agent, saying softly, "I'm—sorry, Mr. Barton. You can depend on us to do all we can."

"X" read the note quickly, while young Coulter looked over his shoulder. Then he reread it more carefully. It was worth a second perusal:

Dear Mr. Barton:

Your son, Fred, is in my hands. You need not be alarmed—this is not a kidnaping. I have taken your son because be is a brilliant student of chemistry and physics, and I need his services.

If your son performs the work I shall order him to do, he will be allowed to live. The purpose of this letter is to request you, as you value your son's life, not to do anything that might endanger it—do not attempt to trace him, or to communicate with the police!

Yours,

The Master of the Monster.

Old man Barton was fuming. "The insolence of him! To dare to write me anything like this! I'll have every policeman in the city on the trail of this mountebank within an hour! Nobody can do this to me and get away with it!"

Jack Larrabie said drily, "If you'd been at the bazaar last night, Mr. Barton, you'd think differently. This monster is no mountebank—he's a deadly murderer. The police can't do any good—he kills them like flies!"

Barton strode up and down biting his upper lip. "What are we to do then?" he cried in desperation.

"We've hired the Hobart Agency," Larrabie told him. "Just sit tight, Mr. Barton. The monster says in the letter that Fred isn't going to be killed. I only hope," he added fervently, "that Fred has the sense to play along with him. He's so damn hot-headed, he's liable to tell this murder monster to go to hell!"

"If he's any son of mine," the steel magnate barked, "that's just what he'll do!"

"X" had remained silent, studying the three of them, at the same time trying to analyze the contents of the letter Barton had received, trying to arrive at a mental picture of the man who had written it.

He nodded shortly to Barton when they left, following the two young men in silence, his mind still concentrating on the problem.

OUTSIDE, in front of Barton's building, he seemed to return to realities again with a snap. He said firmly to the two young men, "I am convinced that there is a deeper motive behind your friend's disappearance than merely a desire to use his scientific knowledge. Though he may be brilliant, there are still many men who are far more advanced in the intricacies of chemistry and physics than he is—men in the great industrial laboratories of the country, for instance. I feel that perhaps that letter was only written for the purpose of lulling your suspicions. It may be that there is some sort of plan to wipe out you four young men; perhaps you offended this murder master in some way—you may have, for you don't know who he is in private life."

"What do you think we ought to do?" asked Ranny Coulter, nervously.

"I think you each ought to have a bodyguard. I will arrange it with Mr. Hobart right now." He made for a phone booth across the street, disregarding their protests.

"Damn it," Larrabie growled, "we came to Hobart because we wanted him to work with us offensively. We didn't come because we were afraid and wanted protection!"

"Nevertheless, you shall have protection. You have given us this case, and we are going to work it our way!"

The Agent's dynamic personality, the assurance with which he overrode their objections, left them no alternative but to agree.

When he was through phoning, he turned to them. "Wait here. Hobart is sending down a man for each of you. There will be some one with you day and night. It is quite possible that an attempt will be made against one or both of you, and I advise you to keep to your homes. Let the agency work on it from now on."

"All right," Larrabie agreed. "We'll stand for the bodyguards, but I'll be damned if we stay home quietly while you have all the fun. Take it or leave it!"

The Agent sighed. "Well, I guess that's the best I can do with you. But if you must expose yourselves, please be careful. If you don't care about your own hides, remember that our operatives are valuable to us—don't place them in unnecessary danger. Now, if you will excuse me, gentlemen, I have work to do."

He left them before they could ask him where he was going, just as a car deposited two of Jim Hobart's operatives on the sidewalk. As he walked up the street, he noted with satisfaction that Hobart had obeyed his instructions to the letter. For another car had pulled up behind the first; and from this second car there stepped two more operatives. These two were poorly dressed, and carried sandwich-board signs, back and front, advertising the virtues of some cafeteria.

The two sandwich men proceeded down the street behind the first two operatives, strolling along with an air of casual indifference which concealed their alertness. They were covering the first two men assigned to guarding Larrabie and Coulter. If the murder monster should attack the young physician and his friend, the monster would be due for a surprise. For those sandwich signs were constructed of bullet-proof, fire-proof steel; and underneath each, conveniently placed on a hook so that it could be brought into action at a moment's notice, was a Thompson sub-machine gun!

The Agent was planning an interesting reception for the murder monster!

CHAPTER XVI

"THE CHARGE IS MURDER!"

THE NEXT TWENTY-FOUR hours produced no new crimes, no new wave of terror. It was almost as if some evil prescience had warned the murder monster that traps were being laid, preparations being made for the reception of its cohorts of crime.

Secret Agent "X" kept unceasing vigil. He knew that this was only a lull before the storm. He spent the time in perfecting his arrangements, keeping in constant touch with Bates and Hobart. Under his orders their operatives flocked into the city from every part of the country and were immediately assigned to stations where it was likely that the monster would strike next. They were instructed not to offer resistance in the event of an attack, for that would have been suicide, but to call either Bates or Hobart at once.

Banks, jewelry establishments, even the subtreasury, had these unobtrusive watchers stationed nearby, on the alert every minute of the day.

Young Doctor Larrabie and Ranny Coulter remained together all day at "X's" suggestion in order to make it easier for their bodyguards. And wherever those bodyguards were, there, not far off, could be seen the two sandwich men, shambling along with their innocuous looking signs hanging from their shoulders.

Larrabie and Coulter even slept together that night at the home of Ranny Coulter's family. The two bodyguards prowled in and out of the house all night, while across the street the two sandwich men kept constant vigil from the shelter of a small private park.

In the morning, Secret Agent "X" paid a visit to the tailoring establishment of Corlear & Son, where he had stopped in the day before. Mr. Corlear himself conducted him into the fitting room, and locked the door, arousing a good deal of speculation among the clerks as to the identity of the mysterious customer.

It was twenty minutes before the Agent left Corlear's. He was wearing a gray sack suit that to all outward appearance differed in no way from the hundreds of other suits Corlear's made and sold. The clerks in the store would have been immeasurably more curious had they known that the mysterious customer had paid two hundred and ten dollars for that ordinary appearing suit!

The Agent stopped in at one of his apartments and changed from the disguise of Mr. Vardis to that of Arvold Fearson, but continued to wear the gray suit. Upon leaving the apartment, he drove downtown, stopping on the way to phone Bates for a report.

Bates had been awaiting his call anxiously. "We've finally got something on Runkle!" he announced. "I put two men on him as you ordered. They picked him up a while ago and followed him to a house in Brooklyn. It's a private house—Number Twenty-two Belvidere Road. Fowler and Grace, the two men who are shadowing him, just phoned in again. There's an empty house next door to Number Twenty-two, and they got into it somehow. They can look into the room where Runkle is sitting. He's there with another man, a gangster named Brinz. They seem to be waiting for someone."

"Who is Brinz?" asked the Agent. "What have you got on him?"

"I figured you'd want to know that, sir, so I've got the file handy. Brinz served a term in the Federal Detention House here in the city for transporting and selling liquor. That was before repeal. He got out eight months ago and hasn't been up to much since. During prohibition he worked for 'Duke' Marcy, but there doesn't seem to be any record of his present connections." Bates added a short description of Brinz, so that the Agent could know him if he saw the man.

"All right," said "X," "I'm going out to Belvidere Road. If Runkle or Brinz should leave the house in the meantime, I want to know about it. But I won't be able to stop and phone you. You'll have to use the broadcast."[26]

---

26 AUTHOR'S NOTE: *Secret Agent "X" has been very reticent about this broadcasting equipment. The reason for this reticence is that he still finds it very useful and does not wish to reveal anything that might help in locating it. Adjusted to the same wave-length as New York police calls, the Agent is able to pick up messages from it with an ordinary radio which is installed in every one of his cars. Thus, if the car should be found by the police and examined, no suspicion would be aroused. The sending set is fitted with a device perfected by the Agent himself, which nullifies the results of the direction-finders of the police and radio authorities who might wish to locate the station. The Agent has not imparted any information to me about this device, except that he calls it a "disperser"—it disperses the short-waves so that the point of their origin cannot be determined.*

"Right, sir. If there's anything new, I'll shoot it out to you."

"Use code A."[27]

"Code A, sir," Bates repeated.

"X" left the phone booth and got into his car. The broadcast equipment was one that he employed very infrequently, in cases of emergency, or where it was impossible to phone for reports. It was a powerful sending set located in Bates's headquarters, sending on the same wave-length as the New York police calls, and for that reason the Agent did not make frequent use of it. But more than once in the past it had been the means of bringing him to the scene of action in time to thwart well-laid criminal plans.

NOW the Agent cut over to the East Side in his car, and crossed the Brooklyn Bridge. Everywhere, as he passed, he saw police patrolling the streets, with drawn, taut faces. Squad cars toured the city with riot guns ready. These men were bravely preparing to meet the next onslaught of the monster, knowing in advance what little chance they had of surviving.

The Agent stopped for a moment to buy a newspaper and saw the headline, "Governor to be asked for troops to reinforce police. City in dread of next attack of murder monster!"

The Agent increased his speed a little after crossing the bridge. Suddenly the radio in his car came to life. The voice of Bates came over the air, speaking slowly. "Station 'X' calling! Station 'X' calling!"

At once the Agent drew a pencil from his pocket, wrote on a pad attached to the dashboard as the voice of Bates continued, speaking in Code A. The Agent drove with one hand, hardly slackening his speed as his pencil wrote down only those words of the mes-

---

27   AUTHOR'S NOTE: *Since messages from the Agent's broadcast system can be received by the police as well as by himself, it is necessary that they be transmitted in code. These codes are constantly changed, and the Agent has kindly consented to reveal the key of Code A, since he no longer uses it. Code A consists of a combination of three languages—French, German, English. Three words are transmitted for each word of the message itself—the other two not counting at all, but serving as camouflage. The first word of the message, for instance, would be a French word, the second a German word, the third an English word. By rotating the order of the languages, the code is further confused for outside listeners, but is comparatively easy to interpret, especially for one with experience in these matters. As an example here is how the simple message, "I see him." would be transmitted. The capitalized words are those that count. "JE freund monkey SEHE when rein HIM esel ami." It will be observed that the order of the languages rotates in this case, as follows: first: French, German, English; second: German, English, French; third: English, French, German.*

sage that counted.

Finally the voice of Bates ceased. The message which "X" had written on the pad stared up at him: "Fowler reports 'Duke' Marcy entered house on Belvidere Road. Fowler returning to empty house next door. Expecting you."

As the Agent drove on, he tried to puzzle out why "Duke" Marcy should be calling on Runkle and Brinz in this out-of-the-way section of Brooklyn.

He left his car in front of a drug store a block from Belvidere Road, and started to walk toward the corner. Number Twenty-two, he knew from a directory he had consulted, would be just around the corner to the left, and he did not want to attract undue attention by driving right up to the house.

This was a quiet residential section, with few people about in the streets. When the Agent was halfway up the block, he noted a large green coupé turning the corner from Belvidere on two wheels. The coupé roared down the street, gathering speed as it passed "X."

The driver, who was the sole occupant of the car, had his hands tightly on the wheel and gazed straight ahead without glancing to either side. "X" started as he recognized that driver. It was Ed Runkle!

In a flash the car had sped past and roared down the street out of sight. But in that instant "X's" eyes had been busy. His keen senses, constantly on the alert, had caught the license number of the coupé. He waited a moment to see if Runkle was being followed by Grace or Fowler, who were supposed to be watching the house on Belvidere Road. But when no other car appeared, the Agent acted instantly. It was important that Runkle should not be lost sight of at this time. It would be impossible for "X" to return to his own car in time to take up the chase. Accordingly, he turned and raced back to the drug store. The clerk behind the counter gazed at him curiously as he tore into the telephone booth and dialed Bates' number. When he got the connection, he spoke swiftly.

"Runkle has just left the house on Belvidere Road, driving a green Stutz coupé, license number L 27-2. He is not being followed by Grace or Fowler. He is probably headed back for Manhattan, so send out men in cars to cover all the bridges. If he crosses into Manhattan, they can pick him up and trail him. This is important, Bates!"

Bates repeated, "Green Stutz coupé license number L 27-2. Right, sir. I'll have the bridges covered inside of five minutes." He said anxiously, "I wonder what's the matter with Grace and Fowler."

"We'll know soon enough," the Agent told him. "I'm going there now."

"X" walked up the street again, turned the corner into Belvidere. Number Twenty-two was the second house from the corner and seemed peaceful enough. So did the one next to it, which was vacant, with a "For Sale" sign pasted to one of the pillars of the front porch. The Agent walked around to the back of the vacant house and tried the rear door. It was unlocked—probably left that way by the watchers.

He entered the narrow foyer behind the kitchen to which this door opened, and was assailed by the musty atmosphere that is peculiar to houses that have been long untenanted. He pushed through to the kitchen, then stepped into the dim hallway. Little light entered here from outside, but his sharp eyes detected a huddled form close to the wall.

He stopped short, scrutinizing the shadows at the far end of the hall, the deep blobs of blackness that lay under the stairway to his left. He discerned nothing lurking there, and took a quick step forward, knelt beside the prone body. It was a dead man. He had been shot through the head at close range; there were powder marks around the wound. The floor beneath the man's head was sopping wet with blood.

The lips of Secret Agent "X" compressed grimly as he recognized the body. It was Fowler, one of the two men who had been shadowing Runkle. Fowler was still warm; the wound was still bleeding. He had died within the last few minutes.

The Agent's fists clenched involuntarily. These men whom he employed were not just impersonal names to him. He had investigated each one thoroughly, knew them, had met them under one or another of his disguises. Fowler had died in his service—another score to be settled with the murder monster

DESPITE the possibility of pressing danger around him, "X" stopped here a moment, paying silent tribute to the man who had died in the performance of his duty. Then, tearing himself back to the business in hand, he stole noiselessly along the hall, seeming to merge with the shadows. His shoes made not the slightest sound as he explored the other rooms on the ground floor, found them empty and deserted.

Still silently, he went up the stairs. At the upper landing he paused, listening intently. No sound greeted his ears. It was lighter here, and he could see that the hallway was empty of life. But an open door at the right drew him toward it. This room was unfurnished, like the rest, but there was another body on the floor.

Brilliant morning sunlight poured into the room, playing upon the face of the dead man, and "X" did not need to kneel beside him to tell how he had met his death. For the gaping, bloody hole in his forehead spoke for itself. And the man was Grace, Fowler's co-watcher.

Fowler and Grace had been killed coldbloodedly, no doubt to allow the killer or killers a free hand in the house next door. The Agent's eyes were bleak as he stepped to the window through which Grace had been watching, and looked across the narrow driveway to Number Twenty-two.

He saw a room there, corresponding to the one he was standing in. It was furnished as a sitting room—evidently Runkle thought that a ground floor sitting room might be too accessible to eavesdroppers.

At first glance it appeared that the room in there was vacant. "X" wondered if Runkle's guests had also departed with the little attorney—but if they had, they certainly had not come in the green coupé with him; for there had been no one else in the car with Runkle.

And suddenly, from that room; across the driveway there came a deep moan as of a man dying in agony.

Almost before that moan was ended, the Agent had swung himself over the sill and leaped to the ground. He landed on his toes, and was in motion at once, running around to the front of Number Twenty-two. The front door was unlocked, and "X" hurled himself through into the dim hallway within. He raced up the stairs to the upper floor, and as he reached the top landing, he saw the bloody, wabbling figure of a man stagger out of the sitting room. In the uncertain light it was impossible to identify him, but the Agent saw that the man held a gun. The gun came up, wavering, pointed at the Agent, and the narrow hallway rocked with the heavy explosions as the man in the doorway fired again and again, keeping his finger down on the trigger.

But "X" had dropped to the floor at first sight of the gun in the man's hand, and the slugs whined over his head harmlessly, burying themselves in the opposite wall. Eight times the gun roared in quick succession; and then, when the Agent knew that the clip was empty, he launched himself from the floor in a flying tackle that brought down the man in the doorway, landed them both in a tangled heap inside the sitting room.

Secret Agent "X" grappled with the man, was surprised to find him offering no resistance; the man lay flat on his back, breathing heavily, gasping, almost sobbing. High above his heart was a bullet wound, and it was miraculous that he had lasted long enough to stagger through the doorway.

It was lighter in here, for the sun came in through the window on the driveway, and "X's" lips compressed as he saw the man's face. It was "Duke" Marcy!

Marcy's eyes were assuming a glassy look. His chest heaved with each breath he took, and he expelled it with a long wheeze. His lips were moving weakly.

The Agent raised his head, demanded, "Who shot you, Marcy?"

The dying man tried to form words, in fact, uttered several faintly, but so low that they were indistinguishable. There was a raucous rattle in his throat, and his head dropped back. He was dead.

From outside now, "X" heard the sound of a police whistle, of excited shouts. There were heavy steps on the stairs, and a uniformed policeman burst in with drawn gun. He covered the Agent, ordering, "Get up, you, and raise your hands!"

"X" shrugged and obeyed. He knew what the policeman thought—that he had killed Marcy.

He said, "I did not kill this man, officer. I heard him groan and ran into the house. I found him here with a gun in his hand, dying on his feet."

The policeman lowered at him. "Yeah?" He kept the revolver steady. "That's a good story. You can tell it to the homicide men!"

Brakes squealed outside, more feet were heard on the stairs. "X" glanced around the room, and for the first time saw another form huddled in a corner where it had been invisible from the window across the street. The man was Brinz—he recognized him from the description Bates had given him.

The Agent's brow wrinkled in thought. Fowler and Grace killed in cold blood; Marcy and Brinz murdered here—and Runkle driving away at breakneck speed. There were puzzling elements here that needed clearing up. Runkle had been in this very room, according to reports; it was inconceivable that he could have gone across to the empty house, shot Fowler and Grace, and returned to do the same to Marcy and Brinz. He must have had assistance, if he were the murderer. In that case, the thing must have been planned in advance—must have been a trap into which Marcy walked unsuspectingly.

Now, the room filled with uniformed figures. A precinct sergeant, several plain-clothes men, and in a few moments, Inspector Cleary, in charge of the Brooklyn homicide division. The policeman who had arrived first made his report to Cleary. The inspector heard it, frowning, then said to the Agent, "What's your name?"

"I am Arvold Fearson, inspector, a private investigator. I did not kill—"

The inspector interrupted him gruffly. "Stow that. You're under arrest, Fearson. The charge is murder. I warn you that anything you say may be used against you!"

CHAPTER XVII

VIA SHORT WAVE

ESCAPE WAS IMPOSSIBLE now. The room was filled with police, they were swarming through the house, and more were coming. "X" permitted himself to be handcuffed, maintaining silence. Nothing he could say now would induce Cleary to release him. Later, perhaps, a method of escape would present itself. Now, he remained quiet while a sergeant "frisked" him.

The sergeant felt the texture of the custom-made suit he wore, and frowned, but said nothing. He ran big hands over the Agent's person, and found the gas gun which reposed in an inner pocket built into the lining of the coat. He examined it curiously, and was about to ask a question, when Cleary, who had been phoning headquarters, returned from the phone.

Cleary told the sergeant, "Commissioner Pringle wants to question this man personally, Frazer. This man, Marcy, was wanted as a suspect in the robot murders, and the commissioner thinks this bird ought to know something about them."

Sergeant Frazer saluted. "This gun, sir—"

Cleary waved him away. "Take it down to headquarters with you and give it to the commissioner. I've got nothing more to do with the case. It's been taken out of my hands."

The inspector was plainly peeved that he had been superseded in the investigation. His mood saved "X" the immediate necessity of explaining away the gas gun.

Sergeant Frazer and two plain-clothes men escorted the Agent down to a squad car in front of the door. Frazer sat in front next to the chauffeur, while "X" was placed in the rear seat between the two detectives.

"Over the Brooklyn Bridge," Frazer directed the chauffeur, "to New York headquarters."

As the car got under way, the Agent saw the medical examiner arrive together with a headquarters photographer. Nobody had mentioned the bodies of Fowler and Grace next door. Apparently they hadn't got to the empty house as yet.

While they traveled toward Manhattan, Frazer leaned forward and turned on the button of the short-wave radio receiver. Several routine calls came over, and then after a few moments these were drowned out by a powerful sending set somewhere. The Agent stiffened as he heard the voice of Bates.

"Station 'X' calling. Station 'X' calling!"

There was a moment of silence after the signal, when the regular police calls became audible again.

Frazer swore. "There's that damn station again! They haven't been able to locate it yet. Some damn amateur. When they locate him, he'll get plenty!"

The detective at the right of the Agent started to say something, but stopped as Bates's voice once more drowned out the police messages.

Slowly the alternate French, German and English words came over the short wave, sounding like nothing but the meaningless jargon of a deranged mind.

Frazer grumbled, "Let him have his fun. They'll let him fix radios in jail when he's caught!"

But Secret Agent "X" paid him no attention. He was concentrating on that message, picking out the words that counted—one French, one German, one English; one German, one English, one French, and so on. Decoding the message mentally required a swift-thinking, keen intellect. "X" could not write the words now; he had to remember each one that counted, and at the same time keep track of the progressive changes from one language to another.

He shut out his surroundings, focused his whole attention on Bates's voice. And while the others in the speeding car made petulant comments, to him those words began to assume significance.

Bates was saying, "Suspicious truck reported opposite home of Randolph Coulter. Have ordered plane number one to go up to circle the neighborhood. Am awaiting further instructions."

Bates began to repeat the message, but "X" had no need to listen. He had decoded the message as he heard it. A truck in front of Ranny Coulter's house—and Coulter and Larrabie both staying there. The truck might be innocent enough, but "X" had a vivid picture of the monster stepping into that other truck when it had nearly caught him in the apartment on Eighth Avenue.

Should he tell Frazer? The sergeant wouldn't believe him, would think "X" was trying some sort of trick. If Coulter and Larrabie were still home, they must be warned against going out, must stay inside the house until the truck had been investigated.

There was no time to be lost. "X" must get away from his captors at once; if the suspicions of Bates's operative were well grounded, then this might be the opportunity that "X" had been waiting for.

In addition, there was another, perhaps more immediate danger looming up. If the Agent were brought to headquarters, he would be thoroughly searched. The things that would be found on him would damn him a thousand times over in the eyes of the police; his bullet-proof vest, his kit of chromium tools, his make-up material. Above all, they must not be allowed to examine Mr. Corlear's suit too closely.

"X" LOOKED up, saw that they were approaching the Manhattan end of the Brooklyn Bridge, and reached a swift decision. His manacled hands moved inconspicuously. His fingers flicked to his tie, came away with a small glass capsule that had laid in an ingeniously contrived pocket of the lining.

Too late, the detective at his right saw what he was doing and reached out to grip his hand, exclaiming, "Say! What the—"

He did not complete the sentence, for the Agent had flipped the glass capsule into the air, over the driver's shoulder. The capsule struck the windshield, shattered; and the powerful, pungent odor of concentrated ammonia gas filled the car.

Frazer and the two detectives began to cough as the stinging gas entered their throats; their eyes clouded with burning tears. The driver, in a panic of sudden agony, let go of the wheel to rub at his eyes, and the car swerved, careened into the rail at the side of the bridge. All four of them forgot completely about the presence of their prisoner in the abrupt anguish which attacked their eyes, noses and throats.

Secret Agent "X" had taken a deep breath as he hurled the capsule, and now he held it while his fingers dipped into the vest pocket of the detective at his right, emerged with the key to the handcuffs. In a twinkling the steel links were loosened and dropped to the floorboards.

The impact of the car against the rail sent them all flying in a heap to the floor, but it was the Agent who acted with the precision

"You're under arrest," barked the inspector. "The charge is murder!"

of a machine. He kept his eyes closed as a protection against the gas, heaved himself up, and twisted the knob of the door. The car had come to a standstill as he leaped out. Brakes screamed as the traffic behind came to an abrupt stop.

The Agent took a deep breath of the clean fresh air, and looked around. Another car had come to a halt beside them, the driver looking over at them with wide eyes. "X" sprang over, wrenched open the rear door, and swung inside.

"Drive ahead!" he ordered with a crisp incisiveness that brooked no opposition.

The driver hesitated only an instant. The Agent gripped his shoulder with hard fingers. "Get going, or I'll throw you out and drive myself!"

The man at the wheel quailed under the quiet threat of that voice. He mumbled something indistinguishable, shifted into first, and put the car in motion.

Behind them came hoarse shouts from Frazer and the other detectives in the squad car. They were not hurt, but they were helpless, blinded for the moment by the gas. An officer was lumbering toward the scene from the Manhattan end of the bridge. He did not even look toward the car that passed him, in which "X" was riding; he had eyes only for the accident farther up.

"X's" unwilling chauffeur slowed up almost imperceptibly, half-turned toward the bluecoat outside. But the Agent divined his purpose at once, pressed the hard end of a fountain pen flashlight into his shoulder blade. "Just keep going," he ordered softly.

The driver obeyed.

As they left the bridge behind, "X" moved over to the right side of the seat so that the man at the wheel could not see him in the rear vision mirror. "Turn left," he instructed. "Drive downtown till I tell you to stop."

The owner of the car did as directed. At the next corner there was a red light. "I'll have to stop for this," he said over his shoulder. "Is it okay for me to—" His voice trailed off, and he braked to a stop with a bewildered expression on his face. Then he pulled over to the curb and swore. For he had been talking to thin air.

As he had slowed up for the light, his passenger had opened the right-hand door and leaped from the car, disappearing into the lunch hour crowd around city hall. The only evidence that he had even been present in the car was a folded twenty-dollar bill which he had placed conspicuously in the slot of the door handle.

CHAPTER XVIII

THE MONSTER PAYS A VISIT

THE AGENT CROSSED City Hall Park at a fast walk, and entered the drug store at the corner of Broadway and Chambers. He looked up the number of Ranny Coulter's house, and hurried into a phone booth, put in the call, hoping that nothing had happened there yet.

He was relieved to hear Jack Larrabie's voice over the wire.

He said crisply, "This is Fearson, Larrabie. Is young Coulter there with you?"

"Yes," Larrabie answered. "We were just leaving to go down to headquarters. Harry Pringle's father, the deputy commissioner, has offered to deputize us so that we can go after the monster. We're sick and tired of sticking in the house and doing nothing!"

The Agent's voice rang with a sudden note of authority as he said, "Neither of you must leave the house till I get there, Larrabie! There is a truck parked outside which may be waiting for you to come out. Do nothing until I arrive. Is that clear?"

"Well—" young Larrabie said reluctantly.

The Agent interrupted him. "On no condition must you go out. I'll be there in less than a half hour. And stay away from the windows, too!"

He hung up without waiting for an answer, but he did not leave at once. Instead he turned his back to the glass door of the booth, set up his portable mirror on the corner of the small shelf where the telephone rested, and set to work on his face. Within three minutes, Arvold Fearson had disappeared. Mr. Vardis now stood in the booth. Though the gray suit was the same, the Agent's whole bearing was different.

As he stepped out of the booth, he no longer walked with the shuffling slouch of Fearson. Instead, he strode erect, with head held high. So perfect was the transformation, that by the very change in bearing he seemed to be inches taller than Fearson had appeared.

Out on Broadway, he met a scene of wild excitement. The street was aswarm with police. Frazer and the plain-clothes men must have recovered by this time from the effects of the ammonia gas and given the description of Fearson.

Plain-clothes men were peering into the faces of every passer-by. The office buildings were being combed by a flood of officers that had been thrown into the district. They were apparently determined that the supposed murderer of Marcy should not escape.

But Mr. Vardis passed unquestioned, for he in no wise resembled the fugitive. He hailed a cab, gave directions to drive to the Coulter home. "If you hurry," he said to the cabby, "you can make it in twelve minutes; I want you to do better than that—I want to get there in ten. And there's ten dollars in it for you."

The cabby grinned, and stepped on the gas.

So far, all of "X's" genius had been futile in combatting this dreadful monster that terrorized the city. He had been forced to fight blindly, depending on chance, waiting for the monster to make a mistake. Even now, as he sped uptown, he realized that there was only one chance in a hundred that the truck in front of the Coulter home had anything to do with the monster. But that one chance had to be looked into. In a battle like this, nothing could be passed by lightly.

The cab made it in ten minutes.

It turned into Madison Avenue two blocks below the Coulter home, and the driver headed north.

TRAFFIC was light at this time of the afternoon, and "X" could see far ahead over the cabby's shoulder. He saw the two sandwich men on the corner in front of the Coulter house, saw the large truck across the street. He consulted his watch, saw that he was well within the twenty-minute time limit and breathed a sigh of relief. He had outlined in his mind a tentative plan for investigating that truck without arousing the suspicions of its occupants, if there were any.

He leaned forward, said to the driver, "When you get up to that corner where the sandwich men are standing, pull up next to them."

The driver nodded, began to slow up. They still had one street intersection between them and the Coulter house. The green traffic light on the avenue turned red, and the cabby braked to a halt at the corner. A block away the sandwich men paced lazily with all the appearance of a couple of down-and-outers working for a day's pay. No one would have suspected them of carrying sub-machine guns concealed under those signs.

Somewhere in the immediate vicinity there would also be the two men assigned as bodyguards to Larrabie and Coulter.

But "X" had eyes only for the truck. At the distance of a whole block, his keen eyes examined it carefully. It was all white, with black lettering on its side, announcing that the "Snow-Cap Laundry Does Your Sheets Like New." It was facing north, away from him, and he could not see the driver's compartment. But he suddenly noted something that caused his whole body to grow tense.

Projecting from the roof of the truck was a short length of metal tube which was curved at the top, so that the opening faced toward the Coulter house. "X" had seen many of these in war times, knew that at the first sight of one of these rising upon the crest of a barren ocean, stark panic had been wont to tread the decks of the proudest ocean liners. It was a periscope such as is used on submarines! Somebody within that truck was watching the house across the street!

It took but a second for the Agent to note this, even while the cab was slowing up for the red light. Now he leaned forward, said tensely, "Don't mind the red light—shoot ahead, quick. If there's a fine, I'll pay it!"

But the driver shook his head. "Nix, mister. It'd be my fourth ticket—I'd lose my license. They're hard on us hackmen."

And then things began to happen.

The Agent saw the door of the Coulter house open, saw Ranny Coulter and Jack Larrabie come out and start to descend the steps to the sidewalk. His eyes smouldered. They had deliberately broken their promise to him, had not waited the full twenty minutes.

And now, almost simultaneously with the appearance of the two young men, the rear doors of the waiting truck were flung open, and a swarm of the stiff-walking, robot-like men deployed into the street. They rushed toward Larrabie and Coulter, silently, purposefully intentful; each carried a silenced automatic.

Secret Agent "X" leaped from the cab. But he was too far away. Things happened too fast.

Coulter and Larrabie had stopped, transfixed, at the sudden eruption of attackers. It was the two sandwich men at the corner who stopped the rush of the robots. Even as "X" was leaping from the cab, they swung their sub-machine guns clear of the sandwich boards, and directed a hail of lead at the attackers. The sweep of their slugs bowled over the robot-like men as if they were ninepins—but did not kill them; their bullet-proof clothing stopped the slugs, though they had the wind knocked out of them by the terrific impacts. Not one was left standing. They littered the gutter, started to crawl back toward the truck. The sandwich board trick had been successful so far.

BUT now there descended from the truck the huge, ungainly shape of the murder monster. Its robots had failed; it was swinging into action itself. It paid no attention at all to the two machine gunners, no attention to the squirming forms of the robots who were creeping back to the shelter of the truck, but lumbered with a dreadful singleness of purpose—straight toward the two stupefied young men on the steps of the house.

The Secret Agent had started to run toward the scene, but he was still almost a block away. A police whistle shrilled near by. Women passers-by screamed, others ran helter-skelter to places of safety.

The two sandwich men frantically shoved fresh clips in their Tommy guns, raised them to their shoulders, and almost as one man they pumped a rapid, steady stream of lead at that horrible figure—to no avail. The slugs buried themselves in the outer covering of the monster, staggering it a little, but not swerving it from its course.

It made a straight line toward its objective.

Larrabie and Coulter turned to run into the house. The monster raised its hand, pointed that deadly finger, and young Coulter, who had been a trifle in the lead, suddenly staggered, and became enveloped in a sheet of flame!

He screamed once, then rolled down the steps to the street, uttering choked cries which quickly changed to incoherent moans, and then died to nothingness as his scorched, crisp body jerked and twitched convulsively and lapsed into pitiful stillness.

Young Larrabie had stopped, aghast, beside his friend. The monster called out in a resonant voice that seemed to rise to the rooftops, "Come here, Larrabie. It's you I want. Come here or die!"

As in a trance, Larrabie approached the monster.

By this time Secret Agent "X" had reached the corner beside the two sandwich men, who were reloading once more, holding their ground regardless of the danger that the monster might turn its dreadful finger of doom upon them too. "X" seized a loaded Tommy from the hands of the nearest, saying, "It's all right. I'm from Jim Hobart!"

He swung the machine-gun toward the monster. His purpose was to wait till the monster got into motion once more, then direct the stream of lead at a spot just above its middle. The bullets could not pierce its protective coating, of course, but if they struck at a point just above the monster's center of gravity, they might topple him over.

But he never pulled the trip of the gun. For the monster suddenly reached out, gripped young Larrabie about the middle, and lifted him off the ground. Then, carrying him under its arm, it returned to the car, not hurrying, turning its massive, hideous head from side to side to survey the situation. To fire the sub-machine gun now would only mean the death of young Larrabie who had slumped in his captor's arms, apparently in a faint.

The injured robots had crawled into the truck, and the monster followed them, unmolested.

"X" watched, helpless to intercede, with bitterness in his heart, as the door swung shut, and the truck got into motion, sped away.

Above, the hum of an airplane motor became audible.

The Agent glanced upward, and his eyes glittered as he saw the huge flying machine circling in the air. It kept its altitude, did not dive, but the radius of its circle increased gradually. Bates had been on the job. Now, if those flyers only did their work well .... Secret Agent "X" nodded grimly to himself. He said to the two sandwich men, "Get rid of those signs—drop them right here with the machine guns—and disperse. Here comes the police."

The two men obeyed quickly, disappearing around the corner, piling into a car which had been parked there. No one in the fast gathering crowd tried to stop them, or noticed them. Everybody was gathered around the still smouldering body of Ranny Coulter, commiserating with his hysterical parents who had rushed out of the house.

Secret Agent "X" effaced himself in the crowd just as the first police car appeared.

CHAPTER XIX

BIRD'S-EYE TRAIL

THAT AFTERNOON THE papers were devoted almost exclusively to the startling events of the day. The murders in Belvidere Road, the horrible killing of Ranny Coulter, and the abduction of young Larrabie were the subjects of excited comment throughout the city.

The police were still searching ineffectually for the truck in which the murder monster had escaped with Larrabie as his prisoner. A radio car had given it close chase for a while, until a small porthole in the rear of the truck had swung open. Through this porthole had appeared the pointing finger of the monster, and the police car had suddenly burst into flames; the two policemen in the car had been burned to death.

No one had seen the laundry truck after that. Examination of records revealed, of course, that there was no such firm as the "Snow-Cap Laundry." It was not understood how the truck could have made its escape with every exit from the city guarded, with hundreds of plain-clothes and uniformed men searching the streets and garages.

With all this bustle and excitement Secret Agent "X" did not concern himself. He was ensconced in a darkened room in one of his retreats, engaged in doing a peculiar thing.

This room was exceedingly large, some thirty feet in length. At one end a white motion-picture screen was hung on the wall. At the other end, Secret Agent "X" was engaged in threading a reel of film into a motion-picture projection machine. This completed, the Agent threw a switch, and the machine began to hum as the reels turned, the arc-light of the projector throwing a beam of light across the room.

The Agent now stood tensely, watching the motion pictures

which were flashed on the screen. There appeared a bird's-eye view of a portion of the city, including that section of Madison Avenue where the Coulter home was located. The Agent saw the frantic, running specks which were men and women in panic, he saw a sheet of flame in the street, and his lips compressed grimly as he realized that this was the burning body of Ranny Coulter.

But his eyes followed the motions of the object that he knew was the murder truck leaving the scene of the crime.

The picture flickered often, darkened sometimes to an indistinguishable blur, but it always cleared, always kept that fleeing truck in view.

These pictures had been taken by an aerial camera built in under the cockpit of the plane which had circled over the scene of the crime. It was one of the two planes which "X" had kept in readiness for just such an emergency. Knowing that the monster used a truck for transportation, the Agent had provided this means of tracing its movements.

He waited tautly, watching the flickering film. The next few minutes would tell whether the camera had been able to follow that truck to its hidden destination—a thing the police had so far failed to do.[28]

On the screen there appeared the vast network of streets that was New York City, with humans that resembled minute ants scurrying everywhere. And through it all the Agent followed the movements of that blob that was the murder monster's truck, speeding northward, then east to the river front where it stopped at a deserted spot.

From the truck there swarmed a number of specks that were men. They were carrying two large flat objects which they fastened

---

28 AUTHOR'S NOTE: *This method of tracing criminals after a major crime has been committed was devised by Secret Agent "X." He found it of such value, that he has permitted me to mention his use of it in this chronicle. He has also instructed me to offer the idea to the New York Police Department in connection with its air division. If the Police planes were equipped with aerial cameras, the procedure would be as follows: Immediately upon the alarm of a major crime such as a bank holdup, all traffic lights in the vicinity of the crime would flash red thus halting the movement of every vehicle except that in which the criminals were escaping. The police plane, taking off at the first alarm, could be over the city in a few minutes, and the aerial camera would then record the movements of the car in which the gunmen were fleeing. Thus, if they succeeded in evading pursuit, the camera would show unerringly just where they had holed up, and the forces of the law could then proceed to smoke them out. The Agent has suggested that the aerial camera would work even better in less populous centers, but there is no reason why it should not work in a large city.*

to the sides of the truck, and then they hurried around to back and front for a moment. Their work over, they climbed back inside, and the truck once more resumed its course, this time proceeding much more slowly, threading its way back into the heart of the city.

The Agent stirred at his spot beside the projector. He understood why that truck had not been traced. The license plates had been changed, and the truck itself had been disguised by fastening thin sheets of metal over the sides. These were probably of a different color, with another name. No wonder the police had lost it—they were still looking for a white laundry truck.

Now the disguised truck proceeded sedately through traffic, passing traffic officers, radio cars, driving boldly to its destination under the very eyes of the entire police force.

Its destination was a street on the west side of town, where genteel brownstone houses rubbed elbows with garages and tall apartment houses. The truck turned in to one of these garages, disappeared from view.

The film continued to wind through the projector, flashing further bird's-eye pictures on the screen. But "X" had no more interest in it. He had turned away into a cubbyhole just off the projection room, where a large-scale map of the city hung on the wall. On this map he was engaged in tracing the movements of the truck, which his photographic memory had recorded faithfully from the film.

In a moment his pencil rested on the exact spot where the truck had disappeared. His face was alight with a strange glow. He had traced the monster to its hole!

CHAPTER XX

HELL'S HEADQUARTERS

IT WAS CLOSE to dusk when a dignified gentleman in a gray suit drove a large and expensive looking sedan into the street on the west side of town where the monster's truck had disappeared.

The gentleman noted, as he drove down the street, that there were several men loitering near the corner. Among them were two whom he knew as Stegman and Oliver.

On the corner was a large apartment house, and next to it was a row of old, three-story brownstones. On the other side of the street there were several garages. The Agent drove slowly, as if not certain of his destination. Finally he slowed up, swung the car into the driveway of a large garage in the middle of the block.

There were a dozen cars on the floor, here, though the space would have accommodated thirty or forty. Several of these were trucks, though none, of course, bore the name of the Snow Cap Laundry. A single attendant, who was built along the lines of a heavyweight prize-fighter, was in charge.

He approached the sedan, looking inquiringly at the driver.

"What is it, mister?"

The Agent descended leisurely from the car, said affably, "I've just moved into the neighborhood and I was looking for a good garage to store my car. What do you charge in here?"

The attendant cast an appraising glance at the visitor, and said surlily, "The boss ain't in, mister."

"Well, have you any idea what the rates are?"

The attendant had half turned away, as if to return to his duties. He stopped reluctantly. "They run around a hundred a month with service."

"A hundred a month!" the Agent exclaimed. "Why, that's almost twice the prevailing rates!"

"That's what we charge, mister. We only take in high class people."

"That's entirely too much," said "X." "I don't see how you can get any business."

The attendant shrugged. "We get along." He turned away once more. "I think it's cheaper up the block. Why don't you try over there?"

"I will. Oh, by the way—"

The attendant stopped once more, annoyed. "What—"

He never finished. For Secret Agent "X" had stepped close to him and, as he turned, delivered a smashing blow to the point of the attendant's chin. The overalled man staggered backward, his eyes growing glassy, and would have slumped to the floor had "X" not caught him and eased him down slowly. He then dragged the unconscious attendant's body over to a corner, where he deposited it.

Now he proceeded to scan every corner of the garage. There was no place of concealment anywhere. The walls were of brick, bare, without any sort of covering that might hide a secret door.

The Agent stepped to the doorway, looked out at the street. Directly opposite was a brownstone house, one of the long row that ran to the corner. They had once been the homes of comfortable families, quiet and refined. Now they all had "furnished room" signs. All, that is, except Number 346, which was the one directly opposite. This one had no sign, and did not seem to be occupied at all.

Secret Agent "X" frowned, turned away from the entrance, and went into the office of the garage, which was in the corner, facing the street. There was no one in the office, but he noticed that the large window on the street was of frosted glass, making it impossible to look in from outside.

There was a desk against one wall, and a table in the center. The floor was of concrete. There were two closed doors in the wall opposite the desk. The Agent tried them. The first opened into a wash room, the second into a closet. It was quite a roomy closet. A dozen new tires, still in their wrappings, were stacked at one side. The rest of the closet was occupied by boxes of inner tubes, cans of oil, and other innocent-appearing accessories of a legitimate garage.

The Agent examined the floor and the walls, but could find no trace of an opening. His face was intent, thoughtful.

Before leaving the closet, he put his hands on the top tire of the stack, tried to lift it. He found that it could not be lifted. It was tied to the others by several lengths of heavy wire. "X" gripped the wire, and pulled.

And the whole stack of tires moved outward, toward him!

They had been resting on a metal plate set just above the floor, which moved on a pivot. Below the plate there was disclosed a circular opening leading down into darkness.

Secret Agent "X" peered down into this opening and saw a set of stairs.

HE was taut now, all his senses keenly alert. No sound came from the garage outside the office, no sound came from the depths below. Ominous silence lay about the place, and the gathering dusk seemed to creep upon him with damp, stifling fingers. Here then, was the lair where lurked this murder monster that had held the city in terror. Now at last, after unremitting effort, after thrusting himself into danger time and again, he was going to come to grips once more with that horrible specter of death that caused men to turn into a living blaze of torture.

The Agent lowered himself into the opening, descended the short flight of steps. It was pitch black in here, but he did not light his flash. He reached the bottom, felt a wall at his right, and followed it. He put out his left hand, felt another wall.

He was in a narrow passage, and his sense of direction told him that it ran under the street, toward Number 346, opposite. He followed the passage for about thirty feet, and found himself before a closed door.

Now he risked the flashlight, saw that the door was of steel, with a small peephole, closed now, high up at the level of the eyes.

He set the flashlight on its end so that the beam was diffused upward, and knelt before the lock, taking out his kit of tools. In less than three minutes, working with absolute silence, he had the door open, stepped through into a lighted cubbyhole.

One of the robot-men was seated here, apparently a guard. He sprang up, hand streaking for the silenced automatic that lay on a small table beside him. But the Agent was faster. He had provided himself with another gas gun to replace the one he had lost earlier in the day,[29] and he fired this full in the face of the startled robot. The man sank to the floor without a moan.

The Secret Agent wasted no time. He knelt beside the inert form, set up his portable mirror and laid on the floor his make-up kit.

His fingers worked swiftly, dexterously, as he modeled for himself a face that was the duplicate of the face of the robot who lay before him.

Finally he arose. His gray suit was of the same cut as that of the robots; his face was an exact replica of theirs. He walked stiffly, opened a door at the other side of the cubbyhole, and stepped through, for all the world another one of those merciless killers.

He was in a short hall, musty and dank with the typical cellar smell. This must be the cellar of Number 346. He passed a rickety wooden door, heard a scraping noise behind it.

The door was fastened on the outside by a staple which he removed. He flashed his light into the dark ulterior, saw a huddled form, tied, with mouth and eyes taped.

He stepped inside, knelt beside the figure, and removed the tape from the mouth, leaving the man's eyes covered. The man was Ed Runkle!

Runkle had not been picked up by Bates' men—in fact he had been lost sight of after "X" had seen him driving away from Belvidere Road. And this was why he had not been picked up again. He was a prisoner of the monster—Runkle, the attorney who had defended the monster's man in court, whom "X" had seen driving away from the slaughter house on Belvidere Road!

WITH the tape off his mouth, the little attorney wet his lips, ran his tongue around the outside of his mouth where the tape had torn the skin. "What do you want of me?" he asked huskily. He wriggled

---

29 AUTHOR'S NOTE: It will be recalled that the Agent's gas gun had been taken from him when he was placed under arrest by Inspector Cleary, and he had not had a chance to recover it when he made his escape from the police car. It was not a great loss, however, for, though the gun in itself was an interesting instrument, it was useless to anyone without the formula for the gas which it discharged. And the police chemists would certainly not have a chance to analyze it, for the moment the gas chamber was opened, the gas would escape, rendering whoever was present unconscious for several hours. As a matter of fact, this is just what did occur, as the Agent learned some time afterward. The incident was related to him some weeks later by Commissioner Foster on his return from Europe, when they met in the Bankers' Club—which was frequented by the Agent in the personality of the wealthy Elisha Pond.

his head as if he could in that way remove the tape from his eyes. "Are you one of the—robots? Talk, why don't you talk! Let me hear you say something!"

"X" kept his ear cocked for the possible approach of anyone along the corridor. He said, "I am not a robot. Answer my questions, but do not raise your voice. How did you get here?"

Runkle's body seemed to stiffen at the sound of "X's" voice. He exclaimed, "If you're not a robot—who are you?" He had seemed to gain courage from the news that this was not another one of the ruthless mechanical-appearing men of the monster. Even his voice seemed to assume a new tone, a tone with a tinge of cunning in it. He repeated the question—"Who are you?"

"Never mind that," the Agent told him curtly. "There's no time now for explanations. If I'm to help you, you must answer me quickly. How did you get here?"

With the instinct of his profession, Runkle began to hedge. "You want information? Why don't you take the tape off my eyes then? When I see who you are, maybe I'll tell you what you want to know."

"X" arose from beside him. "I have no time," he said shortly. "If you won't talk, I'll leave you here." He went toward the door.

Runkle called out in a low, desperate voice, "Wait! Don't leave me here! I'll talk."

The Agent returned, stood above him. "Go on."

"I don't know how I got here. I was driving, out in Brooklyn. Suddenly a large truck cut in front of me, forced me to the curb. The rear door of the truck opened, and a small army of these robots swarmed out, grabbed me and hustled me into the truck. They tied me up this way, and taped my eyes. Then I passed out, and I don't know what happened after that. I came to in here—I don't know where I am." He raised his voice in a thin whine. "For God's sake, get me out of—"

"X" quickly placed a hand over his mouth. "Silence, you fool! Do you want to attract everybody in the place?"

The Agent removed his hand from the attorney's mouth, asked, "Why did you kill Marcy and Brinz?"

Runkle shifted energetically. "God! I didn't do that! I went down to the kitchen to get some drinks for them, and when I got back I saw two of those robots in the hall upstairs, and they were firing their silenced guns into the room where Marcy and Brinz were sitting. I got scared and ran out. I got in my car and drove away from there as fast as I could go."

The Agent bent closer. "What was your business with Marcy?" he asked.

Runkle was silent for a long time. Finally he said, "I don't believe you're here to help me. You're one of that monster's men. You're pumping me!" He lapsed into stubborn silence.

The Agent arose. "You need not answer," he said. "I know what you were meeting Marcy for. Brinz was bringing the two of you together—'Duke' Marcy knew who the Murder Monster is, and he wanted your help to avenge the death of Mabel Boling!" Runkle uttered a gasp of surprise. The Agent turned to the door. "I'm not taping your mouth again—but if you value your life, don't make any outcry or do anything to attract attention. I give you my word that you will be freed before I leave here." Then he added, as Runkle started to protest, "You can rely on it—it is the word of—Secret Agent 'X'!"

Runkle's jaw fell open in astonishment. He was too stunned to speak.

"X" stepped out and continued down the hallway. The hall ended in a cross-corridor; at the end of the corridor was a door, and before the door stood one of the robots with an automatic in his hand. It was too late to draw back, for the robot had already seen him.

"X" advanced in his direction, but the robot seemed to take him for granted. Indeed, there was no reason why he shouldn't, for he no doubt took "X" to be one of his fellows.

He raised his hand, however, motioned for "X" to go back. He was apparently on guard at that door, with instructions to allow no one to enter.

But "X" advanced as if he had not noticed the gesture, until he was within two feet of the other. The robot stepped forward, barring his way, motioning angrily, now, for him to go back.

"X" smiled disarmingly, and fired the gas gun, which he had held out of sight, directly into the robot's face. The guard sagged, unconscious, the automatic slipping from nerveless fingers, and the Agent eased him to the floor.

He stepped over him and tried the door. It was unlocked, and he pulled it open gently, a fraction of an inch, without making a sound.

CHAPTER XXI

FLAMES OF HATE

THE ROOM WITHIN was large, square. The effect of the first glimpse was an effect of whiteness and cleanliness. The walls were tiled, white. A long bench at the opposite wall ran across the full length of the room, except for the spot in the right-hand corner where there was a flat-topped, mahogany, glass-covered desk.

On the bench were retorts, test tubes, microscopes. Racks of tubes containing liquids and gasses were nailed to the wall above the bench. Everything seemed orderly, neat; so neat as to be terrifying—terrifying by the very incongruity of this white-tiled laboratory in the cellar of a rundown house in a run-down district.

The Agent, however, had nothing but a cursory glance for the setting—a glance, though, that embraced everything vital before it rested upon the two characters in the center of the room.

One of those two was young Jack Larrabie. The other was the weird figure of the murder monster.

Larrabie's face was suffused with rage. He was shouting, "Damn you! Why did you kill Coulter?"

The murder monster waddled forward slowly, stopped, facing Larrabie, and standing sideways to the door through which "X" peered. From somewhere in its depths there came the deep metallic voice that the Agent had heard before. It uttered a hideous, inhuman laugh. Then the laughter stopped suddenly, and the voice spoke.

"You seem to forget, Larrabie, that I have the whip hand. Do you know what that means? I will show you!"

Too late, young Larrabie turned, leaped away from in front of that hideous figure. He had not covered three feet before the ponderous, moving finger of the monster rose, pointing at his back. Horrid, sizzling flame burst out around the young man. He screamed once, half-turned, and his face was a mask of hate and dread.

He dropped to the floor, tried ineffectually to beat out the flames by rolling over and over. Now he was enveloped in fire, a screaming, wriggling, sizzling ball of fire.

It had all happened so quickly, almost upon the instant that the Agent had opened the door. Now, "X" flung it wide, launched himself at the monster in a flying leap that caught the gruesome figure amidships. The Agent struck with his shoulder, sent the monster staggering backward so that it would have fallen had it not ended up against the bench. It had gone right through the sheet of flame that enveloped the writhing body of young Larrabie, but had been untouched by it.

Now its dread finger came up, directed itself unerringly at "X."

The monster seemed to be quite at ease, secure in the knowledge that in another instant this intruder would likewise go up in flames. But nothing happened!

From deep within the monster came a rumble of astonishment.

The Agent laughed grimly, and leaped at the monster once more. This time he did not attempt to match his weight against that of the heavily padded and protected form. He seized the pointing arm, twisted around so that his back was to the monster, his shoulder under the padded arm.

He used the leverage of his shoulder now, heaved and twisted. The monster was carried forward for a moment, off balance. And in that moment the Agent lunged against it sideways. It staggered to one side, and unable to recover its balance, crashed to the floor. The Agent had attacked it in its one weak spot—being so heavily padded and protected, it was easily unbalanced; and once on the floor, it could not rise without great difficulty. It was something like the armored knights of old—invincible while on horseback, but at the mercy of the first attack when thrown.

The monster struggled frantically to swing its deadly finger up once more, but "X" deliberately stepped on the padded arm, pinning it to the floor.

The Agent stared down with somber eyes. "You should have pointed that finger of yours at my face—it's the only vulnerable spot. The clothes I am wearing are made to order, of sheet asbestos, specially treated to soften it so it could be tailored into a suit. It is fire-proof!"

The body of Jack Larrabie lay still, a few feet away, smouldering, scorched, a pitiful thing in death, the face now fleshless and charred. Even now, with the spark of life burned out of it, the body twitched convulsively as if it still lived in agony.

THE monster tried to twist itself free of the Agent's foot, which pinned it down. But its very bulk was against it.

The Agent bent swiftly and unbuckled the straps that held the gas mask in place. He jerked it off, and found that the head beneath was nothing but an empty shell of aluminum, covered by the gas-mask. It was held to the metal body by two strong clamps. The Agent undid these, and removed the aluminum shell. Out of an opening in the barrel-like body, where the neck should have been, there stared up at him a pair of venomous eyes, sparkling with hatred.

The occupant of that monster's armor was not as tall as his shell. His head remained within the armor, while the gas-mask and the aluminum head were merely for the purpose of effect. "X" could now see two peepholes, covered with glass, in the padded body. It was through these that the man within had looked at his victims.

The Agent said, "You can crawl out of there now. You're through." His voice was flat, with a strange bitterness. He saw mental pictures of the atrocities at the bazaar, saw the lifeless forms of Fowler and Grace.

The man within the armor spoke, no longer metallically, resonantly, but in a human voice, full of anger. "You fool! What good is this going to do you? You need me. Even if your face is changed, there are enough papers in the safe deposit box to identify you to the police. Wherever you went you'd be recognized as one of the robots—you'd be seized in an hour!" Clearly, he was taken in by the Agent's makeup, believed him to be one of the robots.

At the sound of his voice, Secret Agent "X" had nodded to himself as if in confirmation of a suspicion. He said. "I am not one of your robots, Fred Barton. I am the instrument which brings you to the bar of justice!"

The man within the armor of the monster gasped. "Who are you?"

"X" did not answer. He was unstrapping the padding from the metal armor of the huge figure, still keeping his foot on that arm.

His suspicions were confirmed. The man within that shell was Fred Barton. Fred Barton, who was supposed to have been kidnaped; Fred Barton who had just consigned his friend, Jack Larrabie, to horrible death by fire!

It took fifteen minutes to get him out of that cumbersome suit of combination armor and padding. The Agent was careful to prevent him from using that deadly right arm that controlled the secret of the burning death.

He snapped a pair of handcuffs on young Barton's wrists when he dragged him out of the shell of armor. Barton tried to resist, struggled with maniacal strength. But the Agent twisted his arms in a punishing grip, and tightened the cuffs.

Barton stood there, breathing heavily, his face flushed, while "X" knelt beside the monster's suit, found the tube that ran from the underneath metal finger in the right hand to a compact tank strapped on the inside of the back.

He looked up at Barton. "You were always a clever chemist, Barton. This gas that you use here—it could have made you famous; you would have been hailed as a leader in your field—the discoverer of an invisible gas that ignites upon contact with organic substance! Why did you employ it in this way?"

Barton's youthful face twisted into a leer of malice and hatred. "You've ruined the greatest scheme the world has ever known! In a short time I would have had more power than any king or emperor!" He took an impulsive step forward. "Whoever you are, you must be clever, ingenious, to have fought me this way. Why not join me? There will be little reward for you in turning me over to the police compared to what I can offer you. With the secret of that gas, two such men as you and I could achieve world empire. What do you say!"

"X" paid no attention to the mad offer of partnership in crime. He gazed speculatively at Barton, reflecting that there were strange motives in the world which impelled men to do mad things. This young man, possessed of wealth, education, culture, had turned to crime because of those very endowments which the world envied; surfeit of good fortune had made life empty—boring for him; and his brilliant mind had sought in crime the thrills that his jaded appetite craved.

"X" said aloud, "You had no regard even for your own father. You permitted him to think you were kidnaped—so that you would be free to appear as the monster!"

Barton waved the comment away impatiently. "What of it!" His voice became wheedling; eager. "Will you join me? You and I—nobody could stop us. We could climb the heights of power together!"

"X" shook his head. "And meet the same fate that your other

partners met?"

Barton jerked his head up, eyes startled.

The Agent went on inexorably. "Of course you had partners. You didn't operate on those convicts' faces yourself—it was Jack Larrabie here that did that. And Harry Pringle, too. He planned the jail break because of his intimate knowledge of the layout of the State Prison—his father is the deputy police commissioner."

Barton stared at the Agent, fascinated, as he went on. "And Ranny Coulter—another of your jaded young thrill-seekers. This is his father's house. The whole row belongs to his father. He furnished your headquarters. You were all going to take turns at acting as the monster. But you killed them all, one after the other, when you found you didn't need them any longer."

The Agent spoke bitterly now. He pointed an accusing finger. "Barton, you are the worst of the lot—for you betrayed even your own associates.

"I have no sympathy for you—only for your father, for the fathers of Larrabie, and Coulter, and Pringle. I am thinking of the disgrace, the shame that you four thrill-seeking egomaniacs have brought upon their heads!"

Barton asked fiercely, "Who are you, anyway?"

"You may call me—Secret Agent 'X'!"

Barton's body tautened. He raised his manacled hands in the air, leaped at "X" in a furious, desperate, fanatical onslaught. He brought his joined hands down in a chopping blow at the Agent's skull.

But "X" had jumped inside his guard, so that the steel cuffs glanced off his shoulder. The Agent at the same time swung a hard right fist to Barton's middle, doubling him up. Barton sagged weakly to the floor. There were tears of defeat in his eyes. His breath, taken away by that blow, came in short gasps. His hands fumbled in his vest pocket, came out with a small pellet. They flashed upward, and the pellet disappeared in his mouth. He gulped, and swallowed.

Now he smiled grotesquely. "I've saved you the trouble of calling the police!" he said. "You win, Sec—"

His whole body stiffened, his face became crimson, and he collapsed.

The Agent stooped beside him. He was dead.

CHAPTER XXII

"DE MORTUIS, NIHIL NISI BONUM"

NOW SECRET AGENT "X" worked swiftly, but with purpose. He stepped to the desk, rummaged through drawers, until he found a sealed envelope. He ripped this open, inspected the sheet of paper within. It was headed, "Formula for nitrocetylene." Below it were chemical symbols which the Agent took care not to look at. He did not want the responsibility of possessing the knowledge of that hideous, death-dealing gas.

Slowly, somberly, he ripped the paper to shreds, touched a match to them.

Then he stepped out of that room of horror, into another passage. At the end of this passage was a curtained doorway. "X" parted the curtains, peered through. He saw that the doorway opened upon a platform in a large room. Before the platform, rows of chairs were arranged in a semicircle. And the chairs were occupied—all but two of them, by the figures of the robot-like ex-convicts.

They were evidently awaiting the arrival of their master upon the platform; they must have been summoned for a meeting which would never take place now.

One of the robots noticed the crack in the curtains, started up in his chair. "X" gave him no time to warn the others. He held in his hand three glass capsules, larger than the one he had used in his escape from the police car on Brooklyn Bridge. They were colored red; they contained, not ammonia, but the anesthetizing gas which the Agent used in his gun. He stepped through the curtains, onto the platform, and hurled the three capsules among the convicts.

He did not wait to see the effects; he knew that within a matter of seconds they would be rendered unconscious by that swiftly vaporizing gas, would remain that way for hours.

He stepped back into the corridor, hurried back to the laboratory. There was a phone here, and he picked it up, dialed the number of Jim Hobart's office. When Jim got on the wire, the Agent gave him the address of the house of death, issued swift instructions.

"This is Fearson," he said. "Come to this address at once. Bring with you a large black bag which Mr. Martin keeps in your office. Ring the outside bell, and I will take the bag from you."

That done, the Agent inspected the room carefully. He was seeking the hiding place of the safe which Barton had said contained the descriptions of all those convicts who were lying unconscious in the meeting hall....

IT was almost midnight when sirens sounded before that house of mystery and death. Headquarters cars, squad cars, radio cars filled the quiet street. Police swarmed in from every direction. They were headed by Deputy Commissioner Pringle in person, and they were there in answer to a mysterious telephone call. The caller had instructed them to go to this address in connection with the robot murders.

Commissioner Pringle was the first up the steps, tried the door and found it open. Burly Inspector Burks, in charge of homicide, shouldered past him. "This is my job, Commissioner," he grumbled. He strode into the dark hallway with drawn gun, flanked by two plain-clothes men with Thompsons.

But they met no opposition. Not until they reached the cellar did they know that they had not been hoaxed.

For there they found the laboratory, and on the floor the empty, monstrous armored shell of the being that had struck terror to the city: And close by lay Fred Barton, youthful and innocent looking in death, beside the scorched body of Jack Larrabie.

Pringle said with a catch in his voice, "Poor boys. They died trying to fight the monster. I hate to be the one to break the news to their families!"

From the laboratory they passed down the hall, found the meeting room. Inspector Burks stepped onto the platform, looked down, and exclaimed, "What the hell is this!"

The chairs had been cleared away from the center of the room. Where they had stood, there were now ranged in a long row twenty-five unconscious bodies. And the faces were not the faces of robots, but those of the very men who were being sought all over the country—the twenty-five convicts who had escaped from State Prison!

Inspector Burks leaped from the platform, stooped and examined those heavy-breathing forms. To the chest of each was pinned a typewritten sheet bearing the identifying marks to be found on their bodies—marks which were part of the prison record of each man, and could not be denied.

Burks exclaimed, "These are the robots! Feel their bodies—they're wearing the bullet-proof clothing yet!"

He placed a hand on their faces, cried, "Good God—this is make-up! Somebody's fixed their faces to resemble their old selves. They've been delivered to us on a silver platter!"

He arose, issued orders excitedly. Men hastened in, placed handcuffs on the unconscious convicts. A call was put in for the wagon.

Pringle was trembling with emotion. "I wonder which of these convicts was the ringleader—which of them used the armor of the monster."

"We'll never know," Burks said morosely. "Whoever it was that laid them out here, must have taken out the one in the monster's shell and set him here next to the rest. It makes no difference, though—they'll all burn for murder!"

Pringle sighed. "Well, there'll be no more robot killings. At least Professor Larrabie, and Giles Barton will have the satisfaction of knowing that their sons' deaths were not in vain. They can always be proud that their boys were brave enough to risk their lives against these killers!"

And from somewhere in the distance there sounded the faint notes of an eerie whistle that jerked every man in the room to attention. That whistle was the inimitable signal of the man who was known as Secret Agent "X"—and it seemed to carry through the air the stamp of approval of Commissioner Pringle's words.

The secret of those four young men who had built a tower of terror upon a dream of power would forever be locked in the breast of a single man—Secret Agent "X."

For the sake of their families he had adopted the adage, *"De mortuis, nihil nisi bonum!"*[30]

---

30   *"About the dead let no evil be spoken!"*

BOOK XI

THE SINISTER SCOURGE

Unseen, horrible as the tightening coils of some spectral serpent, the dope ring worked! Those who betrayed its secrets died in the agonies of the green-hued poison death. Those who served it became sweating, shattered slaves. And Agent "X" dared both death and slavery to fight the sinister scourge!

CHAPTER I

HUNTERS OF DARKNESS

NIGHT LAY OVER Chinatown. Night with its stillness, its darkness, its strangely sinister shadows. A blanket of drifting fog, deadening sound and sight, made even familiar objects appear distorted and mysterious. Behind this dank vapor there was tenseness, uneasiness and unusual activity along the narrow, winding streets.

As the fog rolled ponderously through them like the coils of some huge, ghostly serpent seeking human prey, men moved in the gloom and spoke in whispers. Few Orientals were abroad. The men who trod cautiously by dusty shops and dark doorways were white. Their faces were grim. Guns weighted the pockets of many. Automatics were strapped in holsters ready for instant use.

A score of extra policemen had been detailed for duty in Chinatown tonight. Others of the group who so vigilantly patrolled were plainclothes detectives and special agents of the Federal Narcotic Squad. All were hunting the same insidious thing—dope.

Certain habits of the men from the Land of the Poppy Seed were known to them. Suspicions therefore led to this section of the city where thousands of Orientals dwelt.

The few Chinamen who ventured out crept furtively along the pavements, ducking out of sight quickly. Those who didn't were stopped and questioned by alert detectives. They were asked to identify themselves, with business references or immigration papers. If they couldn't they were driven away in patrol wagons to police headquarters for further questioning. Because of the sinister, unseen presence of the dread dope evil, East and West were close to the breaking point tonight.

As the darkness deepened and the fog grew thicker a shadow moved at the end of a narrow, cluttered alley. It became taller, clearer, and suddenly took shape as a man. There was a fence behind the alley. Through this the man had come. So quietly and mysteriously had he appeared that he seemed hardly more than some apparition, a human embodiment of the darkness of the night.

Yet he had the complexion and the sloe-black, slanted eyes of a Chinaman. A lofty, intellectual forehead, broad, high cheek bones, and a tall, muscular body proclaimed that he was one of the proud Northern Manchu race, conquerors and rulers of China for three hundred years.

The tall Oriental moved with catlike quiet and swiftness. He was dressed in a simple black mohair suit. Black, rubber-soled shoes were on his feet. A black, soft hat covered his head. Except for the yellowish moon of his face he was invisible as long as he stayed in the shadows.

He seemed to have a definite objective, a route that he was following. Twice this took him across Chinatown's main streets. At such times he waited with infinite patience until the patrolling cops had turned their backs. Then, swift and silent as a streamer of fog blown by the night wind, he would slip across the thoroughfare and disappear into an alleyway beyond.

In a few minutes he came close to a building that was famous in Chinatown's history. This was a simple three-story, brownstone edifice with a peaked roof. Once it had been a white man's residence. Now ornate bronze dragons graced its four corners. On its front, high above the street, was the insignia of the Ming Tong, powerful Chinese secret society whose influence stretched into every city in the land where Orientals gathered.

In the past, bloody tong battles had raged close to this building. Tides of death had swept around its base when hatchetmen and slant-eyed sharpshooters fought for supremacy. Then peace had come to Chinatown. The tongmen had arrived at secret pacts and agreements. The Ming Tong was now ruled over by the benevolent and aged Lo Mong Yung, father of the Mingmen.

IN the mouth of an alley across from this building the tall Manchu paused. He would have to cross one more street to reach the door of tong headquarters, and two federal men were on patrol there. They were ready to nab and question any members who might come. In the minds of the white men tonight the tong was linked up with sinister narcotic activities. In spite of the wisdom, strength and kindliness of old Lo Mong Yung, they felt that Ming

The stranger gave a wild, blood-curdling shout and leaped madly forward.

headquarters might be the clearing house of the dreaded drug.

The tall Manchu understood this. His eyes glittered. He waited, watching, debating, as ten minutes passed. The Manchu's patience seemed inexhaustible. He appeared able to make of himself a living statue.

A half hour went by. Then, at the end of it, he was rewarded. For something down the block attracted the attention of the federal men. This was a truckload of rice, spices and bamboo shoots arriving at the side door of a harmless old merchant's shop. The federal men suspected apparently the consignment might contain hidden dope.

Seizing his opportunity, the tall Manchu crossed the street as quickly as he had the others. He slipped through the doorway of

Ming headquarters so deftly that he seemed only a breath of the night fog entering.

Yet a voice instantly sounded close to his ear. A flashlight clicked on, and the hard snout of an automatic was pressed against the Manchu's side.

He didn't cry out or jump as a white man might have been expected to do. He stood straight and taut, staring into the lens of the flash, waiting, unawed it seemed by the presence of the gun.

"Where are you headed, fellah? What's your name and what's your business?" The words came from the lips of Detective Bartholdy, veteran sleuth of the city narcotic squad; a man who had spent twenty years of his life hunting dope, and a man who trusted no Chinaman.

The tall Manchu caught a glimpse of Bartholdy's face. Suspicion gleamed in the detective's narrowed eyes. Bartholdy was set for trouble. He had been lurking here to nab just such a visitor. He would never let this man enter the tong without exhaustive inquiries. Valuable minutes had already passed. The tall Manchu in the black suit, notwithstanding his outward calm, was in a hurry.

He addressed the detective in excellent English, but in the slightly nasal, singsong accents of his race. "My name is Ho Ling," he said. "I go about my private business, and that business is harmful to no one."

The detective only pressed the gun tighter. "Yeah? And how do I know that? I don't remember seeing you around here before. I've got a pretty good memory for faces."

"It is not likely, white man, that you would remember the faces of all the five thousand members of my race who inhabit this quarter."

"Don't try to high-hat me, fellah! Show me some identification."

The tall Manchu nodded gravely. He held out a slender but powerful hand with pointed fingertips and nails that were carefully manicured, "This ring," he said. "Perhaps you have seen one like it before. It is the symbol of my tong. I am not a Mingman. I am here in the stronghold of the Mingmen, however, on a peaceful mission."

On the Manchu's third finger gleamed a ring of immense proportions and singular design. A dragon's head of rose onyx was held in a wrought gold setting. Two tiny emeralds sparkled in the dragon's eyes. Its nostrils flared open.

BARTHOLDY grunted and leaned forward, moving his flash so that the rays fell on the strange ring. His intent face was not more than a foot above the ring which the Manchu held high.

"I never remember seeing a ring like that before," Bartholdy said. "I guess—"

He didn't finish the sentence. For the Manchu's long and powerful hand moved imperceptibly. The third finger, as though it had a life all its own, twitched upward ever so slightly. As it did so the tiny, hideous jaws of the onyx dragon opened wide. From them shot a jet of strange, pungent vapor. Straight into Bartholdy's open mouth and nostrils it went.

The cry that rose to his lips was stilled. The Manchu's other hand, working in lightninglike conjunction with the one that bore the ring, wrenched the gun from Bartholdy's fingers before he could pull the trigger.

Bartholdy, gasping and trying to retain his faculties, endeavored to keep a grip on the wall behind him. He could not. Slowly and still soundlessly his body sagged. His knees gave way under him. He sank to the floor and lay inertly; not dead, but knocked out for many minutes by the concentrated essence of a powerful anaesthetic vapor he had inhaled.

The Manchu's expression had not changed. His eyes still gleamed. His yellow face was impassive. Before moving from where he stood he caught hold of the head of the dragon ring, gave it a dexterous twist and snapped it open. The hollowed out onyx, which was merely a thin shell, disclosed a small metal cylinder. The Manchu took this out, dropped it in his pocket. It was empty now. It had done its work. He replaced it with a fresh one, snapped the onyx dragon's head down again.

Then he glanced down at Bartholdy's inert form. It could not stay there. In a moment the two federal men would be back. They might look in the doorway of Ming headquarters and see it.

The Manchu's keen eyes saw a door opening toward the left. He turned the knob, stuck his head inside, and saw that here was a classroom maintained by the Ming Tong and used in the daytime to teach Chinese merchants American business tactics.

In a moment he had transferred the unconscious Detective Bartholdy to this chamber. He left the detective propped solemnly before a desk. Then he moved silently up a long flight of stairs to the building's second floor. He walked down a short corridor and stopped suddenly again, as a voice challenged him for the second time that night.

This was no white detective or federal agent. It was a tall, stern-faced Chinaman, clad in a silk robe with flowing sleeves. His yellow arms were crossed and his hands stuffed in those sleeves.

"Who are you, stranger, and what is your business that you come to the headquarters of the Ming Tong at this time of night?" The Chinaman with the folded arms spoke in Cantonese.

The tall Manchu gave answer fluently, in the same language, as though all dialects were familiar to him.

"Sung, courageous guardian of the portals of this most honorable tong, I come in peace. I would have talk with Lo Mong Yung, venerable father of the Mingmen. Tell him that one by the name of Ho Ling wishes to see him."

The robed Chinaman shook his head sternly. "You appear to know me and call me by name, but I have never seen you before. There are fears and evil whispers abroad tonight. Caution has been impressed upon me by my master."

The Manchu eyed the other calmly. He knew that in those flowing sleeves, clenched in the snaky yellow fingers, were twin automatics capable of mowing him down in a second. He knew that the Chinaman, Sung, had been selected for this post because he had nerves of steel, the brain of a fox, and could shoot with the uncanny accuracy of a born marksman. He nodded and reached into his own coat pocket.

"It is about these fears and whispers that I come," he said.

The other's body stiffened; But instead of a gun the tall Manchu brought a card from his pocket.

"Give the venerable Lo Mong Yung this," he said.

The other looked at it, snorted. "It is blank," he said. "It has no writing on it. What foolishness is this?"

"Give it to him," replied the man who called himself Ho Ling, "Save your questioning till afterwards." There was a strange note of authority in his voice now, and something in his eye that seemed to command the other's respect.

"I will do as you say," the guard said. "But remain here. If you attempt to enter the chamber of Yung before he has given the word, your life will be upon your own conscience."

Deftly removing one of the automatics hidden in his sleeve, to give the impression that he was unarmed. Sung took the blank card and walked through a doorway. He returned a minute later, and stared at the visitor, Ho Ling, with new respect and a little awe.

"You may enter," he said, "Lo Mong Yung, the honored and revered father of our tong, will see you."

THE Manchu passed through the doorway that Sung indicated, swept a curtain aside and found himself in a room that was like an ordinary American business office.

At a glass-topped desk an aged Chinaman sat. His face was withered, parchmentlike. His hands were mere fragile wisps of bone and loose skin; yet his eyes were piercingly bright. He glanced at his visitor, glanced down at a white card lying on his desk, and in those bright eyes was a look of perplexity.

The card, which a moment before when Sung had carried it in had been blank, now showed a black "X," startlingly revealed on its white surface. Under the rays of the light overhead this "X" had come out.

The old Chinaman's voice sounded in the room. It was low, thin as tinkling glass, hardly more than a whisper, but it carried the weight of wisdom and authority.

"I do not understand, O stranger. You come bearing the card of a white man—the only white man ever to be taken into our tong and made a brother of the Mingmen. Yet you are not he. You are a Manchu, and one unknown to me who have seen many men."

The tall Manchu bowed. "O father of the Ming Tong, accept greetings from that white man of whom you speak—and know that I am he, now brother of the Mingmen."

For seconds the eyes of the two men clashed. The ancient Chinaman shook his head.

"The white man I speak of has surprised me with his deeds before. He is a brother of strange ways and remarkable talents. Yet he once did the Ming Tong a great service, and his actions are always based on the good things whereby men live well and honestly. If you are really he, step close and speak in my ear that word known only to the brothers of my tong."

The tall Manchu did so. What he whispered was spoken so softly that it did not carry beyond the desk. Yet it satisfied Lo Mong Yung.

"Now I know," he said, "that whispers I have heard are true. You are he whom they call the 'Man of a Thousand Faces.' You are one who fights the dragon of evil. You are—"

The visitor lifted his hand. "Do not speak it, O venerable father! For even here there may be inquisitive ears. Let it be enough that I am a Mingman come to ask words of wisdom from one who has known many years of well-spent life."

The old Chinaman nodded slowly. "Proceed, O brother," he said. "If the withered brain of this unworthy servant may humbly aid one of illustrious deeds; the honor blesses the revered fathers of my ancient family."

The white man in the guise of a Manchu bowed. It seemed utterly incredible that his Mongolian features, slanted eyes and yellow complexion were all parts of a masterly disguise. Yet this was so, for Lo Mong Yung's visitor was the strange, relentless criminal investigator known as Secret Agent "X," a man so secretive and mysterious that no living soul had ever knowingly seen him unmasked.

IF it were rumored that "X" was in the building, a cordon of police would be thrown around it at once. Machine guns would be trained on the Ming Tong headquarters, the rooms would be bombarded with tear gas. "X" would have to pause in his investigation to save himself. For the Secret Agent, friend of the law in fact, was misunderstood.

Many times he had been accused of crimes that he was trying in reality to prevent. Many times the guardians of the law had looked upon him as a ruthless, dangerous enemy of society, not knowing that he fought always *for* society, against the rabid hordes of the underworld of crime.[31]

He was beginning one of his amazing campaigns now. He was about to fight something that threatened to spread over the whole nation like a relentless, sinister blight. He addressed Lo Mong Yung gravely, still using the flowery language of the East.

"Respected master, an evil visitation has come upon us—something as destructive to men as locusts are to a field of young rice. Unless this monster is strangled before it grows too large; unless the country is freed from its evil spell, no man can predict what may happen. There will be a famine of happiness surely, a collapse of human hopes—perhaps utter ruin. I speak, O venerable father, of the drug evil."

His slender, fragile hands thrust in the great sleeves of his gold-worked, richly embroidered mandarin coat, Lo Mong Yung sat as motionless and inscrutable as the figure of Buddha, wreathed with incense, that squatted in a niche on the opposite wall. Yet the eyes of the aged Chinaman were like fiery coals gleaming from the yellow face of a waxen idol.

"I have heard the story," he spoke at last in his thin voice. "The evil has permeated the privileged class. The wealthy have succumbed to the pitiless power of drugs. Their bodies writhe for the soothing potency. Their children cry to have their crawling nerves quieted. A dreadful narcotic is making maniacs and criminals of people who were as wealthy and respected as mandarins."

Secret Agent "X" nodded. "But these children of misfortune have not sought this degradation. It has seeped into their veins, enslaved them unawares. I have discovered, wise father, through the science of my laboratory, that many brands of expensive cigarettes, candies, even lipsticks, have been treated with a powerful narcotic

---

31 *AUTHOR'S NOTE: A secret pledge to a high government official in Washington D. C. was made at the outset of Agent "X's" strange career. He dedicated his life to the combatting of crime in its most hideous forms. His brilliant and original work as an intelligence agent during the World War, including his extraordinary talent for disguise, made the government select him for one of the most dangerous and strange tasks in existence.*

that has worked subtle power over these victims.

"It is a wily method, a masterly stroke of distorted genius on the part of someone to gain addicts for this insidious drug. Yet no money has been demanded so far as I can find out. The drug is being administered free. This is one thing that makes the law helpless. And it makes the mystery of it all as black as a forest of ebony."

The Agent made a sudden gesture of apology.

"I am presuming upon your tolerance," he said. "I tax your ears perhaps with what you already know. But let me picture briefly how this thing is being spread."

Lo Mong Yung motioned with one withered hand for the Agent to continue.

"A wealthy man may drop in at his club," said "X." "He may refresh himself at the cocktail hour, not knowing that his liquor is adulterated with this strange drug. He thinks the exhilaration he feels comes from alcohol alone. Even the club manager and the regular attendants have no knowledge of the evil force at work.

"But in a week, two at most, our clubman has become an addict. He is no longer human. He is a fiend with a craving that destroys his integrity, an appetite that will make him lie, slander, sell out his partners, even kill, to get more of this thing that has enslaved him. Yet no one knows who is giving this drug out, or why it is being done."

Lo Mong Yung threw out his hands, palms upward.

"It is deplorable," he said. "But why do you confer with my profound ignorance? How may the sum of my blundering experience help you against this blight?"

"Learned father," said the Secret Agent slowly, "is it possible that the poison of some strange plot has eaten into the hearts of our Mingmen? The tong is powerful. It has ways of reaching all levels of society. I ask you therefore, as the honorable head of the Mings, to speak if you have any suspicion of our brothers."

LO MONG YUNG'S expression did not change. He did not show anger. It was not in his philosophy to let the fires of rage destroy the wisdom of his venerable years. His was the power of a placid man.

"Truly, my son," he said quietly, "the burnt child is wary of the fire. And the man who has reached the mandarin's palace does not seek the coolie's hut. The insidious poppy once ravaged our people like a leprosy. We have been the burnt child. But we have smothered the velvet fumes of the opium pipe, have broken the needle of the hypodermic. No longer do Mingmen court the devil dust of morphine that mocks them with visions of lotus blossoms while it shrivels their souls and shrinks them, body and mind. We have left the coolie's hut of poverty. We have sipped the nectar of prosperity. No, O son, the weight of my years be upon my words! No Mingman is guilty of this evil."

The Agent bowed low, and his gesture of humility was sincere.

"Forgive me, most venerable sage," he said, "and accept my deepest thanks for the manner in which you have answered my question. Know, too, that I am happy in the assurance that the brothers of our Ming Tong are innocent of any traffic with this evil. And now I would draw upon your wisdom a little longer. Have you, O father, given any thought as to what man, or group of men, may be behind this strange thing?"

Before he answered "X's" latest question, the venerable father of the Ming Tong arose and crossed the room that was like any business office except that ancient Eastern art mingled with modern Western efficiency. Built into the back wall was a large filing cabinet.

On it stood an enameled bronze incense burner of the Ming Period. Across the paneled wall stretched a scroll of flowers and birds, which "X" knew to be the work of Pien Lan, an artist of the Tang Dynasty, who lived in the eighth century. There were specimens of Chinese craftsmanship; carvings of teakwood, jade, rose quartz and ivory. On the glass-topped desk lay a cinnabar box of delicate design, and chrysanthemums filled a glazed flower vase of the Ching Dynasty.

Lo Mong Yung lighted a coiled joss-stick and placed it before the idol of Buddha, then he seated himself again and spoke in the solemn tones of some Eastern oracle.

"My son, long before the bluecoats swarmed the streets and caused our people to bolt the doors and draw the blinds, I knew that our noble order was suspected. I have sent out many of our brothers to try and pierce the mystery. But we have learned little. It may be that the dragon of a foreign power is breathing fire on America—seeking to weaken the nation for invasion."

The eyes of Agent "X" gleamed as Lo Mong Yung said this. He crouched forward toward the ancient Chinaman with something of the look of a questing hawk about his face and posture.

"That thought has troubled me," he said softly. "If a hostile country is fostering this dread thing, then the leaders must be caught before guns roar and men are mobilized for wholesale slaughter. But possibly a madman, jaded by riches and jaundiced against the goodness of the world employs this treachery to feed his hatred and cultivate his wickedness."

"The suggestion has the color of logic," replied Lo Mong Yung. "Whether it carries the substance of truth, I do not know. I can speak only in feeble conjectures. But I do know of one powerful white drug ring that is like a volcano, rumbling in its depths and boiling with the threat of devastating eruption. We have learned that this ring is combing the underworld for gunmen—for the vicious gray rats and snarling jackals who slew during the prohibition era. Maybe it is behind this blight for some reason we do not know, and maybe it is marshaling forces to fight a competition that threatens its ruin."

The Secret Agent pressed his fingertips together till the nails showed white. His eyes seemed to carry leaping points of fire in their depths.

"O father," he said quickly, "you may have given the lead that will direct me to the heart of this trouble. Tell me where these men gather to plot their wickedness."

Before Lo Mong Yung could answer something disturbed the quiet of the room. The shrilling note of a police whistle pierced the tense stillness of Chinatown. Then a harsh Western voice roared out orders that brought a look of distress to the ancient Chinaman's face. A gun cracked sharply, and somewhere a window crashed shut.

From a lower floor arose a shrill chatter in Canton dialect. Then came a ripping, splitting racket that was almost deafening. Axes were splintering the front doors. The headquarters of the Ming Tong was being raided.

CHAPTER II

UNDER FIRE

IN A MOMENT there was a bang as the door was flung back. Heavy footsteps thumped in the lower hallway. The guard, Sung, began protesting in pidgin English.

Agent "X" heard a snarled oath, then the crack of a fist against flesh and bone. Sung's outburst was cut short. Immediately there was the pounding of steps on the stairs.

The Agent slipped his hand in his pocket and brought out a gun. Lo Mong Yung put a restraining hand on "X's" arm, and shook his head. He did not know that the weapon discharged only gas pellets, which aided the Agent in his captures and escapes, but which did no harm other than render the victim unconscious for a short time.[32]

"One killing in the house of the Ming Tong," said Lo Mong Yung, "and I would join my ancestors knowing that our society would be forever blackened in the eyes of the law. I speak now as the father of the Mingmen. Come!"

It was a command, and the Secret Agent bowed to it, following the fragile Chinaman across the room. Already the police had reached the floor, and were pounding at the door.

The Agent thought he would have to fight, for there appeared to be only the one exit, and the law was swarming in the corridor. But Lo Mong Yung slid his slender hand like a caress over the scroll of Pien Lan, and a long-nailed finger touched the bill of a humming-

---

[32] *AUTHOR'S NOTE: Despite the danger that is constantly his lot, and the many attempts made on his life, Agent "X" seldom if ever kills. He leaves such crude methods to operatives of less intelligence and experience. Then too, a killing would mean a murder charge lodged against him, and while he has the secret sanction of one of the highest Washington officials, public sanction is denied him. This is so because of the secrecy and daring unconventionality of his work.*

bird drawn during the Tang Dynasty, when even Europe was a land of barbarians.

Instantly the filing cabinet moved forward, revealing an aperture through which a man could squeeze. "X" needed no prompting. He was through the opening in a second, and the cabinet was rolling back, leaving him in a vaultlike room lighted by an oil lamp. The room seemed sealed, except for a secret entrance, but the air was fresh, so there was some other means of ventilation and probably another exit.

The Agent was amazed how clearly sounds came from the other room. He carried a small, portable amplifier, but he didn't need it now, for the vault was equipped with a microphone connected with the office. The members of the narcotic squad were in the room. "X" pictured Lo Mong Yung greeting them with the sedate, unruffled graciousness of a philosopher. Lo Mong Yung's voice reached his ears now.

"A violent entrance and a furrowed brow imply an interest which a doddering old heathen like myself does not merit," he said in faultless English and with gentle irony.

A quick retort came.

"Listen, you slant-eyed old fossil! I'm Inspector Bower of the Narcotic Division. We got a tip-off that you had a Chink dope runner cached in here. Bring him out or we'll tear this dump down and sell it for kindling wood."

"Your request fills me with regret," said Lo Mong Yung. "You ask me to perform a task not in my humble capacity to achieve. Had I the power of Confucius I could not lessen my unworthiness by bringing forth the dope runner in question, for he does not exist except in the fertile realm of your excellent imagination. If you will honor me, however, by accepting a glass of Tiger Bone wine, or a choice draft of Gop Goy in which a lizard has taken ten years to dissolve, I will feel that I have made partial atonement. Or, if liquor while on duty is forbidden, perhaps I can tempt you with cockroaches in honey, a delicacy that caused the Emperor Shih-tsu to neglect the affairs of state."

The Agent heard a snarl of laughter.

"That's tellin' him, Lichee Nut!" a squad member said. "The old duffer has you tied in a package and ready for delivery, Bower."

"Search this room!" bellowed the voice of Inspector Bower. "This isn't a tent show. Tap the walls, and if you hear a hollow sound, use the ax. Look in those jugs, too. You never can tell where these slobs may hide dope."

CRASH. Agent "X" stifled the anger he felt as one of Lo Mong Yung's rare vases was knocked to the floor and smashed to bits. He heard the voice of the aged Chinaman rise calmly, "You do injustice to my feeble attempts to honor this visit. You humiliate me by breaking the lesser of my art pieces. That is only a poor offering of the great Chu Tse-min, who went to rest in the dragon's horn during the Yuan Dynasty."

Listening at the microphone, "X" realized from Inspector Bower's mumblings that the Chinaman had taken the wind out of the squad man's sails.

A bulldog sort like Bower wasn't the kind to volunteer an honest apology, but shortly afterward, certain that Lo Mong Yung was alone, he did hustle his men out of the office, leaving Lo Mong Yung to contemplate the ruin of his ancient vase.

Presently the Chinaman touched Pien Lan's scroll again. The filing cabinet rolled forward, and Secret Agent "X" stepped into the room.

"The bull has invaded the China shop, my son," spoke Lo Mong Yung calmly. "But the scattered fragments of Chu Tse-min's vase make me rejoice to think that we still are here to gaze upon them. I believe the honorable official is convinced that I had no strange visitor, that all I entertained were the sad memories of a life misspent in folly and indiscretion."

"I am forever in your debt, O father," said Secret Agent "X," "and I am sorry that I am the cause of this invasion of your sanctuary. But now I must say farewell and bid you long years of full rice bowls and warm coverings."

Lo Mong Yung looked startled for the first time.

"You will stay surely!" he said. "In these poor quarters you have refuge at least. Outside you will be a hunted creature, doomed to become a prey in the ravening clutches of the law."

Agent "X" knew that Lo Mong Yung didn't exaggerate the danger. But he knew, too, that no matter how long he waited in Ming Tong headquarters the police would not be recalled from Chinatown as long as Police Commissioner Foster was shouting for results. Meanwhile the drug evil was spreading. The duty of the Agent was plain. He must find out about this dope ring that was recruiting cannon, and see whether it was behind the mysterious spread of this sinister narcotic.

When Lo Mong Yung understood that "X's" mind was made up, he stopped his protests and gave "X" the address of an underworld

From the hideous jaws of the onyx dragon shot a jet of pungent vapor.

dive and instructions that would enable him to reach the inner circle of the drug ring.

Armed with information that gave him something to work on, "X" left the office of the Ming Tong. The corridor was clear, but he could hear footsteps on the floor below. There was no chance of getting out of the building by the front entrance, and cops were probably at the back door.

At the end of the hallway was a small window. The Agent moved stealthily toward it. He shoved up on the frame. Moisture or paint made the window stick, but suddenly his efforts caused it to fly up with a bang. The noise wasn't loud, but it was thunderous to "X" who wanted to go in silence.

Some one shouted. Others took up the call of alarm. A man ran up the stairs, reaching the landing below as the Agent was going through the window. It was one of Bower's men.

The detective's automatic roared, and the report echoed thunderously through the house. The bullet dug into the sill, but the Agent had catapulted through the window onto the slanting, corrugated terra-cotta roof of a Chinese restaurant designed after the pattern of an Oriental temple.

He intended climbing over this to the flat roof of a Chinese hotel. But halfway up the slanting side he was spotted. Sub-machine guns were trained on him. Inspector Bower shouted for him to give up. The squad chief warned the Agent just once, then barked an order for his men to fire.

The cops began shattering the terra-cotta on each side of "X." It meant suicide to buck such odds. The Agent stopped climbing and slid, down to the eaves of the roof. Through the fog-laden darkness from the street, it appeared that he had been hit. His legs were hanging over the side. It seemed that his belt buckle, caught in the gutter, kept him from falling to the ground.

"We got him," said the inspector harshly. "Keep him covered and climb out there. See what's happened to him. But watch out. We don't know whether he's dead or trying to pull a fast one."

AGENT "X" did intend to pull a fast one, but it had to be exceedingly fast—or fail entirely. He couldn't afford the slightest misplay. Bower had sent two men out on the roof and cops were milling in the street. Others had been sent into the Chinese hotel.

A narrow alleyway separated the tong headquarters from this, but the drop would break every bone in the Agent's body. He was covered from the street and not more than four feet away, a detective had a gun on him.

Before Agent "X" had leaped from the Ming Tong house, however, his photographic brain had recorded that under the eaves right below him was an opened window to the third story of the restaurant. That window figured in his daring plan. But he hung limply until the detective with the gun sprang across to him.

The dick got a footing in the rainwater gutter and a hand-hold on a half-circle of terra-cotta roofing. Agent "X" caught a glimpse of his face. It was Bartholdy, the man he had temporarily knocked out. The detective spoke savagely now.

"Hell! There's that dragon-head ring that crocked me cold as a cod. But you won't trick me again, Chink, not by a damn sight!"

"X" heard Bartholdy suck in a deep breath. The plainclothes cop didn't intend to inhale any more sleep-producing gas tonight. But, to get the ring and prevent the supposed Chinaman from falling at the same time, the detective had to drop his automatic in his pocket.

This he did, still holding his breath. Then he grabbed the Agent by the back of the coat and began slipping the large gold-wrought, rose onyx ring from "X's" finger.

Bartholdy wasn't aware that his prisoner, whom he thought dead or unconscious, held a gun in his right hand which was wedged in the gutter under his body. The swirling, dank fog helped the Agent.

He waited until Bartholdy had removed the ring and exhaled. Then "X" himself took a deep breath and held it. The next instant he whipped his gas gun out and fired at close range. Bartholdy caught the full effect of the anesthetic vapor as he inhaled.

He uttered a faint sigh like a tired man and collapsed. His foot, jammed in the gutter, prevented him from going over the side. The Agent muscled up beside the unconscious detective. Death was close at his elbow. He must hurry if he expected to get away at all. But he wouldn't leave Detective Bartoldy without first making certain that the man wouldn't fall. He insured against this by thrusting the detective's hands and arms under two half-circles of terra cotta. Bartholdy was safe now, far safer than Agent "X."

Men were bounding up the stairs of the Ming House. Bower shouted to Bartholdy and, getting no answer, began giving orders like a general planning an attack.

Agent "X" lowered himself quickly until he was hanging below the eaves, many feet above the street, like a man suspended above the brink of doom. In spite of the curtain of fog the sharp eyes of Bower spotted him.

"He's getting away! Powell—Lorimer—get the lead out of your feet and nab that Chink!"

Because of the danger of hitting Detective Bartholdy, Bower had the good sense not to order another burst of sub-machine gun fire. This was what "X" had counted on. He swung to the window ledge and was through the opening as Detectives Powell and Lorimer rushed to the window in the Ming house. They shouted commands for him to halt, threatened to drop him, but "X" ducked out of sight and ran into a room filled with frightened Chinese.

None of the Orientals tried to stop him. They saw him as a Manchu, a Mingman, and a brother. He opened a door. Three plainclothes men and two uniformed cops had reached the head of the stairs. They hadn't seen him before and weren't sure of his identity. Their hesitation gave "X" a chance to slam the door shut and lock it. Instantly there was an uproar on the other side, pounding on the panels, then the crash and splinter of wood as the officers rammed shoulders against the door.

A Chinaman directed "X" to another exit with a slight shift of his glance. The Agent streaked across the room and was through the door. He raced down three flights to the kitchen and got out the back way before the Chinese cooks recovered from their startled surprise.

He plunged down a twisting alley, vaulted a fence, and sped along the narrow space between two brick buildings, entering the first back door he reached. Here he found himself in a second-hand clothing store. The proprietor jumped up, uttering a startled yell. He made a grab for a phone, thinking evidently that "X" was a holdup man. The Agent gave him a quick shove into a pile of old suits and streaked past him.

HE reached the street door and paused suddenly. For a moment his wild exertions over the past few minutes told upon him. An old wound in his side, received on a battlefield in France, and curiously enough drawn into a scar that was shaped like a crude "X," gave him a twinge of pain. Surgeons at the time that wound had been made by a piece of whizzing shrapnel had predicted that he could not live. But the Agent's amazing vitality and unconquerable will had won out. The X-shaped scar seemed symbolic of the qualities that made Secret Agent "X" a fighter who refused ever to quit.

He straightened now. Then strode calmly out into a street that during the daytime was a main business artery. Behind him lay Chinatown, swarming now with cops and detectives, searching through the chill fog for a mysterious Manchu.

Because there was still a slight chance that someone was on his trail, Agent "X" took a devious route to his mid-town hideout, an apartment furnished with equipment and clothes for his numerous disguises.[33]

He rode a subway to an express stop, walked two blocks crosstown to an elevated, and rode the local a few stations downtown. After that he changed taxis three times, and finally paid off a cab driver a block from his apartment.

Once in his hideout, he went to work swiftly to create a new disguise. He removed the black mohair suit that had fitted the role of a dignified Manchu tongman. In his undershirt and shorts Agent "X" showed a lean, supple, muscular body that had the condition and reflexes of a champion pugilist's.

Quickly he stripped off the makeup which had given him the appearance of an Oriental. Beneath it was a remarkable face that not even his few intimate associates had ever knowingly seen. Strong, distinguished features full of power and character were there. The slightly curving line of the nose marked hawklike stamina. The piercing, brilliant eyes were clear lenses that transferred sharply defined pictures to a highly geared brain mechanism.

Not only was the identity of this man marked with mystery, but there was mystery even in these features. For different lights changed them almost as effectively as did his disguises. Looked at from the front they seemed remarkably youthful. But light falling on them from an oblique angle brought out the maturity of one who had been through a thousand strange and harrowing adventures. Sometimes in overhead rays Agent "X" seemed to have the long sensitive face of a scholar. With light coming up from below, his broad, fighting chin was most prominent.

With dexterous, experienced fingers Agent "X" worked plastic, volatile make-up material over his face, covering the skin first with ingenious flesh-colored pigments. He got up from his triple-sided mirrors after a few minutes and put on a salt-and-pepper cheviot of shrieking design, such as one would expect a race-track tout to wear.

He added patent-leather shoes and spats, and tipped a dove-gray hat on his head so that the rim came just to the hair-line. Over his head he slipped an ingeniously made toupee fashioned in a sporty

---

33 AUTHOR'S NOTE: *Part of the Secret Agent's strength as an investigator of crimes lies in his ability to make quick and complete changes of disguise. For this reason he has used part of his fund in the First National Bank to establish hideouts in many parts of the city, and even in many cities throughout the country. It may be remembered that his Washington hideout served him well when he was combatting the half-breed terrorist in the crime chronicle called "The Ambassador of Doom."*

sailor's haircut, with the back of the neck shaved up to where the thick hair bulged out.

When he walked from his hideout the "Man of a Thousand Faces" had achieved a new character. He was now "Spats" McGurn, professional mobster and gunman, eager to quote homicide rates to the highest bidder.

At a casual glance he didn't look tough. He had slightly thickened one ear and broadened the bridge of his nose to suggest that he had served an apprenticeship in the prize ring.

THE Agent knew his characterization would be more effective if he didn't give himself too tough an appearance. He looked like a person who spent his time in dance halls and pool rooms, one who prided himself on being a classy dresser. But "X" had changed the line of his mouth to suggest cruelty. He had molded his features so that he could if he chose register intense viciousness.

Taking a taxi to the slum districts of the city he got off at a section that did its share in keeping the state penitentiary populated. The Agent's destination was the address given him by Lo Mong Yung. This was a pool room on London Avenue called the "Big Kid's," known to the police as a hangout of small-time gamblers, petty racketeers, sneak-thieves, and loafers who were studying to be criminals. What the police didn't know was that below the pool room, a dope ring was organizing and plotting activities.

The Big Kid's had a small bar, thirty pool and billiard tables, slot machines against the walls, and back rooms for card games where suckers could be cold-decked. The air was blue with tobacco smoke, loud with the click of pool balls and the profane talk of the players.

"X" spotted the proprietor, Dan Sabelli, whose three hundred pounds of quivering blubber deserved the name "big," but who was forty years from being a "kid."

He was a sweating, bleary-eyed, wheezing man, who controlled enough votes to swing the district to his advantage. His pouchy, flabby-jowled, veined face was familiar to police line-ups. He had been indicted sixteen times for crimes ranging from petty larceny to homicide, but had never been convicted. The Agent had business with him, but he took his time.

He looked over the pool players for a while, took part in a couple of games, then deliberately picked a quarrel with a thick-necked giant of a man. "X," as Spats McGurn, insulted the giant, provoked a fist fight and neatly knocked him out with a tricky left and two well-placed rights.

Dan Sabelli, the Big Kid, lumbered over at once, wheezing, puffing, and growling orders to attendants to get the senseless man into a back room quickly. He stepped up to Agent "X" angrily.

"Listen, guy! If you're feelin' tough tonight scram out 'o here! Do you want to have the cops droppin' in and botherin' the boys? That ain't no way to help business! Start lammin' if you know what's good fer yer."

"Sorry, Dan," the Agent apologized. "A mug insulted me and I had to let him have it. He was askin' for it. They can't get tough with Spats McGurn, see? An' before I leave this lousy joint I got some business to transact. You're makin' a book, ain't you? And while I'm here I'm gonna slap on a few bets fer tomorrow's races. The ponies always act right when I'm wearing these rags."

He took the Big Kid by one blubbery arm and led him away from the others. His voice sank to a hoarse whisper.

"I like Iron Man in the fifth at New Orleans tomorrow," he said.

The Big Kid gave a start and studied the Agent with a piercing gaze. "X's" last comment had been the countersign which would admit him to the inner circle of the dope ring. It had been included in the instructions given him by Lo Mong Yung.

"All right, fella," said the Big Kid. "I get you. Take that back door on the right. Go into the fourth room on the left. Wait there."

"X" nodded casually. He lighted a cigarette, sauntered to the rear of the pool hall and wandered down the corridor to the designated room. It seemed to be an ordinary card room, garnished with a round table and a half dozen chairs. On the walls were photos of vaudeville queens and pugilists.

BUT the moment the Agent was inside, the door closed, and there was an ominous click. He did not need to turn the knob. He knew he was locked in.

His eyes glowed more brightly, but his features did not change. He puffed on his cigarette and seated himself at the table. An old pack of cards lay scattered on the circle of green felt; "X" gathered them in, shuffled them, and started a game of solitaire. He was certain he was under close surveillance.

On the back wall was secured a large full-length picture of John L. Sullivan. Suddenly some one spoke and "X" whirled. The voice came from the lips of Sullivan's picture, and those lips moved. Also the eyes were gleaming at him, and they were alive. The Agent saw then that the eyes and mouth of the picture had been cut out. Yet they had been in place when he entered. Possibly they worked on hinges. Now some one was behind the picture, studying him and speaking.

"Who got you interested in Iron Man?" demanded the voice behind John L. Sullivan's picture.

The Agent answered quickly. "Hoppy Joe said I could pick up some nice change if I had the right dope," he said.

The hidden questioner remained silent for a second, apparently deliberating. Hoppy Joe was a Mingman, one of the spies detailed by Lo Mong Yung to ferret out the secret of the dope blight that caused suspicion to be thrown upon the tong. The Chinaman had worked his way into a membership in this drug ring. That was how Lo Mong Yung knew the counter-sign which he passed on to the Agent. There was a chance of difficulties, however, for Hoppy Joe, instead of being a narcotic victim, was in reality a scholarly young Chinese named Shen-nang Ti.

The Agent waited tensely for the man behind the picture to speak. Suppose the Chinaman's identity had been discovered? What if it had been learned that Shen-nang Ti was a spy?

No trace of out-of-character emotion showed in his face, or gestures, however. The hidden man was studying him intently. The Agent was careful to maintain his attitude of insolent confidence as the gangster, Spats McGurn. The cigarette hung loosely from his lip. He raised one eyebrow impudently. Finally the unseen man demanded his name and details of his career.

"Pete McGurn," said "X" at once. "They call me Spats out West. Chi's my home town, but I rode the rails out when the goin' got bad. Down along the Mex border I got to be quite a handy man. Ran snow, coke, a little poppy paste and some heroin. Never bothered with marahuana. That's greaser stuff and not for smart guys like me. I played all the spots from Laredo to Nogales, till the Border got too hot for me. I came North with a nice stake, but blew it on a dame. That's why I want to go to work."

"It listens good," said the hidden man. "Knowing Hoppy Joe shows you got the right connections, and the way you popped that punk out there wasn't bad. But we ain't much on knuckle stuff here. We leave that fer the kids. Can you use a rod?"

Agent "X" snorted and flicked ashes from his cigarette scornfully. "Listen, mister," he said. "Along the Border they do some fancy shootin', an' they call hittin' a silver dollar two out of five at fifteen feet pretty good. Four out of five was my average."

"Yeah! Well, you'll get plenty of target practice on this job, fella. But it won't be silver dollars you'll shoot at, see? Maybe you'll do, Spats, and maybe you won't. If you want the job you can have it. We'll give you a chance to make good. An' any time you want to quit the racket you can do it—via the morgue!"

The Agent heard a scraping sound behind him. A strip of the floor near the far wall was rising. It continued until it almost touched the ceiling. On a level with the rest of the floor was the platform of an elevator. "X" was instructed to stand on this. He did so, and the platform began to sink quickly.

ON the next level, "X" stepped into a cellar room lighted by a small yellow globe. The jaundiced light gave a ghastliness to the pinched face of the rat-mouthed, shifty-eyed little man who greeted the Agent in a high-pitched nasal voice. The twitching muscles and jerking movements proclaimed the hophead.

The guide took "X" down a long flight of stone steps into a winding passageway. Though they were underground, the air lacked dankness of an earthy odor. That was because the walls were of concrete. Somewhere down here, the Agent believed, were dry vaults where narcotics were stored. He wondered if this was the fountainhead from which free drugs poured forth on the country in a deadly, sinister flood.

At the end of the passage, the guide pressed a button that opened a door covered with bullet-proof sheet-iron. Ushered into a brilliantly lighted room, "X" viewed at least a score of men lounging in easy chairs, playing cards or billiards, or reading. The place could have been the clubroom of wealthy men, except for the amazing variety of types.

Pallor and nervousness marked the younger men as drug addicts. Some of the older ones, if they were victims of the habit, showed no evidence that narcotics ravaged their systems. A few of the oldest were of distinguished appearance, and the Agent's impression was that they possessed more than front. Likely they were medical men, outlawed for illegal practices, who handled the details which required professional knowledge.

"This guy is Spats McGurn," the guide introduced "X" to the crowd. "McGurn, make yourself at home. Plenty of reading material around. If you feel hungry, the cook will fix you a snack. Bunks are in the room on your left. Nothing to do but loaf now."

"X" sensed that he was the focal point of frank distrust. In this place, a stranger was under suspicion until he proved himself a member of the underworld by some criminal action. The Agent scowled and sprawled in a chair.

Though he had reached the hideout, he was a long way from success. He was under probation. As far as he was concerned, this clubroom was an observation ward. Experience told him that he might be kept idle for a week or more, while he was watched and studied. During that delay, thousands of people might be enslaved to the insidious drug that was being unloaded upon the nation. Misery and tragedy would stalk across America, while a mobster determined whether "X" was worthy to shoot men down for the dope ring. He had to do something that would win the interest of the leader, that would end his probation at a stroke.

HE picked up a newspaper and rattled through it to the sports section. Behind the raised sheets, he listened intently. The conversation buzzed around the commonplace topics of small talk. He heard nothing about the activities of the ring.

The clock ticked oft valuable time, and "X" was learning nothing. He tried to single out the mob leader, but no one seemed to fit the part. The entire group appeared contented with idleness. This hideout wasn't unlike firemen's quarters, where there was little to do until an alarm came in.

The Agent puzzled over a means whereby he could start something and end this exasperating inaction. Trouble would do it, a quarrel, a fight. These men lived by the gun. It wouldn't take much of an injury to pride or person to make them draw.

Yet he couldn't brush up to a man and deliberately start a dispute. That would be too obvious. Vicious living had made them smart to tricks, overly suspicious. A play that was too open would suggest a hidden motive.

"X" noticed that whenever he rattled his paper, a sniffing, hard-eyed, death's-head of a man reading a book nearby, looked up with a scowl of irritation. The Agent's eyes gleamed. Here was a chance.

He rattled his paper a little more. He gently kicked a table leg in nerve-rasping rhythm. He hummed a monotonous tune, drumming an accompaniment on the arm of his chair with his fingers. To this symphony of irritation he added the most agonizing noise in existence by repeatedly smacking his tongue against a tooth.

Suddenly the hophead sprang from his chair, cursing viciously at "X." He snatched the paper, yelled, "You damn low-life! Go climb in a bunk before I put the heat on you, and shut you up for good. You'd drive a man nuts with them noises. Lay off that one-man band, or I'll bend a gun-barrel over your thick dome."

The snowbird interspersed his tirade with fighting words. "X" hid his satisfaction behind a savage scowl. Leaping erect, he lunged at the man, who sprang to one side and shot a fist at "X's" head.

The blow landed, though the Agent rolled the force out of the impact. He answered with a vicious snarl and swung a chair overhead. Murder instantly flamed in the hophead's eyes. Life had etched no humanity on his repulsive face. There was nothing but greed, and evil, and killing hate cut in the harsh lines.

He went into a fighting crouch, his right hand streaking to a shoulder holster beneath his armpit. The gun had half cleared the leather, when "X" dropped the chair. His own hand darted under his coat and appeared again, clutching an automatic.

The draw was swifter than the eye, a blur of movement, that made the others tense in amazement. "X" actually completed the draw the instant the chair struck the floor.

Usually he carried only his gas gun, but this time he'd packed a real bullet-shooting weapon. A mobster without a killing gun was like a plumber without a wrench. To avoid suspicion in that direction, the Agent had brought a rod along.

Then came the pounding crash of flame-spitting guns, and savage blasts filled the room with ear-bursting thunder.

CHAPTER III

SECONDS OF DEATH

THE REPORTS SEEMINGLY were simultaneous; but one was a split-second late—and that wink of time was sufficient to dispel the shadow of death that hovered over the duelists.

The hophead's automatic suddenly flew out of his grasp as the slug from "X's" gun smashed against the frame. The man was yanking the trigger as the bullet struck, and the muzzle lanced flame while the gun was spinning in mid-air. The lead buried into the ceiling, sending a shower of plaster down on the billiard table.

Cursing madly, the hophead clutched at his hand and shrank back. Fear bulged his eyes, as he whimpered for help. But he did not need help, for "X" was finished with him. A slight bullet groove across the knuckle of the hophead's right thumb was the only casualty. The Agent's astounding display of marksmanship and cool steadiness immediately made him a personality to be respected and recognized.[34]

"ALL right, rat," "X" snarled. "Crawl into your hole and leave the rod work to professionals. You amateurs are always on the receiving end. You're all thumbs. Your kind generally end up on the hot squat."

The Agent addressed the others sarcastically.

"Sorry I disturbed you, gents. Don't like to overstep myself—specially when I've just joined up with a mob. But I ain't the sort to let a guy get funny with me. If they stay off my toes I'm like a milk-

---

[34] AUTHOR'S NOTE: In preparation for just such a situation as this, Agent "X" has spent many hours of practice in secret with guns of all types. In the sound-proof cellar of one of his hideouts he maintains a practice range. Here he has a rack of weapons, including automatic, single-shot target pistols, and Western type revolvers. He has practiced the quick draw as industriously as any sharp-shooting cow-puncher.

fed lamb. That's my story, gents, straight and simple—and now I'll finish my paper."

The hophead had ducked into another room. From the look on the man's face, "X" knew the snowbird still had ideas of murder. But the Agent wasn't worried. As long as he didn't turn his back to his foe, he doubted if the man had the skill or the nerve to get him.

No sooner had the Agent settled himself to listen again behind his newspaper than the others began coming up to comment on his gunwork and to voice profane admiration. The ice was broken. That brief trick had done more to put him in the favor of the mob than any overtures of friendliness or attempts at being a good fellow.

He learned that he had dueled with Teddy Eldon, "one of the best gunmen in the mob when he's loaded with coke and waltzing on air." But the Agent didn't learn about the traffic in drugs.

Later, his rat-faced guide came in.

"You're a quick worker, Spats," the man said. "You've done the shortest trick at bench warming of any new guy. Generally a fella cools his heels for a coupla weeks, sometimes a month, before the chief lets on he knows the bum is alive. But he was watchin' you when Teddy elected you a candidate for a marble slab. Martel wants to see you."

"X" was taken to a luxurious office, with blue, modernistic decorations and furnishings. The carpet was thick, the room air-conditioned, the lighting indirect, and behind a broad desk sat a gross bulldog of a man, an iron-jawed symbol of evil prosperity with a long black cigar jammed in the corner of a square, firm mouth.

Martel was obviously not a victim of the drugs he sold. His eyes were as clear as they were cold. His skin was tanned by the sun, and his walking beam shoulders looked as though they would be more at home in a gymnasium than a night club. He was the embodiment of vicious strength. It would take a hard-fisted, ruthless man like him to handle that nondescript gathering of cokeheads in the big room.

"I'm going to break a rule, Spats," Martel told "X." "I saw your swell work with Teddy Eldon. Just a slug, that guy. A good man for his job, but he'll end up in the death house or be carted to potter's field. You, Spats, you're different. I heard about you freezing a punk upstairs with a punch. You've got brains, enterprise, nerve. You say you've been in the dope racket yourself. Then you know what it's all about. And you know that the main thing in life is *power*."

Martel boomed the word. "I came out of the gutter, Spats. I

never opened a school book in my life. But I've got doctors, lawyers, professors, statesmen, big shots in business, right in the palm of my hand." Martel emphasized this by squeezing a huge, beefy hand into a formidable fist.

"Why?" he boomed. "How is it these mental marvels are kids in my grasp? I ain't a wizard. No! But I control the stuff that makes me a wizard, see? *Dope!* Load a guy with dope, get him to where his nerves are on fire, and every inch of him is crawling for want of a shot, and never mind how high-hat he is—if you control his supply of junk he's your sucker. Dope—*power!*"

MARTEL puffed furiously on his black cigar. "I run a good layout, Spats," he went on, "but now I've got competition, rotten, dirty competition. And I've got to break it!" His teeth clicked as though he were biting off the words.

"Somebody's muscling in on your territory, eh?" said "X" casually, "Have you got a line on them, chief? I don't always treat guys gentle. Maybe I could do your outfit some good."

"You bet you can!" said Martel emphatically. "I don't know who's running this other mob. But, damn them, they're not underbidding me. No, sir! The dirty heels are *giving* the stuff away! I've been gathering cannon. That's why you're here. I've had spies out. A tip just came in. This other mob is bringing an auto load of dope down from up-state. I'm hi-jacking the stuff tonight, and by the holy cow, I'll give the junk away under the Martel banner."

The Agent hid a smile of elation. The mob chief didn't know who was behind this other ring, but he'd said enough so that "X" was no longer working at loose ends.

"I'm sending you out tonight, Spats," Martel said. "You're in the pick of my six best rodmen. On this job tonight depends your future standing with me. I want that load of junk! I'm going to blast that gang off the face of the earth. If they show fight, give 'em the works, see? And remember, a guy with *rigor mortis* don't talk."

That was the interview. A few minutes later the Agent was in a high-powered sedan with five of the hardest-faced men seen outside of a penitentiary. "X" was made to ride in the front seat with the driver. That was a measure of precaution. He was not entirely accepted. The others didn't relish having their backs to him.

The driver was "Fat" Hickman, a homicide expert, who actually had spent six months in the Sing Sing death house, and had finally been acquitted on a technicality. He was dangerous as a rattlesnake, and actually eligible for the electric chair on a dozen counts.

"Them babies are going to give us a picnic, sure enough, Spats," he said. "They enjoy puttin' the heat on a guy to see him fall. When we welcome them to our fair city, put your whole heart into your work. Give the undertaker a decent break."

The talk as they rode along was light and bantering, on the surface. Four of them were so hopped up with cocaine that they could have laughed at a firing squad. Hickman had a natural killer's nerve. He didn't need a narcotic to deaden his mind against peril. The Agent's self-mastery always served him faithfully when danger threatened.

They traveled out of the city about ten miles along the highway north. Then Hickman swerved off onto a macadamized country road. It was a lonely section, a sharp contrast to the congestion and clangor of the city.

"X" looked at his watch. It lacked a few minutes of two. Suddenly headlights pierced the gloom ahead like two gigantic serpent's eyes. The mobsters ducked down. Machine guns were thrust through holes in the re-enforced body of the sedan.

Hickman slowed the car, then stopped it crosswise on the road, so that the other machine would not be able to pass unless it ran into a brush-choked ditch. The car ahead stopped about fifty yards away. The occupant waited. Then he began to back up.

"Picked a blank that time," commented Hickman, starting the machine. "That fella figured we're stick up artists."

When the gunman swung the car to the right side of the road, the other machine gathered speed, and whizzed by at sixty miles an hour. Three times Hickman blocked the road for the wrong car. Then they heard the purr of a high-powered auto traveling at great speed.

"That sounds like business," said the former death-house resident with an evil leer.

He brought the car to a skidding, rubber-screeching stop. A large sedan hummed over the knob of a hill. There was a mad grinding of brakes. Blinding headlights glared on the blue-steel barrels of Tommy guns protruding from the side of the Martel car. Deathly silence prevailed for a few tense moments. Then the lonely, quiet country road became a thunderous battlefield.

Hickman had stopped the right car at last.

THOSE in the other sedan needed no explanation of gun-barrels projecting from an automobile parked across the road. The gunmen in the dope car started hostilities without challenge or interrogation. They knew they were facing hi-jackers. Martel's men had the advantage, however, for their machine was crosswise, and they could blast their foes with a fierce broadside. A Thompson sub-machine gun was thrust into "X's" hands. Grim of face, his eyes gleaming as coldly as the unwinking stars above, the Secret Agent put the weapon into operation. Its roar was savage and intense, but his aim was deliberately wide. The bullets whirred harmlessly into the night.[35]

A thunderous attack from the dope car smashed against the bullet-proof windows of the sedan and ricocheted from the re-enforced body. In time the glass would be drilled through, but before that happened an alarm would go through the countryside, and the clashing mobsters would have the law surrounding them.

Some one in the dope car let out a shriek of agony. Fat Hickman cackled like a madman. His eyes glittered with murderous light, his thick, drooling lips were drawn back in a wolfish leer. Flushed and sweating, he was on his knees, a hulk of viciousness, the stock of his hot and smoking Tommy gun bucking against his fat-padded shoulder.

"We've got 'em!" he yelled exultantly. "That ain't bullet-proof glass. We'll pour so much lead into them babies that the undertaker

---

35   AUTHOR'S NOTE: *During the World War it was the Agent's business, as an intelligence expert, to ferret out the secrets of the enemy. He familiarized himself with the use of all types of machine guns at that time. In the years since he has been a close student of armament, both civil and military.*

will have to melt 'em to get 'em into their caskets. Give 'em the works, Spats! This is our night. We'll collect a bonus fer this job!"

Agent "X" muttered savagely to himself. He had hoped that Martel's men would capture the rival mobsters, or trail their car. But here he was in the thick of what would probably be a massacre. The car would become a shambles, a bullet-wrecked hearse. His five gunmen companions wanted no survivors of the dope car. The thunder of gunfire sounded like an attack on a front-line trench. When the smoke cleared, the road would be strewn with corpses.

The opposing gangsters were hidden. Suddenly a big barrel, thicker than that of a shotgun, was thrust over the bottom part of the shattered windshield's frame. That puzzled "X." Machine gun bullets had been ineffective on the Martel sedan. Certainly buckshot against the car would be like trying to smash a stone wall with a sling-shot.

A terrific, deafening explosion jolted the sedan. The car rocked as though it had been rammed by a truck. Violently thrown against the side of the machine, the Agent struck his temple against the metal crank used to lower the window. He slumped to the floor, unconscious. Luckily his great strength threw off the effects of the blow quickly, or he would have been burned alive.

HE regained tortured senses to find himself alone, deserted in the sedan that had become like a furnace, stifling and searing. The top of the car was a flaming mass, and fire was licking up around the machine. The mobsters were to the left, concealed in the heavy brush and pouring destruction at the dope car.

His vision blurred and his brain hazy from pain, "X" puzzled foggily to determine the cause of the fire. There was a peculiar glow to the flame that was unlike ordinary combustions. He recalled the terrific explosion that had knocked him out. Again he studied the flame—like opals on fire. Then he understood. The rival mobsters had fired a phosphorus bomb.

Already the burning chemical was eating through the top, dripping fire onto the rear cushions. If those flaming globules dropped on "X" they would cling and eat like acid. The poisonous fumes were pouring into the car. "X" was but a few seconds from unconsciousness. He knew it.

Some of the phosphorus had got into the engine, and there was danger of an explosion. Even if "X" did get free, he would be exposed to the menace of Tommy guns. The left forward door was jammed, and the one next to the driver's seat would open onto sure death. Peril cleared his brain. He contemplated the left rear door. That was his one chance, yet near it phosphorus was dripping from the burning top. He had to risk that vicious chemical, or be broiled to death.

The Secret Agent took a knife from his pocket and ripped the leather covering from the front seat. Using this as a shield over his head and body, he climbed to the rear, careful not to step on the phosphorus.

Instantly his improvised leather shield was dotted with fiery particles, but he got the door open, and flung himself from the roaring holocaust into the road. He hurled the blazing covering away, stepped gingerly to avoid phosphorus on the ground, and made for the ditch. A wild shout came from the other car. "X" gave a violent leap. He had been spotted.

While in mid-air a Tommy gun began streaming lead around him. Bullets seared across his back as he fell, but the mobster did not shift his aim soon enough to finish the Agent.

Some of the brush was afire, for the bomb had scattered the phosphorus. "X" managed to avoid the flames as he crawled through the brush *toward* the dope car. That direction saved his life, for the gangster was raking the ditch with machine-gun fire farther down, obviously thinking that the person, if he lived, was making his escape to the rear.

The firing from Martel's men had dwindled with ominous significance. "X" detected only two guns in operation from the side. Then came a piercing outburst that rose shrilly above the savage rattle and roar of the Thompsons.

A man cursed madly. The Agent recognized the voice of Fat Hickman. The killer's stream of oaths was suddenly cut off in a withering blast of gunfire. Another gang execution had taken place. That ended the battle. Possibly one Martel man still lived, but he was not staying to meet the same fate as his companions.

By now the Martel sedan was a mass of flames. Any moment the fire would reach the gas tank. "X" was close enough to be killed by an explosion. As swiftly as he could; he crawled through the bushes. The mobsters, triumphant but begrimed and bloody from the battle, returned to the dope car. The engine started, and the machine swung around to head back the way it came.

Climbing the bank of the ditch, "X" darted to the rear of the machine, and clutched onto the spare tire. It was a desperate risk.

About a quarter of a mile away there boomed a thunderous explosion as flames reached the gas tank of the Martel sedan. "X" clamped his jaws as he looked back at the flaming wreck. To him that demolished car was like a symbol of the destruction that was being wrought to fatten the bank accounts of vicious, greed-mastered men like Martel.

Yet Martel was insignificant compared to the drug menace that was breaking into this racket.

CHAPTER IV

MONSTERS OF EVIL

THE DOPE CAR swung off onto another road, and headed in the direction of the city. Agent "X" quickly took something from an inner pocket of his coat. This was a small, flat object that looked like a pocket camera.[36]

He snapped it open, pressed a black disc attached to a cord to the rear of the sedan, put the cameralike box to his ear and fingered a screw head on its side. At first only a confused blur of sound reached him. He tuned his amplifying device down, selecting the sounds he wanted. And in a moment he began to catch bits of conversation. He learned that a Martel spy had been caught and tortured into talking. That was why the mobsters were prepared for the hi-jackers.

"X" began to grow concerned about his next move when the car reached the city. If the driver took a route through the center of town, "X" would have to get off, for a man hanging onto a spare tire would get the instant attention of a night-patrolling cop. And the Agent didn't like the idea of following in a taxi. The gangsters would surely be watching to see if they were trailed.

But the Agent's worry on this score was dispelled when the car neared the city, for the driver headed toward the river. The auto sped along the dark, deserted waterfront between the columns of a ramp. "X" hoped that one of the men would say something that would give him an idea of their destination. He was riding with killers. If they found him, he would soon be floating in the river.

---

36   AUTHOR'S NOTE: Followers of the published chronicles of Secret Agent "X" will recall that he has made use of this strange sound amplifying device before. The screw, which corresponds in appearance to the film wind of a camera, is a delicate rheostat control. Batteries, no larger than those of a flashlight, are stored in either end. The disc at the cord's end is a tiny microphone, and the cameralike box itself is the earpiece.

The driver traveled within the speed limit, for with their illegal freight, they could not afford to be stopped. "X" believed it was a hot car anyway, stolen for the trip, to be abandoned after it was unloaded.

Drawing near a tumbling down old condemned warehouse, the car swerved to a driveway alongside it, and next to the high brick wall surrounding a packing plant. As the car crossed the sidewalk, "X" dropped from his perch, and darted to the corner of the wall.

The machine stopped a short stretch down the alleyway in front of a small workman's cottage. Four of the men leaped out, scanned the driveway in both directions, and then pulled eight large suitcases from the machine.

If those suitcases were filled with narcotics, the runners had made a very profitable trip, for, computed at current prices, that quantity would sell in the tens of thousands.

It was close to sunrise now. Trucks were rumbling over the cobblestones. Early gangs of dock workers were shuffling to the piers. "X" now knew one of the hideouts. But with dawn approaching, there was little he could do. He might visit the cottage later in the day, disguised as a peddler or a tramp hunting for a hand-out. Or he might wait until darkness. But, in his present disguise as Spats McGurn, his appearance would arouse suspicion. He started to turn away, when some one came out of the cottage.

"X" stepped into the shadows. The mobster started the car, and backed out. The Agent's eyes blazed with excitement. That changed his plans, but suited him perfectly. When the machine neared the sidewalk, he again took his position on the rear tire. But he didn't intend to stay there long.

At the first stop for traffic, "X" stepped to the pavement, walked to the side of the car, and thrust the muzzle of his gas gun through a lowered window. As the mobster turned, a jet of gas sprayed directly into his face. The man gasped, started to curse and go for his gun. Then he collapsed over his steering wheel.

By the time the traffic cleared, the Agent was in the driver's seat, with the mobster slumped beside him, overcome by the gas. "X" drove to another of his hideouts, in the tenement section more than two miles from this spot. The dope runner was still unconscious when the Agent stopped. Putting one of the man's arms over his shoulder and holding the wrist, "X" grabbed him around the waist, and dragged him across the sidewalk. An early pedestrian stopped and stared.

The hophead went into a fighting crouch, hand streaking to a shoulder holster.

"Too much celebration," explained the Agent, and hauled the mobster into the dim and dingy hallway. There "X" got the fireman's grip on the man, and carried him up three flights of stairs.

"X's" place was in the back, a typical tenement double room, shabbily furnished, but with cross-ventilation. It was not the ventilation that had interested the Agent, but the fact that one of the windows was close to the fire escape of the next building, offering a chance of escape in an emergency.

AFTER he locked the window and drew the blinds, the Agent bound and gagged his captive, then went back to the car, which he drove to another section of the city and abandoned. A hot car would draw a cop instantly. He didn't want a blue-coat prowling around the tenement where his hideout was located.

By the time he returned it was daylight and the effects of the gas had worn off. The mobster was conscious and struggling with his bonds. "X" placed some white powders, neatly squared on white paper, on a tray and held them in front of the dope runner. The man was a drug addict, sweating and writhing in his need for easement. "X" removed the gag.

"If you yell," he said, holding the gas gun menacingly, "it'll only be once, understand? I'm not going to fool with you. What is your name? Whom do you work for? Your system is screaming for a shot. Here it is. Enough to make you do a toe dance. Talk—and I'll give it to you."

As Martel had said—dope was power. This man was born a cur and a weakling, but he feared gang reprisal. It took an hour before his tongue began to wag. But when he started, he chattered like a man in a delirium.

"I'm Louie Corbeau. Geez, fella, give me a sniff, just one little sniff! I've got to have it. I'll kill a cop, do anything for you, for one of them decks. I'm dyin', mister, dyin'! Your foot ever go to sleep? Well, that's the way I am. Only a billion needles are stickin' into me from head to foot. Let my hands loose so I can grab onto something. Geez, I can't stand it! I'm goin' nuts. You ain't human, mister. Can't you see I'm dyin' for want of a shot?"

The Agent looked at the man with a coldness that was beyond pity or contempt. Just as this man was a dupe for the leaders of the dope ring, so he was a pawn for "X" in the Agent's grim, relentless drive against that ring. "X" was aloof. Like a great surgeon, he employed his genius for the betterment of humanity, and for this killer and criminal in his power he felt only scorn.

"Corbeau, you can squirm until your nerves crawl out of your flesh," said "X" grimly, "and this morphine will stay on the tray. This is barter and trade. Give me information and you'll get the dope."

"Geez, I'll talk!" blurted Louie Corbeau. "I don't know much. The mob is located in that condemned warehouse at Haswell and Riverfront. I've only been a snowbird three months, boss. Honest! I got hurt in an auto smash up. Went to the hospital. An orderly kept givin' me cigarettes every day. After I was discharged, I nearly went goofy when I couldn't get any. Then a fella told me I could get the stuff to quiet my nerves. I had to join the mob—an' now I'm squealin' on him!"

There was terror in the man's voice. The Agent's eyes blazed. A trace of pity showed in them now. This man was an instinctive criminal, but he had been lured into the clutches of the gang. Here was an insidious way in which the ring worked. When it wanted a recruit, it first made him a drug addict. Once under the ring's control, a dope fiend would commit an atrocity to get a supply of narcotic. Each new addict became an ally of the gang.

"X" questioned and cross-questioned Corbeau. The hophead told the truth, for the Agent's skillful, rapid-fire examination did not trip him. There was no countersign to use, nothing but the mobster's face to admit him to the hideout. The leader of the local organization was a killer named Karloff, he said. "X" obtained also the names and descriptions of the other mobsters. And then he went to work. He gave Corbeau the drug his system craved, and a powerful hypnotic which induced sleep instantly.

The Agent needed the drug addict in a relaxed condition, because the man's face had been so distorted by agony that "X" would not have been able to determine the exact features.

THE Agent brought out his triple mirrors, peeled off the disguise of Spats McGurn, and in a few minutes he molded his plastic, volatile make-up material until Corbeau would have thought he was gazing into a mirror if he had looked at "X."[37]

After changing to Corbeau's clothes, the Agent gagged his prisoner again, manacled him with steel bracelets, and left the tenement. He ate breakfast at a cheap lunch counter, and went directly to the hideout at Haswell and Riverfront. There was no signal. A man entered. If he did not belong, he probably would never get out as he had gone in. "X" walked into the workman's cottage.

It was a three-room shack, actually occupied by a machine operator in the big packing house opposite. The workman, of course, was a mob member, who acted as a blind. The factory man was cooking ham and eggs when "X" came in. He greeted the Agent

---

37   AUTHOR'S NOTE: *The Secret Agent's marvelous ability at disguise is based to a great extent on his knowledge of facial planes. He has the instincts of a sculptor, and I believe he has spent much time modeling likenesses in clay before attempting his own impersonations. It has been rumored also that he was at one time associated with a great character actor.*

casually, calling him Corbeau. "X" nodded.

He had learned the layout of the place from his captive, and he went immediately to a small, windowless storeroom, raising a trapdoor that led into a tunnel. In a crouch he ran along this passage to a flight of steps, which took him into the large cemented basement of the condemned warehouse. The place was apparently the temporary quarters of the drug ring, for it had none of the luxurious furnishings of Martel's hideout.

A number of rooms had been partitioned in the big house. There were tables, chairs, and army cots. A few mobsters were in the main room. A man with the scar of a bullet wound on his right cheek addressed him as Corbeau. From his captive's descriptive, "X" knew this was Gus Tansley.

Somewhere in the building a man was shrieking for help. That was Serenti, who had been caught by the police and questioned. He had talked too much, and Karloff was punishing him by cutting off his drug supply.

At "X's" hideout, Louie Corbeau had gibbered out the story of Serenti, for the latter's fate would be his if it were discovered that Corbeau had told any of the secrets of the ring.

A dark, evil-faced man suddenly appeared at the Agent's side. His approach had been so stealthy that not even "X's" keen ears had caught any sound. The man was Karloff. "X" recognized him by the description Corbeau had given.

"Did you dispose of the machine?" asked the mob leader, speaking with a slight lisp, his voice possessing at the same time a metallic ring.

"Sure, Karloff," answered the Agent, imitating Louie Corbeau's voice. "I always do what you say. Now do I get my shot?"

Corbeau and the others had risked their lives to bring in a supply of the drug that would not have been exhausted by them for years, but the suitcases had been sealed. It would have been worth their lives to have opened one. Karloff kept his men under the lash by doling out drugs only when their nerves began to rebel.

He was a long, somber man, dark and sinister. His wicked eyes were like points of fire. His upper teeth protruded a little, giving him a perpetual leer. Wearing a long black coat and a high stiff collar, he had a funereal look. His black hair was plastered down on his forehead, straight across, like a bang.

"Come!" he ordered, beckoning "X." He repeated the command and the gesture to the others. Then he drifted away like a wraith, the men obediently following.

KARLOFF led them to a group of barred cells that had been strong rooms when the huge, tumbling warehouse was in use. From one of the cells came blood-curdling screams; pitiful, heart-rending wails.

"X" saw Serenti then, the man who had talked too much. He was hardly a man any longer, but a live thing in the throes of exquisite torture. The Agent glanced coldly at Karloff, but the leader's face was a mask that revealed nothing that went on in the cunning killer's brain. "X" marked him as a sadist who feasted on cruelty, who was governed by inhuman traits.

Serenti threw himself against the bars and reached through with a bloody, clawlike hand, pleading for relief: His arm was bare, showing the skin, hard and toughened by countless hypo punctures. Blood streamed down Serenti's face from deep, self-inflicted scratches. In his agony he had clawed himself unmercifully. "X" saw ugly welts and lumps on his head. Mad frenzy had made Serenti pull his hair out by the handfuls. His hands were crimson talons of raw, lacerated flesh caused by clutching the rusted iron bars, and by pawing the rough cement walls.

Nature had made the sufferer fight pain with pain. Serenti had gnawed at his tongue until it was swollen and looked like a hunk of pounded beefsteak. Crimson drooled from his cracked lips. He had slashed his arms with long finger nails. He had torn his clothes to ribbons. The craving for drugs had made Serenti demented; a writhing, sweating, cawing, bundle of rasped and outraged nerves.

"They're eatin' me up!" he screamed madly. "Ants! Big red ants. Millions of them. They're tearin' me to pieces. But I can get rid of them. Pour gasoline over me, Corbeau! Then touch a match to me, Tansley! I'll burn 'em off! I'll burn them big red ants. They can't eat me to pieces. I'll fix 'em."

He babbled away in a nightmarish delirium, while his companions looked on without compassion. A blaze flared in the Agent's eyes. Karloff had the fixed expression of a hideous idol. He showed no sign of emotion. Here was an example of the tremendous power drugs could give a man like Karloff. He was a despot. An addict, deprived of his drug and shrieking for the powder that would end his suffering, would sell his life or take a life for "just one little shot."

Serenti collapsed and clawed at the cement floor. The grinding of his teeth sounded like the rasp of a steel file against granite. He raised to his knees and cried like a lost child. Getting up, he staggered across the cell and pounded his fists against the wall.

"I've got to have it!" he blubbered. "Give me one little shot, Karloff. Just one little shot. Then I'll go out and kill anyone you want. I'm being eaten—alive—eaten alive!"

"Serenti likes to talk," said Karloff softly, his voice almost a purr. "He became very friendly with the cops last week. He even told where one of our hideouts was located. He's been a week without his dope. But we mustn't be too severe. Here, Serenti, here is your shot."

Karloff spoke as gently as a mother to her sick child. Serenti uttered a hysterical cry and threw himself against the bars again. He reached out both hands for the white capsules which Karloff produced.

"You're my friend, Karloff!" he screamed. "You're my best pal, my only pal. I'll do anything for you. Anything!"

Serenti got three little capsules from Karloff. The drug addict gulped them down like a famished dog swallowing a bit of meat. His nerves quieted. He relaxed and leaned against the bars, sighing contentedly. But Karloff was not as kind as his manner indicated.

Suddenly Serenti stiffened. His eyes all but popped from their sockets. His veins bulged and seemed to writhe like snakes. He choked and struggled in a terrible agony for breath. He howled like some wounded creature in the wilderness.

"Karloff! Karloff—you fiend! The—the green death!"

"Yes," breathed Karloff, "the green death."

IN amazement the Agent watched a startling transformation in the pigmentation of Serenti's skin. The tortured man suddenly slumped to the floor. "X" knew he was dead. That was not astounding, considering the treachery of Karloff. But what opened the Agent's eyes was that Serenti's skin had turned green, a horrible, deathly, muddy green—the hue of some dread arsenical poison.[38]

"Come, gentlemen," said Karloff softly.

Not once had the leader scowled or smiled or sneered. Only his gentle voice had the tone of ugly insinuation. He moved away

---

38 AUTHOR'S NOTE: *In his contacts with crime and criminals, Agent "X" has had cause to become a profound student of toxicology. The vegetable, animal and mineral poisons, their effects and antidotes, are known to him. In his own secret laboratory he has made many experiments with snake venoms; and also analyzed exotic, lethal substances from many foreign countries. By these studies he had been able to catch and forestall many hideous murderers.*

with the softness of a cat. In the big room, he handed "X" a small square of powdered narcotic wrapped in white paper. By this time the Agent was cleverly simulating frayed nerves, playing his part of Louie Corbeau. He grabbed the deck of dope, opened it with trembling fingers.

At least, he appeared to open the one Karloff had given him. But right before the sinister man's searching, penetrating ferret eyes, "X" performed a brilliant trick of sleight-of-hand. He had palmed another square of power—a harmless powder. This one he opened, having palmed the one Karloff handed him. Quickly, dexterously he poured the powder on the back of his hand, and sniffed it. Immediately he straightened up, squared his shoulders and smiled.

Karloff was gone. He had drifted away again, his tread as soft as a cat's. The Agent found himself alone with Gus Tansley. After a few minutes of idle conversation, "X" decided that he could learn something from Tansley by skillfully guiding the talk. He worked around to the subject of dope, and the trafficking of this drug.

"What I can't understand, Tansley," he said, "is why we risk our lives, why fellows like Serenti get the green death, all to transport and distribute dope that is *given* away!"

The Secret Agent's eyes were brightly alert. He hoped he was close to a solution of the enigma that had puzzled him all along—the purpose behind the dope ring's free distribution of the dread stuff. His questioning of Tansley was a shot in the dark, but it connected.

Tansley laughed wickedly.

"You're a sappy guy, Corbeau. I figured you was wiser than that."

The Agent waited tensely for Tansley to go on. For a moment it seemed that the mobster would say no more. Then, with the arrogance of one who feels himself in possession of superior wisdom he continued:

"You saw how Serenti was howling for the junk. You know yourself how shaky you was before Karloff handed you a deck. It takes a week to make a hoppy. How many ever get off the stuff?"

The Agent shrugged. He knew that the percentage was very small. The cure depended on the will of the addict, and most of them were weak-willed at the outset. The drug undermined what little moral strength they had, so most cases were hopeless.

"Not many, I guess," answered "X." "But I still can't figure why we're going in for this gift proposition."

"Till America's right in our fist, Corbeau! That's why."

"It don't seem smart, Gus," returned the Agent. "I know a little about dope. I know that a hundred tons of opium are enough to give the docs of the world all they need. Yet more than two thousand tons are being turned out—and a lot of that tonnage is coming to America. We get everybody twitching and jerking for a shot, and guys like this Martel will jump in and cop the business."

TANSLEY smirked. "For a little while, yes," he said. "But it costs a hell of a lot to smuggle dope into the country—and half the junk the peddlers handle is adulterated with about fifty percent sugar of milk. Lots of guys fork over two bucks for a deck, and get nothing but a pinch of salt. But we'll sell the straight stuff—and *underbid* any dope ring in America. Even with all of this free junk we'll make profits the *first day* we start selling. Now do you get the idea, sap?"

Agent "X" nodded. He got the idea all right. A chill seemed to pass slowly through his blood. The free samples constituted a hideous advertising campaign, a build-up for a tremendous sales onslaught that could not fail. In all his experience with vicious criminals he had never run into anything more appalling than this.

The menace of a foreign invasion had been abolished. But in its place was this monstrous, hydra-headed scheme that was just as terrible. And it was not only possible, but too imminently probable.

Agent "X" knew that statisticians claimed that one-fourth of China's four hundred million were opium smokers. A hundred million drug addicts in Asia alone. And every twelfth person in India chewed or smoked opium. What if that fate visited America, a land of highly organized nervous systems, keyed up to the pitch of modern civilization? Would the filth, the squalor, the untold misery of the Far East become the Fate of America?

"X" was about to ask *how* this drug ring could possibly smuggle enough of the stuff in to underbid the other rings, when he noticed a slender thread of wire, colored the mahogany of the furniture, that ran down the leg of the table at which they sat. Quickly he reached his hand under the table and felt a small, hard-rubber disc. A dictograph.

"Yeah," Gus Tansley was saying, "in another month we'll all be on the gravy train. Hell, us that've got in the outfit early will be drawing in so much cash, we'll have to hire bookkeepers to tally each day's take. Gold mines and oil wells ain't in it. They peter out. But a cokehead ain't gonna stop sniffin' till he croaks!"

"You've said enough," spoke a soft voice behind Tansley.

"X," who had been tensely alert, had not heard the approach of Karloff. The chief came out of the gloom as softly as a cloud. There was no anger in his voice, but just a faint reproach that was deadly in its gentleness.

"Corbeau," said Karloff somberly, "you are too inquisitive. Tansley, you are too willing to answer questions. I have listened and I am not pleased. I was not pleased with the way Serenti regaled the police with secrets. You know what happened to Serenti!"

Tansley instantly sank to his knees and clutched at Karloff's legs. He began sobbing, pleading. In a flash all the arrogance had left him. He was a quivering craven, blubbering for mercy, from a man who bad no mercy in his soul.

Agent "X" stood up, aloof, a certain grim majesty in his bearing, his eyes cold with deadly challenge.

"Karloff!" shrieked Tansley. "You—you're not going to give it to us? Not the—green death!"

"Yes, Tansley," said Karloff with his faint lisp. "I'm going to give it to you and Corbeau both. You're gabbing, gossiping fools who have no place in this organization. You'll be squealing next, telling secrets to the police—the way Serenti did. You have earned the green death!"

CHAPTER V

CRIMSON MENACE

THE AGENT LOOKED quickly about the big room. Karloff had forestalled a dash for an exit. There were five doorways, though only one led to the tunnel. Framed in each opening was a vicious mobster, gripping an automatic. They were shaking, drug-famished men, eager for the favor of their chief. They had been companions of Tansley and Corbeau, had laughed and joked and eaten with them, and had risked their lives side by side. But now they would riddle the two with lead, if Karloff gave the word.

The reason was plainly apparent. Mastered by drugs, they had seen the horrible torture that deprivation had inflicted on Serenti. And they were sick, suffering men. No doubt Karloff had promised a bonus of white powder for this job. Karloff had but to nod, and their guns would crash. They were his slaves, for their drug supply depended upon him.

"X" had only a few seconds to save himself from Serenti's fate. If he were not shot at once, the green death would be meted out to him, either in capsule form or by means of a hypodermic. Tansley's end would be the same, too. The mobster knew it and groveled like a cur at Karloff's feet

The Agent hesitated. Even to raise his hand would bring a hurricane of lead. And Karloff was about four feet away. Not much chance of delivering a knock-out punch, either. These mobsters would press triggers before he took a step.

Realizing their advantage they were closing in. Insanity glittered in their eyes. They were palsied, shaking like victims of St. Vitus' dance. Along with the deathly peril which these hopheads symbolized, the sight of them in their loathsome wretchedness was sickening.

The Agent's eyes were magnetic, impelling, hypnotic, as they fixed on the chief with a withering stare.

Karloff felt the power behind those eyes. One shoulder raised in a defensive attitude. He made an apologetic gesture with his hand. Yet there was irony in Karloff's manner. He held the winning card and was gloating in that fact.

Looking straight at him, "X" spoke, still in the role of Corbeau.

"You're a sap, Karloff," he said in a contemptuous voice. "You've got so few brains you have to get tough all the time. A weak sister, Karloff, that's you. Without dope, and a lot of dopies to manhandle guys for you you'd be hanging out in the municipal lodging house."

"X" had deliberately stung Karloff's pride, yet the man was too well-schooled in poker-faced inscrutability to show anger.

"Quite a speech, Corbeau," he said softly. "But I am not a free agent. I must answer to my superiors for the mistakes of my men. So I strike hard and swiftly."

"Yeah—that's what *you* say—and who are these guys that make you jump when they snap their fingers?"

Agent "X" hardly hoped to get information; and Karloff shook his head.

"I do not give away secrets like Tansley here—and like our friend Serenti. Perhaps that is why I keep my job, whereas you—"

That was as far as Karloff got in his explanation. The drug-craved mobsters were close. The Agent suddenly dived in a football tackle, his hard-muscled shoulder striking Karloff at the knees and knocking him to the cement floor. The chief shouted for his mobsters to shoot, but they could not, without hitting Karloff, for he was on top of "X."

The Agent got his gun from his shoulder holster and shot out the lights, utilizing his lightninglike draw. The gunmen rushed toward the fallen pair. Gus Tansley scrambled to his feet and started for an exit. One of the other mobsters took a chance and shot wildly then, and Gus Tansley uttered a scream of agony.

"They got me, Corbeau!" he shrieked. "Right in the guts. Come on, you rats! I'm finished, but I'll take some of you with me!"

Wounded, Tansley acquired the sudden courage that hysteria gives a coward whose doom is sealed. His automatic snarled fiercely. Someone screamed. Karloff was bellowing orders, but they only added to the wild confusion. The Agent was the single person with self-possession. He crawled toward Tansley, guided by the dope fiend's frenzied voice.

"Quiet—and keep down!" "X" said in a low, tense voice. "There's a chance of getting out of here. Shut up—or we'll never make it!"

THE firing had ceased now, for the basement was as dark as a vat of tar, and the gunmen feared shooting one another. Crawling toward the door, "X" half dragged Tansley. The hophead wouldn't have been in this mess except for his talk with the Agent. He was twisted, warped, less than half a man, but possibly there was something still to reclaim, something to justify his life. "X" would get him out of here and to an institution.[39]

The gunmen were clustering around Karloff, who was threatening them with the green death. But their bravado was gone. Darkness and the chance of stopping a bullet took the fight out of them. So the Agent made the door and got Gus Tansley through the tunnel to the workman's cottage. There the drug addict collapsed.

He was bleeding heavily, and "X" realized he was through. So did Tansley.

"I'm a goner, Corbeau," he moaned. "Any of them rats would double-cross a brother or shoot his dad for a deck of coke. Croakin' doesn't seem so hard, but the pain, Corbeau—the pain! Geez! Give me a shot, just one little shot before I go!"

Tansley's body relaxed. A fixed stare came to his glazed eyes. His mouth was half open. Another tragedy had been marked up to the evil of dope? Tansley was through, and his last words had been startlingly significant of the terrible power of narcotics. With death reaching out, Tansley had still been under dope's insidious spell. His only request, before he passed into eternity was the plea of all dope slaves—"just one little shot—"

The gunmen were in the tunnel now. Tansley lay beyond help, so "X" dashed on through the door and down the alley. Shortly he had blended into the surge of the healthy, work-a-day world.

In a fever of excitement he took a devious route to one of his hideouts and began changing his disguise. A desperate plan had come to his mind—one of those strange schemes that made Secret Agent "X's" method of work unpredictable and astounding. He had located one of the strongholds of the gang dispensing the free

---

39   AUTHOR'S NOTE: *In his dealing with the underworld, Agent "X" tries always to be merciful and just. He is fair to his foes. He gives even vicious criminals a sporting chance and the benefit of the doubt—never condemning until guilt is proved. And often he helps unfortunates who have been dragged into the hideous whirlpool of crime.*

A terrific, deafening explosion jolted the sedan.

dope. There were dozens of vicious gunmen there, and a man who was more a fiend than a human being. "X" could not hope to round them up single-handed. And, so great was the peril of the spreading menace, that he could not leave these men to carry on with their devilish work. Something must be done and done quickly, and Agent "X" had made up his mind.

The impersonation that "X" created now was what he called one of his "stock disguises." It was a makeup he had used before in other cities. It would do for the plan he had in mind.

Completely changed in appearance from the mobster Corbeau, he went across the city again to the office of Orrin Q. Mathews, local head of the Federal Narcotic Bureau.

It was early morning, yet the anteroom was filled with people.

"X" saw that he might be kept waiting for an hour or more, and time was precious.

He took a piece of paper from his pocket and a pencil. In a moment he had written a carefully worded note, calculated to arouse the interest of the chief inside. It stated that the writer of the note had important information bearing on the drug evil that was menacing the city. This "X" folded and handed to an attendant with instructions to give it at once to Mathews.

It gained Agent "X" an interview immediately. Mathews was sitting behind his desk, his forehead creased with worry. In the person of Agent "X," now calling himself Biggers, the narcotic head saw a drab-faced man who could have been an overworked bookkeeper. The Agent's walk was shuffling, apologetic. He let his hands dangle at his side. His acting was perfect.

"What is it, Biggers?" demanded Mathews in a gruff voice. "I'm a busy man, as you must know. Have you really something to tell me, or are you just another crank seeking publicity or wanting to spread slander? Every man with a grudge against some one, it seems, is coming here trying to pin this narcotic business on some person he doesn't like. My men are kept busy following false leads. Quick, what is it you have to tell me?"

"X" glanced at a clerk in the room with Mathews. He made a significant gesture with one eyebrow, and at a word from Mathews the clerk withdrew. Mathews and Agent "X" were left alone.

"Now," said Mathews. "Quick, spill it!"

MATHEWS sat back in his chair. He produced a cigar and stuck it between his lips. The Agent smiled grimly. This suited him nicely. He quickly brought a lighter from his pocket—one that he kept for special uses.

"Allow me," he said, snapping it into flame.

"X" lighted the cigar, and as Mathews puffed it energetically, waiting for "X" to begin, the Agent suddenly pressed a tiny lever on his briquet. The flame went out, and there was a hiss in its place. A jet of the same harmless gas that he had used in the dragon-headed ring in Chinatown went into Mathews' nostrils. With a single prolonged wheeze, the narcotic head sank slowly forward on his desk. The cigar dropped from inert fingers. The Agent's anaesthetic gas, potent and concentrated, had acted as quickly as a punch to the jaw.

Holding his own breath so as not to inhale any of the vapors still in the air, Agent "X" dragged Mathews from his chair and stretched him on a small leather couch. Swiftly he locked the door and took his portable make-up materials from the pocket. These included his flesh-colored pigments and tubes of plastic paste that his expert fingers could model with such an amazing skill.

He studied Mathews' features for nearly a minute, then went to work. The disguise of Biggers came off. In its place he built up a likeness of Mathews. He changed to Mathews' clothes, and then, gagging the official, he placed him in a closet. A few minutes later "X" unlocked the door, as like Mathews as though he had been the federal man's twin brother. He poked his head into the next office.

"Hayes," he addressed the clerk who had gone out, imitating Mathews' deep voice accurately. "Send Wells in. Tell Everts to get the Thompson guns ready. I want Creager to drive the car. Have Lorson and McAllister wait down below. We're going to stage a raid that may make history."

The men whose names "X" gave so fluently were members of the narcotic squad whose activities were known to him. The clerk hurried to follow instructions, tense with excitement.

"X" sat back in his desk chair, alert in mind and body. He had had little time to study the characteristics of Mathews. There was a chance that his daring impersonation of the man might be detected by his subordinates. But "X," profound student of psychology, was counting on the excitement of the occasion to cover any slight errors he might make. An important raid would put the men on edge.

Wells was the first to come in. "X" was rustling through some papers on his desk. He did not speak until he had jumped up and grabbed his hat. Wells' face showed no suspicion.

"Just got a tip," said the Agent quickly. "Don't know whether it has much basis or not, but I think it has. A lot of cranks have been yapping their heads off around here, as you know. But this time it looks like I've got something. Down at Haswell and Riverfront. An old condemned warehouse. The tip says it's a headquarters for the dope ring that's been *giving* the stuff away. Imagine that, Wells—snow selling for sixty-four bucks an ounce—and this gang handing it out free! Well, here's a chance to stop 'em—maybe—and confiscate a pile of dope."

"Sounds something like that Serenti tip-off," said Wells. "Maybe it's the same gang moved to a new hide-out. We missed 'em the last time. I hope we'll get 'em now. I'd like to blast the top off a couple of heads to make up for what happened to my pal, Broderick."

The Agent motioned for Wells to come along, Everything was

dovetailing nicely. Wells knew that Serenti had talked, and Broderick, a victim no doubt of the mob that took Serenti's life, was a friend of the federal detective.

They left the narcotic bureau and piled into the car outside, driven by Creager, a man grown gray in the department. For the most part they were silent as the car roared through the early morning streets, but "X" gave clipped instructions which the men memorized before the car stopped a half block from the warehouse.

He detailed two of the detectives to break in the front entrance. Lorson and McAllister he sent to crash in the doors on either side. The Agent took Wells to the cottage.

THE body of Gus Tansley lay where the mobster had died. Wells, case-hardened to violent deaths, gave the corpse an incurious glance and grunted. "X" wondered grimly how Wells would react if he should learn that this man had died a short while before in the arms of the person he thought was Mathews.

The Agent and Detective Wells were the first to reach the basement. The place was deserted, yet there remained evidence of recent occupation. The body of Serenti lay in the cell. The floor of the big room was splattered with crimson, but, to "X's" intense disappointment, Karloff and his mobsters were not in evidence.

"It's the same man, all right," said Wells, gazing at the green, horrible face of the dead Serenti. "They sure took the wag out of that guy's tongue. Must have embalmed the sucker with green paint."

The other federal men arrived, covered with cobwebs, but with nothing to report. On the upper floor they had not found even tracks. Karloff and his men had obviously left via the tunnel and the cottage, taking the suitcases of dope with them.

The Agent, his voice harsh, gave a quick order.

"Lorson, send in word to headquarters. Have the medical examiner come. I want to find out how long Serenti and the other stiff have been dead. The rest of you give this dump a thorough search. Don't miss anything. Knock on the walls, open up the furniture, collect anything you see."

Lorson started for the stairs, but he didn't get far. Suddenly there was a terrific, rocking explosion. The concussion threw them to the floor. Three more detonations came in quick succession, booming blasts that tortured their eardrums and rumbled through the old building like heavy thunder. Then came a smashing, deafening roar from one of the basement rooms.

Instantly the whole building was resounding with the snarl of mounting flames. The crackling above them was savage and intense. A shower of liquid fire had been sprayed over the top of the partition of the basement room, coming dangerously close to the federal men. Some sort of incendiary time bombs had exploded.

The Agent's jaw clamped viciously. He recognized those flaming opalescent globules. Burning phosphorus. Karloff had placed his infernal machines around the building. Undoubtedly some one had been sent to watch federal headquarters, in anticipation of a raid. Corbeau had been suspected of being a spy. That was why Karloff had fled—and left these engines of destruction behind him.

"Come on, men," said the Agent, lifting his voice above the crackle of the flames. "This place isn't going to be healthy in a minute."

Veterans though they were, the sudden explosion of the bombs and the sight of the flames on all sides had had a demoralizing effect on the men. They obeyed the Agent like sheep, and he led them into the tunnel. But halfway through he realized that escape was cut off in that direction. Harsh crackling sounds came from the cottage, too. He rushed forward and raised the trapdoor. A billow of smoke puffed into the tunnel instantly. Fiery tongues licked at him.

He turned, and with the others sped back to the basement. There was no escape above, the old warehouse was a blazing inferno. They were surrounded by fire. Karloff's bombs had been placed with fiendish cunning and thoroughness. They were trapped.

CHAPTER VI

MURDERER'S BULLET

THE BUILDING, LONG condemned, was as dry as tinder. Its rotten old beams and worm-eaten walls burned like kindling wood. The temperature in the basement was mounting to withering furnace heat. Already it was so hot that the sweat dried the instant it oozed from their pores. Every breath of stifling air was like fire drawn into the lungs. Thick, poisonous, suffocating smoke poured into the basement.

None of the detectives thought he would get out of the roaring holocaust except as a sack of charred bones. They were brave men, used to seeing death at close range and steeled to the prospect of going out violently.

"We'll save the folks funeral expenses anyway, boys," yelled Creager. "I'm sorry for you gents who have wives and kids. I've helped send a dozen men to the chair, but I never thought I'd fry, too."

From the street came the shriek and clangor of fire engines. But rescue from outside was impossible. Yet Agent "X" had not given up. He wasn't ready to die. His work was not finished. Too much depended on his living. Cut off from above, cut off from the tunnel, there still must be a way out. One direction remained. That was toward the street in the forward part of the basement.

"Come," he shouted to the detectives. "Grab my hand, Wells. You, Creager, grab hold of Wells. Are you all here? Sing out! That's it! Come on!"

With the federal men close behind, "X" ran to the forward wall. He felt along it until he found the door of a coal bin. He had a flash, but the light wouldn't penetrate the heavy smoke. He got the door open and the men inside. It was comparatively cool here. The air was clear enough to use his light. He flashed it on, directing a beam across the ceiling. Then he gave a shout. About ten feet above was the iron disc of a manhole plate.

"Climb on my shoulders, Wells," he cried. "Shove that cover off."

The Agent crouched. Wells grabbed his hands, stepped on his thigh, and swung around to his shoulders. Supported by the Agent, who clamped powerful hands on the man's calves, Wells experienced little difficulty in removing the manhole cover. It opened onto the sidewalk.

Firemen rushed to help them, and in a few moments the detectives were getting clean air into their lungs. A throng had gathered. The street was strewn with hose. A half dozen companies had been called out. Firemen were playing streams on the blazing building, but their efforts were directed entirely to keeping the fire in the confines of the condemned warehouse.

Reporters, officials, curiosity seekers, began pushing toward the Federal men. "X" had to get away. For all he knew, Mathews had been discovered. Maybe at this moment cops were scouring the city for the impostor who had taken five federal men on a raid.

"Wells," the Agent addressed one of the detectives, "stall off this mob for me. Tell the reporters I'll have a statement prepared at my office. I want to follow down another lead—alone. So long!"

"X" ran along inside the police line. A cop got in his path, and the Agent flashed the federal badge belonging to Mathews. That cleared the way. Around the next corner, he hailed a cab, and rode to the railroad station. He barged through to it, went out a side exit and hurried to one of his hideouts.

Here he changed quickly to the disguise of A. J. Martin, newspaper man. Out in the street again he sped in a second cab to an

office he maintained under this name.

The Agent was bitterly disappointed at the outcome of the raid. The fire had consumed whatever evidence the building might have contained. Karloff and his sinister crew had fled, taking the dope with them. Their whereabouts was unknown even to "X." This troubled him.

HE paced the floor of his office for a moment, then reached for the phone. Posing as a press man connected with a big syndicate, he had a staff of operatives working for him, running down minor leads and obtaining information that was vital to his activities. There was shadowing to be done, routine investigations to be made, and other tasks that any competent man could perform. The dangerous, uncertain missions he reserved for himself.

The man he phoned now was Jim Hobart, an ex-detective, and one of the Agent's most skilled and trusted operatives. He was a bluff, red-headed, rawboned young man. Framed by an underworld czar he had been dismissed from the force on graft charges. Now having got back into the good graces of the police by rendering them service in one of the Agent's cases, he had been allowed to take out a license and open up a private detective agency.

It was known as the Hobart Agency, and no one except Jim knew that A. J. Martin was the real proprietor. Even he did not guess that the man who had helped him and employed him was the mysterious, ever alert Secret Agent "X," whose real identity was an eternal enigma. In his eyes "X" was just what he seemed, a high-pressure newspaperman out to get inside stories of crime.

Under the Secret Agent's direction Hobart had organized a staff of a dozen skilled operatives, men and women in all classes of life and of all ages. By giving a brief order to Jim, "X" could send any one of these men or women out on a shadowing or investigating job. This left his own time free for the really important tasks that no one save himself would have the skill and daring to undertake.

Hobart had been working on details of the drug menace, tracing down the rumor that even the police were being reached by the sinister gang. He answered "X's" call now, his voice crackling with excitement.

"Plenty of things are happening, boss. You sure had the right tip. This dope wave has hit the department. It's hard to believe, but you remember Eddie Broderick? A damn good guy. Rough and tough, but a credit to the force. Well, he's done for, washed up. They found a hypo in his locker, and his arm looks like it was used for a pincushion. He can't explain how he took to snow, except that the thing came to him, and he almost went crazy until some cokey introduced him to the needle."

Jim Hobart was full of news, bad news, showing how the sinister ring was spreading. The police department had been hit by the drug evil. The commissioner had managed to stifle publicity, but he couldn't prevent the facts from getting to a tireless investigator like Hobart. The Agent's operative went on to tell what else he had learned.

Dolph Palmer, a deputy inspector of the narcotic bureau, had been caught pilfering confiscated drugs. He had admitted his evil habits, but claimed that he'd developed a severe nervous affliction that puzzled the doctors, and which could be soothed only by dope.

Bob Lane, on the police force for twenty years, a typical, honest, courageous cop, the sort who walk a beat until retirement, was in prison on a murder charge. He had held up a small drug store, killed the proprietor to get the store's supply of narcotics. There was mystery surrounding his addiction, too. He could give no reason why he used drugs, except that suddenly the awful craving had mastered him.

"It's bad enough when the coppers get on the stuff," continued Jim Hobart, "but when kids take to dope, it's awful. You wouldn't think there'd be cokeheads at the private schools—but take Miss Laurel's place for girls. That's about the most high-hat, hoity-toity outfit in town. A gal has to have blue-blood ancestors, a couple of financial pirates for grandfathers, and an inheritance that'd pay off an army before she gets into the Laurel brain factory."

Hobart paused a moment and the Agent asked a horrified question.

"You mean those child-heirs to millions are taking narcotics?"

"Worse than that, boss," came Hobart's answer. "Their folks have kept the story out of the papers, but last night Miss Laurel's little queens turned out one of the wildest riots in history. One of them got a vial of dope somewhere. Another tried to steal it. She got a paper knife through her ribs. That started it.

"By the time the show was finished, Miss Laurel's dormitory looked like a battlefield. Dope made those gals hell-cats. More than half of them are hopheads. Ten are in private hospitals, and they're all under observation. The papers don't dare print a word, because they'll lose a million dollars worth of advertising from some of the gals' papas."

An intense light shone in the Secret Agent's eyes. The drug evil was raging and spreading like a plague. Cops, children, people of wealth. Dope knew neither class nor creed. With only a week needed to make a drug addict, this insidious, mysterious ring would soon have the whole city in its power.

"X" had to act quickly. The indefatigable Hobart had a long list of crimes of violence attributed to the new dope evil. The Agent stopped him in the midst of his recital. "You've done a swell job, Jim," he said. "Now I want you to try to discover what the drug victims themselves don't know. How did they become addicts? That's what we've got to find out. Keep in touch with the office. I don't know how long I'll be away this time."

He hung up and for a moment sat at his desk in deep thought. A mysterious, brooding figure, hidden behind an impenetrable disguise, the Secret Agent was plotting his course of action against one of the worst criminal rings he had ever faced.

FOOTSTEPS sounded in the hallway outside. Something was dropped in the special mail box attached to the door. The footsteps passed on.

The Secret Agent arose quickly, opened the box and took out a long, thin envelope. It was sealed with wax. The color of the wax told him instantly that it was a confidential report from another of his operatives, one Lloyd Hankins.

He tore the end of the envelope off immediately, spread out the papers inside.

The report concerned Count Remy de Ronfort, a European of

shady reputation whom "X" was suspicious of and had asked Hankins to investigate. De Ronfort was a descendant of a noble French family, but had become a criminal. He had been in America five weeks, according to Hankins' report, but so far hadn't indulged in activities that would interest the police. His time had been spent wooing Paula Rockwell, the fluffy, pretty ward of a retired financier, Whitney Blake.

Charming and aristocratic, de Ronfort was considered a catch for the season's debutantes by their parents, who didn't know his reputation. Hankins' report was brief. He had been shadowing de Ronfort, but had learned little more than what had already been recorded in the society columns. De Ronfort had recently become engaged to Paula Rockwell.

The Agent went at once to his own secret files. He was not satisfied with Hankins' report. He had some data of his own on the man. The count had a long criminal record on the Continent, but the full list of his adventures outside the law was tucked away in the hidden archives of the Paris Sûreté.[40]

The society columns told of de Ronfort's vast country estates in France, but it was recorded in the Agent's authoritative files that the man was penniless, except for what he had made through underworld activities.

He had been associated with dope smuggling activities in Europe. That was why "X" was interested in him. The man was clever, highly educated, with influential contacts throughout the world, and he was a thoroughgoing scoundrel. He had been suspected of purchasing large quantities of crude opium in China and India. Later the police of France had connected him with the activities of a ring engaged in smuggling in the refined products of heroin and morphine. He was said to be a purveyor of narcotics to the rich and black-sheep nobility of several of the world's metropolises.

The Agent's own suspicions seemed justified. The count's conduct had been beyond criticism in America. Yet perhaps he was the power behind the ring now dispensing free drugs. The count lacked neither the ability nor the bent for such a position.

The Agent glanced at a newspaper lying on his desk. He had

---

40   AUTHOR'S NOTE: *To check up on the lives and activites of famous European criminals, the Agent made during use of his genius for disguise on two occasions. Once, impersonating an assistant to the prefect of police, he collected data in the files of the Sûreté. At another time he helped himself to information in the record books of Scotland Yard, disguised as a high official of the C. I. D.*

folded it to a photograph. This was a picture of Remy de Ronfort with Paula Rockwell. They made a dashing couple. There was an announcement of a party in honor of the engaged couple, to be given at Blake's house the following night.

THAT interested the Agent. Temporarily checkmated in his attempt to catch Karloff, he was ready to try any new lead that had promise. A way to meet Count de Ronfort instantly suggested itself. He reached for the telephone, called the city room of the *Herald*.

"Miss Betty Dale," said the Agent when the connection had been made. The girl he had called was one of the few people in the world, besides a high Washington official known as K9, who knew the nature of his strange work. She was the daughter of a police captain who had been slain by underworld bullets. Her contempt for the criminal class was as great as that of the Agent's himself.

A clear, confident voice came over the wire. "Yes, this is Miss Dale of the *Herald*."

A faint gleam appeared in the Agent's eyes. "You're going to the Blake party tomorrow night, are you not, Miss Dale?" he asked.

"Yes, that's right, I've been detailed to cover the affair. Who are you?"

Agent "X" ignored the question.

Instead of answering he asked another of his own. "How about taking Ben Buchanan, clubman and man-about-town, as your escort?"

There was a little gasp, a pause, then a cold note crept into the voice that came over the wire. "I'm sorry, Mr. Buchanan, there must be some mistake. I don't think I've had the pleasure of an introduction. And the first edition goes to press in half an hour. I'm very busy—if you don't mind—"

"You haven't answered my question!"

"No; and I don't intend—"

"X" knew she was about to hang up on him. Betty, golden-haired, pretty as some artist's model, had a will of her own and could take care of herself. He puckered up his lips suddenly, leaned forward and sent into the telephone's mouthpiece a whistle that had a strange birdlike note. It was melodious, yet eerie—a sound that once heard could never be forgotten. It was the whistle of Secret Agent "X." He listened after he had given it. The voice at the end of the wire changed again. It was low and tense now, with a quaver of emotion in it.

"You!" breathed Betty Dale. "I didn't understand—I thought—Of course I'd like you as an escort. You know—"

Confusion made the girl stop; yet there had been warmth, pleasure, expectancy in her reply. Often before she had given the Secret Agent aid in his desperate work. Often they had shared stark dangers together and walked in the Valley of the Shadow side by side. Never knowingly had she seen the Agent undisguised. His identity was a mystery to her as to the rest of the world. Yet she had felt his power, honesty, courage and unswerving purpose. Beside him others whom she knew seemed tame, commonplace.

"Tomorrow evening," she added quickly. "Eight-thirty at my apartment. I'll be—waiting."

THE next night a sleek, high-powered limousine with a chauffeur at the wheel drew up before a big apartment building. Whitney Blake's penthouse was on the top.

In the vestibule below, a liveried doorman helped from the car a girl of decisive, glamorous beauty. She wore a shimmering evening gown of white satin. A black velvet wrap trimmed with fur fell from gleamingly white shoulders. The golden, lustrous hair that was like imprisoned sunlight was set off by a tiara of sparkling brilliants. In spite of her career as a newspaper woman there was an unspoiled freshness about Betty Dale. The strength in her firm little chin and clear eyes only heightened her appeal.

The man who escorted her was broad-shouldered. His formal black-and-white garb was tailored to bring out the lines of a muscular, tapering body. The tan on his face suggested the polo field and the hunting trail. He had the easy poise of a man who had devoted his life to graceful, luxurious, selfish existence. The poise of a clubman, and wealthy sportsman at home in the city's most exclusive drawing rooms. Again Secret Agent "X" was playing a masterly role.

As Ben Buchanan, society gallant, he was just the sort to be welcomed into the gay, sophisticated circle of Paula Rockwell's friends.

A private elevator whisked them to the twenty-second floor. A door clicked open, and they stepped into an anteroom of the lavish, spacious penthouse of Whitney Blake.

The party was already in noisy progress when "X" and Betty Dale were ushered into the large drawing-room. The Secret Agent looked about him. Beneath this atmosphere of luxury and gaiety, it was possible that he might find the sinister footprints of crime.

The lights were subdued. The music was lilting. In the air was a blend of many soft perfumes, from flowers that stood in tall vases, and from the gowns and bodies of the lovely, glamorously dressed women present. Couples were dancing on the front terrace. In the rear, adding a touch of unconventionality to appeal to the younger set, was a swimming pool, made gay with colored lights. Guests in bathing suits were making use of this. Short swims were being mixed with long drinks.

Many times the Secret Agent had mingled with false and boisterous gaiety of this sort. He knew how to appear to be a part of it. Yet in his heart he felt contempt for it. To one who had known the closeness of death in the pursuit of master criminals, to one who had had adventures in the shadowy underworlds of crime, the false thrills and inanities of drunken wit and alcoholic capers were insipid. Betty Dale spoke softly in his ear.

"There's always a mixed crowd at Paula Rockwell's. She's an excitement seeker and social lion hunter, too."

"I rather think she is," said the Agent significantly.

A tall, dark man was coming in from Whitney Blake's private bar. "X" recognized him as Count Remy de Ronfort. A girl ran in from the terrace and grabbed the count's arm. She was a fluffy-haired, doll-faced debutante dressed in blue chiffon.

"There's Paula now," said Betty. "They make a picture, don't they?"

The Agent did not answer. His eyes were upon de Ronfort. The count's smile was ingratiating. "X" could see at a glance that the man had mastered all the social tricks and graces that pass for charm. He had a slight look of dissipation, a slight air of boredom. The small mustache that graced his upper lip was trimmed and trained elegantly. He cut a dashing figure in his evening clothes. Despite his former criminal activities, Remy de Ronfort, in appearance and manner, was as correct as some fashion plate.

Paula Rockwell saw Betty and ran forward, tugging the Count with her.

"Miss Dale," she cooed. "I'm so glad you're here! It's *the* party of the season. Everybody's come. All the worth-while people. You must give it a big splurge in tomorrow's *Herald*. And don't forget my fiancé—the Count. His favorite reading is the news stories about himself. And you won't find *me* dodging any cameras."

Paula Rockwell had beauty of a sort; red lips, dancing eyes. But there was an exaggerated coyness about her. Her face mirrored a shallow, empty mind. She drove twelve-cylinder cars and had a one-cylinder brain.

Studying de Ronfort, "X" saw that the man was playing a part. His treatment of Paula Rockwell was the last word in tact. He laughed at her commonplace sallies, baited her into feeling clever, and made her the center of attraction. Behind his actions was the scheming cunning of a man set to get a rich wife. But what did the Count do for money now? That interested "X."

DE RONFORT murmured polite nothings to Betty. In a moment Paula Rockwell led him away proprietarily to meet some other newly arrived guests. She guided them and the count toward the end of the room. Agent "X" looked in the direction where the engaged couple were headed.

"The old chap in the arm-chair over there in the corner is Whitney Blake," said Betty. "He had a paralytic stroke after the stock market crash in '29. The sight of two million going up in smoke was too much for him; but he still has enough left to buy polo ponies and yachts, for Paula and her Count."

For a moment the Agent's eyes became fixed on the ex-financier, a white-haired, craggy-faced man. Then they switched from him to another man close by and he asked a sudden question.

"Isn't that Silas Howe talking to Blake, Betty? How did he crash a party like this?"

Betty Bale stared, then nodded.

"It's Howe all right. They were talking about him at the *Herald* office this afternoon. He's already campaigning against narcotics. He wants to lead a crusade and grab a lot of publicity for himself. I suspect he's here to make Whitney Blake contribute. He has an apartment in this building and must have crashed the party."

The Agent's eyes narrowed. Even here at this gay party the drug menace was making itself felt. Howe, a famous reformer and temperance man, with a rawboned body and a long nose that seemed especially made to be thrust into other people's affairs, had seen fit to come. The Demon Rum was no longer in the limelight. Howe saw his chance to win notoriety by battling the Demon Drugs.

He began haranguing Whitney Blake now, and the Agent became instantly alert. He moved closer, to overhear the conversation and see what opinions Howe held. The reformer's voice rose blatantly.

"I tell you, Blake, the big-stick policy must be used against the underworld. Catch all the crooks—make 'em tell what they know—

and you'll run this thing to the ground. I intend to form vigilance committees and—" Howe paused to wipe his gaunt, perspiring face "—I appeal to you as a man of wealth to aid me. I have seen the light again. I've come out of retirement. I intend to wipe out the drug evil in America. Contribute ten thousand dollars, Blake, and your fellow citizens will be eternally grateful."

Blake said nothing. He chewed his cigar thoughtfully. Count de Ronfort, standing near-by with a contemptuous smile on his face, addressed Howe.

"You wouldn't take the work of the police away from them, would you, my frien'?"

"The police?" sneered Howe. "What have they done? Nothing, nothing, except bungle. Their feet are bogged down in politics. Graft is a festering sore in their midst. A non-partisan organization must fight this thing. That's why I'm collecting contributions from men like Blake. And I won't take no for an answer. I know that Blake and others like him will back me up when they learn the facts. I know I can depend on them."

Silas Howe had the fire of a fanatic and an egotist. He pictured himself as a knight in armor leading a crusade against evil. His voice rose to the hoarse note of a frenzied orator. People gathered about. Whitney Blake listened patiently for a while, then began to show irritation in the tapping of his black cane. He spoke at last, ignoring Howe's eloquence.

"If the police have bungled," he said, "I don't think you and your vigilance committees will get organized enough to do even that. You're theorists—all of you. Talk can't win against organized crime. I've no desire to contribute money that will be given over in fat salaries to speech-makers. If you want to see some action, Howe, get yourself sworn in as a deputy and join the police or the narcotics bureau. Maybe when hopheads start shooting at you, you won't be so anxious to lead the crusade."

HOWE'S lean face turned crimson with fury. He choked down his anger, tried a wheedling tone on Blake. The ex-financier made an impatient gesture and drew out a fresh cigar which de Ronfort courteously lighted for him. Betty Dale laughed in the Secret Agent's ear.

"Howe has met his match," she said. "He's a publicity hound and Blake knows it."

Agent "X" nodded. He led Betty onto the dance floor. For five minutes they were engaged in the intricate steps of a new tango; then the alert eyes of "X," trained to miss nothing, began to notice a queer change in the guests. His fingers tightened on his dancing partner's arm. His voice was tense.

"Look, Betty, there's something going on here!"

What the Secret Agent had seen was this. Members of the party, who a short time before appeared fatigued with dancing and sodden with drink, now began to show signs of feverish activity. Their eyes were brighter. Their conversation more noisy, their laughter shrill and metallic. A couple bumped into them and made a vulgar sally. Betty Dale grew tense.

"What is it?" she whispered.

"X" had a theory of his own, but he said nothing. He led Betty off the dance floor and they watched and waited. A youth, strangely restless, and circulating through the room, teetered up to them. He had a box of fancy Turkish blend cigarettes in his hand. With a brittle laugh he held this out to the Agent.

"Try one, pal ol' pal!" he invited. "They're good for that tired feeling. They pep you up in a jiffy. See for yourself!"

Calmly the Agent took one; but there was a smoldering light in his own eyes. He touched a match to the cigarette, inhaled deeply, while the youth nodded and smiled.

"Makes you feel good, doesn't it, pal?" he said.

Still Agent "X" said nothing, but at the third breath a sudden sense of exhilaration filled him. He held the cigarette in his hand, said quietly:

"Where did you get these?"

The youth tittered. "A chap in the dressing room gave them to me. Said they were a sort of rejuvenator. And he hit the nail on the head. They're just what's needed at a dumb jamboree like this. Here!"

He held the box out for Betty Dale.

"Pardon me, lady, should have offered them to you first—but they make a fellow forget his manners."

At a sudden warning glance from Agent "X" Betty Dale refused. The Agent had become hawk-eyed now. He did not puff the cigarette again, but he watched the youth closely. The fellow, still in his teens, was obviously a guileless sort. Pleased with the effect of the cigarettes on himself, he was sharing his find with others. He offered a smoke to Paula Rockwell next, and with a coy glance at him she accepted.

The youth struck a match gallantly and held it out for her. But before Paula could get a light Count de Ronfort stepped in suavely. His long hand reached out, drew the cigarette from her fingers. He snapped it in two, dropped it.

"Come, *ma cherie*," he said. "That is Turkish and too exotic for your American taste. One of my own would be better—the kind you have been smoking all evening. One must be consistent in these things."

Paula Rockwell made an annoyed *moue* with her red lips, but she accepted the Count's cigarette.

"You are so masterful, Remy," she said.

Agent "X" had seen this small byplay. His heartbeat had quickened. De Ronfort had known that there was something queer about the cigarettes the youth was offering. Either he had previously tried one himself, or—

"X" did not question him now. He was casually trailing the youth across the penthouse floor. Many guests accepted the smokes he offered. His supply was diminishing. He lit another himself, inhaled hungrily, and came to the side of Silas Howe.

"Have one on me, grandpa," he said flippantly.

THE reformer's rawboned figure stiffened. His face quivered with the righteous indignation of his profession.

"Young man," he said, "your manners are conspicuous by their absence. Treat your elders with respect—and take those filthy weeds away. I never have and never will touch tobacco in any form."

The youth tittered again, and gave a burlesque salute.

"Then I'll keep the rest of these for myself," he said. "Thanks, ol' man, thanks."

He started to slip the box into his pocket; but Agent "X" laid a sudden hand on his arm.

"Tell me about this chap who gave those to you!" he said. "He was in the dressing room, you say. Suppose you introduce me to him."

The youth smiled slyly. "Want a box of 'em for yourself, eh? Well, all right. I never was one to hog a good thing. Come on!"

He led "X" to the dressing room for men, looked about and shook his head.

"The chap's gone," he said. "He must have buzzed out."

"Then we'll hunt him down," said "X" grimly.

He escorted the youth through the various rooms, till the young man began to complain.

"What's this—a walking tour! He's gone, I say. Never saw him before in my life. Now he's breezed out. Here, I'll divvy with you. Can't go buzzing about like this all night."

He took out the box of cigarettes. Agent "X" snatched them from his fingers, watching the young man's face. Indignation alone was expressed there.

"I say!" he cried. "A fine pal you turned out to be. Grab 'em all for yourself. You can't get away with that."

In a moment the Agent's voice grew hard. He stepped close to the man, caught his arm and faced him.

"Don't be a fool," he said, "There's dope in these cigarettes. The tobacco's loaded with it. That's why they 'pep' you up!"

"Dope!" the youth's face expressed horror. "It's rot! Paula Rockwell wouldn't have dope at her party."

"You say yourself you got them from a stranger. He isn't here now. Look, he's passed out dozens of those cigarettes. Half the people here have been smoking them."

"And who are you, a dick?"

"No, a man who recognizes dope when he comes across it."

The youth passed a shaky hand across his flushed face. "I guess you're right at that," he said. "I feel—funny. Like floating away, or getting into a fight, or something."

"Go over and sit down," said "X" firmly. "Say nothing about this to anyone, but if you see that man who passed them out again tell me."

The youth nodded, stumbled toward a seat. Agent "X" turned back to Betty Dale. Just as he reached her side a small, self-effacing man came up. He had a paper in his hand.

"I'm Rivers," he said, "Mr. Blake's secretary. You're Miss Dale of the *Herald*, I'm told. Miss Rockwell said to give you this, a list of tonight's guests. And if there's any other information you wish I—er—will be pleased to give it to you."

Betty Dale thanked the man absently and took the list. There was a grim smile on the Agent's face. Paula Rockwell was seeking publicity, seeking to feed her shallow-minded vanity—while the coils of the drug evil wound themselves about her guests, and the viperlike poison of dope bit into their hearts and minds.

Before the Agent could speak his thoughts to Betty there was a sudden startling racket outside, near one of the French windows leading to a side balcony.

Those in the spacious drawing room stopped tensely in their tracks. Eyes turned, necks craned. Then gasps went up.

For the French windows swung inward, banging against the wall. Glass shattered and shivered to the floor, and framed in the opening a wild-eyed, unshaven man crouched. He stood there a moment, peering at the crowd, blinking at the light. Then he stepped inside, and a woman gave a terrified shriek.

The man had the look of a hunted beast. His eyes were savage, sunken, with a curious haunted expression. The skin of his face was as tight as a death's head. The muscles beneath it twitched painfully. He was sniffing like an animal, with nostrils dilated. His clothing was torn, dirty and threadbare, and one hand was thrust before him rigidly. In the fingers of it was clutched a long-bladed knife.

His eyes swiveled about the room. They focused with an insane glare on the group in the corner, where Paula Rockwell, de Ronfort, Silas Howe and others were grouped about Blake in his arm-chair.

The stranger's breath hissed through clenched teeth. He uttered a shrill, hate-impelled cry and pointed. The Agent started for the man. But the stranger gave a second wild, blood-curdling shout and leaped madly forward, brandishing the wicked sliver of gleaming steel overhead.

CHAPTER VII

MYSTERY MURDER

AT THAT INSTANT a swift outburst came from Silas Howe. "It's one of them!" he cried. "One of the dope ring! They hate me, fear me—and they'd kill me if they could. But I wield a stronger weapon than they. I—"

As he spoke, the lights in the big room abruptly winked out. His hysterical utterance was cut off by a wild confusion of screams and frenzied shouts. There was a rush to get clear of the maniac's path.

Agent "X" did not join this. He stood tensely, trying to pierce the gloom. Then a streak of flame lanced the darkness suddenly. The Agent heard no gunshot, yet an agonized cry followed the streak of burning powder. Something thudded to the floor and thrashed about.

Panic gripped the guests of Whitney Blake. They began stumbling over furniture, crashing against the walls. Some one hurled a chair through the French doors leading to the front terrace. There was a clatter, as a tray of liquor glasses was upset. Persons were colliding with one another in a mad endeavor to reach safety.

Then, as mysteriously as they'd gone off, the lights came on again.

Agent "X" surveyed the room. Sprawled on the floor was the wild eyed man, his tousled head encircled by a crimson pool. His knife had dropped from still fingers.

"X" leaned over the body. He didn't disturb it, but he was able to see instantly that the man was dead. A bullet had caught the stranger in the head.

Excitement gave way to a nervous let-down in the room. A woman laughed hysterically. Another fainted in the arms of her escort. "X" glanced at Silas Howe. The man was trembling with excitement. Beside him, debonair and unruffled, stood Remy de

The whole building was resounding with the snarl of mounting flames.

Ronfort, trying to comfort Paula Rockwell, who was crying noisily. Old Whitney Blake still held his cigar, but his face showed lines of strain, like wrinkles on parchment.

De Ronfort's suave voice sounded in the room, "Most excellent work, M'sieu Howe," he said. "You saved us from a crazy man. He would have carved us up assuredly. You showed preat presence of mind in administering the *coup de grace,* as it were—in shooting him."

Silas Howe looked bewildered, "But—but—" he stuttered, "I didn't shoot him. I'd have killed him willing—if I could have. He was a homicidal, drug-crazed man—and you saw yourselves that he intended to murder me. But I'm not much of a shot and wouldn't have taken the chance—especially in the dark. You're mistaken, Count de Ronfort, it was someone else who slew the vermin."

De Ronfort laughed and shrugged. "You are a modest man, M'sieu Howe. I myself saw you reaching for a gun just before the lights went out. You should take full credit to yourself instead of giving it to another."

Howe started to protest when Whitney Blake's voice sounded.

"Whatever the circumstance we must call the police," he said. "And I must ask that none of you leave this apartment until a checkup has been made."

He sent his man, Rivers, to call headquarters. And as this was being done Agent "X" moved through the crowd, brushing against men and deftly touching them to see who was carrying concealed weapons. But the one man who seemed to have a gun was Silas Howe, and yet the reformer had vehemently denied the killing. The agent's eyes were bright. Betty Dale sensed that there was strange drama in the air.

"Why doesn't Howe admit the killing?" she whispered. "He could claim self-defense. He has nothing to fear."

The Agent shook his head. "Perhaps he's telling the truth. We'll find out soon."

IN a few minutes the police arrived. There were several officers in uniform, the medical examiner, and three men in plainclothes. The sight of one of them made Betty Dale exclaim under her breath and clutch the Agent's arm nervously. This was a pale, sharp-featured man who surveyed the room with a coldly impersonal gaze from piercing gray eyes that gleamed beneath jutting black eyebrows.[41]

One of his men addressed him as "inspector," and with the medical examiner at his side he looked at the dead man for a moment,

---

41   AUTHOR'S NOTE: *The man whose appearance made Betty Dale fearful for the Agent's safety was Inspector John Burks, head of the city homicide squad. It may be remembered that in other of the Secret Agent's encounters with criminals Burks had acted as a barrier in his path by treating "X" as a criminal himself. This was natural, since the inspector had no inkling of the Agent's connection with a high government official.*

then went over and glanced at the French windows.

De Ronfort, poised and talkative, took it upon himself to describe the stranger's entry and the killing. Inspector Burks listened, making notes in a small black book, then spoke in the flat, hard tone that was habitual with him.

"Nobody admits killing him, eh? That doesn't look so hot. There must be more to it than self-defense. If a man broke into my house and got fresh with a knife I wouldn't hesitate to drop him. But if nobody's going to own up to this job, we'll have to find out who did it and why he isn't telling."

Count de Ronfort laughed. "We have a very modest man with us," he said. "M'sieu Howe here is the hero of the occasion. But he is too retiring to claim the credit. I think, however, if you will question him—"

The Count ceased speaking. Inspector Burks had already turned on the reformer and fixed him with an eagle eye.

"Well, what about it, Howe? You've been holding the lid down on this city for a good many years. But I didn't know you'd taken over the job of executioner, too. Tell us how you killed this guy."

Howe shook his head, and his eyes snapped. "I told the Count that I did not do the shooting. He chooses to call me a liar. I have got a gun, but—"

"Ah!" said Burks. He held out his hand. With a sour scowl, Silas Howe fished in his pocket and drew out a small revolver. He gave this to the inspector.

Burks broke open the gun, examined the shells, then squinted through the barrel. Still unsatisfied, he pulled out his handkerchief, thrust it into the gun and twisted it around. Then he examined the cambric intently and shook his head.

"Clean as a whistle. No smoke here, and all the cartridges new! This gun hasn't been fired tonight. You didn't kill this man, that's plain, but you'll have to take a trip to headquarters anyway, and likely pay a fine. There's a law in this state that says—"

Silas Howe interrupted angrily. "I have a permit," he said. "You can't annoy me like that, inspector, though I know you'd like to—after the expose of police graft I made some years ago; but, see here—" he produced a piece of paper, a pistol permit, and waved it triumphantly in the inspector's face. "In the reform work I do my life is in constant peril. What happened here tonight shows that this is true. That man came to murder me, and I want to offer thanks to whoever shot him."

Burks grunted in irritation. His pale face looked still paler. He was in a mood to make trouble for some one. He turned on his assistants.

"I'm going to get to the bottom of this. We'll search every man and woman in this room. This fellow may have been a dopy, but I want to know who killed him. Porter, and you, Kendal, round the folks up. Hunt for a gun, and don't stop till you find it!"

The two detectives snapped into action instantly. Their skilled, experienced fingers went through men's pocket and women's bags and compacts. They were systematic about it, marshaling those who had been searched to one side of the room, keeping the others in a corner. Even Paula Rockwell and Whitney Blake himself were not excluded.

The Count de Ronfort submitted to a search smilingly. Then it was "X's" turn, and, as the two detectives approached him, all color drained from Betty Dale's face. Fear made shadows in her eyes. She had hoped the Agent would make a break before this. Yet "X" could not, for suspicion would have reflected back on Betty, since he was her escort.

Now it was too late—and Betty knew that Agent "X" carried various devices to assist him in his strange battle with crime. She had seen them many times, and the thought that they would be found by the police made her blood run cold.[42]

Their presence on the person of Ben Buchanan, supposed clubman, would reveal him instantly as Secret Agent "X," a man hunted and hounded by Burks as a criminal, and a man wanted by the police of a dozen cities for questioning in connection with crime cases that were still a mystery to them.

Betty Dale held her breath. Deep in her heart she loved this strange, mysterious man whose real face she had never seen. She had hidden her love carefully, pledging herself that it must never interfere with the career he had chosen. But when death and danger threatened him, she found it hard to suppress her emotion.

Inspector Burks stood now with his eagle eyes fastened on the Agent and a gun in an armpit holster close to his hand. And, as the two plain-clothes men reached for the man they knew as Ben Buchanan, it seemed to Betty Dale that she was going to faint.

---

42 *AUTHOR'S NOTE: The Agent's hidden devices are changed from time to time as new emergencies arise in his dangerous, desperate work. But almost always he carries his gas gun, his sound amplifying device, and various materials for quick changes of disguise.*

CHAPTER VIII

SMUGGLER'S SECRET

HOLDING HER BODY rigid Betty Dale watched as the detectives searched him. Seconds seemed to drag as their hands went systematically through his clothing. But all they found was a key, a handkerchief and a wallet containing the identification card of Ben Buchanan. There were mocking glints in the Secret Agent's eyes.

Betty Dale gave a little sigh of relief; but she was puzzled. "X" always carried strange instruments on his person. Now he didn't even have his specially made chromium tools. Yet a short while before Betty herself had seen a cigarette lighter in his hand, the one with the tiny lever that released a jet of anesthetizing vapor.

When the detectives had passed on to another of Blake's guests, Betty glanced at the Agent questioningly. He drew her aside and whispered a quick explanation.

"That bookcase over against the wall," he said. "I'm glad the inspector isn't interested in Greek tragedy. I pulled out a volume of Aeschylus when he wasn't looking and hid certain things behind it."

"X" retrieved his mysterious equipment as dexterously as he had hidden it. Then he turned his attention to the work of the police. Blue-coats had been dispatched to search the apartment. They had discovered the means used by the intruder to reach the penthouse.

A rope had been thrown up over the balcony railing from a set-back ledge on the floor below. This floor held several empty apartments. The man could easily have hidden in one of them, or in a deserted corridor until he was ready to break into Blake's penthouse.

There was no clue, however, as to who had turned off the lights. Apparently no one in the drawing room was responsible. Several switches showed along the walls. Inspector Burks tested them. Each controlled a row of lights, but no master switch could be found in the room. Agent "X" was lynx-eyed with alertness, listening, watching.

The sudden entry and shooting of the wild-appearing stranger had flung a pall of horror over the party. And the mystery of his death was deepening each second.

The medical examiner's statement that the man had been a drug addict started Silas Howe on another harangue.

"That's right," he cried vehemently. "He was a hophead, and he came here to murder me. My life isn't safe anywhere. But danger won't stop me. My course is set. I'll smash all barriers in my fight against the drug evil. You see now, Blake, what great need there is for funds! As a close neighbor of yours I must ask again that you contribute."

Whitney Blake merely grunted. He ignored the reformer's final plea. This dampened Howe's enthusiasm for a while. But soon he singled out a pretty, wealthy debutante who had been to the bar once too often. He began picturing to her the horrors of the drug, stirring her alcoholic imagination, as an aid in soliciting funds.

Agent "X" nudged Betty, and for a time his eyes intently studied the gaunt, leathery face of the reformer.

Inspector Burks began the weary routine of questioning all those in the room at the time of the shooting. He got nowhere. A dozen people had been standing in front of the maniac when he burst through the French windows. Any one of them could have seen his silhouette against the outside glow when the lights went off. Any one with a gun could have shot him. But Silas Howe's was the only weapon to be found, and that hadn't been fired. Unseen, horrible death, like the spirit of evil itself, seemed to be present at the party. Men and women shuddered.

"X" was in accord with Burks's theory that the shooting had been done by some one now in the room. But who was it? He had not forgotten that his purpose in coming had been to investigate Count Remy de Ronfort. Yet the Frenchman seemed the most unperturbed person there. And not even a pocket-knife had been found in his possession.

After the names and addresses of the guests had been taken by the police, Burks announced that they were free to go. But he warned them that any and all were subject to call as witnesses.

"And I won't hesitate to subpoena you, either," he added threateningly.

The inspector was in a savage mood. Some one had turned a common, self-defense shooting into a complicated affair, with possibly a hidden motive. Burks grew more ugly when his men finished searching the body and reported that there were no visible means of identification.

Agent "X," pointing to the man's shoes, spoke with a touch of irony, "Those are custom-made, inspector. They were good shoes once, though they are in bad shape now. Acid or something has spotted and rotted them. Even at that they provide a lead for any detective who knows his job."

Inspector Burks grew purple with irritation. He choked, made a snarling noise in his throat and glared at the Agent.

"A brilliant observation, Mr. Buchanan, but it happens that I am conducting this investigation. I'll thank you not to interfere." His voice was shaky with rage. "X" had put him in an embarrassing position before the crowd, made the police appear inadequate and hurt his professional pride. Burks alibied himself quickly.

"I was coming to those shoes as a matter of routine," he said icily. "The police I can assure you don't need the advice of meddling bystanders to conduct a murder investigation."

Yet in spite of his harsh response "X" knew that Burks would work on the tip. The Agent himself took special note of the shoes. The heels had been built up on the inner part, as is done to help and correct feet suffering from fallen arches. Stamped in German script on the insteps were the words "hand made."

BLAKE'S frightened guests began to straggle out, glad to escape from his place of mystery and death, Agent "X" and Betty left also. "X" had learned all he could from watching. There were certain leads now that must be carefully followed.

He escorted Betty to her door, silent for the most part. She raised her blue eyes to his just before he left her and asked him to promise that he would call her if there was any way in which she could help him.

"I will, Betty," he said, "but—"

He left the sentence unfinished. Before his mind rose a horrible picture of the man who had died in Karloff's stronghold. The man who had fallen to the floor in the agonies of the green death. The hideous shadow of the narcotic ring must not be allowed to menace golden-haired Betty Dale. He took her hand, pressed it for a moment, and turned.

"I'll be seeing you soon," he said gaily. The smiling light in his eyes gave no indication of the inhuman dangers he would shortly face.

In one of his hideouts he changed his disguise to that of A. J. Martin, then went to the laboratory of a toxicologist and brilliant research chemist named Fenwick. Posing as Martin, "X" had made use of this man's technical skill and complex equipment before.[43]

Already in the present case he had made arrangements to employ Fenwick in probing the sinister secrets of the dope ring. Every scrap of evidence so far in the way of confiscated drugs had been turned over to the man.

Small, birdlike, with an almost inexhaustible energy that enabled him to work night and day, Fenwick greeted the Agent.

"How are you, Mr. Martin?"

The chemist was wearing a stained white coat. There was a dripping hydrometer in his hand. A metal pot was boiling on a small gas stove and fumes filled the close air of the laboratory. Agent "X" smiled, but wasted no time in pleasantries, He handed Fenwick the Turkish cigarettes he had obtained at Blake's party.

"These contain a drug," he said quietly. "I doubt if an analysis of them will be easy. There's hardly enough of the stuff to isolate and work on. But do your best, Fenwick."

There was an undertone of tenseness in the Agent's low-spoken words, and Fenwick nodded at once.

"I'll get busy immediately. There'll be a report for you tomorrow, Mr. Martin."

"Good!" said the Agent.

He left Fenwick's place and hurried away. The chemist was only a small cog in the amazing crime-combating machine that Agent "X" had secretly built up. There were many other cogs.

He went to the office which he maintained as the newspaper man, Martin, and picked up the phone. Once again he called Jim Hobart, but this time he asked Jim to come and see him.

The long, lanky operative arrived quickly, removing his hat and exposing his crest of flaming red hair. He had shared many dangers with "X" and had a wholesome respect for his employer, the man

---

43 *AUTHOR'S NOTE: In a hideout of his in the old Montgomery mansion, Agent "X" has a small laboratory and chemical apparatus of his own. But when time is precious he does not hesitate to make use of trained men like Fenwick, just as officials in great police bureaus employ technical experts in many branches of science.*

he thought of as A. J. Martin, representative of a great newspaper syndicate.

"What can I do for you, boss?" he said.

Agent "X" sprawled a leg over his desk, hung a cigarette on his lower lip, and assumed the manner and attitude of a hard-boiled newspaper man. Through clouds of smoke he squinted up at Hobart.

"Have you got a man on your staff, Jim, who can speak French, wear nifty clothes and mingle with the best society?"

Hobart immediately nodded. "Yes, boss. Walter Milburn's the fellow. His mother was French and used to whale him if he didn't talk frog. She sent him to dancing school and after he grew up he got to be the slickest bond salesman going, until folks stopped buying bonds. He can wear clothes like a fashion plate and he's got a Park Avenue manner. On top of that he's turned out to be a good dick."

"Good," said "X" quietly.

He drew a photograph of Count Remy de Ronfort from his desk, along with a brief record of the Count's career.

"I want this man kept under surveillance day and night," he said. "Get Milburn and whoever helps him to give you a daily report on him. Spare no expense. Use your own methods. Tip bellboys, bartenders, waiters, anybody, if necessary—but don't lose sight of him. If you hear of his doing anything funny get in touch with me at once."

HOBART looked at the picture and whistled, "That's the guy who's engaged to old Whitney Blake's ward, Paula Rockwell! They had their mugs in the papers the other day."

"Exactly!"

"And he's an ex-crook and dope runner, you say?"

"Yes! He's been shadowed before, too. See that Milburn does his stuff right."

"Count on me, boss. If Milly pulls any boners I'll clout him so hard he'll think he's a skyrocket."

"Then it may be too late," said "X" quietly.

When Jim Hobart had gone, Agent "X" left the office of Martin and went to a phone booth in a drug store many blocks away. Unknown to Hobart, or anyone else, there was still another detective organization under the Agent's control. This was a staff built up of

Agent "X" threw all his weight and strength into the blow.

seasoned and reliable operatives, interviewed individually by himself under different disguises and recruited from all parts of the country. They were nominally in charge of a man named Bates.[44]

Bates had secret headquarters, established by Agent "X." Day and night either Bates or one of his assistants was beside the phone, ready to respond to "X," the man they knew only as "chief."

---

44   AUTHOR'S NOTE: It may be remembered by followers of Secret Agent "X" that Bates played a courageous part in the case of the "Hooded Hordes." Also in the "Murder Monster," when two of his best men were killed.

The Agent had even equipped Bates's headquarters with a special, short-wave broadcasting radio. From this he could pick up important messages in code on the radio of his own car.

He called Bates now, and the man's voice came to him instantly.

"Yes, chief, is that you?"

"Right."

There was a pause at Bates's end of the wire. He was waiting for the chief to speak. "X" did so at once, using the particular tone he always employed when communicating with Bates's headquarters.

"I want you to send an experienced operative to the morgue," he said. "Tell him to look for the unidentified man who was killed at Whitney Blake's party tonight. He can claim he's hunting for a friend who is missing. His best lead is to trace down this man's shoes. They are custom-made and of a certain type. The maker shouldn't be hard to locate. Hurry on this job. I want you to beat the police."

"O.K., chief."

"And, Bates, send every man you've got on the job if necessary. Look up every place that makes custom-made shoes in the city. Give them the dead man's description. Find out who he is."

"Yes, chief."

Agent "X" hung up. He was throwing both of his highly trained organizations into this battle against the drug menace. Working separately; unknown to each other, both had been enlisted in the same cause. Both were responsible to Agent "X." The expense of his campaign might be great; but "X" stood ready to spend a fortune if he could stamp out the drug blight. The huge account held for him under the name of Elisha Pond in the First National Bank would take care of that.[45]

SIX hours passed, and the Agent received the first of his reports. It was from Fenwick, the chemist, and its contents were disappointing. Hard as he had tried, Fenwick had been unable to make a complete analysis. The drug in the impregnated tobacco of the cigarettes had become blended with nicotine in such a way that its

---

45   AUTHOR'S NOTE *This and a fund to replenish it was subscribed by ten public-spirited men of great wealth at the outset of the Agent's strange career. They had no inkling of "X's" identity; but one of the highest government officials in Washington has put his secret sanction on the Agent's activities. This fund may be used in any way "X" saw fit to fight crime.*

exact chemical nature eluded him. He promised sure results if "Mr, Martin" could obtain a purer specimen of the drug.

"X" called up the headquarters of Bates's and received a message that helped to offset Fenwick's failure.

"We've traced down those shoes, chief," Bates said. "They were made by a German over on the west side of town for this chap who was killed. His name's Alfred Twyning. He used to work in the research department of the Paragon Chemical Company. Looks like he hit the booze, got fired and got to be a bum."

"Good work, Bates," said Agent "X" quietly. What the man had told him checked up with those acid stains he had noticed on Twyning's shoes. But mystery still shrouded Twyning's death. Who had shot him, and what for? "X" snapped quick orders into the phone.

"Get all the information you can on Twyning's connection with Paragon Chemicals. I've heard of the place. It's out in the suburbs. They make tooth-paste, face creams, and stuff like that. Try to find out where he lived. If he left any belongings, search them, any way you can. Get all possible data."

"Yes, chief."

"X" spent the day making the rounds of underworld haunts in the disguise of a sportily dressed crook. It was a stock make-up that he had often employed. It aroused no suspicion. He hoped to run across one of Karloff's men, or hear something that would lead him back to the present hideout of the man who killed with the horrible green death. But if any criminals knew about the dope ring they dared not speak. Terror seemed to have taken the underworld into its icy grip.

Back in the office of A. J. Martin that evening Agent "X" received a message that sent him into instant action. It was Jim Hobart calling. The courageous redhead whom "X" had placed in charge of an agency was excited.

"I'm in a cigar store across from Clarendon Field right now, boss," he said. "I just followed the frog out here in a taxi. This de Ronfort guy has got a plane that he keeps under the name of Pierre LaFarge. Tie that if you can! I heard him talking to some mechanics. They're getting the plane ready now. I don't know where he's going; but he's traveling alone. What's next on the program?"

"Stick close," said "X" grimly. "If you can, slip de Ronfort's mechanics some money to stall on the job. Tell them it's a practical joke and that you want to make him late at a wedding. Something like that. Then charter another plane and stand by. Follow de Ronfort if he takes off before I get there."

The Agent clicked up the receiver. He grabbed his hat and coat and ran swiftly from the office. At the curb he jumped into one of his own cars, a smart, fast roadster with a short wave radio concealed under the dash panel. He was in a desperate hurry, impatient to get through the heavy traffic, and twice he drew reprimands from cops. A motor cycle officer stopped him, but his press card saved him from a summons.

In the suburbs he struck smooth concrete where he could step on the accelerator. He made the roadster surge forward till the engine was roaring as though a giant were imprisoned beneath the hood. Soon he was in a thinly populated section where the road was flanked by rolling meadows. Another mile, and he drove up before a big gate in a high wire fence.

Parking his car at the curb, he hurried through the gate and onto a broad field where he headed toward a bulky line of great, sprawling buildings. These were airplane hangars. "X's" sharp eyes recognized a mechanic lolling against a wall and he shouted to him.

"Get the bus out, quick, Joe! The biplane!"

THE mechanic flung away his cigarette and snapped into life.

"Right away, Mr. Martin," he said. "The open one's in tiptop shape. I went over her this morning. What's happening this time, Mr. Martin? You newspaper guys sure lead a wild life."

The Agent motioned the talkative mechanic to show some real speed. He ran to the hangar. By the time the plane had been pushed out, with a dolly under the tail, "X" was ready, garbed in a suede jacket, with goggles and helmet adjusted.

At this field he kept two planes. This small, single-seater biplane he called the *Blue Comet*. She was a beautiful craft, built with staggered wings, low camber and plenty of sweep-back. Except for her flashy coloring she might have been an Army pursuit job. During the war the Agent had done considerable flying. He had an expert's knowledge of all types of ships, and he'd selected the *Blue Comet* for its speed, climb and maneuverability after exhaustive tests of many other planes.

The Agent climbed into the cockpit as his mechanic wound up the inertia starter. He raised his hand, switched on the ignition, and the engine broke into a smooth-voiced, throaty rumble. For a minute or two "X" leaned back against the crash pad and warmed the motor. Then he signaled the mechanic to pull the chocks. He shoved the throttle forward; the radial broke into a roar and the plane leaped down the macadamized surface of the field, swiftly gathering momentum. It rose into the air as gracefully as a soaring gull, and hurtled up into the night-darkened sky

A short climb and "X" circled around, taking a northern course. The city spread out under his wings. Streets, parks, car tracks, with rows of twinkling electric lights like miniature strings of diamonds. Soon his trained eyes singled out the brilliant air beacon of Clarendon Field. He pushed the stick forward, kicked left rudder to sideslip and kill speed, and made an unobtrusive landing.

Jim Hobart was on the look-out for him. Jim knew the *Blue Comet*. Even before "X" had taxied to a stop, the operative was running beside the plane. Quick and efficient, schooled to emergencies, Hobart didn't lose time on unnecessary preliminaries.

"The guy's just taking off," he said hoarsely. "Over to your left, boss! I stalled his men for a while, but the Count complained to the field management about the delay. The operations guy came out, raised hell with the mechanics, and they sure hustled after that."

The Agent shot a quick glance to the left. "An amphibian!" he said.

Two field attendants were running toward the *Blue Comet*. "X" spoke quickly.

"Steer those birds away, Jim! I don't want any one nosing around. Tell them I stopped by to hand over some important papers to you. Quick!"

De Ronfort's amphibian was already in the air. Off the ground again, "X" immediately sought altitude until he was several hundred feet above the Frenchman's plane. The amphibian was traveling due east. To throw off suspicion that he was following, "X" headed south. Presently he banked the *Blue Comet* and brought the craft up on a parallel course with de Ronfort.

There were other planes in the air, but the Agent had no difficulty keeping track of the amphibian. The Count was heading out to sea.

Below twinkled the lights of the shoreline. In the channel a ship was ocean-bound, leaving a banner of heavy smoke trailing from the stack. In shore were the dark hulks of vessels resting at anchor. About five miles out at sea, "X" saw a blinker flashing on the bridge of a small steamer. Only a few lights gleamed from the portholes. The vessel obviously wasn't a passenger ship. "X" wasn't close enough to make out the boat clearly, but through the binoculars it appeared to be a tramp steamer.

Suddenly de Ronfort's plane swooped down, glided along the water and stopped very close to the ship's side. The night was clear. Cutting off his motor and gliding lower, "X" saw dots that were men at the ship's rail. Something attached to a line was thrown overboard. Peering through powerful night glasses, "X" watched de Ronfort haul an oblong shape aboard the amphibian.

"X's" eyes gleamed. This must surely be contraband of some sort. Probably it was dope. The Agent headed south once more. He banked again, and took a northwesterly course toward Clarendon Field, ahead of the Count. His mouth was grim. He meant to find out without delay, what Remy de Ronfort was smuggling into the United States.

CHAPTER IX

THE SEALED SUITCASE

CONFIDENT THAT THE Count was returning to Clarendon Field, "X" shoved the throttle forward and sent the *Blue Comet* ahead at full speed. He landed, turned his plane over to a mechanic and walked toward the black shadow of a hangar.

Five minutes later the Frenchman's amphibian was taxiing to a stop. De Ronfort stepped out of the plane, tugging a heavy suitcase.

He looked around sharply. While he removed his flying garb, he kept the suitcase between his legs. It was plain that de Ronfort was worried. He snapped at attendants and seemed impatient to be off. As soon as he was free to go, he half ran to the street.

Once more he stopped and swiveled his eyes in all directions. "X" had remained in the shadows. He saw de Ronfort light a cigarette, take a few nervous puffs, and throw it down, only to light another. A taxi driver hailed him, but the Count waved him on.

"X" realized the reason when the Frenchman hired the next cab. This one belonged to a company that had twelve thousand machines, and the drivers were not likely to be federal men or rival mobsters, whereas the first car had been a tumble-down machine with a hard-faced man at the wheel.

As soon as the Count's taxi started, "X" ran to another, an independent cab, and flashed a fifty-dollar bill before the man's eyes, along with his press card.

"Climb in the back seat, old-timer," he said. "Let me take the wheel. Duck down so you won't be seen—and give me your cap."

The cabman sat up with a jerk. "Say, what's the gag? You're flashing stuff that talks big in my language, but I ain't anxious to spend ten years in Sing Sing for takin' it. How do I know it ain't bogus? Was it printed in a cellar over in Jersey?"

The Agent quickly returned the large bill to his wallet. The driver's face clouded with disappointment. But "X" drew out five worn and wrinkled tens.

"Here," he said, thrusting the currency in the cabman's hand. "These bills smell with age. I'm on the track of something big and you're going to ruin a scoop if you don't come to life."

That did the trick. The driver got in back and crouched down on the floor. Wearing the red-and-black cap, the Agent slid into the front seat and started the taxi. A deft manipulation of plastic material gave him a twisted, dented nose. Over his perfect upper teeth he fitted a false set that protruded, bulged his lip, and changed the entire appearance of his face. The other machine was a quarter mile away by now, but the road was a through thoroughfare, and soon "X" was close behind.

He saw de Ronfort staring back anxiously. The Count's expression changed to one of relief when he saw that the taxi seemed to be occupied only by a dumb-looking driver. When they got to the heavy traffic, "X" stayed about a half block behind, though he was careful that the Count's car was on the other side of the cross street when the lights turned red.

The Count's car drove to the heart of the city, and rolled up a side street on the fringe of the theatrical district. The taxi stopped in front of the Perseus Arms, a swanky hotel that catered to celebrities and people of wealth.

The Agent stopped the taxi, hastily remodeled his nose, removed the false teeth, and tossed the cab driver his cap.

"You've earned your money," he said. "But keep mum."

The Agent went across the street and into the Perseus Arms. There was no danger of detection, for the man that de Ronfort had seen driving the taxi had none of the smooth, genteel appearance of A. J. Martin.

The Count stood at the main desk, writing. "X" dropped into an easy chair and watched. A few minutes later a Western Union messenger entered the lobby and went to the desk. The clerk spoke to de Ronfort, and the Frenchman handed the boy a note and a bill. "X" sauntered from the lobby. When the messenger reached the sidewalk, the Agent followed him.

Around a corner, he stopped the lad and flashed a detective badge.

"I'll take charge of that slip, son," he said in a kindly voice. "Just move along and keep quiet. If your boss calls you down tell him that a federal man gave you orders to say nothing. Understand?"

The boy nodded, but his eyes grew big and he looked scared. "X" handed him a dollar bill, then a slip of paper with the address of the Hobart Agency on it.

"Nothing to be frightened about," he said. "If you should lose your job because of this go to the address on that paper and the man there will give you a better one."

When the messenger had saluted and dodged into the crowd "X" looked at the note. It was addressed to one Felix Landru, a man "X" had heard stories of, a sly, slippery underworld character, formerly a Paris Apache, and as sleek and suave as de Ronfort himself. "X" read the note.

"The Peacock has a big supply of rabbit food to dispose of at a commission," it said. "The Fox is asked to get in touch with him at the Perseus Arms as soon as possible."

There was nothing incriminating in that note. The "Peacock" undoubtedly was de Ronfort, while the "Fox" likely was the wily Landru. And was the "rabbit food" the contraband that the Count had smuggled into the country in that suitcase? Dope?

The address on the note was the St. Etienne Inn, a cheap hotel on Bordeaux Street in the French section of the city.

THE Agent immediately took a taxi to the St. Etienne. He obtained Landru's room number from the clerk, and rode the squeaky, slow-moving elevator to the fourth floor. A radio was playing in the crook's room, but it was turned off the instant "X" knocked.

There was almost a minute of silence. The Agent grew tense with uncertainty. He knocked again. This time he spoke Landru's name softly.

The door opened a crack. The room was dark. But the shaft of dim light from the corridor glinted on an automatic in Landru's hand. The crook peered furtively through the narrow opening.

"Landru, quick, let me in!" In a hoarse whisper, "X" addressed the man in perfectly accented French. "The Peacock sent me. He's got a new consignment of rabbit food, but the federals are hounding him. We've got to work fast!"

"*Mon Dieu*, you should not have come here then!" exclaimed Landru, letting the Agent into his room. "Why did he not send the note? Has the man lost all caution, now that he is annexing himself to wealth and influence? Or are you—"

Landru did not finish the sentence. Suspicion leaped into his eyes as he stared at the Agent.

Slam! A slugging fist smashed Landru on the point of the jaw. "X" had thrown all his strength and weight into the terrific, jolting impact. The crook dropped to the floor as though his legs had been cut out from under him.

The Agent switched on the lights. He had wanted to sound Landru out, to get information if he could. But the man was obviously suspicious, and "X" had suddenly thought of a better scheme, one more suited to get to the bottom of Remy de Ronfort's activities.

For a while he studied Landru's sharp-featured face. The crook was a dandy, sallow and dissipated, but well groomed. He wore a Vandyke, and the ends of his mustache were waxed and carefully rolled until they were like spikes.

"X" ripped off the disguise of A. J. Martin. With his vials and tubes on the dresser, he went to work shaping features that were identical to Landru's.

In a few minutes he looked like a smooth, dissolute Frenchman out for a night of absinthe and carousal. He put on Landru's clothes, but wore his own shoes with their secret compartments in the soles and heels that held some of his compact, ingenious equipment.

He entered a telephone booth in the lobby and called up de Ronfort at the Perseus Arms.

"The Fox speaking," said "X." "I have your note, but if you wish to do business with me, you must act quickly. Bring the merchandise to Eddie's place on Nyack Street—you should know where it is—and come prepared to quote a low price. This town is like a powder keg with sparks flying around it. If I should be caught distributing rabbit food, you know that I will be getting my mail at a bastille for years to come. Unless you are reasonable this time, we will not do business."

"I'll be there in a half hour," answered the Count. "I have a choice consignment, and the prices will astound you. At Eddie's Place on Nyack Street."

The Count hung up. "X" nodded to the clerk as he started from the St. Etienne Inn, and the man addressed him as Landru. The Agent hailed another cab, and went to Eddie's Place, an old deserted underworld resort in a disreputable section of the city, formerly the hangout of many dope smugglers. He had only a few minutes to wait.

A CAB stopped near the old building. The Count got out. He

carried the same suitcase that he had taken from the amphibian. His hat was pulled low, his face half buried in the upturned collar of his topcoat, "X" motioned to him, and opened the door of the old dive, using one of his skeleton keys. The Count peered at him suspiciously. Then he grunted relief when he recognized the face of Landru.

"You have picked an outlandish spot, Felix," he said irritably. "I hope you have brought a good supply of money. I want to get this transaction over in a hurry. You seem to think you are the only person who takes risks. I am playing for big stakes. If the law catches me, it is my finish. But you, Felix, you have not much to lose."

"Come on!" growled the Agent, speaking French. "We are losing valuable time with your insulting nonsense."

He lighted the way with a pocket flash. He led de Ronfort down a long, narrow corridor. The place had been closed a couple of years previously for violation of the National Prohibition Act. It was an ill-smelling, rat-infested building that had been the scene of several murders.[46]

In a back room, "X" laid his flashlight on the table, and told de Ronfort to exhibit his goods. The pocket flash was the only means of illumination.

"A fine place!" grumbled the Count. "You might have shown one of my station a little consideration, Felix. You could have rented a room at some lodging house."

"Yes," retorted the Agent, "and have a dozen people see you go in and out! With every newspaper blaring about the drug menace, with federal men and the narcotic squad working night and day, I want privacy when I transact this sort of business."

Remy de Ronfort put the suitcase on the table and opened it. "X" flashed the light on the contents. The case was half-filled. There were scores of small, hermetically sealed packages.

"Each one contains an ounce," said the Count. "Three hundred and sixty of them. Made from the finest China opium, processed in England, and smuggled into America by a French nobleman."

The Agent had to stifle his excitement. Three hundred and sixty

---

46   AUTHOR'S NOTE: *It may be remembered by followers of Secret Agent "X" that he had used this place before. While he was combating the "Death-Torch Terror," he met a crowd of evil gangsters here, preparatory to making a raid on police headquarters, where he kidnaped the commissioner himself. This was done in an effort to learn certain secrets in the police files.*

ounces would retail at twenty-three thousand and forty dollars! And the profit to the Count would be enough to keep an ordinary middle-class family for three years or more.

"Not too much, if your price is right," said "X" casually. "I will not buy any cocaine and very little morphine. How much heroin?"

The Count's face darkened. "Nine pounds of morphine and twenty-one of heroin. That is only half of what I brought from the ship. I am in need of ready money. That's why I deal with a cut-throat like you. The rest I shall keep until I get my price."

THE Agent uttered a grumbling protest. "Nine pounds of morphine! *Nom de Dieu!* Man, you know the call is for heroin! Ninety per cent of the users want it. Anybody who takes morphine is willing to switch to the other. Yet you bring in nine pounds of morphine! Most unsatisfactory, de Ronfort. Nine pounds of morphine! A man of your experience, an aristocrat, bungling like that!"

De Ronfort immediately became the placating, cajoling super-salesman.

"You know I have to take what I can get," he said. "You know how I bring the stuff in. Out there where a coast-guard cutter is liable to bear down on me, I must work for speed. As soon as the stuff is lowered over the side and I have it in the cockpit, I take off again."

The Count was an earnest, gesticulating tradesman now, just one voluble, excitable French merchant talking to another.

"You can sell the morphine for heroin," suggested de Ronfort "Half of your customers will need the stuff so badly, they won't notice what they are taking, as long as it has an effect."

"All right, all right," said the Agent irritably. "You have brought in thirty pounds, apothecaries weight. What is your price?"

"Eighteen thousand dollars!"

The Agent began talking to the wall, as though it were a person. "I tell him to come with his lowest price, and right off, he quotes me eighteen thousand dollars. I'm lucky if I get that retail, and I take all the risk of going to the Bastille for some of the best years of my life. It's an outrage. It insults my intelligence."

"You know that is not true!" spoke de Ronfort heatedly. "You would make five thousand more, even if you sold the pure stuff, and you adulterate it fifty per cent."

"My price is fifteen thousand," said the Agent "If the sum does not please you, lock up your suitcase and we will leave. I'm doing you a favor anyway, offering to relieve you of that load, when the police are on the warpath. You could not dispose—"

The Agent stopped suddenly. Footsteps sounded in the corridor. The Count went white. He grabbed "X's" arm.

"What's that?" he said in a low, tense voice. "Is—is it the police? I can't afford—*Nom de Dieu*—it is worth my life to be caught here! I'm going to marry millions—millions!"

The Count swung "X" around. "Is this a frame-up?" he demanded, his eyes blazing. "Are those some of your twitching, sniffing mob? Extortion, is that it? Going to hold me, and try to extract a ransom from my future father-in-law! No wonder you got me into this forsaken place! But it won't work, Felix. I should have known better than to deal with an Apache. You belong in the sewers of Paris! I'm going to blow your head off, Felix. And I'll make quick work of your band of hopheads."

De Ronfort whipped out an ugly, snub-nosed automatic.

"The police will never connect me, an aristocrat, with the common Felix Landru!" he cried. "You're through, you sewer rat!"

The Agent poked his head out of the door. Several men were rushing down the corridor. A flashlight shone on "X." He drew back quickly, bolted the door. There was a yell. Then a harsh command for him to surrender.

"Don't play games with us, Landru!" some one shouted. "We've got you surrounded. You haven't a chance. You can't beat the federal government! Give up, and you'll cheat the undertaker!"

The Agent turned to de Ronfort.

"You see, my friend, I wasn't trying the double-cross. Now you must trust me. Hurry!"

GRABBING the suitcase of dope, "X" shoved the Count toward a rear window. De Ronfort scrambled through, with the agility of a second-story man. Aristocratic dignity was dispensed with for expediency's sake. "X" leaped through the window. They were in a long, dark alley.

De Ronfort clutched at his shoulder. The man was desperate, devoid of poise, trembling.

"It's my ruin!" he exclaimed. "It means millions lost for me. The place is surrounded. Isn't there *some* way?"

"X" thought a moment. He didn't want de Ronfort caught. For

a man could direct the activities of dope smugglers and peddlers from a prison cell with almost the same ease as he could outside, and without fear of further punishment. With de Ronfort behind bars, "X" would be no nearer to ending the drug menace than he was now. He wanted de Ronfort to continue. By allowing the Count plenty of scope and freedom, "X" might possibly gain information that would aid in finishing the drug ring.

"X" knew how the rear of the old gambling den was situated. He had determined a route of escape for himself, if he needed it. But now those federal men were dangerously near, and he wanted to be certain that the Count got away.

"Over the fence!" he ordered de Ronfort. "On the other side is the back entrance to a tenement. The door is unlocked. You can get through to the street. I'll head these fellows off. I'm not doing this for nothing, de Ronfort. I'm risking my life, understand? When you marry the Blake girl, you will have to make me a nice present."

"You are a rat, Landru!" snarled de Ronfort. "But I will pay! Give me the suitcase."

"Hurry!" exclaimed the Agent. "They're coming. You can't take the dope. If they see you going over the fence, they'll shoot."

That decided the Count. "X" helped him to the top of the wall, and in another moment de Ronfort had disappeared.

When the federal men burst open the door "X" had bolted, the Agent disposed of his gas gun in an ash can. If caught with that on him, the federal men might discover his identity. Packing the suitcase, he sped down the alleyway. They would hear his footsteps pounding on the cement. They would shoot, but the darkness would make accurate aiming impossible. "X" had a chance.

A police whistle sounded. The harsh note made the Agent's body tense. He must not be caught now, just when he seemed to be on the right track. He ran with all the speed he could muster. But he wasn't fast enough. Again the whistle sent out its piercing, warning note.

The mouth of the alley was lighted from the street lamps, and suddenly three forms were outlined in it. They were racing toward "X." He dropped the suitcase, leaped to the concrete fence. A spring, and he was hanging onto the top, muscling himself up.

Guns began to roar. Bullets crashed into the wall. Chunks of concrete, chipped by the smashing lead, struck the Agent's head and body. Men were converging on him. On top of the fence he would be a perfect target. The only escape now, it seemed, lay via the morgue.

CHAPTER X

THE AGENT EXPOSED!

AGENT "X" DROPPED to the alleyway again and raised his hands. In another moment he was surrounded by six men. Immediately the Agent was frisked for a gun. They found the automatic belonging to Landru. The search otherwise was not thorough, because the federal men had him disarmed, and they also had all the evidence they needed. He was shoved along toward the street.

"X" thought ironically how this treatment contrasted to the respect these men had shown him when they had met before. Then they had jumped to his orders, for they were the same federal men from Orrin Q. Mathews' office. One of them was a stranger to him. But "X" had recently saved the lives of the others, when he led them out of that burning warehouse at Haswell and Riverfront.

The men flanking him were Wells and Everts. Creager, Lorson, and McAllister followed. McAllister kept poking a gun in the small of the Agent's back.

"Who's that guy who got away, Landru?" he demanded. "You'd better talk. We've been watching you for a long while, Frenchy. You're going up for a long stretch, but you ought to get the chair! I bet you're the rat who's been peddling hop to girls' schools. You're going to come clean, or we're going to shellac you proper. Me and my buddies damn near got cremated by one of your hop peddlers, and we don't like your breed at all. Down to headquarters, you're going to pick up a lot of lumps and bruises, if you hold back."

"X" was thrown bodily into a big car. The suitcase of dope was tossed in on top of him. He had sized the real Landru up in the few moments the Frenchman had talked. He knew that the dope seller would whine and cringe. So the Agent put on a convincing exhibition of a coward.

"*Mon Dieu*, gentlemen! You make the very great mistake, of a certainty. I don' know why you arrest me! No—I do not! My name is Felix Landru, yes. But I am a Frenchman studying social conditions in America. The *gendarmes* of my country would not treat you so."

"Studying social conditions, are you, Landru?" growled Creager. "I bet you can spot a hophead a block away!"

All the way to headquarters, "X" maintained his protests of innocence. While he was talking, he was puzzling what he should do. These men would have died for him that day he led them from the Karloff hideout. Now they would gladly kill him.

He knew what was ahead. They would put him through a third degree. The plastic material on his face would never stand up under the poundings of a rubber hose. And if one should yank on his goatee, it would come off. He could not afford to have them penetrate his disguise.

It wasn't until he reached headquarters, and the federal men surrounded him in the room where he had first interviewed Orrin Q. Mathews, that "X" conceived his plan. The detectives were actually gloating. They hoped Landru would keep silent, so they could employ the strong-arm routine.

McAllister brandished a strip of rubber hose in front of him.

"Going to talk, Landru? Or shall I begin the softening process? Who was that bird you were with? What was the deal you two were making? Where is the rest of the stuff hidden? Tell us the names of your peddlers. Might as well save yourself a lot of punishment."

"*Mais oui!*" exclaimed the Agent. "I talk—I talk, *m'sieus*. But it must be to one man only. There is too much involved, my friends. Names, names—you would be astounded at the names I would mention. I am but a poor, hard-working man who caters to a great need, *m'sieus*. But my confession will breathe scandal on people who are high up. Take me to General Mathers. Gladly will I talk—for his ears alone. Then *le bon general* will use his own discretion, and my conscience will be at rest"

General Mathers was the head of the Eastern narcotics division. The detectives would have taken "X" before the general, anyway, after the sweating process made him talk. They had a consultation. They were disappointed not to get the chance of manhandling Landru, but they could not beat up a prisoner who was willing to talk.

"X" was taken before the division chief. General Mathers was a hard-faced man with gray hair. Every feature was aggressive. He had fierce, piercing eyes, with pointed eyebrows that looked like stunted horns. He had ridden with Teddy Roosevelt at San Juan Hill, been with Black Jack Pershing on the Mexican border, and helped to break the Hindenburg Line in France. He was a tough old campaigner, and his prize hatred was for dope smugglers and peddlers.

Before the general, the Agent made himself as dejected and wretched in appearance as possible. This man was a strategist who knew all the tricks. He would be savage in dealing with a man like Landru.

"Here he is, general," spoke Detective McAllister with the utmost respect. "We caught Felix Landru on Nyack Street in an untenanted building that used to be Eddie's Place, a gambling hall and a murderers' inn. Men have been on detail watching Landru for two weeks. We nabbed him red-handed, carrying more than twenty thousand dollars' worth of morphine and heroin.

"Landru is wanted by the Paris police on a murder charge. We found an automatic on him. He says he won't talk except to you alone, but two of us will be outside during the interview. We hope you'll call us if he shows the slightest hostility. He's desperate and alone; he may try to kill you, sir."

"Very well, McAllister," boomed Mathers, nodding to the detective. "Leave him with me. I'll know how to handle him no matter what he does. You men are to be congratulated. I hope this man proves to be the ringleader we're after."

DETECTIVE MCALLISTER went out. "X" was left to face the formidable, glowering general. Mathers placed a big service revolver on the desk before him. Then for a full minute he studied the Agent with glaring eyes.

On the desk stood an open box of cigarettes, which gave "X" an idea. He was in a tight spot, and he was fully aware that General Mathers would show no leniency or mercy. The official had a knack of discovering murders that could be charged to the big shots in the dope traffic who had the ill luck to be caught by his men. He considered his work well done when he sent a dope smuggler to the electric chair.

"You said you'd talk to me," rumbled the general, "that was to save yourself some punishment, wasn't it? Very well, Felix Landru, begin your story. Stick to the facts, and don't try to make yourself misunderstood and heroic."

The Agent was twitching and trembling. *"M'sieu,"* he spoke in a plaintive voice. "I suffer so much from the need of a drug. I cannot think, because of my nerves. You will not give me heroin, no. That I do not expect. But, please, *m'sieu;* one cigarette. A smoke will soothe me, and then I will amaze you with names. *Mais oui, mon genéral!* For me—*c'est fini,* the end. One cigarette and I talk."

The general growled, but he tossed a cigarette to the Agent, and shoved a book of matches across the desk. "X" deliberately fumbled the catch. The cigarette dropped to the floor. The Agent bent down and picked the cigarette up. When he stood erect again, the general also was standing, and he had the service revolver leveled at "X."

"Now, try one of your Apache tricks!" rasped Mathers.

The Agent pretended to be deeply hurt. "But, *m'sieu,* you are wrong. I am here, not for tricks, but to tell everything."

"Then proceed."

"X" lighted the cigarette. He had to stall for time. The general still had the service revolver trained on him. Even a step forward might cause the man to shoot. The Agent racked his brain for something to say. He could not bluff a hard-bitten individual like Mathers very long.

Then a knock came at the door. "X" gave a little sigh of relief. In response to the general's growl, a clerk entered, carefully kept out of the Agent's reach, and handed a slip to the chief.

The clerk withdrew. Mathers read the note with a sudden lifting of bushy eyebrows. A sour smile spread over his hard features. He moistened his lips like a tiger licking his chops in anticipation of a kill. He tapped the paper with his fingers, and gazed at the Agent with the cold scrutiny of a scientist studying a laboratory specimen.

"X" did not know what had occurred. He kept his eyes on the general. The gun lay on the desk now. He had to work with lightning speed, or his one chance would be gone.

"You're Felix Landru, the dope peddler, are you?"

"*Oui, m'sieu,* I am Felix Landru," spoke the Agent tensely. Now he had an inkling of what had happened.

The general tossed the slip to him. He read it with a sudden quickening of pulses.

"Felix Landru has just been found unconscious at the St. Etienne Inn on Bordeaux Street. Has a fractured jaw. Fingerprints compared with those on record. They are identical."

"An impostor, eh?" snarled the general. "Not Felix Landru. Yet your disguise is perfect. I think you are a far greater prize than Landru! There is only one man in the world who could do as smooth a job as that. You must be that criminal they call Secret Agent "X!"

CHAPTER XI

THE HAND OF KARLOFF

THE AGENT WAS trapped. Even General Mathers didn't know that he had the secret sanction of a high government official in Washington. And that secret could never come out even if "X" had to go to jail. It was part of the pledge he had made.

Detectives were waiting outside. The general had but to grab his revolver and call them in. Mathers' hand started for the weapon. Immediately "X" pounced forward. He brought his right hand down on the fleshy part of the official's arm.

He jabbed a tiny hypodermic needle into the arm. The harmless but powerful drug had instantaneous effect. It happened so quickly, so unexpectedly, that the general did not think to cry out. Now it was too late. Without making a sound, Mathers slumped into his chair, unconscious.

"X" had obtained the little hypodermic when he dropped the cigarette. The instrument had been hidden in a compartment in the heel of his shoe. The Agent had palmed the hypo, intending to drop it in the sleeve of his raised arm, had the general demanded to see if he held anything except the cigarette.

There was no time to lose. "X" was in an even more difficult situation now. Suppose one of the detectives should look in? The general was merely in a drug-induced coma, yet he appeared to be dead. The man would hardly pause to ask questions. A look at the general, a look at "X," and he would be apt to start shooting.

Noiselessly the Agent locked the door. Strapped around his right leg just above the ankle was his portable kit of make-up material. He set out his vials and tubes. While he studied Mathers' features, he removed the disguise of Felix Landru. He worked feverishly. Men had been talking outside. Now there was a significant silence. "X" knew the reason. The voices had ceased in the office, and the detectives were growing anxious.

To forestall an investigation, the Agent began talking, first in the whining accent of Landru, then in the general's thunderous voice. While he was molding a new disguise, he crept to the window and looked out. There was no way of escape below, but one could grab the window ledge overhead and climb to the floor above—with capture before he got out of the building almost a certainty. "X" had another plan, daring, audacious, one that required cold nerve, great skill, and perfect timing.

He finished his disguise. It was not an elaborate one. He had not the time to work in identical pigmentation and exact features. A close scrutiny would reveal that he was not the general. "X" had to take a chance. He did not change to the official's clothes. Hauling Mathers to a coat closet in the office, he locked him in.

Some one knocked.

"Everything all right, General Mathers?" The voice was McAllister's.

The Agent was tense, dry lipped. His eyes burned with feverish excitement. He was not at all sure that his disguise would get by. Instead of answering the detective, "X" grabbed a chair and deliberately hurled it through the window. The loud crash was followed by the musical clatter of falling glass.

"X" uttered deep, full-throated groans, such as might have come from the general. The detective outside was rattling the knob and pounding on the door. He called to the other federal men. Footsteps beat on the tiled floor of the corridor.

"You can't get away, you scoundrel!" exclaimed "X," imitating the general's thunderous voice.

The Agent snatched up the service revolver, and fired several times at the shattered window. Then he ran to the door and unlocked it. Assistants swarmed in. Posing as the general, "X" was rubbing his jaw, as though he had been struck. He pointed at the smashed window with his smoking gun.

"Out there, men!" he cried hoarsely. "The blackguard slugged me and made a dash for it. But he can't get away. After him, McAllister!"

THE detective already was climbing out the window. Creager was following him. The room was suddenly packed with a milling mob. Attention was focused on the man at the window. That was the Agent's cue.

Picking up Landru's hat, "X" quietly left the office. He went down the corridor to a washroom. There he quickly changed to one of his stock disguises. From a photograph he had seen of Landru on the crook's dresser at the St. Etienne, "X" knew that the former Apache wore the brim of his hat downward. Therefore the Agent turned it up, pulled the hat low on his forehead. Now there was not a vestige of his recent disguise as a Frenchman in manner and make-up.

While the futile search went on in the building, "X" strolled out the main entrance and hailed a cruising cab. De Ronfort had brought only half of his smuggled narcotics to Eddie's Place. That dope was now in the possessions of the Federal Bureau. The count still had the balance. "X" would call on the Frenchman as an emissary of Landru, who was in the custody of the law.

At the Perseus Arms, however, he learned that de Ronfort had checked out an hour before. And he had not left a forwarding address. De Ronfort was frightened. Possibly he was afraid that if Landru was caught, he would squeal. Or he might have left to dispose of his contraband goods in another section of the country. Maybe he was eloping with Paula Rockwell. That scare at Eddie's Place might have shown de Ronfort the need for quick work. Once married, the sly, ingratiating aristocrat would have little trouble maneuvering a joint bank account, or one in his own name, from the rattle-brained heiress.

With the Blake fortune behind him, de Ronfort could easily become the narcotics king of America, wielding the power of an absolute despot. It was a terrifying thought. The Agent pictured millions enslaved to de Ronfort through the tyranny of dope.

Wherever the Frenchman was going, "X" knew he would keep in touch with Paula Rockwell. There was a chance that the smuggler right now was at the Blake penthouse. The Agent returned to one of his hideouts long enough to freshen up and change to the disguise of A. J. Martin. As a newspaperman, he went to the Blake apartment building. But he stopped outside. He would wait. If de Ronfort were there, he might come out. Paula Rockwell had no aversion to newspaper people, yet an interview might reveal nothing of what he wanted to learn.

The dial over the private elevator indicated that the car was at the top floor. At this hour Whitney Blake probably had retired. If the girl was out, the car likely would be on the first door, with the operator waiting for her return. "X" remained inconspicuously in the lobby. One of the public elevators was in use, carrying cleaners and all-night workers.

Close to half an hour later, the Agent's monotonous wait was rewarded by the appearance of Paula Rockwell. She came down in the business elevator with a scrubwoman and a janitor. Why had she avoided the private one? She was nervous, extremely so, and her manner was actually furtive. Evidently her departure was a secret from those in the penthouse. "X" was curious about the reason.

The girl hurried from the building. She held her bag up to shield her face as she crossed the sidewalk. Instead of leaving in one of her own cars, with the private chauffeur, she hired a taxi. The Agent beckoned to another cab, and instructed the driver to follow the car ahead.

Paula Rockwell's taxi took her to a slum section, where she would go ordinarily only with an escort. The machine stopped before the Genoa Café, a cheap restaurant and saloon, where a few, shabby men and slatternly women were dancing to the tinny strains of a battered player piano.

The Agent sauntered into the place a few moments after the girl entered. He ordered a small beer at the bar. At a corner table not far from the bar sat Remy de Ronfort, his suavity gone, lines of worry etched in his handsome face.

PAULA was sitting across from him, holding his hand and talking earnestly. The count had been drinking. His eyes were glazed and bloodshot. A bottle of whiskey stood on the table. He tossed off two glasses of liquor without a chaser. It was hard for "X" to believe that a man, aristocratic supposedly in everything but his scruples, was affected so much by what had happened at Eddie's Place. Had something else occurred in the meantime? "X" could not tell from their conversation, for the tinny, jangling piano drowned out their words.

With a cautious side glance, "X" saw Paula Rockwell hand de Ronfort some bills. There was a hundred-dollar greenback on top. A flash of relief shone in the Count's face. Then he began showing impatience. He tossed off another drink, and jammed his hat on, without thought to appearance. The girl grabbed his arm. Her manner was that of worried protest. "X" cursed the noisy piano. But for that, he might have heard their talk. De Ronfort shook his head and jumped up. He and the girl went to the sidewalk. As they passed the bar, "X" caught a few words.

"But can't you tell me?" the girl was saying. "Are you leaving just because you got an unsigned note of warning? Probably it's some silly crank!"

Then they were out of earshot again. The Count beckoned to a taxi. Paula was in tears now. De Ronfort almost shoved her into the back seat. There was a brief embrace. He motioned for the driver to start. The girl began to weep without restraint.

The smuggler hired another cab. "X" was no longer interested in the girl. She had given him a lead. As soon as de Ronfort's car got underway, the Agent jumped in another taxi. The first car sped through night traffic to Union Station.

De Ronfort rushed into the waiting room and straight to a ticket office. A line of people was ahead of him. "X" waited to one side, his face behind a newspaper. As soon as the Frenchman had obtained his ticket and walked away, the Agent elbowed in ahead of the next buyer, who choked off a protest when he saw the blazing light in "X's" eyes.

"What was the destination of that last ticket?"

The clerk looked curiously at the Agent and shook his head. "I'm not at liberty to give out that information," he said slowly.

"X" flashed a detective's badge. "Give me a ticket to the same destination," he ordered in a low but harsh voice.

"Yes, sir—yes, sir!" responded the clerk respectfully. "With a sleeper, sir?"

The Agent nodded. The clerk pulled a train fare and a pullman ticket from the rack and stamped them.

"Seventeen seventy-six, please. The train leaves in three minutes. Track forty-two."

"X" slapped down a twenty dollar bill and raked up his change with the tickets. He started on a run for the entrance to Track 42. Until now he did not know where his ticket would take him. He glanced at it. Montreal. Out of the country.

The Agent looked up to meet a greater surprise. Four men were slipping through the crowd toward de Ronfort. They had hard, pasty faces, wicked eyes, cruel mouths. They were nervous, almost palsied, and their spasmodic movements added to their vicious appearance.

As Corbeau, the drug-addict gunman, "X" had known them. They had watched Serenti die horribly of the loathsome green death. They had shot Gus Tansley so that he bled out his life in less than a minute. They were the drug-mastered fiends of the somber, sadistic Karloff, and they were after Count Remy de Ronfort.

CHAPTER XII

DEATH TO THE AGENT

PUZZLED, THE AGENT moved close. De Ronfort was starting through the train gate, when one of Karloff's rat-faced gunmen shoved in ahead of him, and pushed the Count back. The smuggler began a dignified protest, but he stopped abruptly when he found himself surrounded by three others. They pulled back their coat lapels and showed badges.

What was it all about? Karloff's men posing as federal officers and nabbing de Ronfort. Apparently the Count was not one of the big dope ring. Yet possibly he had challenged Karloff's authority, and the evil chief was striking in his usual brutal way.

The gunmen rushed the Count across the big waiting room. Trained to avoid scenes in public, de Ronfort went along without protest. But the moment they got him into a sedan, he began to struggle furiously. Physically he was probably more than a match for the four dope-ravaged thugs. Watching from the side of a pillar, "X" saw him slam one of them between the eyes and give another an uppercut that put the man out of the fight.

But the aristocrat's polo-trained physique was helpless before the deadly threat of an automatic. He suddenly ceased his struggles. "X" knew a rod was probably jabbing the Count in the ribs.

De Ronfort still clung to his suitcase. The sedan started. "X" feared there would be gunplay this time, so he did not hire a taxi. Instead, he commandeered a car, turning on the ignition with a specially constructed key for that purpose. If the car was wrecked or bullet-riddled, the owner would get money for a new one from the inexhaustible funds of Elisha Pond.

"X" wanted that suitcase of dope that de Ronfort was carrying. Traffic was thin now, and the sedan sped to a back street where the driver would not have to stop for lights. In a short while they were out of the city and racing along a lonely suburban road. The Agent kept a quarter of a mile to the rear, so that it wouldn't seem that he was following the mobsters. For a long while his attention was absorbed by the pursuit. Then he happened to glance in the reflector above him.

He muttered savagely, clutched the steering wheel until it seemed that the white skin over his knuckles would split. He clenched his teeth. Bunches of muscle stood out on his jaw. His narrowed eyes blazed with anger and excitement.

In the mirror he saw a hard and sinister face, a face that conjured up pictures of sudden and horrible death. Karloff. Karloff was in a car close behind, and that car was crowded with his dope-crazed slaves. Karloff's men were ahead of him and behind him. And there were no roads or lanes branching off.

"X" was hemmed in!

Just then the car ahead stopped by a field. A short way beyond flowed the black waters of a river. De Ronfort was shoved from the car. He still clutched his suitcase. No effort was made to take it away from him. It was pathetic, the way he clung to that supply of narcotics. "X" plainly saw what was to take place. It was the end of the journey for de Ronfort. Surely the Count could not be blind to the significance of the stop.

Yet fear had mastered him. All the fight was drained from him. He was trembling and helpless, as helpless and wretched as Serenti had been before the horrible green death ended his tortures. Yet the count was not a drug addict. Instead, he was a rank, quivering coward. He stood there like an idiot, his eyes seeing nothing. Stupidly he held onto the suitcase, while the drug addicts piled from the car.

The Agent now was in as deadly peril as the Count. There was no escape on either side, sure death behind, and but a sliver of a chance of getting by those mobsters in front. But a desperate situation called for a desperate chance. And that was what the Agent took.

Suddenly he jammed down on the gas. The high-powered car leaped ahead as though impelled by rage and bent on annihilation. "X" held the wheel rigidly, steering straight for the mobsters. Panic froze the drug addicts, they stared pop-eyed at the charging car.

One of them screamed in terror. Frightened witless, they crouched in frenzied fear, directly in the path of the roaring machine. Grimly the Agent exerted more pressure on the accelerator.

He was not bluffing. They had a chance to move. If they chose to stay there, he would run them down.

A SNARLING command burst from the rear. Karloff had poked his head from the other car and was lashing his men with vile oaths. The mobsters came to life. They sprang aside. Fear and hate twisted their faces repulsively. Guns went into action.

The Agent ducked low as the automatics thundered out whining destruction. Lead shrieked by the car. A bullet smashed into the windshield, showering razor-edged splinters over "X." Flying glass cut him, pierced his clothes and lacerated his flesh. But he kept his foot on the accelerator.

The mobsters were at the side of the road, madly raking the car with lead. The Agent whizzed by. Suddenly he slammed on the brakes. The car jumped, skidded sidewise. Before it lost momentum, "X" swung it straight again. The car stopped close to de Ronfort. Men were shouting, cursing. Smoking, flame-spouting guns snarled wickedly. Karloff's car came to a shrieking stop. The mob chief had lost his deadly calmness. He was cracking out orders like a top sergeant. But those orders were not carried out. Drug-starved to make them obedient, the hopheads were gripped by hysteria and no match for the wild, mad confusion.

To their frenzy "X" owed his life. They wasted plenty of lead. Bullets, aimlessly, blindly fired, came dangerously close. The Agent was crimson from glass cuts, but he kept down, protected by the body of the car. He opened the left-hand door.

De Ronfort was standing close by, like a man under the spell of catalepsy. Without speaking, "X" grabbed him roughly by the front of the coat, and yanked him into the car, hauling in the suitcase after him. De Ronfort was just a shivering, teeth-chattering hulk. The Agent shoved him down in the seat, and wasted no time in talking.

A quick shift of gears, and the car bounded forward again. De Ronfort cowered down, actually whimpering. Karloff's car had started up again. It was close behind. Bullets ripped through the back of "X's" machine. He felt a tug at his hat, and knew that if he had been in an upright position, his skull would have been shattered.

The river was directly ahead. A dock led from the road out into the stream. Sudden uneasiness gripped "X." He glanced to the right and left. There was no turn. He was racing at a mile-a-minute clip along a dead-end road.

De Ronfort beside him, uttered a scream of agony. The Agent

turned and saw blood streaming down the man's neck. "X" did not know whether the count had been hit by a bullet or a piece of glass. De Ronfort was shaking like an addict deprived of his drug for a week. A rank, abject coward, he was overwhelmed, crazed by fear.

The Agent's brain worked swiftly. He had never been so close to the finish. Life and death hung on his decision, and he had to make it in a few seconds. Karloff and his gang were no more than a hundred feet behind. Automatics and machine guns pounded away viciously. Bullets thudded against the back of "X's" car, ripped through the fabric of the top.

Ahead flowed the river. Death hovered near in either direction. To pause, to slow down even, meant certain suicide. The Agent could not buck those mobsters in a counter-attack. He would not surrender. He had one other choice. The river. Beneath its surface lay safety—or death. His only chance was to drive straight ahead off the end of the dock.

De Ronforf shrieked when he saw the river so near.

"*Mon Dieu!*" he cried in a voice shaken by terror. "Stop! Stop! Have mercy, *m'sieu!* I will be killed! I do not want to die!"

A low snarl escaped the Agent. The Count was more abject than a terror-stricken child. He was covering his face with his hands. His disgusting cowardice sickened the Agent. He did not want to die either. To him life was a source of unending interest. But a man who lived as hard as he could not expect to die of old age. Long ago he had schooled himself to fight against odds, no matter how overwhelming they seemed, but to accept defeat, when it came, without flinching. To the Agent defeat had but one meaning—death.

The car shot onto the rickety old dock. A triumphant outburst of profane jeering came from the other car. "X" heard the screech of brakes. Karloff's machine had stopped. But the gunfire did not cease.

"X" reached the end of the wharf. De Ronfort uttered a scream and collapsed. The car crashed through the flimsy wooden railing. The Agent clamped his jaws grimly and clung to the wheel. Maybe it was the end. Remy de Ronfort did not want to die, because he feared death, and life offered great wealth. The Agent did not want to die—because there was still so much to do.

The car leaped high, shivering like a thing in agony as it catapulted through the darkness. Then, in a shower of machine-gun lead, it hurtled to the rippling waters of the river.

CHAPTER XIII

A FATAL SHOT

WHILE THE AUTO was in mid-air the Agent got a grip on de Ronfort and the suitcase. The instant the car struck the surface, "X" dived from the open door, tugging the Count with him. The engine stalled the moment the water got into it. There was a vicious hissing as steam rose from the hot metal.

"X" was under. He made a shallow dive, coming up immediately for air. The water revived de Ronfort. The Count was gasping and spluttering. Lights from the Karloff auto shone on the river. The two men were caught in the glare. Wild shouts came from shore. Bullets lashed the water around them.

"Take a deep breath!" the Agent rapped out crisply.

Instead, de Ronfort uttered a shrill scream. The mad, frenzied outburst suddenly choked off. The Count groaned, and then became as still as death. That abrupt silence alarmed "X." In the gleam of the light from the car, the Agent looked at the man. There was a dark, crimson blotch on the side of de Ronfort's head. "X" gnawed at his lip, muttered.

Inhaling deeply, he disappeared again, pulling de Ronfort with him. A superb swimmer, able to hold his breath nearly three minutes, "X" was safe from bullets while he submerged. As he swam downward, encumbered by the limp Frenchman, he kept his eyes open. Looking above, he could see the reflection of the searchlight combing the water. Lead still whipped against the surface. Most of the missiles, he knew, would ricochet. The mobsters were in greater danger of those bullets than he.

Swimming downstream under the water, he soon got out of the range of light. Then he bobbed above the surface again. The spotlight still played over the river. He gulped a deep breath, and went under, continuing downstream, but working in toward the bank.

Soon he bumped into the rotting pile of a dilapidated wharf. He shot upwards into the air, and hauled de Ronfort to the shore under worm-eaten timbers.

Leaving de Ronfort lying on his back, the Agent dived into the stream once more, and swam out to the suitcase that was floating down the river. The shooting had ceased. "X" cast a searching glance at the road. The car was gone. Karloff and his men doubtlessly believed they had killed de Ronfort and the stranger. The Agent got the suitcase and returned to the shore.

Count Remy de Ronfort lay dead.

The wound in the side of the head was from a bullet that had pierced the skull. There was nothing to regret in the man's death except that he had taken along the answers to many questions that bothered the Agent.

He covered the body with debris, and left the place, carrying the suitcase. It was still dark, though dawn would soon be breaking. He wanted to get out of this vicinity before the light came. There was a chance that Karloff had left a mobster behind to watch for the bodies, to see if any clues were found that might lead to the killers.

He thought of Paula Rockwell. There was sorrow ahead for her, because the empty-headed girl would never believe that her Count had been a rotter and a cowardly crook. In his fight against crime, "X" often had to waive scruples himself. Later, he meant to call on the girl—as de Ronfort.

He strode along the road, keeping a careful watch so that he would not be surprised by any of the gangsters. Evidently Karloff was satisfied with the night's work. The road was deserted. It was dawn, and his clothes were dry by the time "X" reached a well-populated suburban district. He did not want to ride into the city now, for he had de Ronfort's corpse to consider. Should the body be discovered, it would be turned over to the police. That would spoil his plans.

So he walked into a Chinese laundry. An oriental in black pajamas greeted him with a gold-toothed smile, and gazed wisely at his bedraggled appearance.

"Allee samee fall in the liver?" the laundryman asked. "Me catchee iron and fixee you ploper. Washee shirt. Do very fine job!"

The Agent nodded. "I want that, O brother, but I come humbly beseeching a greater favor. Is there one in this worthy enterprise who knows of the venerable Lo Mong Yung?"

The Chinese ceased being the humorous little laundryman rubbing his hands and speaking pidgin English. He became a personage of dignity, the honorable head of a family, with the record of his ancestors listed in the archives of his native province for two thousand years. He bowed to the Agent, who returned the courtesy.

"Will the gracious guest who honors the house of Su Kung whisper close the word that will prove his identity?"

"X" leaned over the counter and softly spoke the secret password of the Ming Tong. Immediately the Chinaman's eyes expressed deep respect. To him the Agent was Ho Ling, a revered and honored Mingman.

"O great white brother," he spoke reverently, "my decrepit frame trembles with gratitude over this visit. From the lips of the august father himself have I heard praise of the noble Ho Ling, who wages constant war against the dragon of evil. My heart is near bursting with joy that I may please my ancestors by serving the great Ho Ling."

The Agent acknowledged the honor with the proper humility and explained as much of what had happened as the laundryman Su Kung needed to know. He wanted the corpse of the Frenchman brought in and hidden. Su Kung was a poor man. There was danger of being caught by the police. Even if he was held in jail a short while, his business would suffer, and his family with it. But Su Kung did not hesitate. The honor of serving the white brother of the Ming Tong bulked far greater than the danger in Su King's mind.

A short while later a creaking, rattling, horse-drawn laundry wagon driven by an inscrutable Chinese headed down the little-used road to the old dock. Inside the wagon was Agent "X," disguised as a Manchu. The Agent was glad to find that the river territory was deserted except for men fishing far downstream. "X" ran along the bank to the wharf under which the corpse was concealed. He carried a huge laundry bag. He fitted this over the body, and tied the opening. Shouldering the burden, he hurried back to the wagon, where Su Kung was ready to start the horse back to the laundry.

Cold, aloof hunter of criminals though he was, the Agent was deeply affected by the contrast between this sordid finish of de Ronfort and the picture he recalled of the Count at the Blake penthouse, feigning weariness over the fawning attention of debutantes. Yet the man had been asking for trouble, dealing with drug addicts, all of whom were potential murderers.

Back at Su Kung's laundry, "X" carried the body in the rear room, and locked the door. There he took careful measurements of the corpse, and spent a long period of intense concentration studying the Count's face. The Agent's amazing photographic memory would enable him to reconstruct the face, without any inaccuracies in the features.

Before he left the laundry, he gave Su Kung a large sum of money. In aiding him, the Chinaman had shown bravery almost to the point of foolhardiness, for dealing with a corpse without the sanction of the law was risky business. So Su Kung was enriched by more than he could make otherwise in six months. Beside that, "X" left money to have the body embalmed by another tong member, sealed in a casket, and kept hidden until the Agent was ready to have de Ronfort's death made public.

"X" hurried into the city now, went first to one of his hideouts to perfect his disguise as A. J. Martin, and then to the laboratory of Fenwick, the brilliant research chemist, who was working on the analysis of the doped cigarettes.

The chemist shook his head after he had greeted the Agent. "Still no results, Mr. Martin," he said. "We've been working night and day on those cigarettes, keeping up our tests. Nearly five hundred precipitations already, and we've determined nothing except that the drug has some sort of nitrogenous base."

"I've brought along some more," said "X," opening the suitcase and handing Fenwick two of the packages. "You'll have better success this time. I want a careful comparison made with the result of this analysis and what little you've learned of the doped cigarettes."

Fenwick opened a package and examined the contents.

"Ah! No difficulty here, Mr. Martin! You've got the straight stuff now! Off-hand, I'd say this was morphine or heroin. However, I'll put it through the test."

They entered an elaborately equipped laboratory where several men were busy with test-tubes and Bunsen burners. Fenwick went to work, and it was not long before he got results.

"Just as I thought, Mr. Martin," he said. "One package contains morphine, the other heroin."

"That doesn't help much," said the Agent disconcertedly.

"No," replied Fenwick. "We're still as much in the dark as ever with the cigarettes. Whatever is in them reacts on the human system very much like morphia, though far more potently. But we are certain it is neither cocaine, hashish, nor the active principle of opium. It doesn't respond to any tests for the vegetable alkaloids."

Startling information. The narcotics that de Ronfort had smuggled in were common opium derivatives, whereas the dope distributed by the sinister drug ring completely baffled Fenwick, one of the foremost laboratory technicians in the country.

CHAPTER XIV

SUCCESS—OR A SLAB

WHAT PART HAD de Ronfort played in the dope menace? The dissimilarity in the drugs certainly was evidence that the Count had not been connected with Karloff's mob. Yet why had Karloff taken such pains to get rid of him? Not because he was a rival in the distribution of dope. There were bigger men in this illicit traffic who were unmolested. "X" believed there was a deeper reason, a motive that had nothing to do with gang rivalry.

The Agent returned to one of his hideouts. First, he took a much-needed rest. Trained to fall asleep the instant his head hit the pillow, "X" slept so soundly that a few hours of repose were sufficient. Awakening in mid-afternoon, he set to work molding an elaborate disguise, taking infinite pains with small details.

This time he was a long while before the triple mirrors, laying on a new pigmentation with the painstaking thoroughness of a great artist. When he finished with his vials and tubes, he donned a wig of shiny, curly black hair, and surveyed himself critically.

The new countenance brought a cold smile to the Agent's lips. He had done well. An aristocratic face was reflected in the mirror, clean-cut in profile but with a suggestion of weakness about the month. The face that "X" saw had a slight look of dissipation that sun-bronze had not eliminated. The Agent believed that no one would doubt that he was Remy de Ronfort.

He had taken special care because he was going to see Paula Rockwell, to find out what she knew of the Count's activities, and a woman would be quick to notice any irregularity in the appearance of her fiancé.

"X's" plan was one of extreme daring. Karloff wanted de Ronfort out of the way. The Agent wanted to find Karloff; so, by disguising himself as the Count, pretending that the man had not been killed, "X" hoped to draw another attack from Karloff, and thus track him down.

It was literally courting death, posing as the slain de Ronfort. Karloff or his mobsters would likely shoot on sight. Yet it was a sure and swift way of meeting the sinister Karloff.

The Agent put a bandage on his left arm, which he placed in a sling. He added a few touches to his face to give him a haggard look, and stuck a piece of court plaster over his forehead. Karloff would know something was amiss if he saw de Ronfort without any wounds or signs of emotional stress.

At a public telephone booth, "X" called up Paula Rockwell. A servant answered the ring, but the girl apparently had been close by, for she was talking eagerly over the wire a moment after the servant repeated the Count's name.

"Darling!" the girl cried. "You're all right then? Where are you, Remy? I'm worried sick! Come here to the apartment at once! I won't rest a minute till I see you!"

"No, Paula," the Agent answered. "I must see you alone first. Meet me at the Green Lantern on Oswego Street. Hurry!"

The girl agreed and "X" hung up. His eyes were flashing. Paula perhaps would be able to clear up the mystery of the Count's connection with the dope smuggling ring that was handing the stuff out free. It was possible that de Ronfort had tried to doublecross them and they had retaliated for that reason.

The Green Lantern was the same sort of dingy bar and restaurant as the Genoa Café, and Oswego Street ran through one of the poorest sections of the city. The Agent reached the place shortly before the girl. When the heiress arrived, "X" was sitting at a table, staring into a whiskey glass. He got up, slump-shouldered and dejected, the picture of defeat. But beneath the pose he was tense and concerned.

Her eyes were red and swollen from crying. She grabbed his right hand and clung to it. Then she gently touched the arm resting in the sling.

"You—you are wounded," she said tremulously.

THE Agent nodded. She was a flighty, shallow, empty-headed girl. "X" believed her incapable of any real depth of feeling. Her affection was more for the title than the man. The Agent was relieved to see that she was completely fooled by the disguise. There was a slight shade of difference in his eyes and de Ronfort's, but the girl, beside herself with fear, did not notice the change.⁴⁷

"We must flee!" she said. "We must get you away from those terrorists and revolutionists! Why must we suffer so from those horrible men? I'm frightened to death, Remy."

So that was it. Terrorists. Revolutionists. That was how Remy de Ronfoft had explained his harassment—the reason for going away, the reason for borrowing money—to Paula Rockwell at the Genoa Café. He had posed as the persecuted one, the hounded, hunted noble, the victim of his aristocratic birth, preyed upon by treacherous, conspiring terrorists. "X" immediately took the cue. He was disappointed. Paula Rockwell could tell him nothing about de Ronfort's real activities, because she was ignorant of them herself. But "X" must keep up his role.

"*Oui, ma chère,*" he said in a voice husky with weariness, "the terrorists had me trapped. They caught me at Union Station, and took me into the country to kill me. I fought hard and got away, but—they shot me. It is only a flesh wound as you see."

The girl's cheeks flushed suddenly. "We'll go to South America or China," she said. "We'll disappear from sight. In some far-off place we'll find our happiness, living for each other. I don't ask for anything more, Remy dear. My social life would be so empty, so meaningless, without you. My guardian would send us money. Then, when the terrorists have been put down by the police, we can return!"

"X" saw that Paula Rockwell visioned herself in a romantic role. It seemed as though she were quoting gushy motion-picture dialogue. He wondered if she would feel like a heroine after six months of obscurity in a Shanghai hideout, such as she probably pictured. How much would she have loved de Ronfort without his title? The girl was frightened, but the Agent believed her tears were more the product of hysteria than sorrow.

"I can't go out of the city, Paula," said "X" bitterly. "Every station, every road, every ship will be watched by the terrorists. I am lost, my dear, lost!"

---

47   AUTHOR'S NOTE: *As has been mentioned before, the question of eye coloring is one of the most difficult problems the Secret Agent has to meet in the creation of his masterly impersonations. He has overcome it in various ways: by the use of belladonna solutions to increase the size of the pupils and thus make the eyes seem darker, and by dropping harmless coloring matter onto the eyeballs themselves. The latter method is not wholly satisfactory because a film of pigmentation spreads over the lenses or cornea also. But the Secret Agent is willing to take any pains and run any risk in achieving the desired effect.*

He told of the capture, omitting the part he himself had played, and painting de Ronfort as a hero. No use disillusioning the girl now.

Paula's eyes flashed when she heard the story. It added glamour to her Count. She could not prevent an expression of disappointment, though, when she learned that the China trip was impossible. She was a gullible creature, with merely a surface sophistication that was sufficient for her own trivial set. Knowing nothing of de Ronfort's criminal activities, she believed all "X" told her.

"You must come home," she pleaded. "You need me now. Daddy will know what to do."

"No," responded the Agent. "You are kind, *ma chère,* so kind. But that is too much. Your guardian is a man of position, of wealth. And he has troubles of his own. With his affliction and his age, it is unfair for me to burden him with my problems. Let me fight this out, Paula. It seems hopeless, but I'll face the danger stoutly."

The Agent said that for effect, knowing that the girl would be insistent. He wanted to be seen with her. And, if Karloff had any doubts about de Ronfort's death, he would have spies watching the Blake penthouse. This would further the Agent's desperate plan of using himself as human bait to get on Karloff's trail again.

Shortly he was entering the Blake apartment. The old financier was sitting in his wheel chair on the terrace. Whitney Blake had a guest, and the person was Silas Howe, the reformer.

Howe was still ranting about the drug evil, which was spreading like a plague. Newspapers were filled with murders, riots, scandals laid to the deadly drug blight. Howe had a flare for publicity. Daily he appeared in the headlines with his latest outburst. A dark thought suddenly came to the Secret Agent's mind. Could it possibly be that Howe's vehemence was a beautiful pose, an almost perfect cover? Not one word of suspicion had "X" heard against Howe; but Howe had come carrying a gun on the night of the party. Was it solely fear of the drug ring that made him go about armed?

The Agent watched the reformer closely while the girl blurted out the story of the terrorists. Howe's reaction was one of shock. Either he was a marvelous actor or his manner was genuine, for "X" could detect nothing false in it. If he were connected with the gang that had killed de Ronfort, the long-nosed crusader would know about the shooting. Yet not by so much as the flicker of an eyelid did he betray that he might have such knowledge.

Whitney Blake pounded his cane on the tile floor of the terrace and kept shaking his head while the girl talked.

"Bad," he muttered, "bad. You must stay here, Remy, I'll hire detectives to watch the penthouse night and day. You must have an armed bodyguard."

"I couldn't think of staying here, air," answered the Agent quickly. "It's my own battle. I don't want you and Paula endangered, too. Why, those terrorists might even blow up this building."

Blake mulled over the prospect for a while.

"I'll have to take that risk," he said grimly. "I'll employ more watchmen, and take every precaution. But I insist that you stay. After what you've been through, you need rest and quiet and care."

But "X" refused. There was so much to be done. He wanted to find Karloff's band again. He had proved to his own satisfaction that Paula Rockwell knew nothing of the dead Count's criminal activities.

WHEN the Secret Agent left the penthouse, to the protests of old Blake and his ward, Silas Howe went with him to the elevator.

"Count de Ronfort," said the reformer, "I think you are very unwise to go about in public, while these terrorists are at large. You are in danger of assassination. I beg you to come to my apartment right here in this building. There you will find refuge, and there you will be able to visit your fiancée whenever you like."

The Agent's pulse quickened. He looked into Howe's eyes,

"I am deeply grateful for your offer," he said politely, "but my nature forbids me from imperiling others. I will go to the French consul for advice. Perhaps I will leave the country with a bodyguard via airplane."

Howe's eyebrows raised a little. "X" noticed a sudden flare of interest in the man's eyes. He wished he knew what thoughts were running behind them.

After "X" spoke of fleeing by airplane, Howe did not press him to stay at his apartment. The Agent took his leave quickly.

On the street he got into a taxi. Midway up the block he drew a small mirror from his pocket and held it so that it reflected what was on the street behind him. Then his heart leaped.

Not far behind was a car carrying two vicious-looking men. By their manner "X" knew they were following him! To make sure, he directed the cabman to drive around the block. The other car kept close in the rear all the way.

The Agent's lips tightened to a hard, thin line. A tingle of apprehension went through him. Those men might drive up alongside, and blast away with a machine gun. Then not only his own plans would be defeated, but an innocent cabman would meet death. Such an attack was easily possible. To their minds, they had failed once, and this time they would be out to do a thorough job. Yet he was pleased, too. His disguise had served its purpose. These men must be some of Karloff's gang, set as spies to verify the Count's death.

A couple of blocks farther on, the cars stopped for a traffic light. One of the mobsters got out of the pursuing auto and ran toward a cigar store. The Agent believed he had gone to telephone other members of the mob.

The second man drove on when the lights changed. At the next intersection, a big truck cut in ahead of the gangster car. "X" was quick to take advantage.

He left a bill on the seat of the taxi, and with the truck cutting off the gangster's view, the Agent quietly and dexterously opened the door and slipped out. He moved rapidly through the crowd on the sidewalk and entered a large drug store on the corner.

In a telephone booth, he hurriedly changed to one of his stock disguises, put on a light-haired wig, and reshaped the hat. When he came out he was a blond, with none of the characteristics of a Frenchman.

He rushed out an exit that led into the corridor of an office building. The entrance opened onto the sidewalk below the cigar store the gangster had entered. "X" stood inconspicuously in the doorway of the haberdashery until the mobster emerged from the cigar store.

Then the Agent stepped out and followed the man. Once again he was on the trail of the Karloff gang. What would be at the end of that trail? The finish of the drug ring? Or a marble slab for the bullet-riddled corpse of Secret Agent "X"?

CHAPTER XV

THE BEAUTIFUL GREEN DEATH

THE GUNMAN STARTED crosstown afoot. He was extremely nervous, furtive. One hand thrust into his coat pocket ominously. When he passed cops, he turned his head. He walked at a pace much faster than other pedestrians.

"X" was tense, grim. The man ahead was tortured by nerves frayed from the lack of dope. He was wild-eyed, insane from his deprivation. It would not take much to make him draw his gun and start a massacre. Frequently he looked behind him. He paid no attention to "X" the first block. On the second he fixed him with a suspicious glare for a moment.

The Agent had to walk fast to keep at an even distance behind the mobster, and that was what caused the evil-faced man to single him out. To throw off suspicion "X" stepped into a grocery store and bought a loaf of bread and a few bunches of vegetables. He carried the bread wrapped in its waxed paper, without a bag, and he fixed the other bag so the leaves and stalks of the vegetables stuck out.

It was dark now. On the street he bought a newspaper. Now he looked like an office worker returning home. "X" walked briskly and got close to the gunman again. The gangster turned around, twisted his ugly face into a snarl. Then he noticed the bundles. His face relaxed to its ordinary viciousness, and he paid no more attention to "X." The ruse was effective.

Soon the drug addict reached a factory section. A few blocks beyond was a district of middle-class apartment houses. So "X's" deception still was plausible. The man stopped before a shut-down factory, and waited outside, nervously puffing on a cigarette, until "X" passed by. The gunman eyed him closely. The Agent whistled and walked with the jaunty step of a man whose day's work is over.

He ignored the hophead.

A block farther on, he turned the corner. He disposed of his packages, waited a few minutes, and then peered cautiously around the side of the building. The gunman had disappeared.

Stealthily "X" crept back to the shut-down factory. He was alert in every fiber. Suppose the mobster still was suspicious? He might be lurking in the tomblike gloom, waiting to see if the Agent returned. "X" glanced around carefully. A fog was rolling in off the river, curling its spectral tentacles around the old building. Traffic noise, rising from the avenues, seemed remote, almost ghostly. There was a graveyard silence about this district.

The Agent tried the front door. It was locked. He listened. No sound came from within. Possibly this bleak old building was not the one the gunman had entered. "X" would soon find out. He moved silently to the rear. The back door was locked, too.

"X" brought forth a small leather case that held his intricate tools of the highest grade chromium steel. He took out one that looked like a sail-maker's needle, except that it had tiny pivotal extensions. This he inserted in the lock. He worked it around noiselessly, and then withdrew it to readjust the extensions. The next insertion brought a faint click. He opened the door.

The interior was cold and musty and as black as a cavern. He walked forward, feeling his way like a blind man. He picked a route through a maze of machinery. Frequently he stopped. His keen ears were tuned to catch the slightest sound. Suddenly he heard a muffled scream, one that sent a chill up his spine, for the outcry suggested the agony of fiendish torture. "X" knew he had the right lead.

The scream came again. "X" crept forward more rapidly. He dared not switch on a flashlight. Suddenly he tripped over a small box. His excellent sense of balance enabled him to prevent a fall, but he upset the box. A loud, metallic clangor rang out as iron washers spilled onto the floor.

"X" gritted his teeth. He fell into a tense crouch. A moment of deathly silence followed. Then a shaft of light shot ceilingward from the floor. A man emerged from a trapdoor. He gripped an automatic. The dazzling beam of a flash pierced through the heavy darkness.

The light played on the spot where "X" had tripped. But he had leaped behind a machine. The bright ray focused on the overturned box of washers. The gunman rasped out a savage oath.

The mobster crept forward. Evidently he had just been given a narcotic, else he would not have possessed this courage. The Agent began to circle noiselessly. His outthrust hands touched a board balanced precariously on top of a machine. It fell to the floor with a loud crack.

A savage snarl came from the gunman. He swung around, but before he could shoot, "X" discharged his gas gun. "X" had several gas guns cached at his hideouts. One of them still lay where he had hid it when the federal men had caught him. Instantly there was a thud as the gangster's automatic struck the floor. The man collapsed slowly, soundlessly.

The Agent was at his side. He secured the man's hands behind him, thrust a big gag into his mouth, and left the mobster hidden under a machine.

At the trapdoor, he peered down cautiously. Stairs led into a dimly lighted corridor. Moans and screams and hysterical sobs issued from below. "X" reached the bottom of the stairs. Some one was running along the corridor. The Agent darted to the wall and crouched behind a barrel.

Suddenly the mobster stopped. Every fiber of the Agent's body tensed. Had the man seen him? "X" was too far away to use his gas gun.

"Ain't no use hidin', fella!" snarled the killer. "Stand up and get your mitts in the air, or I'll blast the roof off your skull. If your hands ain't empty, you'll sure die sudden."

SWIFTLY the Secret Agent stuck something in his mouth and closed his lips over it. He got up and walked toward his captor. A leer spread over the brutal face of the gunman. "X" approached him slowly, his hands stretched overhead.

"Now turn around, and march to the council chamber, pally," snarled the mobster. "Karloff is always glad to welcome any uninvited visitors. Guess you've never heard of the green death, buddy? It sure is a picture, watchin' a guy squirm and crawl, while his whole body is turnin' green. You don't live long once it starts workin', but you sure know you're alive and sufferin' while it lasts. Get going—"

While the killer gloated, "X" had drawn in a deep breath. Now the end of a tiny rubber tube protruded from his lips. His cheek muscles contracted abruptly. A thin jet of colorless liquid spurted out of the tube's mouth. The instant it contacted with the oxygen in the air, it vaporized. The mobster gave a startled gasp, clawed at space, and slumped to the floor.[48]

Still holding his breath, so he would not be overcome by the gas, "X" dragged the mobster to a room near by. In this room "X" rapidly disguised himself as his would-be captor. He thrust the man in a steel locker, went out. He did not know the gangster's name, nor his duties. Suppose he should betray himself by a slip-up? Karloff would act on the slightest suspicion. The dreadful green death was an ever-present menace.

Farther down the corridor he stopped before the cell from which the screams had come. He looked in, on a horrible sight. Karloff was dealing out more of his hideous discipline. Two raving hopheads were shackled in irons. In the center of the room stood a table. Chains secured the drug addicts so that they could get within a few inches of reaching a little glass case on the table. That case was filled with a white powder. Heroin. Enough to supply the most confirmed addict for a year. Yet these tortured men could not reach it.

They could not be more abject, more pitiable if they were being burned at the stake. Their mouths foamed up the froth of the insane. One of them gnawed on his wrist. So intense was his agony that he was actually attempting to gnaw it off.

While "X" watched, the madman crunched his teeth down on the bones. There was a sickening crack. Then nature rebelled. The maniac slumped in his chains, his head lolling forward and blood dripping from his mouth.

The other victim of the sadistic Karloff kept swaying and bobbing like one in the wild ecstasy of a primitive religion. His eyes were like agate marbles. They looked as though they would pop from their sockets. His head was almost twice its normal size—from lumps caused by banging his skull against the stone wall. He stared at "X" and uttered a shrill, cackling laugh.

"I'm dying, Hazen!" he screamed at the Agent, naming the mobster who had served as the model for "X's" disguise. "The maggots are finishing me! Look at them! Millions of them. Crawling,

---

48 *AUTHOR'S NOTE: Agent "X" is constantly inventing and putting into use new devices in his warfare on criminals. Before he had surrendered to the mobster he had put a tiny rubber bladder, not unlike a miniature basketball bladder, in his mouth. It had contained an extremely volatile chemical that would render one unconscious instantly when taken into the lungs. He had ejected the vaporizing liquid by pressing his cheeks together and pressing upward with his tongue.*

crawling, crawling!" The madman uttered a blood-curdling shriek, and his body shook under great sobs. "Bring Karloff here, Hazen! I want Karloff! I want the beautiful green death—the beautiful green death!"

A WAVE of nausea surged through "X." He was about to turn away when he was aware some one stood behind him. He swung around, and looked into the evil, funereal face of Karloff. Always that hideous man approached with the stealth of a stalking cat. His dark face showed no emotion.

"Crofton wants the green death, Hazen," he spoke in his soft, insinuating manner, "The beautiful green death! You are young, Hazen, a young, stupid rodman. You are a slug compared to Crofton. He used to be one of the most brilliant chemists in the world. But he wasn't smart enough to know better than to work against our organization. Take a lesson, Hazen. Never be too ambitious. Come, Hazen, the master will soon be here!"

A thrill went through "X." The master. At last, he would see the man whose cunning was devoted to the destruction of human souls and bodies. He followed Karloff into the council chamber. A score of men were congregated there. The atmosphere was tense, electric with excitement. Killers spoke in awed, subdued voices.

At the end of the room was a space partitioned off. Across the front was a sheet of thick glass, and behind the glass, a network of steel mesh such as is found in a bank.

"That is shatter-proof glass, Hazen," said Karloff. "The Big Boss doesn't take chances. No dopies will ever take a pot-shot at him."

The Agent did no talking except to answer in monosyllables. During the wait, he moved quietly about the room, listening intently. He heard much talk that told him nothing of importance. Then he stood near Karloff again. The local chief was giving instructions to one of his mobsters.

"I want you to leave right after the big boss finishes his talk," Karloff was saying. "The stuff will be hidden in ash-cans. If you're stopped, you merely say you're taking ashes to a farm to be used as fertilizer."

The mob chief talked at considerable length. "X" learned that a consignment of dope was to be sent out of the city. Karloff ordered the man to take the load via the Long Meadow Road, a more devious route, but a less patrolled one.

Then a sudden stillness prevailed in the room. Men grew tense.

All eyes focused on the glass shield. Behind it, a door opened. A tall, erect man appeared. He walked with an arrogant stride. A heavy black mask covered his face. Draped around him was a black cape.

For a while he stood back of the bullet-proof glass and surveyed his audience. Then he began speaking in a deep, rumbling voice.

"My message tonight will be brief, gentlemen. I wish to commend the members of this organization, and particularly Karloff, for their splendid and loyal endeavors. We have instituted an advertising campaign that has been a drastic departure from the usual methods. By giving away our product, we have created a demand that will continue to grow to enormous proportions."

The Big Boss explained that the campaign was one hundred per cent successful. A huge market for the drugs had been built up among wealthy and influential people. Daily, police and high officials were being snared into the drug ring!

"Those in this organization who have proved their faithfulness will be amply rewarded," continued the master. "All of you are patrons of our excellent product. If you work heart and soul for the organization, the day will come when you will be pensioned with a fortune and an inexhaustible supply of drugs." There was irony in the man's voice which the Agent did not miss. Beneath suave woods he was showing his sneering contempt of these poor, broken wretches. He went on more harshly:

"I need not tell you the fate of the disloyal. You have seen with your own eyes what happens to them. Remember that Karloff's word is law. He alone is responsible to me for the actions of all the members of our local organization. And remember that you are to co-operate as never before for the big sales campaign which lies just ahead. So far, we have been giving the stuff away. Next we start selling it—and then the golden flood will come in. That is all, gentlemen."

The Big Boss backed out the door. He had not talked long, he had not revealed much that the mobsters did not know, but his presence had been spellbinding, and his words had shocked the Agent. Soon the sale of the drugs was to start. Soon the country would be inundated with a hateful tide of narcotics.

Soon money would be pouring out of addicts' pockets into the coffers of the dread gang. Money—thousands, perhaps millions of dollars would go to build up an organization which should be stamped out like a nest of poisonous, sinister vipers. But who was this man? "X" did not know. His voice had been too much disguised for "X" to penetrate it.

There was a long silence after the master's departure, broken finally by Karloff, who dismissed the meeting.

KARLOFF disappeared into a room adjoining the council chamber. That was the Agent's cue. He quietly slipped out of the big room, and hurried from the building. In the darkness, he changed to a stock disguise which his skillful fingers built up quickly. A little later, in one of his hideouts, he quickly molded the features of A. J. Martin and put on the sandy-haired wig.

He got in his fast roadster and made a swift trip far beyond the city limits. Soon he left the main highway and headed west until he reached a lonely spot on Long Meadow Road.

Stalling the car crosswise on the road about fifty yards around a bend, he waited tensely for the mobsters. A few minutes later he heard the rumble of a truck, the rattle of tin cans. His eyes blazed with excitement. His face grew grim and hard. He changed to a savage, relentless fighting man, fiercely intent on defeating the great evil that was gnawing into America.

Would the truck be supplied with armed guards? Would the odds be too great for a lone man to surmount? "X" got out of his car. He was keyed up to a high nervous tension. Maybe he had but a few seconds to live. He remembered the last time he had faced a machine-load of Karloff mobsters. Would the hopheads throw phosphorus bombs again? "X" did not carry lethal weapons. They would be armed to destroy.

The dope truck careened around the bend. Headlights glared on the stalled car. The driver uttered a profane shout of rage. He jammed on the brakes. The truck skidded half around and came to a screeching stop. The headlights had been gleaming full on the Agent. With the car turned side-wise, "X" was enveloped in darkness.

A machine gun rapped out a wicked tattoo of death. Bullets whined around the Agent. Something pulled at his coat as he threw himself off the road into the bushes. A bullet. He had missed death by a hairbreadth. In the concealment of the underbrush, he plunged toward the dope truck.

Two mobsters manned it, and they were armed with sub-machine guns. The Agent hurled a gas bomb at the driver's face. It struck him on the forehead. The man's wicked snarl was cut short as the potent vapors took instant effect. The second mobster dived from the car. He raked the side of the road near "X" with a fierce volley of lead! Knowing only the general direction of the Agent, he did not score.

"X" flung another bomb. Then a third one. The mobster saw the motion of his hand. He spat out ugly oaths. Then he gasped, choked. A stream of fire and lead poured from the Tommy gun, but the missiles plowed into the dirt road. For the Agent's bombs had struck the gangster. The hophead was already succumbing to the powerful fumes as he triggered the gun. Now he sprawled out on the road, senseless.

Giving the gas time to waft away, "X" then hurried to the truck. On it were loaded a dozen ash cans, heaped up with ashes. The Agent rolled a can off the truck and dumped the contents on the road in front of the headlights. At the very bottom were several small packages. "X" picked the bundles up and hefted them. Probably ten pounds or a little more.

In a few minutes he had the other cans emptied. Each had contained, under the ashes, the same amount of dope as the first. A hundred and twenty pounds, "X" estimated. He gave a shrill whistle of amazement. More than ninety-two thousand dollars' worth of dope. The Big Boss certainly had a business that made the old-time bootlegging of liquor look like a catch-penny enterprise.

While he was working on the cans, "X" had heard the low put-put of motorcycles. Now gleaming spotlights were trained on Long Meadow Road. The motorcycles were coming at racing speed. The Agent hurried to get the narcotics into his car.

He glanced behind the truck. Four motorcycles plunged toward him. The drivers wore olive-drab uniforms, carried guns in holsters. Cops. They swerved around the truck just as "X" was shifting into high. The Agent's car was constructed for a rapid pickup. The motorcycles were close when he jammed down on the accelerator. The car leaped ahead. The cops fired warning shots. The Agent gripped the wheel grimly, kept his gleaming eyes fixed on the road ahead. The officers opened up on the rear of the ear in deadly earnest. If they punctured "X's" tires, he was through.

CHAPTER XVI

CLUES

THE AGENT HAD one thing in his favor. His car could travel at great speed more safely on a dirt road than the motorcycles. If one of the cops got in the way of a large stone, he likely would find himself in the brush the next second, with a few broken bones. But those men were dare-devils.

On the next turn, "X" started down a steep slope. Every hundred yards or so, he careened around a sharp turn. Not once did he ease up on the gas. The motorcycles had to slow down. It would be suicidal for the cops to take those turns at the Agent's speed.

The firing was infrequent now, because the officers had to keep their hands on the bars. "X" swung recklessly around the curves. The terrific driving played havoc with his tires, but that did not matter. All he asked was that they would last until he got out of this danger.

He reached the bottom of the hill. The cops were out of sight, but he could hear their machines. He struck a straightaway. The wheels hit a large plank in the road. The car leaped. It landed with the wheels turned, headed for a ditch. "X" clamped his jaws and fought for control of the car. One wheel went slightly over the edge. He swung hard to the left, brought the auto back into the road.

The cops were just reaching the straightaway when the Agent swerved onto the paved highway. He traveled at roaring speed until he reached the suburbs. Then he slowed to the limit, and headed up a side street. He had thrown off pursuit.

A few minutes later he was in the laboratory of Howard Fenwick, and the great chemist was working over the dope "X" had confiscated. At the Agent's insistence, he was lavish with the narcotic, running a dozen tests in as many tubes simultaneously. When he finished, he was frowning and shaking his head.

"It's beyond me, Mr. Martin," he said apologetically. "I've tried every known test, looked for all the known alkaloids. There seems to be only one explanation. It sounds nutty, but it must be true. The dope is synthetic, made by some method of which I'm ignorant."

"X" frowned, tensed. The chemist's conclusion had almost the effect of a physical blow. Synthetic. No wonder the Federal narcotic men and detectives had failed. No wonder they could not check the poisonous flood of dope when they were looking into the wrong source. They were hunting for smugglers bringing it into the country, whereas the drug was a home product. The Agent spoke harshly, staring straight before him.

"That means the stuff can be manufactured in tremendous quantities and at a low cost!" he said.

Fenwick nodded. "Undoubtedly. The raw materials, whatever they are, likely cost far less than crude opium. The method of synthetic production probably requires much less labor. Besides, the risk of smuggling is eliminated, and also transportation expenses from the Orient."

The Agent was appalled by this astounding revelation. Compared to the man who controlled the synthetic manufacture of dope, the smugglers were dwarfed into mere public nuisances. With this weapon of synthetic narcotics, a person with a twisted, criminal mind could reduce the entire country to his will, unless his evil activities were stopped almost at the beginning. And the gang "X" was fighting was getting ready now to launch its tremendous sales campaign.

FROM the laboratory the Agent hurried to the office he kept under the name of A. J. Martin. His desk was stacked with news stories of the drug menace that had been delivered by a clipping bureau. The story heads explained how the law forces were bungling, how the blight was spreading.

BORDER PATROL CLASHES WITH DOPE SMUGGLERS

—

FEDERAL MEN NAB CHINESE OPIUM CHIEF

—

MORPHINE BROUGHT IN VIA AIRPLANE

—

DOPE-CRAZED BANK PRESIDENT EMBEZZLES $150,000

—

NARCOTICS INVADE THE SOCIAL REGISTER

—

DRUG HABIT CAUSES DEBUTANTE SUICIDE

—

Smugglers, opium, airplanes. The whole detective force was wrong. There were smugglers, yes—and drugs brought across the border by airplane. But the dope plague was not the outgrowth of pioneer methods. The longer the federal men searched on the wrong trail, the stronger the Big Boss was becoming in his bid for despotic power in America.

"X" thought of Twyning then, the chemist killed in Whitney Blake's penthouse. Now that he knew the drug was synthetic, the Agent had a sudden idea of the motive for the homicide, a motive that had little to do with self-defense. Undoubtedly Twyning had been connected with the manufacture of the drug. Could it be that the man had actually discovered the formula?

Suppose he had fought against the illegal use of the synthetic dope? The Big Boss might have made him a drug addict to break his will. "X" recalled that hectic night in the Blake penthouse. A moment before his sudden death, Twyning had headed directly for Silas Howe. That, in the light of his new knowledge, seemed to add weight to his suspicion that Howe might be a possible member of the drug ring.

In any case, the dead Twyning was "X's" next lead. He called Jim Hobart at once, ordering him to learn all he could of the slain chemist. He suggested that Hobart detail Walter Milburn and the nervy Allan Grant, formerly a newspaper legman, on the same lead.

They were skilled operatives, relentless when trailing down information which their boss wanted. "X" ordered that Silas Howe, the reformer, be shadowed also. He set the grimly efficient Bates organization to watch Karloff's headquarters. He was doing everything he could, throwing all his resources into this greatest fight of his career.

Eighteen hours passed with no headway made. Then Jim Hobart strode into the office "X" maintained as Martin.

"I talked to several employees at Paragon Chemicals, boss," said

Hobart. "This fellow, Twyning, seems to have been a pretty good scout. Could handle tough formulas as easy as a kid rattles off A, B, C. Used to work after hours. Sometimes he kept at it all night. Always experimenting. Not a sign of drug addiction. No mixer at all. Didn't know much when it came to anything but chemistry. Some of the laboratory workers spoke of him as a genius."

"Did he talk about his work?" asked the Agent eagerly.

"That's just the point, boss," replied Hobart. "He didn't. He was always willing to discuss the latest discoveries, but not a peep about his own work except, of course, his routine duties. The fellow had been with Paragon Chemicals for years. High-salaried guy, too. Then four weeks ago he didn't show up. That was the last they saw of him, until his body was identified in the morgue."

Hobart's information backed up some of "X's" conjectures. Twyning had been considered a genius, an indefatigable worker, a persistent experimenter. Such a man logically could have come upon the formula for synthetic dope.

Later in the day, Hobart returned with another report.

"I found a lodging house near the Paragon Chemicals plant where Twyning had rented a cheap dump of a bedroom under an assumed name and these were in it," said the operative, handing the Agent a packet of letters. "He used the room, I guess, when he worked late and didn't want to go to his apartment. His rent was paid six months in advance, and the landlady didn't know he was dead. I found nothing about Twyning there, but there's some information in these letters. Silas Howe, that reformer guy, holds majority stock in Paragon Chemicals. Maybe there's something in it."

The Agent leaped to his feet. His eyes flashed. That was it. Hobart had brought in the missing part of the puzzle. Twyning, the chemical genius, the tireless experimenter, had worked for Paragon Chemicals. Silas Howe practically owned the company. Twyning had made this gigantic, revolutionary discovery. Silas Howe had stolen the formula. That certainly seemed logical. Hadn't Twyning, his eyes blazing murderously, come at Howe with a knife?

CHAPTER XVII

A VIPERS NEST

THE AGENT WAS leaving his office when Jim Hobart rushed in for the third time, with Allan Grant close behind. Though the former detective was not the easily ruffled type, he was actually trembling with excitement,

"We've found another gang headquarters, boss!" he exclaimed, "No dirty, abandoned old dump, no dopie hideout this time! We bumped into a ritzy office, full of swank and right up to the minute. I played a hunch and sent Grant to answer an ad in the *Herald* calling for young men and women of hoity-toity social connections. And what did they want! Young society folks to distribute a fancy brand of cigarette among their friends. A smooth-looking dame offered Grant a fat salary to give the stuff away. Grant palmed a couple of smokes. I tried one. Two puffs and you almost hit the ceiling. It wouldn't take many of those cigarettes to make a fellow get a Napoleon hat and start out to conquer the world."

The Agent's face hardened, though an eager light shone in his eyes. More evidence of the master's insidious cunning. Give the Big Boss a few more days—another week at the most—and his organization would be so firmly imbedded that the country's entire law force would not be able to tear out its roots. The death thrust had to be made right away. Within the next few hours. With the drug so potent, with so many people falling prey to the habit, even another full day might mean victory for the Big Boss.

"Splendid work, Hobart," praised "X." "But the real job is ahead if I want to get a scoop for the paper. You two come with me. Where is this office?"

"In the Quinault Building," said Hobart.

The operative named a skyscraper near the center of the city. But it was to another building that the Agent went, one where Silas

Howe kept an office for his vice-suppression activities. "X" learned from the elevator captain that the reformer wasn't in. The three men waited. For once "X" felt that it was wise to have help. Too much was at stake tonight. The happiness, the very lives of thousands. He himself might be killed. There must be someone to carry on the work. But Jim and his aides still thought of him only as Martin, the newspaper man.

Night had spread over the city when "X" saw Howe enter with a couple of prominent social workers. It was amazing how the self-styled reformer maintained his sanctimonious front. For years he had been the bane of theatrical producers and book publishers with his vitriolic attacks. He was in the vanguard of every reform, every crusade.

The Agent waited for Howe to come out. That was two hours later. The reformer's companions were still with him. "X" frowned and tightened his mouth grimly. Possibly Howe would devote this night to social work. The time would be lost, listening to him rage and declaim across the rostrum at a public assemblage. "X" had hoped to follow the man to a hideout where he would see him in his true character.

For several blocks Howe walked with his associates. "X" was disturbed. He had hoped to bear down on this man tonight, but he had no direct evidence yet. Then the Agent's face brightened; Howe's companions left the reformer. The man turned a corner.

A few minutes later Howe was entering the Quinault Building. Now was the time for careful maneuvering, for patience. "X" did not want to put the man on guard by a hasty move. Once more he waited. Soon Howe reappeared.

The reformer's next stop was his own apartment building, the same building where Blake lived. That caused "X" a few moments of concern. Howe had a suite there. Possibly he was retiring for the night.

Then a thrill went through the Agent. Howe did not turn in the front way. He was using the servant's entrance, slinking in furtively. "X" snapped quick orders to his operatives.

"You two watch across the street! If I need you, I'll signal to you somehow. Be on the lookout every instant!"

Pressing himself against the wall, the Agent edged through the deep shadows. He paused in the darkness, watching and listening tensely. Then he darted through the door behind Howe. He made no noise, but he could hear Howe's footsteps far down the corridor.

"X" followed swiftly, silently.

He took out something from his pocket as he moved along. It was a stick of radium paint, unlike any other in the world, and with it he left marks on the wall to guide his men in case he called them. He found himself in a maze of passageways, and there were many doors that could cause confusion.

Howe was walking hurriedly, with the quickness of a man who has something to conceal. "X" sped down the winding corridor, raced into a dark passage, guided by the footsteps ahead. Behind him were the glowing marks of the radium paint, tiny lines and arrows. "X" was alert to his danger, to the possibility of rushing headlong into a trap. His tread on rubber-soled shoes was silent, yet there was a chance that guards were posted, that wicked eyes watched through hidden peepholes.

A door slammed. "X" stopped, peered through the darkness. Was some one coming, or had that been Howe? The Agent went on slowly. He didn't know what lay ahead. He thought of the horrible green death. With success so near, the Big Boss would strike swiftly. The slightest bungle meant annihilation for "X"! He felt his way down another corridor. At the far end, light gleamed faintly through a keyhole. He rushed to the door, listened tensely, then opened it.

A GHASTLY purplish light struck his eyes. Standing in the shadows of an antechamber, he looked into a large room where at least a score of shambling, emaciated men, wearing goggles, were working at long, plate-glass tables under some sort of weird mercury-vapor lamps.

The brilliant tubes glowed and sputtered. The wan and feeble men, moving like automatons, spread thin coatings of a viscid brownish substance over glass plates with long, pliant spatulas.

Before "X's" eyes a strange and amazing transformation came in that thick, tarlike paste. It turned white, although the mercury lamps gave it a purplish tinge. From a glutinous, semifluid material it changed to glistening, powdery crystals.

At last, "X" had the secret. The Big Boss made his synthetic dope by breaking down the molecular composition of some substance, probably a coal-tar derivative that cost no more than crude oil.

The horror of it stabbed through the Agent like an electric shock. Every coating of brown paste was soon changed into white crystals that meant misery, tragedy, death for scores. One coating yielded enough of the poisonous drug to enslave a hundred people. The terrifying sight made "X" clammy with dread.

The Agent had invaded the arsenals of crime kings, stored with bombs of destroying gases. He had been in the laboratories of madmen, where bacteria that wrought loathsome and fatal diseases were sealed in tubes ready to be spread over a defenseless land. But none of those frightful devices quite equaled the deviltry, the fiendishness of the Big Boss. He sent unsuspecting people into a life of the damned, made monsters, abhorrent and inhuman, out of creatures who once were men.

Below the Agent, those human gargoyles, those pitiful, cadaverous slaves, hideous from the ravages of dope, leprous under the rays of the mercury lamps, moved like rusted old machines. Guards stood over them, threatening with automatics and cracking blacksnakes across the thin, bent backs of the shuffling dope addicts.

Suddenly "X" swung around. He was not frightened, but the flesh felt cold along his spine. A sense of acute personal danger had broken through his concentration. His eyes burned with anger as he stared into the cold black bore of a revolver. The brutal, repulsive man behind it had stepped through a panel that had opened in the wall. Murder glittered in his piggish little eyes.

CHAPTER XVIII

A SHOT IN THE DARK

THE KILLER ADVANCED with his gun aimed at the Agent's heart. "Get those mitts in the air and talk quick!" he rasped. "Who sent you in here?"

"X's" mind raced. He was no farther from death than the pressure of a trigger finger. There was no chance of getting his gas gun. A step toward the guard, and a bullet would rip into his heart. The antechamber was dark, but a purple glow from the mercury lamps shone on the guard's ugly face. The Agent smiled. His manner became apologetic. He started to raise his hands slowly.

"Why, I—er—don't understand, sir," he said in a meek voice. "I'm Dudley Smythe of the New England Welfare League. I'm in town for the United Brotherhood Conference that opens tomorrow. I happened to be passing by, and I saw Brother Howe come in the servant's entrance. I hailed him, but my good friend did not hear. Not realizing that I might be trespassing, I followed him. I'm sorry, so sorry, if—"

A vaporizing liquid that turned to tear gas suddenly sprayed over the guard's vicious face. He shrank back, pawing at his smarting, blinded eyes. He uttered an agonized howl that "X" cut short with a savage uppercut that lifted the man off his feet and dropped him in a heap, senseless.

The Agent's talk had thrown the killer off guard, had distracted him, while "X's" hands were slowly moving upwards. But the left hand had stopped at the breast pocket, had clutched at the fountain pen secured there. The pressure of a tiny button had opened a catch that released the tear-gas.

"X" stepped back until the gas dispelled and lost its potency. Then he pressed back into the shadows, and drew his gas gun.

"Help! Quick! He'll kill me!" the Agent cried, imitating the voice of the unconscious guard.

The man's three associates came running at once. And, as they got within range, "X" pressed the trigger of his gas gun and held it down. There was a moment of choking, gasping confusion, and then the gas took complete effect. The first man staggered, tried to retreat, and collided with his companions. The three dropped like sacks of grain.

The Agent went into the room where the drug fiends were working at the glass-topped tables. Against the wall stood boxes containing packets and bottles of dope. The piles extended to the ceiling, enough of the refined product to enslave the entire metropolis.

The wretched creatures under the lamps performed their tasks with slow, mechanical movements, as though they were under an hypnotic spell. They were repulsive, horrible automatons, with all the spirit lashed out of them, beings who lived solely for the dope that was doled out to them in niggardly quantities.

The Agent beckoned to one of the dopies, who shuffled toward him listlessly. The worker's eyes were two feverish spots burning in a fleshless face. The skin had the slate-gray tinge of death. He sniffed constantly. The man was dying on his feet.

"Where is the elevator that your master uses?" the Agent demanded. His voice was harsh. This was no time for gentleness.

The hophead shrank back in fear. "No! No!" he cried. "I can't tell. They'll deprive me of my drug allowance for a week. A week! Do you understand? A week of torture!"

The man was probably not more than thirty, but he had the decrepitude of age, the feeble, piping voice of one in the last stages of senility.

"You won't be deprived of your dope," said the Agent sternly, "but you will get the green death if you don't tell me. The green death, understand! Where is that elevator?"

The hophead all but collapsed from fear. A spasm of shivering, a nervous convulsion, made it impossible for him to speak for a while.

"The green death!" the man gasped, his eyes bulging with horror. "No! Anything—anything but the green death! I'll tell! I'll tell!"

The trembling, terror-stricken man motioned "X" to follow, and reeled into another room. There the Agent found an automatic, self-operating elevator such as is installed in most modern apartment houses. But the entrance to this one was hidden behind a high, green-metal storage cabinet, which the dopie slid back on rollers. The Agent might have wasted precious minutes in hunting for it.

"Are you sure this is the elevator the Big Boss uses?" demanded "X." "If you're tricking me, you'll get the green death!"

The drug addict recoiled in fright. "I'm telling the truth!" He cried in his shrill, feeble voice. "I have seen the green death! I'd do anything to save myself from it."

THE Agent eyed him narrowly. "How much of this drug are you manufacturing a day here?"

"More than a hundred and thirty pounds," was the ready answer, "and what do we get? We who make it! One hundred and thirty pounds, and we get five grains a day! Five grains! Yet each of us makes more than thirty-five grains a day, yet our daily dole is five grains."

The drug addict broke into tears, and his wizened frame, hardly more than a skeleton, retched with great sobs. The Agent looked at him a moment, and then he led the wretched man into the laboratory. He addressed the other slaves.

"You are free men now!" he announced. "The guards are unconscious. They'll be that way for an hour, but you'll never be molested again. Take all the drugs you want. You'll not be harmed. Quiet your shattered nerves! End your torture! Help yourselves, men!"

They stared at him in bewilderment. Then one of them uttered an exultant howl like the savage cry of an animal and dived for the drugs. The laboratory changed into a madhouse, with each dopie scrambling to get his hands on a precious packet. The man at "X's" side wrung his hand, gave him a look that expressed deep gratitude, and then plunged into the mass of frenzied hopheads.

The Agent had had a purpose in turning the dopies loose on the narcotics. It wasn't based purely on sympathy for them and their shattered nerves. It was to keep them quiet, out of the way, while he pursued his grim investigation.

He entered the elevator that he had been shown. He closed the cage and pressed the button that started the car upwards. It seemed that the elevator would never reach the top. "X" half expected it to stop, expected it to be converted into an execution chamber.

He searched for tubes or jets that might flood the car with lethal gas. He found none. Naturally, a master criminal like the Big Boss would conceal his means of destruction. Suddenly the car clicked to a stop. The Agent found himself staring at a concrete wall. Frantically he swung around. His body relaxed in relief. There was a door. His heart thumped. He listened. All he heard was the steady ticking of a clock.

He pushed the door open a little. The lights were on. The Agent poised carefully. He would bob his head in and back again quickly, enabling him to get a glimpse of the room before any one could take a pot-shot at him. Opening the door a little more, he darted his head forward. The room was empty.

It was a large room of a suite, and obviously the abode of Silas Howe. The man had maintained his masquerade even here. The furnishings were expensive but severe. Black was the motif of the decorations. Despite the costliness of the teakwood furniture, the place was as cheerless as a monk's cell.

The Agent searched quickly through the suite. If Howe were there, he was hiding. "X" rushed to the telephone. He would call one of his operatives, and have him order General Mathers' men to raid the stronghold of the dope ring.

But the telephone was dead. Anxiously he hunted for the switch that would connect it again, but he could not find it. Possibly the wires were cut.

Again the Agent had the eerie feeling that eyes were upon him. He ran to the light switch, pressed the room into darkness. He leaped to the window of the apartment.

Far below, on the opposite side of the street, he knew Jim Hobart and Allan Grant were waiting. "X" took a small flash with a powerful lens from his pocket. It had a focusing attachment to concentrate the rays. He adjusted this, then turned it down and blinked it; two longs, a short and two longs. A second passed, and there was an answering blink from below.

Hobart, watchful as the Agent had cautioned him to be, had seen the signal. He returned it, using a special secret code that the Agent had worked out for him and taught him weeks ago. "X" began giving Hobart orders. The time had arrived to smash the whole ring at once, to call in the law and strike ruthlessly, desperately.

"Get General Mathers," he flashed to Hobart. "Twenty men at least. Raid basement! Follow radium lines!"

He sent down instructions for the headquarters in the Quinault Building to be raided, and also Karloff's hideout in the old factory, where the Big Boss had addressed his hirelings. But he stressed the importance of striking hard at the stronghold below first of all. That was the fountain-head of the evil.

"X" heard a faint sound in the dark apartment then. Something scraped on the floor. Outlined at the window, he was a perfect target and knew it. But he had been forced to take the chance. Now uneasiness gripped him.

Madly he hurled himself aside. As he did so, powder flame lanced the darkness. There was a faint, dull pop that told of a silenced gun. A bullet screamed close to the Agent's head, so close that it scorched the skin of his scalp. Some one cursed.

CHAPTER XIX

THE MASTER COUP

TENSE AND ALERT as a crouching tiger the Agent stole along the wall. His photographic mind gave him a picture of the room. He could reach the door without crashing into the furniture. But a squeaking board might betray him. He dared not breathe. The awful uncertainty of whether his next step would be his last made him hold himself rigid.

A draft of cold air fanned the Agent's cheek. Excitedly he felt along the wall. He reached an aperture, a panel that had not been opened before. He had no idea where it led, but he stepped through it into a small, well-like recess. His groping hands felt the cold frame of an iron ladder.

His heart pounded, and there was a sudden, bright light of triumph in his eyes. He climbed quickly, went through another opening into a pitch-dark room. Not even the tick of a clock broke the stillness here. From the street far below came the muffled roar of traffic. Little did those who passed by know the mystery, the weirdness, the peril and tragedy housed in this imposing apartment building.

"X" moved stealthily across the thick carpet, soft as lush grass under his feet. He would get to a switch, throw on the lights. With catlike caution he crept forward. Then suddenly his body tensed.

He gave a start of surprise, almost of awe, as light flooded the room. He stood all but petrified by what he saw. Under his disguise his face muscles stiffened. The fingers of his right hand clenched until they formed a fist.

For, sitting in an armchair and gazing at him with mocking, sardonic glints in his eyes was a white-haired, craggy-faced man, not Howe, but another—Whitney Blake.

The old financier smiled, but not pleasantly. There was a derisive, brutal twist to his thin-lipped mouth. The eyes of the two men clashed. In "X's" was a questing light. Blake's were hard, cruel, uncompromising.

The ladder to Blake's penthouse was proof to "X" that Blake was at least in on the secrets of the dope ring and in league with Silas Howe. Yet the Agent delayed his accusation. He wanted to verify the truth of these new and startling suspicions. Back in his mind for days how had been a vague intimation, unexpressed even to himself, that Whitney Blake might have some connection with the ring. But it had seemed too fantastic to harbor even for a moment.

"I'm after Silas Howe," said "X" quietly. "He must be here. I followed him from the apartment below."

The old financial wolf regarded the Agent with a look of scorn and bitter, mirthless amusement. "My friend, most people in this world know too little. But you, whoever you are, are diffcrent! You know too much—far too much. Your curiosity has thrust you into a situation from which you will never escape."

Blake's expression changed. It seemed that all the bitterness, all the ruthless ambition of his grasping, callous soul writhed across his face. The man's body shook with murderous rage. Agent "X" was astounded at the transformation. Gazing into the financier's eyes was like looking into the black, slimy pit of some pool in hell where living furies lurked. The sudden change revealed the full secret, verified the Agent's suspicions. Whitney Blake was the Big Boss, not the man who had given the harangue in Karloff's hideout, but the guiding force of the great dope ring, the master of the pitiable drug-crazed slaves. His cover, his front, had been an even better mask than Silas Howe's. The man had social position, a nationwide reputation in the financial world. Besides this he was old, supposedly mellowed by age, a donator to many charities, and it was believed that he had an infirmity that made him a helpless cripple.

Much that had puzzled the Agent was cleared up in a flash. He understood why de Ronfort had been murdered, and how Twyning had come to be killed in Blake's apartment.

"You are the man who plotted to wreck the country to satisfy your ambition," the Agent accused in a low, tense voice.

For a moment Blake remained silent, staring at the Agent fixedly. Then he parted his thin lips, showing teeth that seemed like the fangs of a wolf.

"Quite right, my good man," he admitted with contemptuous

indifference. "I intend to make the people of this city dance to the tune I fiddle. Soon the most honored and accomplished people in the country will be subservient to my slightest wish. I will be more absolute in my power than Nero or Napoleon—not by the force of arms, but by the force of drugs. And I will make money—money! Returns greater than that possible on any other investment today. Returns that will more than make up the millions I lost in the stock market crash when fools were in control!"

Inhuman greed shone in the old financier's eyes. "X" spoke harshly.

"But you're through, Blake!" he said. "For your work in spreading the dope blight, you could be sent to the penitentiary for the rest of your life. But there is a more serious charge against you. Murder, Blake! You might be acquitted of killing Twyning on the charge of justifiable homicide. But de Ronfort was murdered. You ordered his death yourself. And there will be witnesses to prove that you engineered the killing."

WHITNEY BLAKE nodded slowly. "I see," he said. "You are a surprising man. You talk as though you had intimate knowledge of my affairs." He spoke with mock admiration. "Yes, I killed Twyning—with my cane gun, as no doubt you have already figured out. A brilliant man—Twyning! Truly a genius. It was he who discovered the secret of breaking down the molecular composition of certain coal-tar derivatives. But outside of the laboratory he was a fool, a child. He wanted to donate his formula to the government—a formula that would have given him greater power than all the military forces of the world. He wanted to give it away.

"Through Howe I had already gained control of Paragon Chemicals. Twyning opposed my plan to manufacture the drug. I had to make an addict of him. He came here to kill me, not Howe, so I disposed of him. Were you at Paula's party? The killing rather livened things up, didn't it?"

Whitney Blake threw back his head and laughed. There was a trace of madness in his eyes. But there was fiendish cunning also. "De Ronfort," he continued. "Yes, I commissioned my efficient aide, Karloff, to dispose of him. A common adventurer! A cheap, sneaking smuggler—and he expected to marry my ward, Paula. It was absurd—and after I found out what he was, I—But never mind that now, my friend. You seem to think I'm an unhealthy influence in this country. What, may I ask, do you propose to do about it?"

There was open mockery on Blake's face now. The Agent's reply to his question was quiet.

"I have already done it," he said. "The federal men have been called out. They are beginning a concerted attack on your organization. Probably, at the moment they are raiding your manufacturing room below. Your reign of terror is over, Blake. Your ring will be smashed!"

Once again Whitney Blake threw back his head and laughed. It was the laughter of a devil. His manner suddenly changed to mock sorrow. "It is very sad," he said, with a shake of his head. "No doubt they are brave men. They have homes and loved ones. Such a tragedy! For you, sir, have only led them to their deaths!"

"What do you mean?" The Agent grew rigid with apprehension.

Blake laughed sardonically. "I can kill them from where I sit, without moving from this chair! You don't believe me, I see. Then look! You came here for Silas Howe! There—see him!"

ONE of Blake's fingers moved ever so slightly. There was a clicking sound. A section of the wall opened outward, revealing a sort of closet. The Agent stepped back in horror. He felt that the blood would congeal in his veins. For there was Silas Howe, the criminal who wore the reformer's cloak. He fell forward into the room, a corpse with the rigidity of rigor mortis already apparent—and his face showed the hideous, poison hue of the green death!

"There he is!" repeated Blake harshly. "A blundering fool if there ever was one! He became overly confident—even careless. He let you shadow him here! I anticipated that he might become a liability in time. He blundered into my hands five years ago when he appropriated for his own use fifty thousand dollars meant for a charitable fund.

"I caught him then, threatened him with exposure, made him grovel at my feet—and afterwards cleared him to put him under obligation to me for life. Now he is dead, killed by me of necessity. But, my friend, he is still useful—just as you, too, will be useful—dead!"

A harsh exclamation came from the Secret Agent's lips. He started forward, eyes blazing. Blake grew tense, alarmed at once. He raised a warning hand, and "X" stopped.

"I know who you are!" said Blake, with a hoarse note of something closely akin to awe in his voice. "You must be the one—the only person I gave thought to as an obstacle to my plans. You must be the criminal known as Secret Agent 'X.' You are a strange man, an interesting man, I have heard. Except for that peculiar twist which makes you an outlaw, go about fighting your own kind, I would like to have you in my organization. But—no! You are an idealistic fool! I have heard that, too."

Whitney Blake leaned forward and glared at "X." "You don't want to cause the deaths of those federal men below, do you? You don't like to kill even criminals. Then don't take another step forward. If you do—they die, like rats in a trap, when I open the valves of the cyanic gas tanks.

"I have taken pains to make it possible for me to wipe out those who do my work—the wretched drug addicts in the basement of this building. And—if you move from where you stand—I shall use the same means on the federal men."

The Agent stifled his rage. He needed a clear mind. He could save himself. But by doing so, he would cause the deaths of many men. He saw by the movement of Whitney Blake's hands that rows of buttons were under the arms of that chair. One of those buttons, "X" knew now, controlled the lights. That was how Blake had plunged the room in darkness the night he had killed Twyning.

Blake laughed softly. "Suppose my drugs are confiscated," he said. "That means only a loss of time. I have the formula. They won't take that from me, because it's in my head. Eventually my plan will succeed. And no one will suspect me. Stand where you are, Agent 'X.' I'm summoning my secretary, Rivers. Remember—a move that displeases me, and I'll kill those federal men in my laboratory."

Blake pressed a button. Soon the quiet-laced Rivers entered. His manner was unassuming, yet "X" knew he was of the same ruthless nature as his employer. He must be or Blake would not have hired him. Probably he was under obligation in some way to his master also, a slave of his own fear like Howe.

"Rivers, take the late Mr. Howe back to his own suite," instructed Blake. "Return immediately. We must dispose of this meddlesome gentleman. He is Secret Agent 'X,' a man of many disguises. Perhaps you have heard of him. Before we give him the green death by hypodermic injection, I'm going to have a look at his actual features. Merely curiosity—an old man's whim."

The secretary bowed, then dragged the corpse through the open panel that led down to Howe's suite.

"You see, young man," said Blake. "I've protected myself against a possible raid. Howe signed a full confession, taking the responsibility for the 'drug blight', as the newspapers call it. For that confession, I promised the poor fool immunity. Strange, isn't it, the man is dead! He looked moldy, didn't he?"

Tense seconds passed while the Agent dared not move for fear of causing the deaths of those men below. Then Rivers returned. He came up behind "X" with irons to handcuff him. Once those steel links slipped over "X's" wrists it would be the end. Yet the Agent grimly held his hands out behind him. If they clicked shut, he soon would look like the man in the apartment below—green, moldy.

WHITNEY BLAKE was trembling with excitement now as he gloated over his distinguished victim. His voice came hoarsely.

"I will assist myself in administering the green death, Rivers. I have a hypo here already. But first I want to see our guest as he really is. First I want to peel that stuff from his face and look at features that ten thousand detectives and police would risk their lives to see."

A surge of deep emotion swept through the Agent. He felt the cold steel touch his wrists. A slight shudder passed through his body—not from fear of his own safety; but because of what those irons symbolized. The shackling, sinister yoke of crime on a whole huge community. Men and women ruined, destroyed body and soul.

It was now or never—one daring, desperate play, or the loss of everything for which he had worked, and annihilation by the green death.

Before Rivers could snap on the cuffs, "X" seized his wrists in a vise-like grip.

Every fiber of the Agent's muscular, powerful, highly trained body grew taut. He bent down, yanked forward like a steel spring suddenly uncoiling. As he did so, the unsuspecting Rivers rose and shot into the air.

The maneuver that "X" had used was amazing but simple. It was an age-old Jiu-jitsu trick of leverage. The Agent had hurled the secretary over his head by means of it. The thing was done with lightning, incredible speed. There was no fumbling, no lost motion. "X's" full power was in the throw.

He hurled the servant straight toward Whitney Blake as though Rivers had been a piece of iron in some weight-throwing contest. The vicious old financier was transfixed with fear, unable to move, paralyzed in his chair.

Rivers catapulted through the air, arms and legs spinning like the vanes of a windmill.

Crack! His head rammed against Blake's in a terrific collision. The chair tipped over backwards. The men struck the floor with a deadweight thud, together. "X" leaped forward instantly and knelt beside them. Expertly he felt their skulls. Possibly they sustained slight fractures. Concussions surely, but they would live to answer to the law for their crimes. Blake would go to the electric chair.

The Secret Agent cut the wires to the buttons under the chair arms. Then he hastened through the panel and down the ladder to Howe's suite. Quickly he searched through the reformer's clothes till he found the confession Blake had mentioned. He read it over tensely. The murdered man had taken the entire blame for the drug ring.

The Agent considered awhile. At the teakwood desk, he spread the confession out and studied the handwriting minutely for seconds. Then he took up another sheet of stationary and began writing with laborious care.

"I am doomed," he wrote in Howe's own hand. "I knew it would come. There is no chance of escape. I am resigned to my fate, but I write this hastily with the prayerful hope that it will get into the proper hands. I have finally discovered the instigator of the horrible drug plague. The human devil behind it is Whitney Blake. Whitney Blake, the financier. From a man named Twyning, Blake stole a formula and method for breaking down the molecular composition of coal-tar derivatives into a powerful synthetic narcotic. Blake killed Twyning. He killed Count de Ronfort, because he did not want de Ronfort to marry his ward. Now he means to kill me. But I will not give him the chance. I am taking my own life. Silas Howe."

The Agent rose and laid the note under a paperweight. Then he propped the corpse of Silas Howe in the chair at the desk with the pen before him. Soon the federal men would come, and they would find the note. "X" was taking away Howe's confession, and in its place was leaving one in what looked to be the dead man's handwriting.

For the first time in his life Agent "X" had committed forgery. Yet it was not for gain, nor to rob anyone. It was to leave evidence that would doom a vicious criminal to the punishment he deserved.

Agent "X" had *forged* the truth.

He turned off the light, went noiselessly from the suite, and passed out into the corridor. From there he went down into the street.

Many police cars were there now, more coming. A cop stopped him, but the Agent's press card under the name of A. J. Martin let him through.

Grim-faced detectives were constantly pouring into the building, following the lines of radium paint that "X" had left. General Mathers' men were at work inside, making the greatest narcotic haul in the city's history.

For a time the Secret Agent watched, eyes glowing. Then he turned away into the darkness, and moved off slowly. A minute passed and his figure vanished from sight—but suddenly a strange, eerie whistle came out of the shadows. It was weird, birdlike, yet pitched in a minor key.

It was the peculiar call of an amazing and enigmatic person—the person known as Secret Agent "X," Man of a Thousand Faces, man of mystery and destiny. It signified that once more the master investigator had completed a relentless campaign against crime. The melodious note faded away as slowly as it had come. The work of Secret Agent "X" was done.

BOOK XII

CURSE OF THE WAITING DEATH

Satan's signals! Those were the lights that gleamed above a bandit pack. Death's own will-o'-the-wisps, with the power of an unseen curse behind them—a curse that made the police stand off, and made Secret Agent "X" pledge himself to battle on the volcano brink of destruction!

CHAPTER I

SIGNALS OF SATAN

THE GREAT PLATE-GLASS windows of Jules Pierrot's Jewelry Shop cracked, split and snapped in a dozen places. Jagged, star-shaped holes appeared. Long slivers of shimmering glass broke away and fell to the sidewalk in a jangling cascade. Near the curb, six masked men, just emerging from a parked sedan, advanced slowly, laying a barrage of bullets before them.

Pedestrians in front of the fashionable store scattered and fled like frightened rabbits. They ducked for cover, sought shelter wherever they could find it.

A girl in expensive clothing, with silver fox furs draped over one shapely shoulder, ran like a mad thing close to the building's facade. She passed near one of the masked bandits. Something gleamed at her white throat; something that caught the rays of the weak winter sun and sent out prismatic colors. It was a big diamond bar pin.

The bandit snarled in his throat like a hungry wolf. He grabbed the girl's slim arm. His hooked fingers flashed forward, closing over the diamond. He ripped savagely, and the front of the girl's dress tore open as the clasp of gold came loose. The bandit pushed her roughly away. She stumbled, fell to her silken knees, then leaped away again and dashed on, screaming fearfully, her high heels clicking over the pavement. The bandit pocketed the precious gem.

Others were already reaching through the shattered windows, scooping the glittering stones from the display racks. The leader of the vicious, marauding gang and one lieutenant, entered the store. Frightened customers, paralyzed with the sound of the din outside and the whining bullets that had glanced through the shop, huddled against counters. Clerks stood white-faced, trembling.

While the gunman guard crouched, with feet apart, the black snout of the sub-machine gun menacing all, the leader smashed a huge display counter with a single blow of a pistol butt. He gathered up piles of sparkling stones, diamonds, rubies, emeralds, sapphires—and dumped them into a canvas sack. His eyes behind the black mask held wolfish greed. His hands were tense as talons as he worked.

Jules Pierrot, owner-manager of the store, seeing a fortune vanishing before his eyes, ran from a back office. He was wringing his white hands, biting his lip, his small, immaculately dressed figure bobbing along. Consternation twisted his pink-and-white face with its carefully waxed mustache.

"Stop! Stop!" he screamed, "Help! Police!" In a frenzy that was almost hysterical he flung himself toward the man who was pilfering the trays.

The machine gun instantly clattered with a ruthless, measured note. Its snout quivered like the black, evil head of a snake lashing itself in fury.

Bullets slapped and slashed against the spotless vest of Jules Pierrot. He gasped, screamed piercingly, and flopped to the floor in a thrashing, grotesque heap. Crimson oozed from his clothing sogging it down. Crimson dribbled from his open, gasping mouth. The bandit leader at the counter calmly ignored the horrible squirming of the dying man. Jules Pierrot kicked pitifully, then lay very still.

Another of the gang came in from outside. The clerks, frozen with fear at the sight of their employer murdered before their eyes, obeyed meekly when they were ordered to open the safe. Some of the shop's most treasured possessions were stored in this. Every flashing stone and bit of gold was scooped into the bandit's pockets or the canvas sack of the leader. Systematically, surely, ruthlessly, the raid went on.

FIVE blocks away from the scene of the crime a small, compact coupé hurled furiously ahead. A man was hunched in it, his knuckles showing hard and white as they pressed the black rim of the wheel.

Under the instrument panel before him a hidden radio blared out police calls. The strident voice of the announcer gave the news of the Pierrot robbery in a numbered headquarters' code.

"Cars seventeen and twenty-six," it said. "Go to Forty-eight Vanderbilt Avenue. Number nineteen. Cars seventeen and twenty-six."

The man at the coupé's wheel wasn't a detective or policeman. He had no official connection with any law-enforcing body in the

land. Yet he knew what No. 19 meant. A store was being robbed. Another crime was being committed in a city already terrorized by the black wave of lawlessness that seemed to be engulfing it.

The coupé driven by the man corresponded to neither of the numbers that the police announcer had called. Yet the concealed short-wave radio beneath its instrument panel was as efficient as that in any official cruiser. The coupé itself was fifty per cent more efficient.

Its tonneau and chassis housed a collection of uniquely strange mechanisms. Sheathed armor plating of finest manganese steel was hidden beneath the enameled aluminum body, making it practical-

In the brief instant when he flashed through space, bullets thudded against the Agent's body.

ly bulletproof. Small racks of tear gas bombs, and flares were slung underneath, ready to be released at the merest touch on hidden levers. A special, electric-field detector behind a sliding panel in the driver's door made it possible for the owner to guide the car along a highway at night without lights, utilizing the presence of parallel telephone wires alone.

Sensitive audiophonic ears in the car's roof could pick up sounds at great distances. These were only a few of the amazing devices that its inconspicuous exterior concealed. Outwardly commonplace, the car was as mysterious as its driver.

Behind the prosaic features of the man at the wheel was hidden an identity that the police of a dozen cities had speculated upon, an identity that the underworld feared and hated; yet knew nothing definite about—the identity of the man called Secret Agent "X"!

Scores of rumors had run rife about him. Plots, by the law and the lawless alike, had been laid to trap him. Dark schemes had been hatched to blot him out of existence, by means of poisons, knives and bullets. Yet he still remained alive, an active menace to evildoers, one of the most daringly unique criminal investigators in all the world. He was a genius of disguise, a master of a thousand faces, a person pledged to ceaseless warfare against the destructive, disintegrating forces of crookdom.

The features showing now formed an elaborate disguise, as impenetrable as scores of others he had worn. Volatile plastic substances, overlaid above flesh-tinted pigment, followed the contours of his own face, yet changed it, so that even his own parents would not have known him. His hair was a carefully made toupee. His features were mediocre and inconspicuous.

Yet the odd burning light in his eyes seemed to hint at personal magnetism and great intellectual powers. Behind that disguised face a formidable brain seemed to be at work—and was. Agent "X" was on the trail of crime again, out to do battle with evil and match his wits against a mystery that was as sinister as it was deep.

The radio before him still sounded, calling the police cars. And, as his own coupé sped onward toward the scene of the crime, he suddenly saw one of them.

A green roadster shot out of a side street, roared into Vanderbilt Avenue. Agent "X" swung around on screaming tires and followed it. The police car's siren was wailing. The men in it were hawk-faced, clean-cut, alert. A sawed-off shotgun was in the hands of one. They seemed ready to do their duty in an effort to save life and property, and beat off a gang of desperate bandits.

The shattered glass front of the jewelry store came into sight. Agent "X" pressed down on the brake pedal of his roadster and tensed. He saw the black bandit car, saw the men with guns standing outside the shop, saw the heap of shattered window glass and the raided display racks. But he was watching the two cops as closely as he was the bandits.

And, as he looked, a strange, seemingly inexplicable thing occurred. One of the killers on the sidewalk turned and saw the approaching police cruiser. He spoke sharply to a companion. The man he had addressed yanked a small pistol from his belt, aiming not at the oncoming car, but straight into the air. His hand jerked. Something shot from the pistol's muzzle.

THERE was a streak in space, a sudden, brilliant flash of green light. A fiery ball like a Roman candle hovered for a moment in the air. It drifted earthward, went out slowly, sparks issuing from it, and two more balls of fire from the pistol's muzzle followed it. These were a bright, livid crimson, like some devil's eyes, disembodied and drifting weirdly through space.

The effect of the three flashes on the police car was instantaneous. Hardly slackening its speed, its siren still screeching madly, it swung around a corner, headed at right angles to the block where the robbery had taken place.

Tense, straining over his wheel, Agent "X" watched and listened. The cruiser's siren, like a mournful banshee wail, was growing dimmer now. Increasing distance lessened its note. There could be no doubt about it—the cruiser had made a deliberate detour at sight of those red-and-green flashes. And Agent "X" had recognized the lights. An experienced airman, he knew a Very pistol when he saw one. It was a device used by flying men to signal their comrades night and day in the sky.

And it had been used as a signal now—a signal for the police not to meddle in what was going on. A signal for them to shy off from the scene of a murderous robbery. They were doing it, too—obeying, for some strange reason, a command from the underworld which they were officially pledged to fight.

Agent "X" could not understand it. Trained to probe the most difficult enigmas, here was a mystery so bizarre and forbidding that it was like a challenge hurled into his very face. If the police were bowing to signals from criminals, what chance did the law-abiding citizens of the city have? Was it graft that made them do it? That seemed unlikely, for "X" had had experience with most of the heads of the department. They were honest, determined men, enemies of his though they might be.[49]

Something unbelievably sinister seemed to be in the wind. Some force, unknown to "X", but hideously real, must have made those cruising cops yield to the signals of a criminal band. And it wasn't the first time it had happened. Other cops in the past week had done the same thing—turned tail and run like rabbits when those

---

49 AUTHOR'S NOTE: *Unaware that Agent "X" has the secret sanction of a high Washington official, the police are continually on his trail. To them, because of his daring, unconventional acts in the pursuit of crime, he is a criminal himself. His identity remains a black mystery. Yet legends of his strange activities are whispered from mouth to mouth. And, since the law does not understand, it hounds him; and Agent "X," a benefactor to society, is ever in danger of imprisonment or violent death.*

mysterious green and red signals flashed. What uncanny power did the underworld wield? Even Agent "X" could not guess.

Their raid accomplished, the desperate men who had robbed Pierrot's Jewelry Shop came out of the store and crossed the pavement. "X" stepped on the gas, racing the car forward again. One of the gang looked up and saw him coming. Once more the Very pistol flashed its green-and-red lights, but "X" paid no attention. He drove straight ahead.

Seeming to sense that here was no cop or detective who could be coerced; seeing a lone man driving a small, unofficial looking coupé, the bandits ran toward their own sedan. One of them stopped long enough to send a burst of bullets toward "X". They punctured the aluminum shell, but stopped harmlessly against the manganese steel beneath. But a cobweb hole appeared in the non-shatterable windshield, and a chunk of lead whistled dangerously close to the Agent's head. Still he came on, a fighting gleam in his eyes, hoping by direct action to find out who these men were and by what mysterious means they had cast a spell over the police.

THE gunman leaped into the sedan. Its door slammed shut. With a screech of gears and a pale feather of smoke from its exhaust it shot away from the curb. Agent "X" followed.

The car ahead seemed to have a super-powerful motor. Its pickup was incredible. In that first minute it leaped away from the Agent. But his small coupé was devised for the highest speeds, also.

He touched a lever beside his hand. This connected the regular feed line with a special tank set close to the car's gas filter. High-test fuel under pressure, containing a percentage of liquid hydrogen, newest of fueling agents, mixed with the gasoline supply. He pressed the accelerator. The small car seemed to hurl itself ahead.

It ate up the distance between itself and the other larger vehicle. A rear window slid up. Once again the black snout of a machine gun quivered and flamed. The gangsters were firing for "X's" tires, not knowing that those innocent black rims had fine-meshed steel screening hidden under the pliable rubber. Bullets hit them but glanced off. The bandit aimed for the windshield again. And Agent "X" rocked the car from side to side with deft twists of the wheel, spoiling the killer's aim.

Ten blocks were traversed. Police cars were conspicuous by their utter absence. The whole department seemed to be lying low. Not even a cop on patrol was in evidence. And then suddenly another large car turned into the street behind Agent "X". He saw it in his rear-vision mirror, thought for a moment it was a squad car. Then he caught a glimpse of an ugly, bloated face hidden by a mask. His heart leaped. Here was evidence that the robbers were part of a large, organized band.

An instant later more proof came. As though in answer to some signal sent out, or as if acting on prearranged orders, a third car swung out of a side street ahead of him. It turned the corner slowly, but instantly put on speed. It was on his own side of the street. He would have to pass it parallelly, and from the open side windows a half dozen gun muzzles projected.

Here were killers regimented and organized to the highest possible efficiency. Here was a death car, waiting to riddle him with steel-jacketed lead. He wasn't even sure that his armor plate would stand such a salvo at close range. Certainly the force of it would destroy his windshield and side windows, and, if a stray bullet didn't lodge in his body, he would have only luck to thank.

But he couldn't stop. The speedometer needle had touched eighty. His tires were making a humming screech on the pavement. His "souped-up" motor was roaring like a Niagara beneath its vibrating hood. To turn a corner or thrust brakes home now meant swift destruction—just as surely as the vehicle ahead stood for grim death. Yet the hands of Agent "X" were steady as rock as he raced forward to meet his fate.

CHAPTER II

THE PALL OF FEAR

A HUNDRED FEET separated him from the car ahead. Fifty. Twenty-five. As the muzzles of the gangster submachine guns lifted to pour a deadly, withering, broadside fire into his speeding coupé, Agent "X" pressed back with his heel at a spot under the seat.

There was a faint click, a whir as a tiny, high-speed electric motor was set in motion. The piston of an air-pump moved with lightning rapidity inside a piece of mechanism as delicately constructed as a watch. A white chemical in solution was sprayed thickly into the interior of the coupé's hot exhaust pipe. At the same moment Agent "X" shoved the cut-out open, leaving a vent directly behind the roaring engine.

Clouds of black, impenetrable vapor shot out from under his car, rising on all sides in a dense curtain.[50]

His coupé was hidden as though a pall of soot had dropped upon it. Through the blackness, the thunderous reports of his unmuffled, "souped-up" engine made a din like a battery of guns going into action. The smoke screen enveloped the gangster car as well as his own, blinding them, preventing any accurate aim.

Agent "X" braked slowly and pulled to the left. There was danger of a sudden, terrible smash-up, if the gangster driver lost his head and made some panicky maneuver.

"X" shut off his engine suddenly, and, in the deathly silence which followed, as his car shot ahead under its own momentum, he heard the shrill scream of brakes as the gangster car was slowed.

---

50 AUTHOR'S NOTE: Agent "X," in this instance, made use of the smoke-producing chemical employed to lay a screen during naval and military maneuvers. A close student of modern military tactics, he has on other occasions made use of wartime methods in his ceaseless battle with crime.

He continued brake pressure himself, driving in utter darkness, with only the instrument board light and his sense of direction to guide him, and he saw the speedometer needle go steadily down.

When his tremendous momentum had been checked, when the car was barely creeping ahead, he swung still farther to the left, guiding the coupé expertly till the fat tires were brushing the curb. The sound ceased in a moment. Agent "X" swung the wheel at once, pulled his coupé into a side street, heading off at an angle from the route he had been following.

He pressed the button under the seat a second time, stopped the pump mechanism and closed the cut-out. Accelerating slowly, he drew out of the black smoke cloud. It had risen to the housetops now. Long, eerie arms of dark vapor, whipped by the wind, seemed a ghostly symbol of the black crime mystery he was battling.

He drove away from the gangsters. No use following them now. The car containing those who had robbed Pierrot's shop would be blocks away. He had saved his life by a comparatively simple trick. The Agent had been ambushed by waiting cars before. He never allowed himself to be caught in the same situation twice. The black smoke cloud was his answer to a danger he had anticipated before it arrived.

The sirens of fire engines were screaming as he drove away from the spot where the smoke screen had been laid. He passed a red truck with men hanging to glittering brass-work, roaring toward the scene of his escape. Some one had turned in a double alarm, thinking the black vapor meant an explosion or a fire. The bells of other engines were clanging. Three fire companies were converging on the spot. None of them guessed that the small innocent-looking coupé they passed had been the cause of it all.

Agent "X" didn't wait to observe the excitement and consternation his smoke screen had left in its wake. It had served its purpose.

He passed two patrolling policemen. They were far from the scene of the Pierrot robbery. Yet he noticed that their faces looked tense and uneasy. They did not stride along with the confident aplomb of their class. There was a furtive, almost apologetic manner about them. Something deeper than the fierce criticism with which the press of the city had been lashing the police department of late lay behind this. The law was falling down. The police seemed to be hiding their heads in the face of the worst crime wave the community had known for years. Murders, robberies, stick-ups, burglaries were occurring night and day. They had been increasing

Agent "X" caught an expression of haunting, lingering fear of Mayor Ballentine's face.

for the past week, and still the department appeared to be doing nothing to cope with the situation.

With a bleak, cold light in his eyes, Agent "X" went to a telephone booth and called a number not listed in any directory. He pitched his voice to a different key, spoke with a deceptive accent, and almost instantly an answer came over the wire.

"This is Bates talking. That you, boss?"

THE man at the other end of the wire had immediately recognized the voice Agent "X" had used. He was Harry Bates, head of an extraordinary detective organization Agent "X" had built up at great trouble and expense. Men and women of various types and from all walks of life were in it. All of them had been secretly investigated by Agent "X." None of them knew that it was his influence and his money, acting through Bates, that held their staff together.

Bates himself had never to his knowledge seen the man he called "boss." Instructions came by phone or radio, money for expenses by mail. The "boss" was only a voice to Bates, and he did not guess that the man he worked for was the mysterious, unknown Secret Agent "X."

"X" talked quickly, hoarsely, now, with an edge of sharp command in his voice.

"Your report, Bates!"

"I've been the rounds, boss, like you asked me to. The mobs are lying low. My men are covering the phony spots, but they haven't picked up anything. It looks like—"

"Are you watching Connie's place and the Escabar over on Ninth Avenue?"

"No, boss, I didn't know that they—"

"Post men there. Tell them to circulate and get friendly. Increase their expense accounts."

"Yes, boss."

"And if you learn anything, broadcast on the dot of every hour using wave-length M, code 26G. Be ready for possible radios from me."[51]

"Right, boss."

Agent "X" hung up and called a second number. This was one listed as the Hobart Detective Agency. It was another of "X's" subsidized organizations, working independently of Bates, having in fact no knowledge that Bates and his staff even existed. It was run by Jim Hobart, a former police detective, dismissed from the department on trumped-up graft charges, and befriended by "X". The voice of the Agent changed again. It was more friendly now, yet still brisk, concise.

"Martin speaking. What news, Jim?"

"None yet, Mr. Martin. I can't find out who is doing the dirty

---

51   AUTHOR'S NOTE: *The Bates organization has been furnished by "X" with a radio transmitting set, also a small, portable receiving set carried by Bates beneath his coat like an armpit holster. Short waves of varying length, corresponding to letters are used as agreed upon. The radiograms are sent out in one of a score of secret codes, devised by "X" himself. The codes and wavelengths are changed from time to time as he is working on a case.*

work. The big gangs are quiet. But there was a pay roll stick-up at Consolidated Wet Wash this noon. Eighteen grand grabbed! And this morning a gang of guys cleaned out the safe of the City Savings."

"I know it," snapped "X" impatiently. "What we must learn are facts—who's behind the robberies, what crooks are operating, where the money's going! How about the Shandley Hotel—are your men watching it?"

"Sorry, Mr. Martin. It's one joint I didn't think of keeping track of."

"Why not? It's a gamblers' hangout. Somebody must be making money, and spending it—possibly at cards. The Shandley is a place you must watch. Send Bailey and his girl friend there with cash enough to crash a game if they get the chance."

"Right, Mr. Martin, I'll do that. You sure keep track of the hot spots."

There was respect, admiration in Jim Hobart's tone. Agent "X" chuckled softly as he hung up. Keeping track of the "hot spots" was part of his strange work. Yet Hobart knew him only as A. J. Martin, inquiring newspaper man. Hobart believed "Martin" worked for a large press syndicate; thought that Martin's concern with crime was in the interest of inside stories for his sheets alone. And Hobart was a willing helper.

But without "X's" supervision, without his vast knowledge of crime and criminals, without his awareness of the darkest, most secret dives of the underworld, neither Hobart nor Bates could get more than routine results. It was Agent "X," Man of a Thousand Faces, uncanny genius of disguise, who moved them like pawns in his ceaseless game of death with the underworld.

He left the phone booth and stopped in passing at a branch post office where he had rented a box under the name of "F. Jones," and where he occasionally received mail. He half expected a letter now, and he wasn't disappointed. A blue envelope was waiting for him, addressed in small, clear writing and carrying a faint trace of feminine perfume. The Agent picked it up eagerly.

IN ALL the world there were only two people who knew the exact nature of his amazing, daring work. One was a man in Washington, D. C., a high official of the government, known to "X" as K9. The other was Betty Dale, blonde and lovely girl reporter on the *Herald*, whose father, a captain of police, had been slain by underworld bullets years ago.

Never had Betty seen the Agent's real face; yet this strange, brilliant man of a thousand disguises had won a lasting place in her heart, and built up an emotion that was deeper than mere friendship.

The blue envelope was from Betty Dale. Yet it was no love letter. It was a report, brief and to the point, addressed simply to "Mr. Jones," Box 29—a name and a number "X" had given to Betty if she ever wished to communicate with him.

"Dear Jones," it said. "I have learned something that I can't even reveal to the paper. Yet I thought you would want to know. I saw an old friend on the force last night. He says that orders have come from higher up telling the police to lay off a certain criminal group now operating and showing signal lights to identify themselves. It isn't graft. It's something very powerful. I don't know what. Please be careful."

That last sentence was the only personal touch. It brought a smile to the Secret Agent's lips. It was proof that Betty was thinking of him not only as a grim investigator—but also as a man, and a beloved friend. Betty, because her father had been in the department, had always been a pet of the police. As a child she had played around the precinct stations. She knew half the cops and detectives in the city by name.

She had been granted interviews with police heads when all other representatives of the press had been excluded. And now she had hastened to inform "X" of the sinister information she had picked up.

Yet it was only more confirmation of what "X" already knew. The police were steering clear of the band that displayed the red-and-green lights. A powerful force for evil lay behind those signals. A sense of menace, almost of catastrophe was in the air. Yet both were shrouded in black mystery.

Agent "X" destroyed the note quickly. It was unsigned, but there was danger that even its handwriting might be traced. There had been times in the past when the black shadow of the underworld had fallen on Betty Dale in a hideous reality. This must not be one of them.

The Agent's lips were unsmiling now. He was troubled. His own operatives, working even under his directions, had failed to ferret out the identity of the signal-using gang. The city's well-known mobs were apparently not active in the present crime wave. It was for him, then, to go straight to the heart of the matter himself.

CHAPTER III

ANGER IN HIGH PLACES

IN ONE OF his secret hideouts, Agent "X" removed the disguise he had worn in his deathly conflict with the bandits. For a moment he appeared as he really was, as not even his closest associates had ever seen him. And the face exposed under the light above his triple-sided make-up mirror was almost as remarkable as the man himself. It expressed character, versatility, mature strength and youthfulness—according to the angle from which it was viewed.

The features were even, the lips firm, the forehead high and wide. From below, the fighting, stubborn chin was most prominent. Looked at from directly in front, the Agent's uncannily intense eyes seemed to eclipse all else. At an oblique angle the faint lines and bunched muscles on his smooth face appeared to be the indelible records of all the strange, harrowing experiences through which he had passed.

He hunched forward now. His long strong fingers reached out. From his materials he selected those he needed, and, from a series of photographs spread out beside him, he proceeded to build up another personality.

The photographs were of himself. They did not depict his real face, but one that he had worn often before—one that was well known in many sections of the city. They were photos of a man called Elisha Pond, depositor in one of the city's greatest banks, member and frequenter of the town's most exclusive clubs, a man seemingly of age, dignity, and solid respectability. No one would have believed for an instant that he and the notorious Agent "X" were one. Pond was put down as a person of important affairs, a director in many companies.

Just how important his affairs were, his acquaintances did not guess. But it was under the name of Elisha Pond that Agent "X" drew out the money necessary to carry on his campaign against crime. It was under that name that he held a fund, subscribed for his especial use, and supervised by one man only, the mysterious K9 in Washington.

When his disguise was complete, that of a strong, quiet-faced, gray-haired man, Agent "X" dressed carefully. Pond, as an individual of means and importance, must always live up to his station.

In the secret pockets of the suit that "X" put on, however, he slipped the many strange devices that he was in the habit of carrying.[52]

When all was ready, he went quickly into the street, using a back exit of the hideout. He walked rapidly several blocks, summoned a taxi and rode to one of the city's best-known hotels.

From the lobby of this he called a wealthy, exclusive institution. This was the famous Bankers' Club, of which Elisha Pond was a member. He asked to speak to Jonathan Jewett, the hard-headed president of the Northern Continent Insurance Co. "X" knew Jewett's ways. Jewett always stopped at the club after work for a cocktail and a chat. The Agent knew furthermore, that Jewett had suffered indirectly at the hands of the gangsters now terrorizing the city.

An affiliate of Jewett's company, handling fidelity, liability and burglary insurance, had been asked to meet policy payments a dozen times in the past week. That meant thousands of dollars loss to the affiliated concern. Jewett should be in a fit mood to be used as a pawn in a plan the Agent's cunning brain had devised. That plan was the formation of a committee to cross-question Police Commissioner Foster.

"X" suggested that Jewett select certain men for the task. With quiet persuasion he stirred the insurance man's emotions, playing on his indignation over the money lost, getting Jewett to agree to his proposal to have Foster, a club member, come down and be put on the mat. It was Jewett himself, however, who suggested that Pond be one of the committee-men. This had been part of the Agent's own plan from the beginning. But he had cleverly let it appear as though it were Jewett's idea.

---

52 AUTHOR'S NOTE: *These are the chemical and mechanical aids in his dangerous work. His gas gun, which can silently and efficiently knock a man unconscious within a radius of twenty feet. His camera-like sound amplifier. His special tool kit; and other small, ingenious devices which he changes from time to time.*

When he sped to the Bankers' Club just before six, the commissioner was already there. Foster looked harried, worried, and was pacing a private rear room tensely. Jewett, tall, menacing, indignant, because of the money his enterprises stood to lose, was glaring at him. Jason Coates, a small, sharp-featured man, who had run unsuccessfully against the present mayor, and hated him and his commissioners, was sneering openly at Foster.

John Harrigan, a financier with large holdings in munitions, was another member of the committee. Christy, a bland-faced broker, was still another.

Foster stared straight ahead of him, meeting no one's eyes directly. A limp rag of a cigar, chewed beyond all appearance of a smoke, hung from his lips.

HARRIGAN was endeavoring to be diplomatic, trying to calm Foster's evident irritation at this move his club members had made. For Harrigan was a friend of the mayor's, a staunch supporter of the present administration, and had been dragged on the committee against his will.

But Foster seemed to feel himself attacked from all quarters. He brushed Harrigan's diplomatic, pleasantries aside. He shot a venomous glance at Jason Coates, then spoke hoarsely, bluntly answering the criticisms that were hurled at him.

"I refuse to admit the charge that my department is inefficient," he snapped. "I've ordered the men under me to do everything in their power. They are doing it, gentlemen. That is all I have to say."

His face whitened as he said this. Agent "X," watching closely, saw that the man was lying. "X" had seen many men lie. The expression on Commissioner Foster's face, the telltale wavering of his eyes, only deepened the Agent's belief that something strange and sinister was wrong with the working of the city administration.

A dead silence followed Foster's speech. In the period that it lasted, the shrill cries of newsboys floated up from the street through an open window.

"Extra! Read all about the big robbery. Storekeeper murdered! Five hundred thousand dollars in diamonds stolen!"

The sound was like fresh fuel heaped on a smoldering fire. Jonathan Jewett struck the table with his fist.

"The citizens of this city will demand a reckoning!" he cried. "You'll find yourself out of a job, Foster!"

Commissioner Foster, holding himself stiffly, stared not at Jewett, but over his left shoulder into empty space—as though he were seeing some hideous specter. He licked quivering lips. His face twitched.

"There's nothing more to be said, gentlemen! If you don't like the way this city's being run—go to the mayor. Perhaps he'll give you satisfaction."

He strode forward hurriedly, jerked open the door and slammed it after him. His quick steps could be heard receding, mingling with the persistent cries of the newsboys still outside, advertising the news of the latest criminal outrage.

Jewett turned on his companions bitterly. His face was screwed into knots of anger. He clenched his fist again. "We'll take him up on that! We'll see the mayor and ask that a change of personnel be made in the police department. If he won't listen, I'll use my influence to see that the city loan he's asking for doesn't go over."

Harrigan looked troubled. "I doubt if you can see his honor," he said. "I happen to know that Mayor Ballantine is a guest on board Monte Sutton's yacht, the *Osprey*."

Jason Coates, political rival of the mayor, nodded and sneered. "I read about that! He's going for a cruise to Southern waters for his health. He's going to run away just when he's most needed."

"But he's changed his plans," said Harrigan hastily. "The cruise has been postponed indefinitely—till city affairs smooth out. His visit to the *Osprey* tonight is a purely social one."

"We'll see what he has to say anyhow!" growled Jewett.

The five of them, in Jewett's private limousine, drove off into the winter night. Harrigan, worried and silent in the face of Jewett's anger, directed the chauffeur. The *Osprey* was close to one of the city's most exclusive residential sections, at anchor in the river near a swanky yacht club.

Jewett arranged for a speed boat to take them out. Bundled in their heavy overcoats, they raced across the dark water, sweeping up to the yacht's companionway.

A score of prosperous looking men and women in evening clothes were sitting in the big saloon. Several couples were dancing on a small polished floor that had been laid in its center. A jazz orchestra, on a raised platform under the shaded lights, sobbed out a melody. Cocktail glasses were clinking. Light conversation and laughter sounded above the music. Monte Sutton's guests were obviously enjoying themselves.

Then "X" saw Ballantine. The mayor's appearance was in sharp contrast to the others. His stocky, broad-shouldered figure was slouched dejectedly. There was a grayish hue on his pouchy face. Wrinkles of worry creased his eyes. His lips were clamped over a cigar. He was solemn, distracted, staring ahead unseeingly, rolling his large shoulders from side to side like a restless bear.

JONATHAN Jewett made straight for him, with Harrigan, the munitions man, running a little ahead, to warn the mayor he had visitors. Ballantine gave a start and looked up uneasily. A combative expression appeared on his face. Harrigan took it upon himself to explain.

"These fellow clubmen of mine have come to make a few complaints," he said. "I told them it wasn't an opportune time; but they insisted. Mr. Jewett, it seems, has an ax to grind."

"You're right, I have," growled Jonathan Jewett. "We saw your commissioner of police a few moments ago, Ballantine. We protested about the inefficiency of his department—and got no satisfaction. Now we've come to make some suggestions. Crime has risen fifty per cent in this city, and—"

Some of the guests were drawing nearer, attracted by Jewett's loud voice. The mayor shook his head distractedly.

"Not here—please! If you want to talk let's go somewhere where we can be alone."

"That suits me," said Jewett.

Monte Sutton, owner of the *Osprey* and the mayor's host, was courteous and diplomatic. With a slightly bored expression on his handsome face, he led them to a small writing room.

"You won't be intruded upon here, gentlemen," he said. "Now get the poison out of your systems."

Coates began to make sneering comments on the general inefficiency of the administration, hinting broadly at graft, predicting that the voters would cast their ballots differently in the next election. Jewett thundered about the rising tide of crime. Harrigan tried to steer conversation into more peaceful channels, and Agent "X," in the role of Pond, stood quietly by, watching and listening.

That the mayor was worried was obvious. There were gray shadows under his eyes. He threw out his hands, and snapped up his head as questions and criticisms were shouted at him.

"Am I to listen to every faultfinder who cares to speak?" he said.

"Am I to alter my policies to suit any committee of citizenry that comes along?"

Jonathan Jewett thrust the evening paper forward, with its screaming headlines. "I don't give a damn about your policies, Ballantine! But this crime wave has got to stop. I've spoken to your police commissioner—and he gave me no satisfaction. If you don't bear down on him yourself, and see about a shake-up at once, I'll use my influence to hinder your administration in any way I can. You might as well know that now!"

The mayor faced his critic. His voice was low, hoarse. "There are factors at work that none of you know anything about," he said. "I'm running this city with the good of all in mind. I'm satisfied that the police are doing the best they can under the circumstances. Commissioner Foster is answerable to me alone—and I find no cause for dissatisfaction in the way he is carrying out his duties."

A stunned silence met this retort. Then Coates gave a harshly sneering laugh. Jonathan Jewett spoke furiously:

"You don't think a police shakedown is necessary then? You are satisfied to let the criminals of this city plunder and murder as they will? You don't want to protect the lives and property of honest citizens? By gad, Ballantine, it would seem almost that you have told the police not to interfere!"

A trembling that was very much like some mysterious, deep-seated terror shook the mayor's body. He clenched and unclenched his hands, swayed his form from side to side.

"I—I refuse to talk any more!" he said wildly.

CHAPTER IV

NIGHT PROWLERS

THAT HE MEANT what he said was evident. The fear that tensed his body seemed to have sealed his lips.

Harrigan was the only one of the group invited by Sutton to remain on the yacht. But he declined, saying he had an appointment ashore.

The committee from the Bankers' Club left as it had come. The members of it formed a silent group as they crossed the black water in the speed boat. Each was preoccupied with his own somber thoughts. But the Secret Agent was the somberest of all.

"X" left the others when the speed boat landed. He refused Jason Coates's invitation to return to the club and discuss politics, turned down Jewett's offer to give him a lift in his car. He gave as an excuse that he had pressing business in the neighborhood. And how pressing that business was, none of them knew...

Much later that night, when the streets were quiet, Agent "X" appeared again. But no one would have recognized him now as the wealthy, dignified Elisha Pond. He was clad in faded blue trousers. Dusty shoes with thick rubber soles were on his feet. A turtlenecked sweater was pulled up to his chin. A cloth cap half covered his face. His features were disguised again, ugly and shapeless now. His brows were heavy, and a black substance that gave the impression of a stubble of beard was pressed into the plastic material forming his face.

He was impersonating a night prowler, a burglar or sneak thief, and under his arm was a worn leather kit containing a set of regulation burglar tools. But these were for appearance's sake only, to be left behind as misleading evidence in case he was chased by the police. His own set of tools, made of the finest chromium steel, and unrivaled by those of any burglar in existence, were the ones that

Agent "X" pressed the muzzle of his gas gun against the man's neck.

would do the strange work he had in mind.

Furtively, using the darkest streets he could find and imitating the actions of a night-marauding thief, he made his way across town. Several times he passed patrolling police. But they didn't see him, so careful was he to keep in the shadows and so soundless were his rubber-soled shoes. But he noticed them—noticed that even these cops on the beat seemed afflicted with some emotional malady.

For they looked uneasy, nervous. They were confused and

strained by orders from headquarters probably—orders which were inconsistent with the duties to which they were pledged. He didn't doubt that they, too, had been instructed to steer clear of any mob showing the mysterious red-and-green signals of a Very pistol.

Agent "X" felt sorry for these men. They must believe secretly that the department they had served loyally for years was going to pieces. They must think corruption had eaten into the lives and minds of the men over them.

It was close to midnight when at last he reached a peaceful, old residential avenue. Prosperous homes lined it. Leafless trees stood in long, even rows.

The Agent walked several times along the block on this street, staring sharply at a certain house, a two-story brick residence, carefully cared for like the others. It was the Ballantine mansion, where the mayor had lived through all his rising political years, and where he still lived, as the city's chief executive. There was a spacious lawn around it, and a sizable backyard.

Silently Agent" "X" climbed a picket fence and stepped onto the lawn. Wraithlike he moved across it, toward a big bay window at the side of the house. His actions were sure, calculated. Once, in another disguise on a different case, he had interviewed Ballantine in the role of a newspaperman. He remembered the mayor's large study, recalled the big safe where Ballantine kept his private and semi-official documents. Surely, here if anywhere, would be a clue to the thing Agent "X" sought.

He went to the big bay window, skirted it and came to an outer door. This was a side entrance to the house, the door used by the mayor in summertime to come out on his lawn and chat with his neighbors over the fence.

With one of his chromium master keys in his hand, Agent "X" came close. There were no lights showing in the house. If the mayor or any of his family were home, they had long since gone to bed. Perhaps Ballantine was spending the night on Monte Sutton's yacht again. In any case, Agent "X" knew how to enter quietly.

BUT at the door he paused. The Fates seemed trying to aid him. The door was not shut, nor even locked. It was open about six inches, and when he looked carefully, he saw something—a man's soft hat—wedged in it to keep it from making any noise in the night breeze.

"X" slowly replaced the chromium tool in his pocket. No use for that now. Here was a strange turn of events. He had come to enter the house only to find that it wasn't necessary. The place was already open.

"X" moved the door slowly, careful to avoid any faint squeak of the hinges. He stepped across the threshold into a hallway, closed the door after him, wedging it as it had been. He moved straight ahead, a flashlight in his left hand ready for instant use, his gas pistol in the other, and every faculty alert.

He had not been in this hall before, but he could guess at his surroundings. The first door at his left would be that of the study, the chamber in which he planned to go. He reached this and found that it was open, too. Then, as he paused and listened, he heard a faint sound inside, a soft, eerie rustling.

Slowly he shoved the door back, and looked into the room. In a far corner where the safe was located a faint light showed, the glow of an electric torch with a paper cylinder over its end to direct its rays in one direction only. This was making a glowing spot on the floor close to the safe. In this tiny arena of light, a man's hands were moving white papers, shifting them and examining them with quick fingers.

He was so intent on his work, so eager, that he had no inkling of Agent "X's" presence. "X" couldn't see his face at first, not until his own eyes became used to the bright spot of light and things around its edge became faintly discernible. Then he started.

His eyes narrowed. He bent forward tensely. For the features of the man before him were familiar. He had spoken with this man a few hours previously. The silent, absorbed figure raiding the mayor's safe in the dark of the night was Harrigan, distinguished member of the Bankers' Club, and enthusiastic investor in munitions.

CHAPTER V

THE SINISTER PLOT

FOR TENSE SECONDS Agent "X" studied Harrigan's face and movements. He was the last man "X" had expected to find here. Yet a possible explanation immediately suggested itself. Harrigan had been on the club committee which went to the yacht to cross-examine the mayor. He had acted as peacemaker, he was a loyal supporter of the party to which the mayor belonged. But it was possible he had grown impatient at the way Ballantine and his commissioners were running the city. It was possible that he, too, had come here tonight in the hopes of finding some evidence which would throw light on Ballantine's strange actions.

Agent "X" watched hawk-eyed. Harrigan was making a systematic examination of the documents the safe contained, piling those he had already looked at on one side, reaching for others at his left.

Agent "X," in his rubber-soled shoes, walking catlike, slowly crossed the floor, till he stood directly back of the kneeling man. He could see over Harrigan's shoulder now, read as plainly as Harrigan himself what documents these were. Most of them were uninteresting; copies of bills submitted to the aldermen, papers dealing with franchises, charters and the like.

Five minutes passed, and a faint noise came from somewhere in the house, as though a restless sleeper had stirred. Harrigan tensed. For a moment it seemed he might get up and go to the door. His hand hovered over his light. But the sound was not repeated. Harrigan went back to his furtive work.

It was then that Agent "X," looking down, saw the paper which Harrigan drew from a black envelope almost at the bottom of the pile. Harrigan opened it like the others. His eyes started to scan the words. But Agent "X," reading faster than the man before him, had already seen a sentence that held hideous meaning. Before

Harrigan had gotten beyond the first paragraph, Secret Agent "X" spoke sibilantly.

"Keep quiet, and raise your mitts, guy!"

At the same instant "X" pressed the muzzle of his gas gun against Harrigan's neck. The man before him let out one whispering gasp. The document fluttered from shaking fingers. His body became as rigid as though he had been turned into a frozen statue.

A second passed. The Agent spoke again. "Get up, mister. No funny business—or I'll pull the trigger of this gat."

"X" turned on his own flash, directing the beam into Harrigan's face. The man's skin had turned putty colored with fear. Caught in such a compromising position, surprised when he thought he was all alone, he was trembling with fright. "X" talked slowly, playing the role of a common criminal, to put Harrigan off the track.

"It seems like I've seen your mug somewhere before," the Agent said. "Ain't you one of the mayor's pals? Tryin' to double-cross the big shot, eh?" He gave a harsh chuckle. "Thought you'd make a little dough for yourself by blackmail maybe. It's a good racket, guy, but you ain't got the guts for it—you white-livered dude."

"I'm not—I—Who are you?"

"Never mind. Stand over there by the wall. Keep your mitts up and your mouth shut. I got a little business in that safe myself. I brought my tools, but I see I won't need 'em."

Agent "X" turned his own flash on Harrigan, saw that the man was obeying orders, standing still, too frightened to do anything else. He put his burglar kit down with a slight deliberate clink so that Harrigan would notice it. He bent forward so that Harrigan might get a look at his disguised features. He made a pretense of going through a compartment of the safe. His other hand was gathering up the paper he had seen in Harrigan's fingers. This he slipped in his pocket, eyes gleaming, and searched hastily to see if there were any others.

At that moment a distinct noise sounded somewhere in the house. Boards creaked above his head. Slippered feet scuffed. Some one had waked and was coming downstairs to investigate. With a sweep of his hand Agent "X" scattered the papers over the floor. He turned, snarled at Harrigan.

"You lily-fingered dub! You've muffed the job—waked the family. Now I gotta lam before they put the finger on me. Stay there till I get out. Don't squawk, or I'll drill you."

His face screwed into the vicious lines of some underworld

night prowler, waving his gun at Harrigan, Agent "X" backed toward the doorway and went out. In a moment he was on the dark lawn.

THERE were lights in the upper part of the house now. Some restless sleeper had been disturbed. But "X" knew that Harrigan had time to make his getaway. He knew the man would take no chances of being found in a position which would ruin his reputation and cause a city-wide scandal. He didn't wait to see Harrigan come out. He could set one of Hobart's men or Bates' to shadow Harrigan if necessary, and see if his purpose in coming to the mayor's study was the one "X" had figured out.

Harrigan didn't interest him at the moment. It was the paper out of Ballantine's safe which made his heart leap. Blocks away from the mayor's house, in the shadows back of an empty store, Agent "X" drew the paper from his pocket and turned his flash on it.

As he scanned the words carefully, his blood seemed to run cold. Here was the answer to the black mystery he had been investigating for the past thirty-six hours. Here was a criminal document containing a message so terrible that even his own fertile imagination hadn't conceived of such a thing. It was typewritten on plain bond paper. It said:

To His Honor, the Mayor:

I have in my possession three hundred pounds of an explosive known to science as nitro-picrolene. This is the world's newest and deadliest detonating agent. A twenty-five-pound bomb of NP is sufficient to raze twenty city blocks.

I have placed a dozen such bombs at strategic points throughout the city. They are concealed beyond possible discovery. Fuse units to be set off by radio impulse are connected with the bombs. From a hidden radio transmitting plant, I can explode these bombs within the space of sixty seconds.

I leave it to your imagination to picture what the results of a dozen such explosions would be. My motives are purely economic. I have selected an underworld executive and a highly trained criminal organization to collect tribute as they see fit. One green and two red lights fired from a signal pistol will identify this group. You will instruct the police not to interfere with their activities. Seventy per cent of all they collect goes to me for the protection I give them. They do not know my identity any more than you.

Being a man of sound judgment and common sense, you will understand that you have no alternative. You must instruct the police along the lines I have indicated. If you do not, the blood of millions may be on your hands.

I have spies everywhere. Any undercover attempt to thwart my plans will only bring catastrophe. Obey, and I will remove the bombs from this city after the group under my protection has collected ten million dollars. Disobey—and destruction will follow.

THE TERROR.

P.S.: As conclusive proof of the truth of my statement, I have placed a five-pound bomb of NP on Baldwin Island. This will be exploded at midnight on December 15. I suggest that you remove the hundred-odd squatters from the island. Give them any excuse you care to. Search for this bomb if you like. You will not find it. But stay away from the island at midnight of the 15th. It will be razed to water level.

The calm, fearful purport of the paper shocked "X". He had dealt with scores of criminals. He had ferreted out crimes, blocked vicious onslaughts of the underworld on law-abiding citizens. But never had he run across a scheme as cold-bloodedly ruthless as this. The lives of thousands, perhaps millions, of unsuspecting innocents had been put in jeopardy that a human monster might enrich himself.

Like terrible, slumbering germs of Death, those bombs lay somewhere among the labyrinthine streets of the city. Like germs that would at an instant's notice grow into a blight of red carnage unparalleled in the country's history.

"X" HAD a vision of great buildings falling down with terrible impact of tons of steel and stone smashing down to break and rend bodies, crush out human lives, kill and maim. Men, women, and little children would be the victims. If what the Terror said was true, no earthquake or giant tornado would leave behind it a more appalling tide of death and desolation.

For a moment emotion choked in the throat of the Agent "X." For a moment a passion of loathing such as he had seldom felt in his career held him in its grip. He was conscious of trembling; conscious of standing there in the darkness with his clenched fists and staring eyes. He had an impulse to go to the nearest great radio broadcasting station and send out a warning to the city's population. If they understood their danger, there would be a general exodus of citizens. They would run fear-stricken from their homes, even leaving their possessions behind to get away from the unseen menace.

But, even as the impulse came, he knew that those who heard would not believe. A few might. Others would be uneasy, but too sluggish to run. Still others, the great majority, would laugh, and say this was only the story of some wild-eyed madman. Nothing so fantastically horrible could exist surely, they would think.

Yet, "X" remembered having read a notice of the squatters being removed from Baldwin Island. The press had kicked up a furor about it. It was an example, they said, of municipal callousness. Without a definite reason, without giving them time to make other plans, the city had swept down and forced the squatters from their shacks. Many with families had protested loudly. Charitable souls had come forward to help them. But there were some among the squatters who stated defiantly that they would not be driven from the only homes they knew. They said they would go back.

And tonight was the 15th! What if some of them had sneaked back? They had no inkling of why they had been driven away. What if a few of the pitiful human derelicts, struggling to keep soul and body together, victims of the great depression, had returned secretly to their homemade shacks? The rest of the world might regard these huts as mere loathsome heaps of old boards, tin cans and stones—eyesores on the landscape. But to those who had built them piecemeal, through long days of toil, they were homes.

Yes, tonight was the 15th, and in a little over an hour the Terror would make good his threat, or fail. If he succeeded, any squatters who had returned to Baldwin Island would be blown into shattered, bloody fragments.

This possibly alone was enough to send Agent "X" out on a mission of mercy. A benefactor as well as an avenger, he could not stand by and see innocent men destroyed.

There was a chance, too, that in a quick energetic survey of the island, with his experience behind him, he might find some clue to those who worked for the Terror. He might even locate the hideous bomb, or find tracks of those who had set it. If there were no squatters remaining, if he could not locate the bomb, then he would be a witness to its detonation—and see if the Terror had been correct in claiming NP as the world's most terrible explosive.

"X" did not make a complete change of disguise. He stopped at one of his hideouts, doctored up his face slightly, then spent a few moments setting in operation an electrical mechanism that was housed in a cabinet standing on a table. When he left it, cogs were turning inside, and a thin, musical whirring came from the cabinet. Agent "X" went into the street and walked quickly to a garage where he kept one of several cars.[53]

In this he sped to an old deserted dock on the river's edge. Its piling was rotting away. It had been declared unsafe for use. Its owner had preferred to close it rather than renovate it.

Agent "X" slipped quietly through a high fence which closed off the end of the dock. He walked out on it, stopped suddenly and lifted a loose board.

A black, cavernous opening appeared. He stepped into this, descended a short ladder, and moved ahead on parallel boarding just above the water level. Walking forward and flashing his light, he came to a spot where a small, swift speed boat was moored.

It rested in a cradle of jute-lined bumpers that prevented it from scraping and squeaking. He stepped into the craft, started the muffled engine, and jockeyed out from under the dock's forward end.

In a moment, the boat was a dark streak in the water, showing no lights, with only a white, ghostly plume of exhaust smoke at its stern.

---

53 AUTHORS NOTE: *For convenience's sake, the Secret Agent owns several cars outside of his special coupé. These he keeps under different registrations, in both public and private garages, always available for the daring activities he is pledged to perform.*

CHAPTER VI

THE DEATH TRAP

SEVERAL TIMES, ON his way, Agent "X" avoided police patrol boats. The harbor seemed full of them tonight. Without lights and headed toward Baldwin Island, he knew he would be stopped and questioned if they could catch him. But when one patrol craft came too close, "X" twisted the wheel, stepped on the gas, and went careening across the oily night swells. The throbbing, sixteen-cylinder auto-type engine under the mahogany hood drove the craft along at a swifter pace than even the fast police patrol boats.

Baldwin Island came into sight at last, a low line of blackness against the faintly lighter horizon. There were other police craft here, circling off shore. Evidently they had been told to stay away at midnight. The mayor must have let slip some inkling of what might happen.

Agent "X" throttled his motor and drifted for a minute, until the nearest patrol boat moved away. Then he gave the engine fuel again, sped on a straight course toward the dark unsightly island.

It rose rapidly above his bow. He slowed the engine at last, twisted the wheel, and slid into a small gravelly beach. In a moment he was on shore, pulling the boat halfway up the beach to prevent the ebb tide from taking it.

Scudding clouds slid across the stars. A faint, wintry crescent of moon cast a cold light. Underneath it "X" got a glimpse of the island. It was a place of ash heaps, dumps, and small storage houses. The largest building on it was a city-owned incinerator. It wasn't a sightly place. Over on the north side were the shacks of the squatter colony.

Agent "X" made toward these, and, when a low ridge had hidden him from the water, he flashed his pencil light. Every few feet he saw evidence that the mayor had made effort to locate the hidden bomb.

Gangs of men had been at work here. Excavations showed in many spots, with fresh earth turned up. Yet obviously the mayor's workers had failed to find it. No doubt the suspense was largely responsible for the mayor's seeming fright.

Agent "X" didn't pause to search for clues now. He'd had dealings enough with criminal minds to know the horrible warped cunning with which they worked. And before he searched there were the squatters to think of.

He came to a slight incline, climbed it, and saw the squatters' colony ahead. Then he stiffened. Not one light showed, but several faint pin-pricks of illumination in the gloom. Smoke curled up from one cracked and rusty stovepipe above a nearby shack. The more daring of the squatters had made good their boast, and returned.

Agent "X" broke into swift strides. It was eleven-fifteen already. There was no time to lose if he expected to get these poor misguided people away. His face was bleak. His eyes snapped grimly. Horror, dread expectancy, seemed to lurk in the night about him on this desolate, barren island, and there were human beings, huddled in the very shadow of possible destruction.

He reached the first shack, burst open the door. There came a low whine, a growl. Then a furry shape bounded toward him. But a quick word from the Agent, and the dog that was about to attack him, paused and stood uncertainly. Something about the tone of "X's" voice and the burning, intent light in his eyes always had an effect on animals.

He looked beyond the dog, saw an old man rising from a box seat before a rusty can being used as a stove. Heat came from the bent sides of the can. The old man had been warming his frail hands above it.

"Hyer—wadda yer want?" he cried. "What's the idea, bustin' in on a fella like this?"

Agent "X" stared at the man silently for a moment. Then he spoke in a calm, friendly voice. "Just dropped in, mister, to see whether you'd cleared out, and to warn you if you hadn't to hurry up."

The old man's face distorted bitterly. "A detective, eh? Get outta hyer, dang you! Sic 'em, Bill!"

The dog, hearing its master's order, growled and bristled, but refused to attack Agent "X." The old man cried shrilly at the animal, but Agent "X" stepped closer, smiling. He reached out and petted the dog, whose hackles instantly went down.

The animal wagged its absurd stump of a tail. It was a mongrel, with a dozen strains fighting in its puny, courageous body. The old man stared in wonder, gulped.

"I never seen Bill take to a stranger like that before," he muttered. "He must have a lotta police dog in him and like dicks."

"I'm no dick," said "X," "I didn't come here because the law sent me. I came as a friend to warn you. Do you know why you've got to leave this island?"

"Can't say as I do. Some damned red tape, I guess."

"No—I wouldn't call it that. The island's going to be blown up—that's why. There's a bomb hidden out here somewhere."

"A bomb—say!" Suspicion came into the old man's eyes. "I wasn't born yesterday, fella. You can't pull a yarn like that on me!"

"X" spoke softly, tensely. "I wouldn't lie to you, friend. You'd better believe me. It's true. Even the cops are afraid to come out near this place. Quick—get away before it's too late!"

THE Agent's hands went to his pockets suddenly. He drew out a wallet, took from it a packet of bills.

"Here," he said quickly. "Take these, friend. They'll keep you and Bill for awhile. Then go to this address—and there'll be a job waiting."

He handed the old man a slip of paper with the name and address of Jim Hobart on it. He would make arrangements to have the old squatter put on his payroll.

"X" left the shack abruptly, saw the form of the old man and his dog hurrying away. "X" himself went on to three other shacks.

In each he found a human being, the stubborn rear guard of the squatter colony. Briefly, tensely, he told them what he had told the old man, gave them money, urged them to hurry. Seeing he was not a cop, impressed by the cash he handed out, they obeyed at once. Kindness had accomplished what threats and force could not.

One more light at the outer edge of the squatter colony attracted him. He walked toward it, came to within twenty feet of it. Then he paused suddenly. For the door was opening and two figures were coming out—a man and a girl.

It was the girl who held "X" transfixed. He stared as though doubting his own senses—stared, and his whole body tensed. For the girl was well-dressed, not like the tattered squatters he had visited, or like the young man at her side who seemed also to be a squatter. She wore a wool suit with a fur collar, a little *cloche* hat, and under its brim a twist of blonde hair showed.

Agent "X" would have known her figure and her walk anywhere. It was Betty Dale of the *Herald;* the blonde and lovely ally who was one of the few persons in all the world who knew about his daring work.

An icy chill seemed to clutch at the Agent's heart. What was Betty doing on this island at this time of night? What was she doing in the very shadow of hideous death?

The Agent stepped back. He puckered up his lips, sent a whistle into the night. It was birdlike, musical, yet with an eerie, ventriloquistic note that made it difficult to locate its source. It was the whistle of Secret Agent "X," his odd, inimitable trade-mark.

Betty Dale stopped immediately. She gave a little gasp of surprise and clutched the leather brief case she was carrying.

"Betty!" said the Agent. "Betty—over here!"

She turned then, said something to her tattered companion, moved away from him and came toward "X." Her eyes were bright. There was a smile on her lips as she approached. In spite of his disguise, one she had never seen before, she came directly to him. He didn't need to introduce himself. She had heard that whistle too many times ever to mistake it

"Why, what are *you* doing here?" she breathed. "Did you know I was around? Did you get my letter?" There was eagerness, happiness in her voice. Her eyes were aglow with a light brighter than mere friendship. There was a flush on her cheeks, not caused by the crispness of the December wind.

"Yes, Betty," the Agent said. "I got your letter, but I didn't know you were on the island till I saw you just now. Why are you here?"

BETTY DALE tapped her brief case with slim fingers. "These squatters," she said, "have been treated miserably. I'm collecting facts for a feature article in next Sunday's *Herald*. I can't understand why the city, yelling about relief to the poor, should hound these people who are hurting no one. The editor of the *Herald* feels just the same. My article will burn the mayor and his friends up. It ought to arouse public opinion. I had to come at night so the police wouldn't see me. Steve, over there, a chap who built one of those shacks, brought me out in his boat. I'm just leaving."

Agent "X" listened to the simple explanation of why she had

come voluntarily into the shadow of destruction. It was one of those strange, ironic twists of Fate which no one could anticipate. He spoke quickly, laying his hand on her arm.

"I see, Betty, but you won't need those notes. The city will understand soon why those poor devils were ordered away. The island is going to be blown up!"

Betty Dale started, paled, and stood very still. Her voice, sounded faint. "Blown up—why? I thought—"

"It's part of a criminal plot, Betty. Part of the thing you spoke of in your letter. I won't explain it all now, but the mayor himself is a victim of it. His hand was forced."

"When—when will this happen?" Betty asked.

"At midnight!"

"Midnight—that's only a half hour off!"

"Exactly. And that's why we must hurry."

Betty came closer, spoke quickly. "There's a young fellow in that shack back there—a friend of Steve's. He refuses to leave. I got most of my notes from him. He's told me how hard things have been. We must warn him, too!"

The Agent nodded. "Wait here a minute, Betty. Steve has a boat, you say. I'll get him to take his friend off at once. Then you can come with me. We'll stand off the island, and watch for the explosion together."

Agent "X" swiftly approached Steve. The tattered young squatter peered at him sharply.

"Say, are you a friend of Miss Dale's? I didn't know she knew any mugs over in this dump! She's a swell kid all right. She's gonna write up in the paper how they treated us!"

"X" repeated briefly what he had told Betty, explained why Steve must leave and take his friend with him at once. The boy's face went white. He pocketed the money "X" gave him dazedly, turned and ran to the shack of his friend, and Agent "X" returned to Betty's side.

"Come," he said. "I'd planned to look around, but there isn't time now. We'd better leave right away."

Betty Dale took his arm. Together they hurried across the ash heaps and piles of dirt toward the spot where he had drawn up his boat. But before they reached it, Betty suddenly stopped and pointed.

"Who are those men?" she asked.

The Agent's eyes recorded the hellish, white-hot flash that seemed to erase the stars and sweep over their very heads.

"X" saw them at the same instant—two furtive, swift-moving figures, just appearing from behind an ash pile. He paused, drew Betty back, and abruptly tensed in his tracks. For a harsh voice sounded directly behind him, a voice that gave menacing command.

"Don't move—either of you!" it said. "I got you covered—and I'd just as leave shoot as not."

"X" OBEYED instantly. He heard shuffling footsteps close behind him, felt a gun against his back. Then the speaker raised his voice and spoke again. "Here's the bird, boys, and a jane with him. Come on over."

The two that Betty Dale had seen came up quickly. They had twisted, brutal faces. Guns were in their hands. The Agent's pulses hammered. His skin felt cold. Left to himself he would have made some swift attack. But the guns were aimed at Betty Dale, also. He couldn't risk a bullet that might snuff out her life.

"Listen," he said harshly, "this is no time for a stick-up. There's a bomb out here somewhere. This island's going up at midnight."

One of the men broke into a cackle of derisive mirth. "Wise guy, eh! You're telling us! Bomb is right—and you and the dame will find out more about it in a minute."

The cords in the Agent's neck stood out. He crouched, made ready to leap. But the quick, brutal voice of the gangster stopped him.

"I don't know who this jane is, but it looks like you like her. Any rough stuff and she gets rubbed out, see? Come on, boys! Put 'em where I told you."

With a single frightened scream, Betty Date tried to break away, crying for "X" to follow. But one of the men caught her instantly. A second man pressed a gun against her back. "X" saw his trigger finger tense. He spoke quickly, hoarsely:

"Betty—don't! They'll kill you!"

Feeling a crushing weight of horror upon him, Agent "X" allowed himself to be led along. These men were spies of the Terror. He realized that, now. Their faces were grim. They, too, were hurrying, anxious to get away from this place. Their actions supported his belief that the Terror's threat was no mere boast. A gun was against "X's" back, also. He didn't fear that, but he was handicapped, made utterly helpless by the knowledge that Betty would be shot down callously if he made a move to save her or himself.

The gangsters veered to the left suddenly, took a narrow, ash-strewn path, and led their prisoners with them. One of them flashed a light. A squat brick building showed ahead. It was part of an old incinerating plant, discarded by the city since the new one had been built. It was windowless, merely a brick storage shed, but it had a strong, metal-bound door. This was open.

The gangsters thrust Betty inside, then "X." They gave the girl a shove which made "X" clench his teeth in fury. The next moment he, too, was forcibly hurled into the shed's interior. The gangster with the guns menaced them an instant. One of them spoke.

"We don't know who you are, guy, but we can make a guess! You seem to know too much. One of the hobos out here told us you'd warned him and the bunch to beat it—on account of a bomb. I guess you'd like to know where the bomb is—and I'm gonna tell you. It's right here in this shed, see? And you and the jane are gonna have a chance to watch how it works. So long, sweethearts! We'll be seein' you in hell!"

Harsh laughter followed this sally. The door slammed shut. A padlock clicked in a staple outside. Then came the sound of footsteps receding.

Betty Dale and the Agent were prisoners, close to the bomb of death—scheduled to explode at the end of a mere twenty minutes.

CHAPTER VII

SECONDS OF DOOM

RIGID HORROR GRIPPED the Agent for a second. He leaped to the spot where Betty Dale had been hurled to the floor and flashed on his light.

She was just getting up. Her voice sounded clear and steady beside him. "I'm afraid I got you in a jam," she said.

The Agent gave a harsh laugh. "It's the other way round, Betty! If I had gone on and left you alone—this wouldn't have happened."

He moved away, flashing his light quickly in all directions. Horror still held him, made his neck and hands feel cold. He wasn't thinking of his own life, or of Betty Dale's alone. He was thinking of those other thousands, millions perhaps, whose existences were threatened as long as this man, the Terror, was active—as long as the dozen bombs remained unfound.

His light paused abruptly, making a round spot at one end of the window-less chamber. A cluster of bricks had tumbled out here. A few broken pieces lay on the floor. Others had evidently been carted away. But what held "X's" interest was a spot above the bricks, on the wall itself, which had apparently been cemented over. The work had been done cleverly, with dirt and soot rubbed in, blackened like the rest of the building's interior. But the sharp eyes of Agent "X," trained to observe minute details, saw instantly that it was only camouflage.

He strode forward, touched the sooty surface with a finger tip, and found hard, new cement beneath the grime. This job had been done within a few weeks. No other part of the building showed repairs. The significance of the thing was obvious. Betty Dale, watching him, understood too. She had followed, was close at his side, staring at the wall in uneasy fascination.

"They said the bomb was in here. That must be it—behind that plaster! Is there any way we can get it out—stop it?"

For answer "X" reached down and picked up a piece of brick. He tapped the cement gently; knew immediately by the sound that it was at least a foot thick, shook his head.

"If we had time, Betty, I could do it. But, there isn't time!"

His light left the wall, returned to the heavy door. No lock showed on the inside. Its oak beams were reinforced with bolted strips-of metal. It would withstand at least an hour's battering— and it was now nineteen minutes of twelve.

Every second counted. Death and time seemed to be working hand in hand against them. The girl sensed the hopelessness of their position, sensed that Agent "X" and she were doomed to die, yet the smile was still on her lips.

The Agent's fingers gripped hers for a moment. He smiled into her eyes, then moved up to that door which seemed an impenetrable barrier. Looking at it now, briefly, speculatively, it was still the time element which baffled him. Given forty minutes, a half hour even, he was certain he could escape from here. The men who had shut Betty and himself inside this room of death did not know evidently with whom they were dealing. They had no knowledge of the strange, ingenious devices carried by Agent "X." They did not guess the full extent of his resourcefulness.

"Hold the light, Betty," he said suddenly. "Keep it on the door."

Feverishly he took out his kit of tools. He scanned them for a moment, shook his head, laid them down. These bits of metal with their goose necks and queer pivotal extensions had served him well for a score of times. With them he had opened bank doors, picked locks that were considered invulnerable in his ceaseless quest for evidence of crime. But they would not serve him now—with only blank boarding to face.

He lifted one foot instead, reached inside his shot sole, and drew out a small implement concealed there. This, too, had performed seeming miracles in its time. At one side of it was a tiny, paper-thin hacksaw, on the back a file, made of a thin strip of black diamond, set in steel-hard cement.

The hinges of the door were fastened laterally, screwed inside the frame. Only their ends showed, and hinged joints themselves, with the metal pivots that held them together. These were welded in, with rounded heads top and bottom. Rust was flaked on them in mantling cakes.

Quickly, energetically, Agent "X" drew his diamond file across them. Under its keen teeth the rust came off. In a moment he had bared the bright metal of the pivot ends. But filing would be a long process. There wasn't time for that.

Time—with that dreaded thing sealed in the wall close by. Time—with every second bringing them closer to eternity. Once the Agent glanced at Betty. A smile of hope, faith, was still on her lips. It clutched at his heart. The girl, who had seen him do the seemingly impossible before, trusted him now, thought that he had found a certain way out. Her hand was steady on the flash. Its beam gave "X" ample light to work by.

WITH tense fingers, he turned the file over, thrust the hacksaw blade against the line where the pivot head and hinge were joined. But rust still clogged the crack, hampered him. He ran and got a piece of brick, came back and knocked violently against the hinge.

Some of the rust came out. He struck the pivot up to give more room. Then, while the slow minute hand of his watch moved upward toward the spot which spelled destruction, he drew the hacksaw blade back and forth.

The sound of its teeth mounted. It snarled, bit into the metal. It rose to a thin wail, like the moan of a frightened animal there in that room of death. The Agent's arm worked like a piston. His breath came in short, quick jerks.

The blade was halfway through now. Rust clogged it further as it bit in. Sweat stood out on the Agent's forehead, though the chill of the December night lay like a pall within that room.

The hacksaw screamed more slowly. It rasped, lurched forward. One of the pivot heads dropped off. He did not attack the head at the other end. He stood erect, moved to the door's top hinge now, thumping it first with the brick, then using the saw again. Once he stopped, asked a question.

"What time is it, Betty?" He tried to make his voice sound casual; tried to hide the eager, fearful note it held.

Betty glanced at her wristwatch. Words seemed to come from

her throat with difficulty.

"Ten minutes to twelve," she said. "Do you think—"

She didn't finish. He didn't answer. He went to work again, more quickly, more furiously than ever; drawing the saw across the pivot in thrusts that threatened to snap the blade; risking all in snarling, lashing strokes. Seconds seemed to be racing. His own pulse-beat seemed to mock him. Then the saw's teeth slid through. The other pivot head came off.

He dropped the saw into his pocket, snatched up one of his small tools. It was a straight bit of steel like a nail set. In his other hand was a piece of brick.

Swiftly, surely, he hammered down on the tool's top, struck the hinge pivot out of the joint. The tiny pieces of metal, which had held them prisoners like iron bars, dropped to the floor.

Agent "X" attacked the door. It fitted snugly. The padlock outside held one end. The wedged sections of the hinges held the other. He dropped to hands and knees, felt along the door's bottom, and thrust his fingers in. Muscles along his back and shoulders rippled as he heaved. Betty had turned the flashlight down. There was no sound in the room, save the Agent's labored breathing. Then the big door squeaked, stirred.

He drew the bottom toward him with a jerk that made the cords on his neck stand out. The wedged hinges came loose. The door broke away from its frame. The padlock staple prevented it from coming entirely free. But he cried out to Betty to step back. He caught the door's edge, drew it inward—and a breath of chill night air came through the opening.

He seized Betty's arm, pulled her from the building. "Quick, Betty! We must run! It's our only chance. The boat!"

He didn't know in which direction the nearest water lay. The prison shed seemed to be in the center of the island. It had no doubt been selected for that reason by the bomb planters, so that the Terror could make good his boast and destroy all. But "X" knew where he had left his speeding boat. His unerring sense of direction told him that.

He led the way, holding Betty's arm. They raced across the ash-strewn ground under the bobbing beam of his flash. He knew it was a race with death, knew that now it must be five of twelve; knew that any instant, if there was a slip in time, a tiny discrepancy, the bomb might explode—and all his efforts would be futile.

Breathless, gasping, Agent "X" drew Betty along, till he saw the gleam of water ahead. Beyond it, far away, the twinkling lights of shore showed, and the lights of boats along the water's surface. He turned a little to the left. There, by that mound of dirt hidden in the shadows, was where he had drawn up his own craft, the boat that would speed them away from this place of waiting death.

He almost lifted Betty from her feet as he guided her. Her breath was coming in quick gasps. Her fingers were clutching him, and suddenly "X" cried out.

"The boat—there it is!"

The slender shadow of the craft had caught his eyes. It lay where he had left it, drawn up on the sand. But even as he saw it and came close, a harsh, bitter exclamation was wrenched from his throat.

Betty stopping beside him, exclaimed, too. For the boat at her feet was not as he had left it. Some one, the men, no doubt, who had imprisoned them in the shed, had been at work.

Rocks lay in the padded interior. Skeleton ribs showed. The boat was useless, shattered beyond repair even if there were time—and, in the blackness behind them, in that prison shed, Death was crouched on its haunches like a black beast waiting to spring.

CHAPTER VIII

THUNDERING HORROR

THE AGENT TURNED on Betty Dale and uttered quick, hoarse words. "We must swim, Betty—swim at once!" Even as he spoke, he reached down, ripped open his shoe laces, drew off his shoes. Betty, following suit, kicked off her pumps and stood in stockinged feet.

The Agent's eyes were bleak. He hadn't told her the nature of that bomb; hadn't said that if the Terror's boast were true the very soil under their feet would disintegrate. There was distance between the shed and themselves now. Betty appeared confident. She was sure they were all right. But Agent "X" knew differently.

The girl was running like a slim nymph toward the cold December water. She flung her wool coat off, tossed her blonde hair back. The rigors of the chill water didn't terrify her. Her young, strong muscles could cope with that. She waded in knee-deep, flung herself down. With long, clean strokes she swam ahead. And the Agent followed. He came close, whispered hoarsely in her ear.

"As fast as you can, Betty! Swim as you never have before! If you get tired—I'll help you."

Her expression showed that she didn't understand his worry. She had proved her swimming ability often before.[54]

"X" didn't try to explain. No time for that now, and no use frightening Betty. The cold water leaped about their bodies. It clung with a chill that almost made their muscles numb. But their long, sweeping strokes held the cold at bay.

Betty turned her spray-wet face. "X" could see the dim oval of

---

54 AUTHOR'S NOTE: *Once, in escaping a horde of Malay prisoners and religious fanatics, Agent "X" had let Betty leap free from a canoe and swim ashore while he led the killers away after him. He'd had no compunction about this, knowing that Betty Dale was an accomplished swimmer.*

it in the starlight, see the clustering blonde curls low on her white neck. He knew that she was good for miles, using her even, racer's stroke that had won her cups in women's championship meets. His own muscles had been trained to endure endlessly. He could stay in the water for hours, swimming on his back if he became tired, floating if necessary. He was as much at home as a seal.

But the dread knowledge of what lay behind them hung like a lead weight around his neck. He stayed close to Betty, with a sense of waiting. There was no telling what minute the bomb might go off. Fast as they were swimming, he wasn't satisfied. He spoke once again, something of the dread he felt in his voice.

"Keep it up, Betty—as fast as you can! Every stroke counts."

They were two hundred feet offshore now. The Agent wished it were two hundred yards. He could almost sense each passing second. He was counting in his mind, keeping track of the minutes. It must be almost twelve! The arch criminal would make it a point to stick closely to his schedule. Midnight sharp would be the deadline.

Far off across the water he saw faint lights twinkling. People were there in their peaceful homes, all unknowing of the danger that lurked so close at hand. Nearer by were the moving lights of boats. Police craft, no doubt, and others going about their accustomed routine.

Then, on a hilltop somewhere on shore, he heard the solemn tones of a great clock booming the hour. The Agent tensed. It must be past midnight. Sound traveled at eleven hundred feet per second. And he heard the clock just striking now—which meant the hour was past—or else the clock was wrong. Surely the dread moment was almost at hand. He had struggled, worked, done his best for Betty and himself. Still they were under the black shadow of doom. Only three hundred feet separated them from the island's shores—only three hundred feet of water beneath them and shuddering death.

HE came close to Betty, reached out a hand to her wet shoulder, felt the warm play of muscles beneath.

"Steady, Betty. I think—"

He did not finish the sentence. He heard the small, frightened cry that Betty gave. It stabbed at his heart. The Agent's eyes recorded the hellish white-hot flash that erased the glow of the stars and seemed to sweep over their very heads. He saw the outline of the island, illumined now. But not the island he had moved on a minute before. The black bulk mushroomed out, spread like a menacing Titan across the blinding whiteness of the light.

And then his ears, receiving impression later than his eyes, heard a sound that was like thunder multiplied a thousandfold. It was a sound that had bulk and substance, a crushing weight of tumbling, fearful reverberations, almost shattering his eardrums.

Instinctively Betty's arms wrapped around him. He held her small, tense body close to his. They were alone in a world of blinding light, of terrible sound, and of earth and rocks that rose volcano-like, seeming to reach to the very sky above.

He got one look at Betty's startled, staring face. He saw her eyes grow big, her teeth set. He could not speak, could not make her hear. He could only hold her with his arm, trembling to think what thing would shortly follow.

For the three hundred feet that separated them from the island seemed pitifully small now. Fringing the black pandemonium of sky-tossed earth, a white line of water showed—like froth rimming the angry, cavernous mouth of some great sea beast. It rose higher and higher—salt water lashed to a foam by the concussion. It mounted, curled and raced toward them, in a roaring tidal wave.

Betty saw it, screamed once, in a surge of fear that she could not choke down. The Agent, seeing that wall of water, believed that it was the end. One thing alone stayed clearly in his mind. He must keep hold of Betty. If it were possible to survive he must not let that fearsome, onrushing fury snatch her from his arms. His hands locked around her. He kept afloat with the scissors strokes of his feet.

But in an instant even swimming seemed futile. For the water was almost to them, curling like a mountain top. There was a trough before it. They slid down into this, and as they did so, Agent "X" cried in Betty's ear:

"Breathe, Betty! Hold it!"

He filled his own lungs till they ached. The water seemed to lift them in a mighty surge. They were borne up, up toward the foaming crest. Then the boiling spray engulfed them. Like straws they were rolled over and over; weighed down, hurled about in a Niagara of churning, fearsome water. More tumultuous than the roughest surf, more exhausting than anything "X" had ever known.

Once he felt a vibration in the water, a compression as though some great weight had struck, and a black something seemed to rocket close at hand. He knew it was a rock, falling from the island, and that the bulk of water above them was all that was saving them from the raining destructing of countless missiles. But his lungs were almost bursting. He feared for Betty. And so, still holding her to him, he struggled upward. It seemed that he would never reach the surface. The boiling foam had subsided now. He appeared to be in still black depths. He held Betty with one arm, pushed with the other, forcing himself toward the surface before it was too late.

Then his head came out. The rumbling roar of the explosion had ceased. The white light had gone, and his half-blinded eyes could not see the stars. But there was still movement all about them—and noise. The water was surging in a vast, sweeping tide. Stones were dropping on its surface in a pattering shower. Debris of all kind was falling.

Something hit "X's" shoulder, made a stabbing pain. A rock splashed close by. Any instant death might come. Yet he dared not take Betty down into the depths again, and there was no assurance that a rock might not strike them under the surface as well as here.

He waited, paddling slowly in a solitude of blackness and death. And then a new menace came. For the tide had turned. He had lost all sense of direction, yet he could tell that in the last few seconds some change in the watery surge had come. The water that had gone out into the boiling wave was coming back, more sluggishly, to sink into the vast hole where the island had been, sink to replace tons of scattered earth. The Terror had fulfilled his threat, razed Baldwin Island to the water level. And now the waters were returning to cover the spot where it had been.

Agent "X" gasped as the tide seemed to reach for them. This was worse than any undertow. And somewhere ahead in the darkness, as the falling rocks began to diminish, he could hear the rushing, roaring sound of a giant whirlpool. It grew louder, closer every instant. He and Betty were being swept back toward it.

This was a new horror. They had lived through the tidal wave. But nothing could survive that sucking undertow. He knew it must be pulling debris down with it—as it would pull them, to crushing depths.

He fought now, snapped into action, brought all the power of his steel muscles into play. He turned over on his back, drew Betty on hers, placed his left arm under her chin, keeping her head up. It was a lifeguard's maneuver, one that "X" had often used. It left his right arm free, the powerful scissors strokes of his legs unimpeded.

He swam as one would swim against a roaring current, swam with the blood pounding in his veins, with every muscle in his body straining like a tautened cord. Yet still the water bore him on. Still in his ears was that strange uncanny roaring. His eyes had grown used to the starlight again. He turned once, a tortured, straining face, and saw the boiling, deadly riptide where Baldwin Island had been. It was toward this he was going, toward the middle where horrors of green sea water were sliding down.

"Betty! Betty!" he called.

She stirred faintly then, as though the sound of his voice were bringing her back from great depths. But the moan that came from her lips ended in a choking gasp. She was on the borderland of consciousness, her lungs half-filled with water. He must fight it out alone, save her and himself, or go under with her to a watery death. The whirlpool could not last forever. The space the exploding island had made must at last fill up. The angry sea must reach its level again.

He fought with the frenzy of a man in the toils of some mighty beast. Yet the current drew him steadily closer. The white froth of the riptide was coming nearer. And Agent "X" almost gave up hope.

CHAPTER IX

THE TERROR'S SIGNATURE

HIS STEELY MUSCLES could not exert themselves forever. His iron will could not battle endlessly against such overwhelming odds. Through seconds that seemed eternities he fought the sweeping, foaming current, till at last the tide, as though merciful to one who had struggled beyond all human endurance, began to slacken.

The Agent's movements toward the snarling edge of the whirlpool slowed. He began to hold his own, began even to make headway against it. Behind him the sea lapsed into a low moaning whisper.

He was conscious of the water's chill then, conscious of the black winter night around him. The cold cut into his very marrow as his own movements slowed. What must Betty Dale be feeling, still and limp in his arms?

He shook her gently. "Betty! Betty! We're all right now."

The faint sound she made frightened him. He turned her on her back, held her chin up, and moved her arms. She made another brief strangling noise. He saw then that he must get her out soon, drive the water from her lungs.

The thought that she was in danger clutched his heart in a grip of fear that all the terrors he had been through had failed to bring. He looked over the dark face of the water. Everywhere whistles were blowing and lights were springing up. Some were moving along the surface—boats.

Agent "X" filled his lungs with air. Not often did he ask anyone for help. Now it was not for himself, but for one who was more than a friend, one who had shared hideous dangers with him and had come through the Valley of Death at his side.

He gave a shout that sped across the water like a gull's wild cry.

Again and again he uttered it, till the wailing siren of a boat gave answer. He saw a light veer then, saw the red and green riding lanterns of a vessel coming fast.

He shouted once more, holding Betty's small face up, moving her arms to drive the cold out. She couldn't swim. She was almost strangled. Perhaps a blow from some passing bit of debris had struck her head. He trod water, keeping her afloat till the approaching craft raced nearer.

He could make out its lines now! It was one of the police patrol boats he'd seen earlier that evening, before the frightful explosion had come.

The blue-white beam of a spotlight whipped across the water, and Agent "X" waved his arm. The light centered upon him and Betty, and the boat swept close.

At the last it veered, then edged slowly toward them, drifting with the wind. Hands reached down from its low deck. Betty was taken aboard first and carried into the small warm cabin. "X" was helped from the water and followed.

Bluecoats stood all about them, men who, had they known "X's" identity, would have snapped steel cuffs on him and menaced him with their guns. But they had no inkling that the mild-mannered stranger before them, in wet clothing, was the mysterious, uncanny Man of a Thousand Faces, regarded by the law as a desperate criminal. The Agent spoke quickly now:

"Get some blankets and liquor at once," he said. "The girl must be attended to."

A heavy-set cop bent over Betty to administer practical first aid, but Agent "X" thrust him aside. This was a job he would trust to no one. His amazing mind held data on many branches of science. Medicine was among those he had studied. He knew more tricks of resuscitation than any of these men around him.

He turned Betty face down on the floor, set to work expertly, moving her arms in a way that forced water from her lungs and started blood surging through her heart. In a moment she stirred and a faint trace of color crept to her cheeks.

Relief swept in upon the Agent now that he saw Betty Dale was safe. For a moment he allowed himself the luxury of forgetfulness, a second's peace after the nightmarish horrors of the past half hour. But the cops' grimly questioning faces brought him back to the sinister mystery of the explosion.

"The girl's Miss Betty Dale of the *Herald*," he said. "She went out to interview the squatters who slipped back after you fellows had driven them away. My name's Ross. We were just leaving when the big noise came. What was it?"

The cops looked at each other quickly. In deliberately querying them first, "X" had checkmated questioning of himself. He kept up the pose of a puzzled witness of some mysterious happening.

"Did the city have dynamite on the island, or what the hell?"

"One guess is as good as another, buddy," said a cop guardedly. "Maybe there was a powder house over on the dump. Who knows?"

Betty Dale was sitting up, talking with the police when "X" re-entered the cabin. They had delved into their emergency chest, provided her with an ill-fitting woman's coat, dress, and a pair of shoes several sizes too large. She exchanged a single, meaning glance with the Agent.

"Please land me as soon as you can," she told the cops. "I'll want to turn in a story to my paper."

The harbor patrolmen nodded. They seemed relieved when the boat finally edged into a small municipal dock.

CROWDS had gathered along the waterfront. Faces were tense with curiosity and apprehension. Questions were being asked in a dozen different tongues.

Betty and the Agent pushed through the buzzing throngs whose interest had been aroused by the mysterious explosion. These people didn't know that the tall man in the wet clothing could have told them more about it than the police. They didn't guess that the two before them had come together through the very jaws of Death.

Agent "X" summoned a taxi and took Betty back to her apartment to change her ill-fitting clothes. He cautioned her not to mention the men on the island or the fact that she had seen the location of the bomb. At the apartment door he said a hurried good-night and gave the cab driver another address. He stopped at last in the middle of a block, paid the taxi man off, and walked a hundred yards farther on. Here he went into the rear door of an empty

house, the same hideout he had visited just before his trip to Baldwin Island.

Even before changing his wet clothing, he strode up to the odd apparatus that stood in a wooden cabinet on the table. It was a special type radio receiver. Simple as the thing appeared externally, it was a monument to the talent of Agent "X" in a field of science which many men made their life work. It represented hours of patient research, amazing inventiveness, and a deep knowledge of the principles of mechanics and radio engineering.

He called it a "radio wave camera," and it was perhaps the only one of its kind in existence—a machine for taking permanent impressions of invisible radio waves. On a large revolving cylinder of white paper, operated by delicate clockwork mechanism, visual records of all the radio waves picked up within a given space of time were made.

The meter length of the great broadcasting stations showed here. Also calls corresponding to amateur stations, police cruisers, ships in the air and ships at sea.

More than five hundred tiny styluses, dipped in red ink and poised above the paper cylinder, were ever ready to descend and make their lines, as radio impulses operated electromagnets beneath them. All the broadcasts of the evening had made visual imprints. Each of those tiny, intermittent red lines corresponded to some orchestra, some speaker, singer or comedian in one of the big studios.

At other points on the white cylinder, code from ships at sea showed. The machine was extraordinarily apt at picking up this, the dots and dashes being plainly visible.

But Agent "X" at the moment was interested in none of these. He shut off the revolving mechanism, drew the cylinder from its drum, and ran his eye along a transverse blue line that had the figure twelve above it.

Twelve o'clock—the zero hour at which the awful bomb had been detonated! Had the Terror been lying? Was it an ordinary clockwork bomb, or had radio impulse really done the work?

The Secret Agent's fingers trembled slightly. His eyes blazed with interest. The Terror had not lied. His talk of radio impulse, like his bomb on Baldwin Island, was no bluff.

There, just one minute before twelve, was a red imprint that one of the tiny needles had made. Four long marks, two shorts, and four more longs. They had been written by a stylus set in action by a wave-length of approximately nineteen meters. They ended just before midnight, did not appear again, and had not appeared before all evening according to the cylindrical chart. As though the Terror had written his signature in blood, those tiny crimson lines on the paper roll were visible proof of his existence.

Agent "X" straightened. He had done what no one else in the city had even thought of doing—made a record of the radio impulse which had exploded the bomb. He had its wave-length now, had proof of the Terror's appalling cunning. He would set one of his operatives to watching that wave-length at all times, in the hopes of locating the point of broadcast.

He changed his clothes quickly. Then phoned the Hobart Agency and listened in to a report from Bates. But neither organization, though they had worked faithfully all evening, had been able to pick up information valuable to "X."

IT was the next morning that the Secret Agent thought of another possible source of information. His methods were often strange. Throughout the city and the country he had made acquaintances in odd places. The underworld knew him only as a legendary scourge. The police considered him a desperate criminal. But to many, to the poor, weak, and down-trodden, he had been a friend and benefactor.[55]

None of these knew his real identity. But, going abroad in one or another of his amazing, brilliant disguises, he had made many loyal friends. In the Chinese quarter he was esteemed as a distinguished member of the famous Ming Tong. As Mr. Martin, newspaperman, he had been a friend and benefactor to many newsboys. In the disguise of a ragged tramp he had delved into the most impoverished

---

55 AUTHOR'S NOTE: *Often in his campaign against criminals, Agent "X" comes into possession of various sums of money, confiscated from the human terrors over whom he wins his victories. He never keeps this for himself. It goes into the fund which he uses to help the unfortunate men, women, and children who have suffered disgraces and poverty through no fault of their own. In one disguise or another, without their realizing his identity, he has given aid in dozens of cases.*

depths of human society, made contacts with beggars, hobos, and down-and-outers. And often, beneath their dirt and rags, he had found brave humor, courage and shining human worth that shamed the upper rungs of society.

Now, because he was working in the dark against murderous criminals, he thought of a man, a friend of his, who lived always in utter darkness.

In his small car, Agent "X" sped down into the narrow, winding streets of the city's tenderloin district. Here squalor and poverty showed on all sides. Here smells rose from the cluttered pavements to compete with the mustiness of the buildings that fringed them. Yet, close at hand, only a few blocks away in fact, was a section inhabited by criminals; with gaudy dance halls, drinking dens, gambling joints, and small unlicensed eating places.

On an alley-like street at the edge of these slums, close to this area of tinsel and crime, Agent "X" stopped. He got out of his car, strolled along the narrow pavement in the role of a plainly dressed young man—with no particular destination in mind. But his eyes were alert. He was definitely looking for some one.

The morning bustle of the section had begun. Pushcarts loaded with fruit, vegetables, and sea food rattled by. The streets were filling up with early shoppers, old women with kerchiefs over their heads, young children sent out to buy a few pennies' worth of food.

The Agent noted all these, but his gaze drifted on. He crossed the alley, came to a wider street at the edge of the criminal quarter, paused at a corner to look in both directions. Then suddenly a flitting smile curved his lips.

A thin, scarecrow of a man with sightless sockets for eyes, was coming down the block. He was walking steadily, surely, along the pavement, with no cane to guide him. His head was tilted back. He was sniffing the cool morning air. Before him, tied around his middle with a piece of string, was a small tray holding a few packets of chewing gum; Agent "X" knew this man.

Thaddeus Penny was his name. Once, disguised as a character, "Robbins," "X" had helped Penny, saved him from being thrown out of his small furnished room for the non-payment of rent. Since then "X" had often met Penny, and the blind beggar was ever grateful to the man he knew only as Robbins.

Agent "X" walked forward now. Penny was blind, stone blind, having lost his eyesight years before in a tenement fire. But, because of his affliction, his wits and all his other faculties seemed to have grown keener. He could walk about without a cane, could read by means of the Braille system, could identify men by their voices and the minute sounds they made.

THE blind beggar suddenly paused as "X" came opposite. He cocked his head to one side, listening. Intelligence brightened his sensitive, sightless face. Agent "X" moved by, watching. Penny turned around then, looked after him, as though those empty sockets were gifted with some strange second sight. But "X" knew the blind man was receiving impressions through his ears alone. He paused, returned, and as he passed this time, Thaddeus Penny spoke:

"Mr. Robbins!" he said. "I thought it was your step. Now I know—you're trying to play tricks on me!"

Unhesitatingly, Penny came forward and laid a hand on "X's" arm. His fingers clasped the Agent's for a moment in a friendly grip.

"Right, Thaddeus," said "X." "You're out early this morning. I saw you and wondered if I could sneak by—but I might have known I couldn't. Let's have a piece of that gum."

Penny was silent for a second or two, his pale, lined face expressionless. He seemed to be listening—or thinking.

"You didn't just stop me to say hello or to buy gum," he said suddenly. "You're worried about something. You're breathing faster and not so deep as usual, Mr. Robbins. Anything the matter?"

Agent "X" threw back his head and laughed—something he seldom did, grim manhunter that he was. But Thaddeus Penny's amazing powers of concentration and deduction always amused him.

"It's lucky, Thaddeus," he said, "that you don't go in for crime. If you did, nobody would be safe!"

"Crime!" said the blind man. "So, that's it! You're always talking about crime, Mr. Robbins." Penny smiled knowingly, staring vacantly into space. "I once told you you were a detective, you remember. Then I took it back, because you don't act like any detective I've ever known before."

"How do I act, Thaddeus?" asked Agent "X" suddenly. Blind as Penny was, he was one man whom Agent "X" suspected of knowing more than he admitted. "X" could come to him in any disguise. It was his voice and step that Penny recognized. But it sometimes seemed that Penny, with his remarkable brain, sensed the strange, magnetic qualities of Agent "X," also.

"You act like a man," said Penny slowly, "who sees farther than any eye could reach. And you act like a man who has a lot to think about."

"The latter is true, anyhow, Thaddeus. I've got a lot to think about. And this morning I'm thinking about crime, as you say." The Agent sank his voice lower then, so that no one passing on the street might hear. "There've been a great many robberies and murders this past week, Thaddeus, a great deal of crime in this town. Some say the police are being bribed. Others say they're scared. I don't know which is right. But there must be criminals who are getting rich and fat. I'd like, for private reasons, to know who they are."

Thaddeus Penny nodded slowly, understandingly. A slow smile overspread his face, a knowing smile as though he suspected the purposes and motives of his friend Robbins and approved of them.

He cocked his head to one side again, listening to all sounds on the block. Then he drew "X" against the wall of a building, leaned close and spoke, his voice hardly more than a whisper.

"I get about a bit," he said, "and sometimes ears are better than eyes. Sometimes I hear and remember things that others quickly forget—because when a man's blind all he has to amuse him are his thoughts. He plays games with himself—tries to fit things together."

Penny smiled and nodded slowly, tapping "X's" arm. "Maybe you've heard of a fellow named Gus Sanzoni. He's been quiet for years, isn't rated as much of a big shot—but they say he made a pile of dough during prohibition. He had cookers working for him on a hundred stills and he had a mob. But when money comes easy, it goes easy, too. I heard that Sanzoni gambled away everything, lost his mob and his power, and had only a night club left. Then, lately, some of the fellows that used to work for him are calling him a big shot again instead of a cheap punk. There's 'Dutch' Wilken, Mateo the Moocher, and 'Little' Dellman among 'em. They seem to feel frisky lately. The girls say they're flashing big rolls. Don't ask me how they get 'em. But when a crook has big money, there's always blood on it. And Gus Sanzoni don't pay men just because they're his pals."

The eyes of Agent "X" shone brightly as he listened. Bates and Hobart had men drifting through the tenderloin section, probably within a stone's throw of him now. Yet they had learned nothing. The lips of the underworld had remained closed to them. It had taken the sharp ears of a blind beggar to hear the whispers that the Agent wanted, the rumors, that might send him in desperate, daring conflict against the menace that lay like a curse of waiting death over the whole great city.

CHAPTER X

A STRAIGHT TIP

HE THANKED THADDEUS Penny quietly, withholding from his voice all trace of the deep excitement he felt. Yet Penny nodded wisely and laid a hand on "X's" arm.

"That's the news you wanted, isn't it?" he said. "It sort of fits in with something you had in mind. You're breathing fast again. I can almost hear your heart beat. But don't go and get into trouble. Even if you're a detective stay away from Gus Sanzoni. He's like the rats that come out from the cellars at night. They run if you go right after them—but like as not they'll turn around and bite you in the back afterwards."

A thin smile twisted the lips of Agent "X." "Don't get into trouble," Thaddeus Penny had said. But trouble was the Agent's daily bread, trouble of the most bizarre and violent sort—trouble that other men would flinch from, but which he had grown hardened to.

"I'll take care of myself, Thaddeus," he said quietly. "Don't worry about me. Suppose you give me a package of that gum."

Agent "X" tossed a nickel into the old cigar box which Penny used as a tray; but along with it he dropped a crumpled five-dollar bill. This maneuver didn't escape Penny's sharp ears, however. The faint rustle of the bill was audible to him.

"There you go again, Mr. Robbins, giving me a cash hand-out! I won't take it, I—"

"Your tip was worth it, Thaddeus. If you don't need the money, give it to some friend who's in a hole. I'll be seeing you later. And thanks again."

Agent "X" walked swiftly away from the blind beggar. He passed one of Jim Hobart's men sauntering toward the tenderloin. But the detective didn't guess for a moment that the person he'd brushed was the power behind his own employer, the man he had to thank for his job and his pay.

In his small, fast car again, "X" sped uptown. Thaddeus Penny had given him a tip which demanded instant attention. The Agent parked his coupé, this time, close to a wide, luxurious drive bordering the river. Not far away was the yacht club where was anchored Monte Sutton's yacht, the *Osprey,* and where Mayor Ballantine had tried to forget his troubles in an atmosphere of glamorous gaiety.

But for the moment Agent "X" had decided to tackle the menace that hung over the city from another angle. He had gone to the municipality's highest executive without accomplishing anything except the crystallization of his own belief that something was radically wrong.

Later he had found the Terror's document in the mayor's home. Now he would delve into the lowest depths of the criminal underworld—in an effort to trace down the Terror's men and make contact with the Terror himself.

Closing and locking the door of the coupé, "X" walked swiftly down a side street and stopped at last before a high brick wall. On the other side of this the gables and peaked roof of an old house showed. Even at a distance there was an air of desolation about the place, an air of disuse and decay.

"X" stepped through a hedge of sparse evergreens. His form blended with the shadows along the wall for a moment. A key grated in an ancient lock. A rusty gate swung open, closed softly—and Agent "X" was in the mysterious, statue-strewn rear yard of the old Montgomery Mansion.[56]

He crossed it quickly to the back of the house that had been closed for years because of the bitter litigation of heirs. Here he descended a flight of stairs to a basement entrance, went inside and climbed more stairs to a butler's pantry.

Under his pressure on a secret lever, one of the big pantry shelves swung out. A door was revealed here, with a large room behind it, a chamber that no one except an architect going over the cubic space of the house would ever suspect. Agent "X" was in a hideout where none had ever been able to trace him.

---

56   AUTHOR'S NOTE: *This particular hideout will be recalled by followers of the case records of Agent "X." In many respects it is the most complete of any he uses. It contains a chemical and photographic laboratory, a set of remarkable filing cabinets and the like. It figured in his thrilling battle with the "Torture Trust," and also when he was fighting that human monster, called by the papers "The Spectral Strangler."*

He went at once to a series of metal cabinets. Here were perhaps the most complete criminological files in the country. Here was data on famous criminals and lesser-known ones that even the police did not possess. Here were odd facts and strange human sidelights which aided the Secret Agent in his amazing work. Fingerprints and Bertillon measurements were included. The files had a cross index system, the result of painstaking hours of labor on the Agent's part. He quickly drew out a small envelope containing the life history of Gus Sanzoni, the man of whom Thaddeus Penny had spoken.

All the facts were given here, many of which "X" remembered. But he wanted to check up and make sure. The Gangster's first steps in crime were recorded; his early thefts as a parcel snatcher. His leadership of a gang of hoodlums. His rise to power during the prohibition era when his business sharpness and brutal tactics made him the head of one of the city's largest bootleg rings. Then the loss of his fortune and his decline into comparative obscurity as the owner of a night club when the repeal law was passed. Names of Sanzoni's mobsters were included.

The Agent quickly found an item that interested him. Two of Sanzoni's former lieutenants, Floyd Kittredge and "Bugs" Gary, were in prison. They had been held in connection with a cop shooting during a liquor raid. Bugs Gary's time was almost up. He had only a month more to serve. His term had been shortened owing to good behavior in prison.

Agent "X" quickly memorized the data on Bugs Gary. It wasn't quite as complete as he would have liked, yet it would serve his purpose. He left his hideout twenty minutes later, satisfied that he had a definite working plan.

THAT afternoon a long-distance call was received in Washington by a man who preferred to be known only as K9. He was an official of the government, so high that a mere suggestion from his lips became a command elsewhere.

For five minutes Secret Agent "X," speaking in a low, guarded voice, and using a private wire straight to Capital Hill, talked to K9. K9 listened and agreed.

The governor of the state in which crime had so strangely broken out and was racing unchecked, received an official government message within the hour. It suggested immediate clemency for the ex-gangster, Bugs Gary.

This message was transmitted to the warden of the prison where Bugs was held. From then on, the wheels of the official machinery, which Secret Agent "X" had set in motion, moved speedily.

Bugs was called into the warden's office. He was told that because of good behavior, the governor had seen fit to shorten his sentence. He was handed his pardon, told that he was now a free man. And, slightly dazed, hardly believing his good fortune, he walked out of the prison gates, with money in his pocket and a new suit of clothes provided by the state on his back.

He didn't notice the inconspicuously featured man in brown, who at once trailed him. The stranger's manner was so casual that even a criminal twice as clever as Bugs would not have suspected he was being followed.

Yet when Bugs went to the station and swung aboard an express bound for the city, the man in brown was on the car, too. He took a seat close to Bugs, keeping the ex-gangster under surveillance through a tiny hole torn in the newspaper which he held before his face.

There was more than mere curiosity in the stranger's eyes. There was studied appraisal. He was watching hawk-eyed every gesture Bugs made. When the gangster asked the conductor a question about the train schedule, the man listened to each syllable of the criminal's voice, storing it away carefully in his memory. At the big Union Depot where Bugs Gary alighted, the stranger strode behind him for some distance, noting the gangster's walk.

Bugs paused for a moment before the windows of a station haberdashery shop to eye admiringly a checked suit of latest cut, and a collection of startlingly bright ties. It was then that the man in brown brushed against him.

Bugs felt a slight prick in his arm, hardly more than as though some tiny splinter of wood mixed with the cloth of his suit had been driven in. He heard the man in brown apologize for being clumsy, then move on—and Bugs thought nothing of it.

But a moment later his legs began to rock and sway under him. Details of the building and people around him began to blur. Bugs opened his mouth to give a frightened cry; but no sound came. His tongue, like his legs, seemed to be out of commission. With a grunt, Bugs Gary collapsed to the station floor and lay there with a surprised expression on his heavy ugly face.

THE man in brown came instantly to his side. He had whipped a black case from his pocket. He looked deeply concerned. A crowd began to gather. The man in brown spoke authoritatively.

"Stand back! Give this man some air, I'm a doctor. He appears to have had a heart attack. Some one help me get him to my car outside. We'll take him to a hospital at once!"

A station attendant gave the required aid. Bugs Gary was carried limply to a small, compact coupé parked outside the station. A few slight dents in its sleek enamel which were carefully patched bullet holes didn't attract the attendant's attention. The man who had said he was a doctor drove swiftly away with the unconscious gangster at his side.

But he didn't go to a hospital. Instead, he drove swiftly to a garage back of a small suburban house. Once inside, he closed the garage door, and carried Bugs through a passageway to the house itself. This was empty. It was another of the Agent's hideouts, and he had accomplished the capture of Bugs Gary by a means he had often used before—the injection of a quick-acting, harmless anesthetic.

Bugs came to after awhile. Still in a dazed state, he found himself handcuffed in a chair and facing a man whose eyes had an uncanny, magnetic intentness. He was terrified at first, but the stranger soothed his fears. No harm would come to him if Bugs answered a few simple questions about his past. Because he couldn't seem to help it under the steady stare of those burning eyes, Bugs Gary did so.

The stranger listened carefully, as much, it seemed, to the tones of his voice as to his words. He made minute examination of Bugs' face and figure, asked him what sort of clothes he liked to wear, his eating preferences, and other odd, personal questions.

At the end of it, the stranger offered Bugs a drink of liquor which the gangster eagerly accepted. He finished it, licked his lips and once more dozed off into dreamless slumber. Though he didn't know it, he was due this time not to wake up for at least thirty-six hours—unless Agent "X" chose to administer a reviving stimulant...

As dusk was again falling over the city, a man, who looked for all the world like Bugs Gary, stepped out of a taxi and swaggered toward the lighted doors of the Montmorency Club. This was the infamous underworld dive whose present proprietor was Gus Sanzoni.

Evening papers had mentioned the fact that Bugs Gary had been pardoned. Whispers had run through crookdom. Bugs would surely be coming back to his old haunts.

The doorman of the Montmorency Club wasn't surprised therefore at the sight of the dapper figure in spats, checked suit and bright tie who came forward arrogantly.

"If it ain't Bugs," the doorman said. "I saw about you in the paper a half hour ago. I thought you'd be coming around to see the boys. You look like a million dollars, Bugs. They must have fed you good up in the Big House."

The man who looked like Bugs flicked ashes from his cigarette and made a fitting wisecrack. All the while he was watching the reactions of the doorman intently. Inwardly he was elated. His disguise made old acquaintances recognize him in the way he wanted. The doorman of the Montmorency Club had no inkling that this man who seemed to be Bugs Gary, was really Agent "X," famous criminal investigator, come to risk death in the headquarters of an underworld czar.

CHAPTER XI

WEBS OF DEATH

A CHECK GIRL took his hat and cane. A strident band was playing beyond the club's polished dance floor, warming up for the evening's work. Few patrons had arrived as yet. It was still too early for slummers. The food at the Montmorency wasn't inviting. It was the hectic, sinister atmosphere of the place that brought men and women from the after-theatre crowds to get a thrill by rubbing shoulders with the underworld.

But some of Sanzoni's hangers-on were in evidence. Two dapper, flat-chested men, with twisted smiles, nodded instantly as Agent "X" came through the door. They were at a table, liquor glasses before them. One got up.

"Bugs Gary himself!" he said. "We heard about you getting on the right side of the governor. Welcome to the old joint, Bugs!"

Behind his outward calm, the mind of Agent "X" was active. His pulses hammered. He knew he was in a dangerous spot. His facts on Bugs' past were brief. He didn't even know the names of these two. Any moment he might say or do something that would betray him. Then their smiles would change to snarls. Their hands would reach for guns.

He wasn't afraid of death. He had rubbed shoulders with the Grim Reaper too often. But he knew now what the strange, sinister mystery that menaced the peaceful life of the city was—knew the horror of those NP bombs. The sights and sounds of the razing of Baldwin Island had etched unforgettable memories in his mind.

He grinned expansively, advanced and shook hands with the gangster. "How are you, boy!" he said, using the accent of Bugs Gary that he had so carefully learned.

"You got your glad rags on, Bugs. You look as if you'd struck it rich in the Big House."

Agent "X" waved a bejewelled hand. "I had a little cash salted away. I thought I'd treat myself to a blow-out now that I'm back on the town."

"Come and sit down, Bugs? The drinks are on us."

A waiter came to take his order; but before the drinks arrived, a glamorous blonde woman came through the door at the end of the big room. She made straight for the table "X" was at, and one of the men beside him spoke.

"There's Goldie, now. She's spotted you right off, Bugs. You always did have a way with her!"

The two laughed significantly, eyeing "X" sharply. And a sudden sense of danger swept over him. There was something in their manner that he didn't quite understand. He had heard of Goldie La Mar, notorious night club hostess and underworld queen. But if she had been an especial intimate of Bugs, his files bore no record of it. His heart beat faster as the woman approached.

Seen closer, her glamorous beauty resolved itself into skillful make-up. Her eyes were heavily mascaraed, shadowed underneath. Her face was powdered thickly, her lips rouged into a dazzling but unnatural curve. Yet she walked with the free-swinging grace of a female panther. She was still a handsome, alluring figure of a woman, sure of herself and of her charms.

"Bugs!" she said. "Ain't this grand! It's like old times to see you back. Your pals thought of you—even when you went away. It seems a long time. How's the boy?"

"Never better. And glad to be back, Goldie," said "X."

He watched the woman sharply. Her eyes held his, lingered, then seemed to find some lack. She pouted, dropped her lids a moment. The orchestra struck up just then. The woman took a step closer, smiled disconcertingly.

"Let's see if you can still hoof it, Bugs—the way you used to. Or did you forget how to shake your dogs while you were breaking rocks?"

It was a command, not a suggestion. Goldie was already close, her powdered arm lifted to his shoulder. He encircled her waist at once, danced out on the polished floor. The woman's heady perfume was in his nostrils. Her supple body was close to his; yet he felt intuitively that he was in the presence of a dangerous being, whose smiling sleekness hid sharp, cruel claws.

Out of earshot of those at the table, Goldie La Mar spoke close to his ear in a husky drawl that held a lingering caress. "What is it,

Bugs, you ain't sore that I hitched up with Gus? You didn't think a girl like me could wait around for a mug forever? You were a good guy, Bugs, but when they railroaded you away, it looked like you was gonna stay for good. I'm a girl who likes nice clothes and things, and Gus is a good provider."

THE beating of the Agent's heart increased. For a moment he was silent, gathering his faculties. The truth came to him. He had ran full-tilt into a complication. Goldie La Mar had been Bugs Gary's moll before he went to jail. Now she was Sanzoni's. He must watch his step. Yet perhaps he could make use of the situation, find out the things he wanted to know.

"A guy forgets how to treat women when he stays in stir," he said. "You don't see 'em there. But watch me warm up if I stick around this joint. It looks like the old days, Goldie, when the boss was running the stuff and sellin' it to the suckers at fancy prices."

Goldie La Mar laughed a brittle, significant laugh. "It's better than the old days, Bugs. You'll like it. There ain't no blue-nosed mugs snooping around to spoil the fun. There's plenty of dough and the liquor's better than it used to be. A girl can drink without growing barnacles inside."

"Sanzoni's running liquor still then?"

"Hell, no! There ain't no money in that—when every soda joint has a liquor stamp."

"What is his racket?"

Goldie La Mar laughed again, mysteriously. "Never mind about that. He's got a lot of things in the fire. But whatever he does is O. K. at City Hall. I guess the guys in the old days didn't know what a wire was or how to pull it."

Agent "X" almost betrayed himself by the tenseness that crept over his body. Then, smiling down at her, he spoke slowly, casually. "Gus always did know how to grease the going, Goldie. You mean he's got the mayor on his side now?"

For a bare instant a glitter crept into the limpid sheen of Goldie La Mar's mascaraed eyes. But the Agent's bland smile disarmed her. She nodded.

"He's got protection—what I mean. The mayor eats out of his hand. And he keeps the dicks in their places. Gus is gonna be the biggest shot there is. And you can't blame a girl like me for fallin' for a guy like that, can you, Bugs?"

Agent "X" forced himself to smile again; forced himself to hide the tense excitement he felt. He was getting nearer the truth now. He spoke softly in the voice of Bugs Gary.

"I can't blame you, Goldie. That's right. You always did know how to pick 'em. Look at me! But one of these days you'll get tired of Gus and—"

Goldie shook her gleaming head coyly. "You and me can be good friends as long as Gus don't get wise," she said. "But I ain't getting tired fast of a mug that pulls in fifty grand a day."

Agent "X" swung the woman into the steps of a fast foxtrot, leaning over her a bit to hide his face from her sharp gaze. He wanted to think.

The dance ended. Agent "X" took the woman back toward the table where Bugs' two former pals still sat. They applauded loudly.

"You and Bugs make a good team, Goldie! It's too bad Gus can't dance like that, too."

Goldie put her finger to her lips and rolled her eyes. "Gus can do other things," she said mysteriously. "And you boys better watch yourselves."

The instant sobering of the two gangsters faces showed the respect in which they held Sanzoni. They assumed poker expressions, fingered their glasses.

"Better go in and see him, Bugs," said one. "He might get sore if you hang out here without letting him know."

"Yes," said Goldie, "run along, Bugs, but act decent. Gus is used to bein' treated right these days. He makes all the boys toe the mark."

"X" hesitated a moment, looking about him.

"The door at the left," said Goldie. "He's got a new hangout now. Go through the hall and up the stairs. His place is right ahead. But knock before you go in."

AGENT "X" followed her directions. He was like a man walking on glass. But the eager, questing light of battle was in his eyes. He entered the doorway at the left of the dance floor, passed through a corridor, mounted a flight of luxuriously carpeted stairs, and knocked at the door before him. A wheezing voice bade him come in.

"X" did so, opening the door and entering a chamber that was a cross between an office and an elaborately ornate den. Great leather chairs stood about. Expensive woodwork made brownish reflections under shaded lights. A period-design of table stood in the center of the floor. And behind this a man sat.

He was a big man, with rounded shoulders and a bull-like neck that hung in flabby rolls over his collar. His small eyes were sunk in pouches of flesh. His lips were moist, red spots in a pile of blubber.

"X" had seen pictures of Gus Sanzoni. This was the man; but he had put on weight obviously. Prosperity had padded his massive frame with an excess of pendulous, unwholesome fat.

He did not seem surprised to see Bugs Gary. He held out a flabby hand, smiled, and waved to a chair. But his fingers were fishily cold, and there was no friendliness in his smile or in the brittle glitter of his small eyes.

"Sit down, Bugs. The boys told me about you getting out. I figured maybe you'd turn up."

Looking at the man before him, Agent "X" felt that he was in for a battle of wits; that he was already on the mat before a relentless, masterful personality who would be difficult to trick or bulldoze.

Agent "X" smiled, met the glittering eyes of the other, all but out of sight in the flesh around them.

"Couldn't stay away," he said lightly. "A guy gets lonely for his old pals in stir."

A laugh that began as a wheeze sounded in Gus Sanzoni's throat. It rose until it was a bubbling peal of humorless mirth that filled the room.

"You like your old pals, Bugs!" he panted. "You got all dolled up just to meet 'em, eh, Bugs? You came back as quick as you could when they let you out!"

Agent "X" nodded, still smiling, but with the knowledge that the man before him was making sport of him for some reason of his own. Then suddenly Gus Sanzoni seemed to rise in his chair, tower like an unwholesome, menacing hulk; his dark eyes aglitter. He leaned forward across the table.

"Don't pull that stuff on me, Bugs," he wheezed. "Don't think you can soft-soap Gus Sanzoni. You didn't get out of the Big House for nothing. You didn't come here because you loved us."

There was silence in the room; tense silence while Agent "X" stared at the other waiting. Gus Sanzoni's fat, almost shapeless hands spread out on the table like a bloated spider's claws. The movement of his small red mouth was venomous.

"I'm onto you, Bugs. They let you out of the Big House for a purpose. You heard I'd taken Goldie. You'd heard I was playing a new racket, and you saw a chance to make some dough for yourself, and maybe square things up. Who's payin' you to be a stoolie—an' spy on me?"

Agent "X" was for a moment speechless. This was a twist he hadn't anticipated. Gus Sanzoni, far from the truth, was yet near enough to upset all of "X's" plans. His disguise had worked; but it had gotten him in as deep as though he had come as an agent of the law.

"You musta gone off your nut, Gus," he said. "I ain't no stoolie. I—"

"None of your dirty lies! I ain't got time to listen to 'em. There's only one thing I want to know. Who's the guy that got the warden to pardon you?"

"Why the governor, Gus. You know the governor has to—"

"Yeah. And who asked the governor to do it? Who's got you on his payroll as a stoolie? Answer me that!"

"You're talking crazy, Gus. You know Bugs Gary wouldn't never doublecross—"

"O. K.," said Sanzoni evilly. "You're a tight-lipped guy! They got you fixed nice! But I got ways to make mugs loosen up when I ask 'em things—and I'll make you beg for a chance to talk!"

"X" didn't see the gangster move. But a buzzer sounded faintly somewhere. It testified to the fact that there was a button under Sanzoni's foot on the floor. Instantly a door at the end of the room opened. Two flint-eyed men with sawed-off shot guns entered. Then, from the sound behind him and the faint draft of air on his neck, "X" knew that others had come in from the rear. He was surrounded, threatened with instant death if he made a move, in the stronghold of as cunning a criminal as he had ever come across.

CHAPTER XII

NIGHT PROWLERS

SLOWLY HE TURNED so that he could see both pairs who menaced him. Those at his back were the same two he had set at table with a moment before—Bugs Gary's pals. But their faces were dead pans now. Their hands gripped black automatics. They would shoot at the merest nod from Sanzoni, send a withering stream of slugs at his body. For that was the law of the underworld—obey the big shot—murder a pal in the interests of one's own career. Like the gray rats that Thaddeus Penny had mentioned, each was out for himself alone. And because Sanzoni had money, influence, they would murder callously at his behest. The gangster's harsh, wheezing chuckle sounded again. "Here are your pals, Bugs. You came to see 'em! Look 'em over! They got a welcome for you—a dose of lead. You'll be glad to talk when they start working on you. Maybe you'd rather unbutton your lip now—and tell me what I asked."

Agent "X" was silent. Whatever he said would be held against him. He couldn't tell Sanzoni what the man wanted to know. Better keep still, and wait for a possible break. But none seemed coming. Sanzoni was experienced in handling desperate, murderous men. He was taking no chances.

"If he goes for his rod, boys, give it to him where he stands. Frisk him, Regio."

A fifth man started toward "X" to disarm him. The Agent's eyes burned somberly at this. There were things on his person that must not be discovered—his strange devices that he carried, his gas gun which would give him away, make Sanzoni suspect that he was not Bugs Gary at all. Sanzoni spoke as the man Regio came forward.

"The boys will take you downstairs, Bugs! They'll work on you there. Shoot your fingers off—like they did Mike Barney's. Maybe you remember Mike! And by the time you've lost a couple of thumbs you'll be willing to talk!

A picture flashed through "X's" mind. A picture of a criminal he had once seen, Mike Barney, trying to light a cigarette with shapeless, crippled hands, a silent, bitter man, reluctant to say what sort of accident he had met with. Now "X" knew.

There was no limit to the unholy cruelty of the fat fiend before him. Sanzoni was laughing, taunting him.

"You won't be such a headliner with the janes, Bugs, when your hands look like chewed-off tree stumps. Mike Barney's gal left him when the boys got through with him. Janes is funny that way. They like pretty things—and a guy with no fingers ain't pretty."

An involuntary tensing of the Agent's muscles made the men with the guns step closer. With a curious, speculative expression in his eyes, "X" estimated the angle that the black guns were pointing. They were aiming low in true gangster fashion. A thin smile curved his lips.

At that moment he heard the brittle laugh of a woman close by, blending with Gus Sanzoni's. He looked up. Goldie La Mar stood in the doorway. Her hands were on her hips. A mocking light was in her eyes:

"You'd better have stayed in the Big House, Bugs. You came asking for trouble—and you've found it!" She turned to Gus Sanzoni "He wanted to know too much when I danced with him a while back. You've got his number O. K. He's just a dirty stoolie."

The gangster, Regio, was close to "X's" side now, reaching out to search him—and find the things that would betray "X" as a far more dangerous enemy to Sanzoni than Bugs Gary could ever be. The muzzles of the mobster killers' guns were held steady, ready to send lead at "X" if he did not submit to Regio's frisking.

An attempt to escape now seemed suicidal; yet, in the fraction of a second before Regio's hands entered his pockets, Agent "X" went into swift, death-defying action.

He lunged forward, sweeping Regio out of his path with one flailing arm. A surprised wheeze came from the lips of Sanzoni. The gunmen killers, obeying the orders their chief had given them, pressed triggers. In that brief instant when he flashed through space, bullets thudded against the Agent's body.

BUT he didn't cry out, or collapse. He hurtled straight on. His movement hadn't been a wild plunge of sheer terror, the panicky, maneuver of a fear-crazed man, as it seemed. It had been a calculated, timed action, based on the confidence of a defensive device which Agent "X" had carried when he came here. This was his special bulletproof vest—a shell of case-hardened manganese steel, with a raw silk stuffing and an outer shell of light-weight duralumin. It was worn like a vest. Once before it had saved Agent "X" from annihilation, at the hands of gangsters.[57]

It worked now. The lead from the sub-calibre machine guns missed him except for a few glancing blows. The .45 slugs from the automatics penetrated the outer duralumin shell, but flattened their noses against the inner steel.

Quick as a flash Agent "X" was on hands and knees before an empty electric wall socket near the floor.

The gangsters, thinking their salvo had mortally wounded him, and hoping to get a dying confession from his lips, held their fire now. This was what "X" had counted on. With a lightning movement, he drew something from his pocket. It was a small, curved bit of wire; a simple, but effective device that had served him well before. He thrust this into the socket terminals under the very nose of Sanzoni's mob.

There was a sputter, a flash of violet light, and every bulb in the Montmorency Club was extinguished as the fuses blew; short circuited by "X's" wire.

In the ensuing darkness Goldie La Mar screamed shrilly. Sanzoni broke into wheezing curses. The gangsters who had been posted to torture or kill Agent "X" bumped against one another and grappled fiercely.

Agent "X," crouched low, could see their silhouettes against the glow of a street light that filtered through a window. A gangster came straight toward him. Agent "X" leaped up, struck a chopping blow to the man's chin, and heard him collapse.

He sprang toward the door then. Sanzoni stepped around from behind his desk and the fist of Agent "X" flashed out to give the fat gangster a breath-jarring punch in his obese stomach.

Sanzoni collapsed gasping over his desk, and "X" sprang through a doorway into the corridor. Pandemonium had broken out in the club now. Shouts, screams, the excited cries of men and women mingled.

---

57 *AUTHOR'S NOTE: This was on the case of the "Octopus of Crime," when Agent "X," on the inside of the Union Bank & Safe Deposit Co., had been surprised by criminals of the Octopus's band. Super-calibre machine-gun bullets, fired at close range, stunned him through repeated blows on his vest, but failed to kill him.*

Straight across the big ballroom Agent "X" sped. He had verified what he had come to learn; verified the truth of Thaddeus Penny's report that these were the men who were spreading terror and death over the city. The same men that Mayor Ballantine was giving protection to. It meant that Sanzoni was the ally of the Terror.

He ran down the stairs, saw the form of the doorman coming in to see what all the excitement was about, and leaped past him into the street.

In a moment he had merged with the darkness. And the night around him seemed heavy with mystery; heavy with the sinister threat of the thing he had learned.

He went to one of his hideouts and paced the floor, facing squarely the problem he was up against. He struggled silently, as a chess player might struggle, trying to anticipate and forestall the play of his opponent.

It was obvious that the impulse sent out to raze Baldwin Island operated only that one bomb. Those other silent eggs of death lay waiting, hidden, for the awful call that would bring them to life also. That call might come on the same meter number—merely another series of dots and dashes—or it might come on an entirely different one. And where were the bombs themselves? How could he find them, now that he knew how the Terror had hidden the one on Baldwin Island and knew also the identity of the Terror's gang?

He got a city map, marked off all the strategic points where bombs would do the most damage. Yet he knew this was only guesswork. It would take days, weeks perhaps, to go over these spots—and meanwhile death and horror hung over the city. Yet if he could only find one bomb, see how the thing worked, learn the exact nature of the new explosive element, perhaps—

The Secret Agent's mind, functioning like some delicate, precise machine, hit suddenly upon a startling conclusion. He believed he had divined one move at least that the Terror might make. One move that, in the light of facts "X" had unearthed, seemed logical and inevitable. To test this belief Agent "X" stood ready to face the thunderous menace of high explosive once more.

CHAPTER XIII

HIDDEN DOOM

LATER THAT NIGHT, between the hours of two and three, Secret Agent "X" approached the Montmorency Club a second time. Sleep was out of the question for him. Restless, dynamic forces drove him on, would not let him be quiet while destruction, fear and horror threatened the community. The thought of those hidden eggs of death, silent and waiting somewhere in the dark city, was a ceaseless spur to his energies.

Since verifying the fact that Gus Sanzoni's gang was active in the crime wave now engulfing the city, Agent "X" had instructed Hobart and Bates to have their best men watch the doings of the gang.

Through both organizations, working independently, "X" had learned that most of Sanzoni's men would be out tonight, ravaging certain sections of the city in a series of bold robberies. This meant that Sanzoni's headquarters in the Montmorency Club would be comparatively deserted. It meant that the stage would be set for Agent "X" to play another surprising role.

Once again he had disguised himself, but not as Bugs Gary. His clothes were black now. His whole face had a swarthy hue. Amongst the shadows he appeared to blend with the night itself. He looked like a burglar or sneak thief once more, as he had on the night he'd gone to Mayor Ballantine's home.

He drove to within a block of the club, left his car parked, and proceeded on toward the spot where the evil Sanzoni, like a fat, poisonous spider, spread his webs of crime. But "X" knew more about the gangster now. He knew that Sanzoni, for all his evil ways, was under the sway of a greater criminal than himself; knew that he was the cat's paw that pulled the chestnuts out of the fire for the Terror. And Sanzoni, who divided his loot with the Terror, must have some way of communicating with his superior, some way of handing over the spoils of his bloody work.

This, however, wasn't the Agent's reason for returning to that place of sinister repute. He had another, more daring motive, based on the startling deduction he had made.

It was late, long after midnight, yet the orchestra in the Montmorency Club was still blaring raucously. Tipsy couples were still moving around the polished dance floor. A few late-comers were still arriving, nighthawks who made a practice of flitting from one gay dive to another.

As Agent "X" shuffled past the front of the club, somber and inconspicuous in his dark clothes, a gay foursome stepped from a limousine. Two youths in high silk hats; the girls in evening wraps, with painted, powdered faces wreathed in smiles. Slummers from uptown. Members of society, possibly, come down to rub shoulders with the city's underworld.

He heard their empty laughter as they hurried into the vestibule. Their mirth would change to gasps of fear, they would run from the place, if they knew what he knew—and suspected the thing he had come to inquire into.

He didn't go to the club's front entrance. Its tawdry, gilded portals were not meant for such as he appeared to be. The doorman, who hours before had welcomed him as Bugs Gary, would order him away now.

A grim smile twitched the Secret Agent's lips. Like a flitting shadow he moved around the side of the building, pausing at a basement doorway. This was below the level of the kitchen. Yet a dim light was burning somewhere inside. He would need all the caution at his command in the thing he planned to do.

He took his kit of special chromium tools from an inner pocket, selected those he needed, and went to work skillfully on the lock. In a moment, under the probing pressure of a small goose-necked bit of steel, it clicked back and the Agent opened the door. He found himself in what had formerly been a luxurious speakeasy. But now it was closed. Now the club had moved upstairs, screaming its tawdriness to the whole world, in renovated quarters above.

Behind the speakeasy were chambers which might contain sleeping quarters for some of Sanzoni's men. "X" did not explore these. Basing his actions on a hunch he had arrived at, he searched for and found a door that led to the building's cellar.

As he opened it, and moved down a stairway toward the dusty room beneath where a light in a wire cage burned, he heard the clanking of a shovel. He reached the foot of the stairs and crouched.

A MAN'S shadow lay like some fallen monster across the floor. It was the shadow of the janitor, fixing the furnace, keeping steam up, that revelers above might have tropic heat.

Agent "X" crept toward him swiftly, silently. When the man turned at last to put the shovel away, the black figure of "X" was directly at his elbow. A gun in "X's" hand was pointed straight at his head.

The cry that the janitor started to give was stifled utterly by the jet of gas that spurted from the gun's muzzle into his open mouth. It was harmless anesthetizing vapor that would merely keep him unconscious for a period of time. He collapsed soundlessly to the floor.

"X" gathered him up quickly, took him to the far end of the cellar room, and laid him on a pile of old burlap. Then he began the quick, shrewd search of the building's basement—which was his real purpose in coming.

For the Secret Agent's amazing deductive faculties had led him to the conclusion that one of the nitro-picrolene bombs might be hidden here.

It was a spot where a man of the Terror's ruthless, systematic character would appear to have reason for laying one of the eggs of doom. Gus Sanzoni was working for him, gathering in the loot to be divided with his master. Sanzoni was a greedy, unscrupulous criminal, a man who would turn on his boss, double-cross him if the chance came. He had not hesitated to double-cross Bugs Gary, take his girl away while he was in jail, and put him to torture when he came back.

And surely the Terror, whoever he was, would make certain that he could wipe out Sanzoni any instant he chose. What better means than concealing a bomb directly under Sanzoni's stronghold?

So certain was "X" that this deduction was right, that he had come prepared with special equipment. Besides his regular tool kit, he carried in one pocket a small leather case containing instruments as compact as they were powerful.

The bomb hidden in the brick building on Baldwin Island had given him his cue. It had been cemented in the wall, and "X" knew that the criminal mind ever works in a routine manner. The gang who laid the Terror's bombs for him would surely use the same means again.

He took a powerful flash and chisel-like scraping instrument from his pocket. With these he set to work. He began systematically at the farthest end of the cellar room. The beam of his light was like a round probing eye. It crept along the soot-blackened walls from floor to ceiling. Again and again at any spot that even slightly aroused his suspicions, he scraped with his edged tool.

Slowly he progressed forward till he had covered one side of the cellar. He went to another, searched over every inch of that without results. A third side followed, and still Agent "X" was persistent, still undiscouraged.

Several times he came to places on the plaster that stirred his interest. Either the soot didn't seem quite as black or something about the surface held his attention. At such times he took a small watchlike instrument from his pocket. It had a tiny needle on its face, slender as a hair. It was a delicate magnetic galvanometer, fashioned to detect minute electric currents produced by the presence of metals.

He pressed this against the suspicious spots, watched the needle eagerly. Once it swung sharply, making his pulse quicken. But a brief scratching on the surface exposed a hidden water pipe.

He went on to the cellar's fourth side, and here he found a small door, held fast with a padlock. This he undid easily. Inside was a square, cool wine cellar, with hundreds of bottles stored away in straw-filled bins. Here was the wine that trickled down the thirsty throats of the criminals and slummers in the gay rooms overhead.

The Agent's eyes gleamed. This room was locked, hidden away from ordinary prying eyes. It was a likely spot to look. He began searching the walls quickly, and almost at once he found a place where the layer of accumulated dust seemed a shade too thick.

To his eager, observant eyes it appeared that this dust had been sprinkled there. His sharp tool scraped it loose. He found that the plaster beneath was whiter, fresher—found that it was a spot like that on the wall of the room on Baldwin Island, where he and Betty Dale had faced awful death.

And when he touched the galvanometer against this spot, the tiny hair-like needle swung instantly upward and remained like a trembling finger of warning. Tense with eagerness, knowing that he might be close to a bomb as terrible as any existing in the world, Agent "X" paused a moment.

LISTENING, he could hear, faint and far away, the throbbing

pulse of the dance orchestra, hear the vibration of moving feet. Men and women were dancing over a veritable hell that they did not even suspect—dancing on Death itself, that lay silent and hidden in that dark cellar.

The Secret Agent set to work quickly. There was an electric bulb above him. He unscrewed it, put a plug in with a long cord attached, and inserted this plug into the handle of one of the tools he had brought. A miniature electric motor, sealed in a sound-proof shell, began to whirl. A cutting point with a rubber cap around it spun at the drill's end. Agent "X" pressed this and the rubber deadened sound against the wall at the fatal spot. This was one of the devices with which he had come prepared, anticipating that he would have to cut through cement.

His sharp, diamond-set drill ate the concrete away. But in spite of all his precautions, it made a faint whining sound—a sound that he knew might reach other ears and attract attention. Because of this he was alert, listening and watching.

But when his drill broke through into a space behind the cement facing of the wall, he forgot all else in his eagerness to find what lay there. He inserted a different blade in his drilling device, a cylindrical type saw, and cut horizontally and vertically, until he could lift a square section of cement out. Then his lips became grim with intensity.

For a sinister metal object rested inside. It was shaped almost like a small fire extinguisher. But it was painted a dull gray, and "X" knew that those strange looking gadgets on the top were for no such humane purpose as the extinguishing of flames.

This was an instrument of hideous destruction, placed there to kindle a holocaust of death and horror such as the city had never known. Its gray metal sides gave no inkling of the deadly stuff it contained. The nature of the new explosive element was unknown to Agent "X," but the mechanics of radio-control were familiar. Such control had been used to guide battleships, airplanes, tanks and cars. Most of the governments of the earth were secretly experimenting with it. It would play a startling part if there came another war. "X" had studied many of the devices already perfected.

New and terrible as the detonating medium of this super-bomb was, the radio-impulse device was built along recognized lines. A few moments of investigation, as he held the terrible engine of death in his lap, convinced him of this.

He took out a small screwdriver, turned it slowly on the bomb's head, knowing that if he made a slip it would spell oblivion for himself and a thousand others. But he made no slip. He removed two screws which permitted the dust-proof cover cap to slip off. Beneath this was the radio-impulse mechanism, the clockwork gear, already wound, to be set in motion by intermittent dots and dashes on a certain wave length.

With steady hands, calmly as though this were nothing more than an old alarm clock he was tinkering with, Secret Agent "X" took a bit of copper from his pocket, and with this wired the clockwork wheels so that they could not turn. The call of death might come now, unseen and sinister in the air. The Terror might try to bring this egg of doom to life, as he had the other—but this was one bomb that would not obey the invisible impulses.

Agent "X" quickly slipped the metal shell back into place, twisting the screws into it to hold it fast. And, as he did so, breath abruptly hissed through suddenly clenched teeth. His hands froze around the gray surface of the deadly bomb. The muscles of his body snapped into rigidity. His eyes flashed sidewise and remained fastened on the oblong of the door.

For, so intent had he been on not making a slip with the lethal bomb, that he had momentarily relaxed his vigilance, neglected to watch and listen. And now the door of the small wine cellar had darkened. Now four ugly, intent faces were framed in it—men of Gus Sanzoni's gang. And in their hands were black automatics, the sinister, round muzzles pointing straight at the Secret Agent's heart.

CHAPTER XIV

SKY PERIL

A SECOND OF tense silence passed before one of the gangsters spoke.

"Stand up, guy—raise your mitts—and don't go for a gat!" he said.

The gesture of a single gun muzzle emphasized the order. Agent "X" obeyed immediately. His hands went up above his head—but they were not empty. They carried the gray cylinder of the bomb with them.

A thin smile curved his lips. His flashing, penetrating eyes held a sardonic light. He remained quiet, staring at the four who had surprised him, and something about his manner held them taut.

The man who had given the order to lift his hands spoke again. "What in hell are you doin' here? You must want a drink bad to steal from Gus Sanzoni! Put that bottle down—easy so you don't break it—and come out. We'll teach you it don't pay to break into this joint."

The Agent spoke quietly then. The sardonic hint was in his voice now. That, and his coolly precise speech, coming from the unkempt figure he presented, made the gangsters hunch forward.

"This isn't a bottle I'm holding. Look again, pal, and see what you make of it!"

The man who seemed to be the leader of the group gave a growling exclamation. "Here, gimme that flash," he said to a man beside him. He grabbed the proffered light, clicked it on and focused its beam on the thing "X" held. His hard, brutal face twisted into lines of puzzlement, and there was a shade of uneasiness in his eyes.

"What in blazes is it? Looks like an oxygen tank—the kind they use on guys that do flop acts at fires."

The Agent's laughter sounded then, humorless, harsh, seeming

The small, cankerlike flame was eating at his 'chute. The ground was five hundred feet below.

to mock his questioner. "Wrong again, pal. It isn't an oxygen tank—and if you don't watch yourselves and go easy you'll all be blown to hell."

Curses greeted this remark, and hoots of derision. "The guy's nuts!" one gunman said. "Come on, boys, let's give 'im the bum's rush. T'row 'im out of here!"

"A dose of lead will fix 'im better," said another.

The leader stood uncertainly, eyes focused on "X" and on that strange thing he held above his head. The Agent spoke again, driving home his point, for he saw that if they were not checked some move on the part of these men within the next few seconds might spell utter catastrophe.

"I'm handing it to you straight," he said quietly, using language that they would understand. "This is a bomb I've got—a pineapple—but one of the hottest numbers you've ever seen. It's the same kind that knocked Baldwin Island off the map this evening. But it's twice as big."

At mention of the explosion on Baldwin Island, fear came into the leader's eyes. News of the thing had reached the underworld. The man spoke hoarsely.

"Lay off him, boys, he's a nut all right; but maybe he's telling the truth. We don't want no trouble here." He took several steps toward the Agent, his gun still centered upon him.

"Now, fella, hand over that pill you got and don't make any fuss about it. You don't want to get drilled even if you are cracked."

The Agent gave a low chuckle of laughter again. The sound was as harshly abrupt as the crack of a whip.

"Turn that gun the other way! If you shoot—this bomb will drop. One bump—and there won't be enough left of you or this building to scrape up. Stand clear—all of you—or you'll get rubbed out."

The Agent moved his right hand, made motions with his fingers close to the round top of the bomb. He seemed to be twisting a screw head.

"I'll start the fuse," he snapped, "if you don't stand dear!"

One of the gangsters, a hophead judging by his chalk-white complexion, made a sudden whimpering sound.

"Geez! Lay off him! Leave the guy alone! A pal of mine was down by the river last night and seen the island go up in smoke. He told me about it—an' if that's the kind of apple that done it I don't wanna fool wit it."

AGENT "X" took the initiative. He moved forward with a menacing motion, and the gangsters stepped back. He was only partially bluffing. He couldn't start the fuse by turning a screw, but, for all he knew, even a slight jar might serve to detonate it. He was using it as a means of escape, playing a deadly game with these hirelings of Sanzoni's.

The leader spoke sharply to one of his men. "Go up and get the big boss," he said. "Ask him to come down here. Tell him there's a crazy guy threatening to blow the place up."

They had backed out into the main part of the cellar now. They faced Agent "X" as he emerged from the wine room.

He saw that these men had no inkling of the truth. They didn't know the nature of the protection that a master criminal had given their boss, Gus Sanzoni.

A moment later there was a creaking on the stairs, then a wheezing sound as the fat criminal, Gus Sanzoni, came down into the cellar. His small, piggish eyes were bright as he spoke in an unctuous, oily tone, thinking evidently that "X" was some half-mad criminal with a new sort of racket.

"Come on now, fella," he said smoothly. "I'll pay you big to take that thing outta here. You're a smart fella, and I like smart guys. You've got a good racket, and I'm willing to come across. Just take that thing out easy, I got guests upstairs." "X" intercepted a flashing signal from fat Sanzoni's eyes. He saw two of the gangsters edging slowly nearer, ready to make a sudden lunge while Sanzoni talked. They thought "X" was some kind of a crazy terrorist. They planned to take the bomb away from him by guile.

"X" spoke again quickly, staring Sanzoni straight in the face. "No tricks," he said harshly, "or none of you will live. This thing can't be fooled with—and I didn't bring it in. It was here already—and has been here for days. Look in your wine cellar. It was sealed in the wall there. I just took it out."

More jeers came, but Gus Sanzoni looked startled.

"Go and see," he wheezed. "You, José, find out if the guy's telling the truth."

A swarthy gangster detached himself from the group and disappeared into the wine cellar that "X" had so lately left. He came back big eyed, and nodded.

"It's God's truth, boss! There's a hole in the wall—a place for that thing to roost in. The cement's been cut away. That bomb must have been there—and this guy took it out."

Sudden pastiness spread over Sanzoni's fat face. His breath seemed to choke him, wheeze in his throat.

"Some one," he gasped, "planted it there—to kill me!" he clenched his big hands, screamed sudden orders. "Search—you fools! There may be others!" His eyes glinted with cunning as he stared at "X."

"You must be a detective," he went on. "You must have got wind of the fact that that thing was there."

There was a moment of silence, then the Agent answered slowly, each syllable falling dramatically from his lips.

"I am Secret Agent 'X,'" he said.

He had reason for letting Gus Sanzoni and his men know who he was. He was gambling with death—staking his wits against the Grim Reaper, not to preserve his own life—but hoping to save the lives of others.

For he recalled vividly the words of the document found in Ballantine's safe. "Any undercover attempt to thwart my plans will only result in catastrophe." The Secret Agent had to think of those thousands who would be brought close to the brink of eternity when the Terror learned that some one was after him. If the Terror suspected the law was on his trail, he might make good his threat—send out the impulse that would plunge the city into the vortex of bloody horror.

But if he understood it wasn't the law, but Secret Agent "X," a man supposedly a desperate criminal like himself, and whom the police had many times tried to capture and imprison, he would take other means. He would try assuredly to kill the Agent as a dangerous rival. But he would see the uselessness of destroying the city's thousands.

THAT was the Secret Agent's mad gamble. Fear for once lay cold against his heart. Fear for the citizens who did not know their danger. Fear that he was playing too reckless a game. What if the Terror should suspect? But he could not think of that— He turned almost fiercely on Sanzoni.

The fat gangster's jaw had dropped at mention of the dread name of Agent "X." The eyes of his men had grown wide. Rumors, whispered along the byways of the underworld, had reached their ears. The pall of impenetrable mystery that lay over the Secret Agent's activities made his character fearsome, awe-inspiring. That fear whitened the face of Sanzoni now. He obviously believed himself in the presence of an arch-criminal, pitiless, enigmatic, inhuman. He tried to speak, but only a wheeze came from his bloodless lips.

One fat hand ineffectually pawed the air.

Agent "X" took advantage of the momentary sensation his disclosure had made. He made an abrupt movement, so quick that none in that room could follow it. His right hand, clutching the deadly bomb, swung down under his arm. His left snapped forward, the gas gun appearing as though by magic in his fingers—its muzzle pressed against the fat belly of Sanzoni.

"Now," he snapped, "you will come with me! I want to talk to you—and if any of your men shoot or try to interfere, two things will happen. First, I'll pull the trigger of this gun. Second, this bomb will drop—and blow you to pieces."

Gus Sanzoni was quaking now. Prosperity had made him soft. Fear had a leechlike hold upon him. He found his voice at last.

"Keep away, boys," he said weakly. "I'll see what—what this man wants. Stand clear of the stairs."

With Sanzoni mounting ahead of him, "X's" gun at his back, the Agent guided the gangster from the cellar and took the bomb with him.

"Out that door," he commanded. "Quick!"

With gangsters trailing them at a respectful distance, Agent "X" prodded Sanzoni along the dark street to his parked car. He took a roundabout route, away from the lighted entrance of the building.

"Get in," he ordered when they reached the car.

For a moment Sanzoni hesitated. A jab of the gun made him jump. "X" threw the car into gear and shot away from the curb, the gun still in his hand. Driving swiftly through the night-shrouded streets, he turned and stared at the fat criminal. There was a look of flashing magnetic power in the Agent's eyes now that evil-doers found hard to meet. Backed by the steady pressure of the gun, it menaced Gus Sanzoni, while the Agent asked a question.

"Who is the man who gives you protection, Sanzoni?"

The gangster's lower jaw dropped. He swayed a little in the seat.

"I—" his breath came to a wheezing end. He began again. "I—can't—tell—you!"

"No!" There was harsh derision in the Agent's tone. "I'll answer that question myself then. The mayor of this city hands it out. Isn't that right?"

Another jab of the gun followed "X's" words. The fat gangster's silence and widening eyes gave mute confirmation to what "X" had said.

"And you've been pulling a lot of fast ones lately, Sanzoni," went on the Agent. "Your men have been having it all their own way, without police interference. Who's the fellow you divvy up with—that's what I want to know? Come on, tell me, or I'll pull the trigger of this gat—and dump you out in a ditch."

This was the kind of talk Sanzoni understood. He had left riddled sodden corpses lying in ditches himself in his time. He saw violent death staring him in the face, and a trembling seized his body. He clenched and unclenched his fat hands.

"I—I don't know," he wheezed. "Honest, I never seen the guy. I just get orders—by telephone—where to leave the stuff. I leave it where he says. He's got the mayor sewed up somehow. The bulls have been laying off my men like you say."

The Agent's face was masklike for a moment. An uncanny judge of human nature, he knew that Sanzoni was telling the truth. This was what he had half expected. This was what the document in Ballantine's safe had led him to believe. Sanzoni himself didn't know who the Terror was. "X" didn't speak again. His purpose in forcing Sanzoni to come along with him had not been merely to question the man.

His gas gun flashed up now, quick as a striking snake. The Agent fired full into the fat gangster's face, cutting off the scream that bubbled to Sanzoni's lips. Sanzoni tumbled side-wise against the side of the car, inert as a bag of meal.

Making sure he was not being pursued, Agent "X" drove quickly to the same garage where a few hours before he had taken Bugs Gary. The ex-convict, formerly a Sanzoni man, was still his prisoner, in the house behind the garage. Now "X" carried the unconscious form of the gangster chief into the same house.

HE got out a hypo needle, gave Sanzoni an injection of anesthetic drug, which would insure his remaining out for at least twenty-four hours, unless the Agent chose to wake him with a counteracting stimulant.

Then "X" left the hideout, got into his car again, and drove away as swiftly as he had come. Time was a precious thing. Time—that Death might be held at bay.

Agent "X" looked down at the gray bomb now lying on the seat beside him. He was carrying one of death's very germs through the night. He would take it somewhere, examine it carefully, make it yield whatever secrets it held. It might hold some clue to the Terror's identity. It was a bet that must not be overlooked.

But in any examination there was danger that it might explode. For this reason he must take it far from the city's teeming population, far from all human habitation. And speed was imperative. The Terror might try to bring things to some swift and ghastly climax.

Hunched over the wheel, knuckles white on its black rim, Agent "X" sped through the night. He had a definite objective now, a definite line of action.

He stopped at another hideout farther up town to make a quick change of disguise. When he emerged, he was no longer a nondescript, unshaven night prowler. He was a sandy-haired, blunt-featured young man, dressed in an ordinary business suit. He was A. J. Martin, newspaper man, connected with a large syndicate. But the deadly bomb lay on the auto seat beside him. The look of strained intensity still showed in the Agent's eyes.

He raced along a wide avenue in the suburbs, drew up at last before a high iron gate with a broad field and low buildings beyond it. With the bomb under his arm, wrapped now in an old cloth, Agent "X" strode to the gate.

A sleepy watchman was on duty. He peered, nodded. "H'yer, Mr. Martin, gettin' an early start this mornin'?"

The Agent merely grunted as he walked toward one of the airplane hangars. Far across the field, lights showed. A truck had come to a standstill. A fast, sturdy mail plane was getting ready to take off for the west.

SETTING the bomb down, Agent "X" unlocked and rolled back the hangar doors. He slipped into a teddy-bear flying suit which he took from a locker, adjusted a suede helmet on his head, slipped goggles over his forehead, ready to be snapped down.

Then he rolled out the small, compact plane that squatted in the hangar like some caged bird. It was swift, powerful, with the staggered wings, low camber and sweepback of any Army ship. It was the Secret Agent's famous *Blue Comet*.[58]

A mechanic shuffled out from the operations office; but Agent "X" had the bomb stowed away, the plane on the deadline and the motor warming before the man arrived.

---

58   AUTHOR'S NOTE: *This ship has aided him in some of his most desperate battles with organized crime. In it he toured the country, landing on airport after airport when he was combating the spread of a vicious secret society known as the DOACs. A skillful pilot, Agent "X" is at home in any plane, but the "Blue Comet" is his own favorite sky craft.*

Five minutes later he took off, sweeping up into the still black sky, carrying in the cockpit with him the metal cylinder that was the concentrated essence of Doom.

He climbed in short, swift spirals till the airport was far below, then headed the cowled nose of his plane northward, toward a lonely mountain field he knew. A rough log building stood there, with tools in it, and some laboratory equipment. Agent "X" had used it before to examine bombs and deadly gases. If any accident should occur, only one life would be wiped out—his own.

He planned to make a swift, thorough examination of the bomb, then return to battle with the Terror, perhaps with knowledge that would aid him in the one-sided fight.

But, with suburban lights still streaking below, some airman's instinct warned "X" to look up. His goggled and helmeted head turned. He stared back along the plane's sleek fuselage, and suddenly his hand tensed on the control stick.

A tiny, ghostly flame had appeared in the blackness above and to the rear. It was not a star; not a signal light on another ship. It was the feather of flame from the exhaust stack of a plane that he could not see. He closed his own throttle a moment, heard the whine of a racing motor.

Then a cry came from the Agent's lips. For, as though the night had drawn itself together, into a vicious, mailed fist, something lashed down out of the blackness. Another flame sprang into sight now. It was greenish, flickering—and above the whine of the unseen motor he heard the staccato reports of a machine gun in action.

He knew in that instant that death was close. The other ship was above and behind. The silhouette of his *Blue Comet* could be seen against the ground lights. His own exhaust plume was visible also. And, with the crackling abruptness of a lightning bolt, the murderous attack came. Only the Agent's quick thrust of the stick saved him from instant annihilation under the first deadly burst.

Bullets crackled through the *Blue Comet's* orange wings. The Agent sideslipped away—but the brief, erratic flutter of the control in his hand conveyed a message of sinister warning. One of his ailerons had been struck. He was already crippled—with a murderer striking for his life.

CHAPTER XV

THE PLUNGE

AT THE MOMENT "X" sensed his ship had been hit, he thought of the bomb. The deadly cylinder was tucked under his seat. It was wedged so as not to fall out—but any instant now it might explode.

If one of those ripping slugs so much as struck it a glancing blow, swift destruction would blast the night. Hours spent over war-torn fields in France years ago had taught Agent "X" all the tactics of aerial battle. As a youthful officer in Allied military intelligence, he had seen service on land, on sea and in the air. For the secret mysterious work of espionage knew no limitations, no frontiers. Only the picked few were chosen. Only the incredibly resourceful and daring survived.

The Agent did not attempt to dive away from that probing stream of lead. To do so would have been to court instant death. He drew the stick back into his lap, shot up in a screaming, hurtling zoom, with the thunderous power of the radial lifting his ship at elevator speed. Then he thrust the control to the left side of the pit as the plane came on its back, attempting a quick wing-over. But that crippled, damaged aileron played him false.

As though a giant steel cable had jerked it, the plane twisted around. It remained on its back, then side-slipped sickeningly. The next instant, as the attacking ship flashed by overhead, it threatened to go into a deadly flat spin.

Agent "X" eased it out gently, adjusting himself to the unequal aileron surface. For a moment the bullets were forgotten. His fight was with the treacherous unstable medium of the air itself—and with a ship that would not obey her controls.

Dread clutched at his heart, dread that he might plunge down into those populous suburbs. Human beings were sleeping down there. Men and women, children and little babies. If his plane, freighted with that sinister egg of death struck, peaceful well-cared-for homes would be transformed into charnel houses.

The killer above him was not considering that. In his savage desire to slay the being who was drawing close to his secrets, he was willing that hundreds of others should die. The Terror had said that his spies were ever watchful. One of them must have reported the theft of the bomb from Sanzoni's headquarters. Perhaps he had men planted among the fat mobster's own gang.

And now the attacking plane had turned, and leaden slugs were coming again. These were tracers. "X" could see their flaming paths. They testified to the flying murderer's efficiency. And he was handling his guns like an accomplished air fighter. Could this be the Terror himself, or was it merely another hireling, a paid gunman of the air?

"X" did not know. White-lipped, blazing-eyed, he was fighting to hold death at bay. By piloting with the stick at an angle, using the full surface of the partially destroyed aileron to hold the wing up, he was accomplishing the seemingly impossible—flying level And this time he side-slipped away, letting the ship fall off on the good wing, and straightening out when the danger was momentarily passed. If he had not been crippled, he could have outflown and out-maneuvered this other pilot, though in sheer, straightaway speed, the attacking ship seemed as swift as the *Blue Comet*. In a moment Agent "X" saw why.

A screaming power dive carried the murder ship below him. He got a glimpse of its silhouette against a body of water, a suburban lake.

His airman's eye identified it at once. It was a seaplane; stubby winged, unbelievably swift. Planes of this type were the fastest in existence, capable of speeds that won all records for velocity. Its twin pontoons were slim as knife blades. Its fuselage was streamlined like a torpedo. He was up against a terror of the air.

It came screaming up at him like some monster hornet with the bright lash of its sting playing an evil spray of fire. The other pilot planned to rake his underside now. That, too, was a fighting maneuver. Agent "X" had seen great German Gothas turned into flaming funeral pyres by the swift upward thrust of a pursuit ship, during the War.

He waited, seeming to hang on slack controls for an instant, then side-slipped again, as the bullets came close. Compared to him, the pilot of the attacking snip was a rank amateur—for all his masterly equipment. But the Agent's shattered aileron was the hazard that made the outcome unpredictable. It seemed to be getting worse, as fabric and cracked metal worked loose.

For all his skilled touch on the controls, the *Blue Comet* was flying like a wounded bird. As he slipped this time, the ship would not straighten out immediately. And, when it did, its cowled nose dropped and it fell into a screaming spin that made black sky and lighted ground blend into a mad, dizzy jumble.

THE Agent fought desperately, sweat oozing out under the clamping curve of his helmet. Twice he stopped the corkscrew turns, sent the ship into a long glide, only to have it spin again. The third time he half rose in the cockpit, leaning far out over the padded coaming, adding his weight to the slender balance of the controls. The ship dived, leveled, and began a long climb.

Savagely, as though sensing that victory was close at hand, the other ship banked and came on. The Secret Agent pressed the *Blue Comet's* throttle forward to the quadrant stop, gave the blasting cylinders of his radial the last drop of gas they could take. The pull drone of the steel prop as it bit into the air rose to a deafening scream. The slanted orange wings rocketed the plane skyward.

But the other ship still had the advantage of altitude. And its hurtling climb was equal to the *Blue Comet's*. But Agent "X" had a plan. If the blind god of Chance favored him, if those raking bullets did not strike him or the bomb, he might yet escape the flying killer by reaching altitudes that the seaplane could not attain. For wing surface must count, given equal horsepower. And he believed his own wings were at least a foot broader.

Yet the hopelessness of his scheme was soon brought home. A steel-jacketed bullet glanced against a flat flying wire with a mocking spang. He presented too good a target. The man in the seaplane could not fly, but he could shoot. And the muzzles of his twin synchronized guns would accomplish what his hand on the controls might not. Those tracers made it too easy for him to point the nose of his ship at the crippled, helpless *Blue Comet*.

With a tug at his heart, Agent "X" made a swift decision. There was one last chance to save himself and the precious bomb—and to save those on the ground below from awful death. If he threw the bomb overboard, or left it in the plane with him dead or wounded at the controls—the result would be the same. An explosion that would surely wipe out other lives when the terrible engine of death struck. Yet if he sacrificed his plane, jumped now, taking the bomb with him—he might win his fearful game with death.

That was the final plan that Agent "X" had evolved. To make use of his seat-pack parachute, hold the bomb in a dizzy plunge earthward. To let the faithful *Blue Comet* crash pilotless, hoping that it would miss human habitation. Even if it struck, the disaster would not be as great as though the bomb were in it.

He braced the control stick with his knee, reached down and drew the gray cylinder from under his seat. Bullets slashed close around him, as though the fiend in the seaplane sensed some trickery, and was making desperately certain that his blood lust were not cheated. One of the crystal, gleaming dials on the *Blue Comet's* instrument panel, a Sperry horizon indicator of latest design, smashed into a myriad needle-sharp particles that stung the Agent's face. The engine gave a sobbing cough as a fuel gauge went next.

Bleak-eyed, holding the bomb beneath his right arm, his hand clamped around it, Agent "X" swung a leg over the ship's side. Never had he so hated to sacrifice a piece of inanimate mechanism. The swift *Blue Comet* had been like a symbol of his power and vengeance over the black forces of crime. Its destruction seemed an omen of his own inescapable defeat. But if in sacrificing it he helped to bring about the Terror's downfall, then the valiant ship would have been lost in a human and precious cause.

The weight of his body unbalanced the crippled plane. It turned, hurled him out—and the next instant Agent "X" was plunging earthward through the still dark sky.

One thing alone was fixed in his mind as his body dropped like a stone through space. The bomb! The deadly cylinder that his stiff arm and clawlike fingers clutched. He had made chute jumps before. The first, years ago over a field near Charlrois, when the high tide of the German advance was engulfing all Belgium in a red wave of fear. And when Agent "X," as a brilliant Intelligence operative, was being dropped into enemy-held territory. Many other jumps had followed in the intervening years. But never had he gone overside with such an engine of death in his grasp.

He made a delayed jump now, did not pull the ripcord till he had fallen a thousand feet below the spot where he had left the *Blue Comet's* cockpit. That was his only chance of escaping leaden death. For he knew the killer would not stop at blasting him from his ship. Guessing his daring maneuver perhaps, the man above, who knew no mercy, would try to complete his work.

Not till the ground with its sparkling lights came dangerously close did Agent "X" reach for the slender wire. Then he tugged it calmly, surely, and felt the harness jerk about his body blisteringly as the pilot chute leaped out and the big envelope of the chute itself blossomed.

His clutch on the bomb was vise-like. The strange silence of his slower descent was as though he had been whisked into another world. But, listening, he could hear the motor of the seaplane, and it seemed to him that the other ship had turned and was swooping down. The ground was only eight hundred feet below him. But he knew that in the next few minutes relentless death would be on his heels again.

CHAPTER XVI

SINISTER CLUE

IT CAME EVEN before he had reckoned. The seaplane was in a power dive. His airman's ears told him that. The ship was hurtling down out of the night straight toward his opened chute. The white spread of it must be faintly visible even in the darkness—presenting a perfect target.

He waited till the engine's roar was echoing almost in his ears—waited till something zipped close beside him in the darkness. It was a tracer he knew. The acrid smell of the phosphorous was in his nostrils.

Then his left hand tugged at the parachute's shroud lines. He gathered them in expertly, spilled air out of the great, white umbrella—and the chute fell off on that side, rocked dizzily and plunged a good hundred feet lower.

The seaplane came around in a snarling bank. He was surprised at the quickness of the maneuver. Its guns were chattering again as his fingers dug into the shrouds. The ground was only six hundred feet down now. The flying killer was desperate to get him. He heard a sound that brought a coldness to his heart. It was the spat of a bullet against the top of his chute. He looked up. A dull glow showed. An incendiary tracer had gone through the fabric, left a burning ring. Here was death in a new guise!

With hands taut as talons the Secret Agent gathered in the shrouds away from the side where the burning spot appeared. He tugged fiercely; let the big envelope sag away, hoping to blow the fire out. But the wind blast was not great enough. It only fanned the slow flame—and Agent "X" knew that he was poised on the very brink of eternity. The small, cankerlike flame festered in his chute. The ground five hundred feet below. The bomb under his arm—and the bullets of the killer above seeking to do still more damage. He must not drop too fast—lest the shock of landing set off the death cylinder he carried. Yet he could not risk another bullet in the fabric of his chute. One more, and the wind that spilled from the holes would increase his velocity to such an extent that the bomb would surely explode when he hit.

Now, before the greedy flame had grown too great, he must stake everything—win or lose.

The plane was coming for him, its guns chattering madly. It had swooped lower, its pilot anticipating another hundred-foot drop on the part of "X". But the Agent gathered in the shroud lines now and clutched them tightly, cutting the chute's surface in half, falling away crazily—pitching downward to what seemed inevitable destruction. But "X" was watching the ground, figuring his odds as calmly as though this were some pleasant outdoor sport he were indulging in.

The pilot of the death ship, thinking evidently that the chute had been destroyed, not supposing that any man would take such chances purposely, held his fire.

Night wind was sweeping the chute toward a lighted avenue. The slender lines of telegraph wires showed. A vacant field was beyond them, with dark shrubbery at its farther edge. There were houses all around, and lights were appearing in them, as sleepers, wakened by the machine-gun fire, got up to see what it was.

Agent "X" held his breath. He was falling at a terrible speed. The telegraph wires were directly below now. Tangled in them, he would not be able to retain his hold on the bomb. It would fall to the hard ground—and that would be the end, for himself and a hundred others in the suburban houses around.

He released the shroud lines then—played his last card, let the chute billow out again. For a second his speed was unabated—and wind whistled through the rent where the sullen phosphorous flame still burned. But the spread of the fabric was still great enough to act as a partial cushion. His calculation had been uncanny. His earthward velocity decreased. The wind carried him over the gleaming wires. The dark turf of the field beyond swept up.

And now "X" got ready for the greatest ordeal of all—the shock when he struck with the added weight of the bomb. He drew his legs up under him, bent his knees to act as springs, pressed the metal cylinder against his middle and doubled up over it, both arms around it as though it had been a football. And the next instant he hit!

It was a moment when all existence seemed to hang suspended; a nightmarish second that he was never to forget. For the wind pulled him off his balance, dragged him over the hard, frozen ground, and the shocks were like some malicious fiend striking out deliberately for the bomb.

"X" ROLLED over on his back, took the full force of the blows against his body, protecting the bomb with his own flesh. And, when the chute caught and stopped at last in the shrubbery at the field's end, he lay dazed for a moment.

Then in the blackness above him he heard the sinister drone of the seaplane again. And it brought him to his senses like the voice of doom. He set the bomb down, drew a knife from his pocket and slashed himself free of the chute harness.

The next instant, as a dark shape hurtled down out of the night, he was sprinting toward the grove of trees, plunging in amongst greenbriar and dwarf cedars as bullets sought to destroy him.

But he knew he could not be seen now. He held the bomb safely, raced deeper into the woods, and the slashing stream of lead that clipped branches and spatted against the ground, swung away. Agent "X" was safe.

But he did not think of that. His desperate, daring work had made him slur over such contrasts. Safety—danger, came in too swift rotation. He only knew there was work to be done, an unheard-of menace to be battled. More than ever speed was imperative. For the Terror, learning how "X" had struggled to preserve the bomb, might suspect that he had some deeper motive than desire to chisel in on Gus Sanzoni's racket. And it was apparent, from the air attack on "X," that the Terror's spies were everywhere; that he had secret knowledge of the underworld.

The Agent got out of his flying suit, wrapped it around the deadly cylinder. He paused suddenly. From far off there came a jarring crash—then silence.

That would be his faithful *Blue Comet*, passing to destruction. It was nothing but a tangled piece of wreckage now. He only hoped that no house or building had been in its path. He could not fly to his mountain laboratory in it. There wasn't time to charter another ship. He was far from an air field.

He emerged from the woods, saw a small, suburban village ahead. It was late, long after midnight. The narrow streets were empty, the houses dark. But a few parked cars stood about, their owners too poor or too niggardly to rent garage space.

The Secret Agent moved quickly toward one. He could not dally with convention. In his battles with crime he used whatever means came to hand, when emergency pressed close. He would borrow a vehicle now, settle with its owner later if there was any loss. Those who unknowingly aided the Secret Agent always received double the value of the service rendered.

One of the cars was a common standard make. A key on the Agent's ring, adjustable to any lock tumblers of a certain size, opened the door and started the ignition. In a moment he was driving away into the open country, with the deadly bomb beside him.

He located what appeared to be a deserted farm, judging by the condition of the buildings, and drove his borrowed car into an old barn. Here he turned up a box and laid the bomb on it.

Using the car's headlights as laboratory lamps he spread out the compact portable tools that had been hidden in his pockets and strapped to his body during the chute jump. There were others that he would have liked to have but with these he had often before accomplished seeming miracles. There were files, a pair of clippers, screwdrivers, a hacksaw, and the goose-necked and pivoted bits of metal with which he opened locks. These would have to do in the strange task before him.

Quietly, calmly, he set to work, removing the bomb's dust cap again, baring the intricate radio-impulse mechanism. A sudden horror filled him as he looked at it. What if the Terror should send out the fatal dots and dashes on a wave-length of nineteen meters just to blast him into eternity? This bomb would not explode, but eleven others might. He would be safe—but a whole city might be bathed in blood and death. For he had figured that all twelve of the hidden bombs must be sensitive to the same impulse.

His fingers trembled slightly as he began to disassemble the ghastly infernal machine. But soon they steadied. Here was work that called for the utmost care and caution. He located the bomb's fuse and a tiny gunlike hammer which could be liberated by clockwork to descend on the detonating cap. He breathed easier when both had been removed.

He examined each piece that he took out, made brief but precise notes on a piece of paper. A micrometer gauge, accurate to the thousandth of an inch, gave him fractional measurements.

He viewed the inner casing of the bomb. It had been made to fit a thirty-seven millimeter shell, such as are used in the new aerial war cannon. The criminal genius who had devised the bomb had merely adapted it for a still more terrible use. And Agent "X" bent forward suddenly. For at the bottom of the case was a manufacturer's mark, stamped into the metal.

The Agent focused a double-lensed magnifier upon it. It was the registered design of an American shell maker—the Schofield Arms Company, a small munitions concern which had prospered recently on orders for light arms and small caliber aerial cannon received from several Balkan States.

The mark itself did not excite "X." He had seen it before during an investigation into the world munitions' traffic, when he had collected data on the giant Skoda works, on the Vickers plants in England, and on a half dozen other European and United States concerns.

What did excite him was a fact stored away in his own memory. For he knew that the Schofield Arms Company was controlled by American interests, American investors, and foremost among them was a man the Agent had talked to only a few days before. This was Harrigan—member of the Bankers' Club and close associate of Mayor Ballantine—who had gone out to interview Ballantine on Monte Sutton's yacht, and had later been caught by "X" rifling the mayor's safe.

CHAPTER XVII

IN DEATH'S STRONGHOLD

EMOTION FILLED "X" as he continued his work. His startling discovery of the clue connecting Harrigan's concern with the murder machine was like a whiplash spurring him on.

He removed the appalling explosive itself next. It was contained in a celluloid case. It was a greenish, greasy acid. The faint fumes coiling from it were like a miasma of death. He buried most of it under the barn floor where he could return for it later. He took out an infinitely small sample to be submitted to chemical analysis. And even these few grains, he knew, could reduce a man's body to a bloody pulp.

He quickly reassembled the empty bomb, did it up again in his flying clothes, and left the deserted farm as he had come.

Grimly he drove through the darkness in the borrowed auto, headed back toward the city. There were still several hours of darkness left. There was much to be done in them.

In the next hour Agent "X" sent out commands to both of his undercover organizations. He commissioned Bates to investigate secretly the Schofield Arms Company and obtain all possible data as to their present activities in high-explosive manufacture. He asked Jim Hobart to locate Harrigan immediately.

Then Agent "X" went to the hideout where Bugs Gary and Gus Sanzoni were still unconscious prisoners. "X" had a move in mind more daring than any he had ordered Bates or Hobart to perform. It was a move that no other criminal investigator in the world would have thought of undertaking—a move that only Secret Agent "X," Man of a Thousand Faces, was fitted to make, by talent and training.

He went to the couch at the side of the room where the gross, slumped figure of Gus Sanzoni lay. Every shade in the house had been drawn. Special, light-proof shutters of opaque boarding had been fitted by "X" on the inside of the windows in the chamber where he had deposited his prisoners. He switched on a small mercury vapor lamp now. Its beam made the room as bright as day. An achromatic globe over the lamp acted as a color-filter in bringing out the natural tints of Gus Sanzoni's fat face.

Agent "X" studied the mobster intently. Sanzoni was breathing slowly and stertorously in his deep, drug-induced sleep. The Agent took a leatherette case of medicines and chemicals from a cabinet drawer. He tied a paper cone over Sanzoni's face, let fall a trickle of blended ammonia spirits in a piece of cotton at the cone's end. The fumes filled Sanzoni's nostrils, entered his lungs.

Three minutes of involuntary inhaling, and Gus Sanzoni was breathing more quickly. His arms moved. His eyelids began to flutter. He had returned to the borderland of consciousness.

Agent "X" took a small bottle from the chemical case. It contained a colorless liquid—essence of sodium amythal. He poured a few drops of this into a whiskey glass of water, tipped back Sanzoni's head, and made the man swallow.

Sanzoni's movements and the fluttering of his eyelids soon ceased. He had come out of the influence of one anesthetic, only to be subjected to another. But this was of a different nature.[59]

The Agent fired low-voiced questions at Sanzoni, and in a moment Sanzoni was giving reply. His answers were mere confused mutterings at first. But, as unconscious nerve centers took control, his voice grew stronger, became natural.

His answers were whining, suave, domineering—according to the questions "X" put to him. And these questions were seemingly unrelated to the criminal case in hand. They were questions concerning Sanzoni's personal habits, his likes and dislikes in food and liquor, his attitude toward politics, his treatment of his men.

Other queries concerning Sanzoni's communication with the Terror followed. "X" verified what Sanzoni had stated previously—that he alone was the one who dealt with the Terror's representative, handing over the Terror's share of the loot, after he had received a telephone call designating the place of delivery. "X" listened to Sanzoni's voice as well as the words he uttered.

Several times he ordered Sanzoni to repeat a sentence. More

---

59   AUTHOR'S NOTE: *Sodium amythal is one of several anesthetics sometimes used by psychiatrists to make patients tell the secrets of their past lives. Under its influence conscious persons will give rational answers to questions put to them.*

than once Agent "X" spoke a phrase directly after the mobster. And the effect then was uncanny. For the Agent's amazing power of mimicry made it appear as though two Gus Sanzonis had spoken. He mastered the gangster's wheezing inflection, copied the involuntary gestures that Sanzoni made with his hands and arms as he talked.

And when he had gotten what he wanted, Agent "X" gave his prisoner still another administration of chemical—a hypo injection this time, of the same sort he had given Bugs Gary. Sanzoni returned to the realm of complete unconsciousness.

IT was then that Agent "X" began one of the most difficult disguises he had ever attempted. Sanzoni was the same height as himself. But there were those roils of fat on the gangster's face and body to be coped with, the baggy flesh under his eyes, the flabby jowls.

These presented great difficulties. Yet Agent "X," as a master impersonator, had anticipated that he would one day come up against such a problem. He had prepared.

In a locked, metal-bound chest in his hideout were sets of padding. Sets such as some great character actor might have possessed. These had been made for "X" by a famous Parisian stage costumer. He selected those which, fastened on, developed the rotundities of Sanzoni.

Then he began work on his own features, first stripping off his present disguise. With his volatile, quick-drying, plastic material he commenced molding the features of Gus Sanzoni upon himself. And here "X" employed the art of the sculptor. He could have done the same thing in clay. He had in the beginning of his strange career made countless experiments with plastic clay, till his powerful fingers had developed an uncanny quickness and accuracy.

Collodion formed one of the basic substances in the materials he used. There were others, known only to "X," blended by a secret formula over which he had worked for months, till he had achieved just the right degrees of cohesiveness and mobility.

He modeled the flexed jowls of Sanzoni; duplicated the bags under the eyes, the thickened, flabby neck, the gross lips. And this padding of synthetic fleshlike material followed the movement of the real flesh beneath. When he smiled the sculptured features smiled also. When he scowled they moved in accordance with the muscular movement beneath. The principle of "X's" disguises was no mystery. The only mystery was the lifelike effect his genius achieved.

For when he arose at last from before his triple-sided mirrors, the twin of Gus Sanzoni seemed to be in that room. And when he removed the gangster's clothes and put them on himself, he seemed to be the real Sanzoni, and the snoring, sleeping man on the couch seemed to be his ghost. The padding over his own firm muscles filled the gangster's oversized suit.

He practised Sanzoni's walk across the room. He addressed the walls in Sanzoni's wheezing, brutal voice. He stuck one of the gangsters cigars between his thickened lips, lighted it, breathed smoke and practised harsh gestures. He was Gus Sanzoni to the life.

But before he left his hideout he added two things to an otherwise perfect disguise. He discolored slightly the plastic material above his cheekbone to look like a bruise. Across his forehead he stuck a small strip of adhesive plaster which seemed to hide a cut. Even the cut was there, a reddish slit in the make-up, in case curious hands should remove the plaster.

TWENTY MINUTES later, a yellow cab drew up before the door of the Montmorency Club, and a man who would have passed anywhere for Gus Sanzoni stepped out. He seemed to be Sanzoni in one of his most evil moods. His heavy brutal features were twisted into a savage scowl. The frayed stub of an unlighted cigar projected from his lips. He flung a coin at the cab driver, turned and clumped sullenly into the club's vestibule.

The doorman had gone off duty now. The last of the guests had finally left. The band had ceased playing. There was none to see Sanzoni's apparent return till he mounted the red plush stairs and reached the floor of the club proper.

But the place was not as deserted as it seemed. A rat-faced gunman lounging outside the door of the club's main room saw the lumbering form of Sanzoni, and gave a hoarse cry of excitement.

"Boss!" he said. "Boss!"

He thrust open the door behind him, called to those inside.

"It's the boss, gents! He's come back! He got away from that guy! He's here."

A score of silent, tense-faced gangsters were gathered in the room. Some had been leaning against the walls. Others sat glumly at tables with whisky glasses before them. Goldie La Mar, Sanzoni's moll, looking old and strained, was pacing the room, smoking endless cigarettes. There was a stampede to meet the returning big shot.

Behind the disguise of Sanzoni, one of the most daring impersonations he had ever wrought, Secret Agent "X" was in a state of hair-trigger alertness. This was a challenge hurled into the face of Fate. This was courting death in death's own stronghold. There was no bullet-proof vest beneath his clothing now. If he made a slip, if one of these men around him, or that nimble-witted woman, learned that he was not Sanzoni at all, but only a clever imposter, guns would blaze murderously. And the menace of the NP bombs would remain to imperil the city. Twice he had escaped close destruction in this building. A third time he had come to make the greatest gamble of all.

Goldie La Mar's voice sounded above the rest, brittle, shrill with excitement. There was relief in her mascaraed eyes. Her painted lips curved in a dazzling smile. She had thought her meal ticket, her prestige in the underworld, had been snatched from her. Now they had returned in the person of Sanzoni.

She flung her powdered arms around Sanzoni's neck.

"Gus!" she screeched. "Gus—we thought that mug had croaked you!"

Her cajoling, perfumed lips tried to cling to his. Agent "X," with an irritable growl, playing the role of a man whose character he had sized up adroitly, flung her away. He made a wry grimace, clutched his shoulder, and winced as though in pain.

"Oh—he hurt you!" said Goldie La Mar. "You've got a cut—and a bruise on your face. How did you do it, Gus? How did you get away?"

Others flung questions at him. He was congratulated, admired, cheered. When he reached the inner room, a gangster shoved a glass of liquor toward him. Agent "X" tossed it off at a gulp; threw out his padded chest a little.

"That bird won't bother us no more!" he said.

"How did you do it, Gus? Where is he?"

"Never mind. Pipe down—all you heels. And you, Goldie—it's time you hit the hay. Clear out. Scram! I got business to attend to."

Agent "X" walked on into Sanzoni's private office. Four slinking gangsters, Sanzoni's own personal bodyguard and lieutenants, detached themselves from the others and followed.

"X" heaved himself into Sanzoni's chair, eyed these men who would have sought to kill him instantly had they guessed the truth.

"How did the work go?" he wheezed.

One of the men, a hatchet-faced, macabre-looking Sicilian, stepped nearer. He drew from his pocket a huge paper packet, laid it on Sanzoni's desk. A half dozen other such packets followed until there was a pile of them.

"It went swell!" the gangster lieutenant said. "Those are all century notes. There are seven hundred of them—seventy grand, and that ain't all." He turned to one of his companions. "Cough up, José," he snapped.

The second mobster disgorged packets of bills from his pockets. The pile on Sanzoni's desk rose. The face of José cracked in a hideous smile.

"We t'ought you wasn't comin' back, boss—an' we didn't know w'at we'd do wid dis stuff. De vault opened easy, but we hadda knock off two guys to keep 'em quiet."

"X" knew that here was more bank loot. Here was more evidence of the black wave of crime that still swamped the city—and would as long as the Terror held the threat of his dread "protection" over Mayor Ballantine's head.

"X" nodded, drew the money toward him, and asked a sudden question.

"Any phone calls for me?"

The men looked at each other uneasily. The one who had first given him the money nodded and spoke.

"Yeah—a guy called you at two o'clock. But he didn't say what he wanted. He sounded sore—because you wasn't here. I said you'd be back later."

Agent "X" didn't reply. He lighted one of Sanzoni's cigars, drew in smoke thoughtfully. But he was inwardly tense. Fingers of dread clutched at his heart. The man who had called had probably been the Terror, wanting to make arrangements for the delivery of his share of the money. Sanzoni had been out. He would not call again tonight, for the cold, gray fingers of the dawn were already stealing in through the window. Agent "X" made an impatient, sullen gesture.

"Scram, all of you. I gotta be alone to think."

It was true; but not in the way they supposed. The gangsters withdrew and Agent "X" went to Sanzoni's big safe. He did not know the combination. But, making sure the doors of his office were locked, he knelt before the safe, listened to the faint clicks of the lock mechanism, and easily opened the door. Inside were other packets of bills, and a small leather satchel—loot no doubt ready for delivery. The cash taken in the bank raid tonight formed an allotment, together with that in the safe. The Terror was impatient to receive his seventy per cent.

But Agent "X" could only wait now. He had made one of the greatest gambles of his life. He was like a man poised on the brink of some terrible inferno. Over those miles of city streets, through which the morning light was filtering, a pall of horror hung. There was a chance that thousands of the city's citizens might never seen another dawn. He himself might not live to see it.

No saying how the Terror might respond to all that had happened. He had known about the Agent's theft of the bomb. He would know also about Sanzoni's capture by the Agent. He must have a spy in the Sanzoni gang. And "X" was depending now on the fact that the Terror would hear of Sanzoni's return. His own statement that Agent "X" would bother him no more must surely reach the Terror's ear. If it did there was hope. If it did not—death, the impulse that would set off the bombs, might come through the air that very day.

CHAPTER XVIII

THE TERROR'S VOICE

IT SEEMED TO Agent "X" that the hands of the clock moved with the maddening slowness of crawling maggots. His nerves were like crawling maggots also. He craved action, yet he must wait, wait! The lives of thousands depended on his caution, his cunning, now. He had entered into the role of Gus Sanzoni. He must make that disguise convincing till the purpose of it was achieved—till he made contact with the Terror, or the Terror's messenger.

He went into the small, windowless den off Sanzoni's office and pretended to sleep. But he wasn't sleeping. His thoughts were active. He was planning his campaign.

The phone in Sanzoni's office, he saw, was an extension. It would be suicidal to call Hobart on it. Other ears would listen in. The underworld was ever suspicious. Yet he must somehow get in touch with Hobart and Bates—learn whether Harrigan had been located and what Bates had uncovered. These details might influence his actions in the immediate future.

He had his lunch sent into his office, ate it somberly, and directly afterwards sauntered out a side exit of the club into the street. Two of Sanzoni's bodyguards sought to accompany him. He waved them off growlingly.

"I got private business, see! After what happened last night I guess I can take care of myself. I don't need you mugs now."

There was a hint of suspicion in their blank faces. Agent "X" had an inspiration. He winked.

"You guys stay here and see that Goldie don't follow. There's a jane I gotta have a talk with—and it's getting so I can't move without Goldie tagging along."

The gangster guards relaxed. This was a simple and understandable explanation of Sanzoni's wish to go for a stroll alone. He had let them think there was another woman.

Agent "X" took a taxi, had the driver speed crosstown. He went into a drug store, called Jim Hobart. The excited voice of the redhead reached him at once.

"Boss, I've been expecting to hear from you all morning! That guy you asked me to locate, Harrigan—has disappeared! He's left his apartment. He ain't at his office. I can't find any trace of him!"

A thin smile curved the Agent's lips under the make-up of Gus Sanzoni. The man he suspected of being implicated somehow in the Terror's activities had taken this time to drop out of sight. That might be mere coincidence, or it might not.

His voice snapped a response at Jim Hobart over the wire. "We've got to find him, understand, Jim! This is something big. You'll know about it later. But keep after Harrigan, question his friends and servants. Find him. And when you do, send out a broadcast in the Z2 code. I may not have a chance to phone you again, but I'll be listening."

Agent "X" snapped up the receiver. Hobart would have been astounded, would have thought himself insane, if he could have seen the man he had just talked to—the man whose voice had been that of A. J. Martin.

Still in the role of fat Sanzoni, Agent "X" walked out of the drug store. He took another taxi to a different part of the city. Here he entered an apartment house where no gangster had ever visited. With a key he took from his pocket, not one of Sanzoni's, but one which he had transferred from his own clothes when he dressed in the mobster's outfit, he opened a door on the second floor. The place was empty, sparsely furnished. It was another hideout of Secret Agent "X."

When the Agent came out he carried a cigar box with him. It was inoffensive. It would not attract suspicion. He had apparently visited a friend, and had been given a full box of choice Havanas.

WITH the box under his arm he hurried back to the Montmorency Club. Goldie La Mar had had her beauty sleep and was up for the day. She greeted him boisterously.

"Where you been, Gus? How you feelin' after the fight last night? Ain't you got a kiss for Goldie?"

She pouted her red lips at him, sidled up to him possessively. Agent "X" gestured her away. He screwed his face into a scowl, spoke gruffly.

"I'm busy, Goldie. I ain't got time for no mushy stuff now!"

Hostility flared in the woman's eyes. Yet he knew that if she wasn't repulsed she would be a pest, interfering with his desperate plans. She snatched at his arm now. "Listen, Gus, you been actin' funny lately." For an instant it seemed to him that he read suspicion on her heavily rouged face. He spoke with swift calculation.

"Lay off me, Goldie! The boys say you got sweet with Bugs last night. You danced with him, didn't you? You two-timing little—"

That brought pallor to her painted face. She shrank away. Her voice was husky, scared. "Gus—you don't think—"

Agent "X" walked on, leaving the woman with something to worry about. His show of jealousy against Bugs Gary would keep her docile and quiet till she learned whether he was going to hold it against her.

In Gus Sanzoni's office, "X" slumped into a chair again, laid the cigar box before him on the desk. He snapped open a little wire catch, raised the lid stealthily. Under the cover, at the top, was a row of cigars wrapped in tin foil. But the gleaming front they presented was only camouflage.

He lifted two of them, moved his fingers deftly on a small rheostat beneath. Finely made, watchlike mechanism filled the remainder of the box. It was a vest-pocket size radio receiving set, operating on two small, but super-powerful, dry batteries. Bending his head he could hear the faint dots and dashes of a secret code message. It was as though a tiny, shrill-winged insect were imprisoned in the box. Three feet away the sound would be inaudible. But Bates was broadcasting a report, and Agent "X" listened. There, in the stronghold of the Terror's allies, he was getting a report from his own men.

A detailed account of the activities of the Schofield Arms Company came from the radio. Bates was a faithful, routine operative, who worked by rule of thumb and could always be depended upon to carry out an order. But his report now was not significant. The Agent changed the dial again, to the wave-length over which Hobart would signal in code Z2 if he succeeded in locating Harrigan. That had been "X's" main motive in bringing the hidden radio here.

He was running a risk in doing it. If its presence were discovered, it would be his death warrant. But death was close, anyway. Somewhere the Terror was waiting for darkness, and the money that reposed in Sanzoni's safe.

The afternoon dragged by. Dusk came at last, stealing across the city like some shadowy, sinister portent. Sanzoni's men came and went; came for orders; came to tell their supposed chief about their murderous, criminal activities. "X" could not tell them to cease their raids. A few innocent citizens must still suffer—that death might not come to thousands. He must appear in all ways to be Sanzoni.

Sitting behind his desk, he gave directions to Sanzoni's evil horde—and waited for the call that would be a command for Sanzoni himself.

Yet the cigar-box radio on the desk before him was silent. Hobart had not succeeded in finding Harrigan. The Agent's campaign against appalling, ruthless crime still hung in doubt.

He got up at last, paced the private office, looked at the lighted streets of the city. Men and women were hurrying by, unaware of the danger that threatened every instant. Others, laughing, elaborately dressed, would come here to the Montmorency Club, to dance and be gay, while doom crept close.

Goldie La Mar stuck her head in once. Meek, blonde and perfumed, clad in a clinging green evening gown, she spoke in sugary tones.

"Ain't you gonna have no dinner, Gus? I had the chef fix up all the things you like. I wouldn'ta danced with Bugs last night—only he asked me to—an' I wanted to find out what he had to say for himself."

AGENT "X" waved the woman away. "Don't bother me, Goldie. I'll eat when I'm ready."

He had his dinner brought into his office again. He nibbled at it, had the dishes taken away, and sat hunched over the desk, apparently in deep thought, but really listening for the insect note of the concealed radio.

Then at ten o'clock the telephone beside him rang abruptly. The Agent was conscious of a slight trembling of his hands as he lifted the receiver. It might be one of a score of people calling the gangster chief, some underworld acquaintance of Sanzoni. But a secret hunch told him that it was not. Personal calls had been few and far between all day. The club's acting manager, a suave-faced young mobster, took care of the routine business.

"Gus Sanzoni, speaking," he wheezed. And as soon as the voice sounded at the other end of the wire, the Agent's body tensed. For the tones of the voice were flat, unemotional, and spoken in a peculiarly measured way. Agent "X," a close student of phonetics, knew that the voice he was hearing now was disguised; knew that it was spoken by a man who did not want his identity revealed—the Terror.

"You were not at hand to receive my second call last night," the voice said. "Why?"

"I—I had to leave!" the Agent wheezed. "I was taken away—by a guy who called himself Secret Agent 'X.'"

There was an instant's pause at the opposite end of the wire. Then the disguised voice came again. "And this man—Secret Agent 'X'—where is he now? What did he want of you?"

Recalling the air battle over the bomb, "X" knew that he must not make the slightest inconsistent statement.

"I croaked him, chief," he said. "I had to—he wanted to chisel in on our racket. He gave me a shot of dope—knocked me out for a couple of hours. I don't know where he went then. When I came to I was in his apartment, but before I could get on my feet again, I heard him coming back. So I laid low. He thought I was still knocked out—then I jumped him. We had a fight—and I slugged him proper. Then I came back here. He had a bomb planted in the cellar. He's a bad guy—but he won't bother us no more. A coffin's the only thing he's got any use for now."

The Agent's knuckles were white on the black receiver of the phone. He was playing a bluff that brought sweat to his forehead—sweat, because he feared for the lives of those teeming thousands outside. His voice sank, became more of a wheeze.

"I'm sorry I wasn't here last night, chief, when you called. But I got some stuff—nearly a hundred and fifty grand. A hundred for you—all in cash."

"Take a cab to the foot of Smith Street," the order came. "Get out, walk across the vacant lot at the right. Stand in the shadow of the big billboard. My man will meet you at ten o'clock. That is all."

The mention of the hundred thousand in cash had done the trick—diverted the Terror's mind from Agent "X." Not suspecting for an instant that any man would attempt such a thing as the impersonation of Gus Sanzoni, he had accepted the Agent's story about his own death. It was now half past nine. In ten minutes Agent "X" would go forth to meet the henchman of the Terror.

CHAPTER XIX

NIGHT MEETING

HANDS CLENCHED TIGHTLY, eyes bleak, Agent "X" started to rise from Gus Sanzoni's desk. Then he stopped. Out of the wooden cigar box before him a faint, insect-like buzz was issuing.

"X" darted a glance toward the door, saw that it was closed and bent down. He recognized at once the dot-dash signals of the Z2 code. This was a special, syllabic code he had worked out with Jim Hobart, forcing the lanky redhead to learn it in many a tedious session with a telegraph key and a buzzer. Picked up by any amateur or commercial operator, its groupings would be unintelligible.

But the message was brief and plain, simple as day to the Secret Agent's trained ears.

"Harrigan located. Visitor on Sutton's yacht *Osprey*. Is expected to remain there as guest until yacht sails on cruise for southern waters."

Patiently, in precise dots and dashes, Jim Hobart began the message again. But Agent "X" lifted the lid of the cigar box and clicked the current off. If any one came in and walked close to the desk, that insect buzz would be a betrayal—and he had heard all he needed to know. Harrigan was on the *Osprey*—probably with the mayor again. Previous reports had informed "X" that Mayor Ballantine was spending a great deal of his spare time on the yacht.

Agent "X" gathered up his cigar-box radio. He walked with it to the black safe in the corner. He again opened the safe, without listening to the lock now, for he had memorized the combination. He took out the black satchel, carefully counted out one hundred thousand dollars, and tucked them away in the satchel's bottom. This left room at the top for his secret radio. He did not want to leave it behind him here.

He closed the safe, put on Sanzoni's hat and coat, and, with the satchel in his hand, he left the Montmorency Club by the side exit again. Several of Sanzoni's gangsters saw him. But he didn't speak, and they made no attempt to follow as a bodyguard. This was proof to "X" that they were accustomed to Sanzoni's nocturnal departures, with the Terror's share of the loot. Perhaps they did not know what Sanzbni carried in that satchel. But he had evidently impressed them with the fact that he was to be left alone when he went out with it at night.

"X" followed the Terror's instructions, took a cab to the foot of Smith Street, a dark commercial thoroughfare that led toward the black waters of the river. Its shops and warehouses were closed now. The cab jolted over rough cobblestones. The driver looked nervously about him when the vehicle stopped.

Agent "X" paid the man, struck off to the right, where he saw the dark expanse of a vacant lot. In the shadow beside a big warehouse loading platform, he drew the cigar-box radio from the satchel. He stooped for an instant, thrust the radio through a broken board under the platform itself. Later, if he chose, he could retrieve it.

There was not a soul in sight. The vacant lot seemed a place of desolation, of possible death. If this were a trap, the Terror could have found a no more likely spot. A thin, vicious cat rattled stones as it slunk out of "X's" path. For a moment its green eyes glared back at "X." This was the only indication of life.

He saw the big billboard the Terror had mentioned rising on the far side of the lot. Its surface showed a ghostly white in the darkness where a faint wash of street light reflected.

Agent "X" picked his way across the lot, every sense alert. He knew it must be close to ten. The Terror's man must be near at hand, somewhere in the darkness. His own figure must be silhouetted by the glow in the street beyond. This was part of the Terror's plan, so that his representative could be sure Sanzoni had come alone.

When the billboard rose directly above him, Agent "X" paused. All around him the darkness was complete. The great bulk of an old factory building rose on his left now, shutting out all light from that direction. Beside him was the smoke-blackened framework of the billboard. A thin streamer of dank mist off the river raced by him in the gloom like a hurrying specter. He heard no sound of footsteps, no indication of human presence.

But, as a great clock in a square blocks away boomed the hour of ten, a voice spoke beside the Agent:

"Give us that satchel, mister."

A SMALL, wiry man, sure-footed and quick as a rat, came out from the skeleton maze of the billboard supports. Without waiting for "X" to reply, his fingers closed over the satchel. He took it and whisked away as quickly as he had come. It was all over in an instant. The Agent had met the Terror's man—and the Terror's man had gone.

But there were grim lights in Agent "X's" eyes. He had come here for a purpose. That purpose was not to be lost sight of.

He picked his way quickly back across the vacant lot. At Smith Street, he turned right toward the river. Suddenly he sped through the darkness like a silent, racing ghoul. His quick brain had been working. The rat-faced man had come from behind the billboard, come from the side facing the water. There was a dark street of deserted stores and few lights at that point, with old wharves to hide on, and innumerable doorways in which to crouch. It was there surely that the Terror's man had gone.

Agent "X" stopped short when he reached it. His rubber-soled shoes had made no noise. His eyes had adjusted themselves to the dim light. There had been rumors that Agent "X" could see in the dark. This was not so; but he had trained himself to make use of any available light beam; of illumination so dim that the average person could have seen nothing.

He did not miss the faint movement a half block away which marked the passing of the rat-faced man. He even got the man's direction—and he followed with the cautious footsteps of a master shadower.

From doorway to doorway he slunk. Crouching at times, creeping Indian fashion across open spaces that he must traverse, eyes never losing sight of the man ahead.

The Terror's henchman looked back once. He could see nothing. His actions indicated that he felt himself safe. Often before he must have met Sanzoni, picked up the loot, and carried it to his master. He had no reason to believe tonight that the man who had come as Sanzoni was any other.

And the course he was taking was parallel with the waterfront.

Agent "X" crept closer, using the opposite side of the street. Dock entrances afforded shadowed shelter here, as did also the parked trucks, silent and still for the night. The Agent was almost opposite the small man now. He paused suddenly as the Terror's representative left the sidewalk, crossed the street, and moved along the river's edge. The man plunged between two covered docks, disappeared for a moment. But Agent "X" was soon at the mouth of the alleylike passage that led directly to the river.

He saw that the rat-faced man had snapped on a flashlight. He was bobbing along toward the black water, the satchel in his hand. The beam of the flash was lighting the ground ahead of him, and abruptly Agent "X" crouched forward, eyes narrowed.

For the thrusting beam of the electric flash had centered on a boat. It was a small boat, painted white. There was faint lettering on its bow.

As the man stooped intently, loosening a mooring rope and arranging his oars, Agent "X," crouched to the ground, coming closer. He held his breath as he made out the name that the letters on the boat's bow spelled. There were six of them, forming a single word. That word was familiar to Agent "X"—*Osprey*.

JIM HOBART'S message flashed through his mind at the same instant as he saw it. Harrigan had been located. Harrigan was on the *Osprey*. And now the Terror's man, with a hundred thousand in stolen bills, was using the *Osprey's* boat.

The Agent could have leaped out of the darkness and made a prisoner of the man. But, so close to his goal, he dared not take chances. There was no saying what the Terror might do if his messenger from Sanzoni did not arrive.

The Agent waited in the darkness, saw the rat-faced man shove off onto the black, sucking tide of the river, heard the faint rattle of the oarlocks as the boat drew away.

He was holding his breath, tense in every muscle. But he turned and sped back to the riverfront street. In a black patch of shadow he tore at his face, peeling off the awkward make-up of Gus Sanzoni. He substituted, from tubes of plastic material that he carried, one of his "stock disguises" that he could fashion by the sensitive touch of his fingers alone.

He drew the padding that had made him bulky as Sanzoni from beneath his clothes. The suit, many sizes too large for him now, hung slackly on his muscular frame. It was not comfortable, it even impeded his movements; but he could not help it.

"X" had prepared for different kinds of water travel from a variety of hidden bases. There was a spot at the river's edge where an old barge had sprung a leak and sunk. The water was shallow. The forward part of the barge was still above the surface. The company owning it had not cared to go to the expense of salvaging it, or having it destroyed. It had been roped off, left to rot. There was a gaping hole in its side where ice cakes in winter storms had battered in the planking.

Agent "X" leaped to the barge's deck from a near-by dock. In a moment he was above the jagged hole in its side. Hanging by his hands he lowered himself, angled his body beneath the deck, and disappeared from sight.

Two minutes passed, and the knife-sharp bow of a small, odd craft appeared. It was a featherweight, Eskimo type kayak—a slender boat made of canvas stretched over a wooden framework. Agent "X" sat in the middle, in a circular cockpit. A thin, double-bladed paddle propelled the craft. Outside of a racing shell, it was the fastest type of one-man boat in the world.

He pushed it from beneath the barge where he had kept it hidden, sent it skimming out onto the river. Swift and silent as a surface swimming seal, he drove it along with expert sweeps of the paddle, rocking from side to side as he dug the blade in.

He paused to listen. The faint squeak of oarlocks reached his keen ears. That would be the Terror's man, rowing toward the *Osprey*. Cutting down his own speed, Agent "X" followed the sound. He could have overtaken the other, reached the *Osprey* ahead of him. They traveled parallel with the city, continued nearly a mile up the river, to the yacht club opposite which the *Osprey* was anchored.

Agent "X" saw the *Osprey's* lighted portholes at last. He started, straining his eyes in the gloom as he came nearer. A feather of smoke showed above the *Osprey's* single funnel. The boat was getting steam up, preparing for departure it seemed, and Harrigan, the man connected with the Schofield Arms Company, from which the inner casing of the radio bomb had come, planned to be among the guests on the contemplated southern cruise.

Agent "X" heard a faint rattle as the unseen rower shipped his oars. He drew cautiously closer, and saw a porthole, near the waterline, darken for a moment. Either the Terror's man had slipped through that, or some one had reached out to take the satchel from him.

Grimly Agent "X" approached the yacht. He circled it once. Faint strains of music reached him. Monte Sutton was having a party again. Men and women were dancing, drinking, laughing, not knowing how close to the black mystery of death they were. For if the stolen loot was taken to the *Osprey* the man who called himself the Terror could not be far off.

Agent "X" saw the row boat tender swinging at the end of the painter. The tide had pulled it out behind the anchored yacht. The rat-faced man had gone aboard. The lee side was the place for "X" to land. But a sailor was patrolling the deck above. Coming close, Agent "X" could see the man's outline against the painted woodwork of the boat. Clad in pea-jacket and knitted cap, the man was dressed against the December chill. He was stationed on regulation watch.

The Secret Agent maneuvered the sharp nose of his kayak close. He edged silently along the yacht's side, pulses hammering. Then he stopped, shipped his paddle carefully. He grasped the end of a thin silk painter in his teeth, and swung up the vessel's side, using the ports as toe and hand holds. In a moment he stood on the yacht's deck, and made his slender painter fast to the boat's brass railing, using an expert seaman's knot.

But as he raised his head, a low voice called a sharp command. The next instant the patrolling sailor leaped toward him, and in the man's hand was the gleaming outline of a gun.

CHAPTER XX

DEATH TO THE AGENT!

AGENT "X" STOOD quietly as the man approached. He did not attempt to run. Did not speak. His attitude was deceptively careless. He slouched against the railing.

But, when the sailor was close, gun thrust menacingly forward, eyes peering at "X", the Agent ducked and plunged forward. So lightning quick was he, that the sailor was unprepared. A chopping uppercut of the Agent's left hand sent the gun spinning over the rail into the water. The Agent's right fist connected with the man's jaw with a swift, clean *crack* that made the sailor sway on his feet, then collapse groggily to the deck. He rolled over, lay inertly, completely out.

Agent "X" stooped, shoved his unconscious body into the shadows by a coil of rope. Then the Agent glanced up at the yacht's funnel again. The smoke told him that the boilers were being fired. The oil-burning furnaces must be heating fast. Steam was almost up. It was nearly eleven now. Perhaps the yacht was to leave at midnight as many liners did. And it could not, must not, leave, with the Terror upon it.

The Agent acted quickly. The time for a showdown had come. He was convinced that all the stolen loot, collected in a score of murderous robberies, was somewhere below decks. He was certain that the Terror was on board.

He turned and raced silently along the deck toward the nearest entrance-way. Through a lighted window he got a glimpse into the main saloon. The dancing couples were there again. Agent "X" bent forward intently. He saw many people that he recognized. There was the puffy, troubled face of Mayor Ballantine. There was the tall grim form of Police Commissioner Foster. There, too, was Harrigan, immaculate in evening clothes, with Monte Sutton beside him, and a black-haired laughing girl on his arm.

There were many from the city's wealthy, political set. This was evidently a farewell party. Ballantine himself possibly was among the traveling guests.

Agent "X" studied Harrigan's face. The munitions man looked white, strained. There were furtive shadows in his eyes. The smile that came to his lips at something his girl companion said was mechanical.

Agent "X" slipped on, passed the lighted saloon, until he came to another entrance. Here he listened for seconds, then opened the door, and entered upon a carpeted passageway inside the luxurious yacht. Familiar with all types of ship design, he made his way forward, surely, swiftly. Any instant he might meet someone—a guest, or one of the yacht's crew. There was no possible explanation he could make. He must count on quiet, secrecy, or a quick, knockout blow if he were caught.

He passed the doors of a half dozen luxurious staterooms. Voices issued from one. He listened a moment, went on; then he came to the door he sought. Behind this was obviously the yacht's wireless room. It was in the forward part of the ship. But there was no sound from inside, no spark in attendance at the moment. The Agent opened the door cautiously to make sure, slipped inside.

He switched on the light, shut the door behind him. There was no bolt. He propped a chair under the doorknob, turned his attention to the radio set. It was modern, complex, complete in every detail; but it offered no problem to the Agent. Radio engineering was one of the subjects he had delved into profoundly.

This was the ship's radio for long-distance sending and receiving. It had keys for the sending of code, a microphone for voice broadcasting. Glittering dials and tubes were mounted on a huge black panel.

FOOTSTEPS sounded in the corridor outside as the Agent stared about. Some one passed the door. Any instant he might be interrupted. The message that he had to send was imperative. He and his staff of organized investigators had worked for days outside the law. Now it was time for the law to be summoned.

And he had the means to do it. Bates had been instructed to listen for messages from his employer. He would be prepared to receive one now, wherever he might be, because he carried on his person one of the Agent's vest-pocket receiving sets.

With deft, experienced movements. Agent "X" switched in the transmitting apparatus, started a generator whirring, saw a bright spark leap across the gaps. He turned down to the short wavelength that would reach Bates, and began tapping the rubber-topped key, sending out the dots and dashes of the secret 26G code. If Hobart should pick up this, it would mean nothing to him. It was for Bates' ears alone.

"Get in touch with police," tapped "X". "Have harbor patrol surround and board steam yacht *Osprey*. Daring criminal and many thousands in loot on board. Speed imperative. Boat leaving soon."

He repeated the message again and again, fingers moving mechanically on the keys, eyes wandering curiously about the room. There was a panel on the side of the wall which he had not at first noticed. He reached up, opened this with his left hand. Inside was a cabinet, filled with more radio mechanism. Squat tubes with silvered caps gleamed in a Bakelite base. Odd-type condensers were visible. A coil of black wire, some sort of a power unit, rose in the center. In front of the whole thing was a metal grille, locked at the bottom.

Agent "X" bent forward tensely, his hand leaving the key of the transmitting set, cutting off Bates' message. And at that instant, as Agent "X" stared aghast at the interior of this mysterious cabinet, the mechanism of which carried a message to his scientifically trained mind, the door of the radio room was thrust inward.

In one and the same movement Agent "X" slammed shut the panel he had opened and whirled to face the door. The top of the chair slipped off the knob. The door swung inward, and "X" saw the faces of two startled sailors framed in the entrance.

He did not give them time to think or question him. He plunged toward them, yanking his gas gun from his pocket. One went down, but the other ducked, shouted—and almost instantly three men in the uniforms of ship's officers appeared. Monte Sutton's boat was well-manned. Agent "X" plunged into the corridor and saw that he was trapped.

Two stewards were coming along the passage from the rear. The three ship's officers offered a barrier in the other direction. The sailor who had dodged his gas jet, leaped toward him with a furious cry—Agent "X" crouched, lashed out with his fist. The sailor's quick feint showed that he was a boxer. He ducked again, flung himself at "X," hammering in with short-arm blows. They clinched, and Agent "X" swung the man bodily, heaved him forward to crash into the opposite wall.

But five others were on top of him now, and far down the passage he heard the hoarse shouts of the guests rising in a bedlam of sound. Agent "X" went down in the carpeted passage under a crashing weight of human bodies. Using a wrestler's technique, he squirmed out from under, got a scissors grip on the biggest of the yacht's officers, and twisted the man on his back. Then something cold and hard was shoved against his neck. A voice shouted in his ear.

"Lay off, feller. Quiet there—or you'll get a bullet in your brain."

The cold thing was the muzzle of a gun. Agent "X" arose slowly. The officer that he had squeezed with the crushing scissors hold lay on the carpet breathless and groaning. The second man seized his arm. The third, still holding the gun against his neck, issued another order.

"Walk forward. No funny business—or you're a dead man!"

Agent "X" was shoved along the passage toward the saloon where the guests were assembled. The orchestra had stopped playing. A tense silence reigned in the big cabin. White, excited faces were turned toward "X" and the officers who held him. The Agent presented a strange figure in the baggy, ill-fitting suit of Sanzoni, hanging loosely now on his powerful frame. His last make-up had been a hasty one. He looked like a tough and dangerous young man.

"We caught this chap aboard, sir," said one of the officers, addressing Sutton. "He's a bad-actor—and almost killed Jarvis."

"Where was he?"

"In the radio room, sir."

MONTE SUTTON swore under his breath. The guests looked startled. Police Commissioner Foster came forward and buttonholed "X," taking the authority of the law into his own hands.

"Now," he growled. "What's the meaning of this? Who are you?"

Agent "X" did not answer at once. He stared from face to face. Harrigan was standing a short distance away, eyes intent and strained. Mayor Ballantine was watching him closely.

"There's a criminal on board this yacht," "X" said quietly. "You're in the right place, commissioner." He looked hard at Mayor Ballantine. "Some of you," he went on, "may have heard of a man who calls himself the Terror."

The Mayor gave a hoarse gasp. His face twitched. Harrigan turned paler. Commissioner Foster shook "X's" arm roughly.

"What are you talking about? Are you crazy?"

"No—not crazy, commissioner! You know that a crime wave has disgraced the city, that the police have been ordered to lie low, and that millions have been stolen. What if I should tell you that the loot or most of it is on this boat?"

Monte Sutton spoke then. "This man must be mad. Take him away, men! Lock him up till we can get him on shore."

Agent "X" fixed his gaze on the yachtsman. Craft was in Sutton's eyes now. His face was hard, lined.

"Wait!" said "X" harshly. "You have an interesting radio room, Sutton! I might ask you to explain several things I found there—but I already understand—"

A transformation came over the face of Sutton. The mask of the dapper society man fell away. He appeared all at once predatory, criminal, vicious. He crouched forward, fingers crooked.

"So—"

Agent "X's" voice rose. "I came to this yacht shadowing a man who carried a hundred thousand in stolen cash. He used the *Osprey's* tender. He came on board the *Osprey*. Now I know who the Terror is. First clues pointed to another man. He is now on board the yacht. What do you know about this, Harrigan?"

Commissioner Foster broke in angrily. "Radio the police, Sutton. This man's a raving maniac."

"No," said Mayor Ballantine suddenly. "I don't know who he is, but he seems to know a lot. I—" He stopped speaking, gave a gasp, for Monte Sutton, dapper yachtsman, had given a sudden signal that the officers of his yacht seemed to understand. They backed away, faces hard. One slipped through a doorway, out on deck. Sutton addressed his guests, staring at Mayor Ballantine.

"So!" he said again, "you decided to disobey the Terror's warning, Ballantine, and you, too, Foster!"

Agent "X" understood that Sutton thought he was a spy, hired by the mayor and his commissioner of police.

Words that were like a scream rose to the mayor's throat. "Good God! You, Sutton—you are the Terror! You planted the bombs!"

CHAPTER XXI

MOMENTS OF TERROR

THE MAYOR'S WORDS had an electrifying effect on the guests assembled in the cabin.

"Bombs!" a woman cried hysterically. "What does he mean?"

"Take me on shore!" another whimpered. "Take me away from here!"

Monte Sutton laughed harshly then. His gesturing fingers swept toward "X".

"This man, this detective of yours, Foster—let him tell my guests about those bombs! Or, no—I will. It's true, my friends, there are bombs—but you will be safer here than ashore. The city is to be blown up presently. You will have a nice view of it from here." Sutton laughed again. His eyes blazed with fury. "I am the Terror!" he cried. "And I am a man of my word! I made a bargain with Ballantine and Foster. They didn't keep it. Let them and others pay the price!"

A BREATHLESS silence followed his words. Then the mayor spoke in a shaken voice. "No, Sutton! God, no! You can't do it! This man wasn't hired by us!"

"You lie!" screamed Sutton. "You tipped him off to come here. And now you'll see what you've done!" He shouted another order at one of his officers. "Get underway! Quick—damn you! We sail at once." When the man had gone, Sutton turned back to his guests, his eyes brutally mocking.

"Harrigan can tell you as much about these bombs as I," he sneered. "The explosive in them came from his company. It was he who told me about it in the first place."

The munitions man made a choking sound in his throat. His face twitched.

"You dirty thief, Sutton!" His trembling hand gestured toward the others. "I hold controlling interests in the Schofield Arms Company. They've been experimenting with a new explosive for months—keeping it dark. It's the most violent thing of its kind in the world—and it was stolen mysteriously a few weeks ago. All our efforts to trace it failed—and now I understand why. I was a fool to mention it to any one—even my supposed friends. But I did—and Sutton was among them! Criminals hired by him made the theft, of course. I half suspected some one was using the explosive to force the hand of the city administration. I even went to the mayor's house and opened the safe like a common burglar in the hopes of finding some evidence. But I didn't guess for an instant that Sutton—" Harrigan's voice trailed away despairingly.

Agent "X," listening, felt a coldness around his heart. Sutton, he knew, was drunk with a sense of his own power—mixed with fury that his plot had been uncovered before he was ready. Now he was on the point of blowing up the city. The yacht was already moving. These men on board, in spite of their dapper uniforms, were criminals, too. Sutton's next words showed his determination to make good his hideous threat.

"In a few minutes," he jeered, "only a few minutes—and all of you will see what those bombs can do!"

Agent "X" spoke slowly, dramatically, a strange smile on his face as he put up a desperate bluff.

"I wouldn't explode them if I were you, Sutton! You may remember that one of the bombs was found. I brought that bomb to the yacht with me. If the others go up—you and your yacht will be blown to hell!"

Sutton turned incredulous eyes on the Agent. He came close and shook a finger in "X's" face. "A lie—another lie! You don't know anything about that bomb! The man who found it is dead. You never saw it. You couldn't even describe it if your life depended on it."

"No?" His eyes fixed on Sutton, the strange smile still twitching his lips, Agent "X" told calmly of the finding of the bomb. He gave a description of the radio mechanism, told in detail how the bomb looked and how it worked. And when he finished, Monte Sutton was white and shaken. He gave another fierce order to an officer who was standing by.

"You hear what this man says? Look all over the ship—find that bomb!" As he spoke, the windows of the saloon were raised. Sailors standing on the deck outside shoved gun muzzles through, covering every man and woman in the cabin.

"You're all my prisoners," said Sutton. "You, too, Foster, head of your damned police—as well as this spy you sent here. If he's not lying we'll find that bomb—and then—"

"You won't get away with it!" Foster shouted. "You'll go to the chair for this, Sutton!"

Sutton, laughing like a demon, walked up and struck the commissioner in the face. Then he turned to Agent "X."

"You will die," he said gloatingly, "but not until you've watched the city go up. It won't be a pretty sight—but it will be something to remember—the grandest fireworks you'll ever see. I—"

He paused suddenly, whirled toward a window. As the yacht moved ahead, something sounded in the darkness outside. It was a moaning wail, like the voice of the night protesting. It rose in pitch—became identifiable as the siren of a boat. Other sirens took up the cry abruptly. They were all around on the black water. The harbor patrol had arrived.

Monte Sutton staggered back. The commissioner of police gave a cry of amazement mixed with intense satisfaction.

At that instant "X" saw the man who called himself the Terror leap toward the wall and press a button that plunged the saloon in darkness. He saw Sutton turn and dash toward the passage at the cabin's end. And he got a glimpse of the man's face in a stabbing searchlight from one of the patrol craft sweeping up. Sutton's features were convulsed. He was in the grip of stark emotion, a raging, unholy devil of a man, lips skinned back from his teeth, fingers clenched.

And in that instant Agent "X" divined Sutton's intent. A cry of horror came from his own lips. Sutton had been defeated in his plot. Yet there was one last coup he could make—a coup that brought beads of sweat to the Secret Agent's forehead. If this happened, his own efforts, his desperate struggles, would have been futile.

He sprang across the cabin after the black shadow of Sutton. All about him was confusion. Men and women were crying in excitement. The sirens of the police boats wailed. The sound of shots as Sutton's criminal crew tried to fight off the law. But in the Agent's mind was no confusion—only cold purpose.

He reached the door of the passageway through which the ship's officers had shoved him a few minutes before. He saw Sutton's figure ahead, a furious streak at the end of the passage. The corridor curved, following the deck line of the boat. "X" lost sight of Sutton for an instant. When he rounded the bend, the man ahead had just hurled himself through the radio-room door.

AGENT "X" after him. The door slammed in his face. He beat against it. Bullets, fired by the human demon inside, ripped through the wood, plucked at the Agent's coat.

Ignoring them, risking his own life that horror might not come to thousands, Agent "X" flung his full weight against the door. It crashed inward; but Sutton was already bent over the instruments in the covered cabinet. A motor-generator was whirring somewhere. Sutton had the metal grille unlocked.

He was reaching for a button inside, fingers taut as talons, eyes gleaming. The man was going to blow up the city anyway, risk the explosion of the bomb that Agent "X" claimed to have brought with him—and commit suicide rather than give himself up to the law.

A gun in Sutton's left hand streaked up. Agent "X" dodged aside as the muzzle lanced flame. Sutton screamed a curse at him, tried to press the gun against his body. Agent "X" battered the gun down and clamped viselike fingers over Sutton's right hand, snatching it away from the radio signal button. Then he crashed into Sutton, knocked the man to the floor.

Sutton was a kicking, clawing, biting fury. His frenzy gave him amazing strength. He tried to sink his teeth into the Agent's arm, reached up with gouging fingers to press out his eyes. The Agent struck with desperate, sledge-hammer blows. His knuckles found Sutton's chin, snapped the man's head back. With a sigh and a groan Sutton relaxed, and flopped back on the floor.

But Agent "X" was taking no chances of his coming to before the police found him. He stooped for an instant, pressed a small hypo needle into the man's arm. That would keep him in a stupor for several hours.

Then "X" went expertly through the man's pockets. In one he found a small-scale city map. His eyes gleamed at this. Red marks showed on it—a dozen of them. Here were the locations of the hidden bombs. One of the marks, at the block of the Montmorency Club, was proof of that. Now the police bomb squad could find them. Harrigan would tell them how to handle the NP bombs. The Agent's work was done.

He stooped down, pinned the map to the front of Sutton's coat, left it on the inert figure. And with it, he left brief penciled instructions to the police, urging that they round up Sanzoni and Sanzoni's gang for the part they'd played in the crime wave. He listed the mobsters' names, added the names of several witnesses. Bugs Gary had done nothing and could go free when he recovered consciousness. But "X" would dump Sanzoni on a certain street corner where the law would find him.

The Agent went to the door then, listened, and stepped out into the corridor. The sounds of shots were diminishing now. The police had overcome criminal resistance. They were boarding the yacht. Soon Sutton's criminals, and Sutton's share of the loot, would be in the hands of the law, too.

No one saw the human shadow that moved out on the yacht's side deck. Crouched and silent in his rubber-soled shoes, Agent "X" slunk across the deck, and down the side of the craft as he had come. The dark and drifting kayak in the water had escaped attention. It looked more like a floating log than a boat.

Agent "X" paused a moment as he stepped into it. Commissioner Foster had come out of the saloon. He was talking to a grizzled captain of the harbor patrol who had boarded the yacht. The captain spoke harshly.

"It's lucky we got your orders, commissioner! This tub's speedy. It would have been out of the harbor in another twenty minutes."

"Orders!" said Foster in amazement.

"Yeah. They telephoned down to our dock from headquarters—said you'd sent a radio out from the yacht here. We got here as fast as we could. Now let's find that loot."

Commissioner Foster did not answer. His face was a mask of wonder and surprise that he took pains to hide. But the Agent's kayak slipped away silently, moved across the black river—and then out of the darkness came a strange whistle. It was eerie, melodious, like the call of some wild night bird—the strange, unforgettable whistle of Secret Agent "X"—man of Mystery and Destiny.

Made in the USA
Lexington, KY
08 January 2011